IN THE FULLNESS OF TIME

Vincent Nicolosi

Fonthill Press
New York

The acid-free paper used in this book conforms to the
guidelines for permanence and durability set by
the Council of Library and Resources and
the American National Standards Institute.

Printed in the United States of America.

ISBN-13: 978-0-692-00464-7

Library of Congress Control Number: 2009932792

Fonthill Press is a publisher of specialty books
of high and enduring quality, intended for
today's readers and for posterity.

Fonthill Press
New York

IN THE FULLNESS OF TIME
In them are revealed the ardor, the hope, the pride of a favored and exceptional people; the high exemplification of the privilege, the power and the vanity of human life.

—**Charles Evans Hughes**
Secretary of State, 1921–1925

PROLOGUE

A Visit to the Tomb

I RETURNED TO President Harding's tomb today, my first visit since three or four weeks ago when I went there to assure myself that all evidence of some recent desecrations had been cleaned away, and that all was respectable once again.

Today I went for an altogether different reason. It is a crisp and beautiful autumn day, a day utterly belying the sorrow that lies across the land. I attended church yesterday, but other than that, I have scarcely stirred from the television set since Friday, an hour or so after lunch, when Mrs. Christian's daughter telephoned from Columbus to tell us that President Kennedy had been shot in Dallas.

I am not ashamed to say that over these past four days I have shed my share of tears, most especially when little John-John saluted his father's coffin as it emerged from St. Matthew's, and to think that today is the poor little fellow's third birthday. Now on every birthday he will hear, somewhere in his thoughts, the cadence of muffled drums.

I sat here late this morning transfixed and, as I watched the gun carriage drawn by the seven white steeds bearing the flag-draped coffin on its slow and stately journey towards Arlington, something stirred

1

within me, a far-off resonance from the sound of those clattering hooves, a distant reflection from that same gleaming gun carriage, which forty years and four months ago bore the coffin of my friend and neighbor, President Warren G. Harding. Without forethought I found myself rising from my chair, adjusting my black tie and coat in the mirror, and drawing on my overcoat and hat. I paused briefly by the panel of windows overlooking the backyard and the Old Forest filled with sunlight, now that the buckeye, maple, and sycamore trees, and most of the ancient oaks, have shed their leaves. For a moment I thought again of that long-ago summer afternoon when the President and First Lady were present in this very room, having graciously called at Tioga to visit and thank my father, who at that time was slowly dying in the bed in the corner. Then, without turning off the television (for it seemed disrespectful to do so), I proceeded down the back stairs, out across the yard to the carriage house, and to my car. And so I made my own slow and stately way around the bend of Mt. Vernon Avenue and along the Boulevard, towards the Harding Memorial.

It was strange beyond words, but not once on the winding, mile-long drive to the tomb did I see a single other automobile, not even at the usually busy four corners. Nor for that matter did I see a single human being anywhere, not even some restless child at play in a yard with his dog. Everyone, the entire world it seemed, was accompanying our young President on his celestial journey. Indeed, I felt more than one pang of guilt for having moved from the television set, but I knew I would not be long at the President's tomb.

I hope you will forgive an old man's pride when I say that I consider the Harding Memorial to be the greatest achievement of my life, and it goes without saying that it will be my most lasting. Indeed, no matter what opinions you may hold of President Harding, I think one fact is utterly inarguable—that his tomb is quite simply one of the finest monuments built since antiquity; in the modern world, it is rivaled only by the Jefferson and Lincoln Memorials. This late morning when I pulled into the little parking area, I sat for a moment simply gazing at the monument in the distance, glowing in the tall trees like a vision from the classical world. Then, with hat in hand, I walked through the clear, cold sunlight and made my way up the long promenade.

It pleases me no end to think that strangers coming upon the Harding Memorial must find it a most astonishing sight. If by some rare chance you are a student of heroic architecture, or classical structures in America, then no doubt you are already quite familiar with the tomb. It is a vast and soaring marble edifice of Hellenic style and Promethean size and splendor. It is circular, what the Greeks called a "tholos," with broad flights of white marble stairs ascending to a continuous colonnade of massive columns encircling an inner cella, or chamber, which is open to the sun and winds. A willow tree grows within the cloister and a hanging garden lines the entablature. At the center of the cella rest two enormous cenotaphic sarcophagi of black granite, surrounded by a thick bed of myrtle, and far beneath these markers, deep within the hermetically sealed concrete vault, lay the remains of President and Mrs. Harding. In spite of its superhuman air, the monument is as peaceful as a grotto in the woods. In all, the Memorial is everything I intended it to be when I first proposed its creation nearly four decades ago. I am confident that the structure will endure for five thousand years. Down through the ages the Memorial will remind people of President Harding, and the character of his little hometown, which built it.

Of course today as I stood there, I was thinking not of the monument's beauty, or for that matter of my own pride. Instead, the sadness and unreality of the day seemed to affect me in unaccountable ways. The assassination of President Kennedy has made me feel once again as if I am passing through history and that history is passing through me. I stood before the cella for nearly twenty minutes before I was aware that even a single moment had passed. My mind ranged back through the years, as it so often does these days, conjuring people and times I once knew. I thought again of how, against all odds, Mr. Harding became President, of how, when he was young (and not so young), people called him, "Nigger Warren." I thought of our long campaign to make him President, and of the night of his sudden death in San Francisco. On this dreadful day I thought of something that I generally make a point of not thinking about at all—the absurd and persistent rumor that the President was assassinated, albeit obviously not with a high caliber bullet through the skull, but with a subtle poison ostensibly ministered by his devoted wife, with the supposed aid of an accomplice. Regrettably, when you deal with President Harding's legacy, you deal with a disproportionate amount of idle gossip and rumor. In fact, it was the same situation during his lifetime, so you can appreciate the challenge this created for us. Regarding the assassination rumor, so far as I'm concerned, it has about the same ring as all the talk nowadays of flying saucers and Martians landing in cornfields. Interesting, but where's the proof? In fact, where's the smallest shred of circumstantial evidence? By my lights, reasoned arguments even from the likes of biographers such as Samuel Hopkins Adams and William Allen White, calling the conjectured assassination "plausible," constitute little more than common gossip notched down to the level of academia.

Some of the President's biographers are just plain scoundrels, more or less. For instance, in the spring of 1947 a seemingly charming young historian, a former airman, arrived in Marion from an Ivy League college in the East. This young man—who called himself Matthias Mende— claimed to be the grandson of a long-dead ambassador to France. He had a picture of himself in his airman's uniform taken with Evelyn Walsh McLean at one of the parties she used to throw for servicemen at her estate in Virginia. Evelyn and her husband Jim—each the heir to a substantial fortune—were the Hardings' closest Washington friends. Jim's hobby was newspapers; he owned, among others, the *Washington Post.* Evelyn's hobby was jewels; she owned, among others, the Hope Diamond. Anyway, as for the young historian, neither a snapshot with Evelyn McLean nor a supposed connection to a long-dead ambassador would ever have given him entrée into Tioga's hermetic little world, but what interested my sister Adeline and me was this fellow's "forthright" admission that he was hoping to make a name for himself by reevaluating Mr. Harding's presidency, via a book analyzing the many wise and important undertakings he carried out in office. To this day I believe that Mr. Mende was altogether sincere in this regard. And I might add that such an approach to the Harding legacy would have been novel indeed, because nearly everyone outside of Marion, *especially* the historians, has conveniently forgotten the vast good and many effective things that the President did while in office. We allowed this young man into our confidence—in fact, into our lives—but soon his true colors began to show. Not only was he a subscriber to the poison theory, he also believed that people were still alive—and living right here in Marion—who supposedly participated in the "assassination."

He never wrote that promised history and, indeed, he himself became woven into the fabric of Harding rumors and legends. One June day he lit out for a visit to Lake Erie and we never saw him again. Matt's "disappearance" brought pain to Adeline and me. And, I might add, it led to the end of a lifelong friendship that we shared with one of our contemporaries, my classmate, Dana Yost.

That young interloper from 1947 was one of the reasons why I refused to speak with yet another of the President's would-be biographers, who just last month was snooping around Marion and leaning on my doorbell.

Obviously, I did not intend to dwell on such irksome thoughts this day, of all days, while standing before the cella in my mourning clothes. As I stood there, a deepening chill stirred me from my thoughts, and I realized that gray wintry clouds were fast approaching from the northwest and that the sun had gone in. I felt a sudden loneliness in that beautiful, desolate place, for I seemed to be the only person alive in the entire world. I adjusted the collar of my overcoat; a glance at my watch indicated that I had now been gone from Tioga for more than half an hour. From my imperfect memories of Washington, I estimated that the President's coffin would soon be crossing the Potomac and ascending the broad rise to Arlington—if it hadn't already. Thus with a little bow to President and Mrs. Harding's graves, I took my leave of them and hastened home for the Burial.

BOOK I

Into the Shadows

I

MONDAY EVENING
25 NOVEMBER 1963
TIOGA

The President Visits Tioga

DARKNESS IS FALLING early and quickly, as it does this time of year, and these four heartbreaking days are at last coming to a close. I kept vigil watching Channel 10 until Walter Cronkite, looking stricken and fatigued, finally signed off just a short while ago with, "And that's the way it is, at the end of a very long Monday, November 25, 1963. Good evening." I do not know if I can ever bear the return of regular programming, so I got up, quickly turned the set off, unplugged it, and settled into my father's green leather chair. I have now sat here for several minutes watching the rather ghostly-looking trees of the Old Forest fade into darkness, while my own reflection slowly appears, equally rather ghostly, upon the darkening windowpane.

Along with the library, this cozy and modest room is one of my favorites in the entire house. This was also my father's preferred room; in fact, although this room was meant as a sitting room, with its panels of windows on three sides and its pleasant views of the Old Forest, he came to use this as his bedroom and, indeed, he died in the same bed in which I sleep. Like the rest of Tioga, the room has changed little through the years. The same windows with their rippled glass, which lend the room a good bit of charm and "character," look out over the old carriage house

8

and over many of the same trees that were alive when my father was in his prime, and the very same lamps and furniture that he knew remain in their places. The portrait of my mother, hand-painted in Cincinnati when she was about sixteen, stands on the night table, exactly where it was on that delightful summer afternoon when President and Mrs. Harding came to pay respects to my dying father.

That was on the 3rd of July, 1922.

I was not living at Tioga at that time. Lucy and I had our own home. Back then, Adeline lived here with Papa, along with Nurse Boyle, who came to us through Surgeon-General Sawyer, having worked for him at his sanitarium on the west end of town. At that time Miss Evelyn Evans, the housekeeper, was still living here. I am happy to report that the former Miss Evans remains housekeeper to this very day, though she became Mrs. Christian about forty years ago, and she remained so efficient through the years that she managed to care for Tioga while raising a family of her own. Anyway, as you can imagine, it was no secret that the President of the United States had come home to Marion for a visit. His motorcade had arrived the evening before from Washington, and on that pleasant summer day all of Marion was draped in flags and patriotic bunting. I was in my office that morning when Adeline telephoned to say that George Christian, the White House Chief of Staff (and a former quarry clerk for my family's company), had just called from his mother's house to ask if it would be convenient for the President and First Lady to pay a little visit to Colonel Hamilton, at around two o'clock, if he was feeling up to it. Well, Dad was feeling as "up to it" as he would ever again.

I am afraid that it was a difficult visit simply because of my father's condition. A stroke had felled him in his sleep five months before, during a snowstorm, and he never rose from his bed again. A couple of other strokes followed, each one cleaving away at his life and functions (and I might add, at his dignity) without spiriting him away, and seemingly without impairing his mind. Throughout that spring and well into the summer he just lay in that bed like a man who had turned into a living corpse. His eyes were as alive as ever, following us with the same intelligence and comprehension as we spoke, just as if he had been sitting at his big desk in the library with his maps and books and balance sheets spread before him.

The Hardings had visited Tioga scores of times during the years, but I suppose it goes without saying that none of those visits was quite like the last, when they arrived as President and First Lady. Ever since the Inauguration, Mrs. Harding had had a genuine—and not unreasonable— fear that her husband would be assassinated, just as his mentor and fellow Ohioan, President William McKinley, had been shot and killed decades before. Thus to placate the First Lady's fears, President Harding's security detail was even more extensive than it otherwise might have been.

I remember Adeline and I were in this very room with Dad and the sun was shimmering in the treetops. I had just helped Nurse Boyle put a new bed shirt on him when we heard Spats, Adeline's little tan and white spaniel, running downstairs causing quite a stir, and then he was at the back screen door barking in his most businesslike tone, the one he generally reserved for tramps or cats on the prowl. I could hear Miss Evans trying to reason with him, and then she called out a greeting, which was answered by a man in the yard. Adeline and I immediately went to the panel of windows to see who on earth was out there, and we saw a local policeman walking along where the yard merges with the Old Forest, and another officer was a little ways into the Forest itself, peering among the trees. I suppose they were searching for any gun-toting Bolsheviks who might have somehow divined that the President was on his way to my family's house. (Earlier that summer the Justice Department uncovered a Bolshevik plot to kill the President by blowing up the White House yacht, the *Potomac*. This was said to be part of their master plan to destabilize the world and bring about "global revolution." Obviously, the conspiracy itself was heinous enough, but it seemed all the more treacherous and perfidious coming as it did after Mr. Harding had sent hundreds of millions of tons of food to the Soviet Union to alleviate the famine then laying waste to their vast nation.)

When Adeline and I went down to await the Hardings on the broad front porch, other policemen were milling about Tioga's park-like grounds, and some were lurking amid the trees across Mt. Vernon Avenue. Two agents wearing blue business suits, looking for all the world like bank managers, waited by the graveled carriage path, and in my mind's eye I can still see another rolling a cigarette, leaning against the rump of the bronze stag that has looked out across the front yard for the past sixty some years. He glanced at us and nodded, and for a moment his eyes settled on Adeline. I remember as we stood waiting on the porch, she said a little something that I forgot for a long time, but which then came back to me with a bit of irony, after a couple of years had passed. In a low voice that no one else in proximity could have possibly heard, she said, "Tristan, do you think all these guards can possibly keep Flossie from doing Warren in? I mean if and when she ever finally gets fed up with his ways."

I smiled. Mr. Harding's private life was, for various reasons, something of a joke between us—as I am sure it was with many other folks in Marion. I glanced at her and we exchanged the sort of conspiratorial little smile we had been exchanging all our lives, over this or that. "Well," I said, "I suppose they'd feel duty-bound to try, wouldn't they? Though they'd best put their own houses in order before they get in Flossie's way."

I hasten to add that Adeline and I both meant what we said strictly as a joke and nothing more.

I also recall very clearly that, as we waited, I was thinking about the job President Harding offered me in a letter that I had received the week before—hand-delivered by Wells Fargo. Dan Crissinger, former president of the Marion County Bank, was now Director of the Federal Reserve. Some sort of position was available at the Reserve and the President wanted me to come out and fill it. Frankly, I was thinking about how to politely turn him down. It would be the second time I had turned down a job with the Administration. Immediately after the elections, the President-elect had asked me to become Superintendent of the National Capital Parks East, but I was not interested in that job either, or in any other job in Washington. I rejected the position in part because we had already achieved our goal—the elevation of Senator Warren G. Harding to the Presidency of the United States. I simply was not interested in going to Washington. Besides, I had some very good reasons to stay here in Marion, and those same reasons were still valid. I needed to tend to my own business, which is to say, to Colonel Hamilton & Son. The economy was brisk in the early '20s, and a building boom was well underway. The local economy was especially strong in 1922, thanks in part to some very lucrative government contracts that had found their way to Marion's industries. And there was another very real issue at stake. So very many of Marion's talented residents—known in certain circles as the "Ohio

Gang"—had gone to Washington to help run the country, that it was a wonder that any of our banks, factories, businesses, or even our schools and hospital had anyone left at the helms. Or for that matter, at the oars. In fact, Argus Finch, my former right-hand man at Colonel Hamilton & Son, was now the Administrator of Public Buildings, and even "Pop" Baldwin, custodian for twenty-some years at the Courthouse, was now overseeing the small army of men who were sweeping the marble floors and changing the light bulbs at the Capitol. Frankly, it annoyed me a little that the President seemed to have forgotten my desire to tend to my own business here in Marion and was persisting in his attempt to twist my arm.

In some ways, I think he was actually trying to make amends with me, man-to-man, for certain personal infractions from about eight years before—back when I still had plenty of pink in my cheeks. I want to stress here and now that I was utterly devoted to President Harding, just as I had been utterly devoted to Senator Harding, and to Candidate Harding. But I had gotten it into my head that it was Warren Harding, the man, who was now trying to make amends with me via the person and prestige of the President. Man-to-man, I would not give Warren Harding the time of day, much less the personal satisfaction of atonement. And besides, President Harding certainly did not need me in Washington; if he had, I would have answered his call. Nevertheless, I hated the thought of having to turn him down anew, so in that way I was dreading the visit.

A few minutes after Adeline and I stepped onto the porch, we heard the low rumble of approaching automobiles and, rounding the distant curve of Mt. Vernon Avenue, the motorcade swung into view, proceeding through the tunnel of overhanging trees. A Marion police car led the pack, two long black sedans followed, and after them came the President's enormous, black Pierce-Arrow limousine, an agent riding on each running board beside the rear compartment; more sedans followed, preceding another local police car. I recall as well that a flotilla of jalopies trailed the motorcade at a respectful distance, crammed with young people, and far behind these a flock of boys on bicycles peddled for dear life trying to catch up, and far in the distance I could see other children and young people running in their wake. It was quite an impressive sight, both for the motorcade itself and for the tide of humanity being swept along in its wake. The lead police car and sedans pulled up along the curb of the avenue in front of Tioga, like sentries, and agents and policemen immediately disembarked and spread themselves over the periphery of the grounds. The other cars of the motorcade parked along the avenue as well.

Only the President's limousine swung onto the carriage path.

The Pierce-Arrow, with gold-tasseled flags fluttering and brass fixtures gleaming, had the presence of a gigantic black yacht floating gracefully up the long drive. It rode so high that not even Adeline, who was an inch or so taller than me, had to stoop in the slightest degree to greet our arriving guests. I had not seen either of the Hardings since I was in Washington the previous summer, and I must say that, looking at them through the windows, I was immediately struck by the changes in each. World-weary is the term that now comes to mind when I think back to how the President looked that day, with bags under his eyes and a somewhat florid hue that lay over his naturally bronzed skin. At first (as usual) he avoided my eyes. And puffy and haggard is how I recall the ever unhealthy but perpetually indomitable First Lady, looking out at us from that plush red and tan interior.

Decades before, Mr. Harding had nicknamed his wife The Duchess. It was a perfect fit.

The Duchess spoke first, calling through the open window even before the Pierce-Arrow rolled to a complete stop. "Aren't we a nuisance? All these agents and such!" When the car stopped, she continued, "I tell Warren, like it or not, it's simply got to be this way. Times have changed—that evil baldy Lenin trying to blow us up! We won't make that mistake again, will we Warren? Helping the Russians!"

President Harding had about thirty years of practice ignoring his wife, and he seemed not to hear any of this. The footmen opened the doors, and the President and First Lady stepped out. I remember that Mr. Harding looked very sporty and modern, wearing a pale green sports jacket with a tan tie, white shirt, white pants, and tan shoes. His usual greeting for male friends was a hearty handshake and a slap on the back, but I was never accorded the latter, owing, I believe, to some stiffness and formality that he perceived in my nature. But he always compensated with a handshake in which he grasped my hand in both of his—something, I noted, that he was disinclined to do with most men. Then at some point, he would lightly, almost timidly, lay his hand on my shoulder. But I remember his eyes more than his warm handshake that afternoon, or his old, familiar, "Hello, Tristan!"

"Welcome, Mr. President."

After initially avoiding my eyes, Mr. Harding scrutinized me in the same hangdog sort of way he had been doing for years whenever, after a time, we came anew into each other's company. As always it seemed as if he was half-afraid that I might hold a grudge against him. And again, as always, he seemed surprised by my cordiality and by the fact that I remained unflinchingly loyal and devoted to him, I mean to the President.

"You know, Trey, you can still call me Warren."

I nodded, and in my mind, I muttered, *Thanks, but no thanks.*

Adeline and the First Lady kissed each other on both cheeks, in the European fashion. Adeline had taught Flossie that custom some years ago, after my sister lived in Paris for two years before the Great War. Mrs. Harding was always keenly interested in such refinements. Indeed, I would go so far as to say that, even as First Lady, she seemed vaguely envious of the way certain people lived and appeared and carried themselves.

Meanwhile the flotilla of jalopies filled with young people was arriving, downshifting and backfiring, aligning themselves on the other side of the avenue, with the cyclists coming up the rear and the children on foot, still far off, running down the avenue. All were doing the best they could to contain their excitement. It was quite a scene.

In those days, two peacocks, Balthazar and Cleopatra, my father's pets, still resided on the grounds at Tioga, and as we came along the little walkway, towards the porch, Balthazar came strutting forward, blocking our way. He lifted and spread his magnificent tail feathers, as if to knock us all flat with bedazzlement. We stood there politely and watched. In fact, everyone was watching. Some of the agents laughed at the spectacle and the young people across the street began to applaud and whistle at his fine performance.

When Balthazar finished with his display, the President said, "Haven't changed a bit, have you old man!"

As we continued across the grounds towards the house, I asked President Harding how his trip was. "Long and bumpy and not enough signposts," he said. "We need to improve the roads in this country, I can tell you that firsthand. The automobile's here to stay and these wagon roads have had their day." Then he asked me about Lucy. (She was expecting a child, and did not wish to appear in public, especially in the company of the President of the United States.) Scores of young people continued to arrive en masse and gather across from the house. Once we were on the front porch, the President waved and gave them a big smile. The crowd wildly cheered, whistling and applauding as if they were at a rally. I found this adulation quite amazing, but I could tell that, by now, Mr. Harding was already very much accustomed to his fame and popularity. I distinctly remember that I was getting ready to broach the topic of the job at the Federal Reserve—to "beat him to the punch," as they say—when the President, still waving to the crowd, said, "So Trey, you got my letter, didn't you?" He threw a kiss to the young people who were now almost wild with elation, and cheering and whistling all the louder. I thought of Dad, paralyzed in his bed at the back of the house, his eyes no doubt moving over the ceiling as he tried to imagine the spectacle going on in front of his house.

"Yes, sir," I said. "Thank you, sir." Then I added, "I bet you get more cheers than Babe Ruth, even when he hits a home run."

He laughed, "Fat chance of that. I'm just President of the United States. He's Babe Ruth." Someone in the crowd seemed to catch his eye. He stared for a moment. Then he glanced to see where his wife was. She and Adeline were still out in the yard. They had stopped to admire the peonies along the porch, and Mrs. Harding seemed to be comparing the blossoms on one of the bushes with the blossoms printed on her dress. In a low voice, the President said, "That girl over there, Trey, the one in the yellow dress, with the yellow hair, don't tell me that's Nell Hypes?"

I spotted the girl he was talking about in front of the gathering crowd, in the tree shade across the avenue. Frankly, I felt a surge of contempt for Mr. Harding, which I am certain that I managed to hide. "As a matter of fact, sir, that is Nell." He was peering intently at the young woman in the distance. "Changed a little, hasn't she?" I said.

"I'll say she has!"

The President stared for a moment longer, and I heard him mutter, "Corn-fed."

He turned to me, and folding his arms, leaned on the banister—one of those man-to-man sorts of stances. "Well, Trey," he said, "about that

16

job. We sure could use a fellow like you out there, and Dan Crissinger, he's very keen on the idea. And I do mean very. Met with him in my office just before we pulled out. Says we can always use an intelligent young man like you, especially with your management skills and such, and your ability to get things done. The only thing that worries me is that it's an indoor job, and you're used to traipsing around outdoors some, so you'd have some adjustments to make."

I glanced back at Adeline and the First Lady. I suppose I was hoping that their presence would somehow rescue me from the awkward situation, but Mrs. Harding was still making her way along the walkway admiring the flowers, seemingly oblivious to the crowds. At that particular moment, I watched her smell the honeysuckle. She closed her eyes and, for a moment, seemed to disappear into the fragrance.

Before I had a chance to speak, the President added, seemingly quite seriously, "Besides, Trey, my Administration could use a few token Democrats. Helps balance things out." We both laughed at his little witticism. Then he added, "But I'm serious, Tristan. Really I am. You did such a mighty job during the Campaign, and during the War, not to mention the success you're having with Colonel Hamilton & Son— no surprise there. Now you should bring those same talents out to Washington. And you know how much Lucy likes DC. You do too, as I recall. So come on out and join the team and we'll set you up in a nice townhouse." He touched my arm so that I looked him in the eye. "I wish you'd take the job, Trey, I really, really do. In fact, I'd regard it as a personal favor."

"Yes," I said softly, "I know you would, sir. Mr. President, once again you have my heartfelt thanks, but you know things aren't good with Dad. You'll see that soon enough for yourself. Besides, the fact of the matter is, sir, someone has to stick around here and keep the home fires burning. Who'll manage Colonel Hamilton & Son if I'm gone? Argus is already out in Washington. We have a major building boom going on right now, right here, and there'll be all Indians around here and no chiefs. So, quite frankly, sir, I think I should stay in Marion."

For a long moment, the President did not say anything. He glanced off across the road, towards the young people. He nodded, "Well, I understand your reasons, and I don't want to twist your arm. Or rather, try to. But do me this honor, Tristan. Think about it for one week. Just think about it. Then telegram me."

"It's you who do me the honor, Mr. President. But I'll gladly give it some more thought and let you know."

After the ladies joined us on the porch, we went into the house. As usual, Mr. Harding stopped before the mirror in the foyer and adjusted his tie, and then we climbed the stairs to the second floor, with Adeline leading the way. She paused in the shadows in the front of the long hallway and said, in a low voice to the President and First Lady, "I just want to make it perfectly clear before you walk into that room that Papa's no longer even a shadow of the man you once knew." I remember that the President seemed winded from climbing the stairs. He was leaning on the little hall table before the mirror (both of which are still there), but the instant he caught his own reflection, he straightened himself. After he caught his breath, he nodded his readiness. When he did, Adeline said, "Brace yourselves." With that injunction, we continued in silence down the long, wide hall to the sunny room at the back of the house.

The President and First Lady had known Dad to be a voluble man of great vigor, congeniality, and substantial strength, especially considering his somewhat diminutive size. Thus even though the Hardings were amply warned about what to expect, I am absolutely certain that both were overcome the moment they entered the room and saw that little white stick of a man lying in the sheets. I suspect that the President had intended, in the back of his mind, to more or less give his old friend some version of his usual slap-on-the-back greeting. But for a long awkward moment after entering, they simply stood in stupefied silence. I mentioned before that I do not believe the strokes had affected my father's mind, but what I really mean is his intellect. His temperament was a different matter. Dad had never been an emotional man, but his illness had transformed him, often rendering him tearful. The Hardings had been warned of this, too. Dad had been watching the doorway as we came in, and during those four or five seconds as the President and First Lady stood there in stunned immobility, my father seemed to struggle within himself—but to no avail. The tears came. That is when the President went forward, his voice breaking as he said, "Oh, Colonel ... Colonel Hamilton." President Harding was not a man with a heart of stone, and I think it is to his credit that tears rolled down his cheeks as he said, "Oh Colonel, I'm so sorry, I'm so very, very sorry." Then the President bent and actually kissed his old friend on the forehead, as if he were a brother, and he moved his fingers through my father's white hair.

Historians like to say that Mrs. Harding was a shrill, hard, and an often-shrewish woman; true, but that was only one side of her. They apparently do not think it important to note that by turns she could be kind, generous, devoted, and loyal to those she held dear. After a moment, when the President stepped aside, Flossie too bent and kissed her old friend—the man who, I might add, so very long ago had indirectly made her marriage to Mr. Harding possible. Touching his cheek, the First Lady said, "There, there Colonel, there now. Warren and I love you very, very much." She kissed him again, and for a long moment closed her tearful eyes and pressed her cheek against his.

All the while, Adeline and I stood off to the side of the room. I was holding my sister's hand.

It is very awkward, of course, talking to someone who cannot respond in any way, but the President and First Lady persevered. I am certain that they anticipated this difficulty, and as such the President seemed to have his words ready. I remember him starting off by saying, "Colonel Hamilton, I want to tell you something. You remember telling me about your visit to the Grand Tetons? And how they should be in the public domain? Well, sir, I want you to be the first outside of the White House and the Department of Interior to know that I'm setting aside four hundred thousand acres, including all of Jackson Lake, for a brand new national park." The President was holding my father's hand. He paused and said, "If it wasn't for you, Colonel Hamilton, I may have set this one out. I had pressure enough from the speculators and bonanza companies to let them come in and take over. Instead there'll be a Grand Teton National Park. I intend to dedicate it myself next summer. And when I do, I'll be thinking of you."

During that visit President Harding also gave Dad a personal account of the dedication ceremonies at the Lincoln Memorial, which had taken place on Decoration Day. Flossie always got her two cents worth in, and she told Dad about the picnic she and the President attended the weekend before with their friends, the McLeans, whom Dad had met (and liked) in

Washington. Dad was a decorated veteran of the Indian Wars in the West, thus he was always interested in military affairs. The President became rather animated when he told us about the experimental aircraft carrier—I believe he called it the *Longly*—and how well its sea trials were going. So well, in fact, that he had decided, just a few days before leaving for Marion, to authorize the conversion of four more battle cruisers into carriers.

Dad followed all of this with keen alertness and interest in his eyes.

Back in those more leisurely days a visit with old friends could encompass hours, but for obvious reasons the Hardings did not stay long, only half an hour or so. At one point, Nurse Boyle and Miss Evans came in together, both shy and giddy, to pay their respects to the President and First Lady, and then they departed, the former leaving a tray of iced lemonades and sugar cookies. Just before the Hardings were ready to say their last good-byes, the President again took Dad's hand in his and said, "Colonel, don't ever think for a moment I've forgotten what you did for us, for Flossie and me, all those long years ago. Why, if it wasn't for you, everything would have turned out different. Who knows, I might be working in a factory right now and living out on the west-end. I am sure that everything, absolutely everything would have turned out different."

Soon the President and First Lady took leave of their old friend, promising they'd hurry back and see him the next time in Marion. That promise was just a nicety. Everyone in this room, including and especially Dad, knew that he would be in his grave the next time the Hardings rolled into Marion—whenever that might be.

Indeed, less than one month later, during the early hours of August 2, 1922, my father, Colonel Anthony Wayne Hamilton, died in the seventy-second year of his age.

Exactly one year later, to the very day, President Harding died in San Francisco.

IF YOU WERE ALIVE forty-three years ago, and of a cognizant age, and even if you have forgotten every other aspect of the famous Front Porch Campaign of 1920, then there is, nevertheless, one thing you surely have not forgotten—the rumor that flew across this nation that Senator Warren G. Harding was part Negro. The "Negro blood rumor" made headlines in nearly every newspaper in the United States, except one—

The Marion Star, which Senator Harding owned. By then I was president of the Harding Volunteers and I can tell you beyond any doubt that the rumor complicated things for us enormously. I can also tell you that the Negro-blood rumor was absolutely nothing new, either for us or for him. Indeed, the rumor had complicated his life since the very day he was born, just as it complicated the lives of his father and Hardings before him. When he was a boy, pupils in the schoolyard dubbed him "Nigger Warren"—and he was subject to their taunts, far more so than children who were actually of obvious African descent.

On his last visit to Tioga—when the President thanked my father—he was essentially thanking him for saving him from one of the many times that the rumor had reared its head. That was in 1890, three years before I was even born.

Believe it or not, the man my father saved Mr. Harding from was Mr. Amos Kling, Warren Harding's future father-in-law.

The Harding biographers always say that Amos Kling was "the town's richest man"—a "fact" that serves to illuminate the utter inaccuracy of their research into the President's life. I can personally assure you, as a lifelong resident of Marion, Ohio, and as a long-standing member of the board of trustees at two banks, that Amos Kling most assuredly was *not* the town's richest man. In those days Edward Huber was by far the wealthiest man in Marion County, and possibly in all of central Ohio. He was founder and president of the Huber Manufacturing Company, which made agricultural equipment that sold throughout the world, and it was he (not John Deere) who created the first gasoline-powered tractor. There was a time when Mr. Huber's company was neck and neck with both John Deere and Case Manufacturing. Believe me, Mr. Huber had the assets to buy and sell Amos Kling many, many times over. However, with that said, I must hasten to add that Mr. Kling was, in fact, a man of considerable wealth and power.

Mr. Kling started out as a lowly clerk in a hardware store, and eventually bought the hardware store. Like my grandfather, he made a good bit of money in Marion during the building boom after the Civil War. He was a land speculator, he was a banker, and along the way he founded the Marion Federal Savings and Loan, which is still thriving a full half century after his death.

Like everyone else in Marion, Florence's father knew all about the Negro-blood rumor. Now I wish to state at the outset that I do not wish to portray Mr. Amos Kling as some sort of villain, for he possessed many, many fine qualities. For instance, at the rear of his splendid house on East Center Street (where the Sunoco filling station now stands) there once stood a beautiful octagonal orchidarium, constructed of plate glass and copper, where he raised rare and exotic orchids of exquisite beauty. He often sent these flowers to folks who had fallen ill, especially in the dead of winter, when his were the only flowers blooming far and wide. I further wish to add that it did not matter to Mr. Kling if the recipients of his precious orchids were white or colored, Irish or Italian, or Protestant, Catholic, or Jew.

Also, Mr. Kling donated the land for the town's original YMCA, and he stipulated that *all* of Marion's citizens be permitted to enjoy the facilities. Mind you, I am speaking here of the 1890s, when Negroes, Jews, and Catholics, and just about every other non-Anglo-Saxon or non-Teutonic person, were excluded from such places.

And who paid for the building of Quinn Chapel, the old African Methodist-Episcopal Church out on Park Street?

Mr. Amos Kling, that's who.

What's more, I know for a fact that no man in this town was more beloved by his Negro servants than Mr. Amos Kling. Thus he most emphatically was *not* some sort of racial villain.

Except, I suppose, when it came to Warren Harding.

I am afraid that I cannot give you any insight as to why Mr. Kling hated young Warren Harding. My father used to say that Mr. Kling's vehemence preceded the courtship by many years. And of course I cannot give you any insight as to why or how, in turn, Florence Kling fell so deeply in love with the young man. Nor can I say a word, with any authority, as to why Warren responded to Flossie. After all, as the dubious part of his history shows, she most emphatically was not "his type." Even back in her youth, the most flattering adjective people could attach to Florence Harding was "homely." She also wore spectacles all of her adult life, was five years Warren's senior, and her ankles were often swollen.

By all accounts, Mr. Harding cut a dashing figure in his youth. He was tall with thick, jet-black hair, chiseled features, honey-colored skin, and striking gray-green eyes. I sometimes wonder whether, in certain less-practical female eyes, his natural appeal may have been enhanced by the very fact that he was also most "forbidden."

I believe that historians are completely on the mark when they say that one of the reasons Mr. Harding won the 1920 election by such a landslide was that women, who for the first time in history had the right to vote, found Senator Harding's robust masculinity especially appealing. (I might add that photographs never did him justice, *ever*—which might give you some indication of his personal magnetism.) By the same token I can assure you that—unlike the election of 1960—no man in this country was swayed to give the victor his vote because he had a glamorous and beautiful wife.

While I am on the subject, let me point something else out. The so-called historians always expect us to believe that Warren G. Harding's "laziness" was exceeded only by his "stupidity." That too is a bunch of bunk. He graduated from Ohio Central College in June of 1882 at the age of seventeen, the youngest in his class. Soon after graduation, he managed to buy the contents of a print shop for exactly thirty dollars, borrowed from his parents, and then he started his own newspaper, *The Marion Star*—which is flourishing to this day. Eight years later, when Florence Kling started courting him, the *Star* had the widest circulation of any newspaper in these parts, the only international news cable within a radius of forty-some miles, and a full-time staff exceeding thirty employees, not including paperboys. All of this before his twenty-fifth birthday.

What I can tell you about the courtship is this: Sometime during the summer of 1890, young Mr. Harding announced in the Social Notes of his newspaper that he was going to Lake Erie for a little vacation, and would be staying at Hotel Victory, on South Bass Island. Apparently, Miss Flossie Kling—already a thirty-year-old divorcee—read the note and followed the young man, whom she supposedly had long had her eye on. Thereafter, a romance ensued.

The romance continued in Marion, upon their return from the Lake.

I know that they managed to keep their romance a secret for a time, but a secret does not stay a secret for long in little towns. Soon everyone knew.

As the story goes, the last to know was Mr. Amos Kling.

At that time, his daughter was living in a set of furnished rooms in the brick house on Greenwood Street, right around the corner from

Mt. Vernon Avenue. Back in those days the independent Miss Kling supported herself by giving piano lessons. The hour that Mr. Kling heard about the romance was the same hour that he visited his daughter's rooms, demanding that she immediately desist from seeing "that nigger Harding boy"—or maybe he said "Nigger Warren." And it is not my literary contrivance to put those particular words in Amos Kling's mouth. My father said that Mr. Kling had been referring to him as such since the very day the young man rode into town on a mule, from Caledonia, in the early summer of 1882. Florence Kling was every bit as strong-willed as her German father. He threatened to disinherit her and she literally ordered him out of her rooms.

A very long time ago I heard that there was some kind of encounter between Mr. Kling and young Mr. Harding. Supposedly it took place in the alley behind the old Star Building, on east Center Street. The former promised the latter that, if he did not desist in courting his daughter, then he, Amos Kling, would ruin Warren Harding, and put him in the poor house.

Warren did not desist and, personally, I believe that Flossie's iron will had something to do with this.

I believe the next couple of months passed quietly. At some point, and I do not know if it was during those quiet months or thereafter, Warren and Flossie even attended Sunday morning church services. Around here, when a courting couple attends church together, marriage is usually not far off. Perhaps Warren had the impression that, because of the quiet, Mr. Kling's threat had been a bluff and that maybe he was going to look the other way.

Then a week or so before Christmas, 1890, Mr. Harding received a letter from a local attorney—from George Copeland, to be precise—informing him that Mr. Amos Kling had purchased all the notes that Warren owed on *The Marion Star*—totaling in excess of nine thousand dollars—and that he was calling every one of those notes due.

Essentially Mr. Kling had just become the owner of a newspaper and the building that housed it. He gave Warren Harding exactly forty-eight hours to either pay his debts or face bankruptcy.

Of course this sort of thing is highly illegal nowadays, but it was far from unusual back in the freewheeling days of robber barons, national and local.

As I said before, I was still years from this world, but I know that young Mr. Harding's sudden predicament became the talk of Marion. There is no doubt that some people were against him, for jealousy or whatever reason, but my father said that most folks were for him and they thought it shameful that Mr. Kling would do such a thing. True, I suppose a fair number of folks were resentful that a "nigger" had far surpassed nearly every other white fellow his age in terms of ambition and success, but by the same token a lot of folks respected him for what he had achieved at a very young age, against considerable odds.

Some of these people did not particularly care if one of Mr. Harding's ancestors, a hundred years before, or whenever, had "jumped the fence."

My father was one of those people. He liked and respected Warren. He also liked his newspaper and had faith in the young man's integrity, hard work, and ability to pay back a loan.

In utmost secrecy he lent Warren Harding the capital to pay off Amos Kling. The secrecy was not because my father was afraid of Mr. Kling; he simply did not believe in making undue trouble, either for himself or others. (The Harding family sent out a rumor that the money came from the Dickersons, some of Warren's mother's people elsewhere in Ohio.)

So you see, my father did, in fact, save young Mr. Harding from the poor house, or at least from a dismal life-sentence toiling in Mr. Huber's or in another of Marion's factories.

In the next few years, Warren Harding endeared himself, via his editorials, to Governor William McKinley, and to Governor McKinley's campaign manager and "king-maker," Marc Hanna. Those editorials were his first ticket into politics.

In other words, if not for Dad . . .

Warren Harding and Florence Kling were married in July of 1891.

For thirteen years Mr. Amos Kling did not exchange a single word with his daughter or his son-in-law. Not even when Flossie and Warren attended her mother's funeral. Finally, as Mr. Kling's life slowly came to its close, he reconciled with both of them, and—Scrooge-like—he spent his last Christmases with them, before setting out by rail for Florida.

In his last years, Mr. Amos Kling became something of a pioneer, building a winter bungalow on what was then still the wild Atlantic coast of Daytona.

On many of his nights in the bungalow, he wrote letters by candlelight to his daughter and son-in-law. (I keep those letters tied in a purple

ribbon in Mr. Harding's desk in the library of the Harding Home.) Mr.
Kling mentions the sticks of red cedar that he nightly burns in his stove
and the lovely fragrance that fills his rooms. He mentions the wreath of
orchids and wildflowers that he wove and dropped into the sea from a
pier in April of 1912, in tribute to the victims of the *Titanic*. He writes of
the call of the panthers in the mangroves, and how he falls asleep each
night listening to crash of the waves and to the rattle of the palmettos at
his window.

Each letter begins "My dearest Flossie and Warren" and ends, "All my
love, Daddy."

Mr. Amos Kling died in Marion in October of 1913, less than a year
before his son-in-law was elected Senator from Ohio, and seven years
before Mr. and Mrs. Harding moved into the White House.

FOR ME PERSONALLY, one of the most annoying rumors regarding
President Warren G. Harding has to do with my sister Adeline. I want
to say forthwith that she most assuredly was not one of the President's
mistresses. This is the plain truth, not the quibbles of an older brother
protective of his younger sister's reputation. I want to set the record
straight once and for all regarding this as well as even worse rumors that
have long besieged Adeline's good name.

This point about my sister leads me to the topic of President Harding
and the ladies. I admit that the President's known history in this area is
dubious, at best, which of course is one of the reasons his history has
stirred up so much embarrassment for us. As Mr. Harding ascended in
power, he began moving in a brilliant world of banquets, movie stars,
kings and queens, and lots of lesser subjects. There is no denying that he
liked girls and beautiful, extravagant ladies, but for whatever his reason,
he usually did his shopping, so to speak, at home. Indeed, every woman
with whom I have ever heard his name associated, for any length of time,
lived right here in Marion, Ohio. Maybe that had to do with the "corn-
fed" quality of our local girls.

President Harding's only publicly known mistress was, of course, Miss
Nan Britton, who lived a stone's throw from his mother's and father's place,
on East Center Street. She had a daughter by Mr. Harding, Elizabeth Ann.
Within a few years of the President's death, Miss Britton lined her purse

to the tune of one hundred and twenty-five thousand dollars in royalties from her tell-all, fireball memoir, *The President's Daughter*. In some ways I hold Dr. George Harding, the President's brother, responsible for this book, and likewise for the terrible turn President Harding's reputation took after his death. I did not know the late Dr. Harding very well. Back in the 1890s, he moved to Worthington, Ohio and opened a sanatorium, which is now operated by his son, also a doctor, and by all accounts, a fine one.

Miss Britton fell on hard times back in the 1920s, after the President and Mrs. Harding were both dead and gone, and she visited Dr. George Harding in his office in Worthington, seeking a lump sum of twenty-five thousand dollars in child support. He contacted me and, as president of the Harding Commemorative Society and executor of the Hardings' eight hundred thousand dollar estate, I strongly suggested that we placate Nan; unlike Dr. Harding, I did not think for a moment that she was lying. Dr. Harding both refused to believe Nan's story and he terribly underestimated what she could and would do. What she did was write a national bestseller. I can say for a fact that *The President's Daughter* did far more than any political scandal to ruin President Harding's reputation. If we had paid child support, as I suggested, then I am virtually certain that history never would have heard from Nan Britton, and President Harding's reputation would have been spared the most precipitous part of its fall. To this day I wish that Nan had known enough to come directly to me.

The last I heard of Miss Britton, she was living in Chicago. So far as I know, she has not set foot in Marion in forty years, possibly for fear of being tarred and feathered and run out of town on a rail by what's left of the feeble old "Ohio Gang." She probably has no desire to return as, to my knowledge, she has no people left here.

I do not know if Elizabeth Ann knows this, but she has a half-brother who is presently living in Columbus. In other words, as has long been rumored here in Marion, President Harding also had a son by another woman. "The Son"—as we generally referred to him back then—spent most of his life elsewhere: up north in Geneva-On-The-Lake, and then out in Boston, and now, in Upper Arlington, just this side of Columbus. The Eastern journalist H. L. Mencken, along with so many others, did everything he could to portray the President as a dimwitted buffoon, and yet, marvel of marvels, Mr. Harding produced a brilliant offspring. Arrian has a PhD in metallurgy—not exactly glamorous, though I think impressive enough. As far as I know, he still works as a scientist and engineer for Battelle Memorial Institute. As for his mother, she moved from these parts at the end of World War II and has resided more than a thousand miles west of here, in the state of Missouri, though I have heard that she would like to move back to be nearer to her family.

As far as I am concerned, Mitzy von Leuckel—Arrian's mother—was by far the prettiest of the President's mistresses. Mitzy actually hoped to become Mrs. Warren G. Harding. In fact, she walked away from marriage with an arguably much more suitable young man because she was bewitched by Mr. Harding and the extravagant hopes of someday marrying him and becoming a senator's wife, and then First Lady. It was not that Mitzy was ever foolish enough to have expected Mr. Harding to ruin his career by divorcing his wife and marrying a woman more than thirty years his junior. Rather, she expected Mrs. Harding to quite conveniently up and die from the chronic kidney complaint that every two or three years would flare up and drag her right to Death's door—only to retreat and wait for another day. That day finally came fifteen months after Mr. Harding's own death. If Mr. Harding had entered the Presidency as a widower, or became a widower while he was in office, then who knows, there may have been a White House wedding—along with a titillating scandal about the bride's Gibson-girl beauty and youth.

I assure you, if that marriage had taken place, then Mitzy von Leuckel Harding would have given Jacqueline Bouvier Kennedy some very stiff competition in the gallery of First Ladies, in terms of beauty and glamour, albeit certainly not wealth or privilege.

In a few short days I shall be seeing Mrs. Blaine—the former Miss von Leuckel—for the first time in about seventeen years. She will be coming to Tioga this Thursday afternoon, along with her only daughter and son-in-law, to share Thanksgiving dinner with me.

I have no doubt that Mitzy's impending visit and the assassination have triggered these long forays into the past.

II

We Were Here

AFTER SITTING UPSTAIRS for an hour or so doing absolutely nothing, I decided to come down to the library and do the same. Actually, I spent some time looking for the key to a small sterling silver box that Adeline kept here in the top drawer of the desk, but having failed once again to find such a key, I stashed the box in the back of the drawer, exactly where I found it after her death. I made a far more thorough search for that key once before and gave up in exasperation, just as I gave up again this evening. I am not even certain as to what curiosity spurred me on. I imagine there are just some old trinkets locked away within and maybe some souvenirs from Lake Erie.

As I mentioned earlier, the library is one of my favorite rooms here in lonely Tioga, just as it was my father's and Adeline's favorite. If you could see the library with your own eyes, I imagine you would know why. Off to my right, from the large desk where I am presently sitting, the north windows look across the wide porch and out across the grounds to Mt. Vernon Avenue. It is not a busy thoroughfare, as thoroughfares go. Every now and then I see the headlights of an automobile whizzing past as it enters or leaves Marion, and then all is still once again. From where I sit I can see, during the daylight hours, a portion of the antlers, heads, and necks of the bronze deer that have looked across the yard since around 1901. Along about this time of year, Adeline used to decorate the stag's horns with garlands of evergreen and red ribbons, and she used to hang a necklace of the same around the doe's neck. I remember one year when

Mrs. Christian bought Santa Claus hats and put them on the deer as a "surprise," while Adeline was out shopping. Secretly, my sister was not pleased, and "lost" the hats when the Christmas decorations were packed up and put away. I believe Mrs. Christian got the point.

When I swivel my chair during the daylight hours, I have a fine view through the triptych of enormous bay windows that look across the side yard to a remnant of the Old Forest. Many of those great oaks and sycamores date back to Indian times, and I am certain that some were alive during George Washington's day. One of my favorite features of these eastern windows is the stained glass elliptical cornice with the figure of a morning lark perched on a limb. During early mornings in late May and through most of June, the sun shines at such an angle as to cast a radiant blur of colored light that slowly moves across the floor, and then along the desktop.

To me, the library is best appreciated when the morning sunshine—something we have precious little of in dark November—streams through the windows with its golden light. The sun brings a warm luster to the dark green linen walls and illumination to my father's fine collection of oil paintings depicting forest scenes and Indian life. My favorite, both when I was a child and now, depicts General Francis Marion seated on a fallen tree with a British general and some Indians, all dining on roasted sweet potatoes. On the wall near the door hang engravings of several ancient monuments, including the temple of Assos in Asia Minor and the Tholos at Delphi, both of which influenced us in our designs for the Harding Memorial. Below these, matted in one frame, are drawings of the four finalists for the Memorial Competition, as well as a charcoal sketch of the tomb executed and given to me back in 1947 by the young historian I mentioned before. Adeline's collection of Venetian masks and sculpted faces is another noticeable feature in this room. They gaze silently from the walls, keeping me company, just as they once kept my sister company. And maple bookcases with beveled glass doors stand here and there, filled with more than two thousand volumes. These cases are of exceptional quality, handcrafted by a colored fellow named Cotton Tully, who worked his entire life for Colonel Hamilton & Son, and was one of our most valued employees. I am proud to say that Dad and I always paid a man what he was worth, and our Negroes and white men earned like wages for like work. In that way, I suppose Dad and I were a couple of radicals.

The only unpleasant aspect of the library is that during the construction of Tioga, while the house was still but a frame, a carpenter working in the upper rafters fell about forty feet, splitting his head open on the base floor, like a dropped watermelon, about eight feet from where I am now sitting. My poor little sister and I witnessed the fall. Adeline was six and I was eight. I have sometimes wondered if maybe seeing that fellow die such a horrible death might have affected my little sister in some way, though I also think it may have increased the bond between us. After Tioga was completed, and we moved into the house, I would sometimes slip into the library alone and stand over the spot where the man died, looking down at the floor while I imagined the hidden bloodstain a couple of inches or so beneath my feet. I knew that if one were to roll back the Oriental rugs, peel away the parquet that's as smooth as butter, and rip up the underlayer of hardwood, then there on the rough-hewn timbers would be the large stain where blood had pooled and soaked into the wood grain. Indeed even as an old man I have found myself, upon occasion, standing there before the desk looking down at the floor, imagining the dark bloodstain hidden away there so long ago.

To tell you the truth, I did that just a few minutes ago when I came into the room. But that, as they say, is neither here nor there.

Today's edition of *The Marion Star* was, of course, still filled with articles on the assassination of President Kennedy, and one of those articles was of particular interest to me. It is about the ways President Kennedy is being memorialized across the United States and throughout the world. It says that President Johnson will issue an executive order on Thanksgiving Day changing the name of Cape Canaveral to Cape Kennedy, and out in New York, Idlewild Airport will soon be known as John F. Kennedy Airport. Yesterday a large square in Berlin was renamed for the President, and the Queen of England is about to commission an impressive monument to be erected somewhere in the vicinity of Westminster Abbey.

Believe it or not, that same sort of global sentiment prevailed in the wake of President Harding's death. Out in California, the largest tree in the world was dedicated to his memory, and a mountain in Alaska was named for him, another in British Columbia, and there's a bridge somewhere in France that bears his name, as well as a street in London. Personally, I think that of all his honors, the President would have been most delighted with Marion Harding High School, and second to that, with the Harding Golf Course out in Hollywood, California. The President loved golf, and his good friend Will Rogers used his influence to have his favorite course renamed for his frequent partner on the links. The President, I might add, liked the company of movie stars, just as President Kennedy did.

Earlier today as I was reading the *Star*, it suddenly occurred to me that the Harding Memorial has the distinction of being one of the last colossal monuments built in the 20th century, and that there will almost certainly be no others. I cannot say that it was the last, per se, because the Jefferson Memorial came along a few years later—which brings me to a little known fact that I am personally quite fond of and cannot help but think of every time I see its image, as I did today during the funeral. You see, the Jefferson Memorial came very close to being the Harding Memorial. What happened was this: John Russell Pope, the architect of the former, submitted almost the exact same design (minus the portico) to the Harding Commemorative Society. It was certainly a strong favorite of ours, but we ultimately rejected it. According to one of those lunatic historians (I believe it was Samuel Hopkins Adams), the reason we turned down Mr. Pope's splendid design was because, if one were to imagine a giant handle sticking from one side, and a giant spout sticking from the other, then what would you have?

A colossal teapot—as in the Teapot Dome scandal.

Get it?

Once again we see the sort of bunk historians have attached to Mr. Harding's true history and record. Now I ask you, if the Jefferson Memorial were the Harding Memorial, then who on earth would look at it and conjure up in his mind a handle and a spout and then come up with a teapot? The very thought is nothing short of utter silliness. We rejected Mr. Pope's beautiful design simply because we preferred Henry Hornbostel's equally beautiful design. Both were exceedingly grand, but our personal tastes—especially my sister Adeline's—simply ran towards the latter. Besides, when I showed Mrs. Harding the designs just before her death, she remarked that the President had once mentioned to her that he would like to be buried beneath a willow tree. We did not feel duty-bound by this request, but the open cella of the Hornbostel design did in fact allow this. Aside from this point, Adeline just happened to know Mr. Hornbostel from her youthful days in Paris, and she greatly respected his work. I might add that all the members of the Harding Commemorative Society were exceedingly pleased when we learned that Mr. Pope's design would be realized in another form and place, with a statue of Thomas Jefferson beneath its dome, instead of Warren Harding.

Unfortunately, I doubt very seriously if our nation will build a monument in JFK's honor that is even remotely comparable to the magnificence of the Harding and Jefferson Memorials. By my lights there is something quite pedestrian in our "Space Age," and I suspect this fact will ultimately preclude the "impracticality" of a monumental tomb. If I had personally known President Kennedy, and if I were a young man again, then (presuming I had Mrs. Kennedy's permission) I would most emphatically undertake the campaign to build an appropriate monument. And I believe I would succeed—even though this is 1963, and decidedly not 1923.

Speaking honestly I would have to say that honoring President Harding was not our only reason for building a tomb of such overreaching splendor. In fact, I have to admit that there was more than a touch of justified spite behind our ambitions. You see, our initial idea for a memorial was something distinguished, but modest, along the lines of the simple block of carved granite that marks the resting place of President Hayes in Fremont, or the sort of elegant obelisk over President Jefferson's grave in Virginia, or the mausoleum that holds the remains of President Zachary Taylor in Kentucky. The Harding Commemorative Society had a variety of such designs in hand, and we were scheduled to make a final decision one Thursday evening in February of 1924, at a dinner meeting in one of the clubrooms at the Harding Hotel. The previous months had been brutal to the late President's good name and reputation—and I might add, by extension, to the good name and reputation of Marion, Ohio. Secretary of the Interior Albert Fall stood accused of fraud for leasing the Navy's Teapot Dome oil reserves to his friend, the oil tycoon Harry Sinclair, who of course made millions on the deal. And Attorney General Harry Daugherty was accused of numerous infractions, including obstruction of justice for his failure to prosecute his friend Charles Forbes, whom the President had named Director of the Veterans Administration. I should pause here to say that one of the many fine accomplishments that President Harding is never given credit for is his creation of the VA. You see, his father was a doctor here in Marion and a veteran of the Civil War, and Dr. Harding had long espoused the establishment of hospitals throughout the nation to care for old soldiers from the Civil War, Indian Wars, and the Spanish-American War. Then of course came thousands of young, battle-scarred and shell-shocked veterans from what was then called the Great War. When Mr. Harding reached the White House, he established the Veterans Administration to build hospitals to take care of the medical and convalescent needs of such men. Anyway, Mr. Forbes, its first director, had quite a scheme going. Shipments of bed linens, towels, medicines, and other such items arrived by trainloads at VA warehouses, whereupon, say, 50 or 60 percent of those shipments were immediately commissioned as surplus, and then promptly sold to private distributors, often on the same day as their arrival. I remember quite distinctly that February day when we were set to decide upon a suitable memorial for the President. That afternoon an article appeared in the *Star* regarding Mr. Forbes' newfound extravagant wealth, and his betrayal of President Harding.

And I also remember that on that very same day, Adeline walked into my office unannounced and came straight to my desk. I immediately knew that something was up; she seldom sullied the soles of her shoes by entering the warehouse and offices of Colonel Hamilton & Son. "Look at this, Trey," she said, handing me an editorial that had appeared in *The New York Times* a few days before, but which had just arrived at her door in the morning mail. "What are you going to do about this?"

I did not make a point of committing the editorial's exact wording to memory, but it referred to Mr. Harding's Administration as something like inept and the most corrupt in American history.

I would be a liar if I said that my heart did not sink upon reading that, especially in such a widely read and prestigious newspaper. Adeline stood (not sat) watching me. When I had finished, she said, "I'll leave this to you, Tristan. I'm sure you'll do something. Daddy would've."

She added, "See you tonight." And walked out the door.

Perhaps in the back of my mind I had already begun to formulate what I really wanted to do all along, which was also what Adeline really wanted us to do. I suppose that editorial assessment merely crystallized our intentions. I took the speech I had already prepared for that evening's meeting and unceremoniously tore it up and dropped it in the dustbin. Then in a matter of minutes I scrawled out a new one on the back of an envelope. As I penned the words, I had in the back of my mind the great Indian mound, hidden in the forest at Goose Pond Farm, our weekend place up in the Sanctuary Lands, north of Marion.

After composing my new speech, I found myself rehearsing in my mind a dramatic gesture that I conceived as a prelude to my address. It was to be the sort of flourish my father might have carried off with great success in his younger years. The Society had already selected five designs as finalists for the President's memorial, and these were to be displayed on a table at the front of the clubroom. It was now my intention, after dinner on my way to the podium, to pause thoughtfully before those modest designs, and then quite abruptly sweep them all to the floor with a single brush of my arm.

For better or worse, some hours later when I actually found myself before the gathered members of Society (a downcast lot, if ever there was one), I was too reserved to execute that flamboyant gesture. Instead, I paused before the nicely framed drawings, and then simply proceeded to turn each one facedown, one by one. By the time I reached the last design, utter silence reigned in the clubroom. I suppose one or two in the gathering may have thought that I was about to say something like, "To hell with it, let's just bury him." But when I reached the podium and glanced at my wife and my sister, I saw a subtle smile come upon Adeline's face and her chin lifted ever so little, as if she had read my mind; as for Lucy, she simply looked befuddled, like everyone else. This is what I said to those assembled:

> *Members of the Society: Since the tragic and untimely death of President Harding a little over a half a year ago, we have stood helplessly by and witnessed the destruction of his good name. We have seen how a small number of his so-called friends betrayed his faith and trust, and the faith and trust of our great nation. In betraying the President, they have become like carrion feeding upon his splendid reputation. Now I am sad to declare that newspapers, pundits, and*

*common people alike, all throughout the nation, are joining in the
ghoulish feast.*

*I say, let us repudiate them. Let us repudiate all those that
now denigrate the President's memory and insult his noble name,
disremembering all that he accomplished in so short a time and all of
the good that he did for our nation and the world. I say, let us spurn
these modest designs and build for him a monument so great that those
who come after us will think us mad for even attempting it. Let all the
world call us fools, if they wish, but let them say it with awe.*

*So I say then, let us build for President Warren Harding, our
beloved friend and neighbor, a monument of insistent ideals, one of
soaring majesty and splendor, a monument that will ultimately bear
witness for him, and for us, down through the ages of the world, saying
at last and forever: **we were here**.*

And that, of course, is exactly what we did, with financial help from
like-minded folks throughout the nation.

Having twice reread my speech this evening, it occurs to me that if
you are like most Americans then you are probably saying to yourself, "So
what the hell did Warren Harding actually do that was so damn great?"

Well, I shall be happy to enlighten you, though you must bear in mind
that the President was in office for less than three years. Eight hundred
and forty-one days, to be exact.

First and foremost I wish to say that it was President Harding—
not Woodrow Wilson, that schoolmaster turned dragonslayer, Hitler's
unwitting and distant enabler—who concluded treaties with Germany,
Austria, and Hungry, thereby bringing a formal end to the Great War.
And it was President Harding who personally conceived and convened
the Washington Conference between the United States, Great Britain,
France, and Japan. This was the very first disarmament conference in all
of history. President Wilson thought that we had actually fought the war
to end all wars, but Mr. Harding did not buy that line one bit. In fact, he
feared that an even greater and more horrific war was looming in the not-
too-distant future, and he hoped to avert that war by easing the rampant
militarization, the armed stillness that continued to grip so much of the
world in 1921 in the wake of the European conflict. Furthermore, President

Harding believed that if a second great war were to occur, and if America were once again drawn in, then we would probably find ourselves fighting in the Pacific against the ambitious and bellicose Japanese (which is why he invited them to the Washington Conference). As part of his peace initiatives the President discarded about thirty warships, but he had long been an advocate of preparedness. Thus even as destroyers were being turned into scrap metal, the first aircraft carriers were being developed. As a senator, Mr. Harding had toured Hawaii, including what was then the relatively small naval fueling station at Pearl Harbor. As President, he had it dredged and developed into a massive base capable of handling a vast fleet of future warships.

And President Harding displayed remarkable personal and political courage. One of his first acts in the White House was to send hundreds of millions of tons of food to the Soviet Union to alleviate the famine then laying waste to that vast nation. Mr. Harding did this out of moral duty, and I know that many in Washington (including his wife) wanted him to do a great deal less—in hopes that the fragile Bolshevik government might come tumbling down beneath the weight of the great famine. I might further add that the relief effort under the direction of Herbert Hoover was vastly effective. It is a simple historical truth that President Warren G. Harding— whose name seems forever linked with this or that dirty scandal—ranks as one of the greatest saviors of human life in the entire history of the world. The deliverance of the people of the Soviet Union is not the only example of the strength of President Harding's convictions. The Negro blood rumor followed him right into the White House. I believe that a less significant man in such a predicament would have distanced himself from any major issue having to do with colored people. But not President Harding. One day in 1923, the citizens of Birmingham, Alabama, sent the President of the United States an invitation to come down and help them celebrate their city's anniversary. To their amazement, he accepted. However, things did not unfold according to their expectations. In front of twenty thousand astonished whites, and ten thousand equally astonished colored people (in segregated seating, of course), President Harding railed the South for its treatment of Negroes, saying that a democracy is not a democracy when colored people do not enjoy the same economic and political advantages as whites. The President demanded this equality in an oration that was certainly the most powerful Civil Rights message delivered either above or below the Mason-Dixon Line by any President living or dead, including Abraham Lincoln. I will add that the President practiced what he preached. His Justice Department waged an active and aggressive war against the Ku Klux Klan and "barbaric lynching," and he demanded that his cabinet officers find good positions for competent Negroes in the federal government, both in and out of Washington.

In spite of a bitter outcry from conservative Republicans (including the First Lady) and Democrats as well, President Harding pardoned Eugene V. Debs, the radical Socialist who had gone to prison rather than go to war. Twenty-some other political prisoners who had violated the Sedition Act of 1918 were set free on that same Christmas Eve, and the radical Debs respected Mr. Harding's political courage for the rest of his life, refusing to speak ill of him—when just about everyone freely did so, with a vengeance.

Not only did the President create the Veterans Administration, he likewise proposed the Department of Public Welfare to expand and improve America's educational system, to aid in the care of the sick, and to propagate child welfare. He prodded and cajoled, and cajoled and prodded the United States Steel Corporation to abandon the twelve-hour work shift and adopt what he believed was a more reasonable eight-hour shift, and when that happened, I think in the spring of 1922, the rest of American industry and commerce almost immediately followed suit. The President also demanded a new law abolishing child labor, after the old one was struck down during the Wilson Administration. He got his new law. And after his long motoring trip from Washington to Marion in the summer of 1922, he called for the Federal government to oversee a national program of highway construction and maintenance. He signed the Highway Act, establishing the creation of the extensive system of interstate roads that now crisscross this nation. In so doing, Mr. Harding brought about the building of more roads than any single man on earth since Caesar Augustus. He created the Bureau of Aeronautics (now known as the Federal Aviation Administration), and he convened the first National Conference on Commercial Aviation. He expanded airmail delivery and pressed Congress for the development of airfields, the development of national air routes, and ways to control air traffic.

He called for the mandatory inspection of airplanes and the testing and licensing of airmen. Likewise he formed the Federal Radio Commission (which latter became the Federal Communication Commission) for the purpose of regulating radio, including the licensing and control of frequencies.

Warren G. Harding—our "worst" President, our "do-nothing" Chief Executive—did all of these things and more during his all-too-brief tenure in the White House. Yet who remembers any of this?

Just a lonely old widower living in a big, rambling house out where the sidewalk ends on the edge of long-forgotten Marion, Ohio.

And I might add that, like my father and sister, I am a lifelong Democrat.

There was a time when the good people of Marion were rather harshly criticized on various fronts (indeed, even lampooned on Vaudeville) for ostensibly viewing the White House as a sort of trophy that we hoped to win for our greater glory. Supposedly our boosterism, envy, and arrogance were such that we collectively came to this conclusion: Since Ohio is already known as the "Mother of Presidents," and since six other communities (including Delaware, only twenty miles south of here) have already sent men to the White House, then why not Marion?

I cannot wholly deny that our ambitions were such, but I ask you, what community, small or large, then or now, would not strongly back one of its own sons (presuming he were a qualified and decent fellow) if it seemed that he might become the President of the United States? Has there ever been a case wherein an American town remained indifferent to one of its own who seemed destined for the White House? Was Canton indifferent to McKinley? Or Springfield to Lincoln? Or Hyannis Port to Kennedy?

I think not.

As far as I am concerned, the accusations that we "chose" Warren Harding and then simply tailored him for the Presidency are ludicrous. If Marion's only goal was to win the White House for one of our own, would we purposely have selected Mr. Harding as our standard bearer, considering all of the rather unique and cumbersome baggage that he came with?

Again, I think not.

As you no doubt have already gathered, some of those hurdles came in the form of shapely young ladies. The most troublesome of the lot (at least during Mr. Harding's lifetime) was most emphatically Miss Mitzy von Leuckel. As I mentioned before, Mitzy will be coming here with her daughter and son-in-law for Thanksgiving dinner. When Mitzy walks through the doors of Tioga on Thursday, November 28th, at around four o'clock in the afternoon, it will be the first time she has set foot in this house since a lovely Sunday afternoon in August of 1914—nearly fifty years ago, a few hours after she and I had returned from church.

III

❦

The Great War Strikes Home

IF YOU ARE AN AFICIONADO OF HISTORY then you need not be reminded that the aforementioned date was the month and year when World War I began in Europe. I assure you that Mitzy's last visit had absolutely nothing to do with that faraway conflict, but two visits that I paid to her, slightly more than four years later, in August of 1918, and then again in October of the same year, had everything to do with the Great War. By then, Marion boys were dying in the trenches of Europe. Mr. Harding had become Senator Harding and, at least to me, he was starting to look very presidential. What's more, the elections of 1920 were fast approaching. President Woodrow Wilson harbored a strong dislike for Senator Warren G. Harding, a dislike that seemed to outrun any political conflict the two men and their opposing parties had ever had. To tell you the truth, I think Wilson would have done almost anything to block Senator Harding's ascent.

Now if I were to come right out and say that Miss von Leuckel was widely suspected of being a German agent, right here in Marion, Ohio, then one might suddenly decide that I am a foolish old man who is not even worth his weight in salt. Quite frankly, I probably am a foolish old man who is not worth my rather meager weight in salt, but I assure you there was a very good reason for us to think that Mitzy was indeed an agent of Kaiser Wilhelm.

I suspect that nowadays when most people think of secret agents, they envision the sort of man recently popularized in spy novels. Now I should say that my reading material does not include that sort of thing, but I have seen such paperback novels with their racy covers lining the racks at Henny & Cooper, our local drug store, and my impression is that those fictionalized agents are something of a cross between Superman and Valentino. When I speak of German agents during and before America's entrance into the European War, I am speaking of another kind of agent entirely.

For instance, in 1915 the members of the Board of Directors of the Huber Manufacturing Company were just about to commence their monthly meeting. The door of the boardroom opened, and in walked a fashionably dressed stranger. Now mind you, I was not present, but the incident became a much bandied about affair in Marion, and besides, I knew every single one of the members of the Board. This fellow introduced himself to the gentlemen as a hardware merchant (I no longer have the slightest idea what he called himself), and then he proceeded to pass his credentials around the table, and unroll his designs. I have always had a mind for numbers, if not names, and I distinctly recall that he offered the Huber company exactly eight hundred and fifty thousand dollars in cash up front, to be delivered by the Guaranty Trust Company of New York, along with the payment of all costs incurred, if the company retooled three of its buildings (he even suggested which three) in order to manufacture armored tractors capable of pulling field artillery. Furthermore, this fellow informed the Board that one of the buildings on the premises was ideally suited for the manufacture of shell casings for field guns and howitzers. Under his plan, shell casings and armored tractors alike would be sold through an agent in Luxembourg to various European powers. When a member of the Board asked exactly which European powers he had in mind, he said that one of the advantages of America's neutrality was that we could sell anything we pleased to anyone we pleased, and that everyone over there was buying. It was glaringly apparent to all present that this fellow could not have known more about the Huber company if he had worked there himself, and when he was asked how he knew so much, he said something to the effect, "Research, gentlemen. Research. The beauty of information!"

Well, I assure you that no book or library in the land contained the kinds of specialized details he knew about the Huber plant, and there was no doubt that his information came from inside the factory itself. When he departed, he left the address of a postal box, I believe in Cleveland, where he could be contacted. Some members of the Board went to the window to watch this mysterious gentleman depart. Looking out upon Greenwood Street, they saw him hastening down the walkway and through the factory gates. He climbed into the back of a long chauffeur-driven Mercedes-Benz.

It is obvious that at least two agents were involved in this incident. The first, of course, was the arms merchant himself; the second, an unseen agent working somewhere within the Huber company. This particular secret agent probably dressed in overalls, carried a lunch bucket, and went home at the end of the day to his wife and children. I would venture to say that he may have been born and raised right here in Marion and had probably never set foot in Europe in his life. I would also venture to say that he was devoted to Germany and acted solely out of devotion to her, and may not have collected a single dime for his information. (Granted, I may be naïve regarding this particular point.) At any rate, scores of men who worked at Huber were of German descent, as was the late Mr. Huber himself. I should add that in the early days of the war in Europe, before America entered the conflict, many were members of the powerful brotherhood called Friends of the Fatherland. I know for a fact that the German network was so sophisticated that information from a factory worker in Marion, Ohio, could easily make its way all the way back to Potsdam, the home of the German emperor, his government, and his rich treasury. Indeed, I do not think it is too farfetched to say that the eight hundred and fifty thousand dollar offer to retool the Huber plant may have emanated directly from Sanssouci, the palace of Wilhelm II and his family.

While Mitzy von Leuckel may not have been an official agent of Wilhelm II, with her very own dossier stashed somewhere in an office on Wilhelmstrasse, Miss von Leuckel most certainly would be considered a traitor under the parameters set forth by the Espionage Act of 1917, as well as the Sedition Act of 1918. And I assure you, if not for Miss von Leuckel's charms and connections, and if not for the benevolence and concern of a certain someone here in Marion, then she no doubt would have done time in the Ohio Penitentiary. Nor can I say for certain whether she was a sort of

Marion-based Mata Hari, communicating military secrets to the German military, or whether she was solely an agent of propaganda. Or both. Now when I speculate as to whether Mitzy was another Mata Hari, I do not for a moment mean that Senator Harding, as a high-ranking member of the Senate Military Committee, would have been foolish enough to divulge to her any secrets of war or state, the way the English officers did with the infamous Mata Hari. Indeed, Mitzy's German sympathies greatly distressed Senator Harding. I have two letters to prove it. What I mean is that, on one occasion during the course of the war, she attempted to lead me—in an indirect but dangerous sort of way—to believe that she may have been up to no good. I suppose one could say that she was thumbing her nose at me, and she did so while she was back East "secretly" visiting her beloved Warren. On yet another occasion, she flaunted her German interests in a most audacious way. That was the time when I visited her in her rooms.

It occurs to me that, before I tell you what happened on these two occasions, I ought to briefly relate a little something about myself and the capacity I filled during the Great War. First off, I regret to say that I did not have the privilege of soldering "Over There." This was due to a youthful history of asthma, a malady I pretty much outgrew with passing time. I cannot tell you the profound depth of shame and disappointment I felt on that spring day in 1917 when I received my medical deferment, and no amount of cajoling or pleas on my part would sway the army physicians. My feelings of shame were made all the more acute because my father was a decorated hero of the Indian Wars and my grandfather was a hero of the Civil War; both achieved the rank of colonel. Indeed, my youthful dream was to be the third colonel in our family. Or even a general. Gladly would I have fought for my country, and if necessary, gladly would I have died (though I would not have been so keen on being disfigured or blinded or made an invalid). Indeed, I even seriously considered crossing Lake Erie, entering into Canada, and joining the Canadian Expeditionary Force. I was ultimately dissuaded by the reality that the Canadians almost certainly would not want me either. Besides, my father pointed out that my condition might easily compromise the performance and safety of others on the battlefield, and that I was essentially putting pride and selfishness before duty and patriotism. I remember he said, "Some men have a greed for valor, Trey. Don't be one of them. They come to bad ends." Senator Harding became aware of my plight and personally stepped in. He saw to it that I would be able to serve my nation right here at home in two very meaningful capacities: as a member of both the War Industries Board and the United States Committee on Public Information. I served in these capacities as a "dollar-a-year man," meaning that I served my country without compensation

On the WIB, I helped oversee the conversion of Marion's plants to the production of war materiel. That German agent who called on the Board members of the Huber Manufacturing Company seemed to have possessed a bit of prescience, for in 1917 we began the manufacture of a five-ton armored artillery tractor capable of crossing the most treacherous landscapes, towing a 4.7-inch howitzer. The tractor, an adaptation of the rugged Huber Phoenix model, would help ensure that our artillery would be able to keep pace with the shock troops once our boys broke through the Hindenburg Line, thus preventing restabilization of fleeing Huns. In all, the changeover of our factories was a rather easy task. It was all logistics, reorganization, and conversion, as well as the marshaling of resources and available labor. In a sense the changeover evolved almost with the progression and beauty of mathematics.

My task on the Committee on Public Information was a bit more challenging. Essentially, I was charged with overseeing the loyalty of everyone within my jurisdiction, which is to say, Marion County. The CPI was more or less a propaganda organization established to ensure that American public opinion unwaveringly supported our involvement in the war, but the Committee was not just some sort of governmental advertising agency, distributing leaflets, posters, and such. The CPI censored newspapers and individuals alike, and it had broad powers of compliance, backed by the Sedition and Espionage Acts. Infringement of either could lead to prison, and charges of espionage could lead to the firing squad. It is now an almost forgotten fact but, to say the least, America during the Great War was most definitely *not* a debating society. The CPI was linked with the Secret Service, whose powers and responsibilities during the Great War far exceeded protecting the President and tracking down counterfeiters. Looking back, I would go so far as to say that some of the powers of the SS (the acronym for the Secret Service before Hitler rendered the use of those initials inconvenient) were occasionally nothing less than sinister.

My tandem positions with the WBI and the CPI made me the Commander of the Marion Branch of the Home Front Army—meaning civilians, young and old, engaged in war work. Looking back, I think it was the most topsy-turvy time that our community ever experienced, even more so than during World War II. The Great War was a bit like the opening of Pandora's Box—out came flying the 20th century. Anyway, my real point is that ladies, when they were not filling in for their husbands or sons or brothers in the factories or the railroads, et cetera, were spending their time folding bandages and knitting, in gray or khaki yarn, things like hot water bottle covers for the Army, along with pullover sweaters, half-finger gloves, socks, and other such items. Of course men too old or too lame for the trenches were also keeping busy, and so were boys. They filled in at the factories as well. They were also spending hours every day in schoolrooms, the gymnastics room at the YMCA, and the dark, heavy paneled clubrooms of the secret societies, where they seemed to talk quite a bit about tanks, aerial dogfights, battleships, and the size and range of cannons, while they too busied themselves with knitting needles on behalf of our boys Over There.

In addition to organizing and overseeing all of the above, my position as Commander also called for me to keep a close eye out for dissenters, aka enemy agents. Miss Mitzy von Leuckel's parents were raised in Bavaria, and both Mitzy and her brother spoke fluent German. Mr. von Leuckel died during Mitzy and Cedric's childhood, and in 1915 or 1916, the mother and brother moved to Bucyrus, about eighteen miles north of here, where he married and opened a bakery which became famous for its cinnamon buns and pumpernickel. I am certain that Mitzy remained in Marion because of her love for Senator Harding. She was standing by, so to speak, just in case the ailing Mrs. Harding happened to be gracious enough to drop dead.

At some point between the summer or fall of 1914 and the summer of 1917, Mitzy lived in Washington. I am not sure of the dates, but I am certain that once the United States entered the war, Senator Harding sent her packing back to Marion because of her pro-German views. She studied history at George Washington University and upon her return, with the

Senator's help, she secured a job teaching American History at the old high school, on the northwest corner of Center and Oak. By all accounts, she conducted her classes with enthusiasm and dedication. This is going to seem like an absurd point to make in 1963, but I had reliable reports that in the midst of the war, Miss von Leuckel was saying "Geshundheit" whenever one of her pupils sneezed, instead of a simple "God bless you."

My reason for pointing this out? Because speaking the German language, as well as the intentional use of words and phrases of obvious Germanic origin, was regarded as an act of sedition and was strictly prohibited during the war. Doing so could result in heavy fines and imprisonment. Indeed, the CPI published a list of words that one ought to avoid, and "geshundheit" was Word Number One. (Someone asked me once what Word Number Two was—it was "frankfurter.") Miss von Leuckel also referred to Daylight Savings Time as "unnatural," and I had it on good authority that, at least for a time, she refused to adjust her watch accordingly. You are probably saying to yourself, "So what!" My point is this: Daylight Savings Time was an innovation linked directly to the war, implemented not only to save coal, but also to create more time at the end of day for gardening and the tonic of athletics, thereby contributing to national health and strength. Grumbling about it qualified as sedition, and legally branded one as an agent of the Kaiser.

Right or wrong, as Commander of the Marion Branch of the Home Front Army, I usually chose to look the other way regarding such minor acts of "treason." Even as a young man I had enough wisdom to know that the war, in spite of its scope, would not last forever, and I knew that when hostilities ceased, I would have to go right on living in Marion with people I had known my entire life. And besides, even if I did not have to go on living here, even if, for instance, I had plans to close up shop and head for Timbuktu, do you think that I would want it on my conscience that I had sent someone to prison just because President Woodrow Wilson had chosen to dispense with the civil liberties guaranteed by the Constitution of the United States of America and the Bill of Rights? Do you think for a moment that I wanted to have a hand in sending to jail the Reverend Cedric Fitchblood of the African Methodist-Episcopal Church, just because in one of his Sunday sermons he cited Jesus as a pacifist? Believe it or not, I know for a fact that in 1918 a Congregationalist minister somewhere in Vermont got fifteen years for a similar sermon; my CPI counterpart was the patriot who had him arrested. (The Vermont minister was to be pardoned by President Warren G. Harding.) Can you blame me for looking the other way when Miss von Leuckel came to my notice yet again—this time for having the audacity to teach the American Revolution in her American History class?

Yes, the American Revolution.

Now you will have to bear in mind that any discussion of the Revolution—presuming it were relatively thorough—would run the risk of casting the British in a less than favorable light. The sentence for doing so?

Fifteen years.

Mitzy quickly developed a first rate reputation as an impassioned and dedicated teacher. In addition, she could be found, without fail, folding bandages in Crawford Hall, the basement of the Presbyterian Church on each and every weekday afternoon between the hours of 3:30 and 5:00, and on Saturday mornings as well.

So I compromised duty to my nation by looking the other way—just as I had done with the Reverend Fitchblood and a few others who happened to speak their minds, in this way or that.

But in August of 1918, Miss Mitzy von Leuckel at last pushed things a bit too far.

She spent several weeks of her school vacation up at her aunt's house on Lake Erie as well as back East, telling folks before she left that she was going to visit kin. But when the Superior in Crawford Hall whispered that in my ear, I was not fooled for a moment. I knew very well, and so did certain others, that Miss von Leuckel was going to engage in sexual trysts with her beloved Warren. Now I would be the first to admit that, on a strictly personal level, this was none of my business, but on a civic level, I think it was very much my business. As I have said, to me the Senator was looking very presidential, though I think you will agree that he would look somewhat less presidential if it ever got out that he was consorting with a mistress. Or two. Granted, the press has never been overly inclined to carry that sort of thing, but it seemed to me that it might make a bit of a difference if the Senator had a mistress of recent German extraction. God help us if, courtesy of the Sedition and Espionage Acts, the said Teutonic mistress qualified as one of Kaiser Bill's agents. I knew very well that if anything ever got out about any of this, then Senator Harding's whole political career would be torpedoed and his possible presidential candidacy, which I was beginning to perceive in the summer of 1918, would be keeping the *Lusitania* company. As for the two lovebirds and the conduct of their affair back East, I suppose that the Senator had rented a suite of rooms for Miss von Leuckel somewhere in Washington, and I have reason to believe that the two of them would go sneaking off on little escapades, probably while Mrs. Harding was at Friendship, Evelyn McLean's estate in McLean, Virginia. To be frank, in spite of myself I sometimes pictured the two of them in my idle thoughts: stepping from a cab in front of a swanky hotel in New York, walking along a beach in Virginia, with him maybe pulling her close, kissing her hair that was as yellow and gleaming as corn silk, the Senator signing false names into the ledgers of cozy hotels up and down the coast.

While Mitzy was out East she was thoughtful enough to send me a picture postcard—the first correspondence I had received from her since Valentines Day, 1914. She sent it to me at Colonel Hamilton & Son, obviously so my wife Lucy would not see it, though there was absolutely nothing personal about this card. Actually, I believed at the time (and still believe) that Mitzy was deliberately thumbing her nose at me in my official capacity. I say this because the postcard did not depict the Washington Monument, Coney Island, the Stature of Liberty, or anything like that. Instead it was a tinted picture card from Port Jefferson, New York, showing the armed merchant cruiser *USS Francis Marion* weighing anchor. General Francis Marion is of course, the namesake of our town. Now I have never been a meticulous saver of correspondence the way Adeline was, so that particular card disappeared decades ago, but I very clearly recall that, in her elegant and flowing script, Mitzy had written something about how it made her heart swell with honor or pride or some such patriotic mumbo-jumbo to see the hubbub of naval activity, the loading of troops and materiel and such.

Again, you are probably thinking to yourself, "So what?"

Well, the point is that just before Mitzy headed East to rendezvous with her lover, I commissioned dozens of school boys—"soldiers" of the Children's Garden Army—with the task of distributing hundreds of CPI leaflets all throughout Marion. One side of the leaflet warned that the Kaiser's agents frequented industrial areas, so citizens should be on the constant look out for people lingering near factories, especially the "hyphenates"—meaning anyone who had ever displayed an inclination to think of themselves as, for instance, German-Americans, as opposed to just plain Americans. The other side warned that naval ports were among the spy's favorite haunts, and that the Kaiser's agents communicated best with their high command from the vantage of coasts, along which submarines prowled. The CPI leaflet warned that a spy could sink a ship with the aid of a strong flashlight, a clear night, and a code.

Four days after I received that card, a German U-boat torpedoed the *Francis Marion* as it steamed across the North Atlantic. I must hasten to add that the ship was sailing out of Southampton, England, towards Port Jefferson, not vice versa. In other words, when I read in the *Star* of the loss of the *Francis Marion*, I regarded the timing as being purely coincidental, for Miss von Leuckel almost certainly could not have had a hand in the tragedy, even if she was Marion's own Mata Hari. Nevertheless, in light of Miss von Leuckel's teasing card and her various other infractions, I decided that it was high time for me to step up and do my duty and confront her in my official capacity, and I was determined to do so immediately upon her return.

She arrived back in town either on a Monday or a Tuesday, less than two weeks after the sinking of the *Francis Marion*, and a week or so before school was set to begin. I remember that some rather sudden and important business had come up that week regarding the manufacture of the armored tractor, though I no longer recall exactly what it was—the nearing depletion of a needed part, I believe, a valve or something of that sort. Yes, I think it was a valve. And besides, another Marion boy died in battle, and the woeful task of informing his mother and sister fell to me. Thus I did not get around to approaching Mitzy until Friday afternoon. Maybe I should have called on her in the privacy of her rooms, but for whatever reason, I did not. Instead I decided to speak to her during my biweekly inspection tour of Marion's war-work facilities. When she did her war work at the Presbyterian Church, she did it standing up, folding bandages and slings at a table in the back of the basement, while the other ladies either sat together in sewing circles doing their knitting, or else at tables folding slings and bandages. I remember when the war began, when we were recruiting for the Home Front Army, Mitzy said to Mrs. Barker, in what I am told was an icy tone, "I do *not* knit."

So she folded.

Mitzy was not really what people nowadays call "anti-social"—not that she ever cultivated large numbers of friends—but for some reason when she had a task to accomplish, she seemed to prefer working alone. I have never been one to make a spectacle of myself, but I remember how I rehearsed in my head the way I would slowly walk up to her—with my boot heels clicking on the stone floor in an authoritative manner and my hands clasped behind me—while she toiled with her back to the door, and thus to me. My footsteps would cease a few yards behind her. After a moment, her chin would rise and her hands would tentatively cease in their folding. Then slowly, reluctantly, she would turn and look over her shoulder, and there I would stand in my uniform, the embodiment of terrible powers. I had also rehearsed various chastising lines that I intended to spring upon her, and I would address her by her formal name, which I had never done in my life. I would say, "So Miss von Leuckel, it seems that in the past four years you have neither gained wisdom, nor discretion. 'Tis a pity, for these are dangerous times." And another line that I had invented was, "Miss von Leuckel, for all of your supposed dedication to Senator Harding, it seems you have no qualms whatsoever about entangling him in your web of Teutonic sedition."

I suppose I should add that Mitzy and I had scarcely exchanged a word since that aforementioned Sunday afternoon in August of 1914, just cursory nods or an occasional "hello" when we had the misfortune of passing each other on the sidewalk. Then came the era of war work, making it necessary for us to exchange a chilly and formal, "Good afternoon." I should add that I always made a point of saying a word or two of well-deserved praise regarding Miss von Leuckel's excellent war work and her devotion to it. This was exactly the sort of praise that I accorded to the other ladies, and the men and boys as well for a job well done.

On that Friday in August, I took special care with my uniform, seeing to it that Nora—our Irish housekeeper—had it perfectly pressed and creased and that my boots had what soldiers once called a "spit" shine. Of course I always appeared in a way that I hoped would bring honor and dignity to my appointed station, but on this particular day, I looked more closely for lint and dog hair.

I remember rain had been falling earlier that day, but the rain had ceased by mid afternoon, and the day was now just dreary and overcast—

the kind of day that used to give Lucy the "blues." And as I have already indicated, that day's sorrows were compounded by the news—telegraphed in on Thursday afternoon—that Marion had lost yet another soldier. Cpl. Orley Boyd had fallen before German machine-gun fire either in, or somewhere near, the village of Ourcq, France. Orley was, by the way, my classmate. I remember when we were children in the schoolroom, the holes in his shoes patched with cardboard, and his safety-pin "buttons," and I remember how proud he stood in his A.E.F. uniform at the train depot, and his smile and hearty handshake when I came to bid him a fond farewell, and I remember how he seemed to see something in my eye; he laid his hand on my shoulder and said, in a quiet voice, "Don't feel bad Trey. You'll be fighting right beside us here at home." That was Orley—generous to a fault, even to someone like me, even if the only thing he had to offer in this life was a kind word. And good God, to think that this world's only bequest to Orley was a white cross above his head in Flanders, courtesy of Mr. Wilson and those quarrelsome old men an ocean away in Europe.

I parked my Oldsmobile in front of the church on Prospect Street, near the alley, some two or three minutes before 4:00 P.M., which would allow me to arrive precisely on the hour. No one was expecting me at that particular time; it was simply the hour I had set for my own entrance. As I sat in my automobile, I took from my jacket the telegram that had arrived that morning from Senator Harding, and I reread it. He asked that I extend his regards to our war workers, and his condolences and "shared sorrow" at the loss of Cpl. Boyd. I had already read it several times, though there were only three lines. I folded it again and put it back in my jacket pocket. In my mind I could see Miss von Leuckel's graceful hands moving in their elaborate motions, perfectly folding one bandage, then another. More than once on my rounds I had stood off to the side speaking to this or that lady, glancing at Mitzy, watching her work. Something in the rhythm of her hands drew my eye, and I distinctly remember thinking that watching her hands was like "watching" music. I know that is an odd way to put it, but that is the way it was.

It is odd the small things the mind retains even after so long a time, and the seemingly large things that slip away. I say this because, as I think back, I have no idea why, but I distinctly remember sitting in my

Oldsmobile watching a family of sparrows bathing in a puddle beneath the dripping elms. They were splashing about like children in a pool, and I thought, "They are as oblivious to the Great War as we are to the moons of Jupiter." As I watched, the harmonica strains of "It's a Long Way to Tipperary" floated over the sultry air from Crawford Hall. A moment later the Courthouse bell commenced tolling the four o'clock hour, and I stepped from my Oldsmobile. The moment I did so, the sparrows flew off and away into the high foliage of an elm. I paused beside my car, looking into the distance and high shadows where they had vanished, and I whispered to myself, "Oh, good God, why Orley?" Something snagged in my throat and my eyes blurred and I caught myself, as I did not wish to allow myself to dwell anymore on that sad reflection. I adjusted my collar and shirt cuffs, smoothed my hair, and stood for a few moments ere I walked across the yard, being careful of my boots. In my mind, I again pictured Miss von Leuckel at the far end of Crawford Hall: her back to the door, her long golden hair hanging down her back in a thick braid, her shoulders moving slightly as she folded bandages; when the other ladies rose at my presence, she would turn, and my eyes would be fastened upon her and something in her would tremble. The heavy wooden doors were gaping open, and as I descended the stone stairs, I heard coming up from the shadows the soft chatter of female voices and the strains of "Tipperary." At the exact moment when the last bell struck, I stepped across the threshold.

The chatter ceased abruptly, as it always did upon my entrance. Or rather, upon the entrance of the Commander of the Home Front Army. At that same instant, I froze, and my heart jumped. Miss von Leuckel was not in her accustomed place. I felt about thirty pairs of eyes looking my way, and the seated ladies, those who were not elderly, immediately rose from their chairs and benches, and those who were standing turned my way. The only other male in Crawford Hall, the schoolboy whose war work was to play marches and patriotic tunes on his harmonica, broke off "Tipperary" and leapt to his feet from the high stool where he had been perched. I gathered all of this in a peripheral way, for my eyes were fixed upon the empty oak-folding table where Mitzy usually worked. It was totally bereft of the neat stacks of pure white cotton cloths awaiting their transformation into dressings and slings. As you can imagine, I had something of a sinking feeling, like a superior who suddenly finds himself both outwitted and outmaneuvered by a subordinate, who was probably wholly unaware of her own accidental artfulness. Fortunately, I have always been very adept at an almost instantaneous recovery of my self-possession following nearly any onslaught of distress, major or minor. Lucy used to say, "You're so smooth, Trey, so very, very smooth."

I do not think she always meant that as a compliment.

Anyway, I am absolutely certain that within a few seconds I had the presence of mind to avert my eyes from the empty folding table and, while still standing one step inside the threshold, I coolly glanced over this scene of arrested female activity.

The floor lamps—I suppose there were at least eight or ten of them scattered about—gave the room a yellowish glow, as if Crawford Hall were lit by scores of candles. I might add that, by my eye, those lamps always gave a nice illumination to the ladies and girls. Most wore mixed ensembles of red, white, and blue, along with caps, similar to what nurses wear today, though I can still see Mrs. Leona Bishop standing with her knitting in her hands, dressed in her husband's blue and gold Interurban uniform. While Guy was in France, she was taking tickets on the evening runs between Marion and Columbus. I glanced once more at the empty table, and then to the Superior's desk off to the left. On the wall behind Mrs. Barker's desk hung the big government issue portraits, behind glass, of President Wilson and General Pershing. In between those hung an even larger portrait of Senator Harding, which I had paid for out of my own pocket. There were exactly twenty more just like it hanging in the places of war work throughout Marion.

As my eyes moved over the scene, I spotted Miss von Leuckel beside a knitting circle, in the far right corner, with Mrs. Barker. Apparently the Superior had assigned Mitzy to another task. She was looking right at me with what I believe was a knowing little smile, as if she had seen me eyeing her empty table and had read my distress. I felt myself blush, and looked away.

Ten or fifteen seconds after I had stepped into Crawford Hall, I bowed to the ladies. They in turn curtsied to me, and the soft rustle of skirts and uniforms filled the room. In a strong, clear voice, I said, "Good afternoon, ladies."

In unison, they responded, "Good afternoon, Commander Hamilton."

I continued: "I have this morning received a telegram from Senator Harding. He asks that I extend his heartfelt greetings to all of you, and he conveys that he grieves with all of us over the loss of our friend and neighbor, Cpl. Orley Boyd." The mention of Orley's name brought an almost palpable stillness into the already attentive Hall. After a pause, I added, "Yet another fine American boy who died a hero's death, slaughtered by the evil Kaiser's marauding Huns." As I said those words, I glanced Mitzy's way, in what I intended as a pointed and cutting gesture, but her eyes were downcast, no doubt with thoughts of poor Orley. I raised both of my hands and motioned for them to be seated. "Ladies, resume your duties, for God and America!"

In chorus, they repeated, "For God and America!"

With those words, the formalities of the Commander's arrival came to an end, and the room once again swung back into a hubbub of activity and harmonica music. Three schoolgirls—who in their innocent way, I think, were a little sweet on me—rushed forward to show me the gains they were making in their knitting skills. I praised them lavishly, telling them that before long they would be showing their grandmothers a few fancy stitches.

As you no doubt have already gathered, I did not march myself straight back to Miss von Leuckel and create a spectacle by accusing her outright of sedition—or for that matter of endangering Marion's hopes for Senator Harding. I simply made my way through the room towards the Superior's desk, doing exactly what I usually did during my inspection tours, circa August 1918. That is to say, I moseyed from sewing-circle to sewing-circle, with my shoulders straight and soldier-like and my hands clasped behind my back as I exchanged courtesies with the ladies, chatting mostly about letters they had received from their soldiers, and about our recent glorious victories at Aisne-Marne and Meuse-Argonne. In retrospect I would realize that there seemed to be something furtive in the hall, as if the ladies were waiting for some drama to unfold. But initially, I had not a clue to this.

I remember how, as I was examining the goods on one of the "finished" tables, the harmonica boy commenced playing a very solemn rendition of "When Johnny Comes Marching Home." His song moved me in a peculiar way. I suppose it was my frame of mind, but in that moment the melody seemed to me like the saddest music in the world. It is odd; I do not remember the boy's name or anything about him outside of that one day. I recall that he had a "bowl" haircut, the kind boys usually got from their mothers or sisters while sitting on a stool in the backyard with an old sheet draped around them, and I recall that he was wearing a gaudy tin ring with a red "gem" that he had probably won at a carnival, or maybe bought at Woolworth's for a nickel. His eyes were closed as he played, like he was somewhere inside his music, and I could not help but wonder, more than anything, how such a sorrowful tune could come from one so young and fair-haired. In a sense I was a bit torn as I stood there. Personally, I found the tune indescribably lovely, but as Commander, I considered going over and telling him to pick up the tempo before the ladies' morale crumpled and they gave vent to all their pent-up tears. But the females in the room were going about their tasks with their usual élan, chatting and laughing quietly, remembering (as they always did) that they were on church premises. I was the only one who seemed affected. And so I listened, pretending to intently examine the stockings for knitting lumps and bumps that I knew I would not find, whilst the sorrows of that old rebel air passed through me like ghosts passing through castle walls. When the tune came to an end, I stood there for a long moment. I thought about going over and discreetly asking him to play it again, in exactly the same way, but of course I did not. I glanced at the portrait of Senator Harding. Then I looked again at Mitzy. She was toiling away, her back to me.

By now the Superior had seated herself at her desk. She was running her fingers down the columns of her ledger, reviewing Crawford Hall's output for that week, readying herself for any questions the Commander might have. Mitzy was working alone, and I could see that she was sorting through books donated for the soldiers. I watched her, debating within myself whether to approach her now, or wait until after I had spoken to the Superior. Either way it would be prudent to speak with her elsewhere; it would have to be outside, as several ladies were knitting within earshot. Mitzy was half in lamplight and half in shadow, with a little gray daylight seeping in from a cellar window up by the steam pipes, near the ceiling. Like the other ladies, she was dressed in an ensemble of red, white, and blue, albeit dark blue, and as she moved, the reflection of the lamplight glistened up and down the braid of her golden hair. To me she looked like one of those pretty maidens in Dutch paintings who manages to look serene and mysterious as she quietly goes about her mundane tasks. The massive, gothic-looking table where she worked was stacked with volumes from the summer book drive. I watched her take an old-fashioned and heavy-looking book from the center; I suppose a history or something of that nature. She carefully dusted it all over and then thumbed through its pages, as if looking for errant notes or markers. She turned to the title page and for a long moment seemed absorbed with the information there, and then she leafed through the pages once again, more slowly. I could not help but wonder what the book was. Then she gently closed it and laid it in the Army-issue steamer trunk that stood open on the floor beside her. I suppose she felt—or I thought she felt—me looking at her, for as she rose, she glanced over her shoulder. But I was not to be caught off guard again. I had sensed, even as she had bent toward the trunk, that she was going to turn and look my way. Thus I was already running another stocking between my fingers, seemingly looking for defects that might give a soldier a blister. I felt her watching me, and as I refolded and laid the pair on the table, I looked up and met her eyes. I believe that I saw contempt. I glared at her, turned away, and headed for the Superior's desk.

Superior Barker was already watching me above her spectacles, and when I stepped up before her, she said, beneath her voice, "So you've noticed, have you not, Commander Hamilton?" She nodded her gray head towards Mitzy.

I felt myself blush, for she had obviously been looking at me looking at Mitzy. "Noticed? Noticed what?"

"Miss von Leuckel's skirt, of course."

"Skirt?" I again looked her way. She was blowing dust from the gilt pages of a volume, and she dusted it ever so lightly with her blue cloth. My eyes went down to the small of her back. The white shirt-blouse was snug against her skin where it tucked into the skirt, just above her narrow waist. I took a long look at her skirt. Suddenly it appeared to be black, not dark blue as I had first supposed. I turned to the Superior. "Why, it isn't black, is it, Mrs. Barker?"

"It is." And with a rather plaintive gravity, she added, "The girl exhausts me."

I looked back at Mitzy. The skirt certainly appeared to be black.

Now in case you have either forgotten or never knew, red, white, and black were the colors of Kaiser Bill's Imperial Germany. As you might imagine, they did not exactly make for a very fashionable ensemble during the summer of 1918. Superior Barker added, "She has the audacity to insist that it's blue. Deep blue, she says. As if I'm color blind! Says all her true blues are in the hamper till washday. So what else was she to do? Says she couldn't do her wash on Monday on account of the fact she was visiting her auntie." The Superior shook her head and made a tsk-tsk sound with her tongue. She leaned forward, looking at me above her spectacles. "Trey," she whispered, "Miss von Leuckel gets bolder by the minute. Sometimes I wonder to myself, Where will that girl's audacity end? Seems to think she has free reign to do exactly what she pleases. But I tell you, what I'm afraid of, is that it's all going to end with a very great fall." She paused and looked me right in the eye, allowing me to unmistakably divine the significance of her words. Then she repeated, "A very great fall." Just in case I still did not get the point, she leaned back again in her swivel chair and glanced over her shoulder, in a reproachful way, at Senator Harding's portrait, then back at me with a hard look, as if I were somehow partly at fault for Mitzy's foolishness. She shook her head and, as if speaking to herself, muttered, "Something ought to be done about that girl, but I'm simply not the one to do it."

Frankly, her words irritated me, and if I had not already made up my mind to speak with her, then I would have put the task off even longer, for I did not want some old woman to think she could manipulate me. I said, "Then I suppose you'll be gratified to know, Mrs. Barker, that I came here today with that exact intention already in mind—having a word with Miss von Leuckel. Not about her skirt, of course, but an entirely different matter. Though I shall speak to her about that as well."

She drew breath, as if alarmed, "You did? What matter?"

I suddenly realized that the hall had grown rather quiet, with the exception of the harmonica music, and that most of the ladies were watching us above their knitting needles, as if they were being entertained, whilst they worked, by a skit they could see but not hear. I nodded to Mrs. Barker, seemingly agreeing to some piece of business we had supposedly been discussing, and said, in a somewhat more audible voice, "Excellent!"

The Superior frowned as I stepped around to the side of her desk, so as to look down at the green-tinted pages of her open ledger. I ran my fingers down a column, scrutinizing the entries regarding the week's output, nodding my head in satisfaction. Superior Barker was gazing up at me as if she had missed something. In a low voice, without turning my eyes from the page, I said, "When I walk away, wait a minute or so, then go over and quietly inform Miss Mitzy von Leuckel that I wish to have a word with her—outside. Ask her to please step into the alley."

"Will do, Commander."

As I was speaking to her, something caught my eye in the ledger. I turned the page to last week's entries, and then to the previous week's, then back to the week at hand. The Superior started into her routine of reviewing the numbers with me, but I said, "That'll do, Mrs. Barker. Just one thing though. Come Monday, I'd like you to take two of the more accomplished ladies from stockings and put them on fingerless gloves. Otherwise we're liable to fall a dozen or so short of August's quota."

"Oh!" She sounded a bit like a hoot owl. She adjusted her spectacles and scrutinized the page.

"There." I pointed to the line entry. I turned the page and pointed to another. "There." Then I did the same with the week before, and said, "And there. Add them up, if you wish."

"Oh, Commander Hamilton! How careless of me!"

"Not at all. There's so many numbers, and it isn't anything that can't be made up. Other that that, everything looks first rate, as usual."

She smiled, like one redeemed. And I moseyed away, with my hands clasped behind my back.

The harmonica boy was just finishing up a tune, so I stepped over to him. He leapt off his stool and saluted me like a little soldier. I told him that he played like Gabriel, and when I asked where he learned to play like that, he blurted out, "From my granddaddy, sir, since dead from drink."

The first words out of his mouth told me why the child was unfamiliar to me.

He had a hillbilly twang that was thicker than cold molasses. His people had evidently come north to find war work in our factories.

He continued, "Gramps was a fifer in the armies of General Lee. His sword's mine now, Sir, and I 'tend to kill me some Huns with it, 'specially

Kaiser Bill. I'd stick it in his belly button"—he jabbed the end of his harmonica into his belly button—"and I'd rip it up through his vitals right into his heart, sir, like this." And he made a violent gesture, as if he were ramming his harmonica up into his own "vitals" and into his heart. His demonstration was so thorough that he even winced in mock pain. When the display was complete, he added, "I'd make his vitals gush out all blood and guts and spill in the dirt and him, he'd squeal like a stuck pig, sir, he would."

I simply stood there looking at that weird little creature, trying to square his grisly desire with the angelic music he had been playing just a few minutes before. I nodded with an encouraging half-smile, "Yes, that's very nice. A soldierly ambition for a boy. Resume."

He hopped back on his stool and launched into an exuberant version of "Dixie"—a song I have always detested.

Just then, I heard the squeaking springs of the Superior's swivel chair as she rose and wandered over to Miss von Leuckel's table. Mrs. Barker whispered in Mitzy's ear. At that particular moment, I happened to be speaking with one of the women, watching the two ladies through the periphery of my vision. Mitzy shot a glance over her shoulder at me. I met her eyes, and she gave me what young folks nowadays call a "drop-dead" look. She laid down the volume she had been dusting and, without the slightest semblance of discretion, turned and hightailed it toward the back of Crawford Hall, her heels clicking with a loud, perturbed flourish down the hall, all the way to the alley door, up the stairs, and out. As you can imagine, the hall had fallen silent, except for the wild playing of the harmonica boy. I closed my eyes for several seconds, filled with embarrassment and self-recrimination for not having foreseen Miss von Leuckel's feminine spectacle—and more to the point, for not having gone to her rooms to speak with her privately. Or at least intercepted her on her walk home and dealt with her at curbside somewhere, in the privacy of my automobile. Frankly, to this day I do not know what possessed me to do things as I did. When I opened my eyes again, Superior Barker was staring at me. She clapped her hands sharply. "Mind your duties, ladies, your duties!"

With my hands still clasped behind my back, and with my shoulders straight and soldier like, I followed Miss von Leuckel, casually walking to the back of the room and down to the end of the shadowy hall, where I climbed the stone stairs to the alley.

As I emerged from Crawford Hall, Miss von Leuckel was standing in the middle of the alley looking down her nose at me, or so it seemed from my rising perspective. I must say, she looked quite striking, even in that dingy alleyway off Church Street. At her back the deep green ivy clung to the red brick wall of Curtzs' old stables, which gave a nice contrast to her golden hair. Her shirt-blouse was open at the neck, not just by one button, but by two, and a red summer scarf loosely encircled her collar, its ends fastened between her bosoms with an ornamental pin, a small American flag. The pin sparkled with diamonds, rubies, and sapphires set in a gleaming base of gold. I knew at a glance that the jewels were genuine, not costume paste. I instantly sensed that the ornament was a gift from Senator Harding.

I planted my boots on the paving bricks about three or four feet before her, and for several seconds we simply stood glaring into each other's eyes. Not for four years had we been face-to-face, four years in which she had borne a son by the Senator and in which I had been married. I must say that Mitzy von Leuckel had the prettiest, brightest green eyes I have ever seen, before or since. In time I would come to think of her eyes as Clara Bow eyes. That was after Lucy and I saw *Mantrap* at the Palace Theatre before the "talkies" arrived, which at that particular time was still several years in the future. I stood gazing into those eyes with something buried deep in my heart. I have no idea what sort of expression I conveyed, if any, but I can tell you that Miss von Leuckel most certainly was not regarding me as if she appreciated the terrible powers of my office. Indeed, her chin was up, and she was regarding me in what I believe was a restrained but contemptuous sort of way, like she was someone of sovereign qualities and associations called into a puddled alleyway to suffer the badgering of a dunce. I thought of the only phrase that I retained from my French lessons in school, though frankly, I am not sure if it came to me then and there, or later: *amour-propre*. I do not know exactly what that phrase denotes to a flesh-and-blood Frenchman, as I have never met one, but as I understand it *amour-propre* has something to do with possessing the pride and confidence of a supreme self.

As for me, I was wondering if Mitzy had at least noticed the brilliant, unsullied shine of my boots.

After several moments, I said, "So, Miss von Leuckel, no doubt you're wondering why I summoned you out here."

"No, Commander Hamilton," she said softly, but with an edge, "I am not particularly wondering anything of the kind."

I believed she was lying, more or less, and I gave a mocking little laugh at her feigned indifference. "Well, one way or another, I shall enlighten you. I summoned you out here . . ."

"If you wish to enlighten me, Commander, then what I am wondering is this: If you wanted to have a word with me in an alleyway, like I was one of your teamsters, then why didn't you simply tell me so yourself? Why have an old woman carry your message ten feet across the room for you? That is what I am wondering." She paused, "Funny, Commander Hamilton, I was under the mistaken assumption that you'd probably outgrown your timidity by now. Especially considering the lofty position Senator Harding has bestowed upon you."

The irony was difficult to miss.

"It wasn't timidity. It wasn't that at all. It was . . ." I am afraid that nothing whatsoever came out of my mouth, and so I stood there, no doubt, looking like a fool.

Miss von Leuckel was good enough to find the words for me. "Just the modus operandi, I suppose, of one in a position of power. Or what-have-you."

I shifted a little from the place where I had so firmly planted my heels. "Miss von Leuckel, I have important things to do before supper; I have the production of armored tractors that's starting to fall behind in production, so I really don't have time for bantering. I summoned you out here, away from the other ladies, to issue you a good stiff warning. And to try to do you a favor."

"And what 'good stiff warning' and what 'favor' might that be, Commander?"

"I think just about everyone in Marion knows all about your tainted history of Teutonic sympathies, and so it seems to me that, in spite of the war, in spite of the fact that boys like . . ." I was going to say, *boys like Orley*, but a slight catch came into my voice and with it, I noticed, a slight change in Miss von Leuckel's eyes scrutinizing mine. After a moment I continued, "In spite of the fact that this week our very own Marion boys are fighting at Meuse-Argonne, you continue to flaunt your Teutonic sympathies, and you do so at very grave risk to yourself and others. Miss von Leuckel, your seditious activities must cease. Or else. I have looked the other way for far too long and I shall look away no longer. Do *not* doubt me."

"Commander Hamilton, I really haven't the slightest idea what you're talking about. 'Seditious activities?'"

"Yes, Miss von Leuckel, seditious activities. And to think that you're the one who used to say that I was always—what was your word? Ah, yes, that I was always 'pretending.' So who's 'pretending' now?"

She ran her eyes down the length of my uniform, to my brilliant boots, and then back up to meet my eyes. "Well, I suppose that all depends on one's point of view, doesn't it?"

"One's point of view!" I said, and gave another curt little laugh. "What I'm looking at now, Miss von Leuckel, is evidence right before my very eyes of sedition. Outfitted in the Kaiser's very own imperial colors." I then made a point of allowing my eyes to do as hers had done and rove freely down between her ample bosoms and the jeweled American flag, to her skirt. I planted my vision firmly on the front of her narrow hips. Mitzy glanced down at herself. My eyes lingered on her lower quarters, even as she looked up at me again. Actually, now that I was out in the daylight, Miss von Leuckel's dress could easily have passed for a shade of dark blue. Nevertheless, when I raised my eyes, I said, "You'd make Kaiser Bill proud, but you'd alarm Senator Harding. Or any SS man who happened by. An SS man would reprimand you on the spot. Why, maybe he'd even arrest you."

"Arrest me for what, Commander, I'm not sure, but if he did, then I assure you, he'd promptly release me. Senator Harding would see to it."

"Oh? Senator Harding's in a position to stop one of President Wilson's SS men?" I gave her a mocking look that, I am confident, clearly conveyed what I regarded as her extreme naïveté in political and security matters. "More likely, he'd start digging all the deeper into your *affairs* and no doubt find them very, very interesting." I paused. "I'm sure President Wilson would make exceptionally good use of the information the SS would find. And why wouldn't he? Finding one of Kaiser Bill's very own agents, and look who she's—shall we say, look who she's 'picnicking' with. What a find that would be for the Democratic Party!"

She glanced down again at her dress, like she was biding a moment's time and rummaging for words to outsmart me, but before she had a chance to speak, I decided to make a bit more hay out of the matter. I found that my tone suddenly and unintentionally grew more urgent. "Wilson hates Senator Harding. Don't you realize that? God help him if you go dragging his good name into your sedition. He'll be finished. Parading around town dressed like a German flag! After everything else you've been up to. Or down to, as the case may be."

"First off, Commander, I am not dressed like a German flag! You and that old biddy in there have been at it, haven't you? That's what the two of you were hiss-hissing about, isn't it? While you *pretended* to look over the ledger!"

"Why, you must have eyes in the back of your head."

"Maybe I do."

"Hmm. Must come in awful handy in your line of work."

She frowned, as if she did not know quite what I meant. She glanced down yet again at her dress and moved her hand along it, as if gently smoothing away wrinkles. "Either I'm color blind, or else everyone else is. My skirt isn't black at all. It's iridium. That's even what the couturiere called it when Warren and I picked out the fabric. Iridium."

I instantly suspected that she was trying to outsmart me with an uncommon word—she who had college courses behind her, while I only had grammar school basics. (I was removed from the schoolroom early on, though throughout my entire life I have continually endeavored to educate and elevate myself, and I am confident that I have succeeded.) I smiled slightly; feeling assured that I had perceived her trick. "That's funny, Miss von Leuckel, no matter what your so-called couturiere says, I think of iridium as having a shade or two more blue in it." The instant I said those words, I discerned the outline of her trap, but it was too late.

She gave a triumphant little smile. "Why, come to think of it, Commander Hamilton, you're quite right. How foolish of me. Iridium *is* a bit bluer, isn't it? Though at least we've established that my skirt is, as you yourself indicate, a shade of blue. And not black at all. What a relief to have that weighty, patriotic question cleared up."

I simply glared at her.

She continued, "I would appreciate it if you'd please inform Mrs. Barker of that fact so she doesn't lose sleep over it."

I said nothing.

"By the way, Commander, did you get my postcard? I sent you a postcard from Long Island."

Amid the controversy about the color of her skirt, I had almost forgotten the real reason I had summoned Miss von Leuckel into the alleyway. "As a matter of fact, that's why I called you out here."

"To thank me for a postcard!"

"Hardly. You sent that postcard to taunt me, didn't you?"

She stared at me. "To taunt you?"

"Yes, to taunt me, and you know precisely what I'm talking about. You send me a picture of the *USS Francis Marion*, and then what happens? Four or five days later a U-boat sinks her to the bottom of the Atlantic. With all hands. "

"Tristan!"

"You may call me Commander Hamilton, thank you." Then I found myself adding, "I am no longer Tristan to you. And I never shall be again."

She studied me. "Commander Hamilton, you don't really think for a moment that I…?"

"Informed the High Command?" I shrugged my shoulders. "I don't know. Like that CPI leaflet that I sent around town says, to sink a ship, all a hyphenate needs is a strong flashlight, a code, and a clear night."

"I send you a postcard of the *Francis Marion*, the ship sinks, and so you put the two together, and you come up me as a mass murderer! Commander, I remember very well that picture of Francis Marion in Colonel Hamilton's library, the one you like so much. That's all I was thinking of when I sent it. That and your loyalty to Marion. Warren calls you 'Young Mr. Marion.' That's why I sent you the postcard. And from that you concoct me having a ship torpedoed on the high seas. Why, for heaven's sake, Commander, what is wrong with you?" She glanced away, "How was I supposed to know a U-boat would sink it and kill all those poor boys?"

Frankly, I was almost convinced that she was telling the truth and that I had misread her intentions regarding her wish to taunt me. I said, "Okay, you sent it because it was the *Francis Marion*. And you sent it to taunt me."

She glanced away in feigned exasperation. "Okay, think what you please. Whatever you please. But do *not* think for a moment that I would wish harm to come to our boys. Why, it's obscene. I stand in there for hours on end, day in and day out, folding bandages for our soldiers, and you have the audacity to say such a thing—Why, Commander, you should be horsewhipped."

After a long moment of silence, I said, "Miss von Leuckel, you may resume your war work, which all of us regard for what it is—exemplary."

I had scarcely budged an inch since I had planted my boot heels on the paving bricks, so my back was still to the church. She, of course, had to have the last word. "But for the record, I'm not the one committing the infractions. Not the real infractions. The ones who are doing that are the ones making a mockery of our Bill of Rights. Of our Constitution itself. *They* are the real enemy agents within our midst."

I had some feelings exactly along those lines as well, but as an officer in the CPI, I was also well aware that hyphenates all too often used such patriotic ruses to cover their seditious tracks. I did not reply, but I made a mental note of what she had just said. She walked past me, towards Crawford Hall, in an apparent state of high-minded indignation and, as she passed, without so much as turning my head a single degree, I said, "By the way, thanks for the postcard—'Mrs. Harding.'"

She paused, just behind me. "You're welcome—Colonel Hamilton— the Third."

I stood staring at the brick wall of the Crutzs' old stables, at the ivy, the water drops from the late rain glistening and dripping from the leaves, perceived through the emptiness of Mitzy's former presence. I listened to her footsteps hurrying down the stone stairs and then vanishing into the hall.

IV

MONDAY NIGHT—LATE

Mitzy von Leuckel

AS I SIT HERE forty-five years later reconsidering those days, I realize that back then I may have been reading a bit too much into things, though I do wish to reiterate that, according to the laws of the time, Miss von Leuckel was arguably conducting herself in a seditious manner. Needless to say, I did not create the laws—as I was to point out to her, and frankly, I suppose I did not do a very good job seeing to it that all of them were enforced. Be that as it may, I still firmly believe that Miss von Leuckel took peculiar pleasure in taunting me in my position, whether it suited her to admit it or not. Indeed, she was to do so again in October in a way that, I think you will agree, was far less ambiguous than the shade of her skirt.

By then the war was winding down and things were going badly for the Germans. I remember they had just lost Laon, their last stronghold in France, but I assure you, the feeling of imminent victory did absolutely nothing to make things more placid. Indeed, the very fact that victory now floated within reach made the entire war effort all the more virulent, both on the battlefield and here at home. What's more, I was also getting it more and more into my head that Senator Harding might actually be a viable candidate for President in 1920, even though he had only been in the Senate for four years. The Republicans had no real front-runners, and it seemed me that the Senator had a shot—albeit a long shot. Others here in Marion were thinking more like in 1924, or in 1928—if ever.

My October confrontation with Mitzy began with a telephone call. I remember it came on a Friday evening around dusk. After supper I had gone out to tend to one of my favorite autumnal chores—raking the yard and burning leaves in the gutter along the avenue. I always found something both brisk and tranquil about this task; it was like rowing a boat along the shore of a quiet lake in the woods, with the added beauty of fire and the fragrance of burning leaves. Anyway, while I was stirring the flames, Lucy called through the screen door to tell me that Mr. George Wiants was on the telephone and wished to speak with me. He was the owner of Wiants Stationery and Book Store on South Main Street. George was of my father's generation, maybe a few years older, and I had known him my entire life. We would say hello on the sidewalk, and whenever I stopped by his store we would have a little conversation, but that was the extent of our association. Thus as I walked across the darkening yard and up the porch steps, I could not imagine why on earth he would be calling me. When I picked up the hand set, after our initial cordialities, he said, "Let me ask you, Commander, are you going to be downtown tomorrow, per chance?" Clearly, he was looking for a Yes. When he got it, he said, "Then do you suppose you could drop by the store for a few minutes? I have a little something to mention to you."

That was back in the days before private lines, when listening in on telephone calls was, for some, a cherished form of entertainment, and so I knew better than to ask him to elaborate. I told him I would be glad to drop by, and when I said that, he added, "Nothing important, just a little something I thought I should mention."

I did not always wear my Home Front Army uniform on Saturdays, but I wore it that day. George had called me "Commander" instead of "Trey," so I wanted to look the part. I donned my uniform and motored over to South Main Street. I might as well mention that Wiants still exists, though George and his wife passed from this world decades ago. I had not really thought about it until just this moment, but Wiants is one of those Marion places, like Tioga, that has scarcely changed since the Great War. Come to think of it, the same brass bell that jingled on its spring as I opened the door on that Saturday morning in 1918, jingled again upon my entry just a few weeks ago, when I dropped in to order my 1963 Christmas cards. The ornate pressed-tin ceiling is still painted silver, and I crossed the same oiled floorboards, past the same oak bookshelves and the same glass display cases that are stuffed with a similar jumble of fountain pens, blotters, rubber stamps, bottles of ink, boxes of Ticonderoga pencils, and things of that order. Even the old National Cash Register at the back of the store is the same, as is the thick glass on the counter that looks as if a permanent frost has settled over it, the result of coins being slid across the glass since the '80s or '90s of the last century. Of course a few weeks ago, I entered Wiants as an old man, but on that sunny Indian-summer morning in 1918, I was all of twenty-six, and I suppose a boyish twenty-six at that.

When the bell jingled, George stuck his gray head from behind a bookshelf and peered out at me. For as long as I had known him, he had sported long sideburns that angled down to his chin in a point, and then angled back up and crossed over his upper lip as a mustache. His whiskers gave him an owlish sort of look, though I suspect this old-fashioned style may have been quaint even a hundred years ago. He said, "Well, you're an early bird, aren't you, young man?" I allowed that I was and he said, "Glad of it. Means we'll be able to talk in peace, I hope. Come on back and have a seat. I got something here to show you."

That morning was the first and last time I ever set foot in that cluttered little cubbyhole of an office, directly behind the rear counter. I believe it must have originally been intended as a hallway leading into the storage area of the back, with the office being stuck in as an afterthought. It's about six feet wide with shelves up one wall and down the other, and a hodgepodge of books, ledgers, papers, and heaven knows what else crammed into every available square inch. George's oak desk was covered with about twice its weight in clutter, and the office had two oak chairs. The second chair was Mrs. Wiants', but on that morning Madge was probably out doing her grocery shopping, which I believe was her custom on Saturday mornings. After we were seated, George asked about Lucy and my father and Adeline. I have no idea what brought about his next comment, but as he reached for a slip of paper, he said, without looking at me, "What a lovely lady your mother was, Trey. One of the loveliest ladies to ever walk down Main Street. Many a time she graced this store with her presence." He looked towards the counter, as if he were seeing her there in his mind long ago. I looked there, too. "So gracious, so beautiful, a great and genuine lady." He shook his head. "Lord, what a pity. Such a pity."

I know it sounds foolish, but after all those years I still sometimes felt "mad at the world" when it came to my mother's untimely death, and it pained me acutely to speak of her during what ought to have been her living years. Thus my only response to his kind words was a muttered "Thank you."

The sheet of paper in his trembling old hand was already absorbing his attention, and his lips were now moving in a labored sort of way as if he were sounding out unfamiliar words. He turned to me and drew his spectacles down his nose with a finger. Smiling slightly, he said, "So, guess who dropped in to see us last night, just before we locked up."

I do not know why people phrased things that way, but back in those days whenever anyone told me to guess who did this or that, the correct answer was inevitably Miss Mitzy von Leuckel. Indeed, I knew this was the case the moment he spoke, with that wry little smile. Nevertheless, my reply was, "No idea."

"Mitzy."

"von Leuckel?"

He tilted his head and looked at me in a playful way, as if to say, *Come on!*

"Trouble," I mused.

He laughed out loud and pointed the paper at me, "That, young man, is exactly what she's looking for. Trouble!" He handed me the paper. "Miss von Leuckel wants me to order this book for her."

I immediately recognized Mitzy's flowing and rounded script. She had written what I remember as having been a rather longish title in the German language. (Regrettably, I no longer have the slightest idea what the title was in German, though after the war, I purchased the book in its English translation. I pulled it from the shelf this very evening.) She had written the author's name beneath the German: "Lieutenant-General Baron Hugo Friedrich Philipp Johann von Freytag-Loringhoven." The name was vaguely familiar because I believe I had read it before in the *Star*, associated with this or that battle. Below the name, she had written the words: "English title <u>Deductions from the World War.</u>"

As I examined the paper, remembering other past things I had seen written in Mitzy's distinctive script, letters and such, and of course that postcard from Port Jefferson, George said, "Miss von Leuckel doesn't simply want me to order it for her, which would spell trouble enough. She wants me to order it in German. Yes, in German! Why, can you imagine all the bells and whistles that'll go off if I try to put that thing through? I leveled with her. I told her it spelled trouble. I even told her I'd have to get in touch with Commander Hamilton about this. You know what she said? She said, 'Mr. Wiants, I don't care if you get in touch with Woodrow Wilson. Someone should. And when they do, they should remind him that this is the United States of America, not Imperial Germany.' She says to me, 'It's a sad state of affairs when an American citizen has to get permission from some sort of commander just to order a book.' And then she says that so far as she's concerned, the very thought of all this quote 'nonsense' is, as she said, 'un-American.'"

Looking me in the eye, George lifted his eyebrows, as if to say, Of course she's right, you know, even though she isn't. He leaned forward, "You and I both know what's going to happen if I try to order that Mr. Baron von Maytag-so-and-so's book in German, don't we Trey? Why, the SS men'll be in here in a flash. And once they start poking their noses around, well, they'll find plenty of dirt to dig in with our gal Mitzy, won't they?" He stared at me, then said, "So what do you say, Trey?"

I looked at the paper and reread the words. "Well, there's no doubt that you're right, George." Then I folded the paper up and stuck it in my jacket pocket. "Tell you what, I'll take care of this from here on out, if that's okay with you."

"You'd be doing me a favor." He studied me. "But what are you going to do, Trey?"

I ignored his question. "What I want you to do, if you will, sir, is just forget about this. And I'd appreciate it if Mrs. Wiants would do the same. If she knows about it."

"It's as good as forgotten by both Madge and me."

As I rose from the chair, he said, "Say, Trey, thanks for coming in." As I shook his long, bony hand, he said, "I'm always more than happy to rid myself of trouble. Even in the form of a pretty young gal like Mitzy." He exhaled and looked towards the counter, as if picturing Mitzy there the evening before. Again, I glanced there myself. Then he muttered, "Gee, I hope she doesn't get sore at me."

"Why would she? You've done exactly what she wanted you to do."

He frowned and studied me. "I have?"

"So long."

A moment later the little brass ball jingled above my head, and I was out the door.

I SUPPOSE I SHOULD TELL YOU a little something about Baron von Freytag-Loringhoven's book. First off, I want to make clear that *Deductions from the World War* would have been readily available in English, even on the very day when Mitzy tried to order it in German. The Committee on Public Information did not ban such books, per se—in the belief that one should understand the mind of one's enemy. (I once read somewhere that General Patton stayed up nights in North Africa studying General Rommel's text on tank warfare.) As I heretofore stated, I own a copy of *Deductions from the World War*. Actually, I waited for about six months after the Armistice before I ordered it, and I did not do so from George. I bought it through mail order. I was reminded of the Freytag book back in the '30s when Germany again started leaning towards war. Essentially, without stating it outright, the Baron seemed to foresee his nation's initial defeat by the Allied forces. But more than anything, he avowed Germany's determination to rearm for the next war just as soon as the first Great War was finished, so that German *kultur* might spread throughout Europe, and eventually, the world. He cited heavy losses, like the Battle of the Marne, as proof of Germany's need to develop advanced armaments. In all, he wove a grim, war-filled tapestry of the future. Obviously, the fellow had more than his share of prescience, and in thinking back, I imagine that Hitler, as a young man, had probably read Baron von Freytag-Loringhoven's book and possibly found some inspiration there. Anyway, that should give you some idea as to what the volume is all about.

Obviously, I knew nothing of this as I drove directly over to Mitzy's on that Saturday morning.

At the time, she was living in a set of furnished rooms on the second floor of a house on Orchard Street, midway between Church and Columbia Streets. Even nowadays I glance at the place when I happen to drive by. Back then the house was nicely painted a sort of tannish yellow and was quite pretty in its ordinary way, though now it is an ugly gray trimmed with white. My grandfather, the first Colonel Hamilton, developed that entire neighborhood back in the 1870s and 1880s. He managed to purchase huge chunks of land after the Civil War, and that area was among the Hamilton family's first developments. Which I suppose tells you more than you need to know about where Mitzy was hanging her silk stockings in October of 1918.

I drove around the block once before I actually parked in front of the house. I sat at the curb looking at her place wondering if she happened to be watching me through the lace curtains, presuming she was up and awake. I did not have the feeling that I was being watched, at least by her, and so I sat a moment longer. The long front yard was carpeted with leaves from the old maples and elms. The owners of the houses on either side had raked their yards along their property lines but apparently Mr. Alexander, who owned the house and lived downstairs, had not gotten around to that particular chore. The hedges along the front porch were bare, and the porch itself looked empty and sad in the way that porches look when the outdoor furniture is taken in at summer's end. I took out my watch: a quarter till eleven. Under the circumstances, not an entirely unreasonable hour to be calling on a lady, unannounced, on a Saturday morning.

As I say, Miss von Leuckel lived upstairs. It was one of those arrangements where the two floors have separate entrances. If you want to visit someone on the second floor, you don't bother knocking on the porch door simply because the person living upstairs could not possibly hear you, so you walk right in to the staircase without any ado whatsoever. I did just that and gently closed the door behind me. I stood in the shadowed vestibule for a long moment wondering if Senator Harding, on one of his visits home, had crept across the porch late at night with his hat pulled down and his collar up, closing the same door behind him. For a moment I almost thought I caught a whiff of the pungent chewing tobacco smell that seemed to attend him, just as a special sweet and pleasant fragrance seems to attend certain ladies. The vestibule was very quiet, with the only daylight seeping in through curtains at the top of the stairs. From where I stood I could see the door to Mitzy's rooms on the left, and the top of a mirrored étagère on the landing, facing the staircase. I climbed the carpeted stairs just as quietly as I could, though I wish to say that it certainly was not my intention to go "sneaking" about. I simply did not want to disturb anyone. Once I achieved the landing, I did not immediately knock on the door, though I do not know why. I simply stood there. Mitzy's door was of carved oak, with an ornate brass lock plate, which had the greenish patina of age, and a matching doorknob that was partially polished from decades of use. As I stood there, I thought of my grandfather and my father, the latter of course still being alive and well at that time, and once again I admired them for always having used fine materials and lasting fixtures, even in modest dwellings. The étagère stood against the wall of the little landing and was part settee and part hat rack, with hooks fastened into the frame on either side of the long beveled mirror. Mitzy's hats and scarves dangled from the hooks in a casual and colorful array, and I had the impression that she hung them there, in part, as a decorative flourish. I thought I heard motion behind the door, but instead of knocking, I sort of leaned my ear towards the door, a move that could have proven itself quite awkward if, by chance, Miss von Leuckel happened to throw open the door just then. As I listened, I heard only silence—if it is correct to say that one "hears" silence. Keeping an eye on the doorknob, I touched the silken tassels of a lilac colored scarf that I had seen Mitzy wearing downtown. I held it to my face and smelled the leftover fragrance of perfume, perhaps a gift from the Senator. I know it sounds odd, but something in the luxurious softness of the fabric impelled me to press the scarf to my cheek and to hold it there for a long moment. I caught my own eye, so to speak, in the mirror, and I instantly let the scarf fall away from my fingertips. I liked wearing a uniform, and frankly, I think it suited me just fine. I straightened my shoulders and smoothed the lapels of my jacket and I studied my face in the mirror. Mitzy used to tell me that I was "handsome." I could not help but wonder if she still thought so. Frankly, I believe that I had not changed all that much since the days when she used to tell me things of that sort. I took my comb from my pocket and began running it through my hair, smoothing and patting it in place.

I was running the comb through my hair when the door flew open.

To this day, I do not know why I wasn't in the least bit startled, but I am glad to say that I was not. Indeed, the door was probably open for several seconds before I even bothered to glance away from my neat hair. Mitzy was standing there framed by the doorway with an astonished look on her face. Her golden strands, I might add, fell in pleasing and curling disarray. Her only visible garment was a royal blue bathrobe. She was clutching the robe closed at her breasts. I do not know what possessed me, but after that momentary glance, I simply turned back to the mirror and continued combing my hair. In my youth, Miss von Leuckel had admired my hair and even, upon occasion, took a special delight in disheveling it in a teasing sort of way, running her fingers through it.

Only after my eyes returned to the mirror did I say, almost as an afterthought, "Good morning, Miss von Leuckel. I trust I didn't wake you."

That's when she blurted out, "Tristan! What on earth are you doing?"

"I am combing my hair."

When I made that glib statement, she stared at me for an astonished moment, and then burst into laughter, though I do not know what she could have found so amusing in that simple statement. "Well, then would you like to borrow some hair cream?"

"Never use the stuff, thank you." I stuck the comb back in my jacket pocket and in the same motion, withdrew the book order, carefully unfolded it, and held it in front of her face—like a sign. "You wanted to see me?"

I think it took her a moment to figure out what the paper actually was. "Oh, I see. Well, Mr. Wiants doesn't waste any time, does he? And neither do you. I order a book on Friday evening and some fellow in a uniform knocks on my door on Saturday morning and sticks it in my face. Like a summons." I instantly withdrew the paper, and as I did, she shifted and leaned on the doorframe, with one bare foot resting atop the other. I felt myself straighten my shoulders. "Come on in, Commander." She stepped aside. "Welcome back to the land of liberty."

I ignored her remark and, with my hands clasped behind my back, I proceeded into her rooms.

I believe that up until that moment I somehow had the impression that Miss von Leuckel was living in furnished rooms, as opposed to an apartment, but that was not the case. Furnished rooms of course have always been the province of itinerant railroaders, day-laborers, young people setting out in life, destitute widows and the like; back in those days, apartments were little more than one step above—meaning you had the goods, but not the house to put them in. As I discovered on that morning, Mitzy's rooms were anything but merely "furnished." In retrospect, I suppose I should not have been surprised by the quality of her things. After all, Senator Harding took good care of his girls; nevertheless, I was a bit taken aback. You will probably think I was a bit malicious, and in truth I guess I was, but the moment I walked through that door, I felt a pang of disappointment to see that Miss von Leuckel was not living in reduced circumstances. During the first year or so of my marriage to Lucy, I used to take delight in the thought of Mitzy living a bare-bones existence—while she sat musing, say, on some hard stool by the window, remembering the splendors of Tioga with its park-like grounds, and Goose Pond Farm with its groves and great Indian mound, and Indian Rock—my family's rustic but spacious cottage on the Catawba cliffs above Lake Erie. Mitzy had been an honored guest in each of our houses, and both my father and Adeline were quite fond of her. But of course life does not always work out as one anticipates, and Miss von Leuckel withdrew from the scene on her Warren's behalf, and her place was soon taken by the young widow who became my life's companion, my dear and devoted wife and best friend, Lucy Richmond Neil. I was a bit disappointed as I entered Miss von Leuckel's rooms and felt the deep carpet beneath my boots, and saw the glint of brass lamps, the French style of the overstuffed pink and gold sofa and matching chairs, and the gilded frames of the mirrors, lithographs, and oils. I thought again, as I often had in the past, that Mitzy constituted an unmonied aristocracy of one. What I saw, within the presence and quality of these furnishings, was an ample display of what I presumed was the Senator's wealth and generosity. (Most people, even in Marion, did not realize how thoroughly well-off the Hardings were. I know for a fact that in 1920, in addition to his government salary, Senator Harding was earning over twenty thousand dollars a year just from his newspaper. In addition, in 1913, Mrs. Harding had inherited more than eight hundred thousand dollars from her once estranged father. This money was kept in various accounts and investments in both their names.) I may be wrong, but as I entered her rooms, I wondered if maybe Miss von Leuckel wanted me, in part, to visit in order to see that she was living quite well. To sort of rub that fact in my face.

Do not think for a moment that I stood there gaping, and do not think that I extended any compliments, either. I pretended not to take notice of anything.

She invited me to sit, whereupon I informed her, "This can hardly be counted as a social call, Miss von Leuckel."

"Well then, suit yourself, Commander, just stand there if you like, but you'll have to excuse me. I have to put some clothes on." She slipped into the bedroom behind one of those tall, four-paneled folding screens—a hand-painted job with a jungle of orchids and tropical greenery covering every square inch. Of course one feels slightly ridiculous standing about in someone's living room, and so at last I sat down in one of the chairs upholstered in heavy silk. As it were, I ought to have seated myself on the couch, facing the front windows. Years later I was to see a Hollywood movie or two, no doubt comedies, though I no longer have the slightest idea what their names were, that had little scenes reminiscent of the awkward moment I endured as I faced Miss von Leuckel's boudoir. There I sat straight and soldier-like with my hands on my knees, as Miss von Leuckel draped her robe over the top of the screen. Needless to say, try as one might, one could not help but imagine her, at least for a fleeting moment, going about the room adorned solely in her "birthday suit." I heard the opening of the chest of drawers, and then the closing, and in a moment, the little clink of a hanger being taken from its rod in the closet. Frankly, I caught myself staring at the screen as if it were not there, whereupon I promptly looked about for a magazine, or for yesterday's *Star*, something with which to decently occupy my mind. I spotted the newspaper on the coffee table before the sofa. When I took it in hand, I was surprised to see that it was not at all current, but from the summer, with headlines announcing the shelling of Paris by Germany's infamous cannon, Big Bertha—which had since been silenced by the Allies. I held the newspaper before my eyes. As I did so, she called out, "So tell me, Commander, how's Lucy?"

"Oh, she's very well, thank you." In my own ears, my voice sounded a bit shrill and absurdly casual.

"Well, I'm glad to hear it. She's as nice as they come." I remember in the old days Miss von Leuckel used to dislike the word "nice," for reasons clear only to her, and so it was rather odd to hear her use it in a way that apparently was a compliment, I think. "Any little ones on the way?"

"None that I know of!"

"Well then, you better get busy." She laughed quietly.

I stayed mum on that one and started reading about the huge howitzer raining death upon Paris from its mysterious lair far in the east, and the desperate Allied attempt to hunt it down. I heard Mitzy's footsteps proceeding down the hall, and she called back, "I'll be right there, Commander. Give me a minute."

I was beginning to feel a little like a well-meaning preacher undertaking a mission to a bordello. As I sat there, I very much wished, once again, that Mitzy and I had shared a different past, or rather, no past at all; as such, our history felt a little like a ghost that was unwilling, or unable, to depart from its former world. I could hear that Miss von Leuckel had gone into the kitchen via another door. When I heard her footsteps coming down the hallway, I stood once again, tossed the *Star* back on the table, and clasped my hands behind my back. She breezed into the room from the hallway bearing a tray with coffee and sweet rolls. "At ease, Commander."

She was wearing an Oriental-looking multicolored gown that hung as loose as a sack from her neck to her toes. I suppose as such it ought to have looked modest, but somehow it managed to appear slightly decadent, though I was at a loss as to discern why. I imagined that the gown was the sort of housedress Mata Hari might have worn. "You came by at the right time," she said, "the coffee was just brewing."

"I've had my fill for the day," I lied, "thank you."

"Oh, have a little more. You only live once. Besides, it's from Jamaica. If you haven't tasted this, you haven't tasted coffee." As she set the tray on the coffee table, she said, "I bought the beans in New York. Warren says it's what the Rockefellers drink."

I wanted to ask how on earth Warren could possibly know what the Rockefellers drink, but I kept mum. Besides, maybe he did know. She poured a cup and added a touch of thick cream, which is the way I have always drunk my coffee, and she handed it to me, along with a sweet roll on a dish. "Mrs. Weaver made these, so they ought to be tasty." After serving herself, she settled in on the couch, tucking her bare feet and legs up beneath her. I stood there with the cup in one hand and Mrs. Weaver's sweet roll in the other, before I too sat down.

She was looking at me with—I do not know what to call it—one of those looks that makes you wonder what someone is thinking. She said quietly, "That uniform suits you, Tristan."

I glanced down at the brass buttons, and I straightened the creases of the trousers. "Well, I just wish it could have been an actual Army uniform, one that I could have worn over there, with the other fellows. But it wasn't meant to be. Just one of those things."

She glanced away. "Yes, just one of those things." She smiled in that sweet way she had and said, "But things have gone well for you. You've done your part on the home front."

I thought of Orley Boyd's last words when we spoke at the depot, that I'd be fighting right beside him here at home. "Yes," I said, "I've done what I could, though I'm ashamed it could not have been more."

"You have nothing to be ashamed of, Tristan." After a moment of silence, she said, "So now tell me, Commander, I gather that you're here to give me another, what was it you said, 'good stiff warning'?"

"No, as a matter of fact, I am not. I tried that once and you ignored me. I'm here to simply ask you to please stop all your risky behavior. You know as well as I do that I've looked the other way, with you and a few others, and I think some people have taken advantage of me, and I don't appreciate it. You must understand, Miss von Leuckel, that I'm not the one who wrote the Sedition Act, or the Espionage Act. And frankly, as you may have noticed, I haven't done a very good job enforcing either of them."

I could tell that I had her attention and this time I saw no faint, smug smile, which is to say, I did not have the impression that the wheels were turning in her mind, preparing clever rebuttals. I proceeded, "Hundreds of people in this country have been arrested, branded enemy agents, and sent to prison, and they've been sent there by men just like me. Who have I sent up? Who? Name one person. No one. Did I report Reverend Fitchblood when he gave his sermon on pacifism? No. Did I send him up when he told his colored folks that Germany had never enslaved Negroes, while all the other warring nations had? No. Did I summon the SS? Again, no. I simply went to his house and spoke with him and asked him to desist. He gave me his word of honor that he would, and he did. And have I reported you for your repeated little and not so little indiscretions, of the very same kind that have landed others in the clink? No, I have not. And it's not because of your . . . your friend."

With her words to George in mind, I added, "As far as I'm concerned, the Constitution and the Bill of Rights are sacred documents, but we're up to our necks in all-out war. And I'm trying to do my job and uphold the oath I took, and at the same time I'm trying to behave nobly and in good faith in a dangerous situation, in dangerous times. So no, I'm not here to give you a 'good stiff warning,' Miss von Leuckel. I'm here to simply ask you to *please* desist. This war will be over soon, thank God, and our boys will be coming home, and after that you can read any damn thing you want, and say any damn thing you want, in English or in German, but for now, I'm asking you, Miss von Leuckel, please desist."

Her face had gone blank and I knew that I "had her." Nevertheless, I lathered it on, though in a somewhat more tranquil voice. "If you won't stop your seditious behavior for me, then maybe you'll do so for Senator Harding's sake." I stirred my coffee with the silver spoon, and without looking at her, I added, sort of quiet and thoughtful, "You know, I sincerely believe that Senator Harding can be the next President of the United States." I took my first sip of coffee, and as I did, I peered at her above the cup's golden rim. She was gazing at me all wide-eyed, like she must have done on her first glimpse into Tiffany's window. I added, "But if that's going to happen, then there are plenty of things we need to keep a lid on. You're one of them. For more than one reason."

I took yet another sip. I must admit that the coffee was indeed quite delicious, though I said nothing regarding this fact.

For the first time since I had launched into my appeal, Miss von Leuckel spoke. "Warren? President? You mean in 1920?"

I nodded.

"Do you really think so, Tristan?" Even when I was young, she often solicited and respected my "reading on things," as she used to call it. Except, of course, when my "reading" somehow encumbered her fun.

"Yes," I said, "I really think so. And why not? Who else do the Republicans have? Or the Democrats, for that matter? And everyone's sick of them."

I watched her face as her initial wide-eyed interest seemed to turn into skepticism. Then she said, "They have Senator Lodge, that's who. Warren says Henry Cabot Lodge will be the next President."

I laughed in the admittedly condescending sort of way that I have always had, when confronted with some foolish notion, which of course is often the case in this world. "I doubt that very much. Lodge is as old as the hills, and he's too out of step, too stubborn. And they say he's a loner in Washington, has too many enemies, even in the GOP. Granted, from what I read, he and Senator Harding seem to get along alright, but it's probably one hand washing the other, that sort of thing. And Wilson obviously dislikes them both, so that puts them in each other's pocket. But lots of people dislike Lodge. I'm no politician, I'm just a builder, but I do read the papers and the magazines, and my impression is that the field's wide open." I paused for emphasis. "And Senator Harding's right smack dab in the middle. The best place to be. And people like him. He fits the bill." I sipped my coffee again, and then I broke off a piece of Mrs. Weaver's sweet roll and took a nibble, giving Miss von Leuckel a chance to think about things. "Of course," I added, "heaven knows that lots and lots of things could keep Senator Harding from being President."

For a long moment, she didn't say a word. "But Tristan, do you really think he's up to it?"

Quite frankly, her doubt—or rather her expression of it—surprised me, and sounded a bit cautious, like she was trying not to have too much hope. "Up to the Presidency? Why, of course he's up to it. Why not?"

She was twirling a strand of golden hair around her finger. "Well, I don't know. Like when I was back East last August . . ."

"Visiting Auntie."

"We were in this hotel in Port Jefferson, where I sent you the card from, when Warren showed me some kind of tax exemption bill, this big thick thing, something to do with Liberty Bonds. He said he couldn't make heads or tails of it, and asked me to read a couple of parts to him, out loud. I did, and then he asks me to explain what I thought they meant. So I ended up sitting down and going through those pages with him line by line, just like I do with a pupil who's having problems with the Federalist Papers, or something." She paused, "It seemed to me that he should've known."

I shrugged my shoulders. "So what? That hardly seems to matter. In leadership, it's one's judgment that counts. And nowadays all the details are done by Boards of Directors. Or in the case of the Presidency, then I suppose the Cabinet. Mr. Harding will have plenty of help with the details. You know as well as I do that he's always had a knack for finding good people and loyal help. Lots of those folks at the *Star* have stuck with him for life. Look at them, he's hundreds of miles away out in Washington, and there they are running his paper like he was right there beside them. I wouldn't dare try that with Colonel Hamilton & Son. Why, I bet Hearst himself couldn't find enough money to hire them away."

"I'm not even sure if Warren would want the job."

"The Presidency! Don't be silly. Of course he wants it. Every man that goes into politics wants it. But there's a big difference. In Mr. Harding's case, he can actually get it, attain it. He's a senator. From Ohio, no less. And on the surface, he has a few things in common with President McKinley, and those things could be very, very useful to the GOP. But of course we certainly won't win the White House if—" I paused. I almost said, indeed, I wanted to say, *if one of his mistresses* . . . I demurred. "We won't win if he's found to have a mistress. Not to mention, as rumor has it, an illegitimate son."

She looked away and I was startled to see her flush red—shamed, at least, by that.

"Especially," I added, "if his mistress is, according to the letter of the law, a German agent. As I said back in August, what do you think President Wilson would do if his Secret Service caught wind of you?" I again took out the book order from my pocket and held it between my fingers, like a piece of potentially incriminating evidence. "Don't you realize that this one little scrap of paper, in the wrong hands, could easily lead to the destruction of your beloved Senator Harding's career? I'm sure he would not appreciate that, nor would anyone else who ever pinned their hopes on him."

With this visit, I think I had finally succeeded in shaming her, and it was a pleasure. After a moment, she said, "It's funny, but Harry Daugherty told him the same thing, that the White House could be his in 1920, if he wants it."

"See!"

"But Harry's a fool."

"He's not a fool. He's a horse's ass, but he's no one's fool. Except maybe his own."

"Well, he's a ghastly man. Anyway, Warren just laughed when Harry said that. He really thinks Senator Lodge already has it all sown up. He told me so himself. Warren should know."

I shook my head. "He's wrong. Lodge walks with a cane. He can't even stand up straight. Why, he doesn't stand a chance. I think maybe the Senator's being modest. Or maybe he can't see the forest for the trees. But with a little luck, and a lot of planning, Warren Harding *will* be the next President of the United States."

I took another sip of coffee. My eyes were fixed on Miss von Leuckel. She was looking out the window now towards Orchard Street. I said quietly, watching her, "Warren G. Harding, President of the United States. Has the ring of destiny, doesn't it?"

Something in her face changed, something in her eyes, and I knew exactly what thoughts were passing through her mind. One of the same thoughts she had been having since 1914: Mrs. Warren G. Harding. But now, maybe for the first time, that thought was walking hand-in-hand with: First Lady. Needless to say, I let her think that. Besides, if Senator Harding actually was elected in 1920, and if Mrs. Harding actually were to die—both distinct possibilities—then, well, who knows? It wasn't as if she was dreaming of marrying the King of England.

"So, Miss von Leuckel, let's start looking forward to 1920. You will stop risking your neck, and thereby the Senator's, won't you?" I paused and quietly mused, "Why, who knows what the future holds. Could be very, very interesting. Like a dream come true."

"Yes," she said, her voice faraway. She was still looking out the window, twirling a strand of golden hair on her finger, nodding as if to her own inner thoughts, and she said, "Yes, like a dream come true."

I stifled a bitter and mocking laugh.

BOOK II

The Hunt for the
Grand Goblin

I

TUESDAY AFTERNOON
26 NOVEMBER 1963
TIOGA

Girl in a Garden at Nightfall

A SHORT WHILE AGO, with Miss von Leuckel still pestering my peace of mind, I retrieved a most rare and interesting volume from its secret hiding place. Indeed, it is so rare that I am utterly certain that no more than three or four volumes can possibly exist in the entire world. In fact, so far as I know, this may be the only one left. Before long, this one too will vanish into the oblivion of fire or flood. Not that the book can do much harm anymore. It is just that I have a strong feeling that a couple of academics, a historian or two, not to mention rare book dealers, are keeping close tabs on me via acquaintances in Marion—though I know not whom. I sense their eyes, so to speak. They are like vultures perched in distant trees keeping a casual eye on an old lion that is still on the prowl, though his fall into the dust is inevitable. Of course what the academics are really interested in is the eventual auction of Tioga's contents, whereupon they will swoop down and pick through my family's possessions, scavenging for any scrap and tidbit having to do with the Harding legacy. Needless to say, they shall find precisely what I want them to find, that and nothing more—and most of that I have already moved to the Harding Home. Other things, like this little volume, I shall feed to the incinerator in the basement, or maybe in due time, on some summer evening at sunset, I shall fling it off the cliffs at Indian Rock and let it be battered to pieces by Lake Erie's roiling waves.

After all, Mr. Harding loved Lake Erie.

As I have already stated, I personally have nothing whatsoever to hide, and I should hasten to add that I have never destroyed, nor shall I ever destroy, a single piece of correspondence that President Harding ever sent to anyone in my family, nor any scrap—incriminating or otherwise—having to do with the Harding Administration.

But I shall do as I damn well please with the other things. I suppose you will think I am mean-spirited when I say that I shall destroy this curious volume, in part, simply for the glee of doing so. Call it plain old spitefulness, if you wish, but do not suppose for a moment that I owe a free lunch, much less a banquet, to vultures.

About this little book—I keep it very well hidden under lock and key, just in case some academic scoundrel ever breaks into Tioga while I am away. I would not put it past them, and they seem to know I have it. I have received at least five letters in as many years from some fellow who calls himself the "curator of the Rare Book Room" at the New York Public Library, begging me to donate my little volume to his library's collection. Why, just last Christmas the fellow even got hold of Hemmerlys Florist and had them send me a big pot of poinsettias wrapped with bright red foil and a bow. I always ignored his letters, though I had no choice but to send the ass a curt thank-you note for the flowers, which of course he immediately followed up with the most groveling letter of all. Worse yet, last year my family's faithful housekeeper, dear Mrs. Christian, received a long-distance telephone call from some kind of book dealer out in New York City telling her that if she could locate the volume "somewhere in Marion," then he would give her, I think his words were, "a very nice chunk of cash, at least five thousand dollars."

Obviously, someone in this very town supplied him with the name of my housekeeper.

Little does anyone know—not even Mrs. Christian—that I also have the original manuscript in my possession, written in the author's elegant hand. Indeed, I also have much of the unpublished last chapter, which is all about Miss von Leuckel, Mr. Harding, their son, and me—along with some mention of Kaiser Wilhelm II. This last and juiciest chapter was in the process of being printed for inclusion in a new edition when the entire lot fell into my hands.

The title of this exceedingly rare and much sought-after little book is *Warren Gamaliel Harding: A Review of the Facts*, written by one William Estabrook Chancellor. Just this past summer I read a little notice in the *Star* that Chancellor had died in a rest home in Dayton, preceded in death by his wife and daughter. Actually, I met his daughter once—along about the time when I acquired the books and manuscript—though I am not altogether sure if he ever knew of this. Anyway, Chancellor reached the advanced age of a hundred and three or four, something like that. He too was an academic, a former professor of history at Wooster College. Like Marion, Wooster is a little town in the middle of nowhere, about forty or fifty miles northeast of here on Route 30.

In an interview in the Sunday edition of the *Columbus-Dispatch* many long years ago, I would say back in the '30s, Chancellor completely disavowed that he had ever written a book about President Warren G. Harding, though apparently, just in case any copies ever managed to surface, he fabricated the outlandish tale that someone had once written such a book, and had "framed" him by maliciously placing his name on the cover and title page, thus making him the enemy of, and he worded it something like: "those gangsters in the Ohio Gang, so called."

I assure you that this is an utter lie and nonsense. Frankly, the lie is so silly that I am not sure why he even bothered telling it. By my reckoning, Chancellor was just a weird and mixed-up little man (with, I might add, a rather pathetic daughter). I am not even sure how he ever managed to achieve "academic success"—so far as I am concerned, an oxymoron if ever there was one. Why, even when Chancellor was haunting Marion, back in the summer and fall of 1920, he possessed a bizarre blend of boldness and skittishness. It was as if he had the mind of a fox but the temperament of a Chihuahua. I might add that he looked like a billy goat—narrow face, sunken cheeks, and gray Van Dyke whiskers. By my lights, he was nothing short of startling.

On page 15 of his book, which is actually the first page of Chapter 1 of *Warren Gamaliel Harding: A Review of the Facts*, Professor Chancellor writes: "Warren Harding has Negro blood in him. He has been ashamed of this element of his blood, ashamed of his own great-grandmother, Elizabeth Madison, and of the negroes that contributed their blood to his great-grandfather, George Tyrone (or Tryon) Harding."

On the next page, he says, "The Presidency is in danger of falling into ignorant hands, for Warren Harding cannot write English that is understandable. His mental furniture is that of a schoolboy."

And a few pages after that:

> *Every man, woman, and child in Marion, Ohio, knows the truth about Warren Harding, and most of them are hiding it because it's a skeleton in their closet. The ones who are most keen about hiding it are the ones who are part of the tight-knit little circle made up of his rich and powerful friends there that want to get him elected so that they can set him up as their puppet President. This way the crooked and ambitious Ohio Gang can rule the country through their colored lackey and get even richer than they already are. Many of them already have money coming out of their ears, for Marion is a rich and ambitious little town, though its shabby north end and its many places of ill-repute reveal its true nature.*

Thumbing through the pages, I see on page 66 an outline of Marion County, which I guess is supposed to suggest a map. Beneath it is the caption <u>Little Africa – Harding Land,</u> followed by the words: "Where for a hundred years has raged a war between the whites and the mestizos."

I have lived in Marion County since the day I was born in 1895, and I have never had even the slightest notion that this Hundred Years War was raging around me. Nor do I have the slightest idea who the "mestizos" are.

A few pages later, I find a small, folded mimeographed sheet with a thumbtack hole in it, from where it was once pinned to my front door. The sheet is a concocted family tree entitled "Genealogy of Warren G. Harding of Marion, Ohio." It is uniformly yellow now, but I remember it being white. Its record is very short, and so there is no reason why I cannot quote it here in its entirety:

Genealogy of Warren G. Harding of Marion, Ohio.

Geo. Tryon Harding
Great Grandfather
(BLACK)

Ann Roberts
Great Grandmother
(BLACK)

Charles A. Harding
Grandfather
(BLACK)

Mary Ann Crawford
Grandmother
(WHITE)

George Tryon Harding, 2nd
Father
(MULATTO)

Phoebe Dickerson
Mother
(WHITE)

Warren G. Harding
Son
(QUADROON)

No issues have been born to Harding, at least none by his own wife, a divorcee, and said by some to be a Jewess.

The Ohio Gang would like for us to think that this is a vicious rumor spread by the Democrats for their own political advantage, but it is no rumor. It is the truth, and the Harding people and the citizens of Marion, Ohio, know it to be so.

These facts and many more are compiled and proven beyond the shadow of a doubt by the distinguished Professor William Estabrook Chancellor, BA, MA, PhD., Wooster College, in his book Warren Gamaliel Harding: A Review of the Facts, *currently available to the American people via agents.*

IF YOU VOTE FOR HARDING, KNOW THAT YOU'RE VOTING TO PUT A COLORED MAN INTO THE WHITE HOUSE!!!

First off, you will notice that in the passage from the book that I cited earlier, Professor Chancellor calls the President's grandmother Elizabeth Madison, but in the above "genealogy" she becomes Ann Roberts.

I shall let the discrepancy speak for itself.

Well, I could go on—but I think you get the idea.

I suppose all this talk about the "Negro-blood rumor" has caused you to wonder just what the devil it's all about, and especially, of course, whether or not President Harding actually was, in fact, a colored man. Or part colored.

As they say, your guess is as good as mine. I will say that Mr. Harding, like his father, was two or three shades darker than most white men, and my father said that when Mr. Harding was young, his thick and wiry hair was raven black. But I've known Scotsmen with similar hair, and like a Scotsman, he had green eyes with a hint of gray tint. As for "proof" regarding his so-called African ancestry, there is none, one way or another. Personally, I pretty much feel the same way about the Negro-blood business as I feel about the assassination theory. And for that matter, as I said before, flying saucers landing in cornfields: interesting, but where's the proof?

Where's even the slimmest shred of evidence?

I will admit that I grew up hearing that the Hardings were colored people. I will also admit that the rumor was so pervasive and enduring that I think a lot of folks believed it, more or less, simply because of the repeated tellings. Indeed, I would go so far as to say that even most of those of us in the "Ohio Gang" weren't entirely sure what Mr. Harding's race was. Not that we ever talked about the subject. And even I must admit that when you grow up hearing a rumor, for years and years on end, it makes you wonder.

But does the fact that a rumor is oft repeated make it true?

Folks used to say that either Mr. Harding's great grandmother or great grandfather was born a slave. Some genealogies, like the one concocted by Professor Chancellor, confirmed this, while others, like one drawn up locally in 1910, utterly contradicted it.

As for Mr. Harding himself, I do not think he ever knew for certain one way or the other, and I think it is to his credit that he refused to speak out publicly regarding the issue. This was strategy, in part, for Harry

Daugherty contended that it was best for him to "remain above the fray," while others of us took care of the dirty work going on down under. This way Mr. Harding remained focused on the issues—the League of Nations, the eight-hour workday, and returning the country to what the Senator always called "normalcy" after all the turmoil of the Great War.

As for me, personally, I never really thought it mattered much whether or not he had colored ancestors. He was a smart man, and decent, except when it came to the ladies. Besides, who really knows what blood any of us may have trickling through our veins? Maybe I am carrying within me the blood of one of the Kings of England, or a Pharaoh, or Moses. Or a traitor, a saint, a thief. Or an African.

And what difference does it make?

I am whom God made me. I am what I do, and I am who I make and remake myself to be. I am what I contribute to the world around me.

I might add that, so far as I know, there's absolutely nothing in the Constitution that forbids a citizen with this or that ancestry from serving as President of the United States, so long as he was born on American soil. I might also add that Mr. Harding was neither the first nor the last to stir up controversy in this area. I have no idea if it's true, so I am not trying to pass this off as gospel, but I distinctly remember that, in the autumn of 1920, when the racial storm was swirling around us, some old-timers swore up and down that sixty years before, people were saying the exact same thing about Abraham Lincoln. And my father told me that there were some very heated debates back in 1896 as to whether or not William McKinley—a first-generation American of Irish stock—should be elected President of an Anglo-Saxon nation. And need I point out that a mere three short years ago, plenty of people were saying that a Roman Catholic had no more business running for President than a Jew?

Anyway, back to Professor Chancellor.

And back to Miss von Leuckel, for it was through her that I made Professor Chancellor's acquaintance.

WELL DO I REMEMBER that pleasant late September evening in 1920 when Mitzy and I spoke again—the first time since our meeting in her rooms, towards the end of the war. I remember it was the night before the Senator took his campaign train, the *Harding Special*, to Indiana. My dear

Lucy and I were dinner guests at Etowah, the home of Mr. and Mrs. George W. King, the Harding's neighbors on Mt. Vernon Avenue. Now I hope you will not think of me as a "name dropper" when I say that the King's dinner party was given in honor of two very special guests, Mary Pickford and her husband Douglas Fairbanks. They had only been married for a couple of months and their trip to Marion was part of an extended honeymoon that included England, Canada, and now the United States. I know that they had stopped off in Miss Pickford's native Toronto a few days before, because I read about it in the *Star*. Along with their fame as movie stars, they had both won great respect and affection all across North America, and in Allied Europe, by raising tens of millions of dollars in war bonds. And now they were lending their voices to Senator Harding's bid for the Presidency. Indeed, several hours before dinner, they had appeared before a vast and almost idolatrous crowd at the Harding's home, each giving a rousing speech through the brass bullhorn (an artifact that we still possess at the Harding Home).

I do not think it is any exaggeration to say that Douglas Fairbanks and Mary Pickford were, at that time, among the most famous people in the world.

I might add that both were greatly taken with Etowah. When they arrived for dinner, they requested a tour of the house and grounds, and were especially taken with Lake Etowah—a former limestone quarry once owned and operated by my family. Naturally, the Kings were more than happy to oblige them with a tour. I very distinctly recall that the newlyweds were planning to build a house out in Hollywood, and they freely admitted that they were "shopping around" for ideas. That house was to become Pickfair, where the elderly Miss Pickford lives to this very day. I do not know what ideas they may or may not have borrowed from Etowah, but I will say that I doubt if even Pickfair surpassed the splendors of Mr. and Mrs. King's home.

Mr. King, a generous supporter of Mr. Harding's various political campaigns, was the president and driving force behind the Marion Steam Shovel Company. He supplied the army of steam shovels that dug the Panama Canal, a project that gave many years of around-the-clock work to hundreds of Marion men, channeling millions of dollars into the town. As a young editor Mr. Harding had helped bring that windfall about via his early political friendships with Governor William McKinley and with the Governor's campaign manager, the "king-maker," Marc Hanna.

I will not bore you with the list of guests present that evening at the Kings' dinner party. Let me simply say that, along with the Hardings, and Mr. and Mrs. Douglas Fairbanks, there were about a dozen others of us present, including my father, my sister Adeline, and of course my wife Lucy. Well do I remember that Harry Daugherty, the Senator's campaign manager, and his sidekick Jess Smith were also present. If one ever beheld the spectacle of those two fellows, side by side at feeding time, then one would never forget it. A fork or a spoon in either of their hands fulfilled about the same duties as a shovel, and neither believed that a full mouth was any excuse for keeping one's mouth shut. But all in all, the dinner was a great success, and quite an extravagant affair, with Dresden china, gleaming vermeil flatware, and sterling silver candelabrum. I have a feeling that even today Mary Pickford, with her long life crowded with brilliant memories, may still have a fond recollection of that long-ago dinner party on a perfect autumn evening in the otherwise woebegone and forgotten place called Marion, Ohio.

As you can imagine, most of the attention was lavished on the quests of honor. I think that America considered them royalty, or something close to it, and frankly, I think that the movie stars held a similar estimation of themselves. Not that they were arrogant; they were simply proud, and their pride was laced with the sort of graciousness that one always encounters in the very best people of their stature. I remember Adeline leaning over to me during the dinner and whispering, "Thank God, Trey, they aren't just 'down-to earth' folks. As if there aren't enough already."

The dinner had progressed to dessert—apple pie with whipped cream. One of the girls was going around the table pouring coffee. I remember Mrs. Harding and Miss Pickford, both divorcees, were having a conversation about dealing with the stigma of that while trying to be exemplars for women everywhere. Douglas Fairbanks was dazzling the rest of us with his account of how they had constructed a temporary railroad in a former orange grove in Hollywood, in order to bring in trainloads of lumber and plaster needed to recreate medieval Arabia for his new movie *The Thief of Baghdad*. Being builders, I think my father and I were particularly fascinated with this, and I distinctly remember Mr. Fairbanks saying that the average cost of those sets, for the time they appeared on the screen, came to more than a thousand dollars per second.

Anyway, I was a bit taken aback when one of Mrs. King's servant girls leaned over my shoulder and whispered in my ear, "Mr. Hamilton, begging your pardon, sir, but there's a lady here to see you. She says it's important."

"A lady? Who?"

I saw her eyes glance towards the Senator, but not at him. He was appropriately absorbed with the guest of honor. She leaned closer to my ear, "Miss von Leuckel, sir. She's waiting in the garden. Says it's important and can't wait. I'm very sorry. I really didn't know what to do."

Adeline, seated to my right, glanced my way at the whispering of Miss von Leuckel's name. She raised an eyebrow, as if to say, Trouble! And then she turned away, so as to stay out of it.

I wiped my lips with the linen napkin and excused myself from the table. As I arose I whispered to Lucy, "Someone to see me. One of the Senator's friends. Be right back."

She nodded, barely taking her eyes from Douglas Fairbanks, spinning his splendid tale about his plaster and plywood Arabia.

I think Harry may have read my lips or sensed something, for he suddenly stopped chewing his pie and whatever else he may have had stuffed in his trap, and I felt his eyes fasten on me as I followed the girl from the room.

She led me down the wide hall, hung with Flemish tapestries, and across the red tile floor of the grand parlor that an Italian painter had decorated with trompe l'oeil frescoes. At that time a high-ceilinged solarium of plate glass and copper was still located off the parlor, and a walk through its interior was like a detour through a little tropical jungle, complete with humid air, fragrant orchids, screeching parrots and macaws, and water splashing into pools abundant with lilies, papyrus, and blue Egyptian lotus blossoms.

The girl walked me as far as the door. "Miss von Leuckel said she'd be waiting out there, sir." She peered through the screen. "I don't see her just now, though I'm sure you'll find her out there somewheres."

I thanked her and stepped out into the pleasant coolness of that September evening. Flocks of noisy starlings darkened the sky, returning to the Old Forest from their day in the country, dining in the cornfields.

I went along the stone walkway towards Lake Etowah, and there, just beyond the hedge, stood Miss von Leuckel. I can still see her in my mind's eye beside the stone statue of a leopard, seated on its haunches. She was wearing a cloak, royal blue in color, and one of those racy post-war dresses with the hem just below the knee—the sort that ladies from the Society for the Suppression of Vices were all up in arms about. I paused in my tracks. She seemed absorbed with the statue. As I said, it was a leopard, or something of that nature, a very large seated cat, its mouth drawn back in a snarl. The creature came up as far as Mitzy's bosom, and her hand was resting on its head. As I watched, she caressed its snout and moved the tip of her finger to the tip of its fang. Somewhere within me I seem to have always nurtured a halfhearted desire to be an artist, for every so often when I behold some scene of enchantment, I think to myself, *Ah, if only I were an artist I would paint that scene.* Thus as I stood there I thought to myself, *I would call my painting: Girl in a Garden at Nightfall.*

"Good evening," I said.

She turned, startled. "Oh, Tristan! I didn't hear you." For a moment, she simply stared at me. "I'm sorry for having to call you from supper. I'll bet it's good."

"Not at all, I'm glad for the fresh air. Besides, I'm sure you have a good reason."

"Unfortunately, I have."

As I walked towards her, I was hoping we would shake hands, for we had not touched flesh for six years and one month. During that time, empires fell and worlds passed away. I stopped an arm's length from her.

She was still appraising me. "Tristan, you look so—so princely."

I gave a little laugh, flattered. "Well, I really don't know about that—"

"No, you do."

I thanked her. Mitzy always liked it when people dressed up. She glanced off towards the house, and I clasped my hands behind my back. "So you and Lucy, you're having dinner with Douglas Fairbanks and Mary Pickford, are you?"

"As a matter of fact, we are. And of course with the next President of the United States. Actually, Mr. and Mrs. Fairbanks have turned out to be very charming people, very intriguing, and quite pleasant. Believe it or not, both are every bit as intelligent as they are good looking. I think you'd like them tremendously. I think they'd like you. You must get Senator Harding to introduce you to them, someday. If events ever arise."

I cast a glance over my shoulder at Etowah, stretching long and massive behind me. I was absolutely certain Miss von Leuckel had never set foot in the place, and probably never would. I said, "And every time I enter Etowah, I'm surprised anew by its many splendors." But the instant I said that, I somewhat regretted it, at least for a moment, because I was suddenly afraid that Mitzy would chide me for my formal way with words. She used to call me a "stuffed shirt," among other things, and would sometimes tease me for my "peculiar phraseology." Indeed, she had even coined a word for my occasional way of putting things; these were "Tristanisms." She might say, "Ah, what have we here, another Tristanism?" But at that moment, I was not sure she even remembered any of this, for it had all happened so long ago, in our youth. She stood peering at the house, as if seeing through its massive stonewalls, picturing the glittering affair ensuing within, without her. "On the whole," I added, "it's been a memorable evening." Eyeing her, I said, "Something tells me it's going to get even more memorable."

"I'm afraid so. Does Warren know I'm out here?"

"Of course not. Just the girl and me. She was very discreet. So—?"

"Well—" She looked behind her, towards the west, seemingly scrutinizing the area, as if half expecting to see an eavesdropper lurking in the cedar hedge. Then she peered off towards Bradford Street, beyond the stone balustrade that rimmed the King estate. "There's such an awful lot of people around. Too many for comfort." Indeed, at that very moment several hundred people, mostly outsiders, waited near the front gates of Etowah, and along Mt. Vernon Avenue, hoping for a glimpse of the movie stars when they departed in the enormous Packard that they'd brought along on their private train. But I should add that not a single one of those onlookers could have possibly overheard a single word we were saying, tucked away as we were, back in the garden. "Tristan," she said, her voice almost a whisper, "something's happened."

"Hmmm," I said. "I suppose I already gathered as much. "

She looked off towards Lake Etowah, at the far edge of the sloping land. "Do you think we could go down there, down by the water?"

Shadows were darkening the lake and the long backyard, and a slight mist was rising over the water. "Why not."

As we started down the footpath, Mitzy said, "Tristan, someone knows."

I do not wish to sound naïve, but I truly did not understand what she meant. After all, there was a lot to know in Marion, Ohio, and the little intrigue between Mitzy and the Senator, and their son, was certainly nothing new. In fact, it was the town's most popular secret. "Knows what?"

"Everything. Absolutely everything. An evil old man. A geezer. A college professor. He knows everything about me and Warren. He knows about Arrian. Why, he even knows what those busybodies were saying during the war. He asked how many secrets I got out of Warren to sell to the Germans."

I felt like saying, *See, what did I tell you?* But I kept my spite to myself.

After a few steps in silence, she said, "I know what you're thinking, Tristan. And you're right. You're always right. It's very annoying, but you are. Maybe you're clairvoyant."

"Clairvoyant!" I laughed. "Hardly. It doesn't always take clairvoyance to see how things are going to turn out in life. Usually it's just plain old common sense."

"I guess that's something I've never had much of, and I don't miss it. It's not always the best feature, you know, and it's certainly not the bravest. Why, we wouldn't be standing here now if Christopher Columbus had suffered from common sense."

I made no reply. I wasn't about to get into some silly philosophical conversation that would have us both chasing our own tails and each other's.

"Tristan," she said, "he even knows about you."

"Me?" For a split second, I stopped in my tracks. Not as an affectation of melodrama, but simply because I was genuinely flabbergasted. "What on earth is there to know about me?"

"More than you think. For starters, about you and me. Our plans long ago." She looked off towards the west where the evening sky glowed pink through the trees. In a quieter voice she said, "And then how the Senator came along."

"So what? Who cares? That's ancient history."

"Ancient history to you and me, maybe. To Warren, too, I suppose. But what would others think? Like tens of millions of voters? And with ladies voting for the first time, what would they think if they heard about it?"

I suppose I should have felt vindicated, but vindication had absolutely nothing to do with our goal of elevating Senator Harding to the White House. If word ever got out that he had engaged in an adulterous affair, or worse yet, that he had split up a young, courting couple, then we would have a fine mess on our hands. "We'd deny it!" I said. "Both of us. Emphatically. As for the Senator, he wouldn't stoop low enough to even comment on such filth. We'd throw it right back in their faces. We'd call it a Democratic conspiracy. One to sully the Senator's good name and Christian character. Not to mention his thirty years of happy marriage." I'm afraid that a tone of bitterness had seeped into my voice, belying my words. I added, "We'd make them eat their words, laced with their own venom."

Mitzy cast me a look. I think my vehemence may have startled her.

We walked beneath the pergola, heavy with the dying vines of summer's purple wisteria, and crossed the plaza to the stone banister overlooking Lake Etowah, with its gathering mists. On the far side, on the cliff walls, the giant face of the stone lion spewed a fountain of water into the lake. Its soothing and faraway sound blended with the uproar of the birds that by now were settling into their roosts in the Old Forest. Upon the water, the fount scarcely ruffled the dark reflection of the surrounding primeval oaks, elms, and maples with their pale leaves, and the darkening sky. It's funny, the hodgepodge of thoughts that such a place can invoke. Yes, I was concerned about the problems at hand, but for a few moments, as I stood there, I thought of how, in our youth, Mitzy and I used to steal into those distant woods, on evenings such as this, and I was thinking of all she had taught me, though I was nearly three years her senior.

Apparently, she was thinking nothing of the kind, for the very next thing she said was, "Tristan, he even knows about the accident."

I did not avert my eyes from the water; on the periphery of my vision I could see her scrutinizing me. "Accident?" I said.

"You know. What they say you did when you were a boy."

"Hmmm, must be an awfully talkative fellow. Anyway, that's the least of my concerns."

"I realize that, but it shows how much he knows."

The smell of a coal fire came from somewhere, and I glanced across the water towards Bradford Street. Someone was standing there enjoying the view. "Be careful," I whispered. "Remember how the lake carries voices."

She glanced about and said quietly, "He knows about the Negro blood, too. But that's no surprise."

That was one of the cauldrons upon which the Campaign was hoping to keep a lid. I turned to Mitzy, "So who is this fellow? What's he want? And why's he telling everything he knows? Though that's a good sign. It shows he's a fool."

"Oh, but he's not a fool. At least I don't think so. He's written a book. He's written lots of books, or so he says. But this one, I'm sure he wrote it. It's about Warren." She was opening the little beaded purse that hung by a strap from her shoulder. "Look here." She read his name from a piece of paper, "Professor William Estabrook Chancellor."

She handed it to me.

It appeared to be the title page from a book. I read it aloud, "Warren Gamaliel Harding: A Review of the Facts."

Beneath Chancellor's name, an imprint of his signature appeared, and at the bottom of the page, the words "Sentinel Press." At first glance, I thought the crisp new page had been neatly scissored away from the volume, which seemed like an odd thing to have done, but as I examined it, I realized that the page had been pulled during the printing process. Neat little pinprick holes lined the left side through which, I presume, binding threads were meant to pass, connecting the pages.

"So, if this is part of a book, then where's the rest of it?"

"Oh," Mitzy bit her lip. "Why, how foolish of me. I didn't think to ask." She looked away, out towards the water. "He's such an awful old man, Tristan. He just found out about Warren and me. From someone around here. He said, 'So where you been hiding yourself, Missy?' He said he thought he'd 'turned over every rock,' and then I 'come popping up like a jack-in-the-box.'"

"Someone in Marion's always doing an awful lot of talking," I said. "But I don't think there's much surprise in that. Or anything we can do about it, either. Except maybe not give them so much to talk about." I gave that remark a moment to sink in, or bounce off, as the case may have been. "So this fellow, he came for a reason. What's he up to?"

Mitzy turned the title page over in my hand; the figure $10,000.00 was written in pencil and underlined twice. "That's what he's up to. He says he'll give me ten thousand dollars if I sign an affidavit saying I'm Senator Harding's mistress." The words Room 202 Hotel Marion appeared further down the page. "That's where he's staying."

After a long moment of stunned silence, I said, "May I hold onto this?"

She nodded and I slipped the page into my pocket.

The swans had paddled over and were now floating below us, apparently waiting for breadcrumbs or something. As Mitzy watched them, she said, "When he wrote that down, I said, 'Ten thousand dollars? That's all?' I think he thought I'd be doing backward somersaults at the mere thought of getting so much money. He says to me, 'That's all! Now looky here, Missy, the truth'll come out one way or another, I'll see to it, so you best take my advice and get rich quick.' I said, 'Well, getting rich has always sounded like a good idea to me. But you looky here, Mister, this is Marion, Ohio, and we happen to be talking presidential politics, not state politics.' I said, 'Ten thousand dollars isn't even worth the governorship, much less the presidency. You want me to sign an affidavit? Then try fifty thousand. I won't even think about it for a penny less.' That's what I told him. And I said that if it comes out in any other way, then I'll sign an affidavit denying everything, and I'll go to court and sue him for slander. And libel. And anything else I can think of. And then I'll get all the money I want, and maybe more, and I said, 'And you'll be making brooms in the workhouse, Mister.' I said, 'And you best not forget something, too, Mister. In a very short time I just might happen to be very close to a certain someone in the White House.' And just for good measure, I said, 'Besides, you have to remember, I'm a schoolteacher. I have my reputation to think of.'" Mitzy had been looking at the swans, not at me. She added quietly, like she was worried, "He says he can get other affidavits, too, Tristan. Plenty of them. Saying I was a German sympathizer. And the Kaiser's agent." She was biting her lip. "But he wants proof about me and Warren. There's only two people can provide that. One of them's running for President."

I interjected, "And the other's hoping to be his First Lady, should Fate be so kind."

"If you were me, an ambitious young lady in my shoes, then maybe you'd want what I want too. And I know you, so don't say you wouldn't.

Besides, it's not really First Lady that I want to be, though that would be nice too; it's Warren's wife."

"He's already got one."

By now I very definitely had the impression that she was not simply watching the swans gliding below us, but that she was also avoiding my eye. And I thought I knew why. "So, Miss von Leuckel, I gather that you've come here looking for fifty thousand dollars from the Campaign? Or is it fifty-five? Or what, precisely?"

I shall not repeat the string of colorful expletives with which Mitzy adorned the evening air. Indeed, her words could have made a teamster blush. But oddly enough, they had no such effect on me. As a matter of fact, I instantly found them comforting. For I realized that Miss von Leuckel, perhaps without forethought or even awareness, had laid before me one of her little traps. By having doubted her "integrity," I had stepped into her snare—somehow making myself look duplicitous, while making her look morally persecuted. Or something.

After summing up her opinion of me, she added, "For your information, Mr. Hamilton, what I came here for is simply to ask you to do something about Professor Chancellor. That's what I want. I don't want one red cent out of this. The only thing I want is for Warren to win the Presidency. Period. After that, what will be, will be."

"Then why on earth did you tell this guy you want fifty thousand—?"

"To give him a run for his money. And to let him know, for his information, that if I were the type of girl who'd go around selling myself, then I certainly wouldn't be doing it on the cheap."

Her logic—including the notion that ten thousand dollars was "on the cheap"—somewhat eluded me, though I was not about to open the can of worms I knew as "Mitzy's logic." I simply said, "I see. How ignorant of me. In that case, I guess we could say that you were just pretending."

"Call it what you will, but sometimes it takes a ruse to get at the truth."

"'A ruse to get at the truth.' Words to live by, though heaven knows where they'd lead. Nevertheless, I ought to remember them."

"Well, I doubt that you will. And even if you do, I doubt that you'd ever live by them." She looked out at the lake, "You've always had too much starch in your underwear, Tristan."

I laughed at her charming criticism (which, by the way, rang true).

"Tristan, what are you going to do about Professor Chancellor?"

I gave a sigh. "Well, I guess there's only one thing to do, at least for starters. Go to Hotel Marion and have a word with him. Then we'll have to take it from there."

"Yes, I suppose so." She looked towards Bradford Street, now filling with shadows. "For some reason, I keep having the feeling that he followed me here." She scrutinized the distance, as if expecting to see the professor peeking from over the low wall surrounding the estate, or peeking from behind one of the elms. I looked that way too, but the only person there was a young fellow enjoying the mild evening and his view of the lake. He took a long drag on his cigarette and then propelled the butt into Lake Etowah. Mitzy said, "Why, maybe he's watching us right now. I think he is, from somewhere."

I gave a little laugh. "How'd you get here—walk?"

"Streetcar. He wasn't on it. Believe me, I checked. Well, maybe it's just my imagination." She wrapped the cloak about her. "He's a reptile," she said. "Otherwise he wouldn't know so much about me. About everything. I bet he's got paid informants right here in Marion. Why, to think of it! Some of Warren's very own neighbors working against him. It's a disgrace."

"That's politics. I'm sure not everyone up in Canton supported Governor McKinley. And I can tell you for a fact that the Harding Volunteers have a very active chapter down in Dayton, with an office only a couple of blocks from Governor Cox's newspaper. Or so I'm told."

(Governor Cox of Ohio, a Democrat, was Mr. Harding's opponent in the presidential race.)

I noticed that the young fellow over on Bradford Street was looking our way. He was a rather "snazzy" dresser, with a straw-boater hat perched on the back of his head in that cocky, sporty way that college boys were wearing them at the time. I presumed he was eyeing Mitzy—for reasons that had nothing whatsoever to do politics. But when he realized that I had my eye on him, he quickly looked away, towards the lion fount. Then he turned his back to the lake and leaned against the wall, like he was "killing time." It suddenly struck me as odd that he wasn't near the front gates with all of the other folks, waiting for a glimpse of Mary Pickford and Douglas Fairbanks, and of course of the Senator.

I glanced over my shoulder towards the house. The dining room windows were glowing golden from lamps and candelabrum. "I should get back," I said. "They're probably waiting for me so they can leave the table."

"'So they can leave the table!' For heaven's sake, Tristan. You're the only one who still pays attention to such things. You and Adeline. That's all changed now."

"That's what you think."

"That's what I know. It's the 20th century now. Not even your father cares about that stuff. Colonel Hamilton never did give two hoots about it anyway. And I bet when you go back in there, Warren'll have a toothpick sticking between his lips. And he's going to be the next President of the United States! Maybe."

"My mother taught us certain things. And the fact remains, Miss von Leuckel, that Lucy and I—we're dining at Etowah tonight, with Mr. and Mrs. Fairbanks. And you—." After a pause, I added, "There's one thing we can agree on—I believe this Professor Chancellor fellow isn't working alone. Not if he's offered you ten thousand."

Mitzy seemed to consider this point. "No, I suppose he isn't. Either that, or he comes from money."

I laughed at the very thought. "Why, from what you've told me, if this fellow comes from money, then I come from Timbuktu."

"Well, he's arrogant and he thinks he's special."

I laughed at her barb.

"Maybe he's with the Democrats," she said. "Maybe he's part of the Cox Campaign."

"I doubt it. But what do I know."

"As a rule, more than one would like. And what you don't know, you seem to pull out of the air, at least sometimes."

I laughed at her mystification of common sense. With Miss von Leuckel, one was either a spoiled brat or a mystic. Or both. As for me, so far as I was concerned, neither came even remotely close to the mark. "I want to go eat my apple pie," I said.

I was just about to walk Miss von Leuckel to the Bradford Street gate and to offer to call a cab for her, but before I could, she laid her hand on my chest. I don't know why, but her touch sent a sort of electric jolt through me. I stood looking into her eyes, looking into mine, and it was like my breath stopped. It is something one feels only in one's youthful years, when touched by the fairer sex. "Tristan," her voice was soft and whispery, "when you see Warren, will you please, will you give him my love?" No sooner had she spoken, than she said, "Oh, my goodness, what am I saying! Why, you mustn't do anything of the kind! If that came out of your mouth, he'd melt with embarrassment. Just tell him—" She removed her hand from my chest and touched her lips in thought. I glanced off towards the Old Forest where the moon was now rising through the trees in the southeast. "Oh, to hell with it, don't tell him a damn thing. I'll see him soon enough anyway, probably, and I'll tell him myself."

"Listen," I said, "I've got to get back in there. I don't want Douglas Fairbanks making passes at my wife. They say he's that type of man, you know."

With that, I turned and walked away, leaving my former sweetheart standing alone in the gathering darkness.

II

Three Figures Materialize from the Darkness

AFTER SEEING LUCY HOME, I pulled the Ford out of the garage and drove to Hotel Marion. Like nearly every place in town, the hotel was nicely decorated—inside and out—with flags, patriotic bunting, and heroic portraits of Senator Harding. I don't believe I mentioned that Marion had designated the streets between the train depot and the Front Porch as being "Victory Way." The GOP provided most of the money, but the Harding Volunteers, with chapters throughout the nation, also provided funds. A colossal triumphal arch (of plywood and plaster, painted in faux marble) spanned the intersection of Main and Center Streets, and white Doric columns topped with gilded eagles lined the entire length of Victory Way. I remember on that particular day that about a dozen delegations of Shriners from throughout the Midwest had marched to the Front Porch behind brass bands. A fair number had their photographs taken on the porch steps with the Senator and Mrs. Harding and Mary Pickford and Douglas Fairbanks.

Now at least a score of the Shriners, along with other guests, were "taking it easy" in the lobby of Hotel Marion, several still donning their red fezzes with the dangling black tassels. Folks were chatting in plush red chairs among potted palms, and I'm sure that many were reading newspaper articles about the Campaign. Scarcely a day went by when Marion was not on the front page of the nation's papers, and often we made the front pages of European papers as well, thanks to the decisive part our nation played in the late war. In fact, I would go so far as to say that, during the summer of 1920, Marion was the most famous little town on earth. Why, I can say with full authority that King George V had heard and read all about Marion. No doubt the hotel guests felt that they were a part of history in the making. A lot of them seemed to notice me as I crossed the lobby, and suddenly I wished that I had changed out of my dinner jacket before coming here.

I did not bother stopping at the front desk. I merely gave a little wave to Claude Uncapher, the clerk, and hastened by. And I certainly did not bother with the elevator. I climbed the stairs, two at a time, and paused at the door of 202. I leaned my ear close and listened for voices, wondering if maybe one of my fellow townsmen just happened to be in that room conspiring with the good professor. But I did not hear so much as a peep. When I knocked, I found myself doing so in a way that I imagined a young lady like Mitzy might knock—I mean sort of lithesome, but emphatic. I suppose I wanted Professor Chancellor to open the door thinking that he would be facing Miss von Leuckel, but instead he would find himself face to face with me. Frankly, my physical presence was not much more intimidating than Miss von Leuckel's, but apparently the good professor had heard a thing or two about me. And that just might work in my favor. In fact, I almost felt as if I wore that old gossip like a mantle. My first knock went unanswered, so I tried again. And a third time.

He was not in.

It occurred to me that very possibly he was seated among the guests in the lobby. I descended the stairs more slowly than I had ascended. I wanted a sweeping view of the folks downstairs. Most of them seemed to be watching me, and I had a feeling that my clothing (and/or the front desk clerk) may have clued them in as to the company I had kept that evening. My eyes swept the room, but I did not spot any likely candidates for what I believed a geezer-academic type might look like—a bit shabby and billy goat-like. Claude Uncapher had his eye on me, like he was hoping I'd come over and give him the lowdown on the dinner at Etowah. I very much wished that we had the lobby more to ourselves. Some of the folks, with their eyes on me, seemed to be making comments to each other. As I approached, Claude said, in a volume that allowed many in the lobby to feel included in his inquiry, "So tell us Trey, is Mary Pickford every bit as sweet and charming in person as she is in the movies?"

Folks fell into a hush, awaiting my reply.

Frankly, he embarrassed me. "Well," I said quietly, "as a matter of fact, she is. And then some."

"She is? And then some!" He followed his words with a whistle. "Why, she must be swell!"

One of the fellows in a red fez was seated near the desk. He was, shall we say, a rather stout man. Indeed, he reminded me of Senator Harding's good friend and fellow Ohioan, former President William Howard Taft, and he probably would have been more comfortable with a davenport to himself, instead of being wedged into a chair. The fellow wore several Harding–Coolidge buttons and ribbons, running up one lapel and down the next. He said to me, "Up close, is her hair more blond or brown? They say it's darkened up."

"Brown. Definitely brown."

Before I could speak to Claude again, and get down to business, the fellow persisted, "And her curls?"

"Well, I suppose you could say they're curly." I took out my watch and studied it for a long moment, which I hoped would serve as a hint to one and all that I did not wish to dawdle.

"Mr. Uncapher," I said, quietly, "have you by chance seen the occupant of room 202? A fellow by the name of Chancellor?"

"I have. Not more than half an hour ago. When they checked out."

"Checked out!" This time it was I who spoke in excess volume, though that was not my intention.

"That's right. Checked out. If you'd gotten here a little sooner, you'd have bumped into them on your way through the door."

The man in the red fez said, "Was that the gray-beard?"

"The same."

I leaned closer to Claude—indeed, close enough to smell the chewing tobacco and coffee on his breath. "'Them'?" I whispered, and then leaned back.

"The old man and two boys. Though I don't think they're his sons. One called him 'Professor.' But I'm not sure about the other."

"They both called him that. I heard 'em." That information was, of course, contributed by the fellow in the fez.

At that very moment the 9:45 blew its whistle as the train rumbled towards the Main Street crossing. "That's probably them passing right now," Claude said, nodding in a northerly direction. "Why, who knows, if you'd run lickety-split, maybe you just might wave 'em down. Wouldn't hurt to try."

"Ha, ha," I said. Through all of my youth, and even well into my young manhood, old men seemed to take a persistent and particular delight in "kidding" me. Indeed, sometimes they would still tousle my hair. Granted, these little annoyances meant that they liked me, but it does not mean that I liked them doing it. Until that moment, I had usually managed to abide such annoyances with a little long-suffering smile. But this time I said, "Mr. Uncapher, you see that guest book there in front of you, sir? Will you please be so kind as to use it to look and see whether he left his address. And if so, may I have it, please?"

Claude studied me over his spectacles, and I am sorry to say that a wounded look came into his eyes. He turned back the page of his guest book, and quietly said, "Sorry, Trey." Then he added, "I guess maybe a certain someone got up on the wrong side of the bed this morning."

Truly, I had not meant to be rude to him. I blew out a long breath. "Maybe it's just been one of those days, sir. Sorry."

He smiled. "I'll bet you have lots of those kinds of days, nowadays, don't you?"

I did not know exactly what that was supposed to mean, but I was not about to ask for an explanation.

Claude was slowly running his finger down the page. "Let's see what we got here."

I spotted the name almost instantly, even though from my perspective, it was upside down. The distinctive signature was the same as the facsimile on the book's title page, with the same big, looping letters. I could tell that Professor Chancellor had written his address beneath it, though I couldn't make out what it was through all his squiggles and filigree.

I did not want Claude to think I was being impatient with him, yet again, so I gave him a chance to spot the name on his own.

I watched his bony finger move down the row. He stopped just beneath the signature, studied the name for a moment and said, "Here it is. This is him. You're in luck." Then he muttered to himself, "Wooster. I got some kin buried in Wooster, somewheres."

He began writing out the information.

I heard the train chugging nearer, whistling and rumbling its way towards the State Street crossing, a mere few hundred yards from the hotel, then that momentary avalanche of sound as the locomotive emerged from between the buildings and intersected the street. I pictured the watchman down the way swinging his lantern in the darkness, and a geezer looking from the glowing window of a Pullman, heading off towards Wooster, or heaven knows where, to do his dirty work. I shook my head in exasperation. I suppose I felt a bit like a cat rounding a corner, only to perceive the flick of the mouse's tail as it slipped into its hole in the wall. Suddenly I was extraordinarily bothered with Miss von Leuckel. So far as I could figure, her little charade about the fifty thousand—giving Professor Chancellor "a run for his money"—had been effective in one way, and one way only: The old man had apparently thrown up his hands and made a beeline out of town.

Plainly put, if Mitzy had kept her big mouth shut, then at that very moment I would probably be up in room 202, having a little face-to-face with the good professor.

When Claude handed me the paper, I looked it over and thanked him. I glanced at the man in the red fez. I was pleased to note that he had dozed off. His hands were folded on his belly. That and his fez gave him the look of a snoozing sultan. Nearly everyone else had gone back to their newspapers, their chatting, or what have you.

I asked Claude to give my regards to Mrs. Uncapher, and then I slipped away.

SENATOR HARDING was and always had been a night owl, so I decided I would go over and fill him in. But I decided to go home first and put the car away. Lucy and I lived only a few hundred yards west of the Hardings, so I seldom drove there. Besides, in those days I never liked pulling into the garage after ten o'clock at night or so, as I didn't want to wake the neighbors. My Ford, like other cars of that era, was a pretty rattley machine. Not to mention the fact that it had a tendency to backfire on the downshift, so I wanted to drop it off before the neighbors went to bed. I had no such worry about waking Lucy. From the first week of our marriage, until the last weeks of her final illness, decades later, my sweet and ever faithful wife always made a point of waiting up for me. And I knew that on that particular night she would be sitting in her favorite chair reading the *Star*, or maybe her *Lady's Home Journal*, awaiting her husband's arrival so that she could continue to effuse about our dinner with Douglas Fairbanks and Mary Pickford, and to speculate about the particulars of their private lives—as she so much liked to do with people she found glamorous and interesting.

After I parked the car in the garage, I rolled the door closed and was walking towards the house. I was going to inform Lucy through the window screen that I was heading over to the Hardings. During our brief walk home from Etowah, I had told her the gist of Miss von Leuckel's story, so she already had a pretty clear notion about the situation. I had walked only a few steps over the gravel drive when a shrill voice somewhere behind me pierced the darkness, "You been looking for someone, sonny?"

I whirled around, utterly astounded, to say the least. I stared into the shadowy darkness, but saw no one. Then I heard the soft swish of footsteps moving towards me through grass, and three figures materialized from the darkness beneath the buckeye tree. For one thing, at that moment the half moon above the treetops was partially hidden by a passing cloud, and so I could not see any details of their faces, not even if they were young or old, only that they were men. They looked a bit like black paper silhouettes, cutouts, pasted on a sheet of black paper. As you can imagine, my mind and heart were racing during those several seconds. My first thought was that they were tramps. I had once had a nasty run-in with tramps. They had been caught pilfering from the coal yards owned by Colonel Hamilton & Son, and I am sorry say that some of my men roughed them up pretty badly. Anyway, in those several seconds as I watched the figures emerging in the darkness, I thought perhaps some of those men had ridden the rails in from "Vagabondia" and that I was finally going to get the comeuppance they had promised.

They stopped, maybe ten or twelve feet from me. If they had come a single step closer, I'd have hightailed it into the house where I kept a loaded pistol in the back of a drawer. I'm sure that a shot or two into the night sky would have reminded them of their manners when it came to the do's and don'ts of calling on folks. The same shrill voice said, "What's the matter, boy? Cat got your tongue?"

It was the middle figure addressing me.

"Who are you and what the hell are you doing in my yard?"

He cackled and I realized he was an older man. "Here I was thinking you'd be glad to see me. Here I was thinking I'd be saving you a bit of shoe leather, me coming to you so you wouldn't have to come lookin' for me. And now you go saying, 'So what are you doing in my yard?' How's that for hospitality!"

At the risk of sounding stupid, I have to admit that I still did not realize who I was talking to, I suppose because I had those tramps stuck in my mind. Besides, the fellow doing the talking sounded like a first-rate hick, not at all like an "educated" man. I said, "You want to tell me what this is all about? Or you want that I should call the police so you can explain it to them? There's several right down the way, and they'll come a-runnin', count on it."

"Well, well, well. You are a fresh one, aren't you? Just like they all say. Fresh and full of yourself. Spoiled, arrogant, ambitious. And nigger loving. That's what they say. You happen to be speaking with Professor William Estabrook Chancellor, BA, MA, PhD. From Wooster College. Ever in the service of truth. And integrity. Words folks 'round here don't cotton much to, seems."

I was, as you might assume, a bit surprised. I certainly was not expecting to see Chancellor coming out of the dark of night in my own backyard, not when I thought he was, at that moment, riding the rails through the cornfields in a Pullman. Besides, I would have expected a different sort of man, in terms of his talk. "I see. Looks like you missed your train."

"Looks like I never intended to catch it, doesn't it? 'Cause if I did, I'd be on it. Shows what you know and what you think you know are two different things."

"So you've written a book?"

"I've written lots of books. Published. Latest one's the most important. About that sambo you call a senator. Someone's got to clear up people's ignorance. Someone's got to educate the populace that a bogus white man is trying to sneak his way into the White House. That a clever nigger-cheat's laying the groundwork to rule over bona fide white men." He paused.

"The revenge of the lower orders. That's what I call it. It's a conspiracy more dangerous than the Reds. Niggers and such using their get-bys to sneak upwards, slow but sure, right here in the United States of America. Parading him 'round the golf links in his knickers and fancy stockings, when he ought to be out by the woodpile wearing overalls and hickory shirts! And now they got him in fine trousers and a collar shirt with his shoes shined. Dressing up that quadroon to use him to steal the White House from the white race! He's got to be stopped, and stopped he shall be!"

Just then, my wife called through the back door, "Trey, what's going on out there? Who's that you're talking to?"

Over my shoulder I could see Lucy in her fancy pink nightgown standing in the darkness behind the screen, the glow of the kitchen behind her. "Just some schoolteacher." I glanced back at them. "And a couple of his pupils, I think. Come to talk politics. Or something. I'll be in a couple of minutes." She did not speak or move.

Chancellor called out, "I'm a college professor, Mrs. Hamilton. Professor William Estabrook Chancellor, from Wooster College. We don't mean any harm, I promise you. These boys here, they're students of history, and decorated war heroes, too. Both of them. Patriots. I'll be grateful if we could have a few words with your husband, if we may, ma'am. I'll be quick about it. No harm intended, I assure you. And we beg pardon for startling you, if we did."

She did not reply, but simply stood framed by the dark screen, looking out.

"Go on, Lucy," I said. "Go on back in and sit down. I'll be right in."

"Seems like an awful funny time to go talking politics in the backyard, in the dark of night."

"I'll be in in a jiffy. Now you go on back in and sit down. It's okay." After a reluctant moment, the pink of her nightgown faded back into the glowing shadows of the kitchen. As I watched I knew she would be lingering by the table, leaning and looking out, making sure that I was safe, and straining to hear our words.

I turned back to Chancellor and his silent bodyguards. By now the moon had come back out, and I realized that one of them was the fellow in the straw boater who had been standing off on Bradford Street a couple of hours before, watching Miss von Leuckel and me.

In something like a loud whisper, or a hiss, the college professor said, just loud enough for me to hear, "That nigger stole your sweetie, didn't he? Back in '14. August of '14, to be particular."

I did not answer.

"Didn't he?"

I did not answer.

"Things would be a lot different now, and for all the rest of your days, if not for that sweet-talking, philandering coon."

I said nothing.

In a slightly louder voice, he said, "And she's not the only one. He nearly broke up a marriage, years ago. I know all about that one. It's in my book. You know about it too, you know all that and more, but still, you want to make that coon President of the United States, just 'cause he's from Marion and available. Just 'cause you and your dad and all your rich friends 'round abouts think it'd be nice to have someone from this skunk-hole town in the White House. And through the Devil's tricks and trickery, and your tricks and trickery, you positioned that coon where he's ready to make the leap. Though the real shame is all of you know as well as I do, nay, even better, that Warren Harding isn't fit. Not racially, not mentally, not morally. Not even fit to be mayor. And to think, that coon stole your sweetie. The one you really . . ."

"Mister, what the hell do you want?"

"What the hell do you think I want? For that lying nigger to stand up and be counted 'mongst the coons. For him to get up there and tell the truth for once. To tell the American people that he's a bogus white man. That he's deceiving the white race and the American people."

I said, softly, "Mr. Chancellor, sir . . ."

"And so are you. You're deceiving them too, you're a traitor to the Anglo-Saxon race, paying niggers the same wages as white men, sometimes more! So's this wicked little Gomorrah, and everyone in it that knows about him but keeps mum and lets him stand up there like a fake McKinley. Warren Harding's a minstrel show turned inside out! A mockery of every white man in this country, Republican and Democrat alike!"

"Mr. Chancellor, sir, if that's what you want, for the Senator to go spreading old lies about himself . . ."

"They aren't lies and you know it. You more than anyone. And you, president of Sambo's Volunteers." He paused and said, with fake thoughtfulness, "The only thing I haven't figured out yet is, if it's you that's got him wrapped around your little finger or him that's got you. Or both." He paused, "Probably both. Yes, indeedy I do think it's both. Nice fit, too."

"Mr. Chancellor . . ."

"It's Professor Chancellor. Or Dr. Chancellor. I'm an ethnologist schooled in scientific ways."

"Mr. Chancellor . . ."

"Killer Trey." Then he cackled again, but in a hysterical sort of way, like he'd gotten himself all worked up and was proud of it and yet that he suspected that he had gone one step too far. "Descendant of conspirators and traitors, on his momma's side—the Blennerhassetts."

I stood silent. The professor had done his cockeyed homework, and it was the first time in fifteen years that anyone had uttered the words "Killer Trey" to my face. I should add that hearing allusions to my mother's people, as well as my old childhood nickname, had an odd, but subtle effect on me. I felt the faintness of a smile cross my lips as I clasped my hands behind my back and walked straight towards him, like a casual killer cornering his prey.

Chancellor fell back, terribly frightened. "Stay where you are! Stay!"

I could almost feel the boys tense up. I took two or three more steps, and then I stopped.

The boy who had been spying on me at Lake Etowah said, "It's alright, Professor. He won't do anything."

"Won't I?" my voice soft and gracious. "And what makes you so sure of that?"

He did not answer.

The other one said, "'Cause you won't, that's why."

"Oh, but I shall. I shall do something. I *always* do something. You'll see. And if you get in my way, football-boy—" Frankly, I wondered how I appeared in their eyes, standing there in the moonlight in my formal clothes, my black tie, glaring at them.

Chancellor hissed, in his old snake of a voice, "Murderer."

"Yes, Mr. Chancellor, sir," I said softly. "Now if that's what you want, for Senator Harding to stand up and advertise old lies and rumors about himself, then why don't you just mosey right back down the alley where you came from and go tell it to him yourself? If you can find my back door, you can find his. Do it."

I started to turn, as if walking away, though I must say that I was not altogether serious, as I desired to know more about his book.

"No! We shan't do that. We shan't negotiate with niggers. We don't even talk with them 'less they know their place, shoeshine boys, kitchen maids, and such. We're respectful of them. Just like we're respectful to any honest white man. Niggers who know their place aren't niggers, they're colored folks, and colored folks can't help but what God made them out to be. But they can stay in their place. And most of them do, the smart ones, that is, the good ones. 'Less nigger-lovers and preachers start putting ideas in their heads. Giving them an inch and pushing them to take the mile. I'll be the first to admit that colored folks got a difficult row to hoe. Far more so than whites . . ."

"Mr. Chancellor, please, I must emphasize, it's past my bedtime. When do I get to read that book of yours? I always appreciate some good bedtime reading. My wife, too. And besides, I'm in need of a good laugh."

"Ha-ha. That book's a sore point with me, so watch it. There it is, all the pages printed up, five hundred of them already bound and ready to ship from Dayton. The other nine thousand five hundred of them ready to be collated and bound, with emissaries standing by, all along the lines from New York to Wichita to Sacramento. Then all of a sudden I find out about Missy and the coon. Missy Mata Hari, like those in the know call her. And their quadroon boy, and all the secrets she got out of that buck to go and sell to the Kaiser. Damn them!" He spat in my yard. "Damn them! If I'd only known! That nigger's got so many cards up his sleeve, I can't keep track! I'll hand him that, all right. Very shrewd."

"What things, precisely, did she sell the Kaiser?"

"I'm researching that. I'd hoped she'd tell me. Says she wants to think about it, then goes tippy-toeing off to see you. That's a spy for you. And a fool. Kissing ten thousand dollars nighty-night, when it'll all come out anyway."

"Ten thousand dollars. That's quite a liberal sum. Your life's savings, no doubt."

"It's not my money. I got backing. Plenty of it. You're looking at three of us standing here, but we're only the delegation sent to try to get things done neatly. There's thousands behind us. Thousands!"

"Ah!" I said, "The Ku Klux Klan."

He did not answer.

"Sentinel Press," I mused, "never heard of it."

"Ignorance. Tends to happen when you get yourself expelled from school at the tender age of sixteen."

I said nothing, nor did I correct his number.

"And I know what you're trying to do, so don't bother."

"Trying to do?"

"Yes. You're fishing. Don't bother. And don't bother faking yourself with me, either. I see through fakers and all their smooth talk and smoke and mirrors. Now here's your homework, buddy boy. Go tell that nigger to own up and tell the truth about his race. Own up to the American people that he's a nigger. Or part nigger. That's all he's got to do. Tell him to fix his speech right and deliver it. He's got till the day after tomorrow. If he doesn't, then everything, *everything* comes out. The flood gates'll open wide and out pops Missy, and the Kaiser too, and heaven only knows what else and who else'll follow. Probably more than either of us can imagine."

The good professor paused, I suppose giving me a chance to speak, if I cared to do so, but nothing came out of my mouth. He continued, "How on earth you can back Warren Harding after what he did to you, to your life, to your manhood, is beyond me. A nigger stole your sweetheart, your betrothed! Right out from under your nose! Just so he could have a little philandering fun! And what do you do about it? You try to make him President of the United States. Changed your life. Ruined hers. Yes, sir. Everything would've been different, but for him. Everything." He paused. "Tristan Hamilton, you disgust me. In some ways, you disgust me even more than that nigger himself. He's just the nigger puppet, you and others like you are the puppet masters."

I said nothing.

He spat in my yard. To his pupils, he said, "Now let's let this young man here get back to his precious wife. And his bed. 'Sides, I got a new chapter to write. Just in case."

He turned, and they headed off into the night.

I stood staring into the darkness, after him.

III

✿

"There Goes Virtue"

AFTER TELLING LUCY what was going on, I headed toward the Hardings. Frankly, I did not feel like talking to the Senator at that particular moment. In fact, when I arrived at that point on the sidewalk where the Harding home came into view, I found myself stopping in my tracks as I mulled over whether to go on, or wait for tomorrow. Until this moment I had almost forgotten that the Harding's front lawn had been covered with gravel, owing to the crowds that gathered that summer and fall. I say this because I suddenly remember that in the moonlight the lawn looked as if snow had fallen there without touching other yards in the neighborhood. The upstairs lights were all dark, though the downstairs windows were very much aglow. I had the feeling that Mrs. Harding had turned in while the Senator was cavorting elsewhere. As I stood in front of Colonel Christian's residence, I took out my watch and read it by the moonlight. I recall the hour was well after ten, around ten-thirty or ten-forty. I felt bad about leaving Lucy, as I knew how much she wanted to rehash her impressions of the movie stars and the events of the evening, and I knew as well that she wanted to be with me, not alone in her armchair, waiting. But obviously the Campaign was facing a very serious situation. Besides, the next morning I had some pressing matters to attend to at Colonel Hamilton & Son, due to the building boom, and the Senator had a busy day ahead as well, with two speeches to deliver. As I stood on the walk, I realized that several men were sitting on the front porch enjoying the mild weather. I had the feeling they were watching me—the man standing off in the tree shadows. At least one of those men would be a policeman. Another might well be the Senator. I instantly resumed my walk towards the house.

I remember that, during those days, I was always careful to approach the front porch along the narrow flagstones, as so that gravel dust would not settle on my shoes. Before I got to the steps, one of the porch-sitters said, "So that's you, Trey. He's out back, if you're looking for the Senator."

I thanked the fellow, without being entirely sure who I was thanking, and followed the flagstones around the side of the house.

"Out back" meant the little white bungalow that the GOP had built for the comfort and convenience of the press corps. It had telephones, a cable, and a number of typewriters and desks, as well as facilities and a little kitchen—everything a reporter in the year 1920 could possibly want. After supper, the bungalow became something of a clubhouse, especially (but not solely) for reporters from the Republican organs. Senator Harding was part of the club. He spent many an evening with the "boys"—not for public relations purposes but simply because he liked the company of his fellow newspapermen. I assure you that they certainly liked him and obviously they liked the idea of being chummy with a bona fide Senator and the possible next President of the United States. I suppose to those fellows—indeed to reporters of any political stripe—Warren G. Harding was like a warm sunny day, compared to the secretive and aloof Woodrow Wilson. Some of those same men had spent the last eight years covering him—or at least trying to. Mr. Wilson was not above shaking his finger in their faces and chastising them, if and when he thought they had been naughty boys—just like the former schoolteacher that he was.

As I walked along the side of the Harding home, laughter and voices came through the screens of the bungalow. The blinds were half-pulled, but I could see through the windows that a card game was in progress, enveloped in a gray cloud of tobacco smoke. The chairs on the narrow porch stood empty, but a policeman was seated in a chaise lounge over in the Christians' backyard, smoking a cigarette. The moment I stepped onto the porch, Laddie Boy, the Senator's little terrier, came barking up to the door. (Today Laddie Boy is as forgotten as any other dog that lived forty years ago, but when he ruled the White House, he was every bit as famous as Lassie or Rin Tin Tin. Indeed, somewhere in the Smithsonian, no doubt in a dusty box deep in one of the most unfrequented caverns of its basement, is a nicely executed, solid copper statue of Laddie Boy, cast from pennies donated by the nation's school children.) After I spoke to Laddie Boy, he stopped barking and was already wagging his tail. No one paid much attention to his yaps, as there were always people coming and going, and he announced most of them. Seven or eight men were engaged in the card game, including the Senator. Each had a cup near at hand, though I had a feeling they were drinking neither coffee nor tea. Harry Daugherty was not part of the game, though his sidekick Jess Smith was sitting there with a smoldering cigar butt sticking from the corner of his mouth, cards in hand. I was never quite sure what position Jess actually held in the Daugherty operations. I know that he had worked for Harry for several years at his law offices in Washington Courthouse, Ohio, as well as in Columbus, although I don't believe that Jess himself was actually an attorney. I know he did some investigative work. I think of him as having been something like a mole or a henchman. Folks used to say that Jess looked a bit like Harry, and so he did, somewhat. Both were overweight, balding, and diabetic, though Jess was Harry's junior by a good twenty years. I know they usually stayed in the same hotel room, I suppose to save money, unless Mrs. Daugherty was along, though Harry usually left her parked in their rather grand home down in Bexley. Anyway, I'm losing my thread here. As I was saying, Jess was part of the card game, while Harry was off to the side with his feet propped on a desk, reading an out-of-town newspaper from the stack at his side. As campaign manager and "king-maker," he read just about every word written every day about Senator Harding—and Governor Cox—often jotting down notes. Sometimes I had the impression that he had friends operating right inside the Cox campaign, which was very possible, seeing how well connected he was in Ohio.

It was not "protocol" to knock on the bungalow door; nonetheless, I did just that, even as I opened the screen. Everyone looked up as I stepped in.

"Senator Harding," I said.

I can still see his eyes above his cards, and the surprise that flashed across them. "Trey!" He glanced at the Seth Thomas wall clock (which to this day hangs in the same place where it hung on that very night forty-some years ago). "Say, isn't it a little past your bedtime?"

I believe my punctuality about bedtime was getting to be a bit of a joke in certain circles. "A bit, sir," I said. I was petting Laddie Boy. "But something's occurred to me, sir, and you know me, once I get something in my head—Anyway, I was wondering if maybe you and me, if maybe we could chat for a moment or two."

The "boys" turned their attention back to their cards, and resumed their chatter. The Senator and Harry cast each other a subtle glance.

I walked out the door again, into the middle of the backyard, and I stood gazing at the moon above the trees. As I did I wondered where Chancellor and his pupils had disappeared to this time. With that thought, I scanned the surrounding darkness filled with the deep shadows: the drooping snowball bushes, faded lilacs, grape arbors, and such. The screen door opened and closed softly. The Senator and Harry had each shed his collar and tie. And there I stood, hours after apple pie à la mode, just as buttoned up as I had been when I first picked up knife and fork.

My eyes fastened on the Senator's eyes as he approached in the moonlight. I think for many years (seven years and ten months, to be precise) my mere presence could sometimes evoke a touch of shame in Warren Harding. Nevertheless, I wish to state that I personally believe in letting bygones be bygones, and I think I was always quite good about separating Warren from the highly capable Senator Harding. And then of course from President Harding. I scarcely dealt with Warren. Indeed, I wanted nothing to do with the cad.

For a moment, I just stood looking him in the eye. "Sir," I said, "Miss von Leuckel sends her love."

I do not think he would have been any more startled if I had slapped him across the face. Even in the moonlight, I could see him turning a splendid shade of purple. That was the first time since August of 1914 that either of us had ever spoken Miss von Leuckel's name in the other's presence. He looked away, jammed his hands in his pockets, and kind of hunched down, like a turtle pulling its head in. He was peering at his shoes with a shake of the head and a sheepish "Aw-shucks-gee-I'm-sorry-Trey" sort of air. Harry crossed his arms and looked back at the bungalow. He started to whistle one of his Irish ditties, but stopped a few notes into it. Laddie Boy was keeping an eye on us through the screen door, his pointed little ears perked.

For a few seconds, Mr. Harding stood there all hangdog, staring at his toes. Slowly and most contritely, he said, "Say, listen Trey, I've always wanted to tell you that I'm awfully, awfully . . ."

"Senator Harding, sir, we got troubles. Campaign troubles." I glanced into the darkness and then nodded towards the house. "Can we talk inside? Mrs. Harding's asleep, isn't she?"

Harry's eyes were fastened on me.

The Senator said, "Troubles?"

"Yes, sir. Troubles. Campaign troubles. Big ones. Can we talk inside?"

He seemed to be searching for something in my eyes, and then I suppose he connected what I had said with Miss von Leuckel. I could see fear come over him. "Oh my gosh!"

"Can we talk inside?"

"Inside?" He glanced at the house, as if for an answer, then back at me. "Flossie might hear us."

Harry said, "Maybe we can take a little walk. Nice night for a walk."

"Yes," the Senator said, "let's take a walk, maybe over by the lake." He scrutinized the ground, like he had dropped a coin in the grass. Then he looked back at the bungalow. His little dog wagged his tail and whined the instant the Senator turned his way. "Let me go get Laddie Boy. He'll be sore if I go without him. He'll know we've gone for a walk."

So the Senator went and fetched his Laddie Boy and Harry went and fetched his Jess.

Lake Etowah, as I believe I have already indicated, was little more than a stone's throw from the Harding home. As we walked along the moonlit sidewalks, I told them, in a low voice, exactly what was going on—about Mitzy's calling me from the dinner table, and Chancellor's calling on her. I handed them the title page, which they paused to look at beneath a street lamp. I told them about the five hundred copies of his book being all printed up and ready to ship, with another nine thousand five hundred ready for binding. I told them of Chancellor's full knowledge, via the generosity of our townsfolk, of the adulterous affair that the Senator and Miss Leuckel were conducting—an adulterous affair which had broken up a young courting couple. (I did not use the word "us," or say "Mitzy and me." I kept my reference in the third person.)

And of course I let him know that Chancellor was well aware of the supposition that the Senator had whispered military secrets in Miss von Leuckel's ear and that she in turn had peddled them to Kaiser Bill.

"That's a damn lie!" he said.

I glanced about. All was darkness and moonlight and leaves drifting down here and there, but I said, "Sir, keep your voice down, please."

Harry muttered, "Jesus, Mary, 'n' Joseph!" And he ran his plump hand over his thinning hair.

By then we were strolling down the sidewalk beside Lake Etowah, tranquil in the moonlight. In a low voice, almost a whisper, the Senator repeated, "I never told her a damn thing. And she never asked me. Not once. Ever. That's the beginning and end of it. I'll swear on a Bible."

"Nonetheless," I said, "I think you'll agree that we have an unfortunate meeting of rumors and circumstances here. Lots of rumors and more than enough circumstances to back them up. And mind you, the good professor's offered Miss von Leuckel ten thousand dollars to sign an affidavit. One stating that she's having an adulterous affair with you."

"She'll never do that." But then after a pause he said, as if to himself, "Unless . . ."

"Unless—?"

"Unless nothing. She'll never do that."

"Hmmm. Probably not. Though of course you know her better than I do. Anyway, Senator Harding, your faith in womanhood is admirable."

As we walked, Laddie Boy was, of course, leader of the pack, with his leash taut. As for Jess, he was holding up the rear with his head sticking between Harry and the Senator's shoulders.

"Chancellor's got backing from somewhere," I said, "but heaven only knows where."

"Yeah?" Harry said, "Well, we'll see if he can outspend the GOP. We got Henry Ford and John Rockefeller in our corner, to name just two."

If we had kept walking along Bradford for another two hundred yards, we would have come to the place where the sidewalk ended, and found ourselves on the winding Indian paths of the Old Forest. So we paused beside Lake Etowah, in almost the exact spot from which Chancellor's pupil had spied upon Miss von Leuckel and me. I looked out across the dark water to that place on the plaza where Mitzy and I had spoken together, just hours before. I pictured her as she had been, at my side at sunset. In turning, my eyes swept over the lake to the darkness of the forest. The arc of water from the lion fount sparkled silver in the moonlight as it splashed into Lake Etowah. The splash had a tranquil, faraway sound that belied our difficulties at hand.

The Senator muttered, "Flossie's going to kill me."

"Yeah?" Harry said, "Well, if she does, there's not a jury in the land that'll convict her. Count on it. In fact, I'll aid in her defense. Without fees."

"I'm not kidding," the Senator muttered.

"Neither am I. And why the hell didn't you think of all this before?"

Jess spoke up. "Harry, there might be someone poking around."

After a meditative moment, Senator Harding offered us an apt Ohio reflection, plaintively uttered, "Sooner or later the birds always come home to roost."

I believe I rolled my eyes, but kept my counsel. Apparently, at the tender age of fifty-four, the commonsense wisdom of that axiom had suddenly dawned upon the Senator, with enlightening clarity.

"It seems to me," I said, "that what we've got here is a war to fight on two fronts. No, make that three. The race rumor. Nothing new there. The adultery business. Not to mention the fact that you broke up a courtship. And now of course the business about you being in cahoots with Kaiser Bill, via your adulterous affair with Miss von Leuckel." I allowed that to sink in and then I said, "I believe that's where we stand."

Harry muttered a very old Anglo-Saxon expletive.

"Oh, by the way," I added, "we do have an out, if we wish, at least from the business about Miss von Leuckel and the Kaiser. All you have to do, Senator, is stand on your front porch tomorrow, or the next day—in short, within forty-eight hours—and tell the American people that you're a colored man. At least that's the deal that Professor Chancellor's offering us. Do that and we're free and clear on the issues of adultery and spying, or so he says." Then I told them about his having just visited me and of his offer to keep mum about Miss von Leuckel and the spy business. "But personally, I wouldn't trust that old man any farther than I could throw him."

Harry said, "That bastard's not only got us over the pickle barrel, he's got us up to our chins in vinegar."

"I'd say more like our eyebrows. And if I'm not mistaken, Miss von Leuckel's not the only one—I mean in terms of the ladies."

After a moment Mr. Harding said softly, albeit with a decided edge, "I told you fellows long ago that you were hitching your cart to the wrong horse, but you wouldn't listen, would you? You just pushed and pushed." His own words seemed to come to him like a revelation. He looked at Harry. "Who the hell didn't listen then? Who?" He looked at me. "Who?"

I averted my eyes.

The Senator repeated, "I said, 'Who the hell didn't listen then?' You knew who I was and what I am, but no—I warned you and you didn't listen." There was a fierceness in his voice that I had never heard before.

Harry raised his hands, "Okay, Warren. Okay. Enough. The incrimination's over. It's getting us nowhere. And you *are* the right horse. That's why the whole GOP's behind you. That's why hundreds of people a day are coming to your front porch and thousands are gathering at your whistle-stops, because they know that you're the man for the job."

The Senator turned away, as if in disgust.

Harry added, "They know that if anyone can turn things back, while keeping them moving forward, it's you, Warren. I suspect that's your greatest talent, with or without your indiscretions." He paused, "You think you're the only leader in history who's ever dallied? It goes with the territory, sometimes." None of us said anything for a few moments, and then Harry added softly, "At least this guy's given us a warning. Yeah, at least he did us that favor, the fool. He could've just sprung this on us then we'd be screwed for sure. And you've always been lucky, Warren, and had a nice way of wiggling out of scrapes, if I do recall."

For a moment we just stood there looking over the dark water. Almost peacefully, the Senator said, "Momma used to say that Lady Luck was on my side, even when the chips were down; 'specially when the chips were down, so maybe you got a point. We'll see."

I had known Mrs. Harding, and frankly, that did not sound like something she would have said—I mean the allusions to gambling—so I said, "Your mother used to say that, sir?"

"Well, maybe not quite like that, but that was the idea. So what do we do now?"

Harry spoke, "Good question, 'What do we do now?'" He was addressing the words to himself. He repeated them, rubbing his plump hands together as he looked over the dark lake. He said, "We got, what, thirty-three days left until November second?"

"Not counting today," I said.

"Lots can happen in thirty-some days. But like a certain Senator I know says, 'You play the hand you're dealt.'" Harry once again rubbed his hands together, like they were cold. I realize in retrospect that that was a mannerism that emerged with Harry when things got tough. "Well," he said, "I guess the first thing we'll do is try to ship a few of these fine ladies off. Fast. And stuff plenty of bills in their pocketbooks so they can shop and shut up."

I said, "Why not ship Chancellor off? Put him on a slow boat to China." Of course, I meant that as a joke, more or less.

Jess said, "The mountains of the moon would be better."

Harry ignored both of us. He turned to Mr. Harding. "So how many ladies are we dealing with, Senator? Eight? Ten? Should we charter a steamer?"

"Ha-ha. That's very funny, Harry."

As a matter of fact, Jess and I could not help but laugh.

"For your information, there's only three. Three that we need to worry about. There's Nan up in Chicago, Mitzy here in Marion, and Mrs. Page. That's it, I think."

"Nan?" I said.

The Senator looked away. "Yes, Nan. Nan Britton. Doc Britton's daughter."

I too looked away. And I was no longer laughing. That was the very first time I'd heard anything about Nan and him. I vaguely remembered hearing that little Miss Britton was infatuated with Mr. Harding, back when she was a schoolgirl, but I never knew that anything came of it. Nan's family had fallen apart after Doctor Britton died, I think along about 1912 or 1913, leaving the family with one foot in the poor house. Mrs. Britton had to send the little boy off to live with relatives. And she and the two girls, both out of school, left Marion before the war. Theirs was the kind of tragedy that was all too common back then, before FDR's Social Security began saving families from such plights.

"Things ended with Mrs. Page several years ago," Mr. Harding said. "But if this guy's walking around waving ten thousand in the air, then I think she could use a vacation. And her husband too. Especially her husband." He looked at Harry, "Jim's the one with the undecorated dry goods store."

Harry nodded, as if he knew all too well. "That store causes a hell of a lot of talk."

"Jim and I used to be good friends, sort of best friends, but he hasn't spoken to me for years, and I doubt he ever will." The Senator sighed, "Sometimes I wonder what's wrong with me."

At that time, Jim Page was the only merchant along the entire length of "Victory Way" who had not decorated his store with flags, patriotic bunting, and the Senator's portrait. Even the vast majority of Marion's Democrats were 100 percent committed to elevating the Senator to the Presidency. But there was Jim. Not talking about it, but quietly spiteful. It caused talk.

I threw in my two cents worth; "Actually, I think Miss von Leuckel might be more valuable to us right here. Just in case she has to vehemently deny things. She's got that down pat."

"Let me ask you something, Senator," Harry said. "Do any of these ladies know about each other?"

The Senator shifted a bit, "Well, Nan and Mitzy, they know about Mrs. Page. Certainly. But they both know that she passed out of the picture years ago."

We waited.

"And?"

"I imagine that Mrs. Page knows about Mitzy. But Nan and Mitzy, they don't know nothing about each other. And heaven help us if they ever do."

"It's enough to make your head spin. Okay, you say Nan's up in Chicago? Let's see if we can hustle her out of the country. To Paris or someplace like that, someplace nice. She can spend Election Day in one of those fancy hotels and shop along the Champs-Elysées to her heart's content. As for Mrs. Page and her husband, your ex-friend, maybe they'd like Hawaii."

"There's no place to shop in Hawaii. They like stores, both of them."

"Then Rome, a place by the Spanish Steps. I'm sure we can make it worth their while. And Miss von Leuckel, well, we'll talk about her later. Now tell me something, Senator, ever heard of this Sentinel Press?"

"Can't say as I have."

"It's down in Dayton," I said. "Governor Cox's hometown. Chancellor said the books are down there, ready to ship. He mentioned it in passing."

"Dayton? Say," Harry said, "you don't suppose our opponent's in on this, do you?"

"No, I don't suppose our opponent's in on this," the Senator said. "Jim Cox is a worthy opponent. He wants to win like nothing else, but he wouldn't stoop so low."

"He wouldn't, wouldn't he?"

"No, he wouldn't."

Harry gave this a moment's thought. "Well, maybe you're right. If he had his fingers in this, I'd probably know about it, I think. But he is a newspaperman. He owns lots of papers. And if he's got lots of papers, then he's got lots of presses. You don't just print up ten thousand books in an alley print shop, do you?"

"No. But I've known Jim Cox for years. I trust him completely."

Harry laughed at this remark, though I personally failed to see the humor.

"Sentinel Press—" The Senator shook his head. "I've been in Washington for six years, mostly, but I try to keep up with the printing business, and I never did hear of this one. And Jim Cox probably is the only one in Dayton with big enough presses to print ten thousand books. Or even five hundred. Presuming it's a real book and not a pamphlet."

"You saw the title page," I said.

"So I did."

I wondered if the Senator was reconsidering his estimate of Governor Cox, and I think Harry was wondering the same.

Instead Mr. Harding said, "I think this Chancellor fellow's lying. That's what I think. I think he's planting a bug in our ear. He wants us to think Governor Cox is involved in this, when he isn't, I doubt. He's hoping we'll do something. And maybe he wants us to think the books are where they aren't."

We stood looking at him.

"I got a directory at the *Star* office. It's got all the printing houses in Ohio listed. Every one of them. And I'm sure if it's—" But then he stopped, abruptly. "Say, what exactly are we going to do? Now wait a minute, what happens if and when we do find those books? What am I getting into here?"

Harry shrugged his shoulders, "Why, what do you think we'll do? See to it that they get put in some place nice and safe."

"Nice and safe? Like a furnace, for instance?"

Again, Harry shrugged his shoulders. "You know anyone's got a big furnace?"

"'Do I know anyone's got—' Now listen to me, Harry, I think we got to remember something here. I'm running for the office of President of the United States. And that's not the way I want to conduct myself. Or my campaign. This isn't Mexico."

"Well, let me tell you something, Senator. You're running for President of the United States. I'm running your campaign. As such, we're running to win, and we won't give any worse than we're liable to get. Besides, with all the impediments we got in our way, we got to play any card we can lay our hands on. Take it or leave it. Yeah, you didn't want to run, but you're running now, so the only way to run is to win." He paused, "'Course if the good Senator would rather keep his fingers out of this pie, then . . . then I guess maybe he can mosey on back home. And let us figure out the particulars." Harry leaned back on the stonewall with that smug, stonewall sort of air that he could sometimes have when he meant business. "Say, Jessie, I bet if you ask the good Senator here, nice and polite like, then maybe he'll let you take a wee little peek in that directory of his. If he asks, tell him we want to print up the notice for a cake walk. We can always arrange a cake walk."

For only the second time, Jess spoke up. "Senator Harding, I was wondering if maybe . . ."

"I keep it hanging from a hook by the corner of my desk. Same hook as the fly swatter. Can't miss it."

Harry laughed, "Good place for it."

"Well," Senator Harding said, "I got a campaign train to catch first thing in the morning, so I think I'll mosey on home, if you gentlemen'll excuse me. That way you can stay here all night if you want, hatching your plots."

He turned and started to walk away into the darkness, back down the sidewalk, toward Mount Vernon Avenue. I can still see the set of his broad shoulders, and the moonlight on his silvery hair. I genuinely admired Senator Harding for his integrity. After a few steps, he paused and turned to us. "Gee, fellas," he said, "I wonder where the plates are."

I'm sure he confounded all three of us. "Plates?" Harry said.

"Why yes, the printing plates. Copper or zinc, usually. The offset. Probably copper." We stood there looking at him. "It'd be awful hard to run a second edition, with or without a new chapter in it, without the printing plates. Plates can take a hell of a long time to make up. None of us has a long time, certainly not between now and November 2nd."

Then Senator Harding turned and walked into the darkness.

Before he was out of earshot, Harry called out, "There goes virtue."

IV

❧

Vacations Arranged for Certain Ladies—
And an Old Maid Is Spotted in the Offing

AS YOU NO DOUBT have already presumed, Senator Harding did not stand up on his front porch the next day, or on the platform of his campaign train, and announce to the American people that he was a Negro. Or a quadroon. Or anything of the kind. Regarding Sentinel Press, it was not listed in that slim directory of Ohio presses that hung on the nail with his fly swatter. As for Professor Chancellor, he was exactly who he said he was, and a bit more. He had not mentioned that he was author of *Our Presidents and Their Office,* but there it was, right on the shelf at our local Carnegie Library. Nor had he mentioned that he was Grand Goblin of the Wayne County branch of the Knights of the Ku Klux Klan. But that too was one of the tidbits that Jess Smith dug up.

It occurs to me that you may be surprised to hear that the Klan was active in Ohio back in 1920, and indeed even right here in Marion, though I should hasten to add that the KKK in these parts most definitely lacked some of the treachery that it has always shown in the South. I assure you there was never a lynching in Marion, Ohio (though I vaguely remember hearing of one out in Marion, Indiana, which is *not* our "sister town" and never has been), though my father once said there was a lynching over in Urbana, Ohio (I think he said) in the '80s or '90s of the last century. At any rate, not once did a flaming cross ever appear in the yards of any of our fellow townsmen. As for the Klan itself, I don't remember hearing anything about it around here before 1918 or 1919, and so I think it was probably one of the many evils, large or small, that flew out (and indeed continue to fly out) of the Pandora's Box opened by World War I. Maybe the Klan's presence this far north had something to do with the many Negroes that came here to work during the War, or maybe it had to do with the popularity of secret societies, or simply the general tendency towards nastiness and violence of all sorts that seemed to rise like a plague from the battlefields in Europe, and contaminate the entire 20th century. So far as I know, Marion's Klansmen limited themselves to the mumbo-jumbo of their coded talk, to dressing up in hoods and nightgowns and sitting in circles, weather permitting, around campfires in the Old Forest, and to carrying torches down Center Street in the 4th of July Parade. Of course all of that would come to an abrupt end after President Warren Harding declared war on the KKK, branding them "terrorists" and "night riders."

I know next to nothing about the Klan over in Wooster, except that the Grand Goblin recruited college boys. I suspect it was pretty much like the Klan in Marion—circumscribed by the fact that everyone and his brother knew who was hiding under those pillow cases, and by the fact that, Ohio being Ohio (as opposed to Alabama or Texas), most of the local Klansmen probably did not particularly wish to offend any of their law-abiding fellow townsmen who just happened to be born, by God's graces, colored folks, Catholics, or Jews.

Though maybe I am being too naïve and kind in my assessment of them and their intentions.

You will recall that Harry told us that his good buddy Jess Smith was "good at digging in the dirt." Indeed, one might have presumed as much, and so he was, to a point. It was Jess who discovered that Professor Chancellor was aka Grand Goblin Chancellor, and that the Goblin had a daughter. I remember the meeting we held at the headquarters of the Harding Volunteers. My family has long owned a certain commercial block along south Main Street, and during the Campaign, my father rented a set of upstairs rooms to the Harding Volunteers for the price of one nickel. At the risk of boring you with a historical footnote, I will pause to say that Mrs. Florence Harding was born in those very rooms, back when Marion was still mostly a wilderness town, in what had heretofore been the Western Reserve. Anyway, my father purchased that block along about 1913 or 1914 from the estate of Mr. Amos Kling, which is to say, from Florence and Warren Harding.

In the early 1920s, we actually thought the "Florence Harding Birthplace" would become a national historic shrine, with a bronze plaque and visitors trekking up the stairs a hundred years hence. But forty years on, I am probably one of the fifty or so people in this entire world who even knows that she was born there.

And I assure you, I am the only one who cares.

Those modest quarters consist of the large front room and a smaller one above the alley. Back in the glorious summer of 1920, we set up an antique crib in the front room, along with a spinning wheel, a pair of rockers, and some pewter candlesticks on a little table with a doily—along with a score of folding chairs that leaned along the wall for use during our meetings. A large portrait of the Senator hung on the north wall, along with a portrait of General Pershing. When Calvin Coolidge visited in July, we rather hurriedly (and temporarily) hung up a portrait of the future Vice President as well, just in case he dropped by.

He did not.

The portrait was just as hurriedly taken down, as Mrs. Harding had expressly forbade that a picture of "that sour pickle of a man" be hung in the rooms where she was born. As to why—your guess is as good as mine, plain old dislike, I suppose.

We—the Harding Volunteers—held our meetings and such there, but the Birthplace was also used by the Campaign, which is to say, by Harry Daugherty & Company, as I so fondly referred to them. The future Attorney General and his helpers kept liquor bottles and shakers locked in the cabinets, out of sight of the more squeamish and law-abiding Volunteers. It is not exactly a recent realization—I noted it even at the time—but I do not remember Senator Harding ever setting foot there, not even when invited by the Volunteers, but as we commented amongst ourselves, climbing stairs seemed to wind him. Maybe that had something to do with the fact that he stayed away.

Forty-eight hours after Chancellor paid me a call, we—the Campaign— had a meeting. I am reminded of the fact that Mr. Harding liked to refer to meetings as "powwows"—including, in time, "Cabinet powwows." Anyway, I do not know why I bring that up, as he was not even present for our meeting; he was on his campaign train somewhere in Indiana, or possibly by then, Illinois.

We had gathered at the table in the back room. George Christian was saying, "So in other words, I guess we aren't any closer to finding the books and plates than we were two days ago. Right, Jess?"

"We haven't found them yet. But that doesn't mean we won't. *Haven't* and *won't* are two different things."

Jess was often given to such profundities.

"And no sign of Sentinel Press?"

"It doesn't exist. At least not in Ohio, Kentucky, West Virginia, Indiana, Michigan, or New York. I haven't been sitting on my hands. I thought maybe Sentinel might publish some of Chancellor's other books too, but that's not the case. All were schoolbook publishers, or big places out in New York. It's a front. Has to be."

I said, "Maybe he made up the name. Considering his viewpoint on things, 'Sentinel' makes perfect sense, doesn't it? Maybe he's having this thing printed privately. When you think about it, what reputable publisher would touch it?"

Harry said quietly, "Lots of maybes flying around. We need facts, not maybes."

"Harry," Jess said, "you really think I've been sitting on my hands? Let me tell you something, this guy isn't stupid, and he's been planning on trouble all along, so he's covered his tracks and covered them good. It's going to take a little time."

"A little time is all we've got. It's all he's got too."

I guess to prove that he had been busy, Jess told us some rather inconsequential things about Chancellor, like the helpful fact that some years ago someone found a stolen Knights of Columbus sword, gilded and jeweled, wrapped in burlap, in the good Professor's office closet at Wooster. According to the Professor, an envious faculty member planted it there to embarrass him. Or maybe some prankster students. Jess also told us some things about Chancellor's work. Obviously, Chancellor managed to get around quite a bit, for according to Jess, he was founder of both the Teachers' College of George Washington University in the District of Columbia and he was founder of the Education Department at Johns Hopkins University in Baltimore, Maryland. I had a little difficulty aligning this information with the old hick and bigot who had sneaked into my yard in the dark of night. I had the impression that, if Chancellor had gone into commerce, then he would probably have been a very wealthy man. Anyway, Jess told us about Chancellor's family, too. Almost in passing, he said, "He's a widower, got an old-maid daughter, a schoolteacher."

To this day I do not know why the tidbit about the daughter caught my ear, but I said, "A daughter? A schoolteacher?"

"Yeah."

"An old maid?"

"Yeah."

"Tell me about her."

"Like I said, she's an old maid. What's to tell?" Jess glanced at his notes. "Teaches home economics in a little berg called Orrville, other side of Wooster. The house there used to be her grandparents' place, I guess. Has a couple of cats, but you've already figured that out. Goes home on Saturdays to help cook and bake for her father, though he has a housekeeper. Daughter's name is Ruby Rose. That's about all I got on her." He turned his eyes on me. "Why?"

I shrugged my shoulders, "Old maids can be interesting, I guess."

"Ruby Rose!" Harry drew the name out and then gave a little whistle, as if he found something tantalizing in those words. Then he added, "Gems and flowers."

"What a hickish name," I said, perhaps with a bit of acid flung from my tongue.

The others looked at me, like maybe they had thought quite differently, but suddenly were not so sure. It is not the best feature to admit about oneself (nor certainly the worst), and it is not something that I have ever intended, but I sometimes had a way, especially when younger, of throwing cold water in the face of other people's tastes and preferences, thus turning something they may have appreciated into something less.

I said, "So how old is this Miss Ruby Rose?"

"Well, I got it scribbled here somewhere. Yes, born 1886. Apple Creek, Ohio. That makes her . . ."

"Thirty-four."

"Now, now Trey," Harry had a smirking little smile on his face, like he was going to tell one of his farmer's daughter jokes. He wagged his finger and said,

"This Miss Ruby Rose, she's a little too old for you. Besides, you're a married man, and we already have enough hanky-panky going on in this Campaign."

I felt my face flush, and I believe a drop-dead look must have risen in my eyes—"daggers" as Lucy used to say. Harry's smirk vanished. "Sorry, Trey. Just a joke. No offense meant."

"Why, none taken," I said, icily. "Not at all."

Nothing more was said about Miss Ruby Rose Chancellor.

We went on to talk about the Senator's mistresses. George Christian told about the generous arrangements already made—twenty-five thousand dollars for Nan, and for the Pages, along with all expenses paid to Europe and back. As for Miss von Leuckel, she would be staying right here in Marion in order to help me deny things, if need be. She would receive twenty-seven thousand dollars, and would be told upfront about the arrangements for Catherine and Jim. But Nan would remain, as they say nowadays, "Top Secret."

At one point, as we wrapped up our discussion of the ladies, Jess muttered, "I still think Chancellor could use a little vacation."

Harry waved the comment away, without a single word. At the time I thought maybe the wave meant, "Don't be a fool."

But in retrospect, I wonder if it meant, "Shut up about that."

V

🌸

Professor Chancellor Makes His Move

VERY LATE THAT NIGHT, Professor Chancellor made his next move.

I woke up early that Saturday morning. I recall the warm aroma of cinnamon rolls filling the house. Back in our youthful years, Lucy used to rise extra early on Saturday mornings and bake cinnamon rolls so we could have them piping hot for breakfast. She was a good woman and a good wife, and I am fortunate and grateful for our forty years together; not a day goes by when I do not think of her, though she's been gone now these six years. Anyway, I was in the kitchen that morning pouring coffee; Lucy had gone out front to fetch the bottle of milk that the Omar man left, every other day, on our step. She called from the porch, "Trey, come and look at this."

I called back, "Look at what?"

"Your friend's been here and left a little something for us."

Needless to say, I had not the slightest idea what she was talking about.

When I stepped out, she tapped her finger on the door, and there was the sheet that I mentioned before— "The Genealogy of Warren G. Harding of Marion, Ohio"—thumbtacked at eye level to our doorframe.

As I stood there reading about the Senator's supposed Negro grandparents and great grandparents, Lucy said, "Next time he shows up in my yard again, don't you dare tell me to go sit down, Trey, 'cause I won't. Just you let me catch that old buzzard crossing my porch again and he'll be looking for a puddle to cool his britches in!"

I took out my pocketknife and removed the tack. "I have a feeling we'll soon be seeing more of these."

"Sooner than you think. Look yonder."

I turned my eyes towards the Verdens' house across the street, expecting to see one pinned to their door as well, but I didn't. Lucy said, "He was a busy little beaver last night." That's when I noticed the tracts scattered here and there in the neighborhood, mixed in with the blowing leaves. Indeed, it looked as if a ream of paper had fallen from the back of a wagon and burst, and the sheets were now scattering about the neighborhood in the blustery wind. The more I looked, the more I saw. They were nearly everywhere one cast one's eye, in the yards, the gutters, and along the sidewalks. I remember looking west, my attention drawn by the clatter of an automobile passing through the intersection that folks have always called "Five Points." When the car passed, heading down Vine Street, its draught drew sheets swirling in its wake. It would be an exaggeration to say that the tracts were as numerous as fallen leaves, but suffice it to say, they were abundant.

"Leave it to a hick to overstate himself," I said.

"Just wait and see what happens if that ol' buzzard comes back 'round here again!"

THE SITUATION was the same throughout much of Marion. The way we figured it, during the wee hours, night riders in speeding automobiles must have roared in one end of Marion and out the other, allowing thousands upon thousands of "genealogies" to blow from their hands into the streets and avenues. A few houses, like ours and of course the Hardings,' had tracts pinned to the front doors—which I suppose was Professor Chancellor's way of "rubbing our face in it."

Nor was Marion alone. The tracts had been spread—albeit in lesser quantities—in towns all along the rails, from the east coast as far as Kansas City, perhaps farther. (I know for a fact copies reached Kansas City, simply because the Huber Manufacturing Company had an agent out there, a Marionite, and he saw young men passing them out on street corners and at factory gates.)

Within forty-eight hours after Lucy called me onto the porch, the once cloistered little rumor that Warren G. Harding had Negro blood in his veins was featured in the headlines of virtually every newspaper in the nation—excepting, of course, the more discreet *Marion Star*. Indeed, if you were around in 1920, and are now of a certain age, then you surely recall firsthand the so-called "Whisper Campaign."

I personally do not know of anything quite like it in politics, either before or since.

My sister Adeline kept several scrapbooks relating to Mr. Harding's public career, from his first run for public office, to the smattering of stories that appeared in the decades after his death—indeed until Adeline's own death. Presently I have here before me the volume regarding the Campaign. Leafing through its last pages, I find a yellowed clipping from *The Dayton Journal*. The clipping is now loose between faded black pages, the paste that once held this particular article in place having crumbled into powder, leaving only grease-like splotches. The headline reads, "Wooster College Professor Ousted for His Lies."

The opening lines of the article read:

> *Right and justice have prevailed, and ere yesterday's sun went down, the* Journal *had in its possession the absolute refutation of the unspeakable assault made upon Warren G. Harding and his family. The evidence is that the truth is what the facts are. The evidence not only indicts the cowardly campaign of vilification, but it declares that the low and indefensible assault upon the Harding name is a lie concocted by the Senator's political opponents and enemies.*

You'll notice, by the way, that the passage does not use the word "Negro," nor does it anywhere else in the text. This whitewashing of the rumor, while reporting it, was the same in many newspapers throughout the land, including most of the Democratic ones. In other words, papers managed to cleverly report the dissemination of the rumor, without mentioning exactly what the rumor was.

But I assure you, everyone in the nation knew.

Let me just say that Harry Daugherty regarded Professor Chancellor's genealogy as being an out-and-out lie and conspiracy financed by the Ku Klux Klan. Jess Smith managed to dig up the fact that tens of thousands of those tracts traveled westward with Governor Cox on his campaign train (almost certainly unbeknownst to him personally) and so that detail blew up in the face of the Democrats rather nicely—from coast to coast.

But you'll recall that we still had other potential annoyances to contend with, including, first and foremost, the book and the plates still hidden away out there, somewhere. It was one thing to dismiss a one-page, cheaply printed genealogy as being the work of a now unemployed crackpot professor, crank, and goblin of the KKK. It would be an entirely different matter to dismiss a two hundred and some page book that named names and was packed with facts and gossip that might at the very least "ring true" (which in fact, much of it does).

VI

A Gentleman Calls on Miss Ruby Rose Chancellor
(Finally)

I DO NOT KNOW WHY, but Miss Ruby Rose Chancellor got stuck in my mind. I am sure that if Jess Smith had managed to track down the whereabouts of the books and plates, then Miss Chancellor's very existence would have passed through my thoughts like a piece of paper riding the wind, but that had not happened. Indeed, after the tracts appeared and the former professor's name landed on the front page of the nation's newspapers, he himself vanished from sight. I knew this because a small army of journalists had gone looking for him, but he had cleaned the junk out of his desk at Wooster College and headed for the hills. There was no doubt in my mind as to what he was up to: He had sneaked off somewhere and was hell-bent on finishing that chapter on Miss von Leuckel. I had this picture of him in my mind: the goat-whiskered geezer sitting at a schoolteacher's dumpy desk in some dingy farmhouse somewhere, his pen feverishly scratching across the page, and as each sensational page was finished, him handing it over his shoulder to one of his pupils, who in turn hastened off to the typesetter.

The way I figured it was this: If we could find the Grand Goblin, then by lying low, we could also find the books and plates.

I have always been one of those fellows who follows Intuition—faithful nag that she is—and so after a day or so I decided to pay a little visit to Miss Ruby Rose. I figured she was bound to know the whereabouts of her dad, and by extension, the whereabouts of his book. And so during

the last week in September, I turned the affairs of Colonel Hamilton &
Son back over to my assistant, Dana Yost, for a few days, threw some
clothes into a small trunk, hung a few spare tires on the back of my Ford,
kissed Lucy good-bye, and chugged eastwards for Orrville.

It would be generous of me to say that poor Miss Chancellor comes
to mind every time I spread my toast with Smucker's jam—the only thing
Orville is known for—but that is not the case. The truth of the matter is,
I have scarcely thought of her during the past forty-three years, except
for last summer when I saw her father's obituary and read that she had
preceded him in death. When and where she died, it did not say, though
something in the wording of the notice gave me the impression that she
died many years ago, probably right there in her brick house on Maple
Lane, where she entertained me during the autumn of 1920.

I remember the first time I saw Miss Ruby Rose Chancellor on a
gray, windswept afternoon with leaves blowing like snow. I parked my
Ford beside a bramble, with her Civil War–era house in clear view, a few
hundred yards away. From there by the roadside, I watched and waited.
Upon my arrival in Orville, I had driven past the high school, but it
was pointless to linger in that setting, as I would not have been able to
distinguish Miss Ruby Rose from other teachers.

I should add that I was still, more or less, mulling over my lines and such
as to how to present myself. I hope you understand by now that I am not, by
nature, a liar, but obviously it would not do for me to introduce myself as
Tristan Hamilton, from Marion, Ohio, president of the Harding Volunteers,
who had come to Orrville for the sole purpose of locating and ultimately
destroying the plates and all copies of her father's scandalous book. Thus
before I even left Marion, I concocted a plan. I decided to present myself as
a graduate of Wooster College, a former student of her dear father's, and
more importantly, as a historian, and a sympathizer with the Klan.

I even arrived in Orrville with "credentials." Before setting out, I dropped
by Wiants Bookstore and purchased the remaining copies of *Lest We Forget:
Oliver Hazard Perry and the Battle of Lake Erie*, by Wellington Boyd.

You see, I now became Wellington Boyd.

What's more, I (Wellington Boyd) had just finished writing a book
on General Nathan Forrest, the Confederate general—a fact (or rather, a
concoction) that I regarded as the cleverest component of my ruse.

I suppose I thought of Forrest simply because my grandfather used to tell me war stories, and as a colonel in the GAR, he had fought against Forrest at Chickamauga. My grandfather admired General Forrest for his superb military prowess, but other than that, he held him in contempt. He was responsible for the Massacre at Fort Pillow, wherein the Rebels slaughtered several hundred Negro men, women, and children. If a military man did anything like that today, then I should hope that he would meet his fate on the gallows.

Instead, General Forrest went on to make a fortune in railroading and became an organizer of the Ku Klux Klan, its first Grand Wizard.

Wellington Boyd's problem was this: The poor fellow was having trouble finding a publisher for his book, because it spoke favorably of the Klan—and no publisher north of the Mason-Dixon wanted to touch it.

So I was wondering if Miss Ruby Rose might put me in touch with her father, who might in turn use his influence to help me see my book into print. After all, like everyone else in Ohio, I could not help but notice that, according to Professor Chancellor's leaflet, he had a book coming out that told the dangerous truth about Senator Warren G. Harding. If he could find a way to publish that, then with his help, surely I could find a way to publish my book on the long-dead General Nathan Forrest.

As for the manuscript itself (should anyone ask), it was up in Port Clinton—Wellington Boyd's hometown—where a lady was diligently typing up the handwritten work.

But of course that was not my only excuse for visiting Wayne County. I had also come down to see if I might render my dear ol' professor any assistance, seeing as to how he was besieged by the press, the crafty Harding camp, and apparently even by my equally dear alma mater—Professor Chancellor's own Wooster College. Or rather his former college.

I thought my concoction was a pretty good one, though I have to admit that I had to rack my brain to come up with it. Of course, in spite of my "dropout" status, I knew enough to do my "homework." And my love of reading has always belied my lack of a diploma. In fact, I had already read various books on Commodore Perry and the Battle of Lake Erie, and my childhood summer days on the Catawba Cliffs, above Lake Erie, had enabled me to take excursions to that part of the Lake where the Battle occurred, just to the north of Put-in-Bay. Regarding General Forrest,

I had read various books on the Civil War wherein his strategies and his sins were given much attention. I also had the vicarious experience of my grandfather having visited him, some years after the war, when he had traveled westward.

I had reviewed these several books on the day and evening prior to my departure, paying special note to small, convincing details, just in case I had to bluff my way through some suspicious inquiry on the part of Miss Ruby Rose.

So, anyway, there I sat in my Ford on that Wednesday afternoon as I peered watchfully through my windshield at the cobbled, leaf-strewn bricks of Maple Lane. That lonely lane stretched into the further loneliness and emptiness that little towns have when they are spread over great spaces, the houses seemingly napping on the far reaches of lawns. The old maples and elms were shedding their leaves like clouds shedding rain, albeit far more visibly and colorfully, and the dull grass of autumn had already vanished beneath their colorful blanket. From my Ford I could see into the rolling brown hills of the country, seemingly just beyond the backyards, speckled with farms and autumn's color. I pulled the collar of my sweater high about my neck, my arms enfolding myself against the chill. Earlier, I had noticed a little restaurant by the water tower "downtown," and oh, what I would have given for a nice, steaming cup of hot cocoa! But like any good hunter, I did not want to miss the first sight of my quarry. Thus I laid low in my "blind," lurking, biding my time. I must say that, in all, I found Orrville to be a pretty little town and, no doubt, a wholesome place to live. Anyway, shortly after three o'clock, a scattering of children suddenly appeared in the distance running home from school, gleefully kicking up the leaves. But after a time the ranks of liberated pupils began to thin. Still no sign of Miss Ruby Rose. I presumed she was keeping some poor child detained after school for some perceived transgression. I imagined her holding his hand in hers and slapping his knuckles with a ruler, and him standing there stoic and defiant, which made her slap all the harder, until silent tears ran down the poor boy's cheeks. Obviously, that was pure conjecture on my part, but who knows—it may have fit the bill.

I was beginning to think that maybe she had sneaked home by a back route, when in the distance two ladies rounded the corner onto Maple Lane. They walked side by side in the near distance. I slunk even lower in my car seat, behind the steering wheel, I suppose a bit like an alligator, its eyes barely a slit above the water, peering at its prey. The wind blew the hems of their long dark dresses and both held their hats in place—large hats of a style that had passed out of fashion, in Marion, after the War. One lady was thin and appeared to be younger, the other big-boned, older. They paused at what I sensed was a leaf-buried path, maybe an old Indian trail passing between yards and trees, where they stood talking. After a minute or two they parted, the younger one following the path, the larger of the two strolling my way, down the walk. And then from my surreptitious place I watched Miss Ruby Rose Chancellor cross her yard. As she did so, an old dog moseyed over from the neighbor's place to greet her. She stood making over it for a few moments, then wearily trudged up her steps, crossed her porch, and entered her house. I sensed that she would live alone there for the rest of her life.

I could not help but notice that she did not use a key to open the front door.

Of course I did not want Miss Ruby Rose to think that I had been lying in wait for her, so I gave her maybe ten minutes to get situated before I slid my wedding ring off, slipped it into my jacket pocket, and stepped from my car.

I must say that I was quite nervous as I traipsed up the flagstones with Wellington Boyd's book in hand and his name on my lips. The old dog that had crossed the yard to greet Miss Ruby Rose now stood under a bush, snarling and leering at me, in spite of my friendly greeting. I am reminded again about how my builder's eye is always watchful, for my nervousness did not keep me from a making a quick appraisal of Miss Chancellor's house, and what I saw was bad news. I recall that the bricks needed to be repointed; indeed, I was virtually certain that plaster and wallpaper damage had already occurred on the interior of the north-facing walls, from wind-driven rain—which possibly had precipitated some rotting in the floor joists. I also could not help but notice that the trim and high copula had been recently painted—by someone who had done a very shabby job. The new paint was already blistering and peeling away from the old, leaving patches of raw wood exposed to the elements. She would be sorry if she didn't do something about that soon—like last summer.

As I have always said, it's expensive to do things cheaply.

I tossed my wind-blown hair from my eyes, straightened my tie, and knocked on her door. I thought I heard a cat meow on the other side. Miss Ruby Rose must have been in the back of the house, or upstairs, for after a minute or so I had to knock again, more forcefully. A few moments later I heard muffled footsteps hastening along a hall. I straightened my shoulders and, Wellington Boyd's book at the ready, I clasped my hands behind my back.

She opened the door.

I smiled. "Miss Chancellor?"

She simply stood there staring at me through the screen with a look of astonishment, mixed with suspicion.

I must say that she was even more matronly than I had expected, and frankly, she had "spinster schoolteacher" written all over her. I repeated, with a smile, "Miss Ruby Rose Chancellor?"

"I don't know where he is."

"Excuse me?"

"I don't know where he is."

I pretended outright befuddlement. "Who?"

"Daddy. My father. And I don't know anything about the trouble, so you can take your notebook and get out of town."

Without removing her eyes from me, she started to close the door.

"Miss Chancellor, wait! You seem to have the wrong idea. I'm not a reporter. Or whatever you think I am."

The door stopped its swing closed, and she scrutinized me through the screen.

"You are Miss Ruby Rose Chancellor, aren't you?"

No reply.

I repeated myself.

"If you're not a reporter, then who the dickens are you?"

"Wellington Boyd, at your service, Madam." I bowed slightly. "I was a student of Professor Chancellor's before the War. I was over in Wooster trying to look him up, but of course he's nowhere to be found, I guess because of all the trouble. But I was wondering, please, Miss Chancellor, if you'd be so kind as to tell me where I might find him?"

The suspicious look flared back in her eyes again. "No, I cannot. Go away." She started to close the door yet again.

"Miss Chancellor, please! Look!" I held up *Lest We Forget*. "I wrote this myself. See, my name's right here. Wellington Boyd. It's about Commodore Perry." Her eyes went from me, to the book, and back to me again. I added, "It was your father's idea. Me writing this book. You see, I studied history with Professor Chancellor, before the War, and he suggested that I write it."

I gave her a chance to reply, but she did not.

"I might add, Miss Chancellor, that your father taught me everything I know about history, especially the presidency, and then some, and I'm very grateful. And now I've written another book, and I need his advice. That's why I'm looking for him, I promise. Besides, I have a feeling that with the Harding trouble, he could use me."

"I told you I don't know where he is." I presumed she was lying. "Daddy left after the trouble began."

"I see. Well, it wouldn't surprise me one little bit if Professor Chancellor was right about Harding."

"Well, it would surprise me."

It had never occurred to me that Miss Ruby Rose might not be of the same mind as her father, so I hastened to add, "Well, you may be right about that. You've no doubt followed the whole affair more closely than me. Frankly, it's of little interest to me, one way or the other."

I could see the wheels turning in her mind, and they were not turning in my direction. "You studied the presidency with my father, but you haven't followed the Harding affair?"

"Well, I mean yes, I have, of sorts, but not too closely." I could feel myself blushing under the weight of my stupidity. I smiled.

She stared. "I don't know where Daddy is."

Suddenly, the door was swiftly closing in my face.

"Miss Chancellor! Please! Miss Chancellor, no!"

But my entreaties were to no avail, and I found myself staring at the shut door. Then I heard her throw the lock with a certain female vehemence. I muttered something under my breath and stood wondering what to do next. I sensed the presence of an altogether cranky, melancholy, and suspicious-minded old/young spinster on the other side, waiting to hear the reassuring sound of a certain gentleman's footsteps crossing her porch and fading forever from her presence down the walk. I resolved that she would hear nothing of the kind. I knocked. Then I knocked again, rather fiercely—so loudly that I thought even the neighbors might hear. "Miss Chancellor," I called, "Please! Please, Miss Chancellor!"

And I knocked several more times.

Finally, the door opened just a crack, with her peeking out. "Stop that! You're acting like a spoilt little boy. Daddy never mentioned you. He always talks about his scholars, but he never said boo about you. And if he told you to write a book, then that's a laugh. He'd never tell anyone that. He'd be afraid it might be better than his."

Needless to say, I didn't know what to say.

And then she added, "He warned me that people like you might be snooping about, and so they are. Two of them already. You make the third. And the most impudent!"

"Miss Chancellor, please. I'm not a reporter. I'll swear to it if you want. Bring me a Bible and I'll swear on it. I am *not* a reporter. Or anything else unsavory."

She stared at me.

"Bring me a Bible, please."

"If you're not a reporter, then what are you? Who are you?"

"I told you. Wellington Boyd. From Port Clinton, Ohio. Up on the Lake. Maybe your father did mention me and you forgot. It was a long time ago. Before the War. Or maybe he never mentioned me at all, I don't know. I guess I kept to myself a bit. Sat in the corner. I was the smart one that other pupils taunted." She frowned, scrutinizing me through the opening. I don't know how to describe her look, like she was divided as to whether to drive me off the porch with her broom, or invite me into her lonely house for tea. "May I come in, Miss Chancellor, please? Just for a moment? I'm not some kind of outlaw. You know that." I shivered. "And to tell you the truth, I'm a little cold, and I don't want to catch pneumonia. Not again. Not like I did in the trenches. The Army doctors said, next time, I'd be a goner. And I barely survived the influenza. One of the lucky ones."

"Then I should think you'd dress more appropriately for the vagaries of the season."

This woman was something else.

She added, "I don't know where Daddy is, so if that's all you want, you're fooling your time away. And mine."

"Well," I said forlornly, "I guess I've wasted a trip after all, all the way down from Lake Erie."

"Well, I guess you have. You should've written ahead. It's common sense."

I laughed to hear myself reprimanded for lacking a quality which Miss von Leuckel had lately chided me for possessing to the extreme. "Yes, you're quite right on that score. Common sense has never been my strong suit. My dear mother—God rest her soul— used to call me a 'will-o'-the-wisp,' a 'romantic.' She was thoroughly right. Miss Chancellor, may I come in, please?"

Something was going on behind those pale, staring eyes, though I knew not what. Suddenly she whispered, "But the neighbors"—as if they might hear—"they'd find it irregular, wouldn't they, a young man like you, a stranger, coming in?"

I smiled and tossed back my hair—a mannerism I'd noticed the summer before in a seasonal laborer, a randy young man working to pay his way through Ohio State. I heard myself (or maybe I should say, Wellington Boyd—cad that he was) half-whispering back, "Why, sometimes a person just has to open the door and not worry about what the neighbors think, don't they, Miss Chancellor?"

She was staring at me, torn and troubled in her thoughts. She touched a strand of hair to her lips. "I wasn't expecting a gentleman caller. I wish I'd known."

I said nothing. I simply looked her in the eyes.

Without further ado, she opened the door, glancing towards the street. I quickly stepped into the shadows of a lonely house, and closed the door behind me.

"This is very irregular," she said.

"Sometimes the irregular is the best part of life." I do not know where that line came from. It just popped out of my mouth. I do not know if I made it up, or if I had read it somewhere before.

Miss Ruby Rose was wearing a faded, flowered housedress that had the appearance of a hand-me-down from her late mother, and ragged pink slippers that ought to have been pitched into the rubbish heap long ago.

The odor of the cats lingered in the place. Indeed, almost immediately they began doing things to my ankles.

Miss Ruby Rose seemed not quite to know what to do with herself, or rather with her "gentleman caller."

To break the awkward silence, and her gaze, I glanced at the dreary surroundings. "Oh, why, how perfectly homey!"

"Do you find it so?"

"Mercy! How could I not?"

"Frankly, I find it a tad bit drab, as it is, but it's the best I can do, at the moment. I often think it could be fixed up just fine for a family. Would you like a cup of cocoa, Mr. Boyd? Hot cocoa and cookies?"

With that offer, I knew I was hitting it lucky, at least for now, and I said, "Oh, that would really hit the spot!"

My hostess invited me to sit in the parlor. Then she nervously hurried away towards the back of the house. Thankfully, the cats scooted along behind her. I had a feeling that in the life of Miss Ruby Rose, callers (except perhaps those of the pupil variety) came along once in a blue moon—if ever.

I inspected the chairs for the one with the least cat hair, and sat down—realizing, by the knobby lumps, why the cats avoided it. Nonetheless, I adjusted myself and stayed put.

My guess was that this house had not changed one iota, inside or out, since the days of Miss Ruby Rose's grandparents. The parlor was high-ceilinged and shadowy with a long, black horsehair couch that had no doubt been hosting people's fannies since the days of Lincoln. As I recall, there were two or possibly three matching chairs, and a matching love seat by the side windows. Drab wallpaper—something like a gray color, or maybe a faded blue, with equally faded flowers—enveloped the room, and a few lithographs hung in frames from old-fashioned velvet cords.

I must say that, as I awaited my hostess, I could not help but feel a bit sorry for her, though I want to note that, so far as I have seen, the plainest of women marry, just like the loveliest, and life does not exclude entrance to the marriage banquet based on looks or station—though it does on a vague, inner something else. What that something else is, I cannot say.

Miss Chancellor seemed to be taking a rather inordinate amount of time in the kitchen melting chocolate and boiling milk. I was beginning to wonder if she had her hands deep in cookie batter, baking up a fresh batch. Then I finally heard a door open in the back of the house, and her footsteps hastening along the hall. She entered the parlor, bearing a tray, with a sort of agitated casualness. I was astonished to see that she had completely changed her outfit, and had combed her gray-streaked hair. Indeed, she was now dressed like Sunday afternoon, ready for the "gentleman caller" who had finally arrived out of the blue. My surprise must have registered, for as I arose, she apparently felt the need to explain herself. "I was doing a little housekeeping when you arrived, Mr. Boyd, and didn't want you to have to look at me in my cleaning dress."

"Why, I hadn't noticed, Miss Chancellor, though I certainly notice now and please forgive me for being forward, but you look lovely!"

She blushed and smiled. "You've picked the most uncomfortable chair in the whole house, Mr. Boyd."

"Not at all." After she served our little snack, hot cocoa and graham crackers, she seated herself on a chair directly across from me. As I stirred my cocoa, I said, "I do hope I can find your father, Miss Chancellor." I made a point of looking her straight in the eye, and said, "He really did suggest that I write a book." As evidence, I tapped *Lest We Forget*, resting on my knee. "I want you to know that, Miss Chancellor, he really, really did."

She studied me for a long moment. "Did he! Then you mustn't be very talented."

Truly, this woman was something else.

"Well, be that as it may, Miss Chancellor, I wrote it and I've written another book, too. One about Nathan Forrest, the Confederate general. But I'm afraid it's proving to be a bit of a hot potato. I mean in terms of finding a printer. You see, he was a great general, a born general, but he was also a founder of the Ku Klux Klan . . ."

"The Klan!" The way she said it told me quite plainly that Miss Chancellor did not share with her father his views on the KKK. For a moment, I even wondered if she knew he was a member, much less Grand Goblin.

"Yes," I said, "the Klan. As a matter of fact, General Forrest was the first Grand Dragon. No one wants to touch my book—"

"In that case, perhaps there is some hope for the human race. In the past several years, I've come to wonder."

"Yes, well, anyway, that's what I'd like to talk to Professor Chancellor about. Maybe he can give me some insight about finding a printer." I thought about mentioning the fact that her father had obviously found a press to publish the book on Harding, as indicated by the leaflet circulating the country, but I did not want to reaffirm her initial suspicions. I continued, "Granted, I should have written ahead instead of just hopping in my Ford and setting off down the highway, but I guess that's the way I do things, sometimes. Like a rambler."

"Truthfully," Miss Chancellor said, "I don't know what to think of either you or your book, Mr. Boyd, or the fact that Daddy never mentioned you, but I can tell you for a fact that I do not know where he is. He sent me a note saying he was going away, but I don't know where, and that's that."

I suddenly had the feeling that she was telling the truth, and that my trip had been a total waste of time. Not to mention the fact that Chancellor might, after all, manage to finish the chapter on Mitzy and get it into his book. "You don't? Really?"

"No, Mr. Boyd, I don't. Really. Daddy goes away all the time and doesn't tell me a thing. It doesn't seem to matter to him that I worry. Like when he was over in Marion snooping around in Warren Harding's life, he didn't say boo about it. I never knew where he was till he got back. I do wish I could help you, but I can't. I won't know anything about it until he comes home. That's the beginning and the end of it. He doesn't care that I worry."

A sinking feeling came over me, as I sat alone with that spinster in her dreary parlor. If she did not know where her father was, and if he did not tell her of his comings and goings, then how on earth was she supposed to know anything about the books and plates? But I am a man of faith, so to speak, and simultaneous to that moment of intense discouragement, I had a small measure of hope that Intuition had not dragged me all the way to Orrville just to share graham crackers and cocoa with a lonesome schoolteacher. In my heart I genuinely felt that surely Miss Chancellor must know something of use to me. I was puzzling over this mystery—and how to gracefully root around for whatever it was, when she asked, "Your father, Mr. Boyd, is he yet living?"

"Yes, thank God. He's a colonel. Fought in the Indian Wars. And my grandfather, he was a colonel too, cavalry. In fact, he fought against Forrest at Shiloh. Grandpa's saber hangs over my bed, unsheathed."

"Why, a soldering family! And you, Mr. Boyd? Have you not followed in their footsteps?"

I believe I fidgeted, as I really did not care to talk about Wellington Boyd's past, simply because I had invented very little of it. Nevertheless, I heard myself saying, "Well, I did my duty, Miss Chancellor. Took a bullet down here"—I tapped my left thigh—"near the village of Ourcq, in France. Lost a friend there too, a boy I enlisted with. We left from the depot together—" Suddenly, I felt a pang of genuine sorrow for my dear, lost friend, Orley. "I'm sorry, Miss Chancellor. If you don't mind, I think I'd rather not talk about that."

"Why, of course, Mr. Boyd."

A long moment of silence followed, in which my hostess sat there intently watching me, with unsaid words.

I was glad she was leaving them unsaid, as I had no interest in her sympathy, and no right to it. I—who had counted stockings and bandages during the War, whilst Orley and the others had gone away to the trenches and died there. But then again, I was at the moment Wellington Boyd, not Tristan Hamilton, and so I was not wholly a cad for conveying his little imaginative history.

"Mr. Boyd," she said, "if you don't mind me asking, I believe you said your mother too had passed into the realm of spirits, did you not?"

Really, this woman struck me as quite an oddball. "Miss Chancellor, I believe I alluded to the fact that she died, yes. When I was a child."

"Mine too."

"I'm so sorry."

"Oh, it's not so bad as that, Mr. Boyd. You realize, don't you, that our beloved dead, so-called, aren't half so far away as we might think?"

I was beginning to see the lay of the land. "Miss Chancellor?"

"I mean to say, Mr. Boyd, that the spirit world is mingled midst our very own."

"I've heard talk of that, lately."

"It isn't just talk, Mr. Boyd, I assure you. It's the truth. The scientific and the spiritual truth."

Let me pause to remind you that séances, spiritualism, and the like were all the rage after the Great War, which had swept tens of millions of souls into the great beyond. None of that business ever interested me in the slightest. By my lights, if there was anything to spiritualism, then it never would have been a fad. If our beloved dead were so readily accessible, then ordinary folks—not just the kooks—would have been checking in on them regularly since Noah's flood, not simply for the past year or so. But in spite of my skepticism, something told me not to let go of the tail of this particular dog. I leaned forward, over my cocoa. "You mean to tell me, Miss Chancellor, that you have actually communicated with the dead?"

"I have, Mr. Boyd. I have."

She uttered those words with such gravity that I had all I could do to stifle what Lucy always referred to as "that condescending little laugh" of mine. Nevertheless, with some effort, I did just that.

She continued, "I communicate with my own dear mother, Mr. Boyd, and you can too. And with your friend, too, if you wish. Death is no reason for being out of touch."

Frankly, this time I could not help but laugh, just a little. "Well, glad to hear it."

"May I ask your friend's name?"

"Orley," I muttered.

"Mr. Boyd?"

"Orley. Orley Hamilton."

"Orley," she repeated. She closed her eyes and, drawing out his name like an incantation, said, "Orley." It was as if she were calling to him, as if his spirit were asleep in one of her rooms upstairs. She opened her eyes, "Mind you, I'm not a medium, Mr. Boyd, but I know one. A very powerful one of great access. Sister Sadie Jones. She lives in a little encampment right outside of town." She paused, as if wondering whether to proceed. Then speaking mostly to herself, she said, "There must be some reason why you found your way to my door."

"I certainly hope so."

"Mr. Boyd, if you're of a mind, then we can go there, together. I wanted to go out there anyway, but had no way, no one to drive me there. Then you came along, out of nowhere. Auspicious!"

I sat there, wondering where this wild goose chase could possibly lead. "Yea or nay, Mr. Boyd?"

I shrugged my shoulders, "Yea, of course. What's to lose?"

She nodded. "Excellent. Mr. Boyd, you strike me as a bit of a seeker, just hopping in your car like that and rambling down the open road, along life's pathways. And now—"

I nodded politely and allowed my gracious hostess to wallow in her silly thoughts.

VII

🌿

Sister Sadie of Mohican Grove

MISS CHANCELLOR DID NOT WISH TO BE SEEN departing from the house with her gentleman caller, and so after our sandwich and baked bean supper, I left via the front door, walked across the yard and back down lonely little Maple Lane, and chugged away in my Ford; whilst along about that same time, my hostess was slipping out the back door, hastening across her backyard and down whatever byways she had to follow to our point of rendezvous—one of those bent, ancient trees from Indian days that had been bowed as a sapling into the shape of an arrowhead, as a trail marker for their hunting and war parties. (Such a tree also stood, until recent years, on the way to Goose Pond Farm.) I remember Miss Chancellor was wearing a colorful scarf over her head, which seemed to give her the mixed air of a sultry Gypsy and an old woman. I had to smile at the peculiar, girlish thrill Miss Chancellor displayed as she stepped into my Ford. In this regard she reminded me of a hooky-playing child who had just escaped the dreary confines of the schoolroom.

As my little Ford was rattling eastward through the Mohican Hills, I was puzzling over how to get back on track regarding her father's books and plates. Meanwhile, Miss Chancellor was rattling on about Sister Sadie's supernatural powers and her first-rate ability to ring up the dead. During a pause in her chatter, I said, "Not to change the subject, Miss Chancellor, but I'm very preoccupied with my book on General Forrest. I really don't know how I'll ever find a printer."

154

"A printer? You said that earlier. I think you mean a publisher. Printers are a penny a peck. I should think you would know the difference."

"As a matter of fact, I believe I do know the difference, and I do mean a printer. You see, I've given up on publishers, at least for this particular book. No one wants to touch it because, as I said, Forrest had his hands in the Klan. Not to mention some lynchings."

"Lynchings!"

"Yes."

"Heavens, then maybe you should have written your book on someone else, on a decent human being."

"Not at all! General Forrest sullied his honor, that's true. But in that way my book will be a warning to doughboys everywhere, north and south—glory in the trenches can be undone by dishonor at home."

"Well—be that as it may."

"Anyway, I've been looking all over Ohio for a printer, one that can take on a book of this size, but I just can't seem to find one." I glanced at my passenger, sitting there in her silk scarf, her reddish nose pointed at the road ahead. "Miss Chancellor, you wouldn't happen to know anything about printers, would you?"

"Hardly. But there's got to be one around somewhere, probably more than one. How else do you suppose Daddy got his book on Harding published? Or rather, printed. His regular publisher wouldn't touch the dirty thing. Neither would anyone else."

"Why, the Harding book! Of course! I hadn't thought of that!" I think my words came out like bad acting, and I felt Miss Chancellor's sharp glance. I hastened to add, "Well, I guess I thought of it, sort of, but . . ."

"You guess you thought of it, sort of! Of course you thought of it. That's why you drove all the way down from Port Clinton. Who do you think you're fooling?"

I paused, chastised. "You're a very bright young lady, aren't you? Perhaps you should be the one writing books."

She glanced my way.

"I mean that."

She made no response, and so I said, "Do you know who his printer is, Miss Chancellor?"

"No," she said coolly, "I do not. You'll have to ask Daddy yourself."

"I would if I could find him, but I have to get back to the Lake! I have to get back to work, soon!" I'd already told Miss Chancellor—over our sandwich supper—all about my family's business interests—building and lumber and coal yards and quarries and such throughout Ottawa County—and how I had written my books on Perry and Forrest during my long evenings, alone. I even told her about Tioga. Or rather I should say, Tioga-on-the-Lake, so to speak. I glanced at her. She was staring straight ahead, looking peevish, and maybe suspicious, too. I did not want her to think me a cad, or doubt my sincerity. "Miss Chancellor," I said, "please don't think me forward, but I was thinking over supper—maybe you could come up sometime and visit us in Port Clinton. Sometime soon. Our house is quite spacious. And I'm sure my father and sister would be pleased to have you—very pleased. Why, I could even show you our cottage. It's only about ten miles up the shore." She was still staring straight ahead, and I did not know what thoughts were going through her mind. "Just think about it, please."

"That," she murmured, "would be very irregular."

"Wouldn't it though! You only live once. Your father, he goes away all the time without telling you. Right? So maybe you should give him a taste of his own medicine. It'll do the old man good."

"If he even notices."

"Do it when he will notice, when he'd ordinarily expect you." I paused, "My little sister . . ."

"Yes, Mr. Boyd. Your little sister, what's her name?"

"Adeline. That was my mother's name too."

"Adeline! Now that's a real pretty name. And your sister, Mr. Boyd, I bet she's every bit as beautiful as her name, isn't she? And your mother, she was beautiful too, wasn't she? I can tell."

"Yes," I said quietly, "she was." I sensed that I now had Miss Chancellor back in my corner, but I must say that I felt a tinge of disgust. Not simply for bringing my mother's name into this, but for all my devious little lies and half-lies to this poor, forlorn woman—all for the sake of covering the Senator's adulterous tracks. Nevertheless, I soldiered on, "Think about it, Miss Chancellor. Think about coming up to see us. Please."

After a reflective moment, she quietly said, "I shall, Mr. Boyd. I shall. Thank you for inviting me. For me, that kind of invitation is a first."

"And maybe by the time you arrive, I'll have found a printer, I hope. That way I'll be able to rest my mind. And enjoy your company all the more! We shall have a nice big dinner. I'll have the housekeeper get out the silver."

"Silver," she said, more to herself than to me, as if the word were a spoken totem to another world. "But as far as the printer goes, I can't help you there. I really can't."

"No? So your father never said anything about it?"

"Never. Not a word. Certainly not to me." She paused. "I'm sure some of his 'protégées' know all about it. His scholars, his pets." She turned to me, "But then again, you know something about that, yourself—don't you Mr. Boyd?"

I said nothing.

"Daddy never tells me a thing," she added. "At least nothing important." After a long moment, she said, "If only I'd been a boy."

I was not about to lend a hand in opening that can of worms.

MOHICAN GROVE was no more than three or four miles outside of Orrville, though it had the feeling of a place entirely unto itself. I remember we'd meandered along a couple of twisting roads through the Mohican Forest until Miss Chancellor directed me to turn down a narrow, unmarked lane cut through towering, ancient trees. After a hundred yards or so, we came to a clearing. And there was Mohican Grove—a misty little coven of ten or twelve clapboard bungalows. They encircled a park-like area where a majestic oak, in what looked to be the exact center, soared like an ancient king above the primeval forest. The place instantly reminded me of a grove out at Goose Pond Farm, albeit a smaller one than this— but ours has a soaring, conical Indian mound at its center, topped by a hemlock, not an oak. As for the bungalows, they were quite new, squat little things, not much bigger than rental cottages. Each was identical with its own dark, screened-in porch and ugly pea-green paint.

I could not help but notice that the cottages had been built too close to the ground. I was somehow certain that cellar holes did not exist at Mohican Grove. Not only that, but from what I could see, the skirting around the "foundations" seemed to lack vents. To make matters even worse, not a single rainspout was anywhere to be seen, and so with each rain, runoff would find its way beneath the cottages.

Whether anyone at Mohican Grove knew it or not, their little community was, even at the moment, rotting away beneath their feet.

The chill wind of the mid afternoon had stilled, and gray smoke now rose in lines from the chimneys.

Sister Sadie's cabin stood beside the meeting house, and as my little Ford slowly made its way around the cul-de-sac, I felt eyes following us from windows, behind the screens of the dark porches. I remember an early jack-o-lantern on the step of one of the bungalows. Miss Chancellor had been rather quiet for some minutes, and the moment we pulled over in front of Sister Sadie's, she said, all of a sudden, "Oh, by the way, Mr. Boyd, there's something I forgot to tell you. Sister Sadie and her husband are colored folks, Negroes. Just to let you know."

"Negroes?"

"Yes, Negroes. I hope that doesn't make any difference to you. They were born slaves, in Florida."

"Florida! Oh, Lord!" I said. Before she could step from the car, I caught Miss Chancellor's hand. "Listen, they don't need to know about my book on General Forrest, okay? They might think I admire him, or something."

"But you do, don't you?"

"Of course not. He was a demon. But does that preclude fascination?"

She persisted. "Well, if he had no scruples, then why would you bothered writing a book about him?"

I squeezed her hand, "Please, Miss Chancellor. Please. I don't want to offend these folks."

She laughed in a gentle sort of way, as if she found my worry odd and charming. "I promise I won't say a word Mr. Boyd!" As she stepped from the car, she added, "But Sister Sadie sniffs things out in a minute. Nay, less. So don't blame me if she soon has you pegged."

As I trudged along behind Miss Chancellor, I could not help but feel a renewed perturbance with Mr. Harding. It was his shenanigans that had led me on this wild goose chase in the first place. Why, at that moment I ought to have been at home, settling down to supper with my wife. But here I was with an unmarried lady, my wedding ring in my pocket, entering the house of strangers in a spiritualist camp.

Sister Sadie called out for us to come in, and when we entered, she was sitting in her rocker with a wooden spoon in hand and, in her lap, a wooden bowl with some kind of broth. Needless to say, on top of everything else I felt instantly embarrassed at catching her like that—in the middle of her supper—though frankly, I do not think such a consideration entered her mind. The first words out of her mouth were, "Missy, fetch Sister Sadie the salt. Ulysses keeps it in the crock 'long the wall."

Miss Chancellor hastened into the kitchen, which was merely a little open cubby at the back. Thus I was left standing in the center of the room, without introductions or acknowledgment of any kind. My hostess suddenly seemed to notice me, and she sat there in her rocker scrutinizing me above a spoonful of broth. Her eyes were not at all cloudy, as one often sees in the aged. Rather they were like polished buckeyes of the richest brown. She sipped her broth, still watching me over her spoon, like I might make a sneaky move. Frankly, I didn't know whether to introduce myself, or simply wait until I was spoken to. I clasped my hands behind my back. "Well," I said with a friendly smile, "I guess the wind's finally died down."

"Did it? Didn't know it was blowing."

Thankfully, Miss Chancellor stepped back into the room with a thimble of salt. "Sister Sadie, this here is Mr. Boyd. Mr. Wellington Boyd. His momma died when he was a little boy and he misses her terrible."

My hostess stared at me, but made no reply—no sorry-to-hear-that, no how-do-you-do, no pleased-to-meet-you. At last she took her eyes off me as she pinched salt into her broth. I had scarcely opened my mouth, but I sensed that Sister Sadie somehow knew that I was a fraud. Either that or she simply disliked the looks of me. Maybe both. I wondered if she disliked me for my shiny, yellow-golden hair. Maybe she saw me as a young rich white man. And maybe she presumed I was either ashamed of being in her house, or that I was finding it quite a novelty, finding myself in the house of colored folks.

When it became obvious that our hostess intended to say nothing whatsoever on my account, Miss Chancellor cheerfully inquired, "So Sister Sadie, where's Ulysses?"

"Called 'round the way. Mr. Wickersham's mule took lame." She gestured with her spoon. "Now you children, scoot them chairs up here near Sister Sadie and sit yourselves down."

I believed that Miss Chancellor was starting to feel a little uncomfortable at having brought me. "Mr. Boyd has a Ford. That's how I got out here. Why, if not for him, I couldn't have come out and seen you, Sister Sadie. Not today."

No reply, only another sip of broth.

"He was one of Daddy's scholars, before the war. Though I only met him just today."

Sister Sadie flashed a look at me, "That so?"

I scrutinized her, trying to look blameless.

"He's from Port Clinton." Miss Chancellor turned to me, "Sister Sadie and Ulysses lived at the Lake for the longest time. On South Bass Island, didn't you, Sister Sadie?"

"We did, dear."

"Most of their lives."

"South Bass?" I said. I had never in my life heard tell of Negroes living on the island. "Is that a fact?"

To Miss Chancellor, she said, "Missy, I best tell you that Sister Sadie's not of a mind to be calling no spirits tonight, so you and your daddy's scholar here done wasted tire rubber."

I believe Miss Chancellor may have been embarrassed, thinking that that is why she had dragged me all the way out here, so I could have a little mystical chitchat with my mother. Frankly, I was relieved to hear that I would not have to go through any of that sort of hocus-pocus. Already I needed a rest from my pretense.

Sister Sadie said, "Folks say that daddy of yours done hightailed it for the hills."

"Yes, they do, but they know as much about it as I do. I think he's afraid of the Harding people. You know Daddy . . ."

"No, I don't 'know Daddy.' And for that I thank my lucky stars. That skunk of a man! T'ain't 'fraid of the devil hisself, but piss scared of his own shadow. If I was you, child, I'd shoot him dead. Tell the 'thorties you took him for a skunk."

I do not know why, but when the old woman said that, she looked at me. Like I too was a skunk that she had already "sniffed out." I looked at my hands in my lap. Suddenly, I very much wished that I had never concocted either my useless nom de guerre or my false reports. Not that the truth, of course, would have placed me a single inch closer to the books or plates, but it certainly would have made for more congenial circumstances. Ironically, there I sat in the company of allies. Miss Chancellor had already mentioned her sympathies for Mr. Harding. And colored people generally regarded the Senator in a friendly way. Not because of the Negro-blood rumor, but simply because he had denounced the tricks that so often disenfranchised them. The Senator had also welcomed Negro delegations to the Front Porch. He readily shook hands with colored folks, and they had their pictures taken side by side with him. And the leaders of their delegations had sat with the Senator in his green wicker porch chairs, sipping lemonade from Mrs. Harding's kitchen glasses.

I might add that colored people also liked Senator Harding because he was, of course, a member of the party of Lincoln—a fact that, in 1920, carried considerable weight—back when the Democratic Party was still linked by long memories to slavery and the old Confederacy.

Anyway, I believed that Sister Sadie had pegged me not only as one of the old "skunk's" protégées (after all, that was how I had presented myself), but also as an agent from the very side I was waging a secret war against. And yet it would not do for me to suddenly reveal my true colors. I would have come across as a deceitful liar (which at that moment, after all, I suppose I was), and as I said, the truth would not have placed me a hair's breadth closer to the books and plates. I was beginning to feel not at all clever.

I kept my own counsel.

I was ignored for a time as Miss Chancellor told Sister Sadie about a mutual acquaintance of theirs, apparently, one of the women who now and then visited Mohican Grove. Needless to say, as the ladies chatted, I did not cast my eyes about the room, but I could not help but notice things. The wall behind Sister Sadie was strung with fishnet, which in turn was hung with several dried starfish and horsefish of various sizes. A mummified baby alligator, with glass eyes, seemed to crawl along the lone shelf behind her. And a framed certificate from the "The Royal Daughters of Abyssinia" hung from a nail.

I was surprised when Sister Sadie suddenly turned her attention and spoke to me. "You familiar with South Bass, young man, hailing as you say you do from Port Clinton?"

"Yes, Madame," I said.

Miss Chancellor quickly told me, almost in a whisper, like we were out of the old woman's earshot, "She doesn't like that, Mr. Boyd. Call her Sister Sadie."

I corrected myself. "I beg your pardon, Sister Sadie. Yes, I know the island pretty well, I guess."

She studied me. "Then you was to Hotel Victory."

"I was. I saw the fire in the sky the night it burned, summer 'fore last."

Actually, I hadn't seen anything of the kind. But Adeline had. She had been summering at Indian Rock, about eight miles across the water from the grand hotel with its thousand or so rooms. In fact, the fire was so spectacular that just about everyone for fifty miles thereabouts saw the roiling orange glow in the night sky.

Sister Sadie was still eyeing me, but no longer in an unfriendly way, more like she was trying to decipher a puzzle. "I toiled there, back in the days. Ulysses too. Him scrubbing pots down in the big kitchen and me boiling sheets in the cellar. Till folks stopped coming like they used to. Assurance."

"Assurance?"

"Folks said t'was 'lectric. Truth to tell, they wanted to collect."

I suppose she was referring to arson, though I had never heard that before, or since. "If I may ask," I said, "what took you to South Bass?"

"What you's askin' Sister Sadie is how'd us colored folk come to plant ourselves on that lily white isle."

I shrugged. "Yes, I suppose that *is* what I'm asking, after all."

A faint smile came to her old leathery lips, and into those dark eyes that, I am sure, missed little or nothing. She took another sip of broth and said, "We walked."

"Walked?" Obviously, she was, as they say, "pulling my leg." Or so I thought. "On water!?" I asked. "Why, that *is* special, isn't it?"

"Not on water, you ninny. On ice. In the wintery-time. Me and Ulysses."

Miss Chancellor said, "Why, Sister Sadie! I never knew that!"

"Now you do. T'wasn't an ordeal we care to recollect much." Thereafter, she seemed to direct her words mostly to me. "We was children. Thirteen and thirteen. T'was the year of Our Lord 1863. Janiary. President Lincoln, his Emancipation had took hold. Me and Ulysses was already husband and wife, married in the Southland by the same master who took the lash to us, quotin' scripture. A man of the cloth. Gave us scars to last till Heaven. We was his to toil and procreate. But he never got a babe from us. We 'scaped north 'fore he got 'em, right through Ohia, 'long the Underground Railway."

"Ohio?" I said. I very much wanted to ask if my hostess had passed through Marion, as my hometown was once a very busy way station on the Negroes' long and dangerous journey into Canada. Tunnels ran under Main Street and I knew of a house on Vine Street, just north of where I was born, that Dad always said had secret rooms. He knew because Grandfather built it. But of course I made no mention of my hometown, lest my inquiry raise suspicion.

Sister Sadie was studying me with those piercing eyes. "That's right, Ohia," she said. "Portsmouth. Chillicothe. Attica. Bellevue. Huron. Marion."

I felt myself blush at the mention of the name of my now famous hometown. Sister Sadie had mentioned Marion last of all—as if for emphasis—when her list's geographical progression, south to north, ought to have placed it after Chillicothe. I looked away.

She continued. "Abolitionists sailed us 'cross the Lake, up Harrowway, to Canada. Poor lil' Ulysses! How he clung to me! Pretty near died a fear, scart all his life of the waves, waves more than the grave. Shamed him terrible, in his own eyes. We made ourselves useful to farmers there. When President Lincoln emancipated colored folk, back down we come. By our feets, this time, o'er the ice. Slept balled-up in buffalo robes, two nights in snow with the wind howlin'. Saw a shining star fall, big 'n' bright as the moon—Jesus foretellin' us our blessings awaitin' us. An' the looks on thems white folks' faces when they seen us comin' 'cross the waste, two lil' pickinnies 'merging from the snow! They had they fishin' lines stuck through holes in the ice. I 'spect they wouldn't a been more surprised was we mermaids skatin' in on our tails. That's how we got there. Walked, if that tells ya."

I nodded, "Walked. So you did."

"Sister Sadie's always been so brave," Miss Chancellor said. "Ulysses too. If he's scared of waves, then it's the only thing."

"Snakes too. But he was a chilt then. Later, he was hisself. But ice never scared 'im anymore than clover. Had frostbit feets. That's why Sister Sadie's got these here canes. That and the rheumatis."

Then the old lady told us of their years as the only Negroes on South Bass, how John Brown, Jr. and his brother Owen—sons of the famous abolitionist, and bachelor exiles on the lonely isle—had befriended them the spring after their long walk across the frozen lake. John Brown taught them their "letters." Sister Sadie told of some of the work they did on the vineyards, and at the summer hotels that cropped up after the Civil War, and how through many years they had lived in a tiny bungalow on a piece of land, on the south shore, owned by John Brown, who bequeathed it to them in his last will and testament.

During her girlhood days on South Bass, Sister Sadie came into her "gift"—in other words, spiritism—though in fact it was Miss Chancellor who pointed this out; Sister Sadie merely nodded when she did so.

Our visit to Mohican Grove lasted no more than forty-five minutes, give or take.

When the time came for Miss Chancellor and me to take our leave of Sister Sadie, after I'd risen from my chair, the old woman leaned forward, as if intently ciphering me, yet again. She reached her crinkled, leathery hand and said, "Child, bring that face o' yours t' Sister Sadie."

"What?" I said.

"Bring that face o' yours t' Sister Sadie. Let her know the smooth of your cheek."

For a moment, I stood stark still, not knowing what to make of this odd request. Besides, I had not shaved since the morning I'd pulled out of Marion—though I assure you, that would not have made me look like a drop-in from Vagabondia. My whiskers have always been nearly as scant and soft as an Indian's, albeit a pale Indian's, one with a thatch of hair the color (in my youth) of corn silk.

Anyway, I bent near and the old woman ran the back of wrinkly fingers along my cheek and chin. As she did so, she seemed to be listening to something far away, and she spoke words that, to this day, I regard as either nonsense or my mishearing, though I have a feeling it was neither. She muttered, "That one like a nigger Saul that stands 'hind thee—"

Suddenly she leaned back into her rocker again. I righted myself, clasping my hands behind my back. Our eyes fastened on the eyes of each other. Something had happened.

"Go get your face shaved in the morning. They's a barber in the square at Wooster. The one gots a white star painted on his window. Get thee t' him, child."

I merely stood in my place, and said nothing.

The old woman held my eyes. "But don't say boo 'bout Sister Sadie. And watch your neck, young'un. He's a prince o' the Klan. And he means it."

She knew. I nodded, our eyes still locked. "Thank you, Sister Sadie. Thank you. It's been an honor."

NIGHT WAS FALLING as Miss Chancellor and I wound our way through the Mohican Forest. The headlamps of my little Ford cast their dim glow before us and the moon peeked through treetops, trying to lend us a helping hand. As we snaked along the winding roads, I thought of how the moon rose over the Old Forest and Lake Etowah, on that evening when Miss von Leuckel came to me with news of Professor Chancellor.

Once back in Orrville, I brought my auto to a halt, as Miss Chancellor requested, a bit down the way from her house, beneath a tree. For a moment, we sat in the idling car, with her looking at me, and me fiddling with the choke, avoiding her eyes.

"Will I hear from you again, Mr. Boyd?"

I smiled a bit sadly into the darkness—Wellington Boyd, called forth, yet again. "Of course, you will."

She seemed to hesitate, "But what if your letter gets lost in the post? I don't know your address."

"Yes, you do. You know my name, right? Well, just send it to me in Port Clinton. Simple as that. Everyone knows us there. We're famous."

I believe it would have given great comfort to Miss Chancellor if I had renewed my invitation of that afternoon, for her to visit my family and me at the Lake. But I was so sick and ashamed of all my lies to this poor woman that no words came to me. Instead I took her hand in mine and looked in her eyes. "Dear Miss Chancellor," I said softly.

I do not know what I meant by that meaningless gesture, though I can assure you that it was the sincerest utterance of my entire trip to Wayne County.

"Why, dear Mr. Boyd. Is anything the matter?"

"No, nothing's the matter. It's just that life pulls us this way and that, and somehow, we do as we're bidden. Or at least I do."

I know that nowadays it sounds awfully quaint—indeed, it was getting so even back in 1920—but I kissed her hand. "Good-bye, Miss Chancellor. I'll send something. I promise."

She touched my cheek, perhaps in imitation of Sister Sadie. "Good night, Mr. Boyd."

I said, "I'm awfully glad I met you."

She stepped from the car, and before she closed the door she said, "We'll meet each other again, won't we?"

For the last time, Wellington Boyd piped up again. "Of course, Miss Chancellor! Count on it!"

As I drove down the dark street, I took my wedding ring from my coat pocket and jammed it back on my finger, resolving, upon my honor, and upon the honor of my marriage, to never remove it in deception again, for as long as I lived.

I turned westward from Maple Lane, and as I did so, I had a feeling that Miss Chancellor was still standing exactly where Wellington Boyd— that cad, that liar and that contemptible ass—had dropped her, and that she would be watching into the darkness long after the rattle of his motor faded into the night.

VIII

✿

Another Little Chat Leads Elsewhere

AFTER ALL OF THIS WAS OVER, Lucy was to ask me what I thought of Sister Sadie's injunction to go to Wooster (where I was staying anyway) and get a shave from that so-called prince of the Klan. In other words, she wondered, was the old colored lady really clairvoyant?

As I told my wife, maybe she was.

But then again, maybe she wasn't.

Personally, after I thought about this, and thought about it again, I did not see a speck of clairvoyance in Sister Sadie's injunction. What I did see was simply a shrewd old woman. She knew very well that Professor Chancellor had "hightailed it for the hills," and she knew very well that he had good reason for doing so. And suddenly, there I was—an utter stranger, a drop-in from out of the blue standing in Sister Sadie's bungalow—in the company of the good professor's spinster daughter. As such I no doubt looked more than a little suspicious to those deeply discerning old eyes. Then Sister Sadie, having turned things over in her mind, planted subtle mention to me of Marion. And in spite of myself, I took the bait: I blushed; that, and no doubt some flicker in my eyes, betrayed me.

Regarding the barber, our "prince of the Klan," I suppose she either suspected, or out and out knew, that he was hooked up with Professor Chancellor. I am sure everyone and their brother over in Wayne County knew the Klansmen's identities. Just as we knew in Marion.

By my lights, none of that constitutes clairvoyance.

It constitutes a shrewd and crippled old colored lady who could, I have no doubt, spin circles around the most nimble of tricksters.

Anyway, as it happened, I could look from my hotel room window and see Gabby's Barber Shop across the square. I could even make out the white star painted above his name, as well as the Cox campaign poster. Now you would think that I could simply walk out the front door of the hotel and cross the square in broad daylight. But that was not the case.

The evening before, when I had returned from Orrville, I just happened to be crossing the lobby, and there sat a portly Associated Press man smoking a cigarette. He was one of the reporters who made frequent use of the bungalow we had built in Senator Harding's backyard.

He might have found it odd—indeed, possibly even newsworthy—if the founder and president of the Harding Volunteers, bearing a false name, just happened to be slinking around Professor Chancellor's hometown.

I suppose I ought not to have been caught off guard seeing a reporter in Wooster, but truth to tell, I was. Yes, the town's name had been appearing on the front pages of newspapers throughout the land, but everyone knew that Professor Chancellor had flown the coop. I simply assumed that the press, by then, had done the same. Indeed, I thought that fellows like the AP man were out running up and down the hills looking for him.

Fortunately, when I had entered the hotel, he had been jabbering away with a couple of other fellows, so I managed to slip past him unnoticed and head up to my room—with the young front desk clerk calling out, as I hastened by, "Good evening, Mr. Boyd!"

I did not wish to "press my luck" again, so the next morning I slipped out a back entrance and negotiated my way, via alleys, to the opposite side of Wooster Square.

I could see Gabby through the broad, plate glass of his front window. He was a tall man, thin as a knife, who looked to be in his 50s. He was dressed wholly in white, from his collar to his shoes. He was busy shaving a fellow stretched on his back in the barber chair.

The moment I opened the door, Gabby's eyes rose and met mine. I gave him a cheerful, "Good morning!" All I got in return was a cool, momentary stare, then a nod. Not the talkative type, apparently. The man in the barber chair was portly and his face was covered with soap. For a nerve-wracking few seconds, I feared that maybe he was the AP man.

But a moment or so later the fellow in the chair said, "Gabby, who's that?"

"You don't know him and neither do I."

I breathed easier.

The portly fellow said, "Let me take a look." He raised his head and shoulders. He said, "Mornin', mister!"

"Why, good morning, sir!"

Gabby said, "If this razor takes a chunk of meat out of your chin, just 'cause you got to pop up and see everyone that walks in the door, then don't blame me!"

His customer paid him no mind. "Welcome to Wooster! You a reporter?"

"A reporter!" I laughed, "Goodness no. Far from it. I got troubles enough of my own without chasing after someone else's."

"Lay back," Gabby said.

The fellow did just that. "If you aren't a reporter, then who are you?"

I settled into a chair along the wall. "Name's Wellington Boyd, from Port Clinton. I must say, though, that I heard all about the commotion being stirred up down here, and truth is, curiosity got the best of me. So I decided to swing through on my way back to the Lake, and see what's what. As it is, there's not a whole lot to see. Pretty town, though."

"What'd you expect to see?"

"Good question. Guess I never been in a town where headlines were being made, 'cept on the Western Front, maybe, but that's different."

"Mister, you want headlines, go to Marion."

I laughed. "I don't want them that bad! Not bad enough to head into— what's that Chancellor fellow call it—what's he call Harding Country? 'Little Africa.' Not bad enough to go on a safari to Little Africa."

Gabby laughed and actually looked at me with a smile.

The fellow in the chair didn't utter a peep, and for some reason, I had the feeling he was a Harding man.

Silence followed. Gabby was anything but gabby. In fact, he struck me as being awfully shut-mouthed. Especially for a barber. I knew that silence would get me nowhere, but the truth is, I could not think of anything to say. Then I suddenly remembered, once again, that it was not Tristan Hamilton who was sitting in that chair in Gabby's Barber Shop;

it was Wellington Boyd. And he was talkative. So the next thing I knew, I stretched, yawned out loud, and announced, "Well, it's a great life if you don't weaken!"

"You can say that again!"

"Take my grandparents," I said. "Both in their eighties, but still keeping their farm going down in Galion. They're out there everyday in the fields pitchin' hay and husking corn and doing what-have-you, getting up at the crack of dawn to milk their cows and feed their hens and such, and neither of them ever mutter a word of complaint. And I've done the same myself, plenty. Just like them."

Without a pause in his scraping, Gabby said, "Mister, you ain't no farmer."

"Didn't say I was. Fact of the matter is, never lived on a farm in my life, 'cept for summers at Gramps'. Farmin' wasn't for us, not my dad nor me neither. We build houses. Up around Lake Erie. Got a lumber company too. And a hardware store. And coal yards. Serving both residential and shipping."

The fellow in the chair whistled. "You sure your name isn't Hanna?"

I laughed at his somewhat ironic (considering) reference to Marc Hanna, the long-dead industrialist and "king-maker" who guided William McKinley into the White House. "No," I said, "'fraid not."

I did not want them to think I was bragging or saying I was rich, so I added, "'Course there's not much work up there. Not where we are. Even in the summer. That's how I had time to write a book. Actually, two books, now."

"Books? You write books?"

"I do."

"What kind of books?"

"History books."

Gabby said, "Several men 'round here write books. I cut their hair."

"Shoot!" I said. "If only I'd have known I'd be talking about it, then I would've brought a copy over so you could look at it. Got a copy right in my hotel room. It's called *Lest We Forget: Oliver Hazard Perry and the Battle of Lake Erie*. Ever read it?"

"Sorry to say I haven't, but I'd like to. You Gabby?"

"Never heard of it."

"I bet it's in your library here. If I do say so myself, I think it's a pretty good read."

Gabby said, "You peddlin' your books door-to-door? That what you're doin'?"

"No, sir, I'm not. I carry it simply because having it gives me hope. Reminds me that I was successful, once, and lucky too—if no more."

A silence followed my mournful words. After a moment, the man in the chair said, "Can't be as bad as all that, Mr. Boyd. May I call you Wellington?"

"Please do."

"Why, you're a young man, right? Bet not a day over twenty-five."

"Twenty-eight."

"Twenty-five, twenty-eight. Point is, you already got a book under your belt. And a family business. Prosperous too. Why, you can tell at a glance you're prosperous. Sounds to me like you got the world on a string!"

I laughed, and I might add that I genuinely liked the fellow. "Well, thanks for reminding me of the good things. But the truth is, I don't have the world on a string. If I did, then I'd be able to give General Forrest his due. He's the one I live for now. General Nathan Forrest. But I've let him down."

I was looking out at the Square as I said those words, while keeping Gabby in the periphery of my vision. At the mention of General Forrest, his hands stopped in their task. He had raised his head and was looking at me. My eyes focused on the square, and I was drifting through my troubles.

My friend in the barber chair said, "Nathan Forrest. That the young fellow with the Rainbow Division—the dandy, wears those capes and such?"

"Wrong war," I said. "That's MacArthur. General Forrest, he's long dead. Though he was one of the most brilliant generals this country ever produced. Unfortunately, he fought on the side of the Confederacy. Folks have forgiven Robert E. Lee, more or less, even old veterans, or at least they respect him, but they haven't forgiven General Forrest. Most've just forgotten him. Those who haven't, don't forgive. I was out to change all that. I wanted to give credit where credit is due. But the powers that be stepped in."

Gabby said, "Mister, you sayin' you wrote a book on Nathan Forrest?"

"I am. Why? You don't mean you actually heard of him?"

"I heard of him, all right, though I never read a book on him. Didn't know there was one."

"Well, there wasn't, till I wrote it. But don't count on reading this one either, 'cause none of those east coast publishing folks want anything to do with it. I'm afraid General Forrest did some things and started some things that some folks don't want to hear about. That is to say, folks back east and up north here."

The fellow in the chair said, "Things like what? What'd he do?"

"Well, for starters, there was an unfortunate incident in Tennessee during the war, at a place called Fort Pillow. Some colored folks got killed there. Quite a few, actually. Though I will add that if they'd minded their place, then nothing bad would've happened to them. That and General Forrest was a founder of the Klan—as in Ku Klux."

"The Klan!" After that, a silence fell over the fellow in the barber chair. Something told me that he himself was not exactly inclined to dress up in a spook clothes and go marching around Wooster Square on 4th of July night with a torch in hand.

By then, Gabby was finishing up with the fellow, dabbing soap trails from his ruddy face. He pulled the lever on the side of the chair, and his portly customer sprung upright.

No one had said a word since I had mentioned the Klan.

He stood up and said, halfheartedly, "Like you say, 'It's a great life if you don't weaken.'" He paid for his shave.

I had been all prepared to pop out of my seat and shake his hand on his way out, but he hurried past me with scarcely a glance, "Nice talking to you, mister."

Then he was out the door. And I was alone with Gabby.

"Well, Mr. Boyd, looks like you're next."

As I settled into the barber chair, I very much wished that my chatty friend, whose ample presence still warmed the maroon leather, had stuck around a while longer.

Gabby said, "Shave or a haircut or both?"

"Shave, please." I did not want this fellow touching my hair.

He leaned me back in the chair, covered me with a sheet, and draped a steaming towel over my face. I heard him stroking his straight razor, back and forth, back and forth, honing it on the strap that hung by my side. I suppose my imagination was getting the best of me, because as he honed his razor, I became keenly aware of my bare throat exposed between my shirt collar and the hot towel. The stroking stopped. I was staring into the white of the towel, and I felt the man standing beside me, holding that gleaming razor between his fingers, staring down at me. He was waiting, of course, for my scant whiskers to soften, but he was also turning things over in his mind, wondering what to make of me, and the business about General Forrest.

I could feel him lean toward me. He said something unintelligible.

"Beg pardon?" My own voice was muffled and garbled by the towel.

I felt him hovering by my ear, and he said it again—something I could not make heads or tails of. I knew then that he was speaking to me in the coded gibberish of a secret brotherhood, testing to see if I was one of the "knights" of the Ku Klux Klan.

"Sorry, sir, but I don't understand."

He snatched the towel from my face, and was staring down at me, "Didn't think you would."

I simply lay there, stuck somewhere between Tristan Hamilton and Wellington Boyd, with my tongue fastened in my mouth.

Gabby came to my rescue. "So Mr. Boyd, tell me how'd you come to know 'bout Nathan Forrest?"

"Ah, General Forrest! Well, I guess you could say I've been hearing 'bout him all my life. My Granddad Boyd—Colonel Boyd—used to tell me stories 'bout him, when I was growing up." As he stood there whisking the soap in his mug, I said, "You see, my granddad, he was a colonel in the GAR, fought against Forrest at Chickamauga. Granddad said General Forrest was an absolute wizard on the battlefield. One of the best soldiers of the war, North or South. Maybe the best. And, I might add, one of the luckiest. I remember him telling me that General Forrest had twenty-nine horses shot out from under him—with him barely getting a scratch. Well, I believed that when I was a child, but as I got older I started shaking my head, wondering. No one's that immune to misfortune. Or so I thought. So when I started my history on him, that was one of the very first things I looked into. Had to, for my own sake, my own satisfaction and curiosity. And you know something? Granddad was right! Twenty-nine horses! Imagine! And him barely getting a scratch! Other men were losing limbs, right and left. Not to mention their lives! And him riding into the end of the war on his thirtieth horse, with scarcely a nick! Someone somewhere was looking after him."

Gabby was all smiles, nodding with satisfaction. Tristan Hamilton thought about interrupting Wellington Boyd and adding the thought that General Forrest's luck was a bequest from Satan, so that he could live for evil in distant days, but I did not, he did not. As Gabby started brushing the soap on my face, I noticed he was wearing a gold ring with a star insignia, like the star in the window. I added, "Granddad said everyone respected General Forrest, even his enemies. Especially his enemies. And that was true too. It was like he sometimes managed to cloak his army in his own invincibility. They'd appear out of nowhere, like they did at Brentwood—in Tennessee—and even though they were vastly outnumbered, they'd ended up taking prisoners. Anyway—I know you're waiting to shave me—after the war, sometime in the '70s, my granddad was passing through Memphis, so he called on his old enemy to pay his respects. General Forrest ended up asking him to stay for supper!"

I paused, "So what do you think of that! And you? You seem to know something 'bout General Forrest. How'd you come to know him, about him?"

Gabby said, scraping my whiskers, "Can't say as I ever knew anyone who ever knew him. Or shaked his hand."

I looked him in the eye, hovering over me, and in a quiet voice, with a sly smile I said, "I bet you're a bona fide knight of the Ku Klux Klan— aren't you? Come on!"

He laughed at my frankness. "Whoa now! Who told you that?"

"Oh, a little red devil."

Actually, he didn't answer my question, so when he paused to wipe his razor, I said, "I don't think there's a chapter up where I'm from. If there was, I'd go run out and join up real quick. If they'd have me. Except I don't want no part of lynchings."

"Well, you do what you got to do. That's the way I look at it. But just the fact that there's knights around can keep most niggers in their place. Not to mention the Jews and Catholics and those foreign immigrants, the folks that don't belong here most. They're the ones more inclined, 'round these parts anyway, to step out of line. Let me tell you somethin', waking up in the middle of the night with a cross burnin' in your front yard is awful conducive to moderation. Sometimes just a noose slung over a tree limb, so as it's hanging there in the morning, nine times out of ten, that'll do the trick. Slitting the throat of a Italian's dog or nigger's dog or horse is another way of getting your point across."

I winced at what he said.

He paused and looked me in the eye, sort of defensive. "You prefer that or lynching the niggers themselves?"

I did not answer.

"Sometimes, dirty work's got to be done."

"Oh, I'd be the first to agree with you on that score."

"No two ways about it. It's like you said, if them niggers at Fort Pillow had kept their place, nothing would've happened. But they didn't. So it did. Wasn't General Forrest's fault. 'Twas their own."

"True," I lied.

"If those niggers ever get the footing, they'll bring this country down. And if you give 'em an inch, they'll take a mile. No, they'll take a thousand! Or ten thousand! Look what they're up to now! Aiming for the White House! And I don't care what folks say, if a man's got a drop of nigger blood in his veins, he's a nigger. Plain and simple as that. Bill Chancellor's right. And Warren Harding's got a sight more than a drop in him, believe you me. Now the whole nation knows! And I'll let you in on a little secret, 'fore long, they're going to know a hell of a lot more. You'll see. And by the way, just ask anyone who's ever seen Harding in the flesh. Looks exactly like what he is. A mulatto."

"So I've heard," I said. "And you know something else? I know a fellow down there, down in Marion, works in one of those factories, he swears it's true that Warren Harding's got more than one lady friend. Right there in town! Sneaks down alleyways at night to see 'em. Supposedly, he's got more than one of them with child. By white women. White ladies! Funny thing is, everybody knows, or so I'm told! Just like they all know he's a nigger! Sidling up with white women! And one of them's a very pretty girl, I'm told. Engaged to be married, she was, to some fellow down there, then 'long comes Nigger Warren! Senator Sambo! And the two of them—!" My voice broke off in disgust; indeed, my pretense was so complete that a certain heated vehemence had come into my voice. "I'll leave it to your imagination. Fornication! Anyway, that's what they say. And now look at him! Running for President!"

"I'll bet she's the one was spying for Kaiser Bill."

"What!"

"You heard me straight. Spying for Kaiser Bill. Folks will know all about that soon enough, too."

"Well, I must say, that's a new one. I'll believe it when I see it."

"Oh, you'll see it soon enough. And it wouldn't be new to you if you were from Marion. They know all about it over there."

I gave him a chance to get some of his work done. When he paused to wipe the blade, I added, "Anyway, that Chancellor fellow, he's doing the country a big favor! You know him?"

"I know him."

"Then you should pin a medal on him!"

"Humph! Back to that book you wrote, Mr. Boyd. You caught my ear. What do you mean those east coast publishers want nothing to do with it?"

"That's exactly what I mean. They want nothing to do with General Forrest. They want him forgotten. Not because he was a Reb, but because he's founder of the Klan, and the fellow behind that so-called nigger massacre at Fort Pillow! To tell the truth, I think they're afraid of Harding too. You know he's said if he gets elected, he's going to make trouble for the Klan. I guess the publishers think that means them too, if they publish my book on its founder. An honest book, I might add, that gives credit where credit is due. Then there may be trouble for the publisher. Not to mention, for me." I gave a thoughtful pause, "You know, in a way, I can't blame them for not wanting to bargain for trouble, 'specially if Harding gets in the White House, why, lord forbid!"

I let Gabby shave me some more, which he did in silence. When he paused to wipe his blade again, I added, "I thought to myself, to hell with them, I'll go ahead and publish it myself. Actually, that was my dad's idea, not mine. What I mean is, he offered to pay the printing bill, if I can find someone to print it up. But I haven't even been able to do that. It's hard to find a printer 'round Ohio who can take on a three-hundred-page book. Certainly none in Port Clinton. None in Toledo either. My wife and I, we like going automobiling, so I thought we'd take a drive over to Cleveland someday and look around over there. But I guess I've just sort of given up."

"Given up! Don't do that!"

"Well, I didn't intend to, but with all apologies to General Forrest, what else am I to do? Blame it on the publishers, not me."

I decided it would be tactical to change the subject, so after a moment's silence, I said, "Pretty little town you got here. I always like towns built around a square. Makes them twice as pretty as they'd otherwise be."

A minute or two later, Gabby said, "I don't think you should give so fast up on that book of yours, Mr. Boyd."

I laughed, "So fast! I could've written another in the time I've wasted trying to publish this one."

"Well, you know something, I know someone who just might be able to help you on that score."

I didn't even open my eyes. "Help me what?"

"Print up your book."

I gave a little laugh and mumbled, "Fat chance of that."

"Your dad's got money, right?"

"Hmmm, I suppose you could say that. He isn't Rockefeller, but he's got money, yes, a little, nothin' special though."

"Said he'd help you, right?"

"He did."

"Well, then maybe 'fore you leave Wooster, you ought to take a jaunt over and see this fellow. He prints up books."

My eyes stayed slumberingly closed, though believe me, my heart was racing. How could such a printer exist in Wooster? Right under my nose! Apparently, Jess Smith, and all of us, had somehow missed him. Yes, I too had poured over the Senator's Polk Printers Directory for 1920, and no such printer was listed in this entire area. As if my mind were drifting elsewhere, I muttered, "Too good to be true. I've gotten my hopes up before, but we'll see."

"Make a point of it." When I did not reply, he said, "You got a car, right?"

"Parked right out on the square."

"Tell you what, Mr. Boyd. I could use a little break, and I haven't ridden in a car since the 4th of July. If you're willing, I can take you there myself. I'd be happy to introduce you to Cal."

"Cal? As in Calvin Coolidge?"

"No, not 'as in Calvin Coolidge!' As in Cal Baily. And he's no Harding man. No nigger-lover either, believe me. Known him all my life. A fine man."

Frankly, I did not like the thought of going anywhere with Gabby, and so I found my mouth staying clamped shut.

"Do it for General Forrest, Mr. Boyd. Make your granddad proud."

IX

In the "Matador's" Museum of Indian Arrowheads and Such

GABBY HUNG A SIGN in his window that said, *Gone out.*

As we crossed the square, I pretended to shade my eyes from the sun, as if the crisp October light bothered me. In reality, I was hiding from the AP man—if he was still in town. A hotel boy was loitering nearby, so I gave him a coin to throw my engine—and to get him off his can.

Then we were off.

Gabby displayed a boy's enthusiasm for riding in an automobile— even my regular Ford. As we drove from Wooster Square, he told me that he did not have a car of his own because he was putting his son through Wooster College and helping his wife's elderly parents "get by." He also said that he'd bought his boy a one-seat jalopy so he could earn money delivering messages for Western Union and making deliveries for the local merchants.

Anyway, I think the fresh air and the automobile ride did Gabby some good—brought him to life, as they say.

We drove west, down one of those lovely Ohio brick streets lined with old trees, the houses set back and far apart, like on Maple Lane in Orrville, but more so. I had driven down the same street the day before, on my way to Orrville, and had taken special note of the neighborhood, as it possessed the charm I envisioned for the Vernon Heights area that I was, at that time, planning for Marion. About three quarters of a mile out, Gabby said, "That's where we're going. That over there." He pointed to a castle-like building of red stone on a broad expanse of lawn.

"That's a printing house?!"

"It's an Injun museum. The printing press is in the basement."

"Ah!" I turned my Ford into the drive, which ran between the museum and an ample, but rather ordinary, clapboard house on the same grounds. A large German police dog, chained to its doghouse behind the clapboard, began leaping and barking at us. The beast looked capable of ripping one's arm off, so I hoped the chain was stronger than he was.

"Run her right over there," Gabby said, pointing, "and park her under one of those trees."

As a rule, I did not like parking on people's grass because of drips from the oil pan, but I figured we would not be long.

I killed the engine near a sign that said Holcomb Museum. The dog—obviously young and vigorous—was leaping and barking quite ferociously, and Gabby opened his door and shouted, "Shut up, Kaiser, it's me!" The dog's ferocious barks changed to whimpers and a few yaps as he strained at the end of his chain, watching us.

For a moment, I forgot Chancellor's book, and just sat looking at the building itself. It really was spectacular—a hodgepodge fantasy of stained glass windows in Arabian arches, a tower, and a couple of turrets spiced with various tidbits of ornamentation—all executed in rustic red stone. "Lord!" I said. "Now that's a building."

"Pretty, isn't it?"

"Very. Come back in five hundred years and it'll still be standing."

"Guess I never thought of it like that."

"It's the yardstick I measure by, ultimately."   ·

When I stepped from the Ford, the dog began barking again, but another shout from Gabby settled him. I glanced at the basement windows—small sets of triple panes along the foundation—and listened for the far-off rumble of a printing press, but I heard only the whining of the police dog, the twitter of the birds in the high branches, and the breeze rustling through the changing leaves.

Gabby told me that Henry Holcomb, who had lived in the clapboard house behind us, was a bachelor-banker, already long dead in 1920. He built the museum back in the 1870s to house his Indian artifact collections, endowing it into perpetuity. (Perhaps I should say or so he thought, as I distinctly remember reading a little note in the "Around Ohio" column of the *Star*, sometime back in the '30s, that Wooster's Holcomb Museum had closed its doors forever because of financial failure.)

The building's only visible flaw lay in its limestone steps—or more to the point, in the earthen foundation beneath the individual slabs. The gravel supporting the steps had shifted in the fifty years or so since the place was built, causing a few steps to sink and tilt ever so slightly. Whoever built the steps had either packed just a shade too little gravel beneath them, or else gravel that was just a little "dirty." I suspected the latter. Either way, the situation would slowly worsen with rain and frost heaves in the coming years.

I also well remember the beautiful intricately carved stone panel above the massive double doors, with its owl perched amid acorns and oak leaves. The doors possessed a medieval look, with massive timbers and enormous, elegant iron hinges. Gabby opened one of those doors and motioned me in with a wave of his hand, as if I were his guest. I entered, but then I said, "Wait. I want to swing it too."

So I backtracked to the threshold, where I slowly opened and closed the door, watching the muscular work of the hinges. I could swing it with my little finger. "Perfect!" I said, more to myself than him. "Look at that. Perfect balance."

"They don't build them like that any more, do they?"

"I would, and could, I assure you, if I had something like this to build."

I ran my fingers along the juncture between the two doors. "Look at that, Gabby. You couldn't pull a dollar bill through that seam, and the doors must weigh half a ton each."

I believe Gabby found my admiration amusing, and maybe a bit flattering too, but I assure you, it was real.

The shadows of the vaulted interior ran far into a great, nave-like hall. Another set of closed, enormous doors led into the back regions of the Holcomb. Above the distant lintel hung what I first took to be the oil portrait of an Indian chief in a heavy gilt frame, and above that, the mounted head of a stag. Display cabinets lined either side of the hall, as well as the mezzanine. Again I listened for the rumble of a press, perhaps printing up ruinous pages about Senator Harding, but again I heard nothing.

Now I must admit that I did not exactly expect to see a crowd of museum goers milling about, ooing and ahhing amongst the display cases, especially with that vicious dog in the yard, though I did expect to see at least someone.

But the museum stood empty and dark, like a church on a weekday afternoon.

"There's no one here," I said in a hushed voice. "No one but us."

"Cal's here. Somewheres. And he knows that someone's here. Kaiser told him so. You wait and have a look 'round while I go dig him up." Gabby started off towards the distant doors. A few steps later, he turned and paused, before he asked, "Say, Mr. Boyd, you do like Injuns, don't you?"

"Do I like Injuns?! Why, I love Injuns!"

He smiled and nodded. "You'll find light switches on the sides of the cabinets. Make yourself to home."

The heels of his white shoes clicked away over the marble floor. I watched his tall, slouched figure slip into the shadows and the great oaken door open and close behind him with a muffled thud. I stood in that great room alone, wondering if my quarry actually lay somewhere behind those massive oaken doors. Or if Fate had delivered me a ruse, if the Sentinel Press were here at all, or for that matter, in Wayne County.

Maybe I was barking up the wrong tree. And even if the press was here, maybe the books were elsewhere, in a warehouse somewhere in Cleveland. Or Cincinnati. Or maybe over in Pittsburgh. Or who knows where.

Colored daylight filtered through the stained glass windows high along the upper walls, between the ornate ceiling and the dark cabinets lining the mezzanine. Each window told a story from Ohio Indian lore. I especially remember the forlorn and broken people in a depiction of the forced exile of Ohio's Wyandot people into the Oklahoma territory, back in the 1830s. Though my personal favorite was of the noble Tecumseh (from whom I take my middle name), standing beside a bonfire addressing the great council of tribes at Chillicothe.

I pressed a porcelain button fastened to one of the heavy oak and glass cases and a little light bulb flashed on, illuminating an array of axes and arrowheads, laid out on purple velvet. Each had its own yellowing identification card lovingly inscribed by a hand that had no doubt long ago "moved on." I remember an exceptionally fine Hopewell blade, about ten inches in length, the largest I have ever seen, before or since. I also remember a warrior's double eagle copper breastplate, so beautifully executed that it might have adorned a centurion in ancient Rome, instead of some Indian brave gallivanting through the hills of ancient Ohio.

Scores if not hundreds of arrowheads, axes, and pipes were displayed in the various cabinets.

To a certain extent, if you've seen one arrowhead, you've seen them all.

Gabby was taking quite a while "digging up" Cal.

And frankly, I was not much in the mood to be standing around poring over Indian relics. Nevertheless, I wanted to put up a good front, so I made my way towards the back, as if I were being watched, feigning fascination—just in case.

My eyes wandered to the large oil painting over the doors. I was flabbergasted to see that the portrait was not of an Indian chief at all, but of a *matador*—adorned in his "suit of lights." A scarlet cape was draped luxuriously from his shoulders, and the fellow held a red-hilted sword, its point in the sand; an exotic, Moorish building arose in a stormy, medieval background. Of course I fully expected to see some long Spanish name— José de la This or That—inscribed on the brass plate, but I was further flabbergasted to read that the portrait was of none other than Henry Holcomb, Esquire. He was a beardless, exceedingly proud-looking young man with fine features and rather long black hair hanging to his shoulders in ringlets.

I was staring at this rather astonishing portrait when a double door swung open.

Gabby gave me yet another scrutinizing look, just like he had given me when I first stepped into his shop. He nodded for me to follow.

Naturally, I had intended to gush on a bit about the displays—as he would have wanted—I certainly intended to ask about Wooster's long-dead bachelor-banker "matador," but intuition informed me that Gabby was no longer quite in the mood for chitchat.

As I followed him down a long hall, he said, over his shoulder, "I'm afraid I may have given you some wrong information, Mr. Boyd. But Cal'll clear it up."

We entered a spacious, high-ceilinged room tucked away and out of sight at the back of the Holcomb, like the kitchen in a substantial house.

A copy of that unfinished portrait of George Washington—the one often seen in schoolrooms—hung on the back wall. Sunlight streamed through high windows, and two massive library tables were spread with books, papers, old topography maps, and a scattering of arrowheads and relics. A large magnifying glass, fixed into an old-fashioned brass stand, stood on one of the tables with a pile of arrowheads nearby. Without being certain what I was even looking for, I glanced about for some hint that this building might conceal the books and plates on Senator Harding, but I noticed nothing of the kind.

Cal Bailey's office was off of this room. We found him seated before a large set of windows. The moment I entered, behind Gabby, the curator rose from his cluttered desk. "Welcome to the Holcomb Museum, young man." He reached across his desk and shook my hand. "Calvin Bailey here, at your service."

I introduced him to Wellington Boyd.

Mr. Bailey was an older gentleman, bald and florid of face and pate, wearing the old-fashioned gold spectacles of an earlier era. He gestured for me to sit, beside the already seated Gabby, who was eyeing me with renewed suspicion. "I'm afraid my friend here may have misled you, Mr. Boyd. Not intentionally, of course, but out of the goodness of his heart, out of his enthusiasm for General Forrest."

"That's right," Gabby said. "Honest mistake."

As you can imagine, I did not know what to make of this sudden change of temper, though I found it interesting. "You mean you don't print up books?"

"Oh, that we do! Little books. One or two every few years. Books like this." Cal reached into a bookcase at the side and pulled from it a slim volume, which he handed to me. As he did, I noticed that he too wore a star ring, like Gabby's—which of course I now realized was the symbol of some kind of a fraternal organization, though to this day I am not certain if it was the Klan. (The old Klansmen here in Marion never wore such rings.) The volume was indeed small, no more than forty pages or so, and the red cover, not much thicker than butcher paper, was decorated with the silhouette of a feathered Indian head. The rather long title had something to do with Indian burial mounds of Ohio, and the publisher was listed as Holcomb Museum, Wooster, Ohio. I thought of the great

Indian mound hidden away in its secret grove at Goose Pond Farm. I knew that our mound would not be in here, unknown, hidden back in its woods. Mr. Bailey said, "My impression is, Mr. Boyd, your book's a few pages longer than that, is it not?"

"Yes, it is not," I said. He frowned at my reply. "Yes, it is, sir."

I fanned through the pages and turned the book over—as if closer examination might offer me some hope that I had slipped into the right place, but of course I found no such hope. Mr. Bailey and Gabby were both eyeing me, and no doubt my disappointment was apparent. "So you definitely couldn't publish a three-hundred-page book—on General Forrest?"

"Not at this time, sir. We're simply not equipped. And as you've already seen, ours is a small museum, with an even smaller press. Though the Holcomb could certainly use the money, I assure you. I might add that it was Mr. Holcomb's wish that we limit our publications to Ohioiana, or to topics about redskins. General Forrest would, of course, fall outside of either category."

I said nothing, my feigned disappointment keen and true.

Mr. Bailey said, quite sympathetically, "Perhaps you could try the Wooster College Press, Mr. Boyd. They're over in the basement of the administration building. Maybe they can help you, though I have a feeling the topic might be a bit of a hot potato for them, when they find out exactly who General Forrest was."

I nodded.

"I'm sorry," he said.

Wooster College seemed out of the question. Jess Smith had looked into the possibility that Sentinel Press was some kind of front for the college press, but that possibility seemed not to exist. In fact, as I gathered, Wooster had always regarded Chancellor as something of a mixed blessing—an inspiring renegade, popular among some students—and I further gathered that, for the college, such a book on Senator Warren Harding would have been more like a red-hot poker than a hot potato.

Both men were studying me. I presumed they were waiting for me to leave.

"Well," I said, "I guess that's that."

Mr. Bailey nodded, "I guess it is."

Rather sadly, I said, "Well, I tried to save General Forrest from oblivion, but I guess it's not in the cards. Maybe some writer in a more enlightened future will remember his qualities. Maybe not. His unmatched courage, his soldiering, his vision for—for America, for the way society ought to be ordered, with everyone in their proper places." For a moment I sat in thoughtful silence, then I added, "And what a shame too, after I interviewed all those folks who once knew and fought with him, folks who had his same pure ideals. Some of those old men have since died, I mean since I talked to them. Others are quickly fading into the land of shades."

I noticed that Gabby was now staring at his hands, and Mr. Bailey, for his part, never had stopped studying me—somewhat as if I was an arrowhead of indistinct provenance that he was still trying to place.

"My father would have gladly paid you hundreds, maybe a thousand dollars. But so be it." I thanked them for their time, and started to push myself up from the chair. To Gabby, I said, "Well, sir, I'll drop you back at your barbershop, if you wish."

"Mr. Boyd, before you go—" the curator said, "Gabriel here, he tells me you also wrote that splendid book on Commodore Perry."

"I wrote a book on Commodore Perry, yes. You read it, sir?"

"Oh, I assure you I did. I read everything that comes out on Ohio history, and I've always been a great admirer of Commodore Perry. He saved us all 'round here from being Canadian, didn't he?"

Actually, I'd never thought of it quite like that, but I said, "Oh, he certainly did."

"I'd rather have George Washington on my dollar bill than the King of England. Any day of the week. But Mr. Boyd, I was wondering if you could tell me something, since I have Commodore Perry's biographer right here in my own office with me. Clarify one little point for me, ere you depart."

"Shoot."

"Commodore Perry, he built his own fleet in the wilderness, did he not?"

I allowed that he did.

"How did he do that?"

"'How'd he do that?'" I said.

"Yes, how'd he do that?"

I knew I was being rather crudely tested, which gave me new hope. "Well, he had all those men there . . ."

"Yes, at Port Sandusky."

"Port Sandusky! No, Port Erie. The fleet was built at Port Erie!"

"Oh my goodness, of course. Port Erie!" He laughed at his own error. "What am I saying!"

It would be an arcane point for most people, but it seemed like an odd mistake for someone who professed to be an admirer of Commodore Perry, and who read "everything" that came out on Ohio history.

He added, "Mrs. Bailey says I'd forget my own head if it wasn't screwed on tight! But really, Mr. Boyd, I never did understand how on earth they could just build a fleet of ships in the wilderness. The warships and cannons and all. How on earth did they do that?"

I smiled, as much to myself as to him. "With great difficulty. The ships came mostly from ash, oak, and poplar trees. All of it unseasoned timber, 'from the stump' as we say in the lumberyards. My family owns a lumber company up on the Lake, like I told Gabby here. Anyway, the cannons had to be dragged through the wilderness. All the way from Albany— with Britannia out there ruling the waves. The sailcloth came from, from someplace. I don't remember where. Buffalo? Yes, Buffalo, definitely. One thing I didn't put in the book, I guess because I didn't think it was quite appropriate, was that when I was a boy, my father and me, we sailed our little skiff—we called it the *Niagara*—we sailed it from Port Clinton, over to Port Erie, and explored a portion of the old forest where Perry's fleet came from. Lots of the stumps from the trees felled by his men are still there. Or at least they were back then. Though heaven only knows now, with so-called 'progress' being what it is."

I added thoughtfully, "Who knows, maybe I never would have written that book, if my father hadn't taken me on that little excursion, along about the summer of 1906 or '07."

(Mind you, the business about us sailing to Port Erie and seeing the tree stumps of Perry's fleet was, in fact, true.)

"Interesting," Mr. Bailey said.

I shrugged my shoulders. "One road leads to another. Anyway, I hope I answered your question."

"Indeed you did, Mr. Boyd. You're obviously very knowledgeable on your subject."

"It rather helps, if you're going to write a book on it."

The rattle and backfires of an approaching jalopy broke the museum quiet. Gabby spoke a name; I think it was, "Eugene."

Mr. Bailey turned in his swivel chair, as a pre-War clunker—one that looked as if it had run interference in both battles of the Marne—rolled up the drive, came to a spirited halt, and the engine died with a couple of coughs and bangs. Needless to say, Kaiser was barking. The car had a Wooster College pennant glued to its door.

Without thinking, I said, "I hope that old rust bucket doesn't throw a batch of sparks and catch those leaves on fire."

Mr. Bailey said, "That's Gabby's boy."

I believe I turned various shades of red.

"Gabriel, why don't you run on out there."

The barber rose and fled from the room, moving more quickly than I'd seen him move before.

The young man was wearing a Panama hat, which he kept perched on his head, even as he crawled through the car window, head first—the door, apparently, being inoperable, possibly due to rusty hinges. The moment the fellow extracted himself, with practiced nimbleness, he turned and sort of crawled right back in, or at least partially so, up to his waist. He hung suspended, with his legs and feet sticking in the air. Cal and I were both staring at this spectacle. The dog was making quite a fuss, though it seemed like a friendlier fuss than he had made towards me. The young man seemed to be fishing something from the floor, his legs moving as he did so, a bit like a swimmer. His father walked up behind him, his feet kicking up fallen leaves. When the boy finally extracted himself, he and Gabby exchanged words.

As they spoke, the young man looked towards my Ford, then at the window of the room from which we were watching. Mr. Bailey leaned forward and gave a hearty wave, which the young man returned. Kaiser was still barking.

I had the distinct impression that Gabby had been sent out there to intercept his son, so he would not come in while I was present.

Mr. Bailey turned back to me in his swivel chair, "Gabby, he works real hard to keep that boy in college." In a quieter tone, as if Gabby might hear, he added, "He's hell-bent on his boy *not* being a barber."

"Yes, sir," I said, "he mentioned his son on the way over."

"He's a good father and a good husband. A good man."

Sister Sadie's words passed through my mind, "And watch your neck, young'un. He's a prince o' the Klan."

Sometimes one doesn't know what to think.

The boy handed his father something.

I suddenly wondered if he was the same fellow who had spied on Mitzy and me across Lake Etowah—and then in the darkness had trespassed into my yard, shoulder to shoulder with ex-Professor Chancellor. If he was, and if he saw me—I touched the revolver in my jacket pocket and leaned further back in the chair.

Mr. Bailey said, "Mr. Boyd, I'd like to ask you for your address."

"My address? I'd be delighted. Any particular reason?"

He dipped his pen in the well. "Reason being—" He shrugged his shoulders, "Reason being, I guess, you simply never know." He slid a sheet of stationery across the desk and held out his pen. "Who knows, maybe we'll be able to accommodate you, someday. And be of service to General Forrest."

I did not understand the ambiguity. Either they could print up such a book, or they could not. "Sounds hopeful," I said. I jotted down Wellington Boyd's address, wondering as I did if the apparently financially strapped Holcomb was planning on buying a big new printing press, and if perhaps Mr. Bailey was open to the idea of taking liberties with Mr. Holcomb's stated wishes.

Or if he was simply lying to me about his outfit's capabilities.

I also wondered if—like a good Ohioan—he was simply trying to be "nice."

All options were plausible.

The sound of Gabby's boy cranking his jalopy began to grind through the quiet. Mr. Bailey turned to his window again. After several muscled turns, the engine kicked in with a rattle and a bang, and the young man quickly wormed his way through the window, feet first. He waved to his father, and drove away. I was terrifically glad that he was gone.

I watched Gabby as he walked towards the building, carrying whatever it was that his son had handed him.

Mr. Bailey said, "So, young man, you'll be pulling out of Wooster today, I presume?"

Actually, I wasn't sure if I would or not. But I could not think of any reason for Wellington Boyd to stay put in Wooster another night, so I said, "That's right."

I heard the back door open, and Gabby's shoes clicking over the oiled floor of the sunny room. Mr. Bailey had already raised his eyes in anticipation when Gabby walked in. Without a word, he handed Mr. Bailey something wrapped in pinkish-brown paper and string—the kind of wrap stationery stores used for magazines and such, back before the days of brown bags.

"You wouldn't be headed back towards the square again, would you Mr. Boyd?"

"I certainly would." Mr. Bailey stashed the parcel in his center drawer. "Got to check out of my room 'fore noon, then it's back to Port Clinton. If I don't have a breakdown, I'll be having dinner with my wife tonight, and sleeping in my own bed."

Thus I took my leave of Mr. Bailey and the Holcomb Museum, and dropped Gabby back at his barbershop.

It is neither here nor there, but I was a bit put out with myself that I had neglected to ask about that curious oil portrait of Henry Holcomb.

X

A Face in Darkness at the Cellar Window

AFTER CHECKING OUT OF THE HOTEL, I drove westward from Wooster Square. I did not know where I was heading, or what my next step would be. I was not even altogether sure if my time in Wayne County had placed me a single inch closer to ex-Professor Chancellor's book on Senator Harding.

I drove again past Henry Holcomb's Museum with its turrets, Moorish flourishes, and stained glass windows. I would have given a silver dollar just for a peek at the printing press through the basement windows—though Kaiser might have tried to slip his collar and make lunch meat of my fanny.

I turned my Ford down the first road that ran north along the museum's western border. I assumed a street or road ran along its northern edge, and I intended to circle the place in order to get a view from the back, but I came upon an apple orchard with only a gated lane used by the pickers. The house and barn stood a quarter of a mile north, and I took the liberty of turning in their drive. The farmer and his wife were in the yard; he was stirring a large kettle over a fire. Even from the road I could smell the wonderful autumn fragrance of apple butter. I stopped to inquire if any of the butter was canned and ready yet, and I remember the lady with the cutting board on her lap, and the horse looking over her shoulder, doing his part to dispose of the cores. I purchased four quarts in Mason jars— one for Lucy, who was quite fond of apple butter on her morning toast, another for Dad and Adeline, one for the Hardings, and one for Dana Yost (my "right hand man" at Colonel Hamilton & Son).

As I departed Wooster, I fleetingly thought of heading back to Marion. I missed my Lucy, and frankly, I was not used to being away from home—unless "away" meant Indian Rock or Goose Pond Farm, but of course they too were home, extensions, in a sense, of Tioga. But Intuition—the nag that had spurred me on this wild goose chase—was still perched on my shoulder, harping in my ear. My mind kept going back to Sister Sadie. I saw her studying me like I was a billboard bearing some cryptic message, then, at last, as if comprehending, issuing her strange injunction that led me to Gabby, and thus to the Holcomb.

I meandered on, past the woods and farms of Wayne County. The more I thought about it, the more I found it odd that Gabby had told me that Cal Bailey could publish a long book, when Cal himself said that he could not.

I assure you that folks in little towns know such things about each other's business.

Why had Mr. Bailey tested me on Commodore Perry, as if he thought I was some kind of impostor or something, a spy perhaps?

And why had Gabby hastened out to intercept his son, as if he and Cal thought it best for him not to come in?

Mind you, obviously if the boy was in fact the fellow who had spied on Mitzy and me across Lake Etowah, who had come into my backyard with Professor Chancellor, then I had to thank my lucky stars that he did not come in. Who knows what events may have transpired had that been the case!

And what, by the way, was in the parcel that the boy had delivered, and that Gabby handed to Cal without comment—who in turn took it without comment and stashed in his drawer?

As I meandered along, I decided that, one way or another, these questions merited a little research. I also reasoned that I had already gone above and beyond the call of duty, so to speak, and that I could now, if I wished, go straight back to Marion, report my suspicions to Harry Daugherty and Jess Smith, and let them and their minions do with it as they would. To tell you the truth, if I had it to do over again, then maybe that is exactly what I would have done. But I cringed at the thought of taking the easy way out and sending others down the half-reconnoitered paths of my wild goose chase.

What if they came across dusty crates of unsold books about arrowheads?

My name would forever be mentioned with a smirk—the well-meaning bungler who, out of cowardice, could only go halfway into the fray, and who had wasted the Campaign's precious time during days of crisis.

Worse yet, what if they entered the Holcomb, bungled the job, and got caught? Frankly, I did not altogether trust either their judgment or their methods.

Thus somewhere between Wooster and the town of Shreve, I knew that I had to return to the Holcomb during the dead of night and try to admit myself into its secret recesses.

But in that case there was Kaiser to deal with, and truly, I did not know what to do about that hothead.

I stopped in the village of Shreve, which by chance had its own hardware store. I have no doubt that the fellow behind the counter was wondering why a well-dressed stranger, coming out of the blue, was stopping by his place to buy three panes of eleven-by-fifteen-inch plate glass, which I had him wrap in paper, and a tin of putty. Any other kind of tools that I might need, like a lantern, a knife, and such, I carried in the back of my Ford.

I wracked my brain trying to figure out how to get around Kaiser. Somewhere along those dusty roads, my younger sister came to mind. Adeline sometimes had trouble sleeping, and I thought of the Watkins' Sleep Powders she used—though she complained how they made her "groggy" the morning after. That is how I came upon the idea of simultaneously treating Kaiser to a tasty ham bone and a good night's sleep. In thinking back, the idea to me now sounds a bit childlike, like something out of TV-land, but for the life of me, I could not think of a single other thing to do. Thus in one of those villages out there— looking at the map now, I think it must have been either Loudonville or Millersburg—I came upon a general store where I found a juicy soup bone, one with lots of meat, and a tin of Watkins' Powders. Once I was back in the open country, I unwrapped the bone on the floor of my Ford and, with my knife, managed to work about a quarter of that little tin of powder into the grain of the meat and the gristle.

That afternoon I had my first blowout. Before fixing it, I changed into the dark clothing that I had the prescience to bring, in anticipation of adventures, and then I stopped at a farm and asked to wash at the well. I also asked the lady of the house if I could buy a hot meal. She sat me down at the kitchen table, handed me a Bible, and proceeded to prepare far more food than I could have eaten in a single sitting. She and her husband were Gabby all over again—as shut-mouthed as the day is long, though I must add that, to their credit, they did not ask me a single question, not even where I hailed from or where I was going. I remember wondering how many words they actually spoke to each other on any given day of the week. I estimated about five.

Suffice to say that, in all, I longed for sundown, or rather for deep night, when I could sneak back to Wooster. At some point during that long and lonely afternoon, I resolved that—no matter what—I would head straight for home after my dirty work at the Holcomb, and "come hell or high water" I would lie beside my Lucy, in our own bed, ere the sun showed its head on a new day.

JUST BEFORE FULL NIGHTFALL I drove by the Holcomb Museum and, expecting to find the place fast asleep, I was surprised to see the lamps burning at the back, both in Mr. Bailey's office and in that larger anteroom. An automobile was parked under the same tree where I had parked that morning.

I turned north, along the darkened orchard road, and doused my headlamps the moment before I was hidden by the windrow separating the Holcomb from the orchard lands. I stopped in front of the gate. It was not so dark that I could not see to undo the latch, but dark enough to give me confidence that my automobile would be hidden by night, and by the autumn-thinned windrow. I was pleased that my little Ford had the good breeding not to backfire as I pulled in and killed the engine.

I sat for a time with my eyes fixed on the Holcomb's distant windows. The waning moon was beginning to show its head, and I did not know whether to be pleased or displeased with its rising, for it would light my way, while simultaneously lighting me. I had in the car a dark watchman's cap with which I intended to cover my yellow hair. I donned it, and quietly stepped from my Ford. I do not know why, but I remember thinking of that splendid dinner—only a few evenings before—when Lucy and I were seated at the same table with Senator and Mrs. Harding, and with Douglas Fairbanks and Mary Pickford. Now here I was lurking in the darkness dressed like a cat burglar, preparing to commit a crime that could easily land me behind the grim stonewalls of the Ohio State Pen.

And I might add, a crime that could derail the Campaign.

I was trembling as I stashed the wrapped panes of glass inside my shirt, beneath my sweater. I gathered the other things I might need—the putty, the knife, and of course the lantern. Then I set out, closing the orchard gate behind me without latching it. I decided to walk along the road rather than cross the yard. In that way I could stay as far as possible, for as long as possible, from Kaiser—whose treat I tucked under my arm, still wrapped in greasy butcher's paper.

The orchard road stretched away like a silvery ribbon in the moonlight and darkness. To the west, towards Marion, a lone cornfield scattered with autumn stubble rolled away into a shadowy, moonlit woods. I was grateful to Henry Holcomb for having the foresight to build his museum at the edge of town so that I did not have to worry myself with neighbors. As for Kaiser, I could make out his doghouse in the moonlight, but I saw no sign of him, which meant he was probably huddled inside in his bed of straw. For the first time I realized that the museum's small basement windows were also aglow. Slowly, as I neared, I heard a far off rumble and clatter. For a moment, I mistook the rumble for a train winding its way somewhere through the Mohican Hills, but as I listened I realized the sound was coming from the building itself—which meant that the press was running. I continued to a point on the road where I had the Holcomb situated between myself and the doghouse, then I crisscrossed back, making my way over the blanket of leaves that covered the sprawling grounds, creeping as quiet as an Indian until I reached the edge of the building, near a basement window.

I suppose if I had been smart about it, I would have taken advantage of the fact that Kaiser was sleeping and tossed the bone in front of his doghouse, then and there. But I did not. I let it fall into the leaves beside me as I slid the wrapped glass from beneath my shirt and leaned it on the foundation. Crouching by the glowing window, I could see two men working at a printing press, one on each side. Actually, from what I could see, the press seemed not that much larger than the one at the Marion Printing Company, over on Owens Street, and it was certainly smaller than Senator Harding's press in the back of the Star Building. I lay on the soft blanket of leaves with my face near the window, but not too near. As I peered in, I had the sick feeling that Mr. Bailey was telling the truth. The press seemed not to have the ability to print up a two- or three-hundred-page book.

But they were printing something.

At first I did not see Mr. Bailey, but when I knelt in the leaves and looked in at a different angle, I saw him over to the side, his bald head shining beneath a hanging lamp. He sat perched on a high stool, crouching over a large table and what appeared to be some kind of wooden tray. He seemed to be consulting handwritten papers, a manuscript.

I lay down on the fallen leaves so that I might have a more comfortable view and, as I peered through the window, I saw among the cabinets and reams of paper and such, two rows of wooden crates—ten in all. As I scanned those crates, I could see that they were filled with black-bound books. I think my heart leapt, because I could plainly see that these indeed were books, not booklets. Thus I could presume that I had been lied to. Here and there the title showed through the slats, but I certainly could not, at that distance, make it out. As a boy lying beneath the summer trees, I had learned a little trick that helps bring faraway objects into sharper focus. If I bend and curl my index finger and peer through the tiny "hole," then the light is refracted in such a way as to bring objects into slightly clearer view, so I did that—but the title still remained indistinct.

Needless to say, after lying there for a while, with my nose, so to speak, pressed invisibly against the glass, I began to wonder just how long it would take before I would be able to go about my work and crawl through the window, instead of simply looking through it. I felt like some sort of wild animal, a fox or something, hidden in the leaves and darkness. The bell in the courthouse down on the square tolled eight o'clock, and by then I must have been lying there for at least half an hour. At first I did not feel the chill, but after a time the night air began seeping through my clothes, like falling dew slowly settling over me. Worse yet, the dampness began to rise through the leaves, then through my pants and coat, then through my sweater and shirt. I probably should have headed back to my Ford and sat tight, until I saw the lights go out, but I didn't want to risk movement. Thus I lay like a fool and shivered. By then the moon had sailed westward, now illuminating the side of the Holcomb where I lay, and of course me.

Kaiser did not stay quietly in his box the entire time. I suppose at some point the breeze must have shifted. Perhaps he either caught a whiff of me, or thought he did; or maybe he picked up the scent of a deer, or some other animal going about its business somewhere out in the moonlight. At any rate, he began to sort of grumble back there, then he barked a few times—not in an angry sort of way, but in an uncertain way, like maybe he had suspicions that something was going on, but then again like maybe he wasn't altogether sure.

That went on for several minutes. I thought about going back and tossing him his bone, but there was certainly no guarantee that my little trick would work. What if the fellow was not to be bribed? What if he was, but the Watkins' Powders took too long to work or had somehow lost their potency after soaking into the meat all day? I didn't know what to do. As I was lying there shivering and deliberating, Mr. Bailey left his stool and headed towards the back of the basement. At first I thought maybe he was going to take care of some personal business, but then I heard the back door of the museum open, and close with a bang. I guess I was unduly startled, for I nearly leapt out of my skin, no doubt rustling the leaves as I did so. At any rate, Kaiser instantly began making a real ruckus. I immediately crawled away from the window and lay pressing myself as close as I could against the cold foundation, with—it seemed to me—the moonlight shining on me like a torch.

I could hear Mr. Bailey say something to his dog, but it brought the animal no calm. Indeed, he was now barking all the more furiously, as I imagined, towards my side of the building. I heard a shuffling of feet coming through the leaves, across the backyard of the museum. I did not know whether to "run like hell" or freeze. I froze, but not before I pulled my watchman's cap about as low as I could, without hiding my eyes.

I watched Mr. Bailey come from behind the museum. He stood there looking westward into the darkness. Then he scanned the grounds beside the museum. I resolved that if he came towards me, I would fly in the opposite direction of my car, circle back through the cornfield, and get the hell out of Wooster when the coast was clear.

But he turned and went back towards Kaiser. It occurred to me that he might set that beast loose. I clutched the handle of my knife. I had never killed an animal larger than a mouse, but if it came down to being mauled by that giant Prussian ogre or using my knife—.

I heard Mr. Bailey speaking to his dog. I lay there trembling, and I think I was more frightened than I have ever been in my life. I slid the knife from its sheath, terrified that any second the monster was going to come roaring out of the darkness straight for me.

But the dog grew quieter. I listened, and I had the impression that Mr. Bailey may have gone into Henry Holcomb's old clapboard house. Maybe he went to tell his wife something.

Kaiser was still growling and grumbling, though he was not carrying on like before.

Ere long, I heard the museum's back door open and close again.

As quiet as could be, I crawled to a place where I could peer into the window again. By the time I had maneuvered myself so that I could see, Mr. Bailey was already perched back on his stool, at the large table where he was working.

Actually, I almost wished that I had been scared off, and that I was now climbing into my car, ready to speed towards Marion, saying, "To hell with it."

I rose from where I was lying, unwrapped the ham bone and then, with knife at the ready (just in case), I crept as quietly as I could along the edge of the museum, towards the backyard. Kaiser had never stopped his suspicious grumbling, though oddly enough, he seemed to grow all the quieter the closer I came to the back corner. I was afraid that maybe he was trying to slip his collar. I was shivering from the cold—and no doubt from fear too—as I paused at the edge of the building. Kaiser was growling—a fierce, low, guttural growl. I steadied myself as best I could, drew a deep breath, whispered a prayer, and stepped into the yard. For an instant, the beast fell utterly silent. He was staring straight at me, with his ears pointed. Then he tore at his chain as I received the full volley of his rage. I should mention that I always had a natural instinct for hurling objects, stones, and such, placing them, more or less, wherever I put my eye. I sent the ham bone sailing through the night air, and saw it land so close to Kaiser that, for an instant, he had seemed to crouch back and draw away, for fear of being hit in the face.

I stepped behind the museum again and stood, breathless, with my body pressed against the wall. He had fallen silent. After a few moments, I peeked around the corner. Kaiser was circling his bone warily, sniffing.

Then he grabbed it and jumped through the door of his doghouse without—so far as I could tell—casting another glance my way.

I thought he might stash his bone in the straw, jump right back out, and have at me again, but I did not see hide nor hair of him again.

I gave a little laugh, victorious, and murmured into the darkness, "Greedy Hun!"

With that, I headed back along the side of the building, scarcely minding the sound of my feet rustling in the leaves.

I had been thinking before that it would be best not to break into the building via the window in the print shop. I had a feeling that it probably had not been opened for years, if ever, and opening it might knock rust loose, and maybe even break the frame. In other words, if I broke in via that particular room, then tomorrow—no matter what I did to cover my tracks—the window itself might betray me.

I slipped along the wall to the next window, and crouched and looked in. Utter blackness. I certainly did not want to go breaking and entering and then find myself in a room locked and forgotten long ago. I walked to the third window, the one nearest the front, and crouched there. I thought I could make out a faint glow, so I lay down in the leaves and cupped my hands against the glass to keep the moonlight at bay. I could barely make out, through an open doorway, a patch of yellow light on the cellar floor, cast either from the printing room or a hall light at the back of the Holcomb. I had found my portal.

I returned to the first window and lay in the leaves again to resume my watch. It sounds rather pathetic, but I actually tried to cover myself with a blanket of leaves to help keep away the cold, to little avail. A scattering of stars, sharp as needle points, poked through the crisp moonlight, and I knew that frost would cover the pumpkins tonight. I sneezed once, and Kaiser, from inside his house, gave a rather lame bark in reply, but that was the last I heard from him. After that, I sneezed once or twice in the crook of my arm.

The courthouse bell tolled ten o'clock, and along about that time—after what seemed like forever—the men brought the press to a cranking halt. I watched one of the fellows take the stack of newly printed sheets from the tray and, carrying the papers on his outstretched arms, disappear from the room. Mr. Bailey followed. I got a pretty good look at the top sheet as he carried them by. The papers were quite large, newspaper-size with many—possibly twenty—book-size pages printed on the topside.

After a minute or two they returned. The other fellow had already begun wiping down the rolls and things with an inky-black rag. Now Mr. Bailey and the other fellow also took up the task of cleaning, talking as they did so. I could only see their mouths moving, and hear the faint murmurs of words. I had to stifle another sneeze; this time they might hear me. After they washed up, they stood around gabbing. At last, in a burst of laughter, they pulled their wraps from the wall and followed each other 'round the corner, towards the back of the basement. The hanging bulbs flickered out and the room went dark as pitch. I heard the door, and their voices, now bantering back and forth with each other as they entered the yard. But not a peep from Kaiser. I smiled at the little trick I had played on him.

At last I heard a couple of cranks of an engine, and then the chug of the motor starting up. A moment later, the car pulled away from the museum, and the sputter of the engine faded down the street, towards town. Then utter silence.

I gathered the lantern, panes, and putty, and headed for the front-most window. I wasted no time in going about my dirty work. The decades-old pitch holding the center pane in place was as brittle as sun-baked mud, and within a minute or so I had knifed it away and was lifting the glass from its frame. Apparently, I would not even need a single new pane, much less three, but as they say, better safe than sorry. My difficulty came—just as I had told myself it would—with the latch and metal frame. I doubt if that latch had been turned in forty years—a fact that reminded me of yet another thing I had neglected to bring: an oil can. Actually, I could have gone back to my car for that, but I was in no mood for a quarter of a mile walk, so I made do. Soon I managed to jimmy the latch loose, and the window creaked open, dropping crumbling bits of rust. The sound was not loud, but I am sure that if Kaiser—poor thing—had his wits about him, then he would have been throwing a fit, and maybe Mr. Bailey soon would have been rounding the corner with a shotgun.

I brushed the leaves clear, struck a match, lit the lantern, and held it into the room. I saw ancient steamer trunks with rusting iron bands, old hat boxes—some covered with velvet, and all covered with dust—

and even more curious, rusting swords and halberds, faded pennants on wooded poles, and several high-back, medieval-looking chairs. Looking back, I now believe the more exotic items may have been stage props. Perhaps Mr. Henry Holcomb had once owned an opera house on Wooster Square, or maybe he had something to do with theater of some sort.

At any rate, climbing through that window was going to be awkward, as I was not exactly practiced at such stunts. I did not know whether to go through head first or feet first, on my back or on my belly. After a moment's thought, I decided I would slide in on my belly, feet-first, as I thought it would be preferable to land on my feet instead of my head. As I squirmed through that narrow portal, I thought of Gabby's son and the agility with which the boy had climbed in and out of his jalopy. Climbing in was not as arduous as it might have been, as someone long ago had been thoughtful enough to place a steamer trunk along the wall, so I was able to use it as a step into the room.

Henry Holcomb must have traveled a great deal, and no doubt he traveled well. From what I saw at a glance, most if not all of those trunks bore in hand-painted words: "Henry Holcomb Wooster, Ohio America." Heaven only knows what was in them. I assure you that I was not about to disturb a single thing, unless I thought it had to do with Senator Harding; if I had seen a gold Spanish doubloon glinting on the floor, I would not have touched it.

Directly across the hall from that room a doorway stood open. I held my lantern aloft and peered in. Actually, I was not altogether sure what I was seeing. It was some sort of long, elaborate machine that seemed to have lots of metal shelves and chains; the thing stood almost from floor to the ceiling. I realized that this was the room into which Mr. Bailey and his helper had carried the stack of printed sheets. Indeed, in the dim lantern light I could barely make out what looked like many such high stacks at the far end of the room, towards the front of the Museum.

I did not wish to become distracted from those crates of books, thus I hastened down the hall to the print-shop room, but just as I was about to go in, a rat scurried over my toes. I nearly leapt out of my skin. I am not ashamed to admit that I have had a lifelong terror—yes, *terror*—of rats. A split second later, after bumping the doorframe, I found myself back in the junk room, perched on the lid of a steamer trunk, like a housewife cowering from a mouse.

I must have stood there stock-still for a good five minutes, holding my lantern aloft, like a statue, scanning as best I could, from my pedestal, the nooks and crannies of alien darkness, looking for beady rat eyes peering at me from their secret places. I heard—or thought I heard—evil, ratlike sounds—squeaks, scrapings, gnawings and such—coming from somewhere in the cellar. I think it was by sheer force of will that I finally stepped to the floor again and made my way back along the hallway. But this time I whistled and scraped my feet so that the basement tenants would, I hoped, take heed and grant me quarter.

This time I leaned and peered around the corner of the print-shop room so as not to risk any unwanted encounters. At that proximity, in the dim kerosene light, the press that I had gaped at for so long through the basement window now appeared to loom much larger, like a mechanical beast slumbering in the darkness.

I turned to the crates stacked with black-bound books. Again I saw the glint of gold letters shimmering through the slats. The rats vanished from my mind as I crept forward, my lantern outstretched. I believe I may have even uttered another prayer. I held the lantern alongside the crates, and there through the slats I read the title: *Warren Gamaliel Harding: A Review of the Facts.* William Estabrook Chancellor's name appeared on the spine. I believe I felt somewhat like Balboa must have felt when he stood on the peaks and saw for the first time the Pacific shimmering before him—exactly where his intuition had told him it would be. I am seldom dramatic, and never intentionally so, but I took one of those precious little volumes in hand and kissed it.

I own it to this day.

In my euphoria, I nearly departed without searching for the copper plates. Actually, I did not have to look far. I found them at the far end of the pressroom, stacked beneath an ink-stained tarp. I saw at a glance that each plate bore the facsimiles of ten pages of text. I scanned the backward written words of the top plate, and quickly found the Senator's name. I "walked" my fingers down the stack of copper plates, counting them. Each plate was protected from being scraped by its fellow by a thick felt sheet. I counted twenty-nine plates, and then glanced at the last page of the volume in my pocket. The book ended with page number 267, and the words, "He is crude, profane, a heavy drinker, vile, and in all ways an example of the powers of darkness." I calculate that about twenty pages of the new chapter had been thus far converted to copper plates.

Thence I departed in haste, not forgetting to replace the windowpane.

XI

"Some Interesting Reading in There"

I CARRIED AWAY with me one other souvenir of my lonely adventures in Wooster—the worst head cold I have ever had in my entire life. Nonetheless, I somehow managed to return to Marion that very night, just as I had promised myself. It is funny—all the little details one recollects when one's mind wanders the winding roads into the past, and yet I seem to remember virtually nothing at all of that middle-of-the-night drive back to Marion. I do not even know how I managed to find my way, as road signs were few and far between back in those days—that is, until President Harding, who very much liked automobiles (and who counted both Henry Ford and Harvey Firestone amongst his good friends), took an interest in improving the nation's highways.

Anyway, my next vivid recollection from that adventure was Lucy's hand lying on my forehead. Her gentle touch awoke me. I opened my eyes, and there she was, my dear and ever faithful wife. I had the feeling she had been sitting by the bed for some time. She bent and kissed me, and then hugged my face to hers, and kissed me yet again. It is good to have been loved in such a way in one's life, even after that love, at last, is called away.

My sinuses felt as if they had been stuffed with cotton, and my mouth was as dry as dust. Nevertheless, I said, "I found them, Lucy, I found the books."

"I know you did. You told me last night." Her voice was soft and quiet. She handed me a glass of water. "Now drink this down, Trey. All of it."

I obeyed. Then I pushed myself up on my elbow, looking for the little trophy that I had borne away from the Holcomb.

But my wife gently pressed me right back down again onto the bed. "You're sick, Trey. Stay lying."

"I'm not sick. Where is it?"

"You are sick, and it's right here." She took Chancellor's book from the night table. "You're running a fever. Do you want me to call Dr. Sawyer?"

For the first time, I looked at the little volume in the light of day, examining the title, the binding, and carefully opening it, as if it were a rare and exquisite volume. "Do you want me to . . . ?"

"No, n-o."

I glanced through the book, and as I did, Lucy said, "There's some interesting reading in there."

"Oh?" I felt a tinge of anxiousness at her words, as I was afraid she was referring to the business about my youthful romance with Miss von Leuckel, and our broken engagement. Of course Lucy knew all there was to know about that, but I did not want my wife's face being rubbed in it. I opened first to the end of the book and scanned for our names in the last chapter. At a glance I could clearly see that it was not about Mitzy and me—and Kaiser Bill; it was just more of Professor Chancellor's ravings about Senator Harding. That is to say, obviously, that the new last chapter—the most dangerous and scandalous—was still in the works, as I presumed it was.

"Lucy," I said, "The books are in a place called the Holcomb Museum, over in Wooster. They're hidden in the basement. Write that down."

She started to laugh, albeit with a bit of discomfort, "Trey! You're not going to die!"

"Well, I feel like I might."

She gasped. "Don't say that! Don't *ever* say that again!"

Obviously, I had meant my little remark strictly in jest, but it was, after all, a thoughtless comment, as Lucy had lost a hale and hearty brother to the influenza epidemic that had visited Marion—and everywhere else in the known and unknown world—during the Great War. Not to mention the fact that she had lost her first young husband to an accident on the rails.

I suppose I should have spoken a few words of reassurance to her, but I was more interested in my little trophy than in my poor wife's concerns. "I found it!" I said, more to myself than to her.

"You're dirty, Trey. I'm sorry to say so, but you're dirty. You got dirt on your face and you got leaves stuck in your hair." She picked out a leaf crumb. "You did something, didn't you? Something bad."

"Something bad, Lucy? I think not. No, I remember doing nothing bad. Not at all. And remember, we're fighting the Klan, I'm sure of it. But yes, I did do *something*. I didn't buy this little hot potato in the bookstore on Wooster Square."

She expelled one of those breaths that often seemed to announce her exasperation with me—and sometimes, her mystification. "In that case, you did something dangerous, didn't you, Trey?"

I said nothing.

"Trey, darling," again she ran her hands through my hair, "sometimes I think you stick your neck out just a little too far for Senator Harding. What if something bad had happened to you over there? People like that are dangerous."

"They had no chance of winning," I lied. "And nothing bad happened. I am not a bungler."

She looked away, like she was remembering something I had perhaps forgotten.

"We're almost there," I added. I squeezed her hand. "Soon everything shall be settled. One way or another."

I will not bore you with a rehashing of the strong, womanly protests and outright tears that I had to endure that morning just to drag myself out of bed and go about my business. Actually, to be more accurate, I did *not* exactly go about my own business that day. A few hours before I had even opened my eyes, Lucy had taken the liberty of calling Dana Yost to inform him that I was back home, but ailing, and would not be into work for at least a couple of days.

I must admit that by the time I had dragged myself through the simple ordeal of a morning bath and dressing, the only thing I really felt like doing was going straight back to bed and sleeping for the next several days. But that was not to be. Fortunately, I still had my appetite, more or less, and the one concession I was able to make to my poor wife's distress was to allow her to ply me with eggs, biscuits, and a "pile" of corned beef hash—the sort of heavy fare her people used to eat. Lucy's calculation was to give me a little strength, and actually I think her so-called "banker's breakfast" did just that. I do not mean to go on and on about a mere head cold. I dwell on it simply because the head cold—or more specifically, my wife's concerns on my behalf—added yet another annoyance with which I had to contend during the Campaign of 1920.

I must say I found it rather amusing that the Campaign—which knew nothing of my Wooster adventures—was still apparently floundering about, trying to decide what could be done about the elusive Professor Chancellor and his equally elusive book. The best they could come up with was an ingenious plan to bribe the fellow—or to attempt to bribe him with one hundred thousand dollars—if they could find him. Fifty thousand would be provided by Henry Ford (as yet, unbeknownst to him), and the other fifty would come from Harvey Firestone, the tire maker, who lived up in Akron.

I arrived at the headquarters of the Harding Volunteers around noon.

Even noon on a sunny day was bit bleak up there. Daylight filtered through the three small windows overlooking Main Street, in the front, and through even smaller windows in the back, over the alley. No side windows existed.

Harry, Jess Smith, and two of their elves—or "staff," as Harry preferred to call them, flunkies on the payroll of the GOP—were sitting around the table in the back room partaking of the thick ham and ketchup sandwiches that Harry and Jess lunched on daily with relish. One of those young men—a fellow whom everyone called "Brownie"—had taken a hunk of shrapnel in the lower part of his face during the Great War, and had lost his ability to speak. To this day, my heart goes out to him, wherever he may be (if he remains among the living). His injuries were such that small children ran from him, and I actually saw, with my own eyes, a dog growl and slink away when Brownie came near. Most adults instantly knew he was amongst the unlucky, hideously deformed brotherhood of veterans known as the "gargoyles," and so they were especially kind to him, while averting their gaze, for their own sake and his. As for me, I did my best to look at Brownie as I would at any man, as did Harry, Jess, and others, including Senator and Mrs. Harding. Indeed, the Hardings were especially kind to him. More than once he sat at their table and in their parlor.

As for the other fellow, Jim Blaine, well, I could never have foreseen it at the time, but three years later that nonentity of a man was to marry, of all people, Mitzy von Leuckel.

Do not expect me to explain that marriage, as to me their union was like one of those motiveless crimes that flabbergasts everyone.

Anyway, in I walked, and the moment Harry raised his eyes and saw me, he called out, "Here's trouble!"

"Depends on how you look at it," I said.

A change came over Harry's face as he gaped at me. "Trey, you're sick!"

I had no idea it was so apparent. "No, I am *not* sick. It's just a head cold."

Now of course they were all gaping. "Well, we have just the thing for head colds. Jim, pour this fine young fellow some head cold elixir." Ordinarily, I would have flatly refused, but not a peep of protest issued from of my lips. Harry patted the chair beside him. "You come and sit down over here, young man. You don't look so good, poor thing. Who knows what *you've* been up to!"

I did as I was told, though I certainly waved aside his prompting to "dig in." In fact, just looking at those greasy ham and ketchup sandwiches made me queasy, especially after a big breakfast.

Harry took a big bite from his sandwich and said, with considerable effort, "So Trey, where you been?—disappearing on us like that into the wild blue yonder."

"Traveling." I sipped the brandy. I must say, it really did "hit the spot," and so I took another.

I remember it was Jess Smith—not Harry—who said, "Traveling! You, Trey?"

Mr. Harding seemed to view me as something of a "homebody"—and I believe he was generous enough to share that impression with everyone.

I was in no mood to give Jess the courtesy of a reply.

"Whereabouts?" Harry asked. "Lake Erie?"

"No, Wooster. Ever heard of it?"

"Wooster?" Jess said. The eyes of all four men were fastened on me. "Did you find him?"

"Chancellor? No."

I believe something of a smirk came over Jess' face, at the thought of my "failure." He did not have much love for me, though I promise you, it was not because of anything I ever did or said to him.

I bent the truth a bit. "As a matter of fact, I didn't even look for him." I took yet another sip of brandy, feeling its warmth slowly radiating from my belly, seemingly warming the cold inside my bones. I savored the feeling for a moment, and then I took Professor Chancellor's book from my pocket and laid it on the table, between Harry and me. As I did so, I said, "I'd almost forgotten how really, really good, good brandy tastes."

For a moment Harry did not notice.

"Never drink cheap," Harry said. The he added, "Well, let me tell you what we came up with, Trey." He took another big bite of his sandwich. I guess I had laid the book on the table with such nonchalance—as if to simply unburden my pocket—that the movement had scarcely registered. Besides, I do not think that books as a rule caught Harry's eye. As he chewed, Senator Harding's name, on the spine, seemed to jump out at him. He instantly stopped and made a slight choking sort of noise. He stared at the little volume, as if disbelieving his eyes. Then he laid the sandwich aside, tidied his fingers on a dirty napkin, and picked the book up, ever so delicately.

Then he turned to me.

Truly, I wish I had a picture of the look on dear ol' Harry's face. I am not entirely sure if Laurel and Hardy were on the scene yet—I do not think they were—but Harry's ample face, pork-stuffed, and that wide-eyed, stuck-pig look could have come straight from Oliver Hardy's repertoire of flabbergasted expressions.

"So," I said, "I found it, the books and plates. I know where they are." I looked at Jess, "Why would I give a damn about Chancellor? I thought it was the books and plates we were interested in?" I sipped my brandy.

Harry managed to let loose with a great, joyous laugh, and—out of the blue—he grabbed my face in his big hands and planted a greasy kiss on my cheek.

"Jessie!" he cried, "He found the damn thing."

I am sure Jess was a bit peeved that it was I and not he who had made the discovery—which I guess he had hoped to do himself, from the comfort of his suite in the Hotel Marion. Jess said, "You've been wanting to do that for years, haven't you, Harry?"

"Trey found them! Jesus, Mary 'n' Joseph, he found 'em!"

"So where are they?"

"Like I said, over in Wooster. But to tell you the truth, the situation is a bit tricky. What I want to do is this—Brownie and me, and Jim here, we'll go over tonight, leave at sunset, and bring 'em back to Marion."

"I'll go with you," Jess said.

"You can't. I have a truck at work, but there's barely room for three in the cab, much less a fourth. Besides, there's going to be lots of heavy lifting, and running up and down stairs and such. It all needs to be done like lightning. Besides, Jess, there's simply no reason for you to go, and it's going to be one hell of a night."

"He's right," Harry said. "You stay here. Better that way."

To Brownie and Jim I said, "A word to the wise, boys—take a *long* nap."

XII

❧

I Was Oddly Pleased That
These Troubles Had Come to Pass

I ALREADY KNEW WHAT I NEEDED, which was not much—the Oshkosh Express truck from Colonel Hamilton & Son, a pair of wire clippers, a little defense—packed again in my coat pocket, just in case— and, of course, another treat for Kaiser. The truck was a little tricky. We had two of them, "twins," one for delivering coal and the other for building supplies. The second, as you can imagine, was cleaner by far. That sort of truck was far too mammoth for the job it needed to do, but at the time, we did not have any smaller models, and so the Oshkosh would have to do. Also, the company name was painted on the side panels in twirling gold letters. Needless to say, advertising our presence in Wooster was the least of my goals. With a little head scratching, I solved that mind twister with a pail of whitewash with some ink dumped in it.

I took my own advice. That afternoon I slept for several hours. Once again, I shall spare you the protestations I had to endure from my loving wife, as well as my useless attempts at reassurance.

We left a bit later than I intended, but as it was, it worked out. Thankfully, the moon was not to be shining on my endeavors that evening. Over the course of that cold October day, one of those great thick banks of leaden clouds crept over Ohio from the northwest, bringing plunging temperatures and—I was afraid—a whiff of early snow. I was very pleased that Brownie knew how to handle a heavy truck—not the most common skill, then or now—and so I let him drive while I rode huddled and

211

feverish between the warmth of my two companions. Lucy forced me to haul along a musty old buffalo robe that had somehow managed to survive from her grandparents' day. It was large enough to partially drape over my companions, a fact that dispelled whatever reluctance I may have harbored in using it.

I might add that we encountered very few other travelers on the long, twisting road to Wooster, which I suppose says something about people's reluctance back then to journey at night, except by rail.

Anyway, at about 11:00 or so, we finally laid eyes on the Holcomb Museum, its dark, castle-like hulk looming against the darkness. The windows, as well as I could make out, were as black as the stones themselves. I thought about telling Brownie just to park the truck along the highway, rather than driving back and pulling onto the gated orchard lane where I had hidden my Ford the night before, but I have always been the careful sort, eschewing heedless taunts to Fate, inviting failure, or worse yet, disaster, and so we "played it safe" and parked it tucked away, out-of-sight, down near the gated lane, albeit not in the lane itself.

As I said before, the moon would not be showing its face on this particular night, but a little of its light managed to seep through the clouds, somewhat like lamplight behind a heavy curtain. The three of us crept quietly down the dark road, limiting whatever comments we had to whispers, so as not to rile Kaiser. When we were parallel to the Museum, we crept across the grounds, with the Museum hiding us from the dog—just as I had done the night before. I found it very odd that we were hearing nothing from him. After all, now there were three of us to smell and hear and bark at. I told Brownie and Jim to wait by the cellar window, wherein we would enter, while I went to toss him his treat.

At the edge of the building, I peeked around the corner. I could see him, thanks to his white chest, which showed ever so dimly. He finally grumbled and barked at me a few times, but his barks were lame, almost as if he were directing a few obligatory yaps at a squirrel in a far field. I remembered what Adeline said about Watkins Sleeping Powders making her feel groggy the day after, and I realized that I had probably sent the poor fellow into a real stupor the night before. I must have given him a dose about ten times stronger than any Adeline had ever taken. He barked at me again, but rather lamely. I felt a little bad at the thought of loading him up with even more. In fact, because I knew we would be driving the truck within twenty yards of his doghouse, I had actually prepared a ham bone that was far more potent than the one from the night before. I suddenly had the sick feeling that I might kill the poor fellow, a thought that had not occurred to me until that very moment.

I groaned and muttered a few choice words that he probably heard, but did not respond to, and I leaned on the building, contemplating this unexpected dilemma. He was, after all, just a brute, an innocent beast caught in the crossfire of human ambition and deceit. I am not a dog killer, even though I am absolutely certain that Kaiser would have gladly ripped my arm off, if his head was clear and if the juicy opportunity arose. After a few moments of deliberation, I took out my knife. It very much annoyed me to get my hands greasy, yet again, especially with no place to wash; nevertheless, I began whittling away some of the meat, where the powders were most heavily packed. Of course I wanted to take away neither too little nor too much, so I had to go by intuition, and mostly by touch, because of the black of night. After I had trimmed what I thought generously appropriate, I stepped into the yard. I suppose my eyes had somewhat adjusted to the darkness, as I could see Kaiser more distinctly than before. He stood at the end of his chain, with ears pointed, watching me. He finally let loose with a volley of yaps, but nothing like the sheer fury of the night before. I even dared venture a bit nearer in order to toss the bone through the darkness with more sureness. As I approached, he lowered his head and snarled in a fierce, guttural way. That's when I tossed the bone. It landed within his reach. He sniffed his treat, left and right, and looked towards me. This time he seemed to hesitate about accepting this unexpected windfall. Nevertheless, in a moment, greed—or something—overruled whatever doubting instincts he harbored in that foolish head of his. He grabbed the bone and toted it into his doghouse.

That was the last I was to see or hear of him, though I am sure he came through the experience no worse for the wear.

I wiped my hands "clean" on the grass and leaves and then we entered the cellar via the same window that I had used the night before, the only difference being that I was able to virtually pop the glass from its frame, owing to the dampness and pliability of the new putty. I lowered the lantern onto the chest I would use as a step, and again crawled in on my belly, feet first. My companions followed. I had already warned them about the rats. They had a good laugh when I told them how I had leapt—ladylike—onto the steamer trunk. I might add that, in their company, I was not half as afraid as I had been the night before, alone. I was fortunate in the fact that Brownie and Jim were every bit as businesslike as I. Both had been soldiers, and it showed. There was no nonsense, no wanting to handle the swords and halberds and such; like me, they were there to get the job done, and get out—fast.

We lit the bare hanging lightbulb in the hall, which would have been more or less indistinguishable, I believe, through the cellar windows. Fortunately, the crates of books and the copper plates were exactly where I had left them the night before. I counted the plates—a total of thirty-one—two more than twenty-four hours before. Thus our little beavers had been busy. The still unbound pages were stacked in that other room, the one I had looked into the night before. I might add that each of those stacks was huge, and all total, there were surely tens of thousands of sheets. In fact, I believed now that Chancellor was telling the truth when he claimed that nine thousand five hundred copies of the book had been printed, but not collated.

We agreed that it would be best to carry everything up then and there, to place it all as close to the back door as possible, so we could swiftly load the truck and be gone, thieving agents in the night.

I certainly had not forgotten about the mysterious envelope that Gabby's boy had dropped off in his jalopy. I had a feeling then—and I certainly had a feeling now—that its contents had some connection to Chancellor's book. So while Jim and Brownie were beginning to carry the crates up, I moved my lantern over that large table in the pressroom where Mr. Bailey had been working. It was quite an array of junk—rusty metal rulers, pencil stubs, paper clamps, pliers, tins of printer's ink, Indian trinkets and such—but there, beneath a carved Indian stone used as a paperweight, lay a small pile of loose-leaf sheets, facedown. Even in that dim light I could make out ever so faintly the dark ink of the handwriting on the other side. When I turned the pile over, it was *not* the words "Chapter XX" scrawled at the top that leapt out at me; it was Miss von Leuckel's name. And there was Senator Harding's name in the line above. I leafed through the chapter, and there, three pages in, I saw my own name. The page reads:

> *The third point in this insidious, corrupt, and treacherous little triangle is one Tristan Tecumseh Hamilton, a glorified carpenter, plumber, coalman, mason, quarryman, surveyor, and all-around fix-it man. He is the spoiled scion of one of Marion's wealthy families with lots of fake aristocratic airs about him that were handed down to him folks say by his late mother, one of the treasonous Blennerhassetts, co-conspirators with Aaron Burr. An accused killer before he even sprouted peach fuzz, "Killer Trey" slipped the noose of culpability thanks to his father's connections and his money. He is an especially ignorant young man who can barely read and write, though he is said to be good with numbers, especially those that have a dollar sign in front of them. Expelled from school at the age of sixteen . . . .*

I read no more. As you can imagine, I bristled at his lies, truths, and humiliating insults. As for him calling me "ignorant"—well, you can judge that for yourself. As the accusation that I had "fake aristocratic airs," I assume that he meant that my mother raised me to carry myself with a certain deportment, to be discreet, and to have polished manners. As for the business that I was "spoiled," well, I would like to know what other spoiled "scion" worked six days a week, and was both willing and able to perform each and every job required of his men—with the admitted exception of his master craftsmen.

And he got the age of my expulsion wrong too.

I folded the manuscript and stuffed it deep into my coat pocket.

I do not think that more than fifteen minutes elapsed between the moment we crawled through the window and the moment when I opened the back door of the Holcomb, ever so quietly. Kaiser did not stir, and the Bailey house was still as dark as night itself. Brownie set off across the grounds with his lantern, Jim stationed himself by the books, and I crept across the yard toward the house. As I did, I cupped my hand over the lantern's globe, glancing at the upper windows—as if I could have seen anyone, even if they had been peering down from those high dark panes.

Once I was alongside the house, I turned up the flame and moved beside
the wall, looking for the telephone jack.

When I found it, I snipped the wire.

Far across the grounds, beyond the distant windrow, the truck's
powerful motor cranked and sputtered to a start, and then its heavy gears
whined as Brownie drove along the road. Meanwhile, I headed for the
back of the house where I unscrewed the light bulb and planted myself
beside the door, waiting for Brownie—and for Mr. Bailey.

To this day, I can still almost hear and feel the terrible rumble of
the truck as it turned onto the grounds. I suppose in part it was my
imagination—I was terribly nervous—but as the truck rolled between the
house and the Museum, the sound reverberated in my ears almost as if
in a tunnel. The back porch window near me rattled and the very ground
beneath my feet seemed to shudder. But then again, maybe it was simply
that my legs were all aquiver. I was suddenly very, very frightened. Indeed,
I distinctly remember thinking to myself: *If I am so terrified of an old man
poking his head from the back door, then how would I have felt in the trenches
facing the Huns, with their machine guns blazing and their mustard gas floating
my way?* But I told myself that if the moment had called, I would have
hurled myself onward into duty, and death.

With a few deft maneuvers, Brownie perfectly aligned the rear door
of the truck with the back door of the Holcomb. I could almost hear—
or at least sense—panicked movement within the house. Brownie leapt
from the truck, leaving the motor running. Then he jumped right back
up on the running board, held his lantern aloft and, holding onto the
door, he looked across the hood, towards me. I suppose he simply
wanted to reassure himself that I was at my post, standing guard. I know
this sounds almost hysterical on my part, and cruel, but for an instant
the dirty yellow light from his kerosene lamp glowed over his disfigured
face and I felt as if I had been looked upon by some hellish fiend from
another world. To this day I thank God that the poor fellow could not
have possible seen whatever horrified expression flashed upon my
countenance.

A light suddenly glowed inside the house. I pressed my back hard
against the outside wall, and I believe I could feel the vibration of footsteps
hastening towards the door. An old woman's voice wailed, "Cal, don't!"

He threw the bolt and the inner door flew open. He shouted through the screen door, "Hey, what you think you're doing there?"

Jim and Brownie were already loading the truck.

Then he literally kicked the screen open and a double-barrel shotgun emerged beside my head. With a lunging thrust, I shoved the barrel upward and simultaneously grabbed the gun and ripped it from his grasp, pulling with such violence that I fear I may have broken one of the old man's fingers. He gave a sharp cry and stepped back, cradling one hand in the other. The old woman screamed.

"Don't move," I shouted. "You move, you die."

"What on earth?"

Mrs. Bailey, standing in her nightdress a few feet behind him, covered her face and began to wail and cry.

"Tend to your wife," I said. "You folks behave, nothing bad'll happen. Step out of line and God help you. We'll be out of here in a jiffy."

Mr. Bailey was scrutinizing me, and then he craned his neck and looked through the window toward Brownie and Jim. I have no idea what he could or could not see from that angle through the darkness, but I assume he knew they were not carting out arrowheads. He was wearing one of those long, old-fashioned nightshirts and bedtime hats, from the pre-furnace days, the kind old men sometimes still wore back then in winter. I am sure that the light shining out from their kitchen illuminated my face, if only dimly.

"You," he said, recognizing me. Then he seemed to spit the word, "Perry!"

At first I thought he was mistaking me for someone he knew by that name.

"You're working for that nigger politician, aren't you?"

"Go tend to your wife."

"I thought there was something funny about you."

That was when I realized that he knew he was speaking to Wellington Boyd.

"Likewise," I said.

He squinted, examining me like I was a riddle he was trying to decipher. "But how in God's name did you find us? Why, I could count them on one hand, those that know."

I laughed, thinking of my good fortune.

"And they're each sworn to absolute secrecy, every one of them." He glanced over his shoulder, at his wife. "Why, Annabelle doesn't even know."

"If you must know, Professor Chancellor told us, though it cost us dearly—fifty thousand."

"What! Chancellor?"

"Yes. Chancellor. He told us."

I think for a split second, he actually believed me, or at least I made him wonder. Then he said, "Ha! I've known Bill Chancellor all my life. Mister, you're a damned liar."

"So what's that make Chancellor? What's that make you?"

Then he suddenly looked off towards the doghouse. "Say, what'd you rascals do to that dog?"

"We didn't do anything, just doped him."

"You poisoned him. And slit his throat!"

"Oh? Like you and your Klansmen do to your colored neighbors, to their dogs? We're not killers. We're not scum. I doped him, that's that."

A moment later the truck's loading door slammed shut. Jim called out to me, "Joe, that's it. Let's skedaddle."

Mr. Bailey solemnly repeated the name "Joe," as if he had just been handed a careless clue, and was letting me know that he caught it. I gave a little laugh at his pompous idiocy.

Brownie was already climbing into the cab. While he maneuvered the truck for our departure, I popped the cartridges from the barrels of the shotgun and tossed them into the darkness. Then I hurled it as far into the distance as my arm could dispatch it—which back in those days was pretty far.

As I headed for the truck, I turned and called out, "Good night, Mr. Bailey. Sorry about your hand. And by the way, sir, go to hell."

"You're a traitor, you know that? A nigger-loving traitor to the white race! You'll see! Damn you! This country's slowly going to hell with all the niggers and dagoes and jackass Jews—all because of men like you!"

I was filled with a sort of feverish and high-strung contempt, as well as elation at our victory, and wholly uncharacteristic of myself, I slapped my backside and yelled, "Kiss it, loser." For a split second an inner demon urged me to stoop and hurl a stone from the gravel path straight at his shiny bald pate. To this day I am thankful that my better angels interceded and I did not.

BROWNIE WAS KIND ENOUGH to drive all the way home and I assure you, driving a truck—especially an Oshkosh Heavy Duty Express—was more exhausting work than you may imagine. It's a little like shoveling coal, especially when it came to turns and shifting the many gears, and the clutch did not exactly respond to a soft touch. As for me, after we found ourselves safely out of Wayne County, I fell fast asleep beneath the buffalo robe and did not wake until Brownie nudged me in the ribs, just as we entered the precincts of eastern Marion. As we passed beneath a streetlight, I managed to glimpse my watch; the hour was about 3:30. I had already put some thought into how we would rid the world of our cargo, and so we headed for Lake Etowah for our first disposal. As the truck lumbered along Mt. Vernon Avenue, towards Etowah, I thought again of the dinner party that Mr. and Mrs. King had given in honor of Douglas Fairbanks and Mary Pickford. That glittering evening had come and gone just shy of a week ago, and yet it seemed like an event ages and ages past. So too did my conversation with Miss von Leuckel, from which this adventure had sprung. As I looked across the way at the dark villa, I thought of the servant girl bending at the candlelit table, whispering in my ear that I had a visitor, and of Mitzy, standing in the garden at sunset in a cloak of royal blue. I thought of Chancellor's pupil, maybe Gabby's boy, spying on us from across the lake; remembering that fellow now brought a smile to my face. His "spy's perch" above the stone balustrade would be a perfect spot from which to dump the plates.

For some reason, I was oddly pleased that these troubles had come to pass.

I do not know why, but I have always had a leeriness of water at night. This was doubly true of the mysterious waters of Lake Etowah, whose very presence I preferred to skirt past sundown—unless the moon was shining high and bright. In Marion the night was even blacker than it had been in Wooster, for the moon, having sailed invisibly behind the heavy veil of clouds, had now slipped beyond the western horizon, dragging along its thin gray glow. As we hauled those weighty printer's plates from the back of the truck, I could not help but think of the thousands of pennies that might have been coined from them, but their material value was hardly of concern to me.

And so we began heaving them over the balustrade and cliffs into the deep black waters of Lake Etowah. Each invisible splash sounded muted and far away, as if it were echoing in an abyss.

After completing that errand, we headed for Tioga. Or rather I should say for the Old Forest behind the carriage house and grounds. Adeline and my father both knew, more or less, what was going on, though I had not exactly come out and told them of my plans to commit burglary. They did know that if all went well, they could expect to suffer through the noise of the truck—and Spats' barks—waking them deep in the middle of the night.

They left the back light on for us.

The truck was of such stature that, as we came along the drive, I could see its high yellowish headlamps reflected in the high windowpanes of the carriage house doors, way at the back of the land. Spats was on his toes, as usual. As we rumbled along beside the house, I leapt from the cab. Already I could hear his piercing barks from a window in my father's room.

A little lamp in the kitchen was aglow, and when I opened the door I was met with the aroma of baked cookies, still hanging in the warm air from hours before. Spats was tearing down the narrow stairs at the back of the house, yapping every step of the way, and I could hear my sister's slippered feet following him down. He was so upset that the fur stood like a brush on his back. I took him up in my arms and spoke to him, and held him so he could see the truck through the window. Brownie was turning around, so the loading door was near the far edge of the carriage house, beside which a trail led off into the Old Forest.

The moment Adeline stepped into the dim light, I saw my mother in her face. Actually, that was not an unusual happening, at least during my sister's young womanhood, though I believe that having read Chancellor's insult of my mother had stirred her nearer to the surface of my thoughts. I might add that, back in those years, people used to say that Adeline could have been our mother's twin; paintings and old photographs confirm this.

"We woke you up," I said. "Sorry."

"So, you were successful?"

"Successful! Why, I even found the manuscript. Everything!"

"Well done. Daddy'll be proud." And then with a bit of trepidation, she added, "Nothing bad happened over there, did it, Trey?"

I thought of Mr. Bailey's injured hand, but I also thought it not worth mentioning, at least not at this moment. "No, nothing bad. All unfolded beautifully."

She smiled. "Dana brought the kerosene over. I had him put it behind the carriage house."

I placed little Spats in her arms. He had settled now.

As I headed for the door, she said, "I had Miss Evans bake cookies for you gentlemen. She put some sandwiches in the icebox too. You'll see them."

"Later," I said. "Thanks."

"Trey, make sure you save one."

I turned. "Save one?" The moment I asked, I realized she did not mean a sandwich, of course, but one of Chancellor's books. I laughed at my foolishness. "Oh, I already have."

She followed me to the back door, cradling Spats in her arms.

Brownie and Jim were unloading the crates onto the leaf-covered grass.

When I was halfway across the yard, Adeline called out, "Oh Trey, by the way, how are you feeling?"

Brownie and Jim both paused and looked across the yard to the back door. Men being men, I presumed they had heard of my sister's beauty. She was barely visible through the screen, so the most they could have seen was a dark, indistinct form.

I gave her thumbs up, "Couldn't be better." I was lying and she knew it, but that was the sort of answer she expected from me, and the sort I expected from myself.

Each of us grabbed a crate and headed for the portal-like opening in the Old Forest behind the carriage house, from which the trail ran. Even with the wicks high in the lanterns, it was almost a blind trudge along the narrow path through the trees. At best, the dim yellow light seemed barely to cleave a little hollow from the darkness. About fifty yards in, we came to the bowl-like indentation that had formed in ages past—whether by Indian hands, or by God's, I do not know. The bowl looked a bit like one of those little craters you see in pictures of the moon, not that I am saying a meteor caused it; just that it looked like that. And for some reason no trees ever grew there, and hardly any brush. We carried the crates to the bottom of the basin and began dumping books, crumpling some of the loose uncollated pages. These we scattered like kindling.

Thus we came and went, from the truck to the bowl, again and again, spreading layer after layer of books and sheets, breaking the crates apart as we emptied them. We doused each layer with kerosene. I suppose in all it took an hour of trudging and dumping before every last book, sheet, and splinter of wood from the Holcomb had been added to the pyre. Then we started in the middle and gave the entire mound yet another dousing.

Each of us prowled along the edges striking matches and flinging them in, setting the books alight, and we flung burning books onto the center of the mound, so that the fire would burn evenly.

Kerosene, of course, is not a spectacular accelerant; it is heavy with oil but in the end it does its job, if not quickly, then thoroughly. As the great bonfire burned, we raked and stirred the edges, constantly pushing the fire into itself. Indeed, before long, I had to run to the house for jugs of water, because the handles of our rakes were starting to smolder.

By dawn, Professor Chancellor's books lay in ashes.

Just as our work was coming to an end, a cold rain began to fall. We headed to the house for cookies and sandwiches, and I brewed a pot of coffee.

∞

The "Negro-blood rumor" faded—not exactly into oblivion, but it departed—and the business about Mitzy, Senator Harding, and yours truly (not to mention Kaiser Bill) never managed to raise its ugly head from those ashes.

On November 2, 1920, on his 55th birthday, Senator Warren G. Harding won the Presidency of the United States by the greatest landslide in American history—a record that remains to this very day.

When Thanksgiving arrived, Wellington Boyd was kind enough to send a card of gratitude, along with a large bouquet of red roses and baby's breath, to Miss Ruby Rose Chancellor of Maple Lane in Orrville, Ohio.

They would be waiting on her porch when she returned to her lonely house from school.

BOOK III

Legacy of Secrets

I

WEDNESDAY MORNING
27 NOVEMBER 1963
TIOGA

A Memory of Thanksgiving, 1923

EARLY THIS MORNING as I was standing before the mirror shaving, getting ready for my doctor's appointment, I heard an interesting report on the radio. At the top of the eight o'clock news our local station, WMRN, reported that the FBI is looking into the possibility that Lee Harvey Oswald may not have acted alone in the murder of President Kennedy. In other words, there is suspicion of a conspiracy. Do not misunderstand me when I say that I had to laugh out loud when I heard that. I said to myself, "Oh, dear lord, here we go again!" And then I said to the old man in the mirror, "History really does repeat itself, doesn't it old man?"

I suppose that by this time tomorrow people will be spreading rumors that maybe Mrs. Kennedy had some involvement in her husband's death. That maybe she was in cahoots with Oswald, that she hired him and took a chance with her own life—sitting there beside the President in the back of his open Lincoln. Maybe they'll say she was jealous over a mistress. Or that she wanted him martyred so he wouldn't look so bad in the eyes of history—after, say, that Bay of Pigs fiasco. Or maybe in the rather freewheeling logic of rumorists, both motives might come into play—that Mrs. Kennedy was jealous *and* she thought it would be nice if the President were martyred, especially with their being Catholics and all.

And let's not forget that President Kennedy was worth millions. And his pretty young widow will, of course, inherit everything.

I suppose you think I am being mean-spirited, facetious, and disrespectful when I say these things about our beloved President Kennedy and our beautiful and gracious First Lady, but my point is those were exactly the things they were saying about the Hardings forty years ago.

I guess only time will tell whether or not we will have yet another crop of outlandish conspiracy rumors, but that report this morning made me realize that the whole tragic and monumental situation is perfectly suited to just such a thing.

I have also of late been wondering whether President Kennedy had a Tristan Hamilton in his life.

I am not flattering myself when I say that. What I mean is some fellow off on the fringes of his life and career, an old friend of the family, maybe from Hyannis Port, or from his Harvard days, someone who did useful things to help him on his way up. Someone who was expedient and well organized, someone both invisible and indispensable. I am sure that the President, in his Harvard circle, had lots of friends who were far more powerful than I could ever have dreamed of being here in little old Marion, a school drop-out with an inherited career as an "all-around fix-it man," as Professor Chancellor said of me. Well, frankly, I doubt very much if such a fringe fellow inhabited President Kennedy's life. After all, what need had he for an axle-greaser? I suppose he was more self-determined and deliberate than President Harding, and certainly he was more worldly and self-confident. I imagine most of President Kennedy's encouragement came from his brothers and his parents. And of course from the beautiful, gracious, charming, and utterly dignified Jacqueline Bouvier Kennedy, the perfect helpmate—revered by every man in America, if not the world.

President Harding had no such familial influence, other than his wife. Though even as I say this I should add that his mother, Phoebe Harding, had an uncanny lifelong belief that her son would one day become President of the United States. I have always thought that his mother's conviction surely permeated and influenced him, though from what I remember, she never directly pushed him in any one direction or another. And mind you, she died in May of 1910—the year of

Mr. Harding's disastrous bid for the governorship of Ohio, and a full decade before the glorious summer of the Front Porch Campaign.

WELL, WITH ANY LUCK, I may live to see another Thanksgiving or two. At least that is what my physician seems to think, and I intend to hold him to it. This morning I received my annual medical checkup from Dr. George Sawyer. Others call him "Doc," but it seems I am just too stiff to use such a familiar and folksy diminutive, even though I have known him all my life. Dr. Sawyer is mostly retired now. He works out of a little office in his residence, White Oaks Farm, and accepts only us old-timers who have been with him for many years. His father was my father's physician, and Mr. and Mrs. Hardings' as well. In 1921, Dr. Charles Sawyer was appointed Surgeon General of the United States and he also served as the President's personal physician. He was with Mr. Harding when the President took ill during the "Voyage of Understanding," and he was at the President's bedside when he died at the Palace Hotel in San Francisco. Dr. Sawyer's signature is on the President's death certificate, certifying that the President died of apoplexy—what we commonly call a stroke.

The main house of White Oaks Farm (which my grandfather and father built) is a rather sprawling bungalow of brick and forest-green clapboards laid out atop a little knoll, in the area called Oakland Heights, just beyond the western edge of Marion. This morning as I drove up the winding gravel drive, I saw in my mind Babe Ruth in his Yankee stripes standing in sunlight over near the duck pond, giving batting lessons to orphan boys from the Children's Home. That was on a golden summer day in 1920. The Babe had come to town to campaign for Senator Harding, and Dr. Sawyer was holding a picnic in his honor. The boys and girls from the orphanage were his "honored guests." I remember that Harry Daugherty and I were standing near the cattails watching the Babe giving lessons, and as we stood there, Harry leaned over and murmured in my ear, "Lord, Trey, I guess this fresh air's getting to me. Could I ever use a wee smidgen of Tullamore Dew!" He nudged me in the ribs and chuckled in that ornery, self-delighted way Harry had; and then he moseyed across the lawn towards the tall oak that once rose near the cistern. He was wearing one of those light-colored summer suits that came into fashion after the war, and he was looking up at the tree like he was scouting for squirrels or something. I had one eye on Harry and another on the Babe, and I saw the sly movement of Harry's shoulders as he pulled the flask from his jacket, uncorked and tipped it for a few long moments, and then stashed it back in his pocket, just as neat and quick as could be.

Today on this gray November morning, forty-three years and about five months later, I glanced to where the future Attorney General had gone to sneak his whiskey. A new building—a warehouse for Pollack Steel—now stands a quarter of a mile or so beyond the Sawyer property, and the tall oak is just an old stump topped with an empty flowerpot, which Mrs. Sawyer decorates with geraniums during the summer.

This morning I recalled yet another occasion at White Oaks Farm, albeit one which I was not actually present to see. It was a day in late summer, 1924, when David Lloyd George, the Prime Minister of Great Britain, came along the winding drive in the enormous Rolls-Royce limousine that he brought from London, complete with driver, mechanics, footmen, etc. The Rolls-Royce was doing most of its traveling in its own canopied railway car on the Prime Minister's personal train. He was in the United States with his wife on a state visit and I suppose he wanted to see a bit of England's lost, rich colony on his roundabout way to Toronto. By then Mrs. Harding was an ailing widow, suffering more than ever from her kidney complaint, and she was spending what were clearly her last days at White Oaks Farm, where Surgeon General Sawyer and his nurses could look after her. The Prime Minister had come to Ohio for the sole purpose of paying a courtesy call on the former First Lady, and to deliver to her good wishes and respect from his King.

This morning I found myself parking my Lincoln in the spot beside the tall cedar hedges where I supposed the Prime Minister's driver probably parked his car. As I crossed the narrow limestone walkway, and then the porch, I imagined Lloyd George crossing those same stones and floorboards, and knocking on the same door.

I think the reemergence of the past over the last several days has been getting the best of me. I say this because, when Mrs. Sawyer answered the door, I had the momentary illusion that it was not she, but Florence Harding, who stood there smiling, saying, "Good morning, Trey, come in. So nice to see you again."

Now before you write me off as an old man who is losing his marbles, I wish to say that there are a few similarities between Mrs. Sawyer and the long-deceased First Lady. Actually, I have noted this fact—on and off—for a couple of decades, though never before had the resemblance struck me with such uncanny force. For a stunned moment, I simply stood looking into the pale gray eyes behind the old-fashioned gold frames, and her eyes were Mrs. Harding's eyes, and the puffy face framed by gray, marcelled hair was Mrs. Harding's hair. I am sure the illusion was furthered by the fact that Edna was wearing an old-fashioned knit shawl draped over her shoulders, and a flowered house dress with a long hem—the very kind that Mrs. Harding used to wear, the sort of dress that nowadays is worn only by old ladies who left their youth in the early decades of the century. I must have stood for a full ten seconds (heaven only knows what idiotic expression was frozen on my face) before Edna reached for my sleeve as she said, "Trey! What is it? Is something the matter?"

Only then did I come to my senses, so to speak, and realize that my mind was playing tricks on me.

I am pleased to say that my perpetually poor memory regarding little domestic things provided me with a very convenient and genuine excuse. I had forgotten to bring the two jars of pumpkin that Mrs. Christian had asked me to deliver to Mrs. Sawyer. She still canned a few things in the old-fashioned way, and I assure you, store-bought pumpkin cannot hold a candle to Mrs. Christian's homemade variety. I slapped my forehead, "Oh heavens, Edna, why, I just realized—I left the jars of pumpkin by the back door. Let me run home and get them, it won't take but a . . ."

"Don't be silly. Just get yourself in here out of the cold."

"But you're going to bake your pies this afternoon, aren't you?"

"True, but I'm on my way shopping so I'll just swing by your place and pick them up. I imagine Mrs. Christian's there, isn't she?"

"And her daughter too," I said, stepping into the house. "Emma Linda's giving us a hand this week."

Edna's eyes widened a little as she closed the door behind me, and she nodded, almost like I had just let her in on a big secret. "Trey, is it true? Mitzy von Leuckel's coming to Tioga? For dinner?!"

I gave a little laugh—I was never surprised at the way news travels in Marion, Ohio. "As a matter of fact, it *is* true, though . . ."

"And how did that come about?"

I smiled at her interrogation. "I ran into Heidi in Kroger's last week. She said her mother was coming in and I invited them, Carl too, of course. Simple as that. And by the way, Edna, Mitzy hasn't been Mitzy von Leuckel for forty years. She's Mrs. Blaine now. She and Jim moved to St. Louis during the war."

"Well, it wouldn't surprise me one bit if she'd had two or three husbands by now, and by the way, she'll *always* be Mitzy von Leuckel. Let me take your coat."

I found her words curious. As I took off my hat and such, I said, "Well, I can assure you, she was married only once in her life, just like the rest of us, or most of the rest of us."

I did not bother to tell her that, according to Heidi, Mrs. Blaine was selling her St. Louis place and planning to return to Marion to be closer to her children, including the President's son, not to mention her grandchildren.

Placing my things in the closet, she said, "I don't remember. How many children did she end up having?"

"Five altogether. Dr. Lang, of course, and then three sons and Heidi, by Jim, though Jim dropped dead a year or so back."

Suddenly, a look of great sorrow swept over her. She laid her hand on my arm. "Oh, Tristan, haven't these been the saddest of days? Just like 1923 all over again, aren't they? Only worse, more tragic. Far more tragic." Her eyes had filled with tears, and she reached into the pocket of her house dress for a tissue.

I suppose I ought to have extended some comforting gesture. Instead, I glanced away—as if I had not noticed her teary eyes—towards the overstuffed chair by the fireplace, where I had last seen Mrs. Harding alive, in November of 1924. "Yes, Edna," I said, "just like 1923 all over again. I can't tell you how much I've thought of those times. Some things seem to run together, don't they?"

Tears choked her voice and suddenly she had the sniffles. "We loved President Kennedy, George and I did, loved him so very much. And those poor, beautiful children, dear God. And Jacqueline, so brave, so much like Florence. Yes, so much like Florence, even if only in that one single way."

I said nothing. I know it sounds spiteful, but I had half a mind to ask if she and George—avid (even rabid) Republicans—loved President Kennedy half so much a week ago as she purported to love him now. And besides, I clearly remember a comment that George made, back in 1960, about the Kennedys being Catholic and how, if the Congressman were elected, the Pope would be calling the shots.

She regained her composure. "You know, I may be speaking out of turn, but George and I, we haven't much use for that Texan. Far as we're concerned, he's no more presidential than Cal Coolidge was. Less so, maybe. Both trying to follow in the footsteps of great men. You know who George thinks he looks like?"

I allowed that I did not.

"Senator Albert Fall, that's who."

Come to think of it, President Johnson does indeed look a bit like Albert Fall—President Harding's Secretary of Interior who brought about the Teapot Dome scandal, leasing the oil fields to his good buddy, Harry Sinclair.

Edna added, "Think about it. All Mr. Johnson needs is a string tie. He's already got the cowboy hat. Can you imagine? A cowboy hat! Well, I suppose we'll just have to wait and see." And then she added, "Well, come on back."

I have learned not to involve myself in political discussions in this deeply Republican town, especially when the subject pertains to Democrats—at least *unmartyred* Democrats—so I kept mum.

George's medical room is in the back corner of the house. As I followed Edna through the sprawling living room—with its heavy old furniture, potted houseplants, Oriental vases, and wall-to-wall carpet—I of course found myself glancing sidelong at the green overstuffed chair wherein I last saw Mrs. Harding. That would have been only days before her death, and several weeks after the Surgeon General's sudden death.

Both died under this very roof.

Mrs. Harding was all bundled up in blankets from neck to toe, her puffy feet and legs raised and resting on pillows on top of a hassock. The marcelled waves in her hair had all fallen into limp strands, and you could see shiny patches where her thin hair no longer covered the scalp. I had come out to show her the four designs we were considering for the

Harding Memorial. She had just given me a box of Italian chocolates for Adeline, and as I was about to leave, she said, "Tristan, you must never doubt that we did the right thing."

Dr. George Sawyer does not look anything like his father. Even in his seventies, George is a broad-shouldered and powerful man.

His father, most decidedly, was not.

In fact, the only moment of humor I recall from the President's funeral occurred at Marion Cemetery when Surgeon General Sawyer, accompanying the widow, stepped from the Pierce-Arrow. Stifled laughter rippled through that multitude of astonished mourners. I can still see Dr. Sawyer and the First Lady, following the coffin into the hillside holding vault on that stiflingly hot August day. He was in his military dress uniform, complete with a dangling saber that he had to sort of leverage by its hilt in order to keep the scabbard tip from dragging through the grass. I do not wish to sound clever, but the truth of the matter is, Dr. Sawyer's diminutive stature and whiskers gave him the air of a cartoon mouse dressed up like Napoleon. The widow towered over him, all poised and serene with her long black veil thrown back, her chin up, and her eyes clear. Indeed, I would venture to say that her eyes were even clearer than Mrs. Kennedy's, whose eyes seemed covered by a veil of mist. I might add that I could not help but think of the Surgeon General this past Monday when I saw the Emperor of Ethiopia, Haile Selassie, following President Kennedy's coffin up the slope at Arlington, standing ramrod straight beside the towering Charles de Gaulle. Though if you yourself took notice of the Emperor, then you would probably agree that, in spite of his diminutive stature, he looked wholly at home in his imperial uniform.

Anyway, as I was saying, George does not look anything like his father. In fact, with his big white mustache and shiny bald head, he looks a bit like a friendly walrus.

But a word to the wise—don't cross him!

He must have been a little late arising this morning, for I sat in the examining room for several minutes, sipping the coffee that Edna had poured for me, its aroma mixing with that medicinal smell that emanates from physicians' cabinets. As you might guess, the medical room has not changed much in forty years. I sat on the same brown leather examining table that was in use during his father's day, and I am certain that the

President himself—no doubt more than once—sat in the very same spot and glanced about at the very same objects. Beside the table sits an oak cabinet with a white marble top, so old that even careful use has not spared it the little nicks and chips brought on by time. And of course atop this table are the usual things—an old porcelain tray with cotton balls, a jar of alcohol, various blue and amber colored pill bottles, and a heavy glass ashtray. George has a curious custom that has always intrigued me. He never throws his calendars away. A wire hangs from a nail on the wall, and a succession of calendars—I would say at least forty-some—dangle one atop the other, possibly going all the way back to President Harding's day. Today, Wednesday, November 27th, had only one notation penciled in, "Tristan 10:00".

Last Friday's notation said simply, "President Kennedy killed"— written by a careful hand in black ink.

But mostly, as I sipped my coffee, I tried to occupy myself with the view from the window. Cornfields, brownish gray this time of year, rolled far away towards leafless windrows, and a flock of starlings were picking through the old stalks. I watched the birds gleaning the fields.

I suppose in a sense I was keeping my eyes averted from the black horsehair divan looming beneath the window.

It was upon this narrow divan that the Surgeon General laid down and died on a September evening in 1924, just after having dinner with Mrs. Harding.

As I concentrated on the starlings, they reminded me of dark-clad immigrant children I had seen long, long ago in New York, during a childhood visit there with my family, while my mother was still alive. Flocks of ragged children were picking their way along the wharves gleaning coal that had fallen, I suppose, during the coaling of ships. Their hands and faces were blackened and they were dropping lumps into cinder buckets and even their pockets. I remember my mother leaned down and said, "Look at the poor children, Tristan. Look at them, Adeline. Boys and girls your own age. You're no better than they, just more blessed. And blessings come gift-wrapped in duty. Never forget that. *Never forget.*"

I have always been pleased that my parents instilled within us the dutiful sentiments of *noblesse-oblige*.

I heard George's footsteps traipsing across the linoleum in the kitchen. The moment before he came through the door, I glanced at the divan—his father's deathbed.

George always saves the chitchat until after his medical work is finished, which is to say, until after he has tried my fortitude with all his probing and poking and his regimen of questions. This morning, after he removed his stethoscope for the day and hung it back on its hook, he peered at me from above his half-moon glasses and said, with chiding gravity, "You know, Trey, if you aren't careful you just might live to be a hundred. So the sixty-four thousand dollar question is: What are you going to do with all those years—I mean if our Maker agrees with me?"

He sat down on the horsehair divan and awaited my answer.

"Well, good question, George. A hundred years? That's another twenty-eight years of being old, so frankly, I'm not sure if that's good news or bad."

"Neither am I, but with a heart and blood pressure like yours, it's a distinct possibility. Of course in my line of work we offer no guarantees. You could just as easily croak tomorrow." He shrugged, as if to say, *So what.* He let out an exasperated sigh, and added, "Who knows, maybe you will. But you won't."

"Well, one way or another, let's make it the day after tomorrow as I have guests coming for dinner. I would be rude to die before that."

He laughed and gave me a little smile, "Guests! So I've heard, Trey, so I've heard! Got a date, have you?"

I probably blushed three shades of red at his insinuation. He stared at me quite amused—no doubt having achieved the desired response—and then he chuckled in an off-color sort of way. At least that's how it struck my ears.

"For heaven's sake, George, you damn fool. What do you take me for? I'm an old man, not a college boy. Besides, her daughter's coming too."

He raised his palms, "Didn't mean a thing, Trey, didn't mean a thing. Say, listen, you sure aren't going to live to be a hundred if you can't even take a joke. A sense of humor's part of longevity."

Then all of a sudden he got serious and in hushed tones, he said, "Mitzy was one pretty gal, wasn't she? Maybe a little too pretty for her own good. Too lots of things, when you think about it. I think she wanted to marry Mr. Harding. I think she was waiting for Mrs. to die. That's what I think. Maybe that's why she got that son out of him, a little guarantee."

He shook his head and seemed to be waiting for me to concur.

I said nothing.

"Don't you think that's what she had in mind, Trey?"

"Since you asked, yes, I believe she did have that in mind."

"Poor thing, talk about delusions. Why, dear God, just look at the life she could have had."

I pushed myself from the examining table. "Things work out one way or another, usually for the best, and it was all a very long time ago."

I picked up my cufflinks from the table, and found myself looking far off out the window.

As I finished dressing, George said, "More coffee, Trey? I'll fix a fresh pot."

"No, I'll be on my way now, thank you. Mrs. Christian gave me a bit of shopping to do, so I better be off. I don't want her cross with me." I could see a darkening coming over the land from the north. "Looks like snow's coming."

He glanced through the window. "That's what they say, coming down from the Lake. Arriving late this afternoon or early tonight. Looks like they might be right, for a change."

As I stood tying my tie, I was looking across the rolling fields. The starlings had flown off somewhere, and I saw an animal moving far away, maybe a cat prowling the furrows. George was watching me, no doubt wondering. I found myself glancing at the divan, and without the slightest forethought, I said, "George, what did your father die of?"

I could sense something like a tautness come over him. I avoided his eyes.

I could feel him staring at me, his eyes boring in, suspicious-like. "My father?" For a long moment, he said nothing more. "You don't remember?"

I shook my head. "Can't say as I do."

"You really don't remember?" There was something sharp in his voice, like I was up to something, and he wasn't about to be fooled.

I shook my head. "No, George. As a matter of fact, I don't remember. Should I?"

"You didn't say a thing to me about memory loss."

"Well, I guess I forgot."

"Ha, ha. Very funny. You could go on Jack Benny."

"George, your father died forty years ago, if it was a day."

Actually, it was thirty-nine years and two months ago, and I knew this very well.

He crossed his arms and just sat there studying me. He didn't answer my question because he knew that I knew the answer. I said, "Heart attack, was it?"

"'Heart attack, was it?' Of course it was a heart attack. Exactly like the President. Died right here on this couch." He patted the horsehair.

The President died of apoplexy. Later, I regretted not having had the presence of mind to point this out, along with George's own apparent "memory loss." There had been some debate about whether the President died of a stroke or of coronary thrombosis. The Surgeon General and the three other eminent physicians attending him debated which it was. Mrs. Harding would not allow an autopsy, and apoplexy won the day. Dr. Sawyer signed the death certificate.

I said, "Now that you mention it, I do remember that he died right here, in this very room."

He was studying me, still wondering what this was all about.

"This week's brought back so much," I said.

Instantly, a change seemed to come over him. "Ah, I see! That it has. Just like 1923 all over again. That's what Edna says."

"But has it brought back a lot of things for you?"

"You could say that, but you have to remember that I wasn't in the thick of it the way you and your sister were." For some reason he changed the subject. "Trey, why don't you get out of town for a while? Go to Florida for the winter. What's stopping you? Get out of that big old house and go down and get yourself a nice bungalow on—where'd that little Marion colony used to be? Where your father and the Hardings and Mrs. Huber and all those classy folks used to go?"

"Merritt Island."

"Yes, Merritt Island. Go there for the winter. Get yourself a bungalow on the beach and some sun and ocean air. A new beginning."

I smiled at the kindness of his suggestion. "Actually, I've been thinking of something like that. Not there exactly, but somewhere."

"Trey, tell me something. Aren't you lonely out there at Tioga?"

I am sure I blushed. After all, it was not the sort of question one ordinarily asked.

He said, "I'm asking as your doctor, Trey. As your doctor, I have a right to know. Are you lonely? It can do things to you. Give you the long-term blues. Depression."

For a moment, I said nothing, and then I said, "Yes, I suppose I am, but I'm a widower. Seventy-one years old. Almost seventy-two. I'm supposed to be lonely, aren't I?"

"Not in my book."

I did not want to continue with this conversation, though I think he did. Abruptly, I took my wallet from my jacket pocket and handed him my five dollars, and as I did, I glanced at the horsehair couch again. I wanted to bring up the Surgeon General's death once more, as it was bothering me, but I did not. Perhaps I should not have mentioned it in the first place, as George has always been unduly touchy about the rumor that the Surgeon General was a conspirator in the supposed assassination of the President. And who knows how he feels about the other old rumor, that Mrs. Harding poisoned his father.

UNFORTUNATELY, IT WAS NOT until after I departed from White Oaks Farm—in fact, while I was in the Thrift Market buying a pound of chestnuts—that I suddenly recalled a little something that George might have found of passing interest, if only I'd had the presence of mind to mention it. Exactly forty years ago tomorrow, the Surgeon General celebrated his last Thanksgiving at Tioga—as did the recently widowed First Lady. They were Adeline's guests, along with Mrs. Sawyer, Reverend Swank of the Epworth Church, and Lucy and me. Perhaps not even the slightest ripple from that remote Thanksgiving would have come back to me if I had not just seen George, but I think what really jogged my memory was digging my hand into that bushel of chestnuts at the Thrift Market.

I was looking for the glossiest, heaviest ones when, in my mind, I saw the First Lady, dressed in widow's black, sitting at the head of the dinner table at Tioga. She was squeezing a nutcracker in her right hand, cracking open a chestnut, saying, "Boy, do I ever love chestnuts!"

Indeed, a little molehill of broken, empty shells was piled beside her on the bread plate, atop the golden damask tablecloth that had been one of our mother's wedding gifts. She added, "Most people would say that chestnuts are chestnuts, but you folks always have the very best right here at Tioga. Far better than Warren and I had anywhere else, even at the White House."

Mrs. Harding may have been right.

Back in those days a big beautiful chestnut tree still flourished at Goose Pond Farm—the country place north of town that Adeline and I inherited from Dad. That tree, said to have been a favorite of the Indians, was one of the last survivors in these parts of the blight that wiped out the trees earlier in this century. I believe that nowadays chestnuts come from Italy. Or at least that is what Mr. Reece—the proprietor of the Thrift Market—said when I mentioned our long-dead tree.

Anyway, the same golden damask cloth that was on the table in 1923 will be in use again tomorrow, when Mrs. Blaine arrives.

In fact, it is already in place.

After I came home this morning from my errands, I rolled back the double-doors of the dining room to look again at the place where the First Lady sat, forty years ago tomorrow. When I stepped into the room, I realized that I had not so much as poked my head in for at least a month. You see, I usually have my meals at the kitchen table, or during pleasant weather, I eat in the little morning room at the back of the house.

It is, I am sorry to say, one of the least used rooms in Tioga, and has been since my father passed away. In fact, tomorrow will be a red-letter day in yet another way. It will be the very first time in my life that I have actually "entertained" at Tioga in a formal way. The only occasions Adeline ever used the dining room were Thanksgiving and Christmas, or sometimes for club, back in the days when she still took part in such activities, in the 1920s and 1930s.

As for my father, he entertained lavishly and frequently, and like so much of Tioga, this particular room has a manly feel—the distinctive handprint of Colonel Anthony Wayne Hamilton. I thought of this the moment I stepped in this morning. Mrs. Christian and Emma Linda had already opened the hot air register and set the table—three place settings on a table which, if the three leaves were inserted, could comfortably seat fourteen. Fresh lemon polish scented the wood, and I heard voices through the kitchen door. Gray daylight was seeping through the western windows, and so the dining room looked forlorn with its heavy shadows. But the moment I turned the switch for the chandelier, the lights in the rose-colored globes drove the shadows back into their nooks and crannies, giving the room an inviting air. Tomorrow with the candelabras lit, and an autumnal centerpiece on the table, the room will be even more cheerful. And I intend to build a fire in the grate.

I have just realized that I have contradicted myself. I said that this is a manly room, but there isn't a whole lot that's manly about rose-colored globes and such.

When I say "manly" I mean things like the large oil above the credenza painted by Edgar Bridgman, a local artist who was an old man when I was a boy. The work, in a heavy gilt frame, shows pioneers hunting a stag with muskets, in what I presume is some corner of the Old Forest. A lone Indian peeks from behind a tree—and heaven only knows what's going through that poor devil's mind. I have considered moving the Bridgman into the library where I might enjoy it every day, but the painting has hung in the dining room since 1900, and this is, after all, Tioga, an unchanging little sliver of the world. And so I am sure the Bridgman will hang where it has until I am dead and gone and the auctioneers cart things out onto the lawn for the Big Sale. I also like the bronze on the credenza. I am not sure where my father came up with this particular sculpture. It is a rather gruesome depiction of a wolf bringing down a stag. As a boy, I used to run my fingers over the wolf's bared left fang that has not yet sunken into the stag's throat, and I did so again this morning, feeling its sharpness on the tip of my finger. Even the dark walnut chairs and table have a manly appearance, with their legs turning into eagle talons clutching a globe. Adeline and I used to play beneath that table, pretending it was a great dragon that would whirl us off to magical lands like Camelot, Medieval France, and Arabia. As I took a long look at myself in the gilt-framed mirror above the fireplace, I realized that I am about the only thing in this room that has changed in the past sixty-three years. The haughty but reserved boy with the corn silk hair, who drove Mitzy to the senior dance in an Oldsmobile coupe, is, of course, no more, but at least tomorrow she will see an old man who has kept himself trim, and who is blessed with a full head of hair—though it turned gray years ago.

As for Thanksgiving of 1923, it was quite an affair.

I remember when the plump turkey arrived for the First Lady in its cage at the depot. It was a gift from the girls of the Conservatory of Music down in Cincinnati, where Mrs. Harding studied piano during her girlhood days. The RKO men were on hand to record the bird's arrival for the newsreels. That moment was, by the way, my last appearance on the silver screen—and there I was, in the auspicious company of a turkey. (During the Front Porch Campaign, I could sometimes catch a fleeting glimpse of myself in the newsreels, my face often partially hidden by layers of men who stood listening to the Senator's remarks or applauding them. I remember once in the summer of 1920, when Lucy and I went to the movies, we saw yours truly leaning out from behind a shoulder. I looked directly into the camera, and then vanished behind the crowd again—though I swore at the time and still swear that I had absolutely no awareness of having done so.)

Anyway, in my last "Hollywood appearance" I was seen walking across the depot parking lot and waving to the camera in those hyperfast movements of the old newsreels. The caption read something like, "A resident welcomes Mrs. Harding's Thanksgiving turkey to Marion." One of my laborers carried Tom Turkey in his cage. He set him on the back of the truck; I jumped in behind the wheel, gave a final wave to the nation's moviegoers, and drove off—not exactly into the sunset, but certainly out of the picture.

I think we were all a little worried that what was supposed to be a happy occasion might turn into a dreary one. After all, the President had been dead for only fourteen or fifteen weeks and various members of his Administration were already under investigation. Not to mention the fact that the rumor mill was churning, and by then what the rumorists were saying had gone from bad to worse.

But in spite of all that, Mrs. Harding seemed bound and determined not to be a depressing presence for any of us. She even told several of what she thought were her husband's favorite jokes—though having known Mr. Harding, I seriously doubt she had ever heard a single one of his true favorites. But then again, I probably hadn't either.

Anyway, a good time was had by all, though I must say that the dinner did have its serious moments—and one or two surprises.

For instance, I distinctly remember that the First Lady herself, who seemed to have been striving for jollity, suddenly turned our little gathering towards a more serious frame of mind. I had done the honors of carving the bird, which sat on its silver tray encircled by shiny red apples and fresh sprigs of greenery—parsley, mint, and such—and we were a little ways into the feast laid before us. Our plates were overflowing with all the delectables of the day—mashed potatoes (a favorite of Mrs. Harding's), cranberry-apple stuffing, creamed onions, buttered snow peas, yam pudding, and a half-dozen other harvest favorites—many of which will indeed make their appearance tomorrow. Prohibition did nothing to stop us from enjoying wine, for my late father's one real hobby was winemaking. He also made sure that Tioga's cellar was well stocked with cases and cases of various liquors and wines before the Volstead Act took effect. On that particular Thanksgiving, we enjoyed an unusually dry Riesling from the Lonz vineyards, up at Lake Erie. Two bottles stood before us on their sterling servers.

After Mrs. Harding had told maybe one or two too many of the President's jokes and after the polite laughter had fallen off, her own gaiety seemed to turn reflective. She was sitting at the head of the table, and I can still see her in her chair—her appetite was not great—and pausing thoughtfully while our forks and knives clicked away. Lucy said, "The President had such a wonderful sense of humor, and he was so sweet, always so kind to the little ones."

"And animals too," Adeline said. "He loved dogs. I still remember tears in his eyes when—Flossie, what was the name of that old hound, the one people said Mr. Crawford poisoned?"

Mr. Crawford, long dead by then, was Mr. Harding's newspaper competitor way back in the early days of the *Star*. "Boone," the First Lady said quietly, "Ol' Boone."

"Yes of course, Boone. Mr. Harding was glum for weeks after that old hound died." And then my sister added, "It's a wonderful man who loves children and dogs."

Reverend Swank said, "Not to mention all creatures great and small, as the Psalmist sings. We all know the story of when young Warren saw the farmer coming along down Center Street in his wagon, clippity-clop, with doves stuffed in their cage so tight they couldn't move. Warren hailed the farmer, bought the whole lot, and paid a pretty penny too, they say, and then he set them free. Now that's a man for you, a true, well-rounded man! Warren was never a brawler, never weak in his manhood, never a man pretending or making a show of manly strength."

Dr. Sawyer said, "I can tell you for a fact, he loved horses. I could tell you a horse story or two about Warren Harding." Dr. Sawyer leaned forward, holding his fork for emphasis, "Warren was as good as an Indian with horses."

"Remember the summer of 1895?" Reverend Swank asked. "Lucy and Trey and Adeline wouldn't, of course, but I think the rest of us do. Hottest on record, and some fellow left his horse tied to a post in the hot sun, the poor thing fell dead, that was over by the Kerr House. Let me tell you, when Mr. Harding found out, he went on the warpath! Outraged, he was! Started a campaign in the *Star* and got the Town Council to pass a law against leaving horses standing in the sun on summer days. Or without a trough nearby." The good Reverend paused in respectful reflection, "Why, even the doves and horses owe Warren Harding a debt of gratitude."

Adeline said, "We should carry on the President's work and get them to start arresting those hillbillies on the west-side who leave their dogs out all night in winter. Some have doghouses, true, but where's the straw? Where's the hide covering the door? As far as I'm concerned, those hicks are criminals. They think if you can do it in south Tennessee then you can do it in mid Ohio. Hillbillies and hicks, the lot of them."

Just then, young Mrs. Christian ever so quietly came through the door—as if she preferred not to be seen—bearing a pitcher to refill our water goblets. But the moment she entered the room, Adeline said, "Here she is! Here's the young lady we owe this day to!" We greeted Mrs. Christian with a little chorus of applause and compliments. She stood blushing by the credenza, almost, it seemed, trying to hide behind it. She had on a crisp new uniform, black with white frills, and she had managed to find time that morning to "do" her hair.

Dr. Sawyer said, "I'm at a loss, young lady, as to how such a pretty little thing like you could put together such a lavish feast single-handed."

"Oh, but Miss Hamilton helped me. She showed me how."

"Scarcely at all," Adeline said, "It was all Evelyn. You've done beautifully, dear. None of this would have happened without you. You're a Godsend, and we thank you."

We each complimented the cook as she moved around the table with her pitcher. When she came to my place, I took her hand lightly in mine and said, "A blue-ribbon job, Mrs. Christian, you could win first place at the County Fair with a dinner like this."

"State fair," Mrs. Sawyer said.

I added, "Colonel Hamilton would be proud of you."

"That he would be," Lucy said. "Trey's dad loved Thanksgiving. Trey's and Adeline's. Loved the holiday times, didn't he Trey?"

"He did." I glanced at Adeline. A touch of sadness had come into her eyes. I winked at her. My "little" sister looked extraordinarily beautiful with her abundant auburn hair sort of folded in layers atop her head, like a Gibson girl, but also like the photograph of my mother, in Adeline's room. For this occasion she wore Mother's cameo and cameo earrings, and Adeline's silk dress—probably fitted in Cincinnati—seemed to be many colors woven into a base hue of gold, like a summer sunset over Lake Erie.

Mrs. Christian quietly slipped back into the kitchen, and after she did so, Adeline whispered, "Tomorrow Evelyn's going to get a bonus in her envelope, and I'm going to give her the whole afternoon off to go downtown and spend it. On herself. She deserves it. I saw the prettiest kid gloves in Uhler's the other day. Has pearls right here." She touched the top of her hand. "Well, I bought those for her, too. She'll adore them."

Mrs. Harding was sitting back in her chair again, looking at the candles, while the rest of us were busy with the feast. Images of little flames were shining on her spectacles. I said, "A penny for your thoughts, Mrs. Harding."

She laughed and picked up her fork. "Oh, Trey, dear, my thoughts are never so valuable as that." Whenever the First Lady spoke, others fell silent. "I was just thinking—thinking how happy I am to be with all of you, and how blessed I am to have such good friends. And yes, I was thinking of the President, too."

"Oh," Lucy said, "if only Mr. Harding could be here. If only!"

"No," Mrs. Harding said, "That's not what I was thinking, dear. I was thinking how it's best that Warren *isn't* here. How it's best that he's gone."

For some reason, the instant the First Lady said those rather remarkable words, I glanced across the table. Almost identical expressions crossed both Dr. Sawyer's face and Adeline's. Both sort of glanced at Mrs. Harding from under their eyebrows, studied her for a moment, and then looked back at their plates, without comment. But then again what is there to say when a widow says that it is best that her beloved husband is dead?

Mrs. Harding said. "Oh, rest assured, I miss Warren. How could I not after thirty years? I miss him more than words can say, but some things happen for the best. Like Momma used to say, 'Everything happens in its own sweet time and place.'" She paused and looked 'round at our faces in the candlelight, and added, "Oh, we had such fun, Warren and me. Such great fun. I often think to myself, what have I got to complain of? And the answer is: *nothin'*. I got nothin' in the world to complain of. My life outran my youthful dreams. For most folks, it's very much the other way around. Back through all those long years when Amos—Daddy—wouldn't speak to us, to Warren and me 'cause I'd married him, back when Warren was first dabbling in politics, I used to think to myself how sweet it would be if someday he actually *did* become President. Yes, I did! Truly I did, believe me! 'Course I never thought for a moment it would actually happen. I thought, 'That would teach Daddy a good lesson!' And then, voilà! Next thing I know, things were happening. Warren's the Senator from Ohio, and next we're riding on the rails to the White House. Alas, Daddy was already dead. Missed it by seven years. Only seven years! What a disappointment! 'Course we reconciled long before he died, but still, what beautiful vindication it would be for Amos to have lived to see it all! To have it smack him in the face! I suppose deep inside, I've never forgiven Daddy. As far as I'm concerned, he committed two great crimes in his life: taking so long to accept Warren and then dying seven years too soon."

Mrs. Harding took a sip of wine. As she did, I noticed that her glass could use a refill. I took the bottle of Riesling from its server and moved to replenish it, but Dr. Sawyer shot me such an emphatic look, that I simply diverted the swing of my arm and added a little wine to Lucy's nearly full glass—as if that had been my intention all along. Mrs. Harding was sitting to the right of me, and Lucy to the left, so obviously this was a ridiculous ruse. The First Lady was never one to stand on ceremony, at least not in the private company of good friends. She said, "Trey, dear—" But the moment she said my name I suppose she remembered whose house she was in. She said, "Adeline, are these the only bottles of wine you have in this house?"

"Goodness no, Flossie, Daddy has enough in the cellar for an army."

"That's what I thought. In that case—" She held out her glass.

Dr. Sawyer said, "Florence, may I remind you of your medical restrictions?"

"You may not. Tomorrow, yes, today no." And there was a chorus of laughter as I poured—a chorus in which Dr. Sawyer disdained to participate, though he did smile, amused. I topped off everyone's wine, raised my glass, and said, "To the President!"

"To the President!"

Then the First Lady said, "Trey, do you know where Warren and I wanted to spend our honeymoon? We went to the Mackinaw Straits, but that's not where we *really* wanted to go."

I allowed that I did not.

"Adeline, you know, don't you, dear?"

"If memory serves me correctly, then I think you once told me Alaska."

"Memory serves you very correctly. Yes, Alaska!"

Lucy said, "Come to think of it, I think I read something about that last summer, in *Harper's*, or one of those magazines. But Mrs. Harding, Alaska? Such a cold and frightful place, all wilderness and snow and wild beasts."

"We'd have gone in July, dear, of course. The month we were married in, not January. It's not so cold then, not like people think, and it's more enchanting than frightful. Like Yellowstone, only more—more something."

"Celestial," the Reverend said.

"Well, not my sort of word, Reverend Swank, but you're right. You've got the right idea. But it was too far, too rigorous in those days just to get there, but Warren and I both, we wanted to go. And finally we made it. Finally, we were there. But I keep thinking, isn't it odd? We'd wanted to go there on our honeymoon, but instead it turned out to be the very last journey of our lives, an epic journey. 'Course I tried to twist Adeline's arm to get her to come with us, when she was out in Washington in July, and then again in Columbus on our fateful trip westward, but she didn't. In retrospect, it was best that she declined."

For a moment I did not catch that, and then I did. Like everyone in Marion, I knew that Adeline had visited the Hardings at the White House, back in early July. In fact, the First Lady had summoned her to Washington. They had also gone to "Friendship"—Ned and Evelyn McLean's estate in Virginia —for the Fourth.

But I knew absolutely nothing about the second encounter, the one in Columbus, which was a bit odd. If Adeline had lunch around the corner with one of her school friends, she mentioned it to me. And yet she had gone to Columbus to see the President of the United States and the First Lady! But did not say a word about it!?

"In Columbus?" I said after a bewildered moment. "On the way westward?"

Usually I am quite discreet and do not inquire into other people's affairs, but I suppose I was taken aback and simply forgot myself. My puzzlement was compounded by the fact that Adeline was now turning nearly the color of the beets in her saucer, or so I imagine her now.

Mrs. Harding answered for Adeline. "Why yes, didn't she tell you? We had lunch aboard the *Superb*, when the train made a coaling stop in Columbus. I told Adeline to pack her bags and bring them along, but she arrived empty-handed. Well, almost so, she did stop by our place and pick a lovely bouquet from my garden, a bit of home for us to carry westward." Mrs. Harding paused, "Why, I told her to bring you folks along too."

(I should tell you that the *Superb* was the Hardings' palace car on the Presidential Express. The *Superb* became a hearse when it bore Mr. Harding's coffin back to Washington after his death at the Palace Hotel in San Francisco, and then back to Marion for burial, or rather committal.)

Anyway, by now I was collecting my wits, not wishing to pry further. "Oh, yes, of course." I lied, "Addy did mention something about that, I believe. What on earth was I thinking?" Dr. Sawyer's keen little eyes were leveled at me.

Adeline said, "Why, Trey, actually I may have forgotten to mention it. I don't remember. After all, I was only there for an hour or so. I felt bad that you and Lucy—that I hadn't—" Her words trailed off.

Mrs. Harding's eyes were on Adeline and a little smile flickered across her lips. Perhaps it was my imagination, but I sensed something vindictive. I believe she knew very well that she had just "spilled the beans."

Mrs. Harding could sometimes take delight in such things.

"It hardly matters," I said. "I forget to mention things all the time. Lucy forgets too, sometimes. We all do." I glanced at my wife. She had this look in her eye like she was bewildered (and perhaps annoyed) by my sister—yet again!

Adeline said, "Trey, you were busy that day with survey teams along the Heights. I didn't think you'd be able to make it, and unfortunately, I neglected to ask. My faux pas."

Lucy sucked in her breath.

"Not at all," I said. "If it was back in July, then it would have been out of the question, impossible for me to get away."

Mrs. Harding said, "One way or another, it was ironic that Warren's and my hoped-for honeymoon became his death trip. But of course when you think of it, Warren was walking-talking irony. Irony made flesh and blood. His whole life was one long irony, from beginning to end. Irony that his friends put him where he was, and irony that his friends put him where he is."

Flossie paused, and let that subtle little bombshell blow us to bits. Quite frankly, I can be a bit slow sometimes, and for the second time in a row, I initially didn't catch the gist of her words, no doubt because I was still recovering from the embarrassment I had unintentionally imposed upon my sister. A palpable silence replaced the sound of clicking utensils.

My wife was looking at the First Lady, who was enjoying her mashed potatoes, and no doubt the effect of her words. Lucy said, "Mrs. Harding?"

"Yes, dear?"

"What do you mean—his friends put him where he was and they put him where he *is*?"

"Why, Lucy, I mean they put him in the White House, and then they put him in his grave. Just that. What did you think I meant?"

What I can only describe as a "roaring silence" filled the room. I glanced across the table at Dr. Sawyer who, as I have stated before, was the subject of unfortunate rumors—like the First Lady herself—regarding the President's rather sudden death. Our former Surgeon General seemed not to have heard a thing, and was seemingly engrossed with some eye-catching sliver of food he was probing with his knife.

"I'm sure his friends didn't intend to put him in his grave, mind you, but they did. They put him there and it's best that he's gone." She gave a sad smile, "And, unfortunately, he's not with us today, at this lovely dinner."

Everyone in the room—in fact nearly every man, woman, and child in Marion, Ohio—had worked very, very hard to put Mr. Harding in the White House. But we had certainly *not* worked to put him in his grave.

As was her wont, Mrs. Harding, seemingly inadvertently, had knocked everyone flat. This feat would be followed, as usual, by her own sudden realization that she had done so. This in turn would be followed by the further protestation that she had not meant to say any such thing. Or had meant to say it in another way.

Now, with the feat accomplished, it was high time to pick everyone up and dust them off—by saying what she had "really" intended to say. Thus she said, "Of course, not for a minute do I mean any of his Marion friends. Above all, no one in this room. Certainly not. Each and every one of you was among the very best friends Warren Harding ever had. Everyone in Marion is 100 percent above reproach. Including the ones who went to Washington with us. It's the likes of Forbes and Fall and Jess Smith that I'm talking about. That gang of thieves. Why, dear Dr. Sawyer here, he's the one that found out about that crook, Charlie Forbes, and all his dirty dealings. Doc's the one informed the President about what was up."

I think we all breathed a little more easily after that.

"That's right!" Dr. Sawyer said. "I caught the rascal red-handed! And told Warren about it too—went straight to the White House and demanded to see the President. Why, I was afraid he was going to have a stroke right then and there, when I told him. But he didn't. It came later."

Mrs. Harding said, "That was the beginning of his troubles. I remember he didn't sleep that night, or for many a night thereafter. The Veterans Bureau, one of his best greatest accomplishments, corrupted, and by the likes of Charlie Forbes. And I'm sorry to say that I'm afraid dear ol' Harry had his fingers in a few pies too. Now I know, Warren loved Harry Daugherty like a brother, in fact, I'd say even more than he loved his brother, but he went to his grave realizing that Harry'd been on the take, that he'd been involved in shenanigans too. And to think he's *still* the Attorney General. We'll see how long Cal Coolidge keeps him! They were all on the take. Every one of them! They're the ones that put Warren in his grave. Apoplexy, yes, but apoplexy brought on by the weight of his friends' betrayals. Knowing what they'd done to him, and to his Administration, that's what killed him, believe me."

She paused, "But I'm proud to say that in spite of them, it was still a great Administration."

"Here, here!" I said—for even then I knew in my mind and heart the scope of the President's accomplishments. I raised my wine glass. "To the great Harding Administration."

And everyone at that table raised their glass and said in unison, "To the great Harding Administration."

After we savored the enthusiasm of those words, Mrs. Harding said softly, "Thank you, Trey. Thank you, my dear, good friends. Warren's dear, good friends."

She sat thoughtful for a long moment, so too did we. I noticed that the candles had burned low.

The aroma of brewing coffee seeped in from the kitchen.

Mrs. Harding said, as if an afterthought, "I know beyond any doubt that when they sweep away the dirt left by the betrayers, they'll see plain and simple that Warren G. Harding was a splendid President. Not just our best-loved President, but also one of the most effective, considering what little time he had allotted to him. History will back me up on that one, rest assured."

"Here, here!" I said.

The First Lady continued, "Warren was great in life, and now he becomes magnificent in death."

Looking back now after forty years, I admit that I am once again mystified as to why Adeline never mentioned that final luncheon with the Hardings. And when I say "never" I mean *never*—for she went to her grave without ever speaking of the issue.

In my thoughts I can hear Lucy saying, "Well, you didn't either, Trey. You didn't *ask* her."

And that is quite true. But I have never made it my business to go prying into other people's affairs, including and especially my sister's.

The reason I found, and find, the whole thing exasperating is simply because that luncheon aboard the *Superb*—and more specifically, my sister's needless secrecy about it—eventually caused, in a roundabout way, her good name to be drawn into the rumor mill regarding the President's death. Now I admit that, no doubt, our local gossips would have seized upon that last encounter one way or another, but Adeline's concealment caused the "secret luncheon" to become, for the rumorists, a most intriguing and significant affair. It certainly set their tongues a-wagging. While news of the encounter was first making its way around Marion, in late 1923, folks here (and indeed Americans everywhere) were still trying to make sense of the President's "strange and sudden demise" as well as things like the First Lady refusing an autopsy, and her personally sitting in a chair all night guarding the room where the embalmers were doing their work at the Palace Hotel. Things of that sort were reported in every newspaper in the land, and I believe you will agree that they have an irregular ring. Needless to say, folks in Marion were especially affected by President Harding's death, and Adeline's faux pas became part of the intricate web of rumor and innuendo spun by the odd circumstances surrounding his demise.

It seems rather obvious that Adeline's entanglement in that web began in the dining room at Tioga on Thanksgiving Day, 1923. I can just imagine Mandy Sawyer mentioning to someone or other that Adeline Hamilton went down to Columbus for a luncheon engagement with the President and First Lady aboard the *Superb*, on its fateful journey westward, and for whatever reason, Miss Hamilton kept that last luncheon a Big Secret, not even mentioning it to her own brother, to whom she was devoted and told everything. Well, Adeline and I may have been devoted to each other, but I assure you she most certainly did *not* tell me everything (nor did I ever expect her to).

I realized this in various ways when I moved back to Tioga after her death and found a lifetime of her letters and mementos. I should add that Reverend Swank also probably mentioned that Thanksgiving conversation to someone, and knowing Marion, that someone surely mentioned it to someone else, and so forth and so on.

And I assure you, my own Lucy could be a bit of a gossip too, especially during her younger years. In fact, I have no doubt whatsoever that she repeated it to her mother and sisters, and you can bet your bottom dollar that those women did not keep mum about it, and so the rumor spread itself, thus making my own wife one of the progenitors of the hearsay.

When the rumormongers heard about the luncheon, they were more than happy to come up with their own theory as to why Adeline had not extended the Hardings' invitation to Lucy and me. My sister had supposedly gone alone to Columbus because she was on a mission to deliver poison into the hands of the First Lady, and she wanted to do so as secretly and as subtly as possible, without drawing her brother into the conspiracy, even in the most marginal way.

The same imaginative folks who had once whispered that Adeline was one of the President's mistresses, now had her as a conspirator in his putative assassination, along with Mrs. Harding of course, and the Surgeon General.

So you are now asking yourself: Why would Dr. Sawyer have needed help gaining access to a poison of some kind, a medication perhaps, potent enough to kill the President, but subtle enough to conceal itself behind other symptoms?

No doubt you are likewise asking yourself: If Adeline used the luncheon as an occasion for the delivery of poison to Mrs. Harding, then why on earth would the First Lady go blabbing about it in front of everyone at Thanksgiving dinner?

My point exactly!

These are commonsense inquiries that rumormongers do not bother to pursue simply because such inquiries instantly blow their pet theories right out of the water.

As I mentioned just a few moments ago, I am afraid that my own wife may have been one of the unintentional progenitors of the rumors. In fact, on that Thanksgiving evening at Tioga, the instant we pulled out of the carriage drive, Lucy started blabbing about our missed luncheon.

At that time we had a sporty little yellow and black Lincoln four-seater coupe, which my in-laws—who were forever talking about automobiles— had nicknamed the "Yellow Jacket." Of course I had known fully well— even while we were still seated at the dinner table at Tioga—that the instant we were clear of Adeline's earshot, Lucy would start harping. And sure enough, we had no more than pulled onto Mount Vernon Avenue when she said, "So, Trey, what do you think of Adeline's luncheon with the Hardings?"

I shrugged my shoulders and pretended as if it puzzled me far less than it really did. "What's to think? It was just a luncheon. She wasn't obliged to mention it, anymore than the Hardings were obliged to invite us."

As I feigned concentration on shifting the gears, I could feel Lucy's eyes on me in the darkness. "But they *did* invite us, and we never heard a word about it. Until today. Not that I mind of course, not really. It's just that it's a little odd, that's all." Again, I could feel Lucy watching me. "You think it's odd, too, Trey. I can tell. How could you not? If it had been anyone but Adeline who did that—well, I don't know what you'd think, or do. I suppose quietly bide your time, and then get even someday. But it was Adeline. And for your information, a luncheon with the President of the United States and First Lady is hardly 'just a luncheon.'"

"I couldn't have made it anyway. Addy knew that."

"You *would* have made it anyway, and you know that. A luncheon aboard the *Superb*! With President and Mrs. Harding! Right down in Columbus! Don't lie to yourself. You would've gone all the way to Tennessee for that, or at least Kentucky, and you know it. And I certainly would have enjoyed it too. It would've been special, especially now, in light of the circumstances."

Her entire air—one of annoyance and disappointment—made it seem as if Adeline's lapse had somehow been my fault. "Besides," she added, "I've never in my life been in a real palace car."

I gave a little laugh. I had once found such naïve admissions charming, but after we were married for a time, they became tedious and all too often took on a grousing sort of ring.

"'A real palace car!'" I said, mocking her words. "If it's any comfort to you, I can assure you that you haven't missed a thing. They're just like a fancy hotel suite, only long and skinny, and as far as palace cars go, the *Superb* is nothing extraordinary. Either Rockefeller or Mr. Ford would throw his baggage in it." I paused, and then added, "You've slept in the White House, in the Lincoln Bedroom. What more do you want?"

"Oh, it wasn't that, Trey. Not really. It's just that it's—well, it's almost like Adeline's hiding something, that's all. 'Course she always is, I think. Why, more than that, you could tell she was hiding something. We weren't supposed to know! And if we weren't supposed to know then no one was. But why? That's the puzzle that puzzles me. Why the big secret?"

"The big secret? What big secret? Hiding what?"

"Well, that's what I'd like to know. But if she isn't hiding something, then why on earth didn't she tell us about the luncheon? Simple as that. You don't have to be Professor Einstein to . . ."

"She told us why. She forgot."

"Oh, Tristan, for heaven's sake—please! I don't believe that and neither do you, and I'm not sure why you're pretending like you do."

She waited a long moment for a reply, but she did not get one. When Lucy realized I was going to give her the silent treatment, she sighed and said, "Oh, Trey, here it is Thanksgiving night, and we're sniping again." In a defeated tone, she added, "Okay, I guess it's not so important after all."

"You're quite right, Lucy; it isn't. In fact, it's of no importance whatsoever. Adeline forgot. Period. End of the matter. Nothing more need be said about it. Ever."

II

Mrs. Harding Burns the President's Papers

WHEN THE FIRST LADY moved back to Marion in September of 1923, she sent ahead many of the things she and her husband accumulated during their Washington years. There were more of these articles than you might imagine, from furniture to clothes to ceremonial swords and even a bona fide totem pole. The little press bungalow was filled nearly to the ceiling. At that time the Millard Hunt family was renting the Harding home. They offered to vacate so that the First Lady could return to her own house, but for whatever reason, she was not interested. They also offered the use of their (Mrs. Harding's) basement and attic, and she stored a few boxes there, but the Hunts were outsiders, and so I do not think she completely trusted them. Thus the remainder of her goods went to Tioga, into Adeline's basement, which was always dry, and into the groom's quarters above the carriage house where the caretaker, Mr. McDuffy, once lived. Those items remained in storage for about three years, until well after Mrs. Harding's death and the execution of her will. The possessions and mementos eventually became the core collection of what is now the Harding Home and Museum. The Harding Commemorative Society oversees both the house and the tomb, of which, as I believe I earlier indicated, I am lifetime president.

The Presidential papers were among the "possessions" that Mrs. Harding brought to Marion, but to a large extent these did not go into storage, they went up in smoke.

I thought at the time and still think that this was a highly irregular and unfortunate action on her part. I have often wondered if such a deed ever happened before in the annals of the American Presidency. Indeed, I looked into it once, as best I could at our local Carnegie Public Library, but I found nothing on the subject. Frankly, I did not really know how to go about looking it up, and I certainly did not want to ask the librarian for help regarding an issue that still raises eyebrows around here. Worst of all, it is an issue that unfairly conjures mention of my name. At any rate, I certainly cannot imagine such a thing happening today. Can you picture, for instance, Jacqueline Kennedy hauling her husband's papers off to Hyannis Port—or wherever she decides to raise her little ones—and then working her way through them, before the fireplace?

Up in smoke go the files marked "Bay of Pigs."

Same with the files containing whatever secret volatile threats (no matter how effective they may have been) regarding the Cuban Missile Crisis.

Into the flames go the papers that have to do with the steel strike, and the classified records regarding the confrontations the President and Bobby Kennedy had with Governor Wallace, that madman. And of course, in this little supposition, the same fate would await other papers—all for the most arbitrary of reasons.

It is a notion rather hard to conceive. But that is exactly what Mrs. Harding did with her husband's papers.

I have always taken this a bit personally simply because the same rumormongers who linked Adeline's name to the President's death, somehow also got their wires crossed on this one, and linked my name to the burning of his papers.

I wish to state here and now, on my honor, that this is absolutely absurd.

If anything, I should be given some measure of credit for getting the First Lady, finally, to stop her destruction.

My involvement with the Harding Presidential Papers began with a simple favor that I did for the First Lady. I believe you will recall that, as the proprietor of Colonel Hamilton & Son, I had trucks at my disposal. Thus upon Mrs. Harding's return from Washington, I took responsibility for transporting her goods from the depot to their storage places. I suppose I should point out that this was not a favor in the strictest sense. The Government was, in fact, going to compensate me for the cost, but by the same token, Colonel Hamilton & Son was not in the moving business. Besides, the economy was flourishing in the fall of 1923, and I probably had a dozen or more families waiting for their new homes to be finished—and the building season was fast fading. Not to mention the fact that I had a long list of people who wanted additions, or needed this or that renovation or repair. And of course many of them wanted the work done yesterday. I will also add that I did not charge the Government a single red cent above my own cost, which is to say that my men got their wages, but my company did not show a profit that day.

Like her husband, Mrs. Harding preferred doing business with friends—the closer the better—and she knew that I would be especially vigilant with her goods.

Thus she asked me to do the job, and I was happy to oblige.

I was a little surprised when, the night before, I received a call from George Christian—who still held his title as the White House Chief of Staff—telling me that he would meet us at the train depot the next morning. I suppose that should have been my clue that there was going to be more to the move than just furniture, clothes, souvenirs, and the sort of gifts that visiting dignitaries give to Presidents.

I was doubly surprised the next morning—which arrived crisply cool and sunny—when we arrived at the depot and there too stood Mrs. Harding's redheaded personal assistant, looking rather dashing if a bit out of place in his Army uniform. Most people called (and still call) this fellow "Major," but I shall call him Rusty Brown, a suitable appellation, and one that does not step on his touchy toes in terms of privacy. He was a decorated veteran from the Great War—a fact that he never quite got over. His father was a policeman, and Rusty himself is now a retired policeman. I might add that for years I drove around town with utmost care, not so much for the sake of obeying every traffic law on the books, but for the sake of not giving Rusty the pleasure of ticketing me.

He never even got to write a parking ticket on me.

Anyway, everyone in Marion of a certain age knows exactly who I am talking about. If Rusty ever wants to step forward and tell his side of the Harding story, especially regarding the papers, then that is his business.

I am not going to do it for him, at least not in any detail. I might add though that part of his story may soon be told for him, whether he likes it or not. My lawyer tells me that that unscrupulous historian, the one who was leaning on my doorbell last month, apparently knows all about the papers, and knows a lot about Rusty—who, I am told, slammed the door in the fellow's face. I have no idea exactly what was or was not said to our new Herodotus in the privacy of certain other people's homes, but I have heard that in the end he was far less interested in those lost documents (or in anything else, for that matter) than he was in the juicy love letters we gave him to keep his hands busy. I say again with relish, what he failed to realize is that, when the time comes, he will face a restraining order on the use or publication of those letters. Anyway, the fellow took the bait, thinking that he had his hands on gold—which of course he did, but then again he did not.

Anyway, as I started to say, Rusty and the First Lady had tagged each crate, trunk, piece of furniture, or what-have-you in terms of its destination, be it Tioga, Home, Press (the bungalow), or Star—and George had already told me that soldiers from this or that regiment out in Washington had been kind enough to transport the things from the White House to the baggage car at Washington's Union Station. A couple of the fellows, I was told, were from the Army Corps of Engineers. The car was then hauled to Ohio and dropped in Marion by the mail train. When I arrived at the depot on that September morning, it was parked on the siding near the locomotive water tower. The car was obviously brand new, gleaming with fresh black paint and shining brass. I had a feeling that it had yet to see a rainy day.

Rusty carried the keys, and after he unhitched the padlocks, we rolled that heavy metal door aside and the three of us climbed in, along with one of my foremen and a couple of the men I brought. The inside of the car was so dark and the morning was so brilliant that my eyes had to adjust. A narrow aisle ran in each direction from the middle of the car to the cavern-like gloom of its ends. The air inside was chillier than the morning air outside, and it had the faint tang of raw wood and straw from the packing crates. The boys who loaded the Hardings' belongings had done a splendid job—obviously a labor of love and respect for the First Lady, for she had always been very kind to the soldiers. Everything was neat as a pin, as if that car had not traveled a single mile, much less several hundred. The contents were all interlocked and stacked ten or twelve feet high in places, bundled into sections with net-walls of heavy rope, the kind they use to keep things from flying about.

A silence fell over us as we passed through that catacomb of worldly goods.

I thought of that sad August day when the Presidential train, draped in purple, pulled onto these very same tracks, bearing the President home for the last time. And I thought of that jubilant, victorious morning in early March of '21 when the Hardings' train pulled away—from this same now-desolate, weed-choked siding—on their way to the Inauguration. Lucy and I, and my father and Adeline, were also aboard. So too were Rusty and George.

My foreman and the other fellows were not part of that circle, but they too had known Mr. Harding, and so I am sure that each of us had our private thoughts and recollections as we moved quietly among the artifacts of his tragic tenure in Washington. It was just a railroad baggage car, but the unearthly feeling of a tomb permeated its shadows. I saw wooden crates stacked upon wooden crates, and more steamer trunks than I could count, some looking like coffins. Carpets rolled up and tied with hemp were stacked on top of things, and here and there the polished glint of a table leg or a chair back showed beneath its protective coverings. An eagle's face, part of what was evidently a totem pole, peeked through the folds of an army blanket. It all reminded me of the tantalizing pictures coming that year out of Valley of the Kings. I suppose I put an end to the collective solemnity when I said to Rusty, "So where are you hiding King Tut?"

No doubt my little witticism falls rather flat today, but it brought appreciative laughter at the time, and a needed change of mood.

A moment or so after making my witty remark, I reached the shadowy end of the car. I was puzzled to see in the shadows a massive wall of wooden crates stacked one atop the other. Each crate was about ten feet long, and was the width and height of a standard filing cabinet. There were about thirty of them, snugly bound against the front of the car with ropes. By then one of the fellows had climbed the ladder on the outside of the baggage car, where the wheel locks are, and he opened the small square aperture that emits air and daylight. Thus I could now plainly see through the shadows that the crates were stuffed with thousands upon thousands of papers—far more than any ordinary human being could possibly accumulate in a lifetime. For some reason the crates gave me a funny feeling, almost as if I were looking upon purloined goods.

Rusty said, "I'm afraid they're going to be mighty heavy."

I don't think I answered him.

I walked forward and looked at one of the tags dangling from the corner of a crate. The word "Star" was scrawled on it in grease pencil, in Mrs. Harding's distinctive hand. The same word was written on the other tags. I became aware that George and Rusty were watching me, and it seemed that they were watching me rather intently. Finally I said, "What is this?"

Rusty answered, matter-of-factly, maybe even a bit flippantly, "The President's papers."

"The President's papers?" I turned and looked at their shadowed faces. Rusty was staring at me, like a challenge, and George glanced down the moment I turned, and studied the floor. "I should think something like this would stay in Washington." Neither of them answered, and then I added, "I didn't know that presidential papers went to their widows."

Rusty said, "These did. In fact, all of them do, if the widows want them. Mrs. Harding looked into it and made sure that everything was done right."

I had a feeling I was being lied to, though of course I had no way of knowing. "Well, I should think they would have gone to the Archives. Or someplace like that. The Library of Congress, maybe. Besides, what on earth is Mrs. Harding going to do with millions of papers?"

"Actually," Rusty said, "I believe she wants them to go to you, Trey. Or I should say, to your Harding Commemorative Society, for your Museum."

"Ah, well that's a different matter." That part, at least, seemed sensible, though frankly, I had never envisioned the Society as being a repository of the Administration's documents. But I was also puzzled as to why the tags were marked "Star." Granted, there were vacant offices on the second floor, adjacent to Mr. Harding's old editorial office (where the President's father had his doctor's office, before he gave up his practice). But the newspaper and its plant were in the process of being sold, and I knew for a fact that, by year's end, or more likely even sooner, the *Star* would no longer be in the hands of the Harding estate. "So why cart them to the Star Building? Why not Adeline's? She has vast amounts of room in that basement. It makes more sense. The newspaper's being sold. We'll end up having to do this same job all over in a month or two."

My point was obviously very sensible, and I could tell that they were both searching their minds for a reply. George said, "Trey, Mrs. Harding wants them at the *Star*."

Rusty added, "She needs to read through them, and it'll take some time, obviously."

"Read through them! Why, it would take a hundred years to read through them."

"Okay, then she wants to *look* through them." Rusty's tone had a sudden edge to it. "Look, Trey, Mrs. Harding knows what she's doing. If she says she wants them at the *Star*, then she wants them at the *Star*. Who are we to question her?" His words and tone seemed to suggest that I shut up.

I suddenly sensed that Rusty and George knew something that I did not, though at the time I could not imagine what it might be.

What's more, I was outside of their circle. Yes, I may have been the founder and president of the Harding Volunteers, and now of the Harding Commemorative Society—but I had not gone to Washington, and they had.

Nor had I gone to war, and they had.

With these thoughts hounding me anew, and with my annoyance over the thought of moving the crates twice, I simply said to my foreman, who was standing behind them, "Well, I guess they go to the Star Building, so let's get at it."

MRS. HARDING ARRIVED IN MARION about two weeks later, after spending much of August and September at Friendship—Ned and Evelyn McLean's estate in McLean, Virginia. More than a thousand people gathered at the depot for the First Lady's bittersweet homecoming, and the very next day, with Rusty at her side (or rather I should say, at her heels), she climbed those creaky well-worn wooden stairs to the second floor of the Star Building and started going through the President's papers.

She did the same for many days thereafter. Mind you, at that time the only people in Marion who had the slightest idea as to what was actually going on up there were Mrs. Harding and Rusty—though there was a clue, and I think I was the first to discern it.

By then we were into the chilly, rainy weather of autumn, and smoke was rising from chimneys all over Marion. Those were the days when the vast majority of folks still heated with coal. Colonel Hamilton & Son, as I believe I may have mentioned at some point, served as the town's coal dealer. As such, I knew who bought bituminous and who bought anthracite. Most people bought the former because it was cheaper and easier to light. But it also burned with heavy, gray-black smoke. The Star burned bituminous. Back in the years when Mr. Harding was still in Marion, I used to pass by the Star Building on my way to and from work, and I would often see his feet propped on the windowsill while he wrote his editorials on a pad, or looked over copy, or whatever else editors do. On chilly days gray-black smoke would come from the narrow brick chimney at the front of the building, to which his potbellied stove was attached.

Two or three days after the First Lady returned to Marion, Lucy called to say she was preparing chili soup—still a novelty in those days of Poncho Villa—and that I should hop in the car and drive home for lunch. I did just that, and on my way up Center Street, I happened to notice Mrs. Harding's enormous black Packard parked in front of the Star Building. I thought about stopping and inviting her along, but frankly, that would mean inviting Rusty, too, so I did not. As I passed, I glanced up at the second floor window, thinking maybe I could glimpse the back of her white head at the window as she sat at Mr. Harding's desk, sorting through his papers.

But I saw no sign of her, only thick gray-white smoke pouring from the chimney.

I must admit that I instantly had a sick feeling. That smoke was not coming from coal; it was coming from paper—from quite a lot of paper.

Now it is easy to look back and say that it ought to have been 100 percent obvious to me that the President's papers were going up in smoke, but that was not the case. After that initial sick feeling, I reassured myself by thinking that, well, after all, Mr. Harding had three, maybe four tall filing cabinets in his office, and several more in other rooms on the second floor. And as I say, his newspaper was being sold, so I assured myself that Mrs. Harding was no doubt simply doing a little housecleaning.

Besides, Rusty had said that the Harding Commemorative Society was going to become the repository of the Harding Presidential papers.

Foolish me, I took the Major at his word and assumed he meant *all* of the papers.

But I guess I must have suspected something, for during the next several days I made a point of driving past the Star Building during the midday hours, when I knew the First Lady would be there. Each time I drove by, I saw pale smoke pouring from the chimney.

It was in this manner that I came to realize that the presidential papers were, indeed, being incinerated.

I know that you are now expecting me to say that I marched myself right up those stairs, knocked on the door, and used whatever influence I might have wielded with the First Lady to demand that she put that darned fire out.

Alas, initially, I did nothing of the kind, and frankly, I am not wholly sure why.

I certainly thought about it, over and over, both throughout the busy workday, and while I was lying in bed at night, staring at the ceiling. I self-excused my inaction with assurances that doing nothing was doing the right thing. I reminded myself that there were probably close to a million papers up there. And of course there are papers, and then there are papers. I assured myself that many probably should be burnt. And better for Mrs. Harding to do it than for me, for the Commemorative Society. What I mean is that, if you have a million papers churned out of an office, be it a factory or the White House, how can every last one be important? In fact, how can even 50 percent be of much importance?

Hundreds of thousands would be "junk," and it appeared to me that every last paper from the Harding Administration had been saved.

Frankly, I suppose there was yet another reason for my do-nothingness. Simply put, I have to admit that when I was younger I had certain squeamishness when it came to facing women of a certain authoritative disposition and age. (I might add that, for whatever it is worth, the President once told me with a wink and an amused smile that General

Pershing himself was "scared stiff of the Duchess." Thus I consider myself in good company.)

Anyway, initially, the only thing I did was drive by and look up in wonder and growing exasperation at that pale column of smoke rising from the chimney.

That went on, I would say, for five or six days.

Then Indian Summer visited us with its blue skies, warm days, and cool nights. During the daytime, smoke stopped pouring from the town's residential chimneys and windows were thrown open to the last warm breezes of 1923. No doubt you have already gathered the fact that, Marion being Marion, everyone knew that the President's papers were not only in town, but that they had gone to the Star Building. In turn, folks going along East Center Street—like myself—soon noticed that lone column of smoke pouring from a chimney during the now balmy days of Indian Summer.

Thus it began to occur to the town that the President's papers were going up in smoke.

I still remember coming home from work late one Thursday afternoon in October—I recall what day it was simply because Dana Yost and I had just done payroll. When I drove by the Star Building, the Packard was gone and only a leftover smidgen of smoke was wafting from the chimney, which meant that Rusty had already driven the First Lady back to White Oaks Farm. I recall that the day was so pleasant that I had even taken the top off my Lincoln coupe. On outdoor days my arrivals home from work were momentous occasions for our little cocker spaniel, Bomber (whose brother Spats, by the way, was Adeline's dog).

On that particular afternoon, Bomber was waiting out front for me, playing in the leaves with the Thorpe children. As usual, he started barking and doing his little celebratory gig even before I entered the drive.

When I turned in, he ran along and followed me into the garage, right up to the door. After all the pats on the head and scratches behind the ears, I turned and headed towards the house.

Lucy was standing at the back door behind the screen—a sure sign that something was up.

I was still several feet from the door when she said, "Trey, have you heard what's going on?"

I knew instantly what she meant. "No, what's going on?"

"Mrs. Harding's burning the President's papers, that's what." Usually when Lucy met me at the back door, she would hold it wide for me, and give me a kiss as I entered. On this particular day she just stood there, door closed, as if blocking my entrance, as if maybe I ought to do an about-face and rush off and have a word with Mrs. Harding.

"Oh, she is, is she?" I said, "And how do you know that?"

I stood before the lower step, waiting for her to open the door, or at least step aside.

She did neither, so I opened the door myself and stepped in. As I passed by her, I planted a quick kiss on her cheek.

She followed me into the kitchen. "Well, Trey, you don't seem very upset about it. You don't even seem surprised."

"Oh? And when was the last time you saw me upset? When was the last time you saw me surprised?"

"When you had to take the papers to the Star instead of Adeline's."

I greeted Nora, our young Irish house girl. Nora had been trained in England, and as such she was the type of domestic who pretended to hear nothing that was not addressed directly to her. As a consequence, Lucy and I found ourselves saying just about anything in her presence, and I always had a feeling that, what she did not hear, Lucy told her. (I regret to say that Nora O'Brian, who did not have a family, died in February of 1926—an event of profound sorrow in our household, one that utterly devastated Lucy, casting her into a sort of quietness that lasted for more than a year. I buried Nora in the Hamilton family plot because, in a sense, she had no place else to go.)

Anyway, Lucy stood by the counter studying me, as I went to the stove to see what was cooking. "You knew, didn't you, Trey? You knew Mrs. Harding was burning the President's papers. I can tell. And you did nothing."

With my back to her, I took the hot pad and lifted the lid from the roaster and smelled the contents. I could feel Lucy's eyes on me.

After a long moment studying my back, she said, "Even if you really aren't upset, Trey, I would think you'd be at least a little concerned. They *are* the President's papers. And Mrs. Harding is burning them. That's not right. And the Major said the Commemorative Society was going to get them, didn't he? So he lied."

273274275276277278279280282284286288289291293294295297298300301302303304305306307308309311312313314315316317318319320321322323324325326327328329330332333334335336337338339340341342343344345346347348349350351352353354355356357358359360361362363364365366367368369370371372373374375376377378379380381382383384385386387388389390391392393394395396397398399400401402403404405406407408409410411412413414415416417418419420421422423424425426427428429430431432433434435436437438439440441442443444445446447448449450451452453454455456457458459460461462463464465466467468469470471472473474475476477478479480481482483484485486487488489490491492493494495496497498499500501502503504505506507508509510511512513514515516517518519520521522523524525526527528529530531532533534535536537538539540541542543544545546547548549550551552553554555556557558559560561562563564565566567568569570571572573574575576577578579580581582583584585586587588589590591592593594595596597598599600601602603604605606607608609610611612613614615616617618619620621622623624625626627628629630631632633634635636637638639640641642643644645646647648649650651652653654655656657658659660661662663664665666667668669670671672673674675676677678679680681682683684685686687688689690691692693694695696697698699700701702703704705706707708709710711712713714715716717718719720721722723724725726727728729730731732733734735736737738739740741742743744745746747748749750751752753754755756757758759760761762763764765766767768769770771772773774775776777778779780781782783784785786787788789790791792793794795796797798799800801802803804805806807808809810811812813814815816817818819820821822823824825826827828829830831832833834835836837838839840841842843844845846847848849850851852853854855856857858859860861862863864865866867868869870871872873874875876877878879880881882883884885886887888889890891892893894895896897898899900

"Why would he lie? And like I told you before, there's millions of papers up there. Millions. I have absolutely no doubt that a lot of them should be burnt. And better for Mrs. Harding to do it than for me, for the Commemorative Society. How can every one of them be of interest and importance? In fact, how can even half be of importance? How? You tell me, Lucy. It's impossible."

Lucy was basically an uncomplicated woman, and it was usually easy for me to argue her into a corner. Indeed, I knew I had stashed her away there already. She stood staring at me, fingering the bib of her apron. "Well," she said, "I just know that it's not right, that's all."

"I'm sure that everything will turn out well, Lucy. Mrs. Harding is of very sound mind."

I excused myself, and as I headed down the hall, Lucy said, "She's not, Trey. She's not of sound mind."

I ran upstairs and tidied up for dinner, though I must say, I felt like something of a cad.

Throughout our long years of marriage Lucy and I maintained the custom of reading together in the parlor after supper. We would usually begin by sharing that day's edition of *The Marion Star*. Then I would generally read a good book, while she preferred one of her magazines, especially the *Ladies Home Journal*. Those decades of shared quiet evenings remain one of the pleasures that I miss most with the loss of my dear wife and life's companion. Anyway, I distinctly recall that two articles appeared on the front page of that evening's *Star*. One stated that the U.S. Senate subcommittee investigating the Teapot Dome oil leases was to hold its first meeting the following Monday, the other that a certain Senator Wheeler, from Montana, was calling for an investigation of the Justice Department. The country was only four or five weeks beyond the month-long period of national mourning for the President, and so his name was not yet mentioned, either regarding Albert Fall, the Secretary of Interior, and the naval oil fields he had so generously leased to his good friend, Harvey Sinclair, or regarding Attorney General Harry Daugherty, who was being accused, among other things, of peddling illegal liquor permits to Chicago bootleggers.

I passed the *Star* to Lucy, having read all the news I cared to read. I took up my book. I distinctly recall it being John Dos Passos' *Three*

Soldiers—though frankly, I could not concentrate, thinking instead how the troubles of Mr. Harding's "friends" seemed to be circling above his grave like vultures.

I knew in my heart of hearts that he himself was blameless, with the exception, of course, of his trifles with the ladies—though that is hardly the stuff of subcommittees.

I could feel Lucy tense as she read what I had just read. From behind her paper she said, "Trey, did you see this?"

"I did."

A minute or two later she put the paper down. "You don't think they think President Harding did any wrong, do you? They don't mention his name, but . . ."

"I don't know what to think. The only thing I know for sure is that Mr. Harding was the soul of honesty, when it came to that sort of thing."

"Trey," she said, as if in sudden comprehension, "*this* is why Mrs. Harding is burning his papers. She's afraid."

At the risk of betraying my own stupidity, I truly had not thought of that possibility until the words came out of my wife's mouth. Nevertheless, I said, "I don't think so, Lucy."

"Of course it is."

I thought about this. "Well, if it's any comfort to you, as I said before, there are millions of papers up there, and I wonder if Mrs. Harding could ever possibly live long enough to burn even . . ."

"Tristan, stop. Why are you saying that? That's sheer nonsense and you know it. Presidential papers are going up in smoke. Mrs. Harding's not well. She's not thinking clearly. She's afraid of all the rumors. And now this." She struck the *Star* with her fingertips, as if in contempt. "I suspect she's burning everything even remotely connected to these oil leases, and to that disgusting Mr. Daugherty. Why, everyone in Marion knows that Mr. Harding was no crook. He would not approve of this. And what if she ends up burning papers that would clear his name? If—God forbid—his name gets drawn into this muck. Tristan, you have simply got to talk to her. You're founder of the Commemorative Society. The papers are supposed to come to you." She paused, and then added, "If Colonel Hamilton was alive, he'd go talk to her, he surely would. He'd see it as his duty. His duty to the President."

For some reason a silence had taken hold of me, and when I said nothing in reply, Lucy added, "Sometimes, Trey, you're like a big jigsaw puzzle to me—with a few of the pieces missing. Or otherwise twisted out of shape."

THE NEXT MORNING I drove down Center Street, and there was the First Lady's enormous Packard parked in front of the Star Building.

And there on that sunny windless day was the now familiar line of gray-white smoke rising from the chimney, against the crisp blue Ohio sky. I swung my little Lincoln in beside the Packard, and when I stepped from the car, I paused in the street to look up at the window where Mr. Harding's feet used to be propped on the sill, as he editorialized about this or that issue, great or small.

There were two ways to reach his office—from the staircase inside the business offices, or via the stairs that went up from the street entrance. I chose the swinging doors of the street entrance and climbed those well-worn steps. I am not one of those people reassured by the clomp-clomp of his own footsteps, and so I did not exactly tramp my way up; nevertheless, those wooden stairs creaked and thumped beneath my quiet steps.

The first thing I saw were four of those long wooden crates, completely empty, stacked along the wall of the hallway. Seeing them gave me a kind of hollow feeling, something like fear, but not fear. Maybe shame. In fact, the burning of the President's papers suddenly hit me like a slap in the face.

I had known about it all along, but I had done nothing.

And Lucy was right—Mr. Harding would never have approved of such a shadowy act, anymore than he would approve of the other violations of his legacy or values.

The frosted-glass window of his office bore the legend that had been inscribed there in gold leaf way back in the vanished world of the 1880s or '90s: The Marion Star, Warren G. Harding, Editor & Proprietor.

In retrospect, I know that I stood before that door for a bit longer than I ought to have. I most certainly was not trying to eavesdrop, or anything of the sort. I was simply thinking of those empty crates, and of Mr. Harding, who had always meant well, in spite of himself, but who now seemed in danger of coming to grief at the hands of the very men he had loved as friends and whom he had trusted most in this world.

I thought about the President's one and only visit home from the White House. He had come into work here at the Star and spent the day editing his newspaper and writing a nostalgic editorial about the joys of home and the beauties of Marion. In truth, I think that by the end of his homecoming, he was utterly dreading his return to the White House and would have gladly resigned his high office and returned to work right here, in this little building—if he could have done so with dignity. I wondered again, as I had so often in the past several weeks, whether or not Mr. Harding might still be alive, if he had never left home. I believe he would have.

Suddenly, I felt a tinge of deep shame for being such a persistent "booster" of his success.

I was standing there thinking—feeling—these things. Quite frankly, I was probably gathering my nerve, too, when I heard lowered voices behind the frosted glass. Suddenly it occurred to me that Mrs. Harding and Rusty had probably heard my footsteps on the creaking stairs, and now sensed my lurking presence in the hall.

Just as I was raising my hand and about to knock, the door flew open—as if to catch a thief.

And there stood Rusty in his uniform with a rather fierce look on his face, which, at the sight of me, turned into a mocking smile. And there before the potbelly stove sat Mrs. Harding on a wooden chair, beside Rusty's empty chair. At a glance I noticed that the stove's grate was gaping, with a vigorous fire flickering within. Files were stacked on the floor near the stove, awaiting their turn in the flames. The First Lady sat as if caught by a camera, holding an iron poker in her hand like a sword or a scepter, looking quite perturbed at the intruder framed in the doorway. The sleeves of her black dress were pushed to her elbows. Her right hand and the sagging skin of her forearm were blackened with soot. I took all of this in, of course, in an instant.

Smiling Rusty spoke first. "Well, well, well, take a look at who's here!"

Mrs. Harding was staring right at me through her gold-rimmed spectacles, but she snapped, "Who? Who's that?" That is when I realized that her vision was failing.

Of course I would have spoken for myself, had I been given more than a split second to do so, but Rusty immediately said, "Why, it's—" He paused, looking me in the eyes with the same cocky boyhood look from the schoolyard, and for an instant I thought he was going to say (as he was thinking), "Killer Trey." But after that teasing moment, he simply said, "It's Trey." He turned to the First Lady. "Mr. Tristan Hamilton himself, Mrs. Harding."

"Tristan? Oh, Tristan!" Her face instantly changed. It seemed to alter from a scowl to a smile in a split second. She jabbed the poker into the fire. "Why, for goodness sake, Trey. You really gave us quite a start. Well, you're here now, so come on in."

I walked through the stacked files, stepping over loose, fallen sheets littering the floor like dozens of pieces of wastepaper that had all missed the can. Some bore the White House letterhead. The First Lady held out her left hand to me, excusing her right because of the soot, and I kissed the back of it. She smelled of smoke and lavender. She said, "It's so dark out in that hall that I couldn't make out who it was. If I told Warren once, I told him a thousand times, 'Join the 20th century, Warren. Hang a light bulb out there!' But do you think he would? I might as well have been talking to the wall. But Trey—whatever were you doing out there?"

I am sure I must have reddened. "Oh, I'm very sorry, Mrs. Harding. I suppose I was just—just remembering, thinking of the President, that's all." Still holding her hand, I glanced at the papers spread about, everywhere on the floor, awaiting the fire. One of them, with the White House letterhead, bore the President's signature—along with the smudge of a heel mark. I stared at it for a moment, a bit flabbergasted, then I looked back at her and said, "I was just remembering back when I used to come here and knock and I'd hear Mr. Harding's voice say, 'Door's open, come on in.'"

She smiled wistfully, glanced into the flickering fire and said, "'Door's open, come on in.' That sums up Warren in a nutshell, doesn't it?"

"Well, now that you mention it—Anyway, Mrs. Harding, I honestly wasn't trying to eavesdrop or anything like that. Please don't think . . ."

"Oh, for goodness sake, Trey. Not at all. You're the last person who'd be up to shenanigans like that. Besides, nothing to listen to in here. Just the Major and me sorting through things. As you can see, we've been busy little beavers."

"Yes, you have." For the first time I openly looked about at the mess. "Very, very busy beavers, indeed."

Messy stacks of files, varying in height from an inch or two to about three feet high were heaped all over the place—on the floor, against the walls, on the tops of the oak cabinets, on every square inch of Mr. Harding's ink-stained desk, and even on the mouth of the old brass spittoon that was already an anachronism and a relic of the President's fading generation. The only items in the room not stacked high with presidential files were the potbelly and the telephone on the wall by the door, but even they were occupied—the stove with a steaming kettle, the oak telephone cabinet with a teacup. Seeing such a mess was a bit odd because Mrs. Harding had always been so finicky that she drove more than one housekeeper to despair by running a white-gloved finger over dust catchers.

She invited me to sit in the empty chair beside her. I glanced at Rusty, as the chair was obviously his. He nodded, and so I sat beside the First Lady. She made inquiry about Lucy and "sweet little Bomber." She mentioned the pleasant arrangements out at White Oaks Farm, how she managed to "stay out of the Sawyers' hair" and how they managed to stay out of hers, and yet they all enjoyed breakfast and dinner together, every day.

Mrs. Harding said, "We don't keep any coffee here, Trey. You know the Surgeon General says I ought not drink it, not with my kidney complaint and all, but we do have a tin of Postum, and the kettle's hot." She turned to Rusty, who was standing by the door, "Major, if you'll wash out Warren's cup for Tristan."

I imagined that Warren's cup was that nasty thing gathering dust and soot on top of the telephone. "Oh, no," I said, "really, I've had my fill for this morning." At that point, I took another opportunity to glance around the room again. "So, Mrs. Harding, I see you're putting things in order."

"It's an uphill battle, but we're gainin'." Then as if I had just reminded her of the task at hand, she said, "Trey, dear, hand me that brown folder please, the one by your foot." I picked up the stuffed folder she had indicated. The words, "War Department – Fort Ethan Allen – Barracks" were written on the tab in India ink. She took out the papers and flung them into the fire. I stared, utterly amazed, as she began stirring them with her poker.

"Funny," she said, still looking into the smoke and flames and curling pages, "but I never hear from Adeline." Her words had the sound of a casual inquiry masking something more probing. She glanced my way, "Why do you suppose that is?"

Truly, I was at a loss. "Oh, well, Mrs. Harding, you know Addy. She isn't the most outgoing person. And besides, I'm sure she wants to give you time to get settled in and adjust yourself to your new situation."

The First Lady seemed to be studying me through her spectacles. I was looking into the fire, watching the flames devour the documents. "Well, she did invite me to Tioga for Thanksgiving, and the Sawyers too, of course, so that'll be nice. I've always loved visiting Tioga. Warren did too. It's—it's really a very special place."

I smiled, "Yes, I suppose it is." A moment of silence came between us, and I decided it was high time to plunge into the task at hand. Still looking into the fire, I said, "Mrs. Harding, may I ask why you're doing this—burning the President's papers?"

She was studying me; I was avoiding her eyes. "So that's why you've come?"

Now I turned to her, rubbing my hands together. "Yes, that's why I've come." As has often been the case in life, once I've confronted an issue, anxiety seems to fuel and embolden me to the task at hand, rather than deter. "In fact, I believe I ought to have come a lot sooner, and quite frankly, Mrs. Harding, I'm rather ashamed of myself that I didn't."

"You are, are you?"

"Yes, madam, I am."

She studied me in a way that made me think she was surprised by my audacity. Then she looked into the fire and stirred the flames. "Tristan, you don't understand."

"I could not help but notice the empty crates in the hall. When we carried them up, I don't think you could have wedged another paper into a single one of them. Now they've all gone up in smoke." Without actually looking at the Major, I glanced his way. He was slouching in a very unmilitary kind of posture beside the door, leaning against the wall with his arms folded. "I was led to believe, by a reliable source, that the

Harding Commemorative Society was going to become stewards of the President's papers. But it seems that that is not to be the case. Indeed, it seems that very soon the only thing left will be their ashes. But the Society is not my main concern, Mrs. Harding, my concern is . . ."

"Tristan, you don't understand. You couldn't possibly understand because you didn't go to Washington with us, did you?"

I did not look away. Mrs. Harding had an instinct for knowing the proverbial chink in one's armor, and once she knew it, she would forever be sticking her long needles in there. But now that I had entered the fray, I was not going to flinch.

"You stayed home, so you don't know what it's like out there, do you? Amongst all those wolves. You don't know how they are or what we're up against. The only thing you know is Marion. Out there, they'll take any little thing and bend it into something it isn't. They'll use everything they can to destroy the President, to destroy his good name."

"Who are 'they' Mrs. Harding? Who will destroy his good name?"

"Why, his friends, his enemies. They're doing it right now, even as we speak. Look at what they've done to him already—implying that it was somehow Warren's fault that Charlie Forbes stole all that money from the Veterans Bureau, forgetting all the good the President did for our soldiers."

That was the very first time I had heard anything whatsoever about Forbes and what would turn out to be the infamous Veterans Bureau scandal.

She looked into the fire. "Charlie Forbes—why, I thought Warren was going to strangle him that day, when he became convinced of his treachery." She gave the burning papers a sharp turn. "Oh, if I had that evil little devil here in this room I'd—" and pulling the smoking poker from the flames, she said, "why, I'd skewer his gizzard with this, I would! And Albert Fall too!"

She composed herself and continued, "Blaming Warren for that evil Charlie's misdeeds! And you wait, you'll see—they'll try to pin him with even worse! Why, it's like blaming the farmer for a few of the bad apples in the harvest. Warren appointed hundreds of men to office. What about William Howard Taft? What about Charles Evans Hughes? And Andrew Mellon? And hundreds more, from cabinet members to village postmasters. What about them? Hundreds, thousands, of honest, decent, upright men, many of them brilliant, 99.99 percent of them as upright as the day is long. Why, of course there's always going to be some worms in the bushel." She was stirring the flames again, and then, like an afterthought, or like an inner reflection that had slipped out, she said, "And now they're saying that the President snuck out to speakeasies in the middle of the night."

She bristled and gave another vicious turn to the fire, and then put her soiled hand to her forehead, in a sad sort of way. The poker was protruding from the stove like a sword from a stuck pig.

That too was the first time I had heard about the President sneaking off to speakeasies; quite frankly, it wasn't something that I found difficult to believe. I said, "The President was a great man, Mrs. Harding. You know that and I know that and so does everyone else in this town, and I'd venture to say that most folks out in Washington know it as well, Republicans and Democrats alike. You can be certain the American people will always remember the President's many, many great achievements."

She leaned forward, so close to my face that I noticed milky cuticles encircling the pupils of her dim eyes. "That," she said, "is exactly why we must protect him from the rabble. That's why we must be loyal and preserve his memory."

"Preserve his memory! By burning his papers? The proof of achievements?"

"Trey, dear," she said quietly, "you're forgetting what they've always done to him. Not just in Washington, but even right here in Marion. Everywhere he ever walked in his life, to and fro. They took one thing and made it another. They took his complexion and made him into a colored man. They took his love of bridge and Parcheesi and called him a gambler, and now this business about him sneaking off to speakeasies and—" Her words broke off, and she seemed to blink back tears—an odd thing indeed for Mrs. Harding. Then, looking into the flames, she said, "The President was great in life, in death he shall be magnificent. Trey, dear, hand me those papers."

Truly, I did not know what to say or do, so I did as I was told and handed her the file she had indicated—"Bureau of War Risk Insurance – Vocational Rehab." She took the offending papers and cast them into the fire.

"Oh, Mrs. Harding," I said, "Please don't do this. Please."

"Tristan," she said quietly, "I am not long for this world, and I don't know what's going to happen when I'm gone. I don't know who is going to try to go snooping through these things. Maybe that horrible Senator Wheeler."

"But what could he possibly find?"

"Something that he'll make into something else. If he doesn't, then someone else will, sooner or later. Count on it."

"So that's what you're afraid of."

"No, that is *not* what I'm afraid of. I'm not afraid of it because it's not going to happen. I'm not afraid of those scoundrels; I merely hate them for what they're trying to do to Warren, to the President, to his glorious legacy. But they're not going to have their way. They're not going to have a thing. I'll see to it. Pass me those papers too, please."

I obeyed, and she threw a handful into the fire.

I leaned back in my chair and watched the flames rise upon the edges, while she stirred the fire. "But Mrs. Harding, I'm certain that others someday, perhaps someday soon, historians and such, they'll want to look at those papers and study the President's achievements. How could they not, after all he did for our nation?"

(I ought to add that I uttered those naïve and hopeful words long before I became acquainted with those rumormongers and liars that so gloriously call themselves "historians.")

The First Lady gave the flames another turn with her poker and said, a bit presciently, "Oh, Trey, to hell with them. You'll learn."

"To hell with them?" I thought of Lucy's words, that the First Lady was not of sound mind. "Why, Mrs. Harding, they can keep the record straight, but they'll need these papers to do it. In fact, papers are all they'll have, I think. They're the signed evidence of what the President did in office, his executive orders and such. Indeed, I'd venture to say they're the only real bulwark Mr. Harding has even now against, as you say, his enemies."

She was looking into the fire. I leaned closer. "Mrs. Harding, let me take the papers to Tioga."

She looked at me, seemingly perturbed. "What good would that do? If they want them, they'll get their hands on them."

"Oh, no they won't. If you do me the honor of entrusting these papers to my keeping, then I swear to God Almighty, that neither Senator Wheeler nor any of his cronies will ever lay their grubby hands on them. Not a one of them, either in your lifetime or after. Even if it comes down to a subpoena, I'll burn them en mass in the furnace. If it means prison for me, then so be it. I'll lay my hand on a Bible and swear to it, if you wish."

I knew I had her ear, at last, and so I continued, "You've said you're going to leave the house to the Harding Commemorative Society. Well, someday when it's a museum, when all of this business with Fall and Harry is long forgotten, I'll move the papers back to your place, and the only people who'll ever see it are historians. Historians who will recognize and appreciate the great things the President did for us, for our nation." I paused. "Mrs. Harding, let me take the papers to Tioga. Please. They'll be safe there. Don't destroy the only hard evidence history has of President Harding's legacy. We must not let people forget. What do you say?"

For a moment, she said nothing, then, "Oh, Trey, I don't know."

A certain virulence had gone from her.

"You have my word, Mrs. Harding. I'll guard them with my life, for all the rest of my days. Or if need be, I'll burn them, just like you're doing. Only much, much faster. Just like I sent that Chancellor book up in smoke. Remember? "

"Chancellor. Yes, I'd forgotten all about that. Well—"

I waited for her to complete her thought, but when she didn't, I said, "You'll have the best of both possibilities. The President's papers forever hidden and kept safe from his enemies, while still being forever preserved for use by his defenders. Available, someday, to those who intend to do right by him."

A change seemed to come over the First Lady. I was sure this change was not in my imagination, and yet I can scarcely describe it, except to say that it seemed as if her will-to-do fell completely away, as if, of a sudden, she slumped into a great, latent exhaustion. "Well," she said, "maybe you're right."

"I am right. I say that not for pride's sake, but for the sake of the President."

I was looking at her, looking into the flames. I leaned towards the stove and was about to close its iron door, when I remembered myself. "Mrs. Harding, may I? May I close it?"

She nodded.

So I closed the grate. It made a clanging sound.

She looked at Rusty, who had been slouching there all that time by the door, listening, obedient. "Major, I think I'll have you drive me home now." Then to me, "The Major and I'll come back and pack these loose papers up tomorrow."

"Oh, no need," I said. "I'll do it for you. You just go home and rest. I'll take care of everything from this point on."

The first thing on Monday morning, we moved the papers to Tioga. They were stored there for many long years in a caged, padlocked room in the basement.

After World War II, I moved them to the Harding Home, where they remain to this very day in the attic, and in the bungalow out back.

III

WEDNESDAY NIGHT

Into the Setting Sun

A SLIGHT AND RATHER INTERESTING CHANGE of plans for dinner tomorrow. Heidi called. Her husband Carl has occasional bouts of arthritis, which lay him low for days on end. He woke up this morning literally unable to get out of bed. Something to do with the weather. In other words, Carl will not be coming to dinner tomorrow, nor will Heidi, who insists upon staying with him. But no, that does not mean that Mrs. Blaine will not be coming to dinner, nor that she will come alone.

Instead, she will arrive tomorrow with her son—which is to say, with President Harding's son!

It should be a most *extraordinary* day, even if Arrian—Dr. Arrian Lang— is, as I suspect, a bit dull and academic. He is not a physician, as I believe I mentioned before, but a "doctor of metallurgy"—if one can imagine that. As for his last name, he was adopted into the family of the great aunt who raised him, I believe it was Mitzy's mother's, mother's sister and her husband—and that is just about all I know of the matter, though I have sometimes wondered if the son has ever contemplated changing his name to Arrian Harding. One way or another, I shall be more than happy to tell him a few anecdotes of his father. It is mean of me to say this, but I am now secretly very pleased that poor ol' Carl has had his bout with arthritis.

As I say, the snow—our first of the season—has finally begun falling across the heart of Ohio. It started around one o'clock with a few flurries and it has turned into a full-fledged snowfall. Now with night coming on, the yard is utterly blanketed and the Old Forest is filling with white. Just before supper, Rob McGregor came out to plow the drive and shovel the walks to the house, and he promises to come by again in the morning. Like Mrs. Sawyer, he already heard that guests are coming for Thanksgiving dinner. In fact, the whole town seems to know that Mrs. Blaine is going to be here. Or at least everyone who was around in President Harding's day seems to know, though the only person I have told about the change in dinner plans is Mrs. Christian.

At this very moment I am sure that scores of school children, with four days of freedom before them, are out at the Harding Memorial sledding down the incline behind the tomb. If I were sixty-some years younger, I'd be right out there with them. I am sure that the President would be delighted that children are enjoying themselves on the grounds of his Memorial. As for the First Lady, well, frankly I have a feeling she would be a good deal less pleased. Indeed, she would probably like nothing better than to get out there with a yardstick and paddle a few fannies, just as she used to do with the paperboys when they were late in delivering the *Star*, or when she caught them "horsing around" in the alley.

As I am sure you have gathered, the assassination of President Kennedy has led me to think quite a bit about President Harding's "strange death." In fact, I would say that I have thought more about it in the past several days than I have in the past forty years. You must understand that, when I say "strange death," I am being somewhat tongue-in-cheek. In reality, there was little if anything strange about the President's death, though that is how a lot of people came to regard it. Granted, there was an oddity or two mixed into the circumstances, like the First Lady sitting up all night "guarding" the room where the embalmers were doing their work. But that incident, obviously, in and of itself had no correlation to the President's death, which was nothing out of the ordinary. Indeed, men die in similar circumstances every day of the week, and no one finds anything in the least bit "strange" about it.

But of course they are not the President of the United States.

More specifically, they are not Warren G. Harding. Mr. Harding had an unfortunate way of spinning rumors, the way mountains spin clouds. Come to think of it, I realize that his death was yet another example of what the First Lady had in mind when she remarked, on that Indian

Summer morning in 1923, that people were always taking one thing about Mr. Harding and making it into another.

There was even a best seller back in the early '30s entitled *The Strange Death of President Harding*. Like Nan Britton's book, it was (and I believe still is) widely available in local libraries. Its author was one Gaston Bullock Means, who once somehow wormed his way into a job as an investigator for the Department of Justice; by turns he also wormed his way into Mr. Harding's rather encompassing Washington circle—though certainly not the inner circle. He was a liar and a swindler, and he became a convicted felon; in fact, he wrote his best seller while in the Atlanta Penitentiary. Back in the 1930s, when I read sections of it, I came to the conclusion that his name "Gaston" was a bit telling, the way names sometimes are. (I'll refrain from trying to make sense of his charming middle name.) Anyway, I merely mention the Means book as a sort of curiosity, one of the sideshows that came as a result of President Harding's sudden death.

Mr. Harding died of apoplexy in the presidential suite of the Palace Hotel in San Francisco on Thursday, August 2, 1923, at around 8:30 in the evening—11:30 our time. Lucy was fast asleep when the telephone rang around midnight. Ordinarily, I would have been asleep too, but on that pleasantly warm night I was reclining on my chaise lounge in the backyard, watching the Perseus meteor shower. Well do I remember the surge of terror that shot through my heart when the telephone rang at that ungodly hour—though I cannot say that I had any idea who it was. I flew across the yard, up the back steps, through the kitchen and into dining room, where the phone hung on the back wall. I picked up the handset on what was probably only the fourth or fifth ring. It was Earl Bacon, who lived several doors down East Center Street from Dr. Tryon Harding. He said that the President's father was going around the neighborhood knocking on doors and calling through windows telling folks the news, that the President was dead.

I ought to say here and now that I know little more about the President's death than the next person, because neither the First Lady nor Dr. Sawyer ever uttered a single word in my presence about the goings on in that hotel suite on that tragic August evening. In other words, I cannot say that she said this or that, nor do I have any comments from the Surgeon General to pass along. No doubt I will further diminish my authority by admitting that I have gotten most of what I know about the President's last days and death from newspaper clippings, books, and to some extent, local hearsay. I believe I mentioned before that my sister kept scrapbooks chronicling Mr. Harding's political career. These books were a hobby of hers, like gardening and collecting the Venetian masks that animate the walls of Tioga with their peculiar, coquettish presence.

Back in the early '20s, Adeline subscribed to a whole roster of magazines and out-of-town newspapers for the sole purpose of clipping interesting articles about the President. In most cases, she jotted the name of the paper in the margins. She then meticulously arranged these clippings and pasted them onto the heavy black crepe paper pages of the scrapbooks. Or in the case of some longer articles, she simply inserted them loose between the pages. More than once this evening I have imagined Adeline in her younger years sitting here at my father's big desk, in lamplight with the bay windows behind her, clipping pages with those big black scissors that are kept to this day in the center drawer. Adeline was meticulous about everything, and it is plainly evident that she measured and calculated the neatest and most presentable way to lay the clippings on the pages. Out of curiosity, I measured a few of the articles this evening in terms of their placement on the paper. Most are exactly centered, with equal margins on top, bottom, and sides, which leads me to the conclusion (for the umpteenth time in my life) that my sister and I really are quite a lot alike. Though I certainly never shrank from society the way she did. Anyway, after forty years (and in some cases more than fifty), most of the clippings have yellowed and grown brittle with age, and in many cases the paste has disintegrated, leaving nothing more than bits of powder and shiny blotches on the crepe, which is now more of a purplish ash-color than black.

President Harding died while returning from Alaska—an exacting journey that he dubbed the "Voyage of Understanding." His cross-country trip and voyage were scheduled to last six weeks. The ambitious itinerary was to include, upon the return, a five-day stopover in Marion. The President had recently purchased the farm where he was born in Blooming Grove. He intended to restore the house and use it as a summer cottage after retiring. Anyway, the cross-country journey and voyage to Alaska had two purposes. A sort of schism had developed within the hierarchy of the Republican Party over the question of whether or not the United States should place itself under the jurisdiction of the World Court at The Hague. The President was an advocate of using the Court to settle international disputes, while most members of his Party denounced it as a sort of super-government, saying that The Hague amounted to foreign meddling in American affairs. The issue became so contentious that several of Mr. Harding's former allies, including Senator Henry Cabot Lodge (father of Richard Nixon's running mate, three years ago), were crossing the country parallel to the Presidential Special, denouncing the World Court. I am telling you this from memory, as Adeline doesn't seem to have included a single clipping regarding the Republicans who were hounding the President's heels, even hinting that he was a traitor.

The President's other official reason for the long journey was that he wanted to undertake an inspection of Alaska. He intended to formulate an entire new policy for the vast territory which, according to an article in *Harper's*, was administered by five cabinet officers and twenty-eight bureaus, many of which were apparently engaged in constant squabbles amongst themselves regarding the territory's riches. President Harding let it be known that he wanted to make use of Alaska's wealth so that its resources would be permanent rather than squandered and ever diminishing.

Well, that was his official reason for going, an inspection tour of sorts. But there was an unofficial reason as well—one touched upon (as you may recall) by the First Lady during our Thanksgiving dinner. Mr. and Mrs. Harding had each harbored a deep longing to visit Alaska. After the President was dead and gone, and after so much bad news had come out, folks said that he had desired an escape there, if only for a time, from the storm that was quietly gathering over his head in Washington. The farther away, the better. And Alaska fit the bill.

So they went.

Much of what I have read this evening, I had either forgotten or never knew. At the time, I had followed the President's trip as closely as I could by reading *The Marion Star* and whatever magazines Lucy and I might have subscribed to at the time. But as for reading out-of-town papers and such, that was Adeline's province, and if she did not lay something in front of me, then I probably never saw it.

I liked a little anecdote that I came across today in a newspaper called the *Emporium*. It seems that the *Superb* was equipped with loudspeakers—or as they put it, "powerful amplification devices"—so that the President could deliver speeches from the rear platform of his palace car. Anyway, somewhere in Kansas a group of farm children were standing by the tracks at nightfall waving little American flags as the train approached. And as it rushed by, they saw the lonely figure of the President of the United States standing on the rear platform, apparently getting some air. When he saw them, he raised his straw hat in greeting. Knowing what I know of rural Ohio in the early 1920s, I can say with some certainty that those farm children in Kansas had probably never even heard a voice speaking to them over a telephone, much less an amplification device, so they must have been dumbfounded by the voice coming out of the train's whirlwind saying, "Your President loves you."

Mr. Harding had a disposition that could be both sweet and mischievous, and I suspect he enjoyed little moments like that.

But there was nothing whatsoever amusing about another event, one that I did know about, but had not thought of in years. The tragedy cast a black pall over the westward journey. While the President and First Lady were attending church services in Denver, four young members of his party, returning in an automobile from visiting the grave of Buffalo Bill, plunged over an embankment into Bear Creek Canyon. One of the fellows in the car was Sumner Curtis, an up-and-coming member of the Republican National Committee. (I remember meeting him during the Front Porch Campaign.) Sumner was thrown and crushed by the tumbling car. The other three men were reporters whose names I did not recognize. They died when the car landed at the bottom of the canyon and exploded in a huge ball of fire. The article in *The Chicago Tribune* said, "The President is deeply disturbed by the accident and the First Lady is strangely affected."

Back in those days people were more superstitious than they are now, and I remember that a lot of Marion folks, including Lucy, regarded the accident as an ill omen. I am absolutely certain that Mrs. Harding did too. She always kept a sharp eye peeled for signs and portents, boding well or ill.

Especially ill.

The clippings of course are placed chronologically, and several pages after the ones devoted to the accident, an article appears about the President in Wyoming. On a sunny morning he stood for a long time on a mountain peak (unfortunately, the reporter does not bother to say which one) near the Continental Divide, gazing out upon the majestic twin peaks of the Grand Tetons. "He removed his hat as if in reverence for the celestial vistas, and a light breeze blew through his white hair." Quoted in the same article is a speech the President delivered that evening:

> *I shall pass from these mountains with a greater reverence and awareness of the Creator, and a deeper desire to be worthy of His best intent. As such, I find it not desirable that the West should fall into the hands of bonanza corporations seeking to exploit this magnificent land for the profit of shareholders. Your President shall stand against them. This I promise you with all my heart.*

Outside of Tacoma, tragedy struck yet again. A backup steam engine following directly behind the Presidential Special was swept from the tracks and down a mountain by a huge landslide, killing the engineer, one Edward Roddy. That very morning, Mr. Harding had given him a lapel pin bearing the Presidential seal. In fact, the President himself had pinned it on him, and Roddy was wearing it when he died. The landslide occurred about forty seconds after the *Superb* had passed the point of the landslide. Thus the tragedy had the trappings of the best of luck entwined with the worst.

The voyage to Alaska was undertaken on the *Henderson*, pictured in several of the clippings. In spite of the ship's phonebook sort of name, photographs of it remind me of the *Queen Mary*. One aspect of the ship's history appealed to my imagination and has never left me through the years. The *Henderson* served as a troop ship during the Great War. As such she was struck by a German torpedo and was abandoned in flames on the high seas, along with her scores of dead. After the Armistice, she was found following the winds and currents near the Arctic Circle, a wandering ghost ship drifting in the high latitudes.

Her dead, mummified by the cold, were aboard. Thereafter, she was reclaimed and refitted.

A clipping from *The Marion Star* dredged up local memories relating to the President's voyage. According to the *Star*, Wiants Bookstore sold one hundred and eleven Rand McNally maps of the Alaskan Territory— much of it, as I recall (having bought one myself), marked terra incognita. And Baked Alaska was being served for dessert all over Marion, including the restaurant at Hotel Harding. In case you're wondering, Lucy fixed the dessert and for a time it became a favorite of hers. Mrs. Helen Kramer, the librarian, was quoted as referring to President Harding as "Odysseus." No doubt that sounds absurdly romantic now, but in a sense, I think she made a pretty good call. I mean that Mr. Harding always harbored portions of both wanderlust and nostalgia, an urge to wander and a great longing for home.

The *Henderson* sailed into lengthening days at the center of her own armada, surrounded by cruisers and fully armed destroyers at both her fore and aft—mostly because of that crafty Lenin. According to one clipping, the President spent most of his shipboard time devoted to untangling the jumbled oddities of Alaskan administration—the fur-bearing animals under the jurisdiction of the Department of Agriculture, the salmon under the Department of Commerce, the reindeer herds under the Bureau of Education. (Yes, the Bureau of Education.) But there was entertainment as well. The Navy Band gave afternoon concerts on the aft deck. When not at work on administrative details, the President usually spent his time writing or reading. Sometimes in the afternoon he played shuffleboard, but favorite among his pastimes were the long bridge games in the stateroom. (I strongly suspect that some of those "bridge games" may have involved poker chips, and I further suspect that plain old lemonade seldom touched the President's lips.) What the articles do not hint at, what folks in Marion would not hear of until after the fact, was that the President seemed to be slipping deeper and deeper into gloom and despair. Mr. Harding usually made a habit of avoiding his own company, but on the voyage to Alaska, he sometimes stood on the deck alone, or spent long hours in a chair, wrapped in a blanket and bundled in his overcoat, staring out at the gray, northern sea. One point not mentioned in any of these clippings is the fact that, during one of those solitary times on the deck, George Christian came along, sat beside him, and asked him twice how he was feeling. On the second inquiry the President gave a one-word answer, "Betrayed."

On the fourth day at sea, the *Henderson* entered Alaskan waters. As they passed the boundary, the men stood on the bow and tipped their hats and the ladies waved their handkerchiefs. It was ten o'clock in the evening, and only then was the sun setting through what was described as "a lilac and violet-colored sky." The Navy Band played the First Lady's favorite song, "The End of a Perfect Day."

The flotilla entered Resurrection Bay through the pillars of the newly christened Harding Gateway, which one correspondent compared to the Pillars of Hercules. While in Seward, the President visited the Harding Icefield, which "stretches away in vast windswept desolation for more than one hundred miles." From Seward, the Presidential party headed northward aboard the Alaskan Central Railway. They rode past waterfalls and "blue glaciers from before the time of Christ." They passed enormous lakes and snow-covered mountains rising into the clouds, and green valleys where daisies blossomed in July's endless daylight. At one point along the way, the President called for the train to stop. He stepped from the *Superb* (yes, the palace car seems to have gone to sea with them) and he stood for a long time looking at Mt. McKinley "sixty miles distant, rising in majestic supremacy and grandeur." The valley was covered with grass and wildflowers, and far away a great herd of caribou stopped grazing to look at the train and the solitary figure of a man. The journalist for *The New York World* commented:

> One wondered what the President was thinking as he stood looking at the mountain named for his martyred predecessor. One could not help but wonder if maybe he was drawing inspiration, in the same way he occasionally does on the mornings when he rides horseback to the Lincoln Memorial and gazes at that great seated likeness of his other martyred predecessor.

Leafing through Adeline's scrapbooks this evening has likewise been informative to me in my capacity as curator of the Harding Home. Only this evening did I discover the source of two of our holdings. One is an oil painting of Mt. McKinley. Naturally, I always presumed that someone gave it to the President during the Voyage of Understanding, but now I know exactly where it came from. It was a gift from the citizens of Fairbanks. The Presidential Special reached that distant outpost at around midnight, in broad daylight, with "the sun and the moon shining side by side on the horizon." In spite of the late hour, virtually the entire town was on hand to greet the President. In a strong clear voice Mr. Harding said, "For the life of me, I don't know whether to wish you Good Morning or Good Evening!"

During Mayor Marquam's welcoming remarks, he gave Mr. and Mrs. Harding the painting, pointing out that Mt. McKinley was clearly visible on the southwestern horizon, one hundred and twenty-five miles away. One clipping states:

> On Wednesday President Harding took a walking tour of Fairbanks. He knocked on the doors of several log cabins and introduced himself. All portals were graciously opened to him and he sat in those charming, rustic houses asking the people what their concerns were and how Washington could help Alaskans help themselves and in turn benefit the Nation as a whole. He also spoke of future statehood, something that is dear to the heart of nearly every Alaskan.

You may recall my mentioning earlier that the possessions Mrs. Harding sent to Marion included a totem pole, which I first laid eyes on that crisp autumn morning in the boxcar.

For forty long years I have mistakenly presumed that the totem pole came from somewhere out West, but this evening I have learned otherwise. Several days after visiting Fairbanks, the Presidential Party was back aboard the *Henderson* crossing the foggy Gulf of Alaska to a place called Sitka, Russia's old colonial capitol. On Sunday morning, the Hardings unexpectedly attended services at a little Eskimo church, instead of the cathedral on the hill, built by the Czars:

> President Harding talked with the Eskimos, who were deeply grateful for his joining them in their little church. He showed great interest in their concerns and one of them arranged for him to have the gift of a totem pole.

In the afternoon, the President and his party stopped at the Cathedral of St. Michael where:

> *Father Pontelarf, for the first time ever, threw open the doors of the inner sanctuary for an outsider. The President and Mrs. Harding and their entourage were bedazzled with the sight of magnificent treasures. These included enameled chalices, candlesticks, monstrances, and jeweled icons of gold and silver. All of these things were gifts of the Romanovs.*

Sitka was the last stop in Alaska. Afterwards, the *Henderson* set sail for Vancouver, where Mr. Harding became the first American President to visit Canada. According to *The Chicago Tribune*, "President Harding's reception in British Columbia was said to be greater by far than that given to the Prince of Wales two years ago June."

AS I SIT HERE on this snowy night reading of the President's dwindling days, it comes back to me that Marion's first inkling that something was wrong did not come from either the *Star*, or Western Union. It came from "Coonie" Christian, mother of the White House Chief of Staff. I remember that the moment the Presidential party reached their hotel in Seattle, George called home. That would have been on Friday afternoon, July 27, 1923. George had two pieces of disturbing news. That morning in Puget Sound, the *Henderson* collided with one of its escorts, the *Zeilen*, in a heavy fog. Oddly enough, the destroyer fared much worse than the liner. George told his mother that it was nearly cut in half, with many, many dead and more injured. After standing still in the fog for several hours, the *Henderson* was finally able to get underway and dock in Seattle. (Actually, the clippings put the death toll at only two sailors, with more than a dozen injured. But the casualty count for the Voyage of Understanding now stood at seven, and counting.)

The second piece of disturbing news was that the President was ill with cramps in the abdomen. Surgeon General Sawyer had assured everyone that it was nothing serious, just a little bit of ptomaine poisoning from a crabmeat dinner held in the President's suite the evening before. I remember that Coonie was very glad her son, good flatlander that he was, and no lover of seafood, had skipped that particular dinner.

I also remember that the next morning the Harding Volunteers met at Redman Hall. We began preparing some simple banners of welcome for the Homecoming, scheduled for the following weekend. That very same Saturday morning another small delegation, including Adeline and Mrs. Christian, motored over to Blooming Grove to tidy up the yard and the old garden at the Presidential Birthplace, and to run a dust cloth over the simple furnishings. As I mentioned, Mr. and Mrs. Harding intended to spend some quiet days at their place in the country. The President hoped to cast a line in the Whetstone Creek, where he fished and swam as a boy.

Needless to say, that morning we still had no inkling as to just how serious the President's illness was.

It dominated the headlines on Saturday, along with the collision of the two ships. While we were busy preparing for the President's welcome, he was bedfast aboard the *Superb*, as his train sped from Seattle to San Francisco.

The next day, the blue and gold Presidential Standard fluttered above the Palace Hotel, where Mr. Harding was now bedfast in the Presidential Suite on the eighth floor. Surrounding streets were closed off, and silent crowds, numbering in the hundreds, kept vigil in front of the hotel. Clippings from the next two days report that he had developed pneumonia, along with a high fever, cramps, and intestinal involvement, and that more doctors were called in, including a heart specialist.

I remember that Marion took on a strange quiet, just as neighborhoods used to do back when someone was seriously ill in a nearby house. I believe it was on Tuesday morning when notice went out by word of mouth that the churches had all gotten together, by some unprecedented miracle, and had agreed to hold simultaneous prayer services for the President at noon. Factories and places of commerce emptied, and every house of worship filled. I know that the Methodist church, which Lucy and I usually attended, had people standing on the outside steps, backed up into the street. I also know that both before and after the services, long lines formed in front of Western Union, as the President's friends and neighbors patiently waited to send him regards and best wishes.

On Wednesday, the headline of a clipping states, "President Passes Crisis; Declared Out of Danger."

The next day, August 2, 1923, *The New York World* announces, "Harding Continues To Gain; Temperature Now Normal; 'When Do We Start?' He Asks."

Thus a feeling of relief and optimism replaced the foreboding of the past several days, and people around here were giving thanks to God that their prayers had seemingly been answered—with the help, of course, of our own, dear Dr. Sawyer.

THAT WAS THE NIGHT, very late, when I lay in the backyard on a chaise lounge, watching the Perseus meteor shower. It's funny the things one starts to recall after forty years, when the mind turns back. I just this moment remembered the meditations that absorbed me as I lay beneath the falling stars on the President's last evening on earth. The second of August was the first anniversary of my father's death, and so certainly my father prevailed in my thoughts, and indeed his death may have been responsible for a certain bleakness of spirit that overcame me. Earlier that summer Lucy and I were told for certain that she would be unable to bear a child, after the miscarriage of our son, Eric Anthony, the year before. We were never to be blessed, in this world, with a child.

To tell you the truth, it hit me hard. I was lying there in the darkness of that warm summer night watching the shooting stars and listening to the crickets, thinking of our little boy, Eric Anthony. Indeed, as I lay there I could almost feel my little boy cuddled there in the chaise lounge with his papa, asking me all manner of questions as we counted the shooting stars, before he drifted off to sleep, safe in my arms, safe from the world. Sometimes my heart used to be near breaking when I thought of my little boy. Indeed, even now—all these long years later—it saddens me that my beloved little Eric Anthony vanished forty-some years ago without ever having lived, and that I am left without even a grave to visit and lay flowers.

Frankly, on that night when the President died, I believe I may have watched some of those shooting stars through quiet, unavoidable tears.

I should hasten to add that I was not thinking only of myself that night beneath the summer sky, with dear little Bomber curled and sleeping on the chaise at my side. I was also thinking of my ailing neighbor and

President—far, far away in San Francisco. I thought of how Perseus was showering light over him as well, even if he could not see the spectacle. I made a point of wishing upon one of those falling stars that the President would have great good fortune, and that soon, very soon, he would be here with us in Marion, resting at his boyhood home in Blooming Grove, his illness behind him and good days ahead. I resolved that bygones would, at last, be bygones, and I pictured him in shirtsleeves and a straw hat sitting on the rock he had once shown me, with his line in Whetstone Creek, maybe saying again, as he once said, "You're a good friend, Trey, and I appreciate that. A far better friend to me than I've ever been to you."

I now remember as well that the President's mother came to mind. Phoebe Harding died in May of 1910, while Halley's Comet was crossing the heavens.

(Until this moment, I have left out of my account two decidedly parenthetical facts regarding the President, and I add them now with reluctance. I haven't mentioned them before for the simple reason that they are so extraordinary as to be unbelievable—even though the first appears in histories of the President. I shall state them without comment or elaboration, and you can take or leave them as you will. First: At the birth of Warren Gamaliel Harding, on November 2, 1865, in Blooming Grove, Ohio, his mother Phoebe Dickerson Harding stated outright that her son would grow up to become President of the United States. She kept on saying that throughout her lifetime, so much so that, after her son entered politics, folks in Marion—even, I assure you, some who had once called him "Nigger Warren"—began thinking that there might actually be something to her prophecy. As for Mr. Harding himself, he came to believe it more and more. The prophecy was mentioned more than once during the Front Porch Campaign, publicly and privately. One night the subject came up while a number of us were gathered in the parlor, and Mr. Harding told us that his mother's prediction "has always hung over my head like the sword of Damocles." He wondered if the prophecy was somehow coming to pass simply because his mother had repeated it so often for so very long to so many people, especially to him, and that it was, as he said, "taking on its own power." Of course I knew Mr. Harding's mother, though I cannot say that she ever mentioned her prophecy to me. Second: Years before the fact, Phoebe Harding always predicted that she herself would die when Halley's Comet crossed the heavens. In the late winter of 1910, she fell, injuring her leg, on her way to the Marion Opera House where her son was about to announce his candidacy—doomed I might add—for the governorship of Ohio. Her leg never healed, and Phoebe Harding died of infection and high fever on a night during the second or third week in May. Halley's Comet was in the eastern sky, plainly visible through her bedroom window. Both of her sons and her husband were at her bedside. She was a Seventh Day Adventist, God-haunted, and self-possessed with the apparent, occasional ability to look into the future and see precisely what lay there. Her last words, upon awakening moments before her death: "He steps from light.")

Anyway, there I lay beneath the falling stars on the 2nd of August 1923 when the telephone rang around midnight. It probably sounds odd now, but those were simpler times with simpler ways and I do not think I had ever before heard a telephone ring at that hour. As I have already indicated, when it did, I felt something like an arrow of dread pass through my heart. By some prescience of my own, I knew it had to do with the President. I sprang to my feet, flew across the grass, up the three back steps and into the house. When I answered, my friend Earl Bacon identified himself. I can still hear Earl's tearful voice saying, "Trey, he's gone. The President has passed away."

For several seconds, I said nothing, then, "Who says so? How do you know that?"

My unintentional abruptness seemed to compose him, at least for a moment. "Doc Harding. He's the one told me. Poor ol' Doc, he's—" and there were tears in his voice again. "He came 'round calling through our screen door saying his boy's dead in San Francisco."

When I replaced the handset, I stood staring through the back window into the darkness for I do not know how long, maybe a full minute. Then I realized Bomber was whining at the back door and Lucy was calling from our bedroom, "Trey, do you hear me? Who was that? What's the matter?" There was alarm in her voice. (Later she told me that she knew the call's message before I actually told her.)

I dislike shouting, even in the privacy of my own home. I let Bomber in, hooked the screen door for the night, and climbed the stairs to our room. I stopped in the doorway and leaned on the frame. Lucy had not turned on the lamp, but my eyes were already accustomed to the darkness, and even if they had not been, the distant streetlight always gave our room a rather pleasant dim glow, like from a candle beneath a basket. She was sitting bolt upright in bed, wide-eyed and looking at me. "Trey, what's happened?"

"He's gone, Lucy. President Harding is dead."

She instantly burst into tears, as I had known she would. I stood there, longer than I ought, simply watching her weep. Then I crossed the room and took her in my arms. She shed her tears on my shoulder, while I stroked her hair. But really there was nothing for me to say.

Afterwards, I telephoned Adeline. When I gave her the news, she was silent for a moment, and then—Adeline being Adeline—said, "Maybe it's for the best, Trey. Sometimes these things happen for a reason."

Again, I truly wish I could say that the First Lady and Dr. Sawyer told me something about the President's last minutes of life. At least then I would have the account of a witness to relay to you, but neither ever uttered a word to me. I am sure George Christian heard all about it, but neither did he ever say a word, at least not to me.

One of the scrapbook clippings reminds me that George was at a banquet in Hollywood at that time, in the temple of the Knights of Pythias, addressing a group of movie stars and studio people, in his boss' stead. In the middle of his address, someone burst into the dazzling affair, in true Hollywood fashion, and announced at the top of his voice that the President was dead. Apparently, George stood there all hangdog and pathetic, running his hand through his hair moaning that he had just lost the best friend he ever had. I used to wonder, once the talkies came out, if some of the countless melodramatic scenes like that one had their roots in the temple of the Knights of Pythias, when Hollywood heard the announcement of President Harding's death.

By all accounts, President Harding died peacefully. Indeed, one might say that his was a comforting death, if there is such a thing. He was not in any pain, nor was he entombed in his own body from the effects of a stroke. He was propped up in bed on a pillow. He had just eaten a few bites of steak and a little spinach. From time to time, he was sipping a "hot beverage."

Mrs. Harding was sitting at her husband's bedside reading from an article by Samuel G. Blythe entitled "A Calm View of a Calm Man." I see here in Adeline's scrapbook that the article, which appeared in the *Saturday Evening Post*, is a mostly flattering piece about the President, some of it sentimental hogwash. I will quote some of it here:

> *He is neither noisy nor brilliant, in the showy acceptance of that term. He is not loud and declamatory. He is a modest and calm man with a philosophy that has worked out. Under Harding's guidance, the country has moved forward and is now the only legitimately prosperous country in the world. Labor is universally employed at high wages. Money is plentiful. All lines of business are flourishing. And there is no other country in the world of which this can be said.*

Perhaps the First Lady had just read a similar passage for, as the papers of the day and later histories report, when she paused and looked up to see if the President was tiring, he said, "That's good. Go on. Read some more."

The instant he said that, a change swept over his face. His hand shot out, his body shuddered terribly, and then he seemed to collapse into himself.

Mrs. Harding sprang to her feet, the magazine falling to the floor. She ran into the corridor calling, "Dr. Sawyer! Dr. Sawyer!"

Within seconds, the Surgeon General and one of the attending physicians rushed in from an adjoining suite and were at his bedside.

The President died moments later. The First Lady was holding his hand.

As I have mentioned before, she did not shed a single tear, and indeed proclaimed, "I shan't break down. I shan't!"

And she did not.

IV

⚘

Immediately, a Plague of Rumors

I CANNOT SAY FOR CERTAIN when the rumors that the First Lady had poisoned the President began in the rest of the country, but I know for a fact that they were circulating in Marion within forty-eight hours of his death. On Saturday, August 4th, to be exact. I remember that the heat wave that had blistered Ohio for three weeks had begun to abate on Thursday, and now the weather was perfectly brilliant, oddly belying the sorrow and tragedy that engulfed the town. Colonel Hamilton & Son was closed both Friday and Saturday out of respect, and we would not resume business until Monday morning. (Of course we would close again for the Funeral, but that was nearly a week away.) We of the Harding Volunteers, soon to be known as the Harding Commemorative Society, had spent all day Friday and much of that night hastening plans to drape the town in mourning. But on Saturday I had to attend to some pressing business matters.

I believe I may have once or twice mentioned Dana Yost. He was the fellow who stashed the cans of kerosene behind the carriage house at Tioga that night in October 1920 when we burned Chancellor's books. Regrettably, he had a weird falling out with Addy and me in 1947, but I shall tell you of that later. Dana was my lumberyard manager after the Great War, and I guess you could say he became my all-around "right-hand man" after Argus Finch, one of our former employees, went off to Washington to join the Administration. (President Coolidge invited him to stay on, and Argus never lived in Marion again.) Dana was an excellent worker, and was always uncomplaining about the many tasks at hand.

His sense of organization and inventory was impeccable, and when he used a typewriter, his fingers flew like the wind; however, I would have to say that his social wisdom was decidedly deficient. He sometimes had a basic lack of good old common sense. He was also a devoted gossip—a most unseeming flaw in a man, so far as I am concerned—and as such he was an effusive conduit of any rumors and tattle that happened to be making their way around Marion. It seems to me that Dana was a magnet for such talk. He was gregarious and would hear things that I would not have heard in a million years, even if I spent all day with my rump parked on a bench on the Courthouse lawn. If I scolded him once, I scolded him a thousand times for telling me things about people that I did not need to know, did not want to know, and could not have cared less about. But all my chiding and scolding never shut him up, not when he had some juicy tidbit to relate. I suppose if we had not been classmates, then his tongue might have been a bit more tied down around me, his boss. By the same token I must add that Dana was always unfailingly discreet when anyone else was present, and to this day I am certain that, until 1947, I was never a subject of his gossip; indeed, in those early days he was utterly loyal and protective of me. During our youth and young manhood, he sometimes seemed a little too loyal to me. He was a funny mix. I read once somewhere, a long time ago, about a man who was streaked with lavender and soft spots of violet. I did not know exactly what that meant, but I did know that it somehow captured Dana.

At the time of the President's death, Colonel Hamilton & Son was engaged in the decades-long process of developing Marion's well-to-do eastern suburbs, known as Vernon Heights. On what would have been Monday the 6th of August 1923, I was slated, as I recall, to "walk the lines" in the company of some fellows from the utilities, along a section of land to the east of what is now Vernon Heights Boulevard. (On Tuesday the 7th, a large delegation of Marion folks, me included, would head for Washington to attend the National Funeral, and then escort the body home to Marion.) In terms of the utilities, some last-minute details needed to be worked out with the grids, survey maps, and such, especially with the water company—hence my presence in the office that day. And Dana was kind and devoted enough to come in and help me with these matters.

When the Courthouse bell struck noon, he took some coins from petty cash and walked over to Price's Market, the little corner store near the lumberyard, to pick up some cold pop and fried, thick-cut baloney sandwiches. Mrs. Price's market was more than just a neighborhood store. It was a gathering place where folks sat around talking on the steps and porch furniture, or inside around the flour and pickle barrels, and stove. I seldom ventured there, but Dana liked any excuse to run over and pick up this or that for us. He still lived with his parents, and I think he was a bit lonely, and the folks at Price's seemed to like him.

On that particular Saturday, I was listening for his footsteps. I had skipped breakfast, but my appetite had returned as the morning wore on. About a half an hour or so after he left, I heard his shoes crunch-crunching over the crushed gravel. I was working at the big oak table along the north wall of my office, facing Quarry Street, with some specifications and a survey map spread before me. I was surprised to hear his footsteps coming directly towards my window, it seemed, instead of heading for the door. He stopped just below my sill and called up through the screen, "Say, Trey!"

There was something giddy in his voice, and muted, like he wanted me to hear, but did not want anyone else to hear—not that a single other soul was present within at least five hundred yards. I stepped to the window. There he stood looking up at me, a brown bag in the palm of each hand— our lunches—like he was carrying flower pots. He was wearing his turtle shell sunglasses. Sunglasses were not at all common in Marion in 1923, nothing like today. In fact, I do not remember anyone else around here ever wearing them back then, other than Mitzy von Leuckel—though I may be wrong on that score.

"What?" I said.

"You are absolutely not going to believe what they're saying about Warren's death."

For a moment I said nothing. Ordinarily, I would have reminded him that I could not care less what "they" were saying about anything. And after that reminder, he would have gone right ahead and told me anyway. But this time I said, "Oh? So what are they saying about 'Warren's death'?"

He glanced over his shoulder and then distinctly but quietly said, "Poison."

"What?"

"You heard me. Strychnine, I suspect." He held up the brown bags and, with a smile said, "I got the baloney."

I must say that Dana had never before captured my attention in quite the same way, though for some reason I did not want him to have an inkling into this. I sat right back down at my table and huddled again over the survey map, with my back to the door—just as I had been for the past two hours. I heard his footsteps cross his outer office, and he was speaking even before he came through the door. "Trey, listen to this, it makes perfect sense. It's an illumination. Really it is. An illumination of you-know-who's discreet—evil!"

I glanced over my shoulder, "What kind of pop did you get me?"

"Now I want you to think about this, Trey, before you go dismissing things out of hand, as is your custom and your wont. First and foremost, do you or do you not think that Flossie was mad with jealousy over Miss von Leuckel?"

I said nothing, pretending absorption with my map. By the rustling of the paper I could tell that he was taking our sandwiches out of the bags and laying them on my desk.

"Not to mention that she's equally furious about Miss Nan Britton, and who knows who else. But Warren having his girls visit him in the White House! If Marion caught wind of that, then so did Flossie. And let me put it to you plain—both of them probably got a pretty good look at the Oval Office ceiling."

"Dana!" I snapped, "I'll not have you talking about our late President in such a despicable fashion."

"As if what I say or don't say will make his habits less despicable. Come on, Trey. You know all this better than I do. There's no doubt in my mind—there ought to be no doubt in anyone's mind—that she, our beloved First Lady, ex-First Lady, if you please, is perfectly capable of murder." He paused for dramatic effect. "Yes, Trey. I said murder! With a capital M."

"That's absurd."

"Oh?" He paused. I heard the cork pop from one of the bottles. "Say, are you going to come over here and eat this or are you going to sit there all day looking out the window?"

I got up and went to my desk. Dana had laid out our sandwiches, using as plates the thick, pinkish butcher's paper they were wrapped in. "You're always so incredibly naïve about things you choose to be incredibly naïve about, Trey, and so incredibly shrewd about everything else. It's the damnedest thing I ever saw! But anyway, think about it, it makes perfect sense. There's a very good chance Flossie poisoned him. Why, even people who seem utterly normal and utterly incapable of killing someone are very often perfectly capable doing just that."

I raised my eyes from my sandwich and looked at Dana in—how shall I say?—a most significant way. After all, in 1923 there were still people in this town who no doubt thought of me as "Killer Trey." He fell silent under my loaded gaze and blushed crimson. I took a swig of root beer to hide my smile and delight at his embarrassment.

"Trey, I didn't mean it like that, what I meant was—Well, you know what I meant. Now let's take Flossie. Okay, picture this. Would you really truly feel totally safe if you had, God forbid, a wife like that? And if, say, she found out that you were still sowing your wild boyhood oats at the tender age of fifty-five? Would you feel safe sleeping in the same room with her after she found out about little Miss Britton and little Miss Mitzy? Or would you feel safe eating food that she cooked up? And tell me this, Trey—" and he leaned towards me, over his still untouched sandwich.

Before he could utter his question, I said, "You know your sandwich is going to get all cold while you're blabbing on, and then you're going to be whining about it tasting greasy."

He took a bite, and while chewing his food, he said, "So tell me this, young Mr. Hamilton, did it cross your mind as you read the paper, as to why Flossie refused an autopsy? Very strange. And why, by the way, did she spend all Thursday night sitting outside of the room where they were embalming him? Sitting there in a chair, guarding the door until the undertakers rolled him out in his nice shiny new coffin."

"Keeping vigil." I had read those words in the *Star*. "Mrs. Harding was keeping vigil."

"I'll say she was! Like a hawk keeps vigil."

"Dana, you're speaking of the First Lady."

"Does that somehow mean that we are not speaking about Flossie Kling Harding? And another thing—they had a point over at Price's—

think about the President's death. The doctors were in, as they said, 'consultation.' In medical circles that means disagreement. 'Well,' says Dr. Sawyer, 'Looks to me like we have here an apoplectic stroke. Everything that I don't know about medicine cries out to me, apoplectic stroke! And I'm sure we can all agree, Gentlemen, that apoplexy looks ever so nice on a death certificate. When in doubt, write apoplexy. That's my motto. Hand me the pen.' Says another, 'My dear Dr. Sawyer, are you saying you don't know a heart attack when you see one? Why, it's plain as day. His heart locked up on him.' Says another, 'But I beg to differ with both of you gentlemen. Remember, our reputations, such as they are, are at stake. The whole world is watching. We are doctors of medicine, not politicians, so we should record the truth and say what we really think. And what we really think is that the ol' boy was poisoned. Of course we can fudge a bit on the details and call it accidental poisoning. Accidental ingestion of arsenic because someone got ornery and accidentally sprinkled it in his peas. Or accidentally spilt a thimble full in his bootleg gin.'"

Said I, to humor him, "Where and how, pray tell, dear Dana, could the First Lady have possibly laid her hands on arsenic, without anyone knowing? Though mind you, when you came to the window you said strychnine."

He shrugged his shoulders, "Strychnine, arsenic—" And smiled like he was ready for my question. "Where'd she get it? Why, where else? Dr. Sawyer himself. He's Surgeon General. He can get anything he wants. Anything! Besides, let's not forget, he is and always has been a homeopath. That's all those guys use is poison. Got bowel storms? They'll be happy to give you enough belladonna so you'll be flat out, and—voilà! no more muss and fuss."

"I don't think that's quite how it works."

"Tut tut tut, dear Trey, that's exactly how it works."

"But arsenic—or something like it—wouldn't that look kind of odd? The President's personal physician ordering arsenic from a drug store?"

"Why bother with arsenic when you got belladonna? Or what have you?" Dana thought for a moment. "Or maybe they had an accomplice. That's how these things get done. Keeps the major players' hands clean."

"Then I suppose Dr. Sawyer was also furious about Mitzy and Nan, since it seems he was in collusion with Mrs. Harding in the assassination of the President of the United States. At least that's how Dana Yost and the sages at Price's Market figure it. Right?"

He leaned back in his chair and took a swig of his root beer. "Well, I admit some details do need to be worked out, but the theory is sound, I assure you."

"Not to worry. I'm sure you'll be working them out ever so diligently."

He nodded. "The point is, Trey, that maybe Flossie and Doctor Sawyer were in collusion, and maybe, just maybe, they were closer than we think. Or have the stomach to think." He leaned back in his chair and winked at me. I looked away, and laughed at the comical absurdity of either of them engaging in illicit love. Dana said, "It's possible. It's very, very possible." His voice became suddenly and strangely quiet, almost thoughtful. "You know, Trey, odder things than Flossie and Doc Sawyer happen. In fact, much, much odder things happen every night of the week, right here in straight-laced Marion."

I looked away, out the window, towards the meadow and the railroad tracks beyond.

Dana added, "Anyway, if Dr. Sawyer is in cahoots with Flossie, in any way, shape, or form, then he damn well better watch out, because he'll get his, too."

By now, we had both finished our sandwiches, and the hands of the big wall clock were moving on toward one. I rolled up the pink butcher's paper and threw it towards the waste can on the other side of the room. It plunged straight in, without even touching the rim.

Dana whistled. "That's our Trey! Never misses his mark!"

V

WEDNESDAY AFTER MIDNIGHT

Mrs. Harding Previews
"A Tomb Fit for Caesar"

AS YOU HAVE ALREADY GATHERED, the First Lady was, in fact, sometimes lacking in sound judgment. Indeed, from time to time she was utterly blind to the possible consequences of her actions. When she burnt those thousands upon thousands of Presidential papers, hoping to protect her husband's reputation, what she really did, of course, was indirectly indict him, in the eyes of many, and arouse suspicion regarding her own character. And God only knows why she refused an autopsy. Now I admit that a lot of people from her generation were of the belief that autopsies are a desecration of the dead, and I know some religious folks who still believe that they are blasphemous inquiries of God. But as far as Mrs. Harding goes, I doubt that either of these notions crossed her mind at the Palace Hotel when she announced, minutes after the President's death, "No autopsy. Don't even utter that accursed word in my presence. I'll not have them slicing up Warren."

So that was that.

Historians have always taken the assassination rumor very seriously. For instance, I have just pulled from the shelves Adeline's copy of a book that I read and enjoyed one summer about thirty years ago, *Only Yesterday*, by Mr. Frederic Hamilton Allen. The book was very popular back then, and I know for a fact that even today it is required reading in the eleventh grade American History classes at Harding High School. Of course I generally have no use for historians—and mind you, they have earned every ounce of my contempt, but I enjoyed Mr. Allen's book and I regard *Only Yesterday* as an engaging history of the 1920s. Unfortunately, in terms of President Harding, the author proved himself to be just another sensationalist rumormonger.

On page 135 of the First Edition, which I have here before me, Mr. Allen calls the assassination rumor "very plausible."

Through the years, tens of thousands of people have read those words, and taken his opinion seriously, including the children at Marion Harding High School.

Now what are those youngsters going to think of their town's homegrown First Lady when they read that?

I have also pulled from the same shelf a thicker volume entitled *Fighting Years*, written by Mr. Oswald Garrison Villard. I read this book, too, back in those years, though it made less of a lasting impression on me than *Only Yesterday*. I suspect this particular book has been out of print for decades, and I think Mr. Villard—the late owner of *The New York Evening Post*—is now mostly forgotten, but in his day he was a well-known, prolific, and much talked about author. (I read somewhere a long time ago that he was also mountainously wealthy, so much so that he lived in a gilded palace in New York City.) Anyway, on page 501, these words appear:

> It is a fact that Harding's letters in his own hand bring tremendous prices—because—so the dealers say—after his death his widow begged or bought every letter of his and then destroyed them, along with thousands of his papers. I am one of those who lean to the belief that there was foul play in his death and that we shall probably never learn the truth. It is, however, an extraordinary coincidence that Surgeon General Sawyer died just as unexpectedly and as suddenly as did the President under precisely similar circumstances. Mrs. Harding was a visitor in his house at the time. The New York Times reported that at the time of his death Mrs. Harding was a guest in his house.

Needless to say, Dana and the other rumormongers—historians among them—had a veritable field day with that accident of history—the fact that Mrs. Harding just happened to be in residence at White Oak

Farm when Dr. Sawyer died of apoplexy. When that happened, I do not think Dana could have been any more tickled if he had won the Irish Sweepstakes. I believe he thought it proof that he possessed not only the gift of gab but also the gift of prescience.

About six weeks after Dr. Sawyer's death, as I was leaving my office, heading over to White Oaks Farm to visit the very ailing First Lady for what turned out to be the last time, Dana raised his finger and said, quite gravely, "Trey, whatever you do, do not eat or drink anything that that woman proffers." I laughed and told him that he was being foolish, and he said, "I am serious, Tristan. Deadly serious. That woman's lost her marbles, and she was mean as a snake to begin with. She can't be trusted. No food. No drink. Period. Promise me!"

I laughed and started to walk out the door, when he said, "Trey, I said ..."

"I promise you I'll return as fit as a fiddle."

Anyway, this evening Mr. Villard's mention of *The New York Times* sent me flipping through Adeline's scrapbooks again, and sure enough—after clippings about the growing scandals, the Congressional hearings, "The Conspiracy of the Ohio Gang" (about the folks in Marion supposedly having tried to take control of the government), the scathing editorials about our plans for a colossal memorial, etc.—after all of those clippings, and more, I found in the last pages of the last scrapbook Dr. Sawyer's obituary from the *Times*, dated September 24, 1924.

I immediately noticed that this particular clipping was distinguished in one minor way from all the others. Namely, in this clipping, Adeline had underlined something. Naturally, I read these words first:

> *General Sawyer's death was almost identical with the manner of death of the late President Harding when General Sawyer was with the President in San Francisco. Mrs. Harding was at White Oaks Farm when General Sawyer was found dead.*

Now I am not going to sit here and speculate as to why, thirty years ago, my sister underlined those particular words, and only those, of all the tens of thousands—if not hundreds of thousands of words—that are packed into these bulging volumes. Indeed, as I sit here pondering the question, I must say that I have not a clue.

I should make clear that my only agenda here is to set the record straight regarding President Harding and his history and accomplishments, and to do so by telling the Truth. In short, it is not my intention to lie or cover up anything. In fact, to prove my point, I shall forthwith "put my money where my mouth is" and admit that I am personally responsible for a couple of inaccuracies in the aforementioned and intentionally quoted *Times* article—as well as every other newspaper that used Associated Press sources to report on the Surgeon General's death. What I mean is this: The Harding Commemorative Society had taken it upon itself to be the intermediary between the late President's circle here in Marion, and the remnant of the press corps that still reported on that circle. I use the word "remnant" loosely. In fact, there was only one AP man that was still around at that time, and he was merely moonlighting for the cables, while he worked full-time for the *Star*. (That reporter, incidentally, happened to be Jim Blaine—the man who became Mr. Mitzy von Leuckel.) It was not the custom then, any more than it is now, for reporters to go knocking on the doors of bereaved families, no matter the stature of the deceased. By default, the moment Dr. Sawyer died, I became spokesman for his family. As such, I gave out the information that I thought appropriate, and no one contradicted me.

Obituaries throughout the nation stated that on the afternoon of September 23rd, 1924, Dr. Sawyer complained to his son that he was not feeling well, that he took some medicine, felt considerably relieved, that he then went and lay down on a couch in his office, talked to Mrs. Sawyer, dozed off, gave a start, and died.

That is not exactly the way it happened.

Once again, I cannot speak from firsthand experience because I was not in the house at the time. For that matter, contrary to the newspaper reports, neither the Surgeon General's son George nor Mrs. Sawyer was there. George was in his own house on Bellefontaine Avenue. As for Mrs. Sawyer, she was visiting her sister in Galion. Now before you too start jumping on the rumor bandwagon, let me say emphatically that the First Lady was *not* alone in the house with the Surgeon General, anymore than she was alone with the President in that suite of rooms in the Palace Hotel. A nurse was right there in Dr. Sawyer's office with him. And the housekeeper, who had personally prepared and served supper, was but a few steps away in the kitchen.

What happened was this: Mrs. Harding and Dr. Sawyer had been dining together and were just dipping into their chocolate puddings when he suddenly took ill. He complained of lightheadedness, excused himself, and made his way back to his office where he lay down on the horsehair couch. Mrs. Harding, of course, had already summoned the nurse, who was there doing whatever it is that nurses do in such circumstances. By then, the First Lady (who herself was obviously not at all well) was sitting on a chair beside her old friend when he gave a start and died.

And no, she was not reading to him.

I think it is probably clear from the unfortunate, coincidental circumstances why I chose to doctor a few of the details that I gave to the press. I simply wanted to deflect some of the embarrassing suspicion that I knew would inevitably be cast upon poor Mrs. Harding's head. By the same token I may or may not have erred in another way. I did not think it appropriate to tell Blaine, the AP man, that Mrs. Harding strongly encouraged the Sawyers to have an autopsy. They politely demurred. The Surgeon General had long been suffering from high blood pressure and so Mrs. Sawyer saw no point in an inquest. Nor did George, who in his bereavement found the thought most upsetting—having assisted in autopsies during his medical school days. Quite frankly, I would have altered a few more details if that good-for-nothing Jim Blaine had not known fully well that Mrs. Harding was living out at White Oaks Farm. I admit that my doctoring of the facts may not have been 100 percent aboveboard, though I would hardly call it deceitful.

Of course the folks in Marion soon learned that the information I provided was not 100 percent accurate; unfortunately, outsiders gradually learned that as well. In looking back, I suppose I made a regrettable mistake. At best, my ruse simply blunted some rumors that would soon cut even deeper into the Harding legacy. And mind you, I paid for my ruse. My doctoring of the facts has always been one of the pieces of bait that has drawn historians to me through the years. It was as if I had donned apparel made of flypaper.

As the saying states, "No good deed goes unpunished."

I suppose another thing that eventually drew the historians to me was the unfortunate rumor and gossip that my sister Adeline was Mrs. Harding's accomplice in the supposed assassination of the President. I have often thought that, if the First Lady had kept her big mouth shut during our Thanksgiving dinner at Tioga, if she had not mentioned Adeline's luncheon aboard the *Superb,* then no one would have ever connected my sister's good name with the assassination rumor.

According to the rumormongers, that luncheon in Columbus was when Adeline handed over the poison to Mrs. Harding.

WHEN I LAST SAW the First Lady, about eight or ten days before her death, and a couple of months after the Surgeon General's death, I was already well aware of the rumor that my sister was her accomplice in the putative assassination of the President. At least the rumormongers credited Adeline with a charitable motive, more or less. To my knowledge there was never any suggestion that Adeline involved herself with the First Lady's supposed jealousy, nor that she aided Mrs. Harding and Dr. Sawyer in an illicit romance. I guess Adeline somehow did not quite fit into that particular picture.

But she fit quite well into the rumor that soon took its place and has endured through the years.

In this later view she was participating in what one might call the President's sanctifying martyrdom. That is to say, the First Lady had concluded (according to the rumormongers) that if Harding were dead, then people would feel sorry for him and would not blame him for the corruption in his Administration, news of which—she knew—would all too soon reach the public. Of course, in the summer of 1923, before the presidential party set out on the Voyage of Understanding, Mrs. Harding was aware of the grave problems besetting the Administration. According to our theorists and logicians, Mrs. Harding put a bug about those misfortunes into Adeline's ear, asked her to go out and shop around for some poison, preferably something subtle, and Adeline obliged her, dropping it off during that luncheon aboard the *Superb.* In one version, Adeline—an accomplished horticulturist—actually concocted this poison herself, either from flowers growing in Tioga's gardens, or else from plants she gathered from the Old Forest. The charitable motive was this: If President Harding were to die in office, while he was still vastly popular and well-loved, then his popularity would either remain fixed in time and never change or else grow as a result of his martyrdom.

After all, decent folks (except for the likes of Dana Yost) do not speak ill of the dead.

I wish to say on the First Lady's behalf that—contrary to what folks were bandying about at the time—she most certainly had not "lost her marbles." I also have proof that she was not desperately intent upon ridding the world of my sister, thus ensuring her silence after Mrs. Harding's own death. I will be the first to admit that the evidence I am going to lay before you is circumstantial at best and would not exonerate Adeline in a court of law, but I think the evidence easily passes muster in the court of common sense.

The First Lady herself, I might add, handed this evidence, to me.

I remember that gloomy day in November of 1924 when I saw Mrs. Harding for the last time. Indeed, that remote morning at White Oaks Farm, almost exactly twenty-nine years ago, was very much like the leaden morning we endured today. I suppose the overcast sky, the unchanged nature of White Oaks Farm, and of course my own preoccupation with the death of the President all contributed to the trick my imagination played upon me this morning when, for an instant, I imagined it was Mrs. Harding who had answered the door, instead of Mrs. Sawyer.

I had gone there to show her the four finalists in the national design competition we held for the proposed Harding Memorial. I suppose that I wanted her blessing, so to speak, to go ahead with the matter, though frankly, we intended to build a magnificent tomb for the President whether we had the First Lady's blessing or not. I spoke on the telephone with her the day before, and she specifically said that she wanted to see the designs. But Lucy wondered whether my visit was in the best of taste. She was one of those well-intentioned souls who adapt an aspect of false cheer around the dying, I suppose as a means of trying to make them think that very soon they'll bound out of bed and go shopping or something. (I am sorry to say that Lucy never lost her own terror of death, not even during her last painful days, a time when many people seem to put such fear aside as they prepare to meet their Maker. I held her hand to the last, but could not go with her, yet, to the land she was traveling to.) Lucy made a point of saying that I was going to White Oaks Farm to show a dying woman a picture of her own tomb. My response was, "So what?"

In the 1870s my grandfather established the Hamilton family plot out at what was then the new Marion Cemetery. Thus countless times my mother and father both saw the scrap of earth wherein they would be buried, long before they were laid there. The same can be said of Adeline, and I might add that every time I decorate poor Lucy's grave, and the graves of my beloved family members (and Nora, our dear housekeeper), I see that patient patch of earth wherein my own bones shall someday lie. What is more, I even see the little headstone with my name already chiseled into the granite, along with my year of birth, a hyphen, and 19__, awaiting the year of my concealment. I hardly consider any of this a problem, and I do not walk away from my grave-to-be in the least bit "down in the dumps." Indeed, it cheers me. After all, I am once again turning my backside to my own grave and skittering back into the land of the living.

Anyway, I ignored Lucy's silly quibbles and took the designs out to White Oaks Farm, though I admit that initially I left them in the car. The First Lady was covered with several blankets, her legs propped high upon pillows which in turn were piled on a hassock. A pair of slippers lay on the rug beside her. Mrs. Harding's eyes were closed and her lips were sort of pinched together, like she had a pain somewhere. Her hands lay folded on her lap. An aspect of sorrow, of leave-taking, permeated the room. For some reason the heavy draperies were drawn against the wan daylight, and so the only illumination came from the lamp behind Mrs. Harding's shoulder, and from the small flames licking away at the log behind the fire screen. Within those walls it seemed more like evening than morning. Her face was puffier than usual. She had always been most attentive to her hair, carefully keeping its thinness disguised with marcelled waves that gave her a much-needed touch of elegance and femininity, but now those waves had fallen flat, and I could see dull white scalp gleaming through pathetic strands. And I think for the first time in my life, I saw Mrs. Harding without her spectacles—it was jarring in an unexpected way. I whispered to the nurse, inquiring if her patient remembered that I was coming, and I was assured that she did, and that she was awake. I do not know why, but for some reason as I stood there I thought of the story that Mr. Harding told George Christian and me in his parlor one pleasant evening back in the summer of 1910, about how twenty years earlier, bold young Flossie Kling had followed him by train, boat, and carriage all the way to Hotel Victory, on South Bass Island, where in the afternoon he encountered her on the walkway above the cliffs overlooking beautiful Lake Erie. She had stood beneath a parasol with violets in her hair. Thus began the romance that led to their marriage and to the long unfolding of their lives together. Here, I thought, slumbered the sad ending of that bold long-ago young woman's curious history.

I walked softly across the carpet towards her. As I did, Mrs. Harding opened her eyes, but it was as if her naked eyes were trying to distinguish something moving in the darkness. She seemed not to focus on my face but on the air around me, until I was a few feet from her. Then she smiled and suddenly seemed very much alive. "Why, Trey, darling, you're here! You didn't forget me, did you, my darling? Ever faithful, ever kind."

I bent and kissed her cheek. "Mrs. Harding," I said, "dear Mrs. Harding." She smelled of camphor and something else that I could not place. "So are they keeping you comfortable?"

She made a little motion with her shoulders and forced a wounded kind of smile. "As best they can. But really, at this juncture, there's only so much they can do. I'm certainly comfortable now, and young Dr. Sawyer has no qualms whatsoever about giving me all the morphine I need. I suppose I'm a—what's that horrible word?"

I knew the word she was thinking of, but I did not want to say it.

Then she remembered, "A fiend," she said. "Like an opium fiend, but it hardly matters now." She squeezed my hand. "But enough of me, Trey, darling. How are you? How's Lucy? How is sweet little Bomber?" She paused, "And Adeline? You must tell me of Adeline."

I may have blushed when she asked about my sister. Adeline rarely came to see her. I knew for a fact that she had not been out since Dr. Sawyer's death, back in September. The nurse brought me a Chippendale so I could sit by Mrs. Harding's side. "Everyone's well," I said, adjusting the chair. "They all send their love." I paused, and hoping to divert the conversation from Adeline, I said, "Bomber caught a rabbit the other day and—well, there was fur all over the backyard. Lucy was very put out with the little guy. Made him sleep on the back porch for two nights running, and believe me, he knows what he's being punished for."

The First Lady bit her lip and shook her head. "That little dickens! But it's not his fault. If you'd keep him on a string, that wouldn't happen. It's your own fault for letting him run loose like that. Besides, he might get run over by a speeding automobile someday. Then there'll be tears. Lord forbid." But as usual, Mrs. Harding was not to be sidetracked. She paused, "Trey, Adeline hasn't come to see me. Why is that?"

This time, I know I blushed. I could feel the fire in my face.

"Why, I didn't mean to embarrass you, darling. I was just wondering if maybe you knew. I just don't understand Adeline, that's all. She knows I'm not long for this world. And it's not like I'm on the other side of the country. I'm on the other side of town." She shook her head, and tears seemed to come into her eyes—another first—and with that astonishing sight, I knew that I was being counted on to give a full accounting to Adeline of these sad goings-on. "Why, I used to take her downtown when she was a little girl and buy her nice gloves and powders, after your mama died. Now she's forgotten me, in my old age." She bit her lip to keep from crying, and shook her head. "And another thing, why isn't she married? Just turned thirty, still unmarried! What on earth's going to become of her? She's going to be an old maid for sure."

It seemed to me that Mrs. Harding had always been somewhat critical of my sister, though I really never understood why. Since becoming a widow, the First Lady had grown increasingly harsh in her criticisms. As for me, I cannot say that I felt comfortable sitting there being a foil for aggrieved remarks about Addy. I said, "Well, I worry about her too, Mrs. Harding, but that's about all I can do, isn't it? I certainly can't tell her to get married or . . ."

"Too rich and too spoiled. Too good for everyone, including America's First Lady. Former First Lady—though I might add that Warren's term in office has yet to expire, even if he is dead, so to hell with the Coolidges. And Adeline's far too pretty, too. It's made her vain. And living out in that big house with no husband to look after, and no little ones to raise. She only has herself to think of. That's her problem. Only herself to consider. She's going to be an old maid, you wait and see. In this world beauty only goes so far and lasts so long. You'd think she'd know that, tending flowers and all. And even if she went out and got married tomorrow, it would still be too late for children. Or almost. It'll never happen. Never." She paused, and I knew what she was going to say next. She used to say it in front of her husband every chance she got; the comment always cast Mr. Harding into a sullen kind of silence. She said, "It's a great sadness to me that Warren and I never had a family. All those long years as husband and wife, but where *are* the children? Where *are* the children? Where's Warren Harding, Jr.? He'd be such a good and nice looking boy, just like you, a good friend for you, and a good son for me. Where is he? And where's his little sisters and brothers? President of the United States and no heirs! No one to carry on the family name! And here I sit—alone in old age." I looked away, into the fire, and Mrs. Harding glanced about and said to herself again, as if demanding an answer from who knows whom, "Where *are* my children?"

To tell you the truth, I almost felt like crying.

Perhaps Mrs. Harding saw this in me, for she said, "Oh, Trey, I'm sorry. Don't feel bad. The world is what it is." After a pause, she said, "I do go on, don't I? You didn't drive out here to listen to some crabby old woman, did you? Poor thing. All in all, I've had a good run. It's just that—" She paused. "But I really do worry about Adeline. Really I do."

"Yes, Mrs. Harding, I know, and I'm sure she appreciates your concern."

"It's just that she's so—so very exasperating."

I determined that I would not say one more word so long as the discussion focused on my sister and her supposed faults, so I leaned back in the chair and looked up at the old-fashioned print on the wall—a picture with a sympathetic-looking lion with its paw on a fainted maiden.

The First Lady said, "There's some chocolates there, Trey," nodding towards a fancy box on the little table beside her chair. "Help yourself."

I instantly thought of Dana's injunction, delivered less than a half an hour before.

"Thank you," I said, and I leaned towards the candy. "Hmm. Are there any particular ones you'd recommend, Mrs. Harding?"

"Well, I can only nibble on one every now and then, but I imagine they're all good. You might fancy those fat round ones, the ones with the leaf stamped on them. They're filled with a nice jam, and I think some kind of liqueur."

I tried one. "Delicious."

"Then take another. Take a couple. But don't get fat."

I took one more. "Superb!" I said. She gave me a funny look. I smiled to myself, relishing the thought of reporting this to Dana. That is to say, if I lived long enough to do so!

She said, "Italian chocolates are always the best, at least in my book. So much better than our waxy American variety. The Prime Minister himself sent them to me, through the Italian Ambassador in Washington. Actually, Orlando remembered I like them and sent me two boxes. But I can't eat them. So remind me before you go, I'd like to give one to Adeline. I know how much she likes rich things from foreign lands." The First Lady paused, and with obvious resentment said, "I'll still be nice and remember your sister, even if she's forgotten me. Shame on her."

I said nothing, and I must admit that the rumorists must have gotten to me, for her desire to give Adeline a box of chocolates did in fact give me a touch of suspicion.

Suddenly Mrs. Harding seemed to remember the topic that we had spoken about on the telephone. "Why, Trey, where's the designs for the President's monument? You said you'd bring them out."

"Oh, that's right!" I do not know why, but I glanced around me, pretending as if maybe I had laid them on the floor beside me, or on a table. "Oh, I believe I left them in the car. Do you want to see them, Mrs. Harding?"

"Well, of course I want to see them, you young fool! What's wrong with you? Why would you leave them in the car when I'm in here? Go right out there and get them, and be quick about it. You know I'm not long for this world!"

I laughed, and obeyed.

I HAVE JUST REALIZED THAT, up to this point, I have said scarcely a word about the colossal monument we envisioned, so I think, before I tell you further about my last encounter with the First Lady, that I should interrupt myself and say a little something about what we had in mind. And when I say "we" I mean President Harding's friends and neighbors here in Marion. Officially, as you know, we were known as the Harding Commemorative Society; unofficially, as I believe I have already indicated, we were known as "The Ohio Gang"—a phrase sometimes decorated in those days by various expletives. It seems odd and yet strangely fitting that we had to endure such a low, outlaw type of designation, when in fact we had such high-minded vision, and yet that irony and incongruity are typical of so much having to do with Mr. Harding's tragedy. Nevertheless, I might add that it was not particularly important to us what our critics said of us, or thought of us, for we were collectively filled with—that French term again—*amour-propre.*

While news of the scandals was raging, and while the rest of the nation was preoccupied with corrupt and degenerate men (not a single one from Marion), we were familiarizing ourselves with classical architecture. Members of the Society studied drawings and photographs of the Parthenon in Athens, the temple of Assos in Asia Minor, of Silinus in Sicily, and Corcyra in Corfu, as well as the Tholos at Delphi and the Mausoleum at Halicarnassus. And mind you, this was not just an "elitist pastime of the wealthy members of the Ohio Gang"—which seemed to be the overall opinion of editorial writers and our critics-at-large. Virtually every man, woman, and child in Marion took an interest in this endeavor, just as nearly every one of them contributed something. Engravings of ancient buildings were produced by the hundreds, courtesy of Marion's secret societies—both the Masons and the Patriarchs Militant of the Odd Fellows. Believe it or not, these renderings became objects of keen interest in factory yards and classrooms and across porch rails and over dinner tables.

I will not go so far as to say that the names of ancient architects were on the lips of butchers and welders, but I will say that many of us, especially the members of the inner circle of the Society, familiarized ourselves with the works of Callicrates and Ictinus, Vitruvius and Theodorus of Phocaea. To us, their names had the same familiarity as the names of foreign generals during the Great War, and we learned words like *ellipsoid* and *entablature, cella* and *peristyle.* The columnar orders—part of every school child's education—suddenly took on local relevance.

In the brochure *Guidelines for Architects Participating in the Design Competition for the Harding Memorial,* which we sent to interested architects, I wrote:

> *We do not expect you to innovate; we expect you to fulfill. It is the intention of the Harding Commemorative Society to conceive and raise a splendid monument. Granted, this monument will not be the issuance of a heroic or spiritual age, least of all that; rather, it will represent a transcendent impulse insinuating itself into modernity, here in our anomalous little town.*

As I have already made clear, our aspirations added to the ridicule already leveled at us by newspapers, ordinary people, and politicians throughout the land. For the most part, they took the view that we were vainglorious and antiquated, a bit pathetic and vastly pretentious. I might add that, by my dim lights, that is the way ordinary people all too often view extraordinary, "impractical" endeavors—especially in an age of impaired vitality, when personal gain alone, or war, or nothing at all, evokes profound commitment and enthusiasm. Yet in one sense I will allow that our critics were correct. Yes, Marion would build out of pride, out of defense and defiance, but as I see it, we would also build out of principles and ambitions that, in a manner of speaking, rose from slumber and walked among us from the epoch of Herodotus and Pericles, from the time of Augustus, and the age of L'Enfant and Jefferson.

Although Marion—and more to the point, the Harding Commemorative Society—became objects of ridicule, there were nevertheless some folks who perceived at least a glimmer of the true nature and spirit of our aspirations. Some sent us donations after they had read of our plans to build a colossal, anachronistic tomb. I recall very clearly that one donor was a retired professor of classics at Harvard University; he sent us five hundred dollars—an extraordinary sum of money back in 1924. My favorite quote ever uttered about Marion and its people—and there were lots of them back then—is pasted in the front of Adeline's scrapbook, copied in her hand. It came from Secretary of State Charles Evans Hughes, speaking after the President's funeral. He said of us:

> In them are revealed the ardor, the hope, the pride of a favored and exceptional people; the high exemplification of the privilege, the power, and the vanity of human life.

If I had it to do over again, I would have carved Secretary Hughes' words in the cella of Harding Memorial. After all, when you think of it, the monument was as much ours as the President's.

As for the placement of the tomb, well, we have Adeline to thank for that. She gave us a parcel of land she inherited from Dad, and it is the perfect setting—on the southern-most edge of town, adjacent to Vernon Heights Boulevard and the road to Columbus. That land comprised an

Indian mound and one of the last vestiges of primeval trees then growing within the town's precincts. A day or so before my last visit to Mrs. Harding, I took the designs out to that wild and woodsy land and tried to visualize, as best I could, each of the designs in that setting. In my imagination I sensed the coalescence of trees from the Old Forest and marble columns of The Tomb, in a setting near crossroads where it would awe all who would enter and leave the town for a thousand years to come, and beyond.

Posterity would know that once we were here.

ANYWAY, BACK TO THAT MORNING, and to the four designs that I took to the First Lady.

They were rather large, and if I do say so myself, they were very nicely displayed. You see, not only was the First Lady going to view them, but the following week they were to go on public display in the Great Rotunda of the Courthouse, and so we wanted them to look as handsome as possible. I had each matted in a gold frame behind glass, and each measured about thirty-six inches by about twenty-six, more or less. (To this day they are stored in their elegant black cases in the Harding Home, though copies of the same drawings in miniature hang right here in the library at Tioga.) That morning, before I left my office for White Oaks Farm, I arranged the designs in the order that I wished to show them to Mrs. Harding—my least favorite first (if that is the correct way of stating it, for in some ways I liked them all), ascending, of course, to my favorite.

They were quite an armload, but I managed to bring them in from the car all at once. This time when I entered, Mrs. Harding had donned her spectacles and was watching the door, waiting. I think she was expecting me to come in with a few loose pictures or something. She looked surprised, and as I crossed the room, she said, "Goodness, Trey, what on earth?"

"The designs! Framed. We do things right around here, you know."

"Yes," she said after a moment, "we do, don't we. But you're going to rupture something you value if you aren't careful, and there's nothing right in that."

I laughed at the First Lady's way with words, "Well, I don't think we need worry ourselves about that—but just wait till you see them!"

Now that I was in Mrs. Harding's presence, with the designs, I became very keen on showing them to her, and I felt a little peeved with Lucy and her qualms. Had she not stated them, then I may have brought an easel or two to properly display the designs. Now mind you, these renderings were not at all technical in nature; essentially, they were drawings complete with trees and landscape, as well as a human figure or two to give dimension. I leaned the cases against a lamp table. I pictured myself holding them one at a time, like placards, with a hand gripping each side, and my chin sticking out over the top, as I peered down awkwardly pointing out this or that. It suddenly occurred to me that if I stood there like that, then I would look like one of those barefoot boys from the west-end who, back in the old days before the movies, used to walk around downtown holding placards, announcing the coming of circuses, itinerant spectacles, and such.

I glanced around. Two straight back chairs stood by the wall. Unlike the Chippendale, they had no arms. I moved the Chippendale aside, and stood the straight backs in its place, with the First Lady watching, quite intently. I could tell she was very curious and befuddled by the elegant, intriguing cases and their contents, and by what I was up to. Like everyone else in America, she knew that we were planning a grand monument, but knowing and seeing are two different things—and I sensed that she had not, at that moment, the slightest idea how grand they really were. Indeed, I do not think she had the slightest inkling that we were aiming for something that would rival the Lincoln Memorial.

As I lifted the first design from its case, I initially kept it concealed from her. Then I placed it on one of the chairs, and stepped back. "Oh!" she said, "Oh, my goodness!" I did not say a word, but placed the second on the chair beside it. "Good Lord!" she whispered, as if looking into the Grand Canyon or something. She stared at them, literally wide-eyed, for a long moment, looking back and forth between the two. "Lord!" she said again. She looked at me, and then back at them. "That's for Warren? Don't these go too far, Tristan? Why, he wasn't Napoleon. He wasn't Alexander the Great. Warren was just plain ol' Warren."

Quite frankly, the First Lady's words rather irked me, but I endeavored to conceal this. "Mrs. Harding, he was President of the United States. And the greatest President since Abraham Lincoln. Think of it. He was and you know it. That fact is what these designs are all about. That and his martyrdom." She shot me a look, like a dart, as if I too had joined the rumorists. I hastened to add, "The President died in office, from the profound burdens of high office. Hence, I say again, martyrdom."

"Yes, I suppose so." She looked back to the designs. Almost speaking to herself, she said, "Apoplexy. From the burdensome anxiety and nervousness of being President. American nervousness."

"Precisely."

And then she said, "Trey, they really, really are beautiful, in and of themselves. Magnificent!"

I smiled at the thought of the two designs still in their cases. Laying my fingers on the frame of the first design, I said, "This one's by Edgerton Swartwout, from Brooklyn, in the city of New York."

She made a face, as if a bad smell had entered the room. "Swartwout—what kind of a name is that? Sounds foreign."

The First Lady never much cared for Jews and Italians and such, in-cluding—and most especially—Anglo-Saxon Americans with a "hillbilly" drawl. In this regard she was utterly unlike her husband, who knew what it was to be the object of intolerance. By virtue of his sweet nature, Mr. Harding accepted everyone.

"Frankly, Mrs. Harding, I have no idea what kind of a name it is, but I'm sure that he's an American, just as you and I are American, no matter what his background happens to be. Besides, I think you'll agree that it's the design that's important." I laid my fingers on the second. "This one's by Paul P. Crest—nice English name—from San Francisco." I moved to the side and stood admiring both. I realized my hands had somehow wormed their way into my pockets, so I took them out and clasped them behind my back, hoping that the First Lady had not noticed. I must say that both designs were very stunning, especially when they did not have to compete, side by side, with the Hornbostel and Pope designs, both of which still resided in their cases.

"You'll notice," I said, "that in the center of the Swartwout drawing, we see a wide stone staircase ascending to a plaza where the tomb itself rises." As I spoke, I pointed to the details. "The tomb consists of a great circular masonry substructure with a single metal door leading into the sepulcher. A second level consists merely of columns holding up a dome, and a hollow space within the columns, beneath the dome and above the sepulcher. The door, of course, would be bronze. Mrs. Harding, notice how, on top of this structure, we have what's called a peristyle—encircling columns—in this case Doric columns, holding up a dome. My problem with this design, one of them, as splendid as it is, is that these columns here encircle nothing. There's nothing within the cella—that's what this circular area inside the columns is called, this inner precinct. Now the Athenians would have placed a statue or something like that in there. If by chance we chose this design, then I think we'll commission a statue of the President for that area. But I'm concerned that the statue would not be visible from a distance, and only from certain angles."

"Yes. Now that you point it out, I see exactly what you mean. You have a good eye, Trey. It wants something up there, doesn't it? It's like a hollow crown. Not a very good symbol."

I laughed. "No, not a good symbol at all. You'll notice, Mrs. Harding, that the Crest design is similar, though perhaps superior in certain ways. In this design, we see twin magnificent staircases ascending to a broad, sweeping plaza. In the center, at the near front edge of the plaza, a great, elevated statue of the President presides over the panoramic setting. As you can see, he's seated, just as Lincoln is seated in his Memorial at Washington. Behind the President, back upon the plaza, the Tomb itself rises—a square, open temple-like structure of massive square columns, entablature, and high roof above the sarcophagi."

I gave her a moment to take it all in, and then said, "Grand, isn't it, Mrs. Harding?"

"Very. I like it better than that Swartwout fellow's."

"Me too. I like its vastness." Each of the architects had submitted a few pages of explanation regarding his design. Of course I had read these over quite carefully, and I was finding myself cribbing their words into my own comments to the First Lady. I said, looking admiringly at the Crest design, "It's all sky and wind over masonry, vastness and tranquility. Imagine the echoing plaza, the sunlight and glaring marble, and in its season, the snow howling through the cella. And mind you, Mrs. Harding, this is the only design in which we'll see right angles. The others are based on circles. Circles within circles, with round columns placed in the context of circles." I allowed the First Lady to take another long look at the two designs.

Then I said, "Allow me to set these below for now so I can show you our other two finalists."

I leaned the first against the fronts of the chairs, on the floor, and then slid the Hornbostel design from its case. I discreetly concealed it from her for a moment, and then I placed it on the chair. The First Lady seemed to catch her breath in amazement, but said nothing. I took the Pope design from its case and placed it beside the other, and stood back. She gazed speechless at each, which was, mind you, beautiful, extravagant, transcendent, and utterly colossal.

I think if either structure had been built in antiquity, somewhere by the Aegean, then like the Parthenon, it would be known today throughout the civilized world. Incorporating some phrases that I had read in a book on classical architecture, I said, "I think you'll agree, Mrs. Harding, that in both of these designs we have a blend of Aegean precedents, Hellenic purity, and Alexandrian immensity."

After a long moment she said softly, "Well, again, I really truly don't know what to say." She paused, staring at the two heroic designs, and then she turned to me. "Tristan, are you really sure this is appropriate? In some ways this is even more incredible than Warren becoming President. Or I should say, more fantastic. Are you really sure this is—merited? I mean especially with all they're saying."

"Quite sure, Mrs. Harding, quite sure. We're all very sure, and committed. Either of these monuments will last five thousand years—at least. Either will be beautiful even in decay, when our age is an age in remote antiquity. How long will the rumors and gossip last? And bear in mind that not one word has ever been uttered to implicate the President himself. Not one. Only those—those others. His so-called friends, from elsewhere. Those outsiders who slithered in. And besides, Mrs. Harding, a great monument will speak volumes about those of us who supported the President—as opposed to those who betrayed him. So yes, I am quite sure that they're appropriate. Besides, we owe this to the President, for all he accomplished in so short a reign, and we owe it to him out of vindication. Now, allow me to continue."

Without giving her a further chance to speak, I placed my hand on the first design, and said, "This one's by Henry Hornbostel, of Pittsburgh. I might add that Andrew Carnegie himself chose Mr.

Hornbostel to design the Carnegie Institute of Technology, in that city."

Again, I pointed to the details as I spoke. "In this drawing, we see two long parallel walkways that intersect great lawns bordered by trees, leading to a colossal, circular tomb of glistening white marble. Notice the broad staircase ascending to the massive colonnade of Doric columns encircling the cella, which is open to the sky. A willow tree grows within, and hanging gardens encircle above, along the entablature, that's the part up here, supported by Iconic columns."

I gave her a moment to take it in, and then I continued, "We liked this one well enough to ask Mr. Hornbostel to draw an enhanced interior view for us, simply because, of the four, it seems the most detailed. I'm sorry to say that it hasn't arrived yet. But you see, Mrs. Harding, if you look closely you'll notice that only the front third of the cella is open. The sides and back are all enclosed by this circular marble wall. Yours and the President's names and dates will be carved there, and I was thinking maybe a quote or two from his speeches as well. At the center of the cella there'll be two great cenotaphic sarcophagi, set amid a garden of myrtle, and of course the weeping willow. I say cenotaphic because the remains will actually be placed below."

What I did not tell the First Lady was that hers and the President's coffins would be welded into vaults, which would in turn be sealed into a concrete burial chamber that extended deep into the earth, and this chamber would be filled in with thousands of tons of concrete, essentially encasing their remains in stone. "Grand, isn't it?" I said.

"Well, yes, Trey. Extraordinary, really. Astonishing. But Trey—"

"By the way, the Hornbostel is Adeline's favorite."

The First Lady looked at me. I was moving my hand to the last design, but before I could speak she said, "Why?"

"Why what?"

"Why is it Adeline's favorite? What did you think I meant?"

"Oh." I thought for a moment and realized I really didn't know. "I guess because she likes the hanging gardens and such, the myrtle and willow tree and the hanging vines. You know how she likes that sort of thing."

I continued on to the last. "This one's by John Russell Pope, of New York. I think you might find it interesting to note, Mrs. Harding, that

Mr. Pope designed your friends' home out in Washington, Ned and Evelyn McLean's place, their townhouse."

"Evelyn's? Really? I know that house! It's such a magnificent place, Trey. Adeline knows it too. She's been there."

"Yes, she told us about it. Quite a place, as I understand."

"Beyond belief. Like something the Vanderbilts would live in."

"Well," I said, tapping the golden frame, bringing the conversation back to the point, "This too is Mr. Pope's handiwork. And if I do say so myself, his design is nothing short of exquisite in every detail. Notice how the reflecting pool seems to double all that we see, trees and sky, and most of all, the monument itself. By the way, I don't know if you can tell, but these are cherry trees around the walkway, with willows, elms, and of course buckeye trees further back. And look at that little man on the walkway there, added for proportion. Incredible. As you can see, we are not dealing in miniatures here. Notice the three broad marble staircases ascending from the walkway along the reflecting pool. You can see here that both sides of the great center staircase are flanked by kneeling angels, bending towards the tomb. The monument itself rises like a great circular Hellenic temple, with a continuous colonnade of Doric columns uplifting a massive dome, which—as Mr. Pope himself pointed out—'seems to float in lightness.' You'll notice, Mrs. Harding, that this structure is also open to the winds and sunlight, except for two partial walls back here, surrounding the cella. Mr. Pope proposes that we carve excerpts from the President's speeches back there. Of course, as you can see, in the center we have the two massive sarcophagi, as in the Hornbostel design. Difference being that, with this monument, the remains would actually be placed within them, as opposed to burial beneath. Mind you, Mr. Pope suggests in his written comments that the remains could indeed be placed below, and the sarcophagi done away with entirely, replaced by a bronze or marble statue of the President— an idea that I personally am very keen on. And speaking frankly, I don't much care for these kneeling angels. They're too—too angelic, or something. Victorian, I guess. Never been keen on angels. And after all, this is a classical monument. How on earth did kneeling angels get in the picture?" After a pause I said, "Well, Mrs. Harding, what do you think? Which design is your favorite?"

The First Lady was studying the renderings, but it was almost as if her mind was elsewhere. Finally, she said, "Well, I don't know, Trey. Really I don't."

She looked at me. "The President did a lot of good in office, didn't he?"

"Considering his abbreviated tenure, I'd call that an understatement."

"And I think more than anyone you know how concerned I am about his legacy."

"Just as I am."

"But maybe as his wife, his widow who knows every little thing about him, not all of it good, maybe I know a bit too much. I'm just having a little bit of trouble reconciling Warren with all this. I mean our Warren. Yes, the Warren who called for the disarmament conference . . ."

"The first in history," I added, "and hopefully not the last. An extraordinary innovation. Visionary. A meritorious act of genius, really."

"Yes, that's what they say. And he formally ended the Great War, and founded the Veterans Bureau, and all that. But still I'm having trouble reconciling the other Warren, our Warren, with all this. " She looked at her hands. "With kneeling angels and Doric columns and hanging gardens."

"The kneeling angels will go. You have my word on it."

"Yes, but . . ."

"And don't you think, Mrs. Harding, that Mary Todd Lincoln could have said the same sort of thing about her husband? After all, she did his laundry." The moment I said that, I regretted it. It has never been my custom to make such domestic allusions. I endeavored to immediately change the direction of my point, as if I had never made it. "He was a complex man, Mrs. Harding, a very complex man."

"Warren? You got the wrong man. Warren was about as complex as a schoolboy."

I made no reply.

She looked back at the designs again. "Yes, a monument befitting his high office and achievements, but a Herculean tomb!"

"Mrs. Harding, I remember you told me something once. You said, 'The President was great in life, in death he'll be magnificent.'" I nodded towards the designs. "These represent true magnificence in death. I admit that Mr. Harding was all too human, like President Lincoln, and maybe he was a simple man, also like President Lincoln—though actually, I prefer the word *common*—in its best sense. Both were men of the people who ascended to the highest office in the land and did extraordinary things. Indeed, President Harding carried out some of the most progressive and bravest measures since Teddy Roosevelt. That's a fact people are already forgetting." I laid my hand on the Pope design. "This will remind them. This will never let them forget. Ever."

The First Lady's eyes were fixed on me, and then she smiled slyly. "You're very smooth, Trey, aren't you? You know you are. You really should have come to Washington with us. You'd have been a great success. I'm sure Cal Coolidge would still be putting you to great use."

I sensed (I think) some contempt from the First Lady in her last words, as everyone knew how she felt about the Coolidges. I said, "I have better things to do than work for that old sourpuss."

She laughed and then repeated, "So smooth."

"I'm smoothest when I personally have nothing to gain."

"True."

"And mind you, Colonel Hamilton & Son builds houses and commercial structures. Why, we couldn't build something like this any more than we could fly to the moon, so I won't earn a cent from this. Not one red cent. I wouldn't if I could."

"Oh, Trey, I didn't think that for a minute."

"And needless to say, my name will not be carved anywhere on this tomb. In a hundred years, when I'm sleeping in the Hamilton family plot, no one, absolutely no one, will remember that a long-forgotten fellow named Tristan Tecumseh Hamilton had anything whatsoever to do with the magnificent memorial to President Harding across the way."

The First Lady nodded and said, "No doubt that's true too."

She was gazing at the designs when she suddenly seemed to think of something else. I could see the thought cross her eyes, and just as suddenly, she laughed bitterly, and said, as if to herself, "Nigger Warren!" She said the words again, and added, "Indeed!"

"You know something," she said. "Daddy's grave, there on his own private little knoll in Marion Cemetery, it looks right across the way, towards Adeline's land, where the President's monument will stand. Why, think of it—Daddy will get to spend eternity looking at Nigger Warren's

Herculean tomb. Serves the old fool right, though he did change in the end, but still—"

I said, "Your favorite design, Mrs. Harding?"

She pointed. "That one. The Pope design."

I smiled, "A perfect choice! Mine, too. You have excellent taste, Mrs. Harding. Personally, I think it's the most splendid of the four."

"Though I do have to say that I think Warren might have preferred the Hornbostel. It has that willow tree and the gardens. You remember that time when we came home in July from the White House, when we called on your father? Well, we visited his mother's grave early that very morning. Mom and Dad's too. We didn't take the Pierce-Arrow, but another car, a Ford or something regular. We snuck out with just one guard. Warren drove. Anyway, when we were at the cemetery, the President told me that he wanted to be buried right here in Marion 'beneath a nice shady tree.' I think a willow would be just the thing."

"Well, I suppose we couldn't go wrong with either one." I glanced at the clock on the mantel. "Goodness! I've been here quite a while, haven't I? And I told Lucy I'd be home for lunch. Besides, I'm afraid I've tired you out."

She waved her hand. "You have, but so what. Soon I'll get all the rest I need."

"I'll stop by and see you next week, and I promise not to stay so long." Already I was beginning to slip the designs back into their black cases.

"Oh, Trey, I do wish Adeline would come out and see me."

"I'll speak to her."

"No, don't bother. Why, you'd think she was afraid of me or something." I glanced at the First Lady. I do not know what little clue or indication I thought I might or might not see in her face, but she was just a puzzled and lonesome old woman gazing at her frail hands folded on her lap. I felt sorry for her. She continued, "Why, Brights disease isn't catching. Adeline should know that. I wonder what's wrong with her. Oh, I just recollected—"

She leaned over the little lamp table and struggled with the drawer, trying to open it. I immediately stepped around and slid it open for her. She lifted out a box covered with shiny gold foil, tied with golden ribbons. "Here," she said, "these are for Adeline. If you'll give them to her, please. I think she'll like them. Tell her they're from Orlando himself."

"Yes."

The First Lady took a bright silver dollar from a little saucer inside her drawer, and turned it over, examining the coin. Then she said, "And on your way home, I want you to stop by Schaffers and get a pound of the very best chocolates you can buy for you and Lucy."

"That won't be necessary, Mrs. Harding."

"I know it won't, but please. Take the money and do me the favor. I want you to have something nice too, but make sure that Adeline gets these." I stared at her. I would be a liar if I said that a feeling of suspicion did not descend upon me. Mrs. Harding continued, "I hope I don't offend you, Trey, but I think your sister would appreciate genuine Italian chocolates more than most folks would. I mean with her taste, so worldly and all. You understand, don't you? She's so particular about things. Other folks aren't so hard to please as she."

"Yes, of course."

"And another thing." She reached back into her little saucer and took out a nickel. She examined it and, I think, must have found it too dull or something. She put it back and fished out another, a shinier one, and examined it. Then holding it out to me she said, "Here. On your way home tonight, I want you to stop by Mrs. Price's and pick up a nice soup bone and give it to little Bomber. Maybe it'll take his mind off the bunnies for a while."

I laughed. "Will do."

After I loaded the designs into the Lincoln, I came back in to say good-bye. I bent down and kissed the First Lady on her cheek. "I'll come back and see you again next week. That's a promise!"

She took my hand and looked at me in a funny kind of way. "Tristan," she said, "you're a fine young man. You and your family have always been so good to Warren and me, from the very beginning, to the very end—and I know, beyond the end."

I felt a little tug at my heart and I attempted a smile. "I consider it an honor, Mrs. Harding."

"Tristan, you must never doubt that we did the right thing."

Frankly, I wasn't sure what she meant. "I never doubt, Mrs. Harding, never, unless doubt is called for."

She was looking at me long, like she was committing her present image of me to memory, forever.

"Good bye, Mrs. Harding. See you next week."

She did not reply.

I kissed her hand, turned, and walked out the door.

The following week I was standing before the First Lady's gray metal coffin. She was dressed in a blue gown—of a hue the American public once called "Harding blue." The marcelled waves were back in her delicate hair and she wore a cameo on a matching velvet ribbon at her neck. Whenever I have stood before the dead, I have wondered what secrets and lost histories they bear away with them into their graves, into eternity. I wondered this even more with the First Lady, just as I had with the President.

Less than two years later, their coffins were lowered into the deep, impenetrable vault of the tomb designed by Henry Hornbostel, because it enabled the fulfillment of the President's wish to be buried beneath a shade tree, and then the coffins were meticulously locked and sealed away forever. Only dynamite could begin to crack open their deep and private sepulcher—at the expense of the million-dollar tomb, this landmark beyond all reckoning.

A shady willow grows in the cella, carpeted by myrtle; ivy from the high entablature drapes upon white marble, offering an inner cloister of peace and tranquility.

I never gave Adeline the Italian chocolates.

After work on that November day, after I dropped by Price's and bought a ham bone for Bomber, I stopped by Schaffers and bought two pounds of the finest chocolates money could buy—at least in Marion, Ohio. One I brought home to Lucy and Nora, as a gift from the First Lady. The other I used to replace the contents of the fancy box she had asked me to give to Adeline.

In short, I stuck my sister with counterfeit chocolates. Frankly, I have a feeling that she never touched them—just as she never visited the First Lady at White Oaks Farm.

As for the genuine Italian sweets, I ate them myself. Every last one of them. I quartered each, and then halved the quarter so that I was eating them one tiny piece at a time. I tasted each nugget carefully, lingeringly, before swallowing, trying to detect some odd or bitter taste, some burning sensation on the tongue, or on the tender wall of the cheek, which I thought might be the telltale imprint of poison. I ate two pieces on the day the First Lady died, over the course of several hours, two more on the day when I saw her lying in her coffin, and a couple more on the day of her funeral, when her casket was placed along side the President's, in their temporary crypt at Marion Cemetery. I always took the precaution of eating those delicious chocolates with milk and bicarbonate of soda at my reach. I had once read in a book that these are anecdotes to poison, though I doubt the correctness of this now.

Obviously, I am pleased to say that the rumorists were 100 percent wrong. Not once did I have the feeling that I was nibbling cyanide, or anything of the sort, and I am ashamed of myself for having even a sliver of doubt about the First Lady.

Or for that matter, by inference, my beloved sister Adeline, Mrs. Harding's supposed accomplice in the putative assassination of the twenty-ninth President of the United States—the great Warren G. Harding.

BOOK IV

Land Filled with Ghosts

I

THANKSGIVING—PREDAWN
28 NOVEMBER 1963
TIOGA

The Silver Casket

THIS MORNING I made a most perplexing discovery.

I believe I mentioned some days ago that, after my sister's death in 1959, and after I moved back to Tioga, I found a locked box, a small sterling silver casket, in the top drawer of her desk. The key was missing for years—that is, until this morning. Though frankly, I now rather wish I had not found it. Perhaps I have been too absorbed with the past and maybe I am reading a little too much mystery into the box's contents. Either way, I now seem to be faced with a most baffling question. And I believe it is a question that I have no hope of answering. As with so much else, my sister took the answer to her grave.

I am not even quite sure what prompted me to look for the key in the place where I found it. I have heard that sometimes secrets are revealed in dreams. Maybe so, but if I had a dream last night, then I do not remember it—though I have no other clue as to why I sprung from my bed, first thing this morning, charged down the hall into Adeline's room, lit the lamp, and raised the lid of the cedar chest.

Actually, I searched through some of those boxes in the months following her death. In fact, I distinctly remember opening the very box where, this morning, I found the key. The moment I raised the lid, I saw the World War II era photograph of Matthias Mende, standing with another airman, and between them stands Evelyn Walsh McLean, wearing the Hope Diamond. When I first stumbled upon this picture four years ago, I was confounded to see that it had fallen into my sister's possession. At the time, I suppose I did not want to be reminded of Mr. Mende, so I simply closed the box and returned it where I found it, without digging deeper into the contents or considering it again. Until this morning.

Last night I went to bed late, after sitting in the library into the wee hours rehashing President Harding's death. I slept rather fitfully and then awoke in the pre-dawn darkness. As I believe I may have mentioned, I sleep in my father's bed in the room at the back of the house where the President and First Lady last visited him on the 3rd of July 1922. My bed is, of course, the bed in which my father died. I was floating in that nether world between half-asleep and half-wakefulness and Mitzy was walking up the carriage drive on a summer afternoon fifty years ago. In her hair dappled sunlight flickered, glowing through lush trees that were mature long before our time. Then we were sitting in candlelight in the dining room and crickets sang out of the darkness. Somehow it was both summertime and Thanksgiving Day and Mitzy was impossibly young and lovely again and I was twenty-two and time had circled back to its beginning.

Through my blankets I felt winter's chill. Remembering the snow, I raised myself on an elbow. The snow was falling through the darkness— one of those silent windless snows. A blanket of white as thick as a thatched roof in rural England lay over the carriage house; through the veil of white I could see snow clinging to the bark and the limbs of trees in the Old Forest, giving them a ghostly and floating presence. Again I thought of the dead—of President Kennedy out in his new-made grave at Arlington, of my beloved Lucy, of Adeline and my parents slumbering in their graves at Marion Cemetery, of poor Nora, our housekeeper, and even Orrin de Pue, the carpenter and drifter who fell from the high beams and died way back in the chilly spring of 1900, when Tioga was just a skeleton of fresh timbers rising against the sky. In the winter darkness I saw again the sudden jerk of his arm, his hand flying towards his temple, and his body tumbling through the bright spring air. His scream merged with the scream of my little sister, and his head burst upon the floor like a watermelon dropped from a high place. Rather than lay him in a potter's grave, Father dug into his own pocket and buried him in a fine coffin, near the Hamilton family plot. His tombstone told all we ever knew of him: *Orrin de Pue – Died April 25, 1900.* (My father even had to hazard a guess at the spelling of the man's name.) And I thought of the President and Mrs. Harding deep in the vault of their hero's tomb; I saw them in their coffins again—the lavender hue of their lips, and the undertaker's heavy rouge on their cheeks, and I saw the shadow drawing over their faces, in the last light of this world as the coffin lid closed and snapped shut forever. I saw in my mind the massive columns soaring into the darkness, the snow filling the cella, blanketing the granite cenotaphs in purest white.

It was then—and do not ask me how or why—that I thought of Matthias Mende and remembered that picture of him in the cedar chest down the hall, and I thought of the locked sterling box.

The conjuncture was startling, like remembering a rendezvous scheduled long, long ago. The sort of consideration that suddenly opens your eyes and shakes the sleep right out of you. I am not claiming clairvoyance here, though I suspect that everyone has such moments, when Intuition prods one in the ribs, points her finger, and says, "Go that a-way!"—like when I drove to Wooster decades ago, purely on a hunch.

I flung back the covers, sprang from bed, and hastened down the hall towards my sister's room.

I no longer had the slightest idea which box in the cedar chest held that photograph, so I had to start popping lids right and left.

I came upon the now-yellowed silk christening gown worn first by my mother and then by my sister. I opened a box with two porcelain dolls, and another with table linen woven and embroidered by monks in Venice. I found my great-grandmother's Book of Common Prayer, and an ancient Anglican hymnal from the Church of St. Mary Magdalene in Bath, England.

Eight or ten boxes in, I lifted a lid and there was Matthias wearing what appears to be a lady's scarf wrapped around his head, like an Oriental turban. He looks a little bleary-eyed—not exactly an uncommon state for him. He wears an airman's uniform and so does his anonymous friend. And between them, looking late middle-aged and homely, stands Evelyn Walsh McLean, wearing the Hope Diamond. In the picture Evelyn is considerably older than she was the last time I saw her, on that hot August day in 1923 when we buried President Harding. The gem glitters darkly at her neck. The fireplace mantle is decorated for Christmas. I remember articles in magazines such as *Look* and *Life* about how Evelyn opened her estate in Virginia and provided lavish entertainment for our troops. I also remember wondering if she ever thought of her friends (or I should say her lost acquaintances) way out here in long-forgotten Marion.

I found another picture of Matthias in that same box. He was very proud of this picture and so I am surprised that he parted with it. He is standing before the wing of his P-51 Mustang. He looks scarcely old enough to drive a car, much less pilot a fighter plane at four or five hundred miles an hour. The photograph was taken at an airfield in England; I believe Matthias said at Leeds. He is thin with light tousled hair and that mischievous smile. I wonder, was he setting out or returning from protecting bombers and hunting for Hitler's Messerschmitts?

At the risk of a further digression, I will mention a couple of other items I came upon in that same box, though they have nothing whatsoever to do with Matthias. They have to do with my sister Adeline, of whom I have said so very little.

The box held three letters she sent to my father and me from Paris, where she lived for about two years from the spring of 1912 to the summer of 1914. I also came upon a brown envelope stuffed with sepia snapshots from her years abroad. I certainly remember her sending infrequent letters home, but never before had I laid eyes on a single one of these pictures. I am not even sure if my father saw them. I lingered over two in particular.

According to the penciled inscription on the back, one is: *Claire et I avec Bernart devant notre petite maison sur la rue de picot le 14 du 1913 Juillet.* So this was Bernart—whom I do not believe I have here mentioned, though I regard him as one of the few loves of my sister's life. And this morning was the first time in my life that I ever laid eyes on him, or rather on his image. My sister spoke to me of Bernart once, and only once, and that was out at our parents' graves on a spring morning in 1947. He was the only one I had ever heard her say that she might have married, but for the fact that he died in the Great War. I remember that, after Claire's letter arrived announcing his death, Addy closed herself in her room for days. I wondered then and wonder now if the boy was her lover—and I do not simply mean her paramour, I mean her *lover*. As I say, my little sister had secrets. As for Claire, she was Claire de Troyes, Adeline's friend and housemate. To my knowledge Claire was the only close contemporary female friend that Adeline ever had. Yes, there was Flossie Harding and there has always been Mrs. Christian, but the one was much older and the other somewhat younger, and Mrs. Christian was a beloved employee rather than a *friend*. As for the photograph, all three of the young people were about the age of nineteen. The photograph was taken in the courtyard of the little stone house where Addy and Claire lived on Rue Picot, somewhere in Paris. The house has a small balcony opening into the trees, and two narrow stone pillars stand to the right and the left of the double front doors. A face with angel wings appears to be carved into the stone above them. Bernart is a very handsome boy with abundant black curls, though I wonder if he could not afford the regular services of a barber. He wears a high-buttoned suit, with his shirt open at the neck. There is something mischievous in his dark eyes and faint smile. He stands between the girls, Claire on his right clutching his arm, and Adeline on his left with her head on his shoulder. The three are surrounded by greenery, with sunlight streaming through here and there. Adeline, like my mother, was partial to expensive clothes, and both girls are wearing, in a casual sort of way, what appear to be pricey gowns.

Adeline mentions Bernart in one of her letters that I came upon this morning. She writes:

> I do not want you to think that I have become Bohemian or emancipated because I have not, but we often entertain some of our friends that we meet in the Academie. These are French, American, and English, and they are of both sexes. Most of them live on the Left Bank and are just getting by but they are never gloomy and they are never imposing or resentful.
>
> Sometimes on the weekends they come over and we have some cheese and meats and bread and Bordeaux put out for them which they soon devour. They are all so very bright and clever and we talk about wonderful things in a mix of French and English so that everyone can understand. They are so very "chic" even though they are struggling. We usually end the evening at a decent hour, usually with a number of songs. Claire will play at the piano and we sing along and usually one

of the young gentlemen brings a violin. One of our friends is a curly-haired youth named Bernart de Vaqueiras. He plays the violin very gorgeously. No one sings when he plays, we just listen and hope against hope that Time will lose its way and forget us forever and that he will not stop, and then we lament when he does.

I return to his image and wonder, if not for World War I, would this fine young fellow have become my brother-in-law? If so, where would they have lived? And would he have gotten regular haircuts? Or would he have been like Dad, caring little for the scissors and less for the comb?

Alas, we shall never know. I remember my sister once speaking of "unfinished lives"—of which there have been tens of millions during this tragic century.

The second photograph I lingered over includes only the two girls, taken at Mont-Saint-Michel. Adeline inscribed the back of this photograph in English: *Our last outing. June 1914. Spent the night on the Mont.*

The girls are huddled close together against the wind on what appears to be a gray sunless day. They stand arm-in-arm on the strand with the island rising in the distance and the desolate wastes stretching as far away as the eye can see. Both wear long, wind-blown cloaks. There are no smiles in this photo. The loose hood of Adeline's cloak is up, and her chin is raised, her eyes fixed on the camera; Claire gazes up from lowered brows. Hindsight tells me that in June of 1914 the Great War was lurking near and that the ocean would soon come between them. Maybe on that sunless June day at Saint-Michel they already sensed the end of their *belle epoch*, and their youth. Their friendship too, I suppose, for Adeline returned to Europe in the mid-'20s and visited Claire, but by then her former housemate was married with a family, and so far as I know, they lost touch forever thereafter.

I wonder if Bernart took the picture, but I do not think so as he is not mentioned in a letter that Adeline wrote regarding the outing:

> *I believe one of the handsome guardians must have taken a liking to us as I noticed him watching us in the nave. He took out his timepiece once or twice as if he had an engagement and then he came and asked*

how strong our legs were. Claire and I both found the question irregular but amusing. He continued and asked if we would care to ascend the tower and watch the sea's return. This is a famous spectacle known far and wide in France, and so who were we to say no to such an offer? It is one that is surely not tendered to every pilgrim who wanders into the Abbey. With a huge skeleton key he unlocked a small, heavy wooden door in the Chapel of St. Martin and led us up spiral stairs, so giddy and winding, up and up to a landing in the open air surrounded by a forest of pinnacles, gargoyles, and sky. At low tide the naked floor of the sea stretches for miles like the flat of a desert. Many a pilgrim has gone astray on those wastes, lost in the fog, and they've been swallowed up in the quicksand, while the sea has overtaken others when it comes back like a rush of wind. The ancient town was far below us with its clustering stone houses and its vines and fig trees, and we could see the tiles and gables of the inn where we stayed, the Tete d'Or. We were up there for maybe ten minutes before the moon was just so, and our guide said, Un moment seulement, dames. Alores vous verrez. In other words, he was telling us that in a moment we would see a spectacle. And very soon, Ecouter! And from far off and away, the terrible rumble of the onrushing sea, a high white wall of foaming water consuming the wastes, and the waves rushing in from miles and miles away, rushing and rushing faster than wild horses to overtake each other. Then soon once more the Mont was an island in the swirling sea. The spectacle was truly breathtaking.

Having rested and ascended thus far, our guardian led us again in another ascent to the windy platform of the Tour des Fous, four hundred feet above the sea. Claire and I clung to the parapot and each other for dearest life. Even at that giddy height, the Archangel was still far, far above us with his sword pointed towards the high heavens. We could see the rock of Tombeleine and the coast of Brittany, and we looked towards Paris, and Europe stretching far away, and then I turned and looked across the vast Atlantic, homeward. I thought of both of you, Daddy and Tristan. I thought of Tioga, I thought of home.

After dwelling on these mementos and a few others of lesser note, I found the sterling key in a corner of the box. The instant I laid eyes on it, I knew the lock to which it belonged. Thus I hastened down the stairs into the library.

BEFORE I GO FURTHER I think it best to tell you something about Matthias Rory Mende, "that flyboy"—as Mrs. Christian used to say. I first mentioned him a few days ago—the fellow who came here in the spring of '47, the young historian who hoped to make a name for himself by reevaluating Mr. Harding's presidency. To this day I believe that, at least in this regard, Mr. Mende was sincere in wanting to discuss the President's achievements. Indeed, perhaps Mr. Mende was sincere in all regards.

Matthias also believed in the poison theory, that the President was assassinated.

One thing I may not have mentioned is the rumor of foul play in Matthias' "disappearance," or at least in his departure. The reason my fifty-year friendship with Dana Yost came to an abrupt and tragic end was because he harbored the bizarre notion that my sister and I had something to do with the "disappearance" of Matthias Mende.

Nothing in the strange and curious annals of the Harding history could be further from the truth than the idea that Adeline and I collaborated in Matt's "disappearance."

Frankly, I loved the boy.

And I might add that I think Dana's fantastic notion of "foul play" was conceived in the wilds of a deeply troubled soul. I was sorry for Dana, and I was sorry for Addy and me, at the loss of a decades-long friendship. The simple truth is that one June day Matthias Mende lit out for Lake Erie and never returned.

Anyway, to Matthias: I very well remember the spring day when he came into our lives. As president of the Harding Commemorative Society, I have always kept a close eye on the Memorial, visiting the tomb several times a week, ensuring that all is in order—that the groundsmen have neatly trimmed round the base and trees, or in its season, shoveled the snow from the marble stairs. They have my strictest orders to never, ever use salt—I even make a point of touching the stone where they have shoveled, and then tasting my fingertips, as a way of checking up on them. In short, I tend to all tasks required for the respectful care and preservation of one of our nation's most beautiful monuments. I do whatever I can in the here and now of my fleeting tenure to ensure that the edifice has an unwavering setting-forth into what I hope will be its "everlasting voyage through time"—just like the Parthenon or the Temple at Karnack. As I mentioned during my last visit with Mrs. Harding, soon the day shall come when not a soul in this little town, much less on this earth, will know that one Tristan Tecumseh Hamilton had a single thing to do with this supreme temple to the dead.

Easter must have come early that year, as I am certain that it was a day or two after Easter Sunday, in early April. The hyacinths and forsythias were just coming into bloom and the sun shown warm on the grass, still a few weeks shy of its first mow. As I pulled my Lincoln into the area set aside for parking, I was surprised to see, in the distance, someone sitting on the lawn between the parallel walkways in front of the soaring tomb. I could not imagine what on earth the fellow could be doing. The Memorial is not a park, though its beautiful grounds might suggest as much, and we do not encourage the spreading of beach blankets and such on the grass, not even on the 4th of July. And it occurred to me as I stepped from my automobile that mine was the only car in sight. In other words, the fellow had either walked to this lonely spot or else someone had dropped him here. Somehow I sensed that he was not from these parts. He seemed occupied in some solitary way, though at first I had not a clue as to what he was doing, as his back was to me. I have always been blessed with acute vision, and so as I cleared the berm of the knoll, I could plainly see that the fellow was quite young, perhaps of college age. As I neared, I could also see that he had a long, drab military coat draped over his shoulders like a cape, its tails cast behind him on the grass. At first I thought maybe he was reading a book, but as I drew nearer I could see his blond head—his gaze—tilt upward, settle for a few moments on the tomb, and then downward toward his lap: up again, down again. When I noticed the slight busy movement of his arm, I realized he was drawing a picture.

I slowed my pace.

He was sitting Indian style—with his ankles crossed and tucked beneath his legs. I recognized his coat as being that of a noncommissioned officer. When I was almost parallel, when I had a pretty good view of his picture, I paused. The sole of his shoe, the one turned my way, had a hole worn in it. A rather expensive-looking leather portfolio lay in the grass beside him. If he knew someone was observing him, then he did not acknowledge the fact, at least not at first. I have no great eye for art, but even I could tell from ten or twelve yards that the young fellow possessed talent. He was working in charcoal. I watched as he added shadows to the cella. After a moment, he turned, not at all startled; his eyes settled on me.

"Good afternoon," I said.

He smiled and nodded, but did not speak. I mistakenly took him to be about twenty-one years of age.

Without ado, he resumed his work. I had found his smile friendly enough to be inviting, so I crossed the grass for a closer peek over his shoulder. I liked his picture; indeed, I liked it very much. He seemed to capture something secret in the Memorial, something that was there but not there—what you might call the spirit of the place.

He looked up. "So what do you think, sir? Like it?"

"Ah, very much."

He smiled and resumed his work in even greater earnest.

Frankly, I wanted to ask if he would be willing to sell his picture when finished. I had a feeling he could use the money, but at the same time I did not want to come across as some vain, middle-aged fellow willing to wave cash around, so I kept mum. (Soon he would make a gift to me of his picture, and the drawing now hangs in the library.)

I headed back towards the walkway.

When I was several steps away, he called out, "Sir, you wouldn't be Mr. Hamilton, would you?"

I looked back and examined this young stranger anew. "I am Tristan Hamilton. And you are—?"

"Matthias Mende."

I repeated his name to myself and crossed the grass to extend my hand.

"Well," he said, glancing apologetically at his charcoal blackened fingers.

I assured him, "I used to deal in coal, young man, so you certainly needn't fret about that."

He gave his friendly, boyish smile again, wiped his fingers on a rag and we shook hands. "What an honor," he said, "shaking hands with a master builder."

"What!" I gave a little laugh at the young man's naïveté. "Master builder! Gracious! A builder, yes, but a master—Why, I'm scarcely a carpenter."

He studied me. I remember my sister once mentioning that artists see things that others do not, and I wondered what this stranger saw in me. He pointed his charcoal stick toward the Memorial. "No carpenter built that."

The marble tomb soared before us like something built by giants in the ancient days of the world.

"True, but neither did I. I was neither builder nor architect."

"Just its *sin qua non*."

Frankly, I had no idea what that meant (until I went home and looked it up), so I simply said, "Well, that may or may not be the case. You aren't from around here, are you, Mr. Mende?"

"Call me Matthias. Matt, if you please. I hail from New Jersey. A place called Elberon."

"Elberon." I shook my head.

"Near Long Branch. By the sea. But now I'm a Princeton man. Ivy League. Working on my Masters."

"Ah, a university man." His coat was draped over his shoulders, cast behind him a bit like swept back wings. "Air Corp?"

"Yes, sir, 4th Fighter Group. P-51."

"A Mustang!"

"Yes, sir."

"Well!"

He raised his blue eyes skyward. "I miss her something terrible. You get shot at and shot up, but she keeps flying, she roars like an eagle and brings you home, then comes the war's end and you got to leave her behind, like a sweetheart. And you know what they did with her, those bastards? You know what they did with her, sir? They hired a bunch of out-of-work Krauts to cut her up and turn her into scrap. Now isn't that something?" He shook his head in disbelief and sorrow. "It just wasn't right. Out-of-work Krauts! Nazis! I mean who won that damn war anyway!"

I gave a sympathetic nod, though I did not quite see it that way. I glanced back at the little parking area, playing host to my car, and my car only. "And now, I gather, you're relying on a somewhat slower means of transport."

He laughed. "Well, I guess you could say that!" He stuck up his thumb. "I see. So what brings you to Marion?"

Again, with his stick of charcoal, he gestured towards the tomb. "That."

"That? The Memorial? Just to draw a picture of the Harding Memorial?"

"That too." He started shadowing the cella again, as if reminded of his mission. Without looking my way he said, "Actually, it's President Harding brings me here."

I instantly knew he was up to something. "Oh, and how is that?"

He shrugged his shoulders, "Some folks go to Valentino's tomb. Some to Harlow's. Me, I've come to President Harding's, at long, long last." He paused, and then added, "I guess you could say I just love the guy. Always have."

Now I had heard it all.

"Yes, of course," I said. "Well, pleased to meet you, sir, and I do hope you enjoy your stay in Marion."

I turned away, leaving him frowning, perhaps startled, as I hurried across the grass. When I was eight or ten paces away, he called out, "Mr. Hamilton," I glanced back. "I knew someone who knew President Harding. And I think she knew you, too."

I waited, but I realized the fellow required my participation in his little guessing game, "And who might that be?"

"Mrs. McLean."

"Evelyn?"

"Who else?"

"And how did you know her?"

"USO."

As I believe I may have mentioned before, there had been pictures and articles in magazines and the Sunday supplements about her kindness to our troops. "Yes, of course, at Friendship." I thought that a certain smug knowing look came in his eyes.

Again he gestured his charcoal toward the Memorial. "Yes, sir, you did a wondrous thing here, Mr. Hamilton. All honor is due to you."

I nodded to this curious young man, wondering what it was he wanted from me, and then I walked away.

I went about my "walk-around"—as I have always thought of my inspections, and as I did, I suppose I glanced Mr. Mende's way from time to time, even as I tried to ignore his presence. Ordinarily, I would make my way back to the car by circling along the tree line at the bottom of the knoll, as a means of searching for litter blown in from the highway and scattered amidst the woods. Indeed, I ought to have done just that, but I did not want the fellow to misconstrue my exit and think me rude for avoiding him. Thus I departed along the walkway. We had already exchanged our good-byes and pleased-to-meet-yous and such, thus as far as I was concerned our mutual business was finished. Besides, I did not want to interrupt his art again. As I came parallel to him, I scarcely nodded.

"Oh, Mr. Hamilton, sir!"

I stopped.

"You wouldn't be heading back to town, would you?"

Frankly, I did not want to have another conversation with this fellow, and I certainly did not want to give him a lift. Besides, his drawing of the Memorial was still unfinished. "But your drawing, Mr. Mende, what about your drawing?"

He laughed, "I'll finish it tomorrow, or the next day, weather permitting. I promise!"

Obviously, I had no choice but to give the fellow a ride, so I said, glancing around, "Well, come along then."

He tucked his sketchpad into his portfolio and quickly gathered his pencil box and things, as if he were in danger of missing a departing Greyhound. After he pushed himself from the ground and started toward me, I could see that he had a slight limp, and I suppose for an unguarded moment, I stared. He read my mind. "Shrapnel. Hot flack. Over Saint-Nazaire." He bent and tapped his left calf, "Jerry got me here. I could smell my own flesh burning even with all that wind roaring through the hole."

"You walked out here?"

"Hitched."

"Oh, yes. Of course."

"Could've walked if I'd been of mind to, but what's the sense?"

"From where?"

"Hotel Marion."

"Ah, Hotel Marion." By then the old hotel had grown decidedly seedy—pool tables in the lobby replacing the plush velvet furniture and the potted palms and ferns of yesteryear, and now the front desk doubled as a bar, selling beer and liquor. On summer days you could smell the stench of stale beer from the sidewalk. Personally, if I were a traveler, I would have slept in my car before crawling into a bed in that seedy dump.

Matthias Mende could be refreshingly direct—at least on the surface. We had no more than pulled onto Vernon Heights Boulevard when he said, "So Mr. Hamilton, I'm told you have no use for historians."

"Historians? Sir, as a matter of fact, I do not, and I will add that in these parts they've earned our contempt."

"In that case I guess I best keep it to myself that that's exactly what I am, or at least that's what I aspire to be."

I glanced at my young passenger, with the headstones of Marion Cemetery passing by in the window. Professor Chancellor, William Allen White, Samuel Hopkins Adams, Mark Sullivan and those other jokers who had poked their noses into Marion had an entirely different air about them. Yes, a bit down-at-the-heels like this one, but a bit like chewed-up cigar butts too. Compared to them, this young fellow was a firecracker. "So *that's* what you're doing here."

"The truth comes out. Always does sooner or later, doesn't it? I came to set the record straight on President Harding."

I did not say a word.

"I mean to tell the truth about him. That is, if you'll let me look at his papers, sir."

Again, I said nothing.

I might add that a lot of people consider presidential papers to be public property and therefore open for public inspection, like books in a library. They are not. Or at least President Harding's are not. His papers are the property of the Harding Commemorative Society, and I am their sole custodian, just as Mrs. Harding herself stipulated by word and by will.

Mr. Mende continued, "Granted, Warren G. Harding was no Abraham Lincoln, but he was certainly a James K. Polk."

"James K. Polk!" If the fellow was trying to impress me then he might just as well have said Groucho Marx. Why, I scarcely even recognized the Polk name, and I could not even attach a bearded 19th-century face with his scarcely recognizable name. I vaguely remembered an old timer, long,

long ago—an old man who worked for my grandfather—telling me that he had fought in "Mr. Polk's War"—meaning the Mexican-American War. Other than that, I drew an utter blank.

"Yes, sir. James K. Polk. One of our nation's greatest Americans and one of our most effective presidents. Extremely capable and efficient to a T, but significantly underrated, I'm afraid. Though at least James K. Polk hasn't been done in by history. Just forgotten. Everyone remembers Warren G. Harding. Or maybe I should say, everyone remembers his cronies. They forgot him. Or never knew him. Not as he really was anyway. Truth is Warren Harding was a very fine, effective president, and the way I figure it, if I can set the record straight, then who knows, maybe I'll win the Pulitzer Prize."

I glanced at this young man who seemed to grow ever more astonishing with each minute.

"My advisor at Princeton, Dr. Klaus—nice Kraut name—Manfred Klaus, no less, though he's been in this country forever, even studied under Woodrow Wilson, anyway, Professor Klaus says it's a tall order for me, but I already have a track record. And if I can pull it off, write a book that proves some good things about Harding, then maybe he can get me a chair at Princeton. Meaning a job. In fact, believe it or not, I've already got a contract for the book."

He pulled an envelope from his coat and proudly held it up, as if it were cash to back up his point. "A book, sir, on President Warren G. Harding. How 'bout that!"

"And so you've sought me out," I said.

"That's right," he said with a smile. "You've got the President's papers, I've got the talent, I've got the connections, and I've got the drive and ambition to do something with them. But none of this is *solely* why I want to write about him. I also want to do it for him, for President Harding. It's just not fair what they've done to him. As far as I know, no historian ever made the slightest move to write the good things, did they?"

"Hardly. It's always been the same, Mr. Mende. Teapot Dome, poker games in the White House. The Negro-blood rumor and the poison nonsense, and Nan Britton, too, of course. And of course the others too, or so they say. That's all the historians ever come here to ask about, and that's all they ever write about."

To tell you the truth, I threw in the business about "and of course the others too" as a kind of play. The only writer to dig up Mitzy's liaison was Professor Chancellor. Miss von Leuckel was now Mrs. Jim Blaine, and by then she was living in St. Louis. As for Nan—the notorious and best-selling author of *The President's Daughter*—she and Elizabeth Ann were said to be holed up in Chicago; by then the President's daughter would have been about thirty years old. Essentially, most of Mr. Harding's women had disappeared (at least the ones that I knew about).

Mr. Mende said, "I would like to say, Mr. Hamilton, that I'm not interested in the Negro-blood business, but I am, sir, a bit. By that I mean, I'm intrigued, and I don't see the shame in it that others see, maybe because I've got Cherokee blood in me. Don't let the blond hair fool you, I'm no purebred either, but one way or another, the colored business is not a thread I wish to pursue—honest I don't. For one thing, I'm not a genealogist, and even if I was, Marion's the wrong place to go rooting around for those kinds of things. Even Blooming Grove isn't the place. You'd have to start in Pennsylvania, so any historian who came here asking about that, he'd simply be looking for rumors, not facts. And I'm not interested in Nan Britton or any of *the others*—as you so provocatively say, sir. Let the muckrakers dig them up. I'll never ask you or anyone else about the ladies, let alone try to see them. I mean, what do I care about what other people do with each other in bed? People should mind their own business about things like that." He paused. "I'm interested in President Harding's presidential history, what he did while in office and his tragic legacy, and I'm interested in doing justice by him and seeing justice done. I'm interested in bringing his record to light and making the connections between things. I'm on President Harding's side. Really I am."

As men say in the building trade say, this curious young man certainly "talked a good job."

"Mr. Hamilton," he said, "may I presume to lend you some food for thought?"

He was already digging in his portfolio. He withdrew some kind of publication and laid it on the car seat beside me, and then he dug out another, and laid that on the seat too. At a glance, I could read the names, *The Burlington Quarterly* and *Sequoia*. I had never heard of either. Both were the sort of magazines that had a table of contents printed on the cover instead of pictures.

"Here's my name right here," he said, tapping his finger to one of the entries. "This one's on Polk, and this one here, in *Sequoia*, it's on Franklin Pierce. You can read them if you like. That way you'll know that I'm not talking through my hat. And when we stop, I'll show you the contract, if you like. From Lippincott. Very prestigious."

"Mr. Mende, how old are you—if I may ask?"

"Twenty-five."

My son would have been his age. I said, "Ah, twenty-five. I took you for even younger."

He ran his hand over his chin, as if feeling for signs of a beard, which, I think, were not exactly forthcoming. After a moment, he said, "You think I'm too young, Mr. Hamilton? Too inexperienced, maybe? Well, what were you doing when *you* were twenty-five, sir—if I may ask?"

"Same thing I'm doing right now, running the family business. Though back then there was a lot more of it to run."

"*And* you were making a President."

"You got your historical facts jumbled, Mr. Mende. Already. I was thirty when Mr. Harding was running for President, if that's what you mean."

He sighed. "Mr. Hamilton, I have no idea how old you are, or were, sir, but I do know that Warren Harding's supporters started dreaming of the presidency long before you were twenty-five. Right? His mother was dreaming of it on the day he was born, supposedly."

"There's no 'supposedly' about it, she was. In fact, I'd say she foresaw it, not dreamed it."

"I might look young, sir, but if I may say so, the war made me older than you'll *ever* be." He seemed to reconsider his words. "No disrespect intended, sir."

I think Mr. Mende took my natural reticence—and maybe my questioning of his age—as a negation, for he said, "Well, if you won't let me see the President's papers, then I guess I'll just have to write about my great-grandfather.

"Ah, always good to have options."

After many seconds of silence, he said, "He was General Horace Porter. Ever heard of him?"

"General Horace Porter—can't say as I have."

"You see, that's the big problem. No one has. He played his part, but always in the shadow of great men, nothing that would warrant his own history. My great-grandfather was in the room with General Grant at Appomattox when Lee surrendered, if you can believe that. Not to mention the fact that he'd been beside Grant throughout the war, or at least through most of it. Was his aide-de-camp, and was more or less the same thing after the war, too, when Grant was running for president. You see, Grant didn't like making speeches, so great-Granddad did it for him, sometimes. Lots of times, actually, while Grant just sat there listening, or maybe thinking of something else. Great-Granddad was Assistant Secretary of War, then vice-president of the Pullman Car Company, then director of the Equitable Life Assurance Company, and so on and so forth. And then he was Ambassador and Minister Plenipotentiary of the United States to France under McKinley and Teddy Roosevelt. And he made *lots* of money, believe me. But not a one red cent of it ever came down to me, not one, damn it."

"I'm sorry to hear that," I said. By then we were passing the Ackerman apartments on one side and the Ohio Theatre on the other, drawing close to the corner of State and Center Streets, the young man's destination. I pulled along the curb. No sooner had I brought my Lincoln to a stop than he slipped the ring from his finger and handed it to me. "That's the only thing I have of General Porter's. The only thing I ever got in this world from those days. Why, to think of it! And he had so much. So very, very much."

An antique coin of pinkish-gold was set in a filigree ring of heavy yellow gold.

"That's Alexander the Great," he said. "The coin itself is two thousand three hundred years old. My great grandmother, Elsie, had it set in a ring after the Civil War as a victory gift and to commemorate great-Granddad's coming-home."

I examined the face of Alexander. He was in profile, with abundant curls. "It's striking. What are those?"

He leaned over, and I touched the profile with my finger. "The curved back things," I said.

"Ah, rams' horns." Then he pronounced two very foreign-sounding words that I could not remember now if my life depended upon it. I did not ask for a translation, and he did not proffer for one.

I handed his ring to him. "Well, young man, if that's your *only* legacy from General Porter, then I'd say it's quite enough."

"Well, a very fine point, sir! A philosopher's point." He kissed the ring. "My lucky charm. I like to think it was Alexander got me through the war, along with God, of course, and *Orpheus*. That's my Mustang. That *was* my Mustang. They were my trinity. They saw to *my* homecoming."

I realized that I rather liked this young man, and I was not particularly impatient for him to leave; nevertheless, I left the motor running. I took up one of the publications, spotted his name on the cover and read aloud, "*James K. Polk: Westward Expansion and the Enforcement of Manifest Destiny.* Matthias R. Mende."

"That's me. The R's for Rory."

I rifled through the pages. I could feel the young man studying me intently, as if considering something. He said a bit tentatively, studying me, "Mr. Hamilton, you wouldn't by chance want to come in for a cocktail, would you?"

I had no intention of entering Hotel Marion under any circumstance. "Thank you, Mr. Mende, I would not." Then I added, "I look forward to reading your articles. We'll take it from there, but don't count on anything. If you want, you can come 'round and see me tomorrow at the Harding Home. Can you make it at 3:00?"

The young man smiled that charming smile of his—which I have a feeling had earned him certain advantages in life. Clearly, he regarded his appointment as no small victory, for he kissed his ring again, made a V with his fore- and middle fingers—all in a jubilant instant. He reached across the seat and vigorously shook my hand. "Thank you, Mr. Hamilton, thank you so very much!"

I had to laugh at his sheer eagerness. "Mr. Mende, please! Don't jump to conclusions. I merely said I'd read your articles. I've seldom given access to the President's papers, you know, and when I have, I've regretted it."

"You won't this time—and that's a promise. Reading the articles is plenty for me. You'll like them, you'll see. You'll *definitely* like them, and besides, I'm just thanking you for giving me a hearing. I'm not presuming a thing." He stepped from the car, flashed that smile, and said through the open window, "I'll do right by you, Mr. Hamilton, I promise. I'll do right by President Harding. I promise I will, upon my honor."

With that said he slapped the roof of my Lincoln, as if it were the rump of a horse and, as if on his prompt, I found myself driving away.

HAVING TOLD YOU of my first encounter with Matthias Mende, I believe you will now appreciate how startled I was when I unlocked my sister's sterling silver casket and there, among some personal trinkets and things, lay Mr. Mende's ring.

Frankly, a chill shot through me like a knife and I think I must have sat for a straight ten minutes without moving a finger. The profound intrigue woven into the Harding history had even me grasping for answers, at least for a few bewildered minutes. In true Harding-history fashion, I was wondering if maybe we have yet another skeleton stashed somewhere in the closets around here. Or as Dana Yost seemed to think—a skeleton buried in the endless wilds of Goose Pond Farm and the Sanctuary Lands.

I do not know how or why Adeline came to possess that young man's ring. But after sitting here this morning in the predawn darkness, I believe I have conceived of at least one very reasonable explanation. And I am sure that I could think of one or two more, if I troubled myself, which I do not intend to do. Mr. Mende, ever lacking funds, probably borrowed from Adeline and she no doubt accepted his ring as collateral.

Simple as that.

As for why he never came back to claim it, well, that is something he would have to answer for himself. I will add that I have known his kind before. I mean the will-o'-the-wisp fellows like that. They start something with enthusiasm and the next thing you know, their mind wanders and so do they. Some leave their work undone, some leave precious things behind. When I was growing up a Scandinavian fellow lived out on the west-end in one of the houses my grandfather built. His wife awoke one morning and his place in the bed was empty, both his wedding ring and his watch lay on the night table, and the gate at the end of the yard was unlatched. The children—I believe there were three of them—lay asleep in their rooms. The fellow was never seen or heard from again. After a year or so his wife started calling herself a widow and she answered one of those old-fashioned ads that lonesome bachelors and widowers out West used to place in the papers. Eventually, she and her children moved to Nebraska or Kansas, or some place like that, and she remarried.

Matthias left behind a lot less than that Swede did.

And I want to assure you that my sister was not some kind of thief or criminal. In fact, I would swear on a stack of Bibles that she was a lady of impeccable honesty and integrity, *and* she was very kind to Mr. Mende. Adeline employed Matthias at a fair wage and she allowed him to live rent-free above her carriage house, and my sister and Mrs. Christian now and then called him in for lunch or dinner. It was Adeline's idea to lend him the keys to Indian Rock, our cottage on the Catawba Cliffs above Lake Erie, because he had a great curiosity about the Great Lakes, which he had never seen. Matthias had a penchant for swimming at night and had no qualms whatsoever about going out alone. To this day I am half-convinced that Matthias Mende drowned somewhere off the Catawba Cliffs.

I have another theory too—that he hightailed it out of Marion to get away from Dana Yost.

II

❧

I Heard the Crow Caw My Name

THE SUN HAS FINALLY RISEN, though you would scarcely know it. On summer mornings, first light peeps through the trees of the Old Forest and slowly fills the library with a wonderful glow part golden, part green—a light that makes me happy to be a part of morning and the world, even if I must enjoy that light alone. I love the smell of the forest and the yard on such mornings. And the birds make quite a racket out there. But I assure you, none of that is the case in November. As I sit here now, a white and shadowy gloom fills the forest and I am tempted to wonder if a single bird sings for a thousand miles. Adeline's once-magnificent gardens, where Matthias once toiled for twenty hours a week in the spring and early summer of '47, are now buried in a blanket of snow, a few skeletal stalks and the gnarled trees standing bare here and there.

Later today, Mitzy von Leuckel—Mrs. Jim Blaine—will step into this house for the first time in fifty years—and she will arrive with the President's son, which is to say that I ought to have more compelling things to think of than a drifter who appeared out of nowhere and vanished back into nowhere, years ago. I suddenly realize that I have mentioned Mrs. Blaine rather often here, but I wish emphatically to state that, after I began courting Lucy back in 1916 (we were married the following year), I hardly ever thought of her again. Indeed, I do not think I tell too tall a tale when I say that she has come to mind more in the past week than she did in the past fifty years. I know that I have more than once alluded to her last visit to Tioga, but if I am to mention any, then I prefer to remember the

happier times, such as her first visit here in June of 1912. I had the house
to myself that day—Adeline had already sailed for Europe, and Father was
somewhere else for a few days, probably Goose Pond Farm, or Indian Rock.
Mitzy and I had just started "seeing each other," and being a rather randy
young man, I may have intentionally waited until my father was away to
invite her over for her first visit. That day we met up at McKinley Park for
a picnic. She brought the sandwiches, though I felt bad about that as the
von Leuckels were struggling. Mitzy's father was dead by then, and she and
her mother and little brother Cedric lived in a rented house over on Pearl
Street, near Columbia. That was long before the days of Social Security. Mrs.
von Leuckel was a teacher at the Olney Avenue School. And Cedric, at the
age of about fourteen, became the man of the house and had to give up his
schooling in order to work all night and much of the day in a bakery. That
was the way things were back then for all too many people.

It was after our little picnic that Mitzy first visited the house.

We took a shortcut through the Old Forest, hiking over the rolling
Indian trails, and it was all great fun. I remember how the hem of Mitzy's
dress kept snagging on twigs, and more than once I had to stoop and
loosen her hem, which afforded a glimpse of her ankles. To this day, in
my memory, I can still see her summer shoes, their lilac-colored lace
and shining brass buckles that belied her family's circumstances, and I
do not think a Vanderbilt girl would have been ashamed to stroll down
Fifth Avenue in such elegant footwear. After getting snagged one time too
many, Mitzy said, "Oh, Tristan, to hell with it. You're just going to have to
look at my legs." Whereupon she hiked her dress and held it well above
her knees. Her legs were as white as ivory and as shapely as those of a
maiden's in a painting. She was quite pretty, and as I say, it was all great
good fun.

Today when Mitzy and the President's son arrive, she will find many
things exactly as they were on that summer afternoon in 1912. The massive
rectangular mirror that hangs in a gilt frame in the foyer is the same mirror
she paused before in her youth, though the glass has darkened a bit and
grown spotted with age, like so many of us. I can still see Mitzy standing
before the glass, running her hands down her girl-slender sides and hips,
turning herself this way and that with her chin up as she touched her
exquisite and abundant hair. Back then I possessed the boldness and

vitality of youth. I laid my hands on her shoulders, I kissed the smooth skin of her neck. She murmured, "Later, Tristan. Show me the house. I want to see the house and I especially want to see the *notorious* library."

My father used to keep the high double doors closed, so I rolled them back, and the mild, leathery fragrance of books, wood, and old things met us. I do not think that Mitzy had ever been in such a room. Compared to other such rooms I have seen, Tioga's library, like the house itself, is decidedly small-town and modest, but if you lived in a clapboard house on Pearl Street, then the place might have seemed like "something else." I remember she ran her fingers over the desk, over the bronze griffin and silver and crystal inkwell, and she murmured, "Yes—yes. Exactly like this." She touched the curlicues and edges of the shelves, pausing here and there before the titles. She asked to look at one. I was not paying much attention to books, back then, though if memory serves me then it may have been Herodotus. She leaned close to the painting of the two Indians gliding through reeds in a canoe at Goose Pond, the one in back paddling, the other kneeling in front, raising his bow and arrow just as geese rise against the sky from the shallows, the sun low on the horizon.

In the center of the room Mitzy lifted her eyes toward the chandelier and I studied for a moment the beautiful hollow of her throat. Without looking at me, she said, "My mother says that your mother was a Blennerhassett."

For a moment, I said nothing, and then, "A what?"

"A Blennerhassett."

"Ah."

"Was she?"

"Is that what they say?"

"Momma said that."

"Then it must be so. Mothers n'er err, do they?"

After a moment of thought, she said, "One doesn't know what to think."

"When that happens," I said, "I suppose it's best to take things at face value. Take the cash and let the credit go."

She made a face, as if only half-listening. She began circling beneath the chandelier, maybe observing her own reflection circling in the hanging brass ball. She shifted her eyes toward the ceiling, then down to the rug, woven in Persia long ago. She ran the toe of her lilac-colored shoe along the intricate designs, the silk—no doubt brought from Cathay, along the Silk Road—darkened and blanched as the light on its threads rippled and altered.

She turned to me. "He's here, isn't he?"

Before I could even say *who?* she said, "Show me where he died."

She meant Orrin de Pue.

Mitzy had never mentioned the matter before, nor had she ever mentioned my mother.

I said, "Right about where you're standing. As a matter of fact, you're probably standing right smack in the middle of his blood."

"Oh!" She looked towards her feet and lifted the hem of her dress to her knees, as if suddenly realizing that she might be situated in a pool of blood. I laughed at her silly gesture. Again in her low whispery voice, with something of a thrill, she said, "You killed him, didn't you, Trey? You killed him!"

I did not answer.

"Didn't you? You can tell me. I'll never tell a soul, no one ever, I swear to it. Don't be afraid. Tell me! Tell me you killed him. You killed a man. I know you did!"

Something in her, something very deep in her, desired that I say yes. I raised my chin, and with my hands clasped behind my back, I approached her. In my imagination, I wore the mantle of a killer. Come to think of it, I believe I used those same words before, affected the same air that I was to convey eight years later on that autumn night when I approached Professor Chancellor and his two pupils trespassing in my backyard—after the old rascal called me "Killer Trey." I stopped a few inches from Mitzy's face, near enough to smell the rosewater scent. I touched my hands gently to her cheeks and, like a hypnotist, I drew her nearer. Looking deeply in her eyes, I said, "Yes."

"Yes, what?"

"Yes, I did."

"Did what?"

"Yes, I killed him."

"Oh!" she gasped in horror. Her fingers flew to her lips as she recoiled from me in absolute horror, falling back onto the desk. "Oh, how awful,

Tristan! You killed a man! And you're proud of it!" Tears came to her eyes. "You killed a man!" I sensed that part of her being was acting out some scene she had once read in a book, or seen on the stage or something, that she was sincere in her demonstrated horror. "But why?"

"Why? Well, I don't know why. I guess I just did it, that's all. Can't say I even meant to. Remember, I was only eight. It was just a lucky shot, a lucky misfortune."

"Oh, but it doesn't matter, does it? You killed a man! That's what matters. Are you at least sorry for your crime? For your horrible sin?"

I gave a little laugh, mocking her drama—not the man's death.

Now she threw herself nearer to me and ran her fingers over my chin, cupping my cheek in her palm, she said, "Tell me, Tristan, how you did it? Tell me how you killed him. What was his name?"

I lied, "I don't remember."

She asked me again, but I did not answer, and then she said, "Oh, the poor thing! Tell me *exactly* how you did it, *exactly* how you killed him!"

I was not prepared for this moment, though I must say, I found it fun. I shrugged. "There's nothing to tell, other than what you've already heard, I'm sure. Addy and I were playing by the tree line. Right out there, as a matter of fact." I pointed through the bay window. "See where the great oak stands? Right around there, to the right of it, I think. I twirled the stone in my slingshot, twirled and twirled it about and let it fly. It was black and shiny, the stone was. I'd spit on it to make it shine even more. That's that."

"Just like young King David! In the Bible! Just like David and Goliath!"

I laughed at her charming idiocy. "Well, I never thought of it quite like that." I glanced toward the ceiling. "He was up real high, far away, so very high and far away. Usually I couldn't hit the broad side of a barn at ten paces, but something happened that day, I don't know what." I paused and looked away, through the windows, not really caring to go down this road again; nevertheless, I continued. "It was like, for a few seconds, something took over my hand and my eye, my whole being and loosened that beautiful stone from the sling at just the right moment in just the right way. Or maybe I should say the wrong way. Anyway, I watched it fly. I thought I saw it disappear over him. But his arm jerked toward his head and he dropped his hammer. Then he fell." I paused again, looking through the window, "That's it. That's that."

"Oh, Tristan, how horrible! But nothing more? Didn't he scream? They say he screamed."

I was still looking off, through the window. "I think so. Yes, he screamed. Addy certainly screamed. She screamed and screamed and ran into the woods and I ran too. Deep inside, I think she never stopped screaming. It was hours before they came looking for us."

"So it's all true then."

"I think so. Yes. It's all true."

I was still looking through the library windows, off into the trees, off into the green shadows of the Old Forest, thinking of my little sister. "I think it affected her. I think it affected Addy. Maimed her."

"Maimed her?"

"Did something to her. Made her odd or something. Made her—made her *strange*. I'm sure of it."

She averted her eyes, but only for a moment. "Poor thing. Poor, poor thing."

Mitzy kissed my lips and ran her fingers through my hair and pulled my body close to hers in sympathy. "Poor thing," she murmured. "Poor lost little boy."

And then I showed her the rest of the house.

HAVING BROUGHT THE SUBJECT UP, I feel that I am now committed to an explanation of the purported part I played—or did not play—in Orrin de Pue's ill-fated end.

I want to confess that I lied somewhat to Mitzy in my confession. I know it might sound a bit lame, but I think that almost immediately the stories and rumors of that day became all jumbled up in my memory so that I honestly have never known for sure whether or not I killed Orrin de Pue. I know that sounds remarkable, but it is true.

What happened was this, more or less: Like many boys at that time, I owned a slingshot, though unlike others, I was disinclined to hurl stones at rabbits, stray cats, crows, and other of God's creatures—including human beings. I slung them at tree trunks, boulders, and windowless sheds, things like that—and I was a child and certainly I was not a very good shot.

Likewise I did not even know Orrin de Pue, so I certainly had nothing against the poor man. Afterwards, they said he was something of a vagabond, a tramp, what we would nowadays call a drifter. Vagabonds were quite common back then. They would work for a few weeks, live in encampments at the edge of town, and then collect their pay and head off into a world that people once called Vagabondia—a somewhat mythical land of freight cars, hayricks, campfires, and, I suppose, its own peculiar form of romance and freedom. I think men back then became tramps because so many of them could not abide the notion of spending their lives in the infernal factories—and I do mean *infernal.* I remember once, when I was a child, riding down David Street with my mother, past the Marion Steam Shovel, and seeing through the windows a cascade of fire and molten metal, and my mother calling it, "Vulcan's workshop." Anyway, my father ordinarily hired vagabonds only as day laborers, to shovel coal, load wagons, and do manual labor, but at that time several of his skilled carpenters were still off on adventures in Cuba and the Philippines due to the Spanish-American War. Thus my father used some qualified itinerants in skilled positions.

On that spring day in 1900, Tioga was but a skeleton of new timbers rising from its new-made clearing in the Old Forest. Several carpenters were straddling the high beams pounding away; one was Orrin de Pue. Something happened. He lost his balance and fell fifty-some feet onto the rough base timbers of what would become the library's floor.

According to one of the carpenters—a resident of Marion who was straddling the beam beside him—a wasp had flown amongst them. Orrin de Pue tried to shoo it away and, in so doing, he either lost his balance or else he actually got stung, and then he fell.

But the next day one of Mr. de Pue's fellow citizens from Vagabondia, who had been milling timber on what is now the front yard, paid a visit to the sheriff. He told him that he saw Colonel Hamilton's boy—i.e., yours truly—slinging stones, and he said that I slung one at Orrin de Pue and hit him. And that's what caused him to fall.

No one else, except for maybe my little sister, saw me do that—*if* indeed I did that.

In fact, Mr. Bacon—the old man who fought in "Mr. Polk's war"—came forward and told the sheriff that he had tried to teach me how to use a slingshot and to hunt with it, just as he had done as a boy during pioneer days, but according to him, I could not hit the broad side of a barn from ten paces, much less a man fifty-some feet up and thirty or forty yards away. In fact, he doubted that even he could have done so back in his glory days of his youth, when he could knock a pheasant out of the sky, or so he said.

With my hand on a Bible, I denied slinging a stone at Orrin de Pue.

My father refused to allow the sheriff to question my six-year-old sister.

The sheriff dismissed the matter, but the story—with all of its ambiguity and with a tramp as its source—stuck.

That is how I became "Killer Trey."

Likewise, that is how I became ostracized from the company of other children, and that is why, as a boy, I was spat upon, why I was struck by more than one stone or snowball hurled at me in the schoolyard and from behind trees as I walked home. And mind you, my humiliations were not only from children—well do I remember a certain elocution teacher who openly mocked the silken "gambler's" vests I wore as an adolescent boy, using me as an example of "boyhood sin." She lived on the far eastside—before the water system extended that far—so in honor of her humiliations and excesses, I crept out there one fall night and turned on the garden spigot. I even donated a hose, so the sound of water splashing full-force would not alert her. Next morning, when she endeavored to cleanse herself of her filth, lo and behold she would have found that her cistern had run dry in the night.

I was driven from the schoolroom before receiving my diploma; that is why I began the strenuous and vindictive process of self-education and cultivation—which I assure you did not cease at the age of eighteen, and which, I further assure you, has far exceeded the educations of most college boys, and which vigorously continues to this very day. How many dropouts, indeed, how many "scholars" do you know who have read Xenophon's *Cyropaedia*?

How many have even heard of it? Or him?

Who knows—had I gone to the university, then maybe I would have read it as it had been written, in classical Greek.

Somewhere along the way "Killer Trey" developed his own (my own) recollection of that spring day in 1900, be it fictitious or real. In this memory I am off by the tree line, near the ancient oak that I pointed out to Mitzy. I am scouring the dirt and leaf meal looking for the perfect stone. Little Addy is nearby playing with her baby doll, Jenny. My search yields a smooth and beautiful stone, black as obsidian, which I clean on my shirt and polish with my spit before tucking it in the sling. As I begin twirling, feeling the stone's strange, willful tug at the end of the leather thong, I cast my eye about for a target, something *more* than just another tree trunk. A crow crosses the sky and caws my name; as I follow its passage, the men on the high beams enter my ken, and the crow vanishes. In my memory—my imagination—the centrifugal force of the twirling stone suddenly generates its own—how shall I say?— its own unearthly power, at least in my remembering imagination. My eye settles on one of the men. He wears a railroader's blue blouse. He pauses in his pounding to swat at something, maybe the wasp that the other carpenter would blame. In my peripheral vision I see my little sister pause in her play, in her fussing with Jenny's hair. Her eyes settle on me, as if something in my nature startles her. The momentum of the twirling stone pulling at my fingers gains more and more insistence and power, and the man in the blue blouse seems to come into super focus, as if all distance between us has vanished. I see the stubble covering his face, I see the scattered nicks from recent shaving accidents. At the perfect moment, I unleash the stone and it hurls like a demon towards its mark. I see it strike his temple. His hand jerks violently upward and the hammer drops, and then he tips, like a drunkard falling off a horse. He screams on his long plunge. With perfect calm I follow his descent and watch as his arms flay in an attempt to stop himself, and then his head explodes like a dropped watermelon on the heavy timbers.

I WOULD LAY MY HAND ON A BIBLE and swear that I do not know whether the account I have just related springs from imagination or from memory. Though I think you will agree that it stinks more of the imagined than the remembered. How could *anyone* possibly see the stubble and shaving nicks on a man's chin from so great a distance?

And yet I swear that I saw them and still see them in my mind. Whether my recollection comes from imagination or vision that was momentarily and bizarrely super-enhanced, I cannot say.

How could an eight-year-old boy who "could not hit the broad side of a barn" possibly strike a man from that great distance—and strike him with such force, and in the temple, no less?

Well, if I did kill Orrin de Pue, if I stole his long, unfinished years, then I regret it beyond all telling and I ask the Good Lord for His forgiveness.

If I did not, then I regret the cruelty, ostracism, and deprivation that I suffered as a child (and to some extant thereafter) for something I did not do. I regret the theft of an ordinary boyhood and I regret the theft of my diploma *and* the theft of the Ivy League education that my mother—dead before this incident—so wanted for her son to have.

Indeed, I wanted that education for myself—almost more than anything.

Either way the incident happened; I am terribly sorry that my baby sister witnessed such a horrific tragedy.

And something else has always disturbed me regarding that incident: the fact that my father did not peel away the bloodstained floorboards and lay down new ones. The blood was simply wiped away, and I believe that whatever brain tissue and hair and such that they managed to scrape together was simply carted off with the rest of him and placed in his coffin. But the blood of course spread over the wood and soaked into the grain, leaving a stain that looked somewhat like a rose opening its petals. Forgive me for this display of honesty, but as a boy looking down at it, just after the accident, I thought the stain rather pretty. As for why my father did not bother to replace those boards, I have not a clue. The one time I asked him about that (after the house was completed and we were living here), he said, "But Trey, it's part of the house, the same way blood's part of a battlefield. They didn't shovel away bloody soil at Gettysburg, did they? And then cart in new? Would you have them do that?"

Well, no, but—

But what can you say to that kind of logic?

Actually, even at the time what I really wanted to say to my father was, "You mean to say, Father, that if someone bled all over the carpet and stained it, you wouldn't replace the carpet because now the blood's part of the carpet and part of the house?"

But I did not "talk back." Besides, by then it was way too late. Tioga was complete. Orrin de Pue's blood was and is forever sealed beneath a layer of hardwood floorboards, and still another layer of parquet, and these beneath the Oriental rug.

I BELIEVE THAT EVEN Matthias Mende came to know the story of Orrin de Pue; in fact, I know he did and rest assured, I know who told him. Matthias came to know many things during his brief sojourn in Marion, Ohio. My impression is that, like many people who elicit confidence, some of his information came to him via the subtle and cunning art of *not* asking questions—or at least by knowing which ones to ask and which to leave unspoken, so that information would flow of its own accord. To that extent, the boy was no fool.

In fact, so far as I recall, at least at the moment, Matthias asked me only one pertinent question during his three months or so in Marion, and that question came about two weeks into his stay here. But I suppose I am once again getting ahead of myself.

I should say first that, as you have no doubt gathered, I did give Matthias access to President Harding's papers. He worked in the old press bungalow behind the Harding Home, where I set him up at the oak desk in the light of the north window, the desk where Harry Daugherty used to sit with his feet propped and with the stub of a cigar sticking out of his mouth, as he scanned newspapers, reading articles about the Campaign. I remember how amused Matt was with the burn marks along the desk's edge, left there by Harry's careless smoking habits, which I might add, did not amuse Senator Harding anymore than they amused me. During the first days of Matt's research I sat with him for two hours at a stretch, or I should say, I sat across the room from him so as to give him some "breathing room," and so I could simultaneously assure myself that he did not get sticky fingers with any of our documents. I admired the young man's powers of concentration. It seemed to me that he would become so involved as to virtually disappear into his work. I can still see him seated at the desk with a stack of yellowing documents before him, with his tousled yellow hair glowing in the afternoon light, his lips moving now and then as he read this or that page. Sometimes I would see the flicker of a smile and I would wonder what tidbit from those years had amused him.

I became fully confident that he would tell the truth about President Harding. Indeed, I never lost that confidence. Thus I allowed him to search through the papers at will and he was free to copy anything he wished. Matthias always arrived at the bungalow with a neat stack of seven or eight notebooks, a box of yellow pencils, and one of those small metal sharpeners. He did not like his pencils dull, and I remember how scrupulous he was about the parings, making certain the flecks fell into the wastebasket that he kept beside him for that purpose. Nor did he like his pencils short. When he had written one down to three or four inches, it would find itself being flung into the can. Sometimes he seemed to copy almost as much as he read, placing his notation in this or that notebook, depending, I gathered, upon its particular subject matter. Sometimes he seemed to abruptly remember my presence, as he would look up from his work, nod and smile to me across the room, and then just as abruptly sink back into the documents and notebooks, and into his scholar's silence. I never pried into what he was finding, copying, or thinking. His diligence and his deep interest in the President engendered my trust, and I suppose endeared him to me in some unexpected way. I wanted this boy to do well by President Harding, and I wanted President Harding to do well by this boy—to help procure for him that chair at Princeton, as he said, and whatever measure of fame a historian can stir up for himself.

I imagine it was the fourth or fifth afternoon into his work. I was sitting across the room reading the *Star* when I felt Matthias' eyes on me. When I glanced up, he was indeed watching me, but he glanced away. I thought perhaps I had discerned an inquiring look in his eyes. For a moment I suspected that perhaps he had come upon some compromising passage in the President's documents, but a moment later he met my eyes again and said, "Sir, I've been wondering, do you and Mrs. Hamilton have children—if I may ask?"

"Ah, certainly, you may." I lay down the paper. "We had a son. But he died as a baby."

He reddened. "Oh, I'm sorry."

Scarcely anyone but Lucy and I had spoken of our boy since the miscarriage a quarter of a century before, and even then very few people—

especially men—seemed to comprehend the enormity of our loss; indeed, in the conception of others the miscarriage might as well have been some fleeting illness from which Lucy soon recovered and then went on her way. I was scarcely in the picture. Our son, not at all.

"What was his name, your son's?"

I don't know why, but his inquiry moved me in the strangest way. I tossed the newspaper aside and knew that I would not return to it.

"His name was Eric Anthony. Eric Anthony Hamilton. I thought about naming him Eric Antonio, I liked the sound, but it was too foreign and my father's first name was Anthony, so Anthony it was. Eric would have been your age now."

Something came into his eyes, though I have not a clue as to what that something might have been. "Do you mind if I ask what happened?"

"Mind!" I gave a little laugh, though I do not think it was "that habitual, condescending laugh" of my youth, which Lucy long ago ridiculed out of me, for good reason. I said, "I appreciate your interest in my son. So would my son." I paused, and then repeated the words, "My son." I did not say to him—nor have I ever said it to anyone, for that matter—but to me those are the two most beautiful and moving words in the English language. And I said again, "My son. My son. Eric Anthony Hamilton."

I found myself rising. Frankly, I felt like crossing the room and sitting across from the boy, from my new, young friend. Instead I found my feet carrying me towards the north window. I stood looking out across the long backyards of distant houses where bright forsythia were coming into bloom. I am not in the habit of talking to people with my back to them, but I guess I simply was not thinking, because so situated, I began telling the young man about the frantic phone call I received at work from Nora, our young housekeeper, and the call I placed to George Sawyer, doctoring son of the Surgeon General. I told Matt of my frantic drive home, of the maddening wait for a train at the Main Street crossing—a freight train, no less. I told him how, when I finally reached home and ran in the back door and up the stairs, Lucy was on the floor in the bathroom, ghostly pale, her lower quarters in a pool of blood and I do not know what else. I remember that blood seemed to be everywhere, all over the toilet and in the water as well, and the sink was streaming with blood. Nora was kneeling at Lucy's side, and a couple of women from the neighborhood were crowded into the bathroom with bloody cloths in their hands. My wife's mother and sisters and Doctor Sawyer soon arrived, and after bathing her we carried her to bed.

I was still standing with my back to Matthias, looking at the bright forsythia, green and yellowing. "It was over so quickly," I said. "I know it sounds foolish, but at the time I don't think I fully understood what had happened. Why, I don't even know what they did with my son." I paused. "What do you suppose they did with him? That's something I've never, ever been able to figure out."

I turned to Matthias, his eyes wide and fastened on me. "What do you suppose they did with my son, Mr. Mende?"

But this young man, who had flown against Hitler's Luftwaffe and lived to tell the tale, found his mouth dropping and he quickly shook his head—too timid or embarrassed or simply unable to speak.

"You and Eric could have gone out chumming around town together. If, God willing, he too had made it back from the War, like you."

Mr. Mende said nothing.

I continued, "Well, I suppose I've answered your question anyway, haven't I, young man?"

Matthias said, "Oh, Mr. Hamilton, I'm so sorry. I'm so very sorry."

This time I nodded to him. His gaze stayed fixed on me for a long moment and I thought I saw a hint of tears in his eyes. I had wanted to tell him that my mother died during the birth of my stillborn baby brother, but I thought that one sad story from me was quite enough, and so we returned to our own affairs. He returned to his notebooks and I quietly left for the day, entrusting him to work in solitude, for the first time, with the President's papers.

I knew that Matthias was fond of coffee, and so the very next day, on my way to the bungalow, I stopped by the market and purchased a tin of Maxwell House, along with a bottle of cream, a box of sugar, and some coffee rolls. Lucy had an extra percolator at home, and so I brought that along too, along with some battered cups that our household could easily forfeit.

After loosely watching over him for a few more afternoons, I asked a couple of guides from the Harding Home, two of the old ladies who worked for the Commemorative Society, if they would take turns in the bungalow acting as guardians of the presidential papers. I instructed Mrs. Carter and Mrs. Fetter not to disturb our young friend, but I do not think they had the wherewithal to oblige me, old women being what they are. Maybe they felt compelled to tell him their own recollections of Mr. Harding, which I am sure he would have welcomed, though probably not during his research time. As he had made clear from the first, the White House years constituted his realm of purpose. Or maybe they asked Matthias about himself. I remember that Mrs. Fetter in particular had a way of reminding any young unmarried man who happened along that he would not be a spring chicken forever. And I might add that she had an available and, as far as I was concerned, homely granddaughter. Anyway, I soon gathered that Matthias did not like having the old women around. Indeed, he referred to them as "the biddies" and "my keepers."

After a week or so, I called off "the biddies" and hung a key for the bungalow on a little hook behind the yew tree. Thus I allowed Matthias Mende to work alone at whatever hours he wished, with full access to the Harding papers. Along about that same time, he gave me the completed charcoal drawing of the Memorial. I had it framed, of course, and it hung in my office at Colonel Hamilton & Son until the day I sold the company and retired. Presently, as I may have mentioned before, it hangs here in the library at Tioga, near an engraving of the Tholos at Delphi. Young Mr. Mende exerted such trustworthiness and charm upon me that soon I even invited him home for supper. He was so amenable and charming that Lucy felt bad about not having had the girl get out the bone china, even if it wasn't Sunday supper. That was the first of many dinners he had at our house.

III

🌸

A Bouquet of Garden Flowers

AT THAT SAME TIME Adeline was interested in finding a school boy to help with her spring gardens, and Matthias was in need of funds and so, as I said, I arranged for him to work part-time at Tioga. And to save the fifty cents or so per night that he was paying at the fleabag Hotel Marion, he took up residence in the rustic quarters above the carriage house, in the rooms where my father's colored groom—Mr. Cotton Tully—lived way back at the turn of the century. This arrangement placed him within walking distance of the Harding Home.

All of this came about in spite Adeline's leeriness of outsiders and her reservations and suspicions regarding Matthias.

As I mention before, he took up in some fashion or another with Dana Yost.

Now you may recall that I mentioned Dana before. He was my friend and classmate who worked for us at Colonel Hamilton & Son back in the '20s—the gossipy fellow who sallied forth for baloney sandwiches on that fine Saturday after the President's death, and returned bearing the rumor of poison. That one. Alas, poor Dana is years gone now. He became a heart cripple and died back in '55, though in '47 he was still going strong. He married a girl from Bucyrus and they had two fine, manly sons, identical twins, Jason and Wyatt. The boys were once inseparable and it was not until they grew up, got married, and went on their separate ways that I could tell them apart. Anyway, Dana's abilities outgrew Colonel Hamilton & Son rather early on, though he would remain involved with my family in a business sort of way for many years thereafter. In November of 1926 he went to work for the Marion Steam Shovel Company as Chief of Inventory, keeping track of everything from the smallest nuts and bolts to "buckets"—the shovel part of a steam shovel—most of them would hold about the capacity of an automobile trunk, but one or two were large enough to scoop an entire two-story house out of the earth, basement to chimney. But no shovel on earth could encompass the sprawling ranch house in which Dana and Margaret raised their boys on Vernon Heights Boulevard. Colonel Hamilton & Son built that house, I might add. I sold the land to Dana at market value, but I let him have the house at a generously slim margin above cost. That may have been one of the reasons why he felt obliged to remain with Adeline and me in a business capacity. As you may have gathered, my sister and I inherited considerable real estate holdings, both commercial and residential, and we added to our holdings throughout the years. People seem to have this notion that landlords always live on "Easy Street," that we just sit back and collect the rent, but I assure you, that is nowhere near the truth. The grass must be mown, the leaks fixed, the rents collected from truant tenants, and a long list of other duties performed—none of them pleasant and few of them easy. Dana began managing those duties for us back in 1921 when Argus Finch resigned from our company to go to Washington. Dana managed property for my sister and me until the summer of '47 when Matthias left us, and our friendship vanished with him. I sent Dana flowers during his illness and a note bearing well wishes and regrets, but he never replied. In deference to his feelings, I did not attend his funeral, though I sent flowers.

Adeline had long ago ceased wanting anything to do with him, living or dead.

It was simply one of those pathetic reversals of a lifelong friendship that one occasionally hears about in this world. And I might add that Adeline and I were the ones who were wronged, considering the slander-ous rumors and insinuations Dana spread during and after the summer of '47. Though I assure you, not once did I ever add whispers or even a knowing nod to the shameful things people said about him—neither then, nor before, nor after.

To this day I am pained to think that I was best man in his wedding and that he was best man in mine (by default more than by my genuine choice).

Of course this reversal would not have come about but for Matthias, though it would be equally slanderous of me to lay blame on his shoulders. In this particular case our historian was more or less an "innocent bystander"—except by then he was no longer even a bystander, simply because he was gone. I believe I may have mentioned that he had a penchant for skinny-dipping at night. He told me so himself. He used to work until well after dark in the bungalow, sometimes past midnight, and on occasions, according to him, he would sneak over to Lake Etowah and go for a plunge. He knew that Warren Harding swam there in his youth and I think he fancied the parallel. When Matthias told me about those midnight swims, I thought it my duty to caution him about the dangers of swimming in old quarries and of going it alone, but he just laughed.

But as usual I seem to have gotten ahead of myself. I assure you, quite a few things happened before Mr. Mende lit out for Lake Erie. For one thing, as I stated, he became my sister's gardener.

BACK IN THOSE DAYS Tioga's gardens were unequaled in Marion. Granted, the Kings' gardens at Etowah had once been far more lavish and extensive, but by 1947 Mr. and Mrs. King were long gone, and so too their gardens, like flowers of bygone summers. Tioga's setting was far more modest—no terraced beds, no grand walkways leading to stone staircases descending to gaily painted rowboats in a private lake inhabited by swans. Adeline's gardens ranged over level ground, and they mainly occupied the side and backyards, hidden from Mt. Vernon Avenue by a hedge of English hawthorn. Perhaps with the exception of the orchid bed, there was nothing "moneyed" about Adeline's gardens. Virtually anyone with a patch of land, time on their hands, and the blessings of a green thumb could have cultivated gardens every bit as lovely. Mind you, my sister had no qualms about spending five dollars for an ornamental tree and heaven only knows how much she spent on some of her orchids. Some were literally hand-delivered by special couriers and agents. Mostly, though, the beauty of Tioga's gardens came from nickel-and-dime plants and the care my sister lavished upon them—that and some inner connection she seemed to have between herself and God's creation, be it of the plant or animal kingdom. In looking back I realize that my sister's gardens reflected her life—old-fashioned and abundant, exquisite and romantic, exotic and homegrown, all hidden away on the far side of tall hedges denser than any man could penetrate. Nowadays Rob McGregor spends his Saturdays from April to October looking after the grounds, but things are not the same. I am no gardener. I care for flowers about as much as I care for bowling, or Persian poetry for that matter, and so the beauty of Tioga's gardens has long gone for the most part, as I so quaintly said before of the Kings' gardens, like the flowers of bygone summers.

I remember a little visit that Adeline, Matthias, and I had in her gardens. That was on a spring afternoon just after he started working here, which was a week, maybe a little more, after he inquired about my son. I had gone home for lunch that day and I knew that he was scheduled to be attending to his chores at that hour, and so on my way back to Colonel Hamilton & Son I swung by to see how things were going. I parked my car beside Mrs. Christian's gray DeSoto. Matthias, Addy, and her little Scotty, Muldoon, were all in the back gardens. Two were working; one was loafing. The little loafer promptly popped his head up above the grass and then came bounding and yapping through the spring grass to greet me. Matthias was on his hands and knees beneath the rose bushes tossing last winter's bedding into the ancient wooden wheelbarrow. Smoke rose from back in the Old Forest, from the bowl-like hollow where Brownie, Jim Blaine, and I burned the Chancellor books deep in the middle of an autumn night, more than a quarter of a century before.

The summer of '47 was the summer when Adeline first tried her hand at orchids in the great outdoors. When I arrived she was breaking the earth with a pitchfork, making a new bed. My little sister had long cultivated orchids on windowsills and in the sunroom at the back of the house, but until that year she shied away from the hazard of planting them in her gardens. Addy once said, "They're temperamental, orchids are, disliking the company of lesser flowers. *All* flowers being lesser. Including other orchids."

Orchids well-suited my younger sister.

Adeline was wearing her wide-brimmed straw hat with a blue bow; it is still in a hatbox upstairs. I think she bought the hat in France and I can easily imagine a lady wearing it in gardens in Aquitaine or Bordeaux, or someplace among the lavender, wherever it grows. "So you've come to check on us, Trey, have you?" she called.

"I have. I thought someone should."

She laughed and Matthias smiled over his shoulder, but kept working, just as he had kept right on sketching that day at the Memorial.

"Matthias wants to learn all there is to know about gardening, don't you Matthias?"

Adeline cast an inscrutable glance my way, as if I were privy to discern some meaning beyond the apparent—whatever the apparent was. If anything, I somehow found her words vaguely rude.

The young man must have sensed something too; he froze for a moment. And then, "But why not, Miss Hamilton? If gardening's what I'm doing at the moment, then why not learn all I can about it? Especially from one so accomplished."

"I quite agree," I said. "100 percent. No question about it."

"He's a fine worker," Addy said, "very fastidious. If he's half as earnest at rewriting history, then Warren and Flossie will rest a lot easier in their graves when he's finished, we can be sure of it."

"Rewriting *miswritten* history, Miss Hamilton. Correcting omissions and righting the wrongs, lots of wrongs."

In the bright sunlight of spring the gray strands, long since coming into my sister's chestnut hair, seemed more numerous than they had through the long winter light, inside. "Trey," she said, "your timing is impeccable. I'm sure Matthias and I could both use a break now. Let's sit down and enjoy the moment. If we keep our fingers crossed then maybe, just maybe, Mrs. Christian will bring us some refreshment."

"I can only stay for a minute," I said.

"Work will wait. It always does. Just like tree stumps. A beautiful spring day, like youth, never waits. Besides, you own the company."

Three stone benches decorated my sister's gardens—indeed, to this day they remain in the exact same place where they have always been. She seated herself on the bench that faced her future orchid bed, and the moment she did so, little Muldoon leapt into her lap. She touched the empty place beside her on the stone. "Sit here, Trey, please. For the first time since last year, I can sit out here with my brother. The long winter's over and now we're in the garden again."

Our young friend was still tossing mulch. He was wearing yellow leatherwork gloves. But for the dirt sticking to them, they matched his hair. I wondered if he was aware of that fact. "Matthias, please," Adeline said. "Even the young need rest. And besides, it's exhausting just watching you. Even, I've noticed, when you're sitting quiet in a chair."

He laughed, tossed one or two more handfuls of mulch into the wheelbarrow and then sort of collapsed right into the mulch bed in which he was working. He lay down, stretched out, and turned his face towards the sun, eyes closed.

On the previous weekend, just after I'd first brought Matthias to Tioga, Adeline immediately followed up the meeting by calling to report that the young man greatly resembled me when I was his age. She was wondering, had I noticed the resemblance?

I had not.

I will say though that I suppose back in my youth my hair was similar to his, before it turned gray. But I will also add that at least I knew the benefits of a comb.

"Trey, Matthias was asking this morning about Mr. Kling's orchidarium. I said he'd have to speak with you. You're the one used to help Mr. Kling out there, when he got old and infirm, weren't you?"

"I was. I went over after school and helped him as best I could. I'd carry things around, jugs of water and trays of soil and things that he could no longer handle on his own. He mixed everything himself. Back then you couldn't go off to the feed and grain store and buy bags of ready-made fertilizer the way you can today. You had to make it yourself. Mr. Kling wasn't afraid of getting his hands dirty."

"Like you, Mr. Hamilton. As for me—" He looked at his own leather work gloves.

I think I blushed. "I didn't mean it like that. I wasn't—"

I think he was amused by my embarrassment, for he laughed and said, "I know you didn't, sir. Relax. So what was it like, the orchidarium?"

I was charmed by the young man's curiosity and seeming innocence, which by some miracle had outlived his harrowing experiences in the War. "Well," I said, "mostly I remember the fragrance—that wonderful perfume of orchids. It was like a little glassed-in Garden of Eden, a stone's throw, I might add, from the tracks of the Erie."

"Jay Gould's railroad," Matt said. "You know, he kept orchids too. Raised them himself. They said he wouldn't let anyone else near them, not even his most trusted servants."

"I didn't know that."

"There's nothing like the fragrance of orchids," Addy said. "Next to orchids, lilacs smell like turnips."

"Well," I said, "in my book, next to orchids, lilacs smell like lilacs. The fragrance of spring."

"What'd it look like, the orchidarium? Was it big?"

"Not really. No bigger than a sunroom, I suppose, though it was quite pretty, a special little place, so quiet in there, just the occasional drip of water. You could enter from the back of the house without setting foot in the great outdoors. It was all plate glass and copper, octagonal in shape. Mr. Kling's orchids came from afar, far, far away, from Costa Rica and Madagascar, the South Seas, from the foothills of the Himalayas and heaven knows where else. I actually remember—I saw it with my own eyes, mind you—I once saw a swarm of butterflies hovering at the windows, just like they wanted to come right in and light on those flowers. Why, they must have thought they were in Kandamoor. It was magical, in a natural sort of way."

Adeline added, "I remember the day you came home and told Daddy and me about that. I think that's when I first became interested in orchids, though I guess I didn't do much about it until years and years later. I was in Paris when Mr. Kling died. Daddy wrote to tell me so I could send condolences to Flossie, to Warren too. They became very close, you know, in Mr. Kling's last years, Mr. Kling and Warren. At least the historians got that part right. Why, you wouldn't have known that Mr. Kling once hated him, his own son-in-law. And mind you, Daddy said, *hated* him."

"Lucy and I took Father to the funeral," I said, "I remember the leaves were falling at the cemetery and swirling around our feet when we followed his casket up that little knoll where the Klings are buried. It was one of those old-fashioned funerals. The horse-drawn hearse, the black horses wearing purple plumes and medallions, and I remember yellow leaves falling on the coffin while the minister prayed. It was so black and polished that you could see yourself reflected in the lid. I looked away. Mr. Harding had been campaigning for the Senate way down in southern Ohio, traveling by chartered steamboat and meeting people in those little towns along the river. Mr. Daugherty managed to get in touch with him and Flossie and they hurried straight home. I remember his opponent,

Mr. Hogan, a Catholic as I recall, suspended his campaign until Warren was back in the running. Those were the days, good politics being like good sportsmanship."

Adeline said, "Flossie never forgave Amos for dying before Warren's victory. He died something like eighteen or nineteen days before the election, I think, and she was half-convinced he did it on purpose, just to spite her. She once said to me, 'Three weeks! Three measly weeks! After eighty-six years, he couldn't wait another three weeks? Why, he was quite thick enough with the devil to buy that much time, and plenty more!' That's what she said!"

We all had a good laugh over that recollection.

"People around here couldn't help but wink at the old man's timing," I said. "And I couldn't help but think, in those last years, that Mr. Kling loved his son-in-law just as much as his daughter."

"More. Amos *always* loved Warren. Why do you think he hated him so much?"

Matthias gave her an astonished look, but said not a word. I had utterly forgotten, until that moment, that Adeline had mentioned to me something along those lines years and years before. I let it pass the first time and I let it pass again. Sometimes the most baffling things flew out of my sister's mouth and just sort of slapped you square in the face. One couldn't make heads or tails of them, and I'm not sure if one would want to.

She said, "I know for a fact that the only reason Flossie supported women's suffrage was because she thought it would help Warren come to power. She was right. What would her father have thought of all this? 'Nigger Warren!' Indeed!"

The young man leaned forward, wrapping his arms around his knees, obviously delighted to be talking about President Harding with people who knew him and knew him well, the inner circle of the "Ohio Gang," no less. "It *is* a wonderful history, isn't it! From beginning to end. Not that I'll be tackling the Negro-blood question, of course, but still, something that wonderful ought to go in, just a little. Don't you think?"

"No, I do not," I said. "Remember, young man, your stated mission. Besides, that part's been done already. You don't even need to mention it."

Matthias, looking remiss, studied his gloves.

Muldoon raised his head and sprung like a shot from Addy's lap. Mrs. Christian was making her way down the back steps, bearing a tray with a pitcher and glasses glittering in the sun. Muldoon dashed yapping across the grass and danced about her feet.

"Such a commotion!" she cooed. Mrs. Christian always loved Adeline's dogs every bit as much as Adeline did. Indeed, Mrs. Christian regrets that I have never adopted a dog.

I rose and greeted her with a kiss on the cheek.

"I thought maybe you folks could use a little lemonade to wet your whistle, and here's some ginger cookies too."

She served us and slipped Muldoon a treat from her apron pocket. We thanked her and when she left, Muldoon followed her back and into the house.

"Miss Hamilton," Matthias said, "where'd you live in Paris?"

"Ah, where did I live in Paris—? Well, Mr. Mende, it's been so long I scarcely even remember. Just how well do you know Paris?"

"Not well enough, I'm sorry to say. Is it possible to know Paris well enough? I was there after the Krauts ran. They stationed us in a villa way out near the Père-Lachaise, where Victor Hugo's buried, him and lots of others. I guess I've been thinking of the city ever since. Seems like one of those places that kind of gets under your skin. Why, even the Nazis loved Paris. Look at General Dietrich—disobeyed Hitler's orders to blow it up, before they hightailed it back to Krautland. Only decent thing the Nazis ever did. I guess that's Paris for you, even the beasts get misty-eyed over it."

Addy said, "I do hope it hasn't changed much, though how could it not? Why, just look at Marion. How far we've traveled from where we were, all the while going nowhere. And we're far from the known world." She paused. "Those were my best years, my Paris years. I knew even then they were destined to be so, and thus I lived accordingly. Then came the first War and swept it all away. That and lots more—taken at the flood."

"What a century," Matt said, "and to think, it isn't even half over."

A silence followed.

I glanced at my watch. It was past time to be on my way, but I had no pressing appointments, and the April sun was so warm, so pleasant, and besides, I could not remember the last time my sister had mentioned her years in Paris.

"So where, Miss Hamilton, where did you live?"

"Where did I live? I lived on the little rue Picot. I bet you don't even know where it is, do you, Mr. Mende? I shouldn't think so anyway."

"Can't say as I do. Maybe you can help me."

"Off the Avenue Victor Hugo, near the Arc de Triomphe, in what they used to call the American Colony, though really there was no such place."

"Holy cow, small world! My great-grandparents lived right around there. My great-grandfather—" The young man glanced at me. "Maybe Mr. Hamilton told you."

"I did. Your great-grandfather was ambassador to France. And lots of other things too, as I recall. General Horace Porter."

"Yes, Trey mentioned that."

"General Porter lived in a huge marble chateau a short walk from the Arch. During the end of the War we were way out in the Twentieth, but I used to take the Métro in and get off at Victor Hugo. You head up the Avenue Victor Hugo and it's off to your right on a beautiful side street, 33 rue Villejust, though I think it may be called rue Paul-Valery now. I used to walk up there and think of my great-grandparents in a big fancy carriage, or the Prince of Wales and people like that arriving in the courtyard. Off to the right, there's a little carriage entrance, and lots of notables entered there." Now he glanced off into the distance and shook his head. "I missed all that. Fifteen hundred guests—that's how many great-Grandfather and Grandmother used to entertain at once. And that was just in the ballroom! Sounds like something out of the movies, doesn't it? When I saw the place it was all dark and forlorn. People around there said a family of rich Jews had lived there, Spitzer, I think, and the Germans sent them off and they were never seen or heard from again. Even stole their art and shipped it all back to Germany. God only knows—"

He shook his head and we were silent, the images of Auschwitz, fresh and forever in mind.

"You know," he said, "I bet there's one thing you might remember about General Porter, something he did that was very famous back then, that is if you were old enough to note it. My grandma told me it was really, really big news. Remember how they managed to find the lost grave of John Paul Jones, father of the U.S. Navy, over in Paris, and bring him back and bury him at Annapolis?"

"I remember that," I said. "I absolutely remember that. I was probably ten or eleven at the time. There was lots about it in the *Star* and the magazines of the day. I guess it was the sort of thing that catches a boy's eye."

Matthias was smiling. "See, I knew you'd remember that. That was great-Grandfather! General Porter was the Sherlock Holmes that figured out where the body was hidden—or I should say, lost. Exhumed him and brought him home on a destroyer. Took him five whole years and $35,000 of his own money to find him, but he did it. Why, even the little burial ground was lost. A laundry had been built over it. But when they finally dug him up, there was no doubt it was John Paul Jones because of the epaulets and buttons and things, even the hair." He paused, "My great grandfather did *all* of that. And me, well—" Matthias examined his ring.

"Your John Paul Jones is Warren G. Harding," I said.

"Yes! Very true! Thank you."

The telephone rang far off in the house. We could hear the jingle-jangle of the bell through the kitchen screens. "Now who?" Adeline said, looking toward the house.

My sister received very few telephone calls, and she often seemed slightly miffed when one finally arrived.

A moment later, Mrs. Christian cracked the screen door. "Miss Hamilton," she called, "Mr. Yost is on the line."

"Dana," I said.

"Shall I tell him to call back?"

"No, I'll be in."

Really, I should have used that as my cue for heading back to work, but I still had half of my lemonade left, and besides, sitting in the warm April sun was turning out to be quite pleasant. I started to say something to Matthias, but a look had come over his face, like recognition, but something else too. Only in retrospect would I realize that he and Dana had already struck up a friendship of sorts. That young man moved briskly through life.

Matthias must have caught something in my eyes too, as he quickly glanced away. I wanted to ask him if he knew Dana Yost, but I mistakenly thought that to be impossible.

I sipped my lemonade and nibbled a cookie.

"Mr. Hamilton," the young man said, "may I ask you a question, sir? And I hope it doesn't give you the wrong impression, or make you mad or something."

"Hmmm," I said, not altogether eager to reply, "well, I guess we'll never know unless you ask, will we?"

"No, sir."

"Well, shoot."

"OK." At first he studied his hands, but then he made a point of looking me straight in the eye. "Tell me, sir, do you think there's anything to the poison rumor?"

Suddenly, I had a feeling that maybe I had made an error in opening the Harding Papers to this young man. "So, you're going to start barking up that tree, are you?"

"Oh, no, sir, not really. Like I said, I'm on the President's side, I promise you, I swear to God, and my interest is realigning President Harding's reputation with his achievements, based on the documents you've so generously opened to me. But by the same token, it *is* a viable question, don't you think, sir, considering?"

"No, Mr. Mende. I do *not* think it is a viable question, considering. That rumor was started by gossips, long ago. It has been perpetuated by gossips, unto, evidently, this very moment. I suggest you take care not to sully your young, unsullied reputation as a historian with the likes of their company. Stick to the facts you find in the boxes and don't go digging into that manure pit." I was startled by my own vehemence. I am sure my young friend was too. In a more gentler tone, I added, "Mind you, Matthias, Mrs. Harding didn't help matters by refusing an autopsy, but you have to understand that that was not a regular thing back in those days, any more than it is now, and she was old-fashioned, to say the least. That's how all this got started. President Harding died of apoplexy, just as his death certificate states. If not that, then a heart attack. One or the other."

He nodded.

I took another sip of lemonade and added. "Let me tell you something about his last visit to Tioga, on the 3rd of July, 1922. He and the First Lady were home for the Marion Centennial and they came out to see Father, Colonel Hamilton. Dad suffered a stroke some months before, and was lingering. After the President climbed the staircase, the one at the front of the house, he was as red as an Indian. You could see it even in the shadows. And he had to stand there for a full minute or two leaning on the hall table, just catching his breath. Why, Adeline even offered him a chair, which he declined. Mrs. Harding said, 'Too many cigars.' Which wasn't true. But soon he was okay, and we went and sat down and visited Father in his room. In that room right up there."

I gestured toward the sunroom, above the back door, beneath the mansard roof.

"I didn't think anything of it at the time, but clearly the President had heart troubles, or high blood pressure. Maybe both. Thirteen months later, he was dead. So much for poison."

The young man nodded as if in agreement, though frankly, I was not at all convinced that he was in *complete* agreement.

"President Harding was *not* assassinated," I said, "take my word for it."

I wondered if young Mr. Mende was privy to the gossip that my sister had supposedly delivered poison to Mrs. Harding during the summer of '23, when she lunched with the Hardings aboard their palace car, on their way Westward. In that moment I remembered Matt's acquaintanceship with Evelyn Walsh McLean and the fact that both Evelyn and Adeline were present at that luncheon table.

"Either a heart attack or a stroke, Mr. Mende," I said as I stood to go. "It all stands to reason."

SPEAKING FRANKLY, I want to say that I somewhat lied to Mr. Mende. I will therefore admit that, in theory, President Harding could have been poisoned. But I think you will agree that *could have been* and *were* are two different things. I wish to appeal to common sense, whereas the rumorists (including, of course, the historians) have always appealed to one's thirst for sensationalism and the extraordinary.

Part of the stupidity of it all is the fact that neither the Marion gossips nor the academic gossips were ever able to decide upon certain basics that they continue to bat around to this very day. For instance, the kind of poison allegedly used to assassinate the President.

Now you will recall that I have already discussed in some detail the President's last days and moments on earth and nowhere did I say (thank heavens) that Mr. Harding went into horrific convulsions, that his back arched and his belly rose high from the bed, and that a fearful death's grin came upon him—these being the symptoms of death by strychnine. And yet in the days and weeks after his death, that was the poison of choice settled upon by the Marion gossips.

Now in order to make some of the more senseless parts of this story sensible, I am going to have to do exactly what the rumorists have always done: I am going to have to presume. For instance, I am going to presume that at some point someone (perhaps my old friend Dana Yost) went to the trouble of simply looking strychnine up in an encyclopedia or something, thereby discovering that death by strychnine did not fit the reality of the President's death. My impression is that, for several months after the President's death, arsenic or cyanide became the favorite recipe of dispatch in rumordom—these poisons accommodating themselves much more nicely to the symptoms of a natural death.

Furthermore, I believe that the gossip took a new turn after Thanksgiving 1923, when Mrs. Harding "spilled the beans" about Adeline's luncheon aboard the *Superb*. To this day I am utterly convinced that if the First Lady had simply kept her big mouth shut then my little sister's good name would never have been dragged into all of this nonsense.

Adeline's surprise entrance into the President's final journey, and thus into the poison arena, added further to a dilemma that the Marion gossips were already wrestling with: the slight difficulty, or at least the awkwardness, of someone (Adeline, for instance) running out to one of our local drug stores and purchasing a deadly dose of arsenic or cyanide. Yes, poisons and the like were less regulated back in those days than they are now, but I know for a fact that druggists in this town always had a strict code regarding such sales. They had to know the person who was purchasing the poison and I know for a fact that our druggists also kept scrupulous records of all such sales, along with signatures. To my knowledge anyone could take a look at these records, if they simply asked to do so. And mind you, I have a feeling that the gossips, the salesladies and such in the drugstores, took a very close look at those lists after wild rumors began to circulate that President Harding had been assassinated with poison.

If my sister's name had appeared on such a manifest, then I assure you that even I would have heard about it. The same can be said of the authorities, who have ears too, but who, to my knowledge, never took the slightest interest in the rumors about my sister, at least not overtly. But gossips are by nature a dedicated and inventive lot, and if one rat hole gets plugged, they will surely seek another.

When the rumorists were unable to connect Adeline with arsenic or cyanide, they concocted an even more inventive scenario. Picture her in her (and/or Mrs. Harding's) garden on a July morning in 1923. In this rumor my sister makes her way along the paths, over the steppingstones, gathering a basket of flowers for the President and Mrs. Harding's luncheon table. Per the rumorists, this thoughtful and common gesture is not entirely unsolicited. She has, by some prior agreement with the First Lady, included in the bouquet some purple foxgloves—one of Mrs. Harding's favorite flowers. Now as you may or may not know, the leaves of the purple foxglove are the source of digitalis.

Digitalis is, of course, the drug that enables chronic heart patients to plod along a bit longer. But like so much else in life, digitalis can very easily be too much of a good thing. A few nibbles from the spinach-like leaves can be as deadly as cyanide and arsenic. As a poison, digitalis attacks the very organ that it might otherwise restore. Its initial symptoms include nausea, vomiting, intestinal disturbances and exhaustion, and its final symptoms can be that of apoplexy or a heart attack.

Believe it or not, I have known since I was a small boy about the dual nature of foxgloves. When Adeline and I were small, our mother used to take us for walks on pleasant evenings before my father arrived home for supper. That was before Tioga was built, back when we were living in the brick house on Vine Street. Usually we followed the path through the trees to Lake Etowah—then called Lafayette Lake—before George King built his stone mansion, but sometimes we walked over to Dr. Sawyer's medicinal gardens on South Main Street, where the Carnegie Public Library now stands. His sanitarium, today an apartment building, stood across the street. He moved his operation out to White Oaks Farm when the automobile became prevalent, as the backfiring of cars struggling up the South Main Street Hill, or coasting down in gear, used to disturb his patients, sometimes sending the more nervous ones into seizures. Some of his medicines came from his own beautiful, well-kept and spacious gardens. I especially remember the giant sunflowers, taller than a horse. He had a big patch of watermelons too and people saved seeds for him. He used them for a kidney elixir, though I have no idea what he did with the sunflower seeds. My mother loved the brilliant red and purple poppies with their glossy petals. From these he derived opium and morphine. And then there were the foxgloves, from which he extracted digitalis for weak hearts. I distinctly remember when Dr. Sawyer had a fence built around the foxgloves after one of the neighbor's milk cows wandered over, munched a few stalks, and died in the alley.

The summer after the President's death I asked Addy, as much in passing as I could, what flowers she had taken with her to Columbus that day; she said, "What flowers?! Trey, that was a whole year ago! Whatever was in bloom, I suppose. I'm not like you, remembering every little thing."

By her own admission my sister did indeed take a bouquet to the Hardings, but the gossips like to fancy that she took some purple foxgloves and that the First Lady somehow fed the leaves to her husband.

No doubt mixed with the spinach leaves of his last meal.

After Matthias disappeared, the rumor went around that the young historian was going to propose, in his book, the exhumation of President Harding's remains for the purpose of conducting forensic tests for poison.

Now perhaps to you that does not sound all that farfetched. In theory I suppose it is not, but as is so often the case, reality and theory do not always walk hand-in-hand. As I have already made abundantly clear, the President's remains do not lie in anything resembling an ordinary grave. Mr. and Mrs. Harding's coffins rest on twin catafalques in an enormous concrete humidor vault similar to a pharaoh's burial chamber. I believe that the most impenetrable ancient chamber would be more easily breached than the sepulcher of President Harding's tomb. Think of it as a tremendous bank vault that, once sealed, can never be reopened. There is one possible key of course, as I said before, and that key is dynamite.

I wondered then and wonder now whether Evelyn Walsh McLean and Dana Yost ever mentioned the idea of exhumation to young Mr. Mende. I remember a profile of Mrs. McLean that appeared in *The Washington Post*. That was not long before our Victory in Europe. As I recall, the article was mostly about her war work, but it also touched upon her rich but tragic life, her ownership of the infamous Hope Diamond, her devout Catholicism, and her recollection of Washington figures, especially President and Mrs. Harding. According to the article, Evelyn and Florence and Warren and Jim were all the very best of friends. I know for a fact that Adeline read that article in the *Post*, but I have never come across the clipping in any of her scrapbooks. The interview also touched upon the people in Marion, and Mrs. McLean was quoted as saying something like, "I suspect that the Marion Gang had its own reasons for entombing President Harding the way they did."

What Mrs. McLean and Matthias talked about at Friendship is anyone's guess, though I have absolutely no doubt that she said something to him about Adeline and me. Possibly, she was the one who planted the first seed of wild speculation in the young man's mind.

IV

An Interesting Favorite

MY SUSPICIONS THAT DAY IN ADELINE'S GARDEN, about Dana and Matthias knowing each other, were soon confirmed. Not long after that, on a Friday night, I saw Dana plying the young man with whiskey and cigarettes at the Saratoga Lounge. I had taken Lucy and old Governor Dan Crissinger out to dinner. Frankly, I was counting on the Governor to remember the Harding Commemorative Society in his will, as we receive not a cent from the government. Lucy and Dan were baseball fans—Jackie Robinson and the Brooklyn Dodgers were in the news—and they were having a friendly argument about whether Negroes should be allowed to play in the major leagues. Lucy saw no harm in it but Dan thought it would be bad for baseball to go mixing things up like that. He was a very old man and managed to go out on the town so long as he had a cane and a helping hand. Perhaps you will remember me mentioning him some days ago; Daniel R. Crissinger was the Governor of the Federal Reserve for both Presidents Harding and Coolidge. The Governor and President Harding were boyhood friends who used to swim together in Whetstone Creek. Dan still sat on the Board of Directors of the Marion County Bank and, as such, he never lost (nor would lose) his keen interest in banking and finance.

Officer Hoffman, of the Marion Police Department, had warned Dan in no uncertain terms not to drive anymore, so Lucy and I picked him up at his place on the Heights. We spoke of Matthias in the car on the way over. I had previously arranged for Matt to interview the Governor and

I had even dropped him off at the Governor's house. That was a couple days before. On the way to the Saratoga, the Governor was telling Lucy and me how impressed he was with the fine young man, with his knowledge of the President, and his conviction that history had overlooked his achievements. Apparently the Governor was very generous with his recollections and in taking time to show Matt various mementos of his Washington days.

As we made our way across the Saratoga's dining room, through greetings from our fellow townsmen, I was stunned to catch sight, through the haze of cigarette smoke, of young Matthias sitting cozy in a dark booth with Dana Yost. They were so deep in conversation that they did not see us come in. Both had highball glasses before them. Like most gossips, Dana was a bit of a show-off. I saw him give his pack of Lucky Strikes a quick and clever flick of the wrist, so that a few cigarettes popped up, just like you see in the ads on TV. The young man reached for one in a very familiar sort of way and then Dana took a cigarette for himself. He lit both from the same match. Seeing them together gave me a funny feeling. After Lucy and I got Dan situated, I made sure that my back was to them. Frankly, I was not even aware until that moment that Matt was a smoker; later on when I questioned him about that, he tried to tell me he was a "social smoker, not a habitual one."

Heretofore, I had thought that a lady's line.

At some point thereafter, I was to wonder if they had been huddled over there in the dark, all chummy like, gossiping about the poison rumor.

After we were seated, Lucy leaned my way. "Trey, did you see who's back there?"

"Who?"

"Dana. And he's with your historian. What do you think of that?"

I shrugged.

"Now where do you suppose the two of them hooked up?"

"Knowing Dana, at the bar."

After we ordered, the Governor broached a subject he had apparently been saving for a dinner table assault. With a mix of pity and perturbance, he said, "You miss a lot in life, don't you, Tristan?"

I knew very well where he was heading with that one; Lucy gave me a here-we-go-again sort of look. I said, "So I've been told. But I suppose every time a train pulls out of the depot and we aren't on it, then we're missing out on *something*. Aren't we, Governor?"

"Maybe, but then again, we're not talking about a train ride. We're talking about a land-office business; literally, government money being shoveled out by the bushelful. And you're missing out on it. Why, it's the biggest damned building boom since the '20s! And you're sitting on your hands while those Conley boys pick your orchard clean." He raised his scotch as if to emphasize his point. "They'll do just that if you don't *do* something, Tristan. You got to *do* something. And do it fast."

Before the War three of the four Conley boys worked for me, the eldest, Jamie, as a foreman. Two went to the Pacific and one to Europe. Carl, the third of the brothers, is buried somewhere in the South Seas. The youngest, Steve, went to the Philippines and came back different. Jamie told me his little brother was sent out on "quid pro quo missions" against the Japs. Supposedly, his squad did everything to the Japs that the Japs did to our boys, including gutting them alive and subjecting them to decapitation—though I take all that with a grain of salt. Before the War, Steve was an ordinary boy, which is about all I can say regarding him, but he came back unordinary. In 1947 he was getting into trouble right and left with the police and just about everyone else. I think he turned out to be the best customer that Old Dutch Beer ever had. He left town in the late '40s, with the sheriff hot on his tail, and that's about the last I ever heard of him. Jamie and Conrad were the Conley boys who were "making a killing" through the construction of little two- and three-bedroom look-alike bungalows, for the former GIs, on postage stamp-sized bits of land in a new development on the far north side of Fairground Street.

Mind you, I had *not* lost out entirely on that building boom. The Governor forgot to mention that the Conley boys bought their lumber from me—by the boxcar. Essentially though, that was none of his business, so I let him jabber on.

"A land-office business, Tristan, that's what's slipping through your fingers. And with all that land you own, you and your sister, why, you could start your own suburb."

"I already did. You live in it."

He looked as if I'd slapped him. "Well, yes, that's true, but I mean a new one, a low-priced one, one for the GIs."

Lucy gave me a small smile and a wink to impart forbearance.

I said, "Governor, there's Cadillac dealers and there's Nash dealers, but how many of them sell both? None, so far as I know. It pays to know your niche and stick to it."

For a second my words seemed to give him pause. Then he waved that liver-spotted old hand of his, as if shooing a horsefly. "No, no, not at all, Trey. You got it all wrong. Your dad wouldn't have said that, I promise you. Nor your granddad either. Colonel Hamilton wasn't too damn proud to build all those houses for the Steam Shovel men, back in the Panama Canal days. He saw it as his civic duty. He did it as a Marion booster. And he made a killing too."

Dan seemed to think that his former status as Governor of the Federal Reserve imparted him with a God-given right to stick his nose into other people's business, and I believe he thought that my thinly-veiled interest in his estate, on behalf of the Harding Commemorative Commission, gave him some license to rattle me at will.

I shall tell you what was *really* on his mind. You see, Colonel Hamilton & Son did business with the Marion County Bank, whereas Conley Construction was doing business with that out-of-town upstart, National City Bank. I can say with absolute certainty that if they had plunked their money down on the tellers' counter at the Marion County Bank, instead of hauling it across the street, then this discussion would never have taken place *and* the Governor's altruistic concern for my business would have gone the way of dirty bath water.

When I made no reply, he said, "Lucy, can't you talk some sense into this man of yours?"

Lucy wore the frozen little smile she always affected through political discussions and anything else that made her either uncomfortable or bored. After a reluctant moment, she squeezed his hand. "Oh, come on Governor, what do I know about building houses? I leave all that up to Trey. And he's done a pretty darn good job of it too, I'd say. Why, I'd have to be out of my tree to meddle." She gave a thoughtful pause. "Besides, Trey, I was under the impression that the Conleys bought their lumber from you, don't they?"

I nodded, "They do."

"Well, in that case, Governor, it hardly seems as if Trey's missing out completely. That's a lot of lumber, at least by my reckoning."

I smiled at my dear, devoted wife. "I'm fifty-four, Governor, ready to coast a bit."

"Fifty-four! Wait till you're eighty-five then you'll know how damn young that really is. And what pays isn't sticking to your niche, it's being flexible and changing with the times, and it's certainly *not* missing out on all that HFFA money that I got flowing into the loan departments."

I almost laughed aloud at that one—as if decades later Dan Crissinger was still pulling strings out in Washington, and with the Truman Administration, no less. Indeed, I have my doubts as to whether Harry Truman ever heard of Dan Crissinger, or if he even remembered that a little place called Marion, Ohio, was once a big spot on the map.

"You know, Trey," he continued, "I'm just looking out for your best interests. Tell me when I haven't."

I nodded.

My wife jumped in with an inquiry about one of Dan's grandchildren who suffered from "sugar," thereby mercifully turning the conversation. And she kept it turned through the rest of the meal.

Sometime later, during cake and coffee, young Mr. Mende appeared beside our table. His hands were jammed deep into his blue jean pockets and he was looking a bit bleary-eyed, like he was starting to float through the evening. "Sorry to interrupt," he said, "just wanted to pay my respects."

"Mr. Mende," Lucy said, "we're glad to see you don't spend *all* your time with those crates of papers, aren't we Trey?"

"Absolutely."

"I saw you over there. Looks like you've got yourself a new friend."

It seemed to take a moment for the words to reach him, as if they echoed far off in his thoughts and he was gathering them in, in his present fumbling sort of way. His eyes flickered toward me and flickered away. In my thoughts I saw Dana pouring him another Jim Beam and I *knew* that he had been chatting up Matt about the President, and no doubt, the rest of us, the "Ohio Gang." Sometimes, in the warmth and assurance of booze, Dana had used those two words with all the remoteness of an outsider. I hoped that maybe Matthias was endeavoring to set Dana straight about the facts, and not vice versa. After a moment, he said, "Oh, you mean Dana, Mr. Yost."

Dana was at the bar paying the bill.

"You met him here?" Lucy asked. "At the Saratoga?"

I shot her a glance—the same fruitless glance I had been casting my wife's way for thirty years, the one that said, *For heaven's sake, Lucy, mind your own business.*

Obviously, the young man had more than one whiskey in him, though he was pretending mightily that he had none. "No, madam, he picked me up. Out near where your place is, Governor Crissinger, sir. Out there. I was hitchin' a ride."

The Governor's eyes were not as sharp at they used to be, except, I believe, when it came to reading ledgers. I am not entirely sure that it registered who the young man was.

"Governor," I said, "it's Matthias Mende. You know . . ."

"Matthias! Oh, well of course, I know! Our historian!"

The young man smiled at his friendliness. "That's me, sir, at your service!" He made an awkward old-fashioned half bow. Then he grabbed the back of my chair.

Lucy glanced at me with the half smile of someone enjoying the amusing spectacle of a harmless drunk. The Governor was unfazed. He added, "Historian *and* fighter pilot. You'll need both those skills around here, young man, if you're going to tackle poor ol' Warren's story. Young man, when we arrived for the Inauguration, and some of us stayed around to help out, the Democratic newspapers in this country had a field day accusing the President of nepotism. The *Independent* called us 'colonizers.' Truth is, Warren'd have been a hell of a lot better off if he'd filled *all* those offices with upright and honest Marion men instead of crooks the likes of Daugherty and that damn Senator Fall!" He glanced at me and added, as if in confidence, "I don't know if you're quite aware of this, Mr. Mende, but the President and I tried to get Mr. Hamilton here to join us in Washington but he declined, thought he ought to stay home and mind his own business, so he could make a killing."

The young man nodded, but I think the words somewhat blew right past him, like something in the wind, then he said, "Oh."

A moment later, I felt a gentle squeeze on my shoulder.

Dana and I had known each other too well and too long to shake hands. On this particular evening I simply nodded my greeting. He gave Lucy a quick kiss on the cheek and he shook the Governor's hand, "Hey, neighbor."

Lucy said, "Say, Dana, looks like you found someone to teach you a bit of history here."

I fixed my eyes on Matthias and said, "And not vice versa, one hopes."

He may have been plastered, but I saw my words register in his eyes. I wanted to add something about associating with gossips—for decades I had been chiding Dana for his jabber, and indeed I could call him a gossip to his face without offending him—but I kept my mouth shut.

Dana said, "So, Trey, you couldn't pry your sister out of that big old house of hers?"

"Didn't try."

Lucy added, "To come to the Saratoga! That'll be the day!"

My little sister spent her adult life refusing to adapt to what she regarded as a world in precipitous decline.

"You know Adeline," I said. "She won't set foot in a restaurant where there's a jukebox. If and when we drive to the Neil House, we'll call her, but how often do you feel like driving an hour and then some just to spend five dollars on supper?"

Dana laughed and patted me on the shoulder, "That's right. Save those nickels, young man. You never know when . . ."

"So where's Margaret?" I glanced at Matt, as if the young man should have been her. "You leave her home tonight while you . . ."

"Vice versa, I'd say. She ran off with the Catholics to play bingo; that's what happens when they move into the neighborhood. Say, Lucy, does this young fellow remind you of anyone? Governor does he?"

I cannot say why, but Wellington Boyd came to mind, my former imposter-self. I have never liked being told that I look like this person or that person. Lucy, of course, had figured that out long ago.

She shook her head, as if without a clue.

Dana gave a helpful hint, "Someone in the here and now who's also someone in the long ago."

Lucy shrugged. The thought of excusing myself crossed my mind, though I have a perpetual dislike for being seen walking into public restrooms.

"Why, he looks a bit like Trey did! You mean you really don't see it?"

"Well," Lucy said, "maybe a little, I guess. But maybe it's one of those things, you know, in the eye of the beholder."

"But just look at him!"

I glanced at Matthias again. His reddened blue eyes were fastened on me, and it was a funny look he was giving me. I do not think he was merely considering the fearful possibility that this is how he might appear deep in middle age. I think something else glimmered in his eyes.

Again, I looked away.

The Governor asked Dana about one of the mammoth steam shovels being manufactured for a strip mine in West Virginia.

Matt touched me on the shoulder and ever so quietly said, "Good night, Mr. Hamilton." He touched his forehead as if to tip a hat. "Mrs. Hamilton," he said, "Governor Crissinger."

Lucy said, "Matt, you have got a way home, don't you?"

"I'll be okay. If you'll excuse me, please. I have to get some air."

Whereupon he headed for the door.

"He may be plastered," she said, "but he's a real gent. Hope he's not going to get sick."

Dana's interest in West Virginia strip mines instantly flagged with the young man's departure.

"Well, Trey," he said, "I'm afraid that historian of yours has had a bit too much to drink. Can't let him get run over, can we?"

With that our Good Samaritan beat a hasty path for the door, in hot pursuit.

Lucy and I looked at each other. She raised an eyebrow.

The Governor said, "Clever fellow, Dana. You know, *he* should have come out to Washington with us. We could have used a smart, executive-type like that."

"On the contrary," I said, "I think quite enough went on out there without having that one along for the ride."

ON MY WAY HOME from work the following Monday—I remember it was mid May— I dropped by the bungalow expecting to find our historian with his head buried in yellowing documents and the crates yawning before him as he scribbled away in his notebooks. He was nowhere to be seen, though clearly he had been there. A couple of files lay neatly stacked on the desk and one of his notebooks lay open. An unfinished cup of coffee waited in its saucer. I touched the china—stone cold. In addition to the notebook that lay open, others lay closed, one atop the other. (In case you are wondering, I did *not* take a peek into any of those pages.) Naturally, I thought nothing of the fact that Matthias had stepped out. Perhaps he had gone for a bite to eat, though he usually packed himself a cold meat sandwich and an apple or something like that. After all, I presumed that not much money found its way into his pockets. And besides, the closest corner store was several blocks away.

Generally, every other Monday afternoon I returned Lucy's books and mine to the Carnegie Public Library, and so I headed for South Main Street. My favorite corner in the Library has always been the old Ohio Room, a cozy little quarter off to the side in the back and down a long and shadowy hallway. Windows line the top of the room in such a manner that only the sky and the high branches of an old sycamore are visible; daylight is abundant but the world's distractions pass muffled and unseen. I guess such rooms appeal only to a certain sort of individual, for generally I had the place all to myself. For the most part, I did my reading at home in the evening with Lucy, but sometimes, after a busy day at work and before heading home for supper, I would park myself at the long oak table, beneath the painting of William Henry Harrison battling the Indians at Tippecanoe. To this day I go there to read out-of-town newspapers; to skim through books that appeal to me, but not enough to go carting them home; and to leaf through magazines, looking at the pictures. Particularly, I am fascinated by the ads for foreign houses in a couple of the architectural magazines. I have always admired the pictures of the occasional baronial mansions and estates listed on the market in Scotland. Some, back in those days, sold for far less than the spacious houses that Colonel Franks & Son built on Vernon Heights Boulevard. I fantasized about buying one and of Lucy and me moving there, but obviously, that never happened. And I suppose it is just as well, though as Dan Crissinger so aptly pointed out, I miss out on a lot in this life. For better or worse, I believe that is the case for most of us. This wide, wide world finds so many of us staying at home—but that too is part of life on Earth.

That day I picked up one of those architectural magazines from the rack, near the librarian's desk, and made my way through the forest of bookshelves and passed down the little hallway to the cozy quiet of the

Ohio Room. I was surprised to see, in the same chair where I usually parked myself, Matthias Mende, back and side to me, jotting in a notebook. Several books lay open before him. His concentration was such that he was utterly unaware that someone was observing him. I was equally surprised to see that he was wearing a new beige "golf" jacket. And I noticed he was sporting a new pair of cordovan "loafers," of the emphatically casual variety so popular with young men after the War.

To tell you the truth, as I stood unnoticed I had the distinct feeling that our historian was up to something. And that he was ensconced back here hiding whatever it may have been that he was up to.

I considered flitting away as unnoticed as I had arrived. But I wondered what he was doing. What's more, I thought I had a right to know. And why he was, apparently, consulting published books on the President when *he* was the sole Harding historian ever to have full access to the White House papers.

After another moment, I cleared my throat, "Why, good afternoon, Mr. Mende."

He whirled around as if I had jabbed him in the ribs with a dagger.

I do not think he could have looked more astonished if I had materialized out of thin air. (Later on, as I was driving home, my wit—or what passes for my wit—belatedly kicked into gear and delivered what I regarded as a very clever line: "Mr. Mende," I would have said, "you make me feel like the Messerschmitt that never got the best of you.") Instead, I said, "I beg your pardon. Didn't mean to startle you."

"Oh," he said, "why, not at all, Mr. Hamilton."

I believe that something nervous instantly came over him. Again I had the uncanny recollection of Wellington Boyd and the way he so cleverly and deviously fooled poor Miss Chancellor and those other folks over in Wooster. I had no intention of having the tables turned upon me. With my hands folded behind my back, grasping the magazine I had picked up, I walked to his side and with, I believe, a hint of menace and knowing, I peered over his shoulder to the notes he was taking. Or to the notes, I should say, that I thought he was taking.

He was not writing in his notebook, he was drawing pictures in it— pictures of flowers. "Flowers!" I said. "Why, you're drawing pictures of flowers!"

A gardening picture book with black and white pictures lay open before him, along with an open tray of colored drawing pencils. The books stacked before him had nothing to do with Mr. Harding. They were gardening books. And a volume from an encyclopedia.

He glanced at his notebook as if to verify my observation. "Yes sir, flowers."

Mind you, these were not the tedious doodles of a wandering mind; rather, they were beautifully, imaginatively executed flowers in shades of purple and green. The picture took shape in my perceptions. "Foxgloves," I said.

After a moment, he said, "Yes, sir, foxgloves. My sweetheart's favorite."

"Hmm. An interesting favorite. And an interesting addition to your notebook."

He was studying me, studying his picture. "I've been thinking of her a lot lately. We're going to get married, once things get settled, once I get my degree and such. Getting that job at Princeton is the key, with the help of my book on President Harding."

I nodded, "Everything in its own due time."

I drifted over to the Harding shelf. I could feel his eyes fastened upon me, and my inward eyes, so to speak, fastened upon him as I looked over the histories—something I guess I do just about every time I enter the Ohio Room—surveying the wreckage of our dreams manifested in print. Here was Gaston Bullock Mean's *The Strange Death of President Harding* and Nan Britton's *The President's Daughter*. And in their Dewey-decimal appointed places, the long line of others: Samuel Hopkins Adam's *Incredible Era* and William Allen White's *A Puritan in Babylon*, both of which speculate on the supposed poisoning of President Harding. And here was *The Road to Normalcy* by some fellow named Bagby, who I never met, and *Albert B. Fall and the Teapot Dome Affair* and books on the Daugherty scandals, and books on the sacking of the Veterans Bureau and the other various aspects of the Harding history. And taking up their tiny niche were the GOP campaign biography and Sherman Cuneo's little booklet *From Printer to President*—the sort of down-home book that pats its subject on the back, while it gives itself a congratulatory pat as well.

With my back still to him, I said, "By the way, Mr. Mende, what is your book to be called?"

"Lately you seem to have stopped calling me Matt, Mr. Hamilton. Any reason in particular?"

I turned. I could not help but notice that he had closed his notebook. "I have? Why, I hadn't noticed that I'd ever called you anything *but* Mr. Mende, Mr. Mende."

"I like it when you call me Matt. You can trust me, sir. I promise you. President Harding *needs* me. I can change the perception of his legacy. And I shall. I promise. You have my . . ."

"And the title of your book?"

He paused, as if in exasperation. "Haven't really decided on it yet, not for certain, but I've been thinking, maybe something like: *Unheralded Triumph: The Untold Side of the Harding Presidency.*"

"Unheralded Triumph! Why, President Harding in a nutshell! Very clever of you."

He smiled at my apparent approval. "Kind of matches your tomb, doesn't it, Mr. Hamilton? And maybe matches you as well."

I laughed, not entirely sure what he meant. "Okay, if you say so."

FINDING MATTHIAS' RING has served to remind me, on this snowy morning, just how estranged my sister and I actually were, in a certain way. Yes, Adeline and I saw each other once or twice a week, and yes, we spoke on the phone every few days, and indeed I was the one—the only one, save for Mrs. Christian—there to hold her hand when she lay on her deathbed. But other than that, I guess you would have to say that we were, in a sense, intimate strangers. Or at least deeply intimate beings lacking in a certain intimacy. Here we were, brother and sister, lifelong residents of the same little town, she living all but a handful of her sixty-five years in this very house, and there I was, living forty-two years on the same avenue, half a mile away, just around the corner from the house in which we were both born—and yet, in so many ways, my sister was, and is, a mystery to me. If she had lent money to Matthias and if she had accepted his ring as collateral, then why on earth didn't she mention it? And no, she was not being "discreet." She lent money to Mrs. Christian and mentioned it to me; she lent money to the Cohen boy, after his father died, so that he could finish law school, and told me about that too; and I know of an array of other such private loans she floated through the years—all of them, so far as I know, interest free. And to my knowledge the loans were always made on trust, which is to say, without collateral. But then again, of course, those people were Marionites, *not* drifters. Perhaps the loan to Matthias was just one of those things that never quite got mentioned, and I suppose she simply forgot about his ring being here in the desk. My sister accumulated a great many beautiful things in her lifetime, many of which I did not lay eyes on until after she was in her grave, when I executed her will, and perhaps his ring was just another one of those unrecorded trinkets that seemingly disappeared from the records of existence, forgotten and unmentioned, into the drawers and locked cabinets of Tioga.

These considerations serve to remind me of a summer night a year or two into my marriage—back when our housekeeper Nora was still alive. Come to think of it, that was the summer when Lucy was expecting, early in her pregnancy. We were both hoping that our first-born would be a son. Lucy allowed me to choose the name, if we had a son, and with her complete agreement I chose Eric Anthony; if we had a daughter (an equally wonderful possibility, more or less), she would choose the name with my help and agreement, and we chose Adana Victoria. That night Lucy and I had Adeline and my father over for dinner and afterwards I drove the two of them back to Tioga. When I returned home Nora was tidying up the kitchen and Lucy was resting on the porch swing in the darkness. For long summers my wife and I sat through countless evenings, together side by side on that swing. We dusted it off each spring and watched for the first lightning bugs to appear—one of those monumental little milestones in the year—and we were there when the crickets first began their song, and there too when they began to fade. Some evenings we spent a couple of hours on that swing, sometimes talking much of the time; other times, most times, just enjoying the silence and the calm of each other's company. On that particular night when I sat down I laid my hand on her belly, as a young expectant father might do, somewhat reaching toward his future child.

Lucy lifted my hand to her lips, kissed my fingers, and then placed my palm and fingers in a slightly different way. "Here," she said, "right here."

I could feel, or thought I could feel, the semi-ghostly movement of our unborn in his little unreachable world at my fingertips. "Yes," I whispered and ever so softly I tapped a little greeting to our baby.

I wondered about the evening we had just spent together, Lucy and I, and Adeline and Dad. My wife and sister were so extraordinarily unalike that I used to worry, especially during those early years, whether she appreciated my sister's company, and vice versa.

Lucy was like wheat, Adeline like emeralds—I read that analogy long ago in a book.

"So, little wife," I said, kissing her cheek, "did you enjoy yourself this evening?"

The glow from the parlor filtered onto the porch, illuminating her smile. She kissed my cheek, as if in gratitude for my concerns, "I certainly did, Trey. Colonel Hamilton is so kind and Adeline so dear."

"Excellent," I said, watching the vast armies of lightning bugs, as silent as falling stars, ferrying their tiny lanterns to and fro through the summer night.

"What was it like, Trey, when the two of you were growing up, you and Adeline?"

"What was it like?"

"I mean were the two of you close? Were you playmates?"

"Oh, absolutely, very close playmates. Especially after Mama died. We didn't have much else except one another, living way out there. Father, yes, but—well, you know."

"Fathers don't make good playmates. They're providers, not playmates. I know."

"Yes, I suppose that was it."

My hand was still on my wife's belly. After a few moments, I announced, "But I shall make a good provider *and* a good playmate. And most especially, a good husband *and* a good father. I shall not shirk, rest assured."

She laughed, without mocking me. "Oh, Trey. But fathers are always too tired from work. And you work very, very hard."

"Yes." I remembered my father's long hours in the library, after he returned from his company—the high doors always open, when he was there, but he always seemed quietly engaged, somewhere beyond us. "Well," I said, "It doesn't have to be that way. I shall be different."

Again in the darkness I could see my wife smile, as if womanhood gave her an insight that I did not possess.

"And if we have a little girl, Trey, will you play dollies with her?"

"If we have a little girl—well, if we have a little girl, then yes, I guess I shall try to do that."

We sat silent for a time, and then Lucy said, "I sometimes think that you and Adeline really aren't on the closest of terms, are you? Not really. Not in adulthood, anyway."

I studied her silhouette in the darkness, against the warm darkness of trees, not understanding what she meant. "But I think we're quite close. What makes you say that?"

"Oh, I don't know. The little things. I can't put my finger on it, but as they say, in the little things you read the larger tale."

"Like?"

"Like the politeness between you, it's like the courtesy of adult friends more than—more than the closeness of brother and sister. And the stuffiness too, the way you both seem to hold back when you're around each other. The way you never cross a certain line, never dig into each other's lives." I started to say something, but Lucy said, "She never asks about us, does she? She never inquires."

I thought of the annoying and sometimes presumptuous intimacy that Lucy had with her sisters, the way they cackled and carried on in the kitchen like hens in the barnyard, the way they sometimes huddled around the table all whispery, as if sharing secret notes, things linked to their womanhood and their marriages. Lucy's two sisters, Marge and Nell, did not much care for Adeline, and I sensed that the feeling was mutual— not that they ever crossed paths much, generally only once or twice a year. As for Adeline and Lucy, I always suspected that my younger sister harbored unspoken opinions regarding my marriage to Lucy Richmond Neil. Like my father, she had been fond of Mitzy von Leuckel, at least until Warren Harding came along, and Mitzy had a certain flourish as well as a few other items that Lucy lacked. Though by the same token, Lucy had qualities that Mitzy was in want of, like devotion and fidelity. Anyway, as for her point that Addy never *asked* about us, I said, "But our business is not her business, nor hers ours. Besides, we're all grown up now. We're not supposed to be *that* close anymore. A marriage is a marriage. Besides, what exactly should she be asking about us? You aren't implying—"

"Tristan! For heaven's sake, no. I don't mean our marriage secrets. I'm talking about—I don't know what to call it. I'm talking about *talking*. I don't know, Trey. I'm not clever with words, like you, but it seems to me that something's not there. Though it's mostly her doing, not yours. She's just one of those people. Guarded, I guess you would say. Smooth as silk, but guarded. I think she keeps things secret that no one else would even consider secret."

Lucy's words rang true and we were quiet for a time. "Maybe when she gets married," I said. "Maybe after she has a husband and a family of her own, maybe then she'll be . . ."

"Addy will *never* marry. She'll never have a family. I'd bet my bottom dollar on it."

I think I was and was not surprised. During the summer of 1919, Adeline would have been twenty-four years old, with her twenty-fifth birthday looming in September—cutting it a bit close for boarding the marriage train, but not at all impossible to catch it before it left of the station. And I might remind you that she was an extraordinarily pretty lady (and indeed would remain one throughout her entire life). "And what makes you say that?" I asked. "Plenty of girls her age play catch up, many with far less to offer than her. Why, look at Flossie. She didn't marry Senator Harding till she was thirty years old, and he turned out to be a pretty darn good catch, didn't he?"

"We could talk all night about *that* one, couldn't we, dear? But the thing is that Addy isn't Flossie. She doesn't want what Flossie wanted. She isn't *fierce* like Flossie is. She lies low in the long grass, as Mama says. Name one single fellow in this town that Adeline's ever received more than once or twice, much less cast her net for."

I said nothing because there was no one to speak of.

"It's as if no one's ever quite good enough for her, no one 'round Marion anyway. Maybe she should go back to Paris now that the War's done. That's what she should do. I'm glad she lives close by and all and I'm glad she's there for your father, but still, she should go back, for her own sake, for her own life. Who knows what would happen far away like that."

After a silence, Lucy added, "You know, Trey, I sometimes wonder if she was more herself over there than here. I think some people have it in them to go away and live elsewhere, and when they don't—Maybe when things change out at Tioga, maybe when the generation changes, she'll take some of that money of hers and cross the Atlantic again—but I doubt it."

"I doubt it too," I said. "She is where she is ever going to be."

V

❧

Decoration Day, 1947

NOT LONG AFTER the day when I encountered Matthias in the library, Adeline and I had quite a little chat about him—actually, about other things as well. This conversation occurred at the Hamilton family plot in the Marion Cemetery where we had gone to tend the graves for Decoration Day. Apparently, Addy and Matt had a little tête-à-tête a few evenings before, and their chat in turn led to ours. I believe Matt had been dropping hints about wanting to see Tioga's library, and so Addy invited him in. She gave him a glass of whiskey and even leant him two antique tomes from Father's shelves: the 1840 edition of Henry Howe's *Historical Collections of Ohio*—the volume having to do with Marion County—and the 1883 *History of Marion County Ohio*. These books are, of course, on my shelves to this very day.

I wish I could say that I was present that evening as I believe their exchange, whatever it was, gave rise to my sister's suspicions of him. Indeed, knowing Adeline, I wonder if the invitation and the glass of whiskey were somehow linked to notions she perhaps already harbored. In other words, maybe she simply wanted him to relax and loosen his tongue. I believe I ought to point out that my sister's suspicions were themselves always to be regarded with suspicion. Without rhyme or reason she would get the strangest notions into her head about this or that person; one of her tenants, perhaps, or a bank officer, or the pretty young girl who worked in the Thrift Market—that this person was an embezzler or that person an adulterer—or some unsavory notions of that ilk. Here is a perfect illustration of my point: During the War she concocted the notion that a certain German-Jewish gentleman, a photographer who was renting one of her commercial properties on South Main Street, was a Nazi spy.

Predictably (at least in hindsight), this particular "Nazi spy" lost virtually all of his European kin in the ovens at either Auschwitz or in one of Hitler's other satanic mills.

As for Addy and Matthias' discussion, I can say only that it had to do with the luncheon aboard the *Superb*, when the Presidential Train made a coaling stop in Columbus on that summer day in 1923.

But once again, I am getting a bit ahead of myself.

As I mentioned, not all of our conversation had to do my sister's growing suspicions. Indeed, much of it would be quite pleasant, and Addy would even tell me things about herself that I knew scarcely anything about—like her "magical years" in Paris before the Great War.

As was our custom, we drove to the cemetery first thing on the Saturday morning before Decoration Day. Adeline and I rode in one car, Lucy and her sister Marge followed along in another. Adel and I always decorated the Hamilton graves while Lucy and Marge decorated the Richmond and Neil graves. After our cemetery chores, we would head for breakfast at the old Mohawk Grill, where Warren Harding dined through much of his life. We carried out that springtime ritual for decades on end, though I am the only one left now. These days I pay Rob Roy to carry out that task for me. After I am gone, the weeds shall grow around the stones.

Marion's cemetery is as peaceful as a grove sequestered in a forest, with the headstones and soaring trees stretching into the rolling distance. On May mornings the grass glows like fields of emeralds, and with so many flowers in blossom, the honeybees come and go like tiny merchants ferrying gold. In older parts of the cemetery, towards the back where the Hamiltons are buried, the knolls are punctuated with 19th-century obelisks, some rather grand, like Mr. Amos Kling's, and some with statues that are quite distinguished, like my mother's.

Anyway, I was unloading the wooden trays with the little terracotta pots of petunias and marigolds from the car trunk, while Addy had gone ahead with the trawls and things. When I caught up she was standing before Mother's statue. After Mother died in childbirth in 1899, along with an infant son, Father hired an Italian sculptor to carve a life-size statue of her, a monument in white marble. With a parting glance over her left shoulder, and with a faint and haunting smile on her lips, she ascends six stone steps, the train of her gown brushing along the stairs. In her right hand she holds a sprig of hyacinth.

"Too young, too young," Adeline said, looking up at our mother's departing glance, "decades and decades too young. A lifetime too young."

Adeline wasn't really speaking to me, but I said, "Two lifetimes too young."

"Ah, yes, Trey. Two lifetimes too young. Our little brother, our poor little brother, he might be here with us now, mightn't he? Whoever *he* was, or would have been. We'll never ever know. Lots and lots of things we'll never ever know."

I said nothing.

When I'm at Mother's grave I sometimes picture her as I last saw her in her coffin in the darkened parlor of our old brick house on Vine Street. She and my baby brother were buried in the same glossy, black casket and I can still see them in their matching white gowns, she in the full beauty of young womanhood and he with his tiny head resting on her breast. I was perched on an Ottoman and Father was standing behind me. I tucked my little carved bunny rabbit beneath her fingers, a gift for my mother so she would not forget me. Father was holding Addy and she began to cry hysterically. The air was heavy with the scent of flowers and people were gathered in the shadows behind us. A sad-looking gentleman in a black frockcoat waited like a footman at the end of the coffin. Someone—I believe it may have been Mrs. Florence Harding—lifted my little sister from Father's arms and carried her out to the waiting coach. I could not take my eyes from my beautiful mother and I felt Father's gentle touch on my shoulders, tugging me away. Somehow I thought that Momma's death was his fault, not "God's will" as he had said. I wanted to shrug his hands away, but I knew my mother would be annoyed with her "little gentleman." Secretly I wished that he were the one lying in that coffin, not Momma, not my baby brother. He murmured, "They're but asleep, Tristan. Asleep in God's arms."

Even now, sixty-five years later, I picture Momma and the baby unchanged in their closed room in the earth, dimly glowing in supernatural light.

Adeline said, "Daddy ought to have given him a name, oughtn't he, Trey?"

"Yes," I said, "he should've." I laid a tray of flowers at our mother's feet, and I added, "Surely they had one picked out."

"It would have made him more—I guess it simply would have made him *more.*"

I began arranging the little pots in the proximity of where I thought the flowers might look prettiest. Addy walked around Mother's statue. The sculptor—one Nicola Giancola (his name is carved in little letters in the base)—had been so magisterial in his art that, thirty or forty years before, the statue could have passed for an exact likeness of Adeline; having been Momma's little look-alike, she had posed for the sculptor so he could mimic her features, matching them with pictures of our mother. Addy was gazing up at Mother's face as she traced her long fingers along the folds and textures of the marble gown, here and there colonized by moss and the web-like intrusions of time upon marble, already slightly melted after a half century of rains, snow, and sun.

"Momma," she said, "you'd be right at home in the Père-Lachaise."

I smiled at the compliment paid our mother. To the sculptor too, of course.

She sighed, "What a shame you never got to Paris, Momma, what a vicious shame, all those unfinished years, all of that life stolen from you."

I was struck by my sister's melancholic words and by something in her voice, a tinge of longing.

Soon we were together, sitting in the grass, clearing the weeds that had grown in the little flowerbed since last May. Addy had spoken of Paris some weeks before—on my visit to Tioga when Matt was there. I had wanted to hear more about that long-ago unfinished chapter in my sister's life, so I said, "Addy, do you ever wish you'd gone back to Paris after the war, or at least after Dad died?"

"Well, I did, Trey, didn't I?"

"I mean to live. To live and stay."

"Oh, I don't know about that. I suppose I wish that sometimes. If you live your best years, your magical years in a place like Paris, if you blossom into yourself there, then I suppose you always want to go back and live again. But—"

I wanted to tell her that it was not too late, but it was. I do not know what took hold of me next, no doubt something in the beautiful spring morning and the intimacy of my younger sister and me working side by side in the vicinity of our ghosts, for I found myself asking something that I had always wondered, "Addy, if you had gone back, or if not for the war, do you think you may have married?"

She laughed, I presume at my uncharacteristic boldness. "Well, Trey, now *that* is a question! And no beating around the bush about it either."

I thought about taking my inquiry back, but instead I found myself pressing on. "So do you or don't you? Maybe things would have been different for you."

"Oh, things would have been different alright, you can count on that." She stopped digging in the earth and looked off into the distance, across the graves and into the Old Forest. "You know a young man loved me once, over there, don't you? Loved me forever and ever long ago. A very, very special young man! Did you know that, Trey?"

"Sort of. Something gave me that impression once. Though you never said."

"Funny to be talking about him now, after all these years, and out here, of all places. He was a very important boy, a very, very special boy. And I loved him dearly and he loved me. And he died at Verdun."

She began digging with an almost angry vigor. I remembered the letter from France and her shutting herself into her room for days, and Father standing at the bottom of the stairs, below her room, whispering to me about the letter in French.

That would have been sometime in 1916.

I said, "So who was he, Addy? Tell me about him."

"His name was Bernart. He was only a boy, though I thought of him as a young man, but he wasn't, he was only a boy, a child, and he died at Verdun. That's what they say anyway. He was most unsuitable to be a soldier, *most* unsuitable—like throwing a puppy into the sea. I don't think he was afraid of dying half as much as he was afraid of injuring his hands, his fingers. He wanted to be a great musician, a violinist—and he would have been, and in fact he was on his way already at the age of eighteen. Ah, when he played, Trey, when he played, you'd have thought you'd died and gone to heaven and were listening to an angel play. And to think—to think what they did to him!"

If Lucy had been telling this story, tears would have been rolling down her cheeks by now—as happened, for instance, when she spoke of Nora, or of my predecessor, her young first husband Hezekiah Neil, who died in his youth in a gruesome coupling accident on the Erie. In fact, Lucy would be faithfully decorating his grave on that very morning, while Addy and I would soon be decorating Nora's.

She continued, "Died before his twentieth birthday! Murdered! And for what? For nothing! Those evil, *evil* old men. Every last one of them—Clemenceau and the Kaiser and Lloyd George. Wilson too. Fancied himself some sort of "knight in shining armor on a white steed." Truth is, he'd placed himself at Satan's disposal—him and his idealism. Mass murderers all. And not a one of them much better than their prodigy, Hitler. Why, they should have hung the old men who stirred the trouble and spared the seed of Europe. And America too. I hated them then, I hate them now. *Hate* them!"

My sister seldom got so worked up about things, especially if they weren't in her own backyard. But I suppose that sooner or later the greater world seeps into even the most cloistered lives. I said, "Your friend, Adeline, tell me about your young friend."

"Yes, forgive me." She spoke his full name again, and then she repeated it: "Bernart Laurant de Vaqueiras. He never got much older than he was when I last saw him. I wanted to bring him here, him and my dearest best friend, Claire. I wanted to bring them both to Marion. I knew Daddy would have approved. They would have been refugees from the war and Daddy would have been very pleased to be their protector. I pictured all of us living at Tioga, with me translating back and forth at the dinner table, and Bernart playing for us afterwards—though I don't think either of them would have cared much for our Lake Erie wines."

I wondered what Father would *really* have thought of Bernart if he had fled the war and left the fighting and the dying to his brethren. I wondered too what the rest of Marion would have thought of hosting a foreigner that had cut and ran, especially after we entered the War to fight alongside them. I said nothing of these points.

Adeline continued, "But it was all a caprice, a castle in the clouds, yet another might-have-been that never was. Bernart would have had to sail as a castaway because by then they wouldn't let him leave. They were already gathering up all the young men they could find so they could send them off to the German machine guns. Claire, she stayed in Paris and after the war married a fellow old enough to be her father. We didn't see each other again till 1925, that summer when I went back. Needless to say, everything had changed, herself included. Her husband was a wealthy banker. Three or four babies and another on the way. That was the last we ever communicated. Not even a Christmas card. I guess the girls we'd been before, no longer were, and so—. It was now a different world, not just a different time and place, but a different world, *un monde disparu*. And Paris too had changed."

We were both quiet with our own reflections on the comings and goings of the world.

She continued, "Poor Bernart was twice lost to the world. No one ever knew exactly where he was buried so I couldn't even lay flowers at his grave, if he had one. I had to content myself with lighting candles in a couple of Catholic churches—not exactly my cup of tea. Not his either, mind you. At least not when I knew him, before the trenches. After that, who knows. Oh, Trey, what a world! Mothers and babies and young men dying, and vile old men like Wilson living on and on into their evil old age."

My son, Eric Anthony, had come to mind, my little boy who never was, not even a grave that I could visit and decorate—my beloved son that I had never laid eyes on, my little boy, twice lost.

We worked in silence and, finishing our parents' graves, we moved to Grandpa and Grandma Hamilton's graves.

Once we were settled there, Addy said, "And now Tristan, it's your turn to tell *me* something." She paused, long enough to make me think that I was about to get a comeuppance for my boldness, perhaps a might-have-been inquiry measuring my life with Lucy compared to a long-ago someone else who had slipped away down the long corridors of the past. Instead, she surprised me. "What do you *really* think of that historian of yours?"

"That historian! Of *mine*, no less!" I laughed, maybe a bit nervously. "I take it you mean Matt?"

She said nothing.

"Ah, so you have doubts, do you?"

"No, Tristan, as a matter of fact I have *no* doubts. None whatsoever."

"Hmm. By the way you say it—so you think I erred. Get to the point, Addy. What's up?"

"Ask him. There's more to Matthias Mende than meets the eye."

I thought of the afternoon when I saw him at the library. I had said nothing whatsoever about that little encounter. "Meaning?"

"Meaning, I wonder if he has—what's that expression? Covert agendas."

"Ah! Well, puzzle no more. He has. He wants a cushy teaching job at Princeton so he won't have to work for a living."

"And mind you, Mrs. Christian calls him 'that flyboy.'" In my sister's book, Mrs. Christian was regarded as an expert judge of character. She added, "And I wonder about him and Dana—those new clothes and new shoes and things."

"What! Him and Dana?" I stared at her, her face partially hidden by her straw sunhat. "New clothes and things! What on earth are you talking about?"

"Why, haven't you noticed? I sense a connection."

I took a moment, attempting to deduce, via the ofttimes dim lights of my wit, the possible implication of her words. "You mean you think he's moonlighting for Dana and Margaret?"

"Oh, for land's sake, Trey!" She shook her head in obvious exasperation and sighed as if in pity and frustration.

But as you can well imagine, I was simply bewildered by the point she was trying to make. "Well, if that's what you're thinking, then think again, because he's not. Two jobs! Why, he wouldn't want to get his hands *that* dirty. Besides, that would cut too much into his time at the bungalow. Believe me, Matt's looking out for the President. And he's not only looking for a Princeton job, he's looking for a bestseller too. And the sooner the better. President Harding's his ticket to Havana."

"Trey, dear, when your eyes are open, they're *wide open*, but when they're closed, well, they're very, very closed."

I was even more bewildered by my sister's double-talk. I said, "Listen, Addy, if he's got a little extra change jangling in his pocket, it's because his mom sends him money. His sweetheart too, maybe. Their letters arrive by general delivery. I've taken him to the post office myself and waited in the car while he picks them up. He goes every Friday. Took him last Friday, in fact."

"So where do you suppose he goes when he slips down the carriage path after midnight just about every night of the week, walking west?"

"Why, to Lake Etowah for a swim. I've warned him about that. I wouldn't doubt that he goes to the bungalow too, after his swim. Addy, historians are queer birds, and they keep queer hours."

"Yes, they do, don't they? I tell you, Trey, something's going on between him and Dana."

Suddenly, I was struck with unaccountable squeamishness, something like fear and apprehension and revulsion all rolled into the same nauseating ball in the pit of my stomach. Evidently, evidence of this passed over my face.

"Okay, Trey, forget it. I'm sorry. I didn't mean to upset you. We'll let sleeping dogs lie." And then she added, as much to herself as me, "And appropriate others as well."

As far as I was concerned, my parents and grandparents' graves were finished, so without a word I got up and carried a tray of flowers to Nora's grave and another to Orrin de Pue's. He's buried over by the gravel drive, outside of the Hamilton family plot.

I wanted to forget my sister's weird words. I bent and brushed from Orrin de Pue's headstone the residue of last summer's leaves and mowings, glancing at his lichen-encrusted name and date, April 25, 1900. I began pulling weeds, thinking of the vast wars and the tumultuous century, nearly half over, into which he had never set foot. I thought of his lost and all but nameless history, the mysterious past of a drifter and a vagabond who had died unknown long, long ago. And I wondered again if folks somewhere out there, way back in the years, had ever sat on the porch watching for him to reappear in the distance, coming down the road again. Odd, but Addy and I had never talked of the tragic day when he fell from the high timbers. Not once, ever, in all the long years and decades. It was like a shared secret between us, a secret held so close that we did not even whisper of it to each other.

I found myself murmuring his name into the morning's silence as I tidied his grave, fleeing my sister's words.

I presumed Addy would tend to Nora's grave while I decorated Orrin's, as I certainly didn't need any help, but soon came the softness of her footsteps rustling through the cool grass. And there she was in her long blue dress settling herself beside me. I was afraid that I had been discourteous to my sister, so I said, in the vein of conciliatory small talk, "All finished over there, Addy?"

She said, "Believe me, Trey, I know one thing for certain about Matthias Mende—he's got cards he's not showing."

"Ah, I guess I misjudged him. Is that what you're saying?"

"Not at all. We simply underestimate his—his capacities, his range. On the one side, our little friend is quite convincing. I wouldn't have given you a hill of beans for President Polk, that is, until I read that article of his. Now I'm convinced Polk was one of our ablest presidents. But for better or worse—most likely for both—young Mr. Mende is very ambitious. And ever so determined. As for his scruples, well, I suspect they're entirely of his own invention. I know you don't want to hear this, Trey, but his interest in Warren is not strictly limited to whatever he digs up in the bungalow."

Needless to say, President Harding's reputation has suffered greatly at the hands of unscrupulous historians and I certainly did not relish the thought of that happening again—especially as a result of my own complicity and largess. But the truth is, at that point I still truly believed in Matt—in spite of such minor annoyances as his expressed interest in previously covered aspects of the President's life and death. Besides, I felt devotion to this young man who had served his nation so nobly and so well against Hitler's Luftwaffe, and by the grace of God had lived to tell the tale. Likewise, in spite of some rather vague doubts, I felt devotion to his career, to helping him prosper and make something of himself. Obviously, I guess you can say that I simply liked the fellow. Anyway, I said, "But, Addy, he's 100 percent on the up and up, 100 percent on the President's side. I *know* he is! I've sounded him out on this, completely. Why, if I were a betting man I'd lay a hundred dollars on him. No, make that five hundred. I'd lay five hundred on him!"

"He *is* on the President's side, Trey. I know that too. But you wait and see. He's going to stir up trouble, just like Nan Britton did. And don't forget, even little Nanny was on the President's side. I am telling you here and now, Trey, that young man's got something up his sleeve."

I was struck by her words and tone. "And what, exactly, might that be?"

"The poison rumor. I have a feeling he buys into it lock, stock, and barrel. And believe me he's *not* going to leave that stone unturned—not if he's allowed to continue. Who knows what he'll write. Who knows the effect his words will have."

That recent Monday afternoon in the Carnegie Library passed through my mind yet again, with him in his new clothes bent over a meticulous and beautiful drawing of foxgloves—executed in one of his Harding notebooks. Not for a moment did I buy his remark that he was drawing foxgloves because they were his sweetheart's favorite flower. But neither did I allow that one moment to obviate, in terms of my trust and regard for him, the dozens of hours he was spending each week pouring dutifully and scrupulously through the Presidential Papers.

I said, "So what am I supposed to do? Take away the bungalow key just because you've decided to be suspicions of him, just like Mr. —?" I mentioned the name of her Jewish tenant, the so-called "Nazi spy."

"This was different. I never said he was going to write a book and stir things up."

"Yes, but you were wrong—100 percent wrong. And you thought you were 100 percent right. Now listen, Addy, if you don't want Matt out at Tioga anymore, then just say so and I'll find another situation for him."

"You'll do nothing of the kind. And what's that have to do with anything anyway? I simply wish he wasn't so sneaky, that's all. And I wish he'd stick to his stated intentions. But you watch, Trey, he won't. Creeping off in the darkness!"

For a fleeting moment I saw myself on that autumn night way back in 1920—in the guise of Wellington Boyd—creeping through the darkness across the great yard at the Holcomb Museum, on Mr. Harding's behalf.

She continued, "But I don't want him going anywhere. He stays at Tioga. He's a good worker, and I want him right there. Besides, I want to put in a flowerbed out back at Goose Pond Farm and burn that pine tree that fell last winter. Either that or drag it off into the woods. It's unsightly." She added, "And look who he's chumming around with, getting an earful. And heaven knows what else." After a moment, she said, "So Trey, do you want him to open our million dollar tomb?"

I literally laughed out loud at that one. "Open our million dollar tomb!"

"Laugh if you like, but I'm telling you he'll set them off. You wait and see. After that, anything can happen."

"I'm not following. Set *who* off?"

"The authorities, of course. Who else? The police, the coroner. Maybe even J. Edgar Hoover himself. Who knows! We're dealing with a President of the United States. And our little Matty may give us all a run for our money, not to mention a bit of a surprise. After all, he's quite the clever one, very wily and very, very sly. And we both read those articles of his. He's very convincing. Duplicitous. Do you want him tampering with our tomb?"

"Adeline, I can promise you this, they'd take one look at the blueprints and go home. They can't possibly open that vault. It would be useless to try. And based on what? On suspicion? On rumors? And the tomb is our property, literally, the property of the Harding Commemorative Society. They'd need a search warrant. A search warrant based on what?"

"Don't kid yourself. They'd get it. And it's not like he's buried at the bottom of the sea. The President's body is right there, twenty-five feet down. Difficult? Yes. Impossible? No. It'll take jackhammers, bulldozers, and a month to do it, but they'll get in. Wait and see."

Both then and now, I do not think my sister was thinking rationally.

"Over my dead body," I said. "And I mean that literally. I'll stand in front of any bulldozer that dares come across our grounds. Why, they'll have to roll right over me. After they do that, then maybe they'll get in. Maybe not."

She laughed at me. "Trey, dear, just let me ask you one little bitty question. How many men do you think it'll take to pick you up—all one hundred and fifty pounds of you—and simply cart you off someplace else? Like out to a waiting paddy wagon, for instance? You ever hear of impeding a criminal investigation?"

For a moment I said nothing, and then, "But Addy, just listen to what you're saying! You have this whole scene concocted! And imagine this—just suppose they do. Then what do you think they'll find down there? Mr. Harding's been dead for a quarter of a century. His coffin was left above ground for a couple of years—years, mind you, with long hot summers. Why, Sherlock Holmes couldn't find anything inside that coffin, just dust and bones and maybe a few scraps of a gray cotton suit. And those would tell no tales. Don't you think they'd figure that out even before they moved a single shrub? Those boys aren't stupid.

Besides, the truth is those bones could tell no tales—even if there were any to tell, which there aren't."

"That's what you think. They can use microscopes and such and run all sorts of tests nowadays. True, there are no tales to tell, but if our historian writes something compelling, then they might think there is. Do we want them disturbing the sacred privacy of the dead? Especially the President and First Lady! Tristan, think about it. It would be an abomination, a sacrilege of the highest order. And don't forget for a single moment that you're Warren and Flossie's executor. You're the only one they have now still walking on this earth and they trusted you. You can stop the interlopers now, but you can't stop them later, not after Matt publishes something provocative and stirs things up."

We finished up with Orrin's grave and headed for Nora's—silently. What was usually a pleasant and even peaceful task, a task that had begun so intimately, was turning out to be quite a confusing and exasperating little row.

As I crossed to Nora's grave, I looked down the way, over the rolling knolls and headstones. Lucy was on her hands and knees decorating her first husband's grave. I had known Hezekiah Neil, but not well. I remember him as a sweet hillbilly sort of boy, very kind and polite, with a pleasing smile. A couple of times through the decades I had offered to move his remains to the Hamilton family plot. That way Lucy could someday lie between the two of us, but she always seemed uncertain about the idea, and so it never happened. As I stood watching, she seemed to sense my presence and looked toward me across the sunny land. We waved and I blew her a kiss. I wondered what thoughts were passing through her mind over there.

At Nora's grave, it felt as if Addy and I were slightly peeved with each other. I finally said, "So tell me, Addy, where'd you come up with all this about Matt—connecting him to the poison rumor and J. Edgar Hoover and his goons coming out here with jackhammers and bulldozers to open our tomb?"

"Mock me if you wish, Tristan, but something could come of it and you know it."

"Where'd you come up with all this?"

"From him, who else? I put two and two together and got him. Him and Evelyn Walsh McLean."

"Evelyn!" Evelyn had not set foot in Marion since the First Lady's funeral in 1924.

"Much surprises you, Trey, doesn't it? You do know, don't you, that she never thought much of us? Her with her Eastern airs and Western money. Why, who were we in Marion compared to the likes of her? Big fish in a little bitty pond. That's what she thought of us. I know jealousy when I see it, and jealous she was—of me and Flossie and our friendship. I don't know what it was about her, like she thought she couldn't be a member of our little ladies club or something, our ladies club of two. Everyone made such big fuss out of that friendship, like we were Ruth and Naomi. Someone actually said that to me once, you know. I didn't know what they were talking about. 'Just like Ruth and Naomi.' I had to look it up in the Bible. What a laugh. Yes, Flossie taught me lots of things when I was small, I won't deny it, good, ladylike things too, and yes, she bought me pretty gloves and dresses and such and I thank her for that, thank her from the bottom of my heart. But then she turned around and charged me recompense for the rest of my days."

I laughed at her exaggeration. "For the rest of your days? Are you saying that Flossie, decades in her grave, is still bending your ear with little injunctions?"

She paused in her work, the business of her hands suddenly stilled in thought. "Yes, that's exactly what I'm saying."

After a moment, I said, "But you loved Flossie, and Flossie loved you."

"So what? I love my dogs. She loved hers too. Neither here nor there in the final calculation of things." Addy tossed her trowel onto the ground as if she'd had quite enough of this beautiful morning. She leaned back on the cool grass and looked up at Mother's statue, rising in the sunlight and shadows, with a hyacinth in her hand, climbing those marble stairs as if into Heaven. "Oh, Trey, if only Momma hadn't died, if only she'd lived on and on, the way she ought to have lived on and on into ripe old age, like Daddy, then things would be different, wouldn't they? Everything would be different."

A pang of grief struck me almost like a bolt of lightning, an unaccountable sorrow that I do not think I would have felt had I not been amid the graves of our loved ones. My hands ceased in their labors, as if of their own paralyzed volition, and I was glad that I was positioned so that my sister could not see my eyes. But with equal rapidity I managed to retrieve myself, and when I had, I said, "Well, I suppose some things would be different, Addy, but what things, exactly, do you mean? Like what?"

"That's a question for the angels. Though I should think things like—well, things like *everything*. That's what." After a moment, she said, "Matt showed you those pictures of him and Evelyn at Friendship didn't he?"

"He did. Seems quite proud of them, too. I think Evelyn was the one who put him on my trail. I had the distinct feeling that he knew all about me before he even set foot in Marion. You too."

"Count on it. I had him in the other night, you know. He was curious about the library. I think he would have been happy to spend days there, curled up in Daddy's leather chair with some of those books. He's an odd one, so bookish but so bon vivant too. I picture him in bed with books, and much more. One can't tell where one thing ends with him and the other begins. As I sensed he would from the first, he wanted to know all about the last time I saw the President and First Lady. But I wasn't fooled. I knew very well what he knew."

"Aboard the *Superb*," I said, "that luncheon."

"Yes, Evelyn was there. He wanted to know what we talked about and such. How would I remember what we talked about? I said, 'I am not my brother. Mr. Hamilton's the one with the mental archives in this family, not me, and he wasn't there.' He even wanted to know what kind of flowers I took."

"Flowers?" I pretended bewilderment, astonishment.

"Yes, flowers. He seemed to know that I took flowers, and he wanted to know what kind."

I lied, "I didn't know you took flowers."

"Yes, you did."

I said nothing.

"I told him I didn't remember. But it was July, so it certainly wasn't hyacinths, or chrysanthemums, for that matter."

Just then we heard Lucy and Marge's voices as they crossed the grass, carefully stepping so as not to tread on the graves. I was both glad and slightly peeved that this conversation was to end.

Lucy was bearing the last potted little flower in her keeping, the precious one she always held back to plant with her own hands at the grave of our lost and ever-beloved Nora.

VI

THANKSGIVING
LATE MORNING

Land Filled with Ghosts

I HEARD MRS. CHRISTIAN calling my name. In the here and now I
heard her calling my name.

She gave me quite a start. Indeed, I am afraid that I too gave her quite
a start.

I was sitting here in the library so absorbed in my thoughts and
ruminations that I did not even hear her and her daughter arrive. The last
thing Mrs. Christian does every evening before she goes home is prepare
the percolator for my morning coffee, and the first thing I do every
morning when I get up is come down and plug it in. This routine has
been played out since the day I moved back to Tioga in 1959, and it was
played out long before that during my sister's lifetime. I always manage to
roust myself from bed early, winter or summer, and I do not recall the last
time I was still in bed when Mrs. Christian arrived.

Nor was I today of course.

I was sitting right here in my chair looking through the bay windows
towards the falling snow, my thoughts inhabiting a spring morning years
ago—Lucy coming through the sunlight with Nora's special flower and
Addy breaking off her comments about Matt—when suddenly I was
rousted from my thoughts by Mrs. Christian's frantic voice calling my
name.

I needed a few moments to recollect myself. I could hear her going through the upstairs hallway calling my name. Indeed, I believe she probably hollered out three or four times before I finally answered, "Mrs. Christian, for heaven's sake, what is it!"

"Mr. Hamilton!" she called.

"I'm down here!"

Frankly, at first I was quite put out with her, running through my house on this tranquil morning, bellowing my name at the top of her voice.

In a moment I heard the soft, quick thump of her footsteps on the carpeted stairs.

When she arrived in the wide double doorway, she looked as she did a couple of weeks ago when she saw a mouse scurry across the kitchen floor. She had not even taken off her coat and muffler. "Oh, my goodness, Mr. Hamilton!" Tears welled in her eyes upon the sight of me. "Thank God, you're alright! You gave me such a terrible fright!"

I must have stared at her in total bewilderment.

"Your coffee! You never touched your coffee. Why, it isn't even plugged in and I thought—" She started to whimper. "Mercy! I didn't know what to think! You've *never* done that before. Never."

Then I understood. "Oh, Mrs. Christian, I simply forgot. I'm sorry. I didn't mean to frighten you."

"Forgot your coffee!" She stood scrutinizing me as her daughter, having crept through the downstairs hallway, now peeked around the doorway, as if to verify that I was, indeed, still amongst the living.

"Good morning, Emma Linda," I said. "I would wish you both a Happy Thanksgiving, but I hardly think that's in order this year. Perhaps a Thoughtful Thanksgiving."

Emma Linda nodded, but her mother has a way of ignoring all distractions, and once she smells something fishy (or thinks she smells something fishy), she is not to be deterred. "Forgot your coffee?"

"For heaven's sake, Mrs. Christian! *Yes*, I forgot my coffee! Please!" She continued her examination of me. "And no, I am *not* sick. In fact, I'm fit as a fiddle, so fit that Dr. Sawyer just warned me yesterday that I might live to be a hundred—if I'm not careful."

She eyed me with suspicion, or at least bewilderment, as she began pulling off her gloves. "In that case, you better have your coffee."

I agreed, and on that note Emma Linda unpeeked herself from the doorway and departed down the hall for the kitchen.

"Oh," she said, as if in realization. "Nervous about Mrs. Blaine and her son coming over, are you?"

"Absolutely not!" I looked away, deep into the snowy woods, and then at Matthias' ring, at the face of Alexander the Great.

"Mrs. Christian, do you know who was here for dinner forty Thanksgivings ago?"

"Forty Thanksgivings ago! Mercy, I can't even remember who—Oh, that would be 1923, wouldn't it? Why, I imagine Mrs. Harding then."

"That's right, forty years ago today. Her last Thanksgiving on this earth. Your first Thanksgiving at Tioga, as I recall." I pictured her again as she was then, a shy young girl with hands as delicate as lilies. She was about fifty pounds lighter with silken hair, and she was standing by the kitchen doorway in her gray uniform and white apron, blushing while we applauded her for the feast. "A most momentous day all around," I said.

She seemed to be remembering as well. "Old Dr. Sawyer was here too."

"Yes. That was his last Thanksgiving as well. Lots of 'lasts' that year, Mrs. Christian, *and* some notable firsts. Now why don't you go hang up your coat and things and when the coffee's ready, bring us both a cup. Emma Linda can join us too, if she pleases. It's been one hell of a week."

Mrs. Christian and I regularly visit over morning coffee, albeit at the kitchen table, not in the library. "Very well," she said, "but then I have my work to do. And you have yours to do too, don't forget."

And then she made her way down the hall again and I turned towards the Old Forest and the falling snow.

Later I will go into the cellar and dust off a couple of bottles of wine, and tote logs in from the back porch. Then I shall light the fireplaces so that the grates are blazing bright when Mitzy and the President's son arrive. It seemed as if I have been sitting here for ages, but the clocks throughout the house began chiming nine o'clock, and so my duties will not need to be carried out for several long hours, seeing that Mrs. Blaine and Dr. Lang are set to arrive at four o'clock. I cannot help but wonder if lateness is still one of Mitzy's hallmarks. She once left me standing for forty minutes one cold autumn night in the rain. Well, there again, in the interest of truth I must step forth and correct myself: I was not actually standing in the rain; I was sitting in my father's Buick, parked at the darkened place on Pearl Street where we had agreed to rendezvous. But even if Mitzy is still somewhat as she was in her youth, I suspect that the fastidious Dr. Lang will corral his mother over here in a timely fashion.

In this long week of bewilderment, I have a question that I very much would like to put to Mitzy, though frankly, I do not need to do so. Plain old common sense delivers the answer without asking a thing.

In spite of that, I would still like to say to her, "Mrs. Blaine, do you regret your choices?"

Or a more appropriate statement of the matter might be: "Mrs. Blaine, to what extent do you regret your choices?"

I know just as surely as I am sitting here now that she must surely regret her youth—investing her young womanhood in Warren G. Harding, in the hope that Flossie would hurry up and die so that she, Mitzy, could marry her Warren.

And then, miracle of miracles, she would wake up some fine morning and find herself the wife of the President of the United States—a sort of 1920s Jacqueline Bouvier Kennedy.

Unfortunately, Mitzy's marriage to Jim was, I am sure, a bit of a disappointment. In short, I am afraid that, for Mitzy, life has been one long disenchantment, brought about by her own folly. I sometimes think that all of the dreams and ambitions of her youth—adulterous dreams and ambitions, mind you—are buried in that marble tomb at the edge of town.

And then, of course, along came the long remainder of her life.

I could have told her what lay ahead with Jim, if only she had asked me. It was simply in the cards, or rather within the man himself. His flaws were thoroughly obvious from the first. Obvious in his idleness and in the low regard in which he held himself, obvious in his penchant for drink—beer at that. Why, to think how vain and worldly Mitzy once was—the teacher who carried herself like a Gibson Girl—and to think how ordinary everything at last turned out for her. By my lights, Mitzy's life unfolded from a vast and early breach of common sense that has imposed its merciless consequences upon her to this very day—without granting her so much as a smidgen of absolution. Actually, that is not altogether true, for she does have three very fine sons and a daughter, and several grandchildren.

But that does not negate one simple fact: that our First-Lady-who-never-was became the most common of housewives, spending her life in clapboard houses on modest side streets in Marion, Ohio, and then, no doubt, in a similar situation out in St. Louis.

Why, to my knowledge, Mitzy cooked her own meals, scrubbed her own pots and pans, and did her family's laundry throughout her entire life. And to think that as a girl she was so vain about her nails. Not that there is anything wrong with any of that—but she so badly wanted something else (or so it seemed).

I firmly believe that everything that has ever come about in Mrs. Blaine's life in the past fifty years springs from the fact that, on a certain Saturday evening in the late fall of 1913, Senator-elect Warren G. Harding, standing by potted palms at a reception at Hotel Marion, kissed her gloved hand. I was standing at her side, oblivious to the moment and its eventualities. From that moment on, as I would later learn, she was in the thrall of a handsome, middle-aged, married man.

WHEN I HEARD the pitter-patter of Mrs. Christian's footsteps in the hall, I turned from the snowy windows.

Bearing the coffee tray into the library, she said, "I cannot tell you what a fright you gave us this morning, Mr. Hamilton."

"But Mrs. Christian, you did. You did tell me. And I cannot tell you how much I appreciate everything you do for me. Including, I am sorry to say, worry."

She set the tray on the side table and poured our coffees. We spoke of the snow and how pretty it was, though she was plenty glad that Emmy was doing the driving today. As she said, if not for Thanksgiving, if not for the fact that Mrs. Blaine and the President's son were coming to dinner, then she would have stayed home and I simply would have had to fend for myself, though by the same token she was *plenty* pleased that the dining room was being put to the use for which it was intended for the first time since, well, for the first time since Miss Hamilton died—and it didn't get much use even then. And that was a shame.

I handed her Matthias' ring. "Recognize this, Mrs. Christian?"

She examined it, turning it in her fingers. "Very pretty. Do I see something engraved in the band, Mr. Hamilton? I left my specs on the counter."

"Some Latin words and the initials HP."

"HP?" She examined the ring anew, apparently trying to place the initials into the context of her extensive familiarity with my family. "I would have guessed it was Colonel Hamilton's, or maybe your grandfather's, but HP?" She shook her head. "I guess someone on your mother's side. I don't know much about those folks. That was long before my time. Looks very old though."

"Civil War era. Actually, the setting's a gold coin that goes back more than two thousand years, before the time of Christ. The face there, that's Alexander the Great."

She repeated the fabled name, with appropriate awe.

"So do you recognize it?"

"Can't say as I do. Course like I said, I don't know much about your mother's people." She handed it back, "Why don't you wear it? You ought to wear it. That's what it's for. And it's so pretty."

"It doesn't belong to me. It's not mine."

She frowned. "Not yours?"

"You remember the young man who came here after the War? Lived in Mr. Tully's rooms above the carriage house?"

"That historian, or whatever he called himself?"

"Yes, Matthias Mende. He worked as a gardener, remember?"

"The flyboy. How could I forget. Mr. Yost's friend. The one who was always sticking his thumb out and going places on it."

I smiled at her summation of him. "Yes, that one. The ring was his."

"His! But then why—?" She did not finish her question.

"That's precisely what I would like to know. I found it this morning in the silver box. This silver box." I took it from the middle drawer. "Remember, I was looking for the key after Adeline died? Well, I found it at the bottom of a cardboard box buried in the cedar chest upstairs. Then I found the ring." I held it up, as if presenting evidence.

Her face seemed to go blank and she leaned back, as if away.

"Mrs. Christian, do you know by chance how and why my sister got hold of Mr. Mende's ring?"

She did not answer for a long moment. She averted her eyes, glancing through the window at the falling snow, then back at me. "How would I know? I barely remember him. Why would I know?"

"Frankly, I don't know, but I thought if anyone might, it would be you. Adeline never told me a damn thing about this. I open this box this morning and here it is, staring me in the face. Why, I nearly fell out of this chair. I mean, what on earth was *she* doing with it? That's what I'd like to know."

Mrs. Christian said nothing.

"That and I'd like to return his ring to him, if I can find him."

She said nothing.

"Mrs. Christian, would you mind telling me what you're thinking? Frankly, I'm rather desperate for sensible answers."

"Let sleeping dogs lie. Let the past bury the past and keep it buried. That's what I'm thinking. Don't dig it up. Don't even try. You can't anyway."

Now for a moment, it was my turn to say nothing. But I felt the need to offer my own accounting of this, I said, "I wonder if Adeline ever lent him money. Maybe that's why she had it. Collateral."

She sipped her coffee, her eyes fixed on me over the rim of the cup. And then, after a time, she said, "Come to think of it, now that you mention it, I think maybe she did say something 'bout that, a long time ago. That fellow was a bad pill, unsavory. You couldn't miss it. Besides, I've never cottoned much to drifters, to barflies and men of that ilk." She took another sip of her coffee, "Now if you'll excuse me, Mr. Hamilton, I have a turkey to roast, potatoes to peel and mash, and about everything else that you can imagine. And dinnertime will come 'round soon enough."

She nodded and, with her coffee, departed from the library and into the back of the house.

I COULD HAVE WAITED until mid-afternoon to build the fires, but the day is perfect for a blazing hearth and so before my bath I gathered wood in from the cold back porch. Afterwards, in the early afternoon, I lit fires in the dining room and here in the parlor where I am now watching the dancing flames. If the snow were not falling so, and if Mitzy and Dr. Lang were not coming for dinner, then I would take a drive to Goose Pond Farm and look around out there. For what, I do not know. For one thing, I have neglected the shed I built in 1912. The rain came through the shingles, damaged by the wind, and rotted some of the joints and beams, and so I am wondering how it is holding up under this snow. Before I sold the business, I should have sent a couple of fellows out to fix the roof and replace the damaged wood, but there were always people who needed more important jobs done.

Actually, I was out at the Farm a week ago today, November 21, 1963—the day before that most infamous of days. I cannot say that Matthias Mende came to mind out there—indeed, he was a very long way from my mind—but I certainly thought of Mitzy, having already invited Heidi to bring her mother here for Thanksgiving.

Now that I think of it, Matt did pass through my mind, albeit a bit like a leaf blowing by in the wind. I remember crossing the backyard and glancing at the now overgrown area where Addy had him dig a garden, and for a fleeting instant I recalled the Sunday afternoon in June when we took him out to the Farm and dropped him off for the purpose of preparing the bed for that now long-vanished garden. Dana came along for the ride. I allowed Matt to bring a box of presidential papers with him; his plan was to do his yard chores in the morning and his research in the afternoon and evening. He was going to stay a week or so and then he would hitchhike to Lake Erie (Addy and I even lent him a key to Indian Rock and drew up a little map for him); thereafter, he would return to Marion and continue things as before. That Sunday at Goose Pond Farm was the last time I ever laid eyes on Matthias Mende. And as events transpired, it was the last happy moment in my lifelong friendship with Dana Yost.

I have never paid much attention to jewelry and ornaments and such, especially on men, and I only wish now that I had made a note as to whether Matt was still wearing his ring that day.

On that gloomy afternoon last week I walked through the wilds that had once been Goose Pond. That whole area once held quite an allure for Mitzy. Out in that area Captain Pipe and his fellow Indians blinded, flayed, and burnt Colonel William Crawford to death, his bones scattered by wolves.

Mitzy thought the entire region "haunted."

One of her charms was that she had thoughts and interests that few other girls entertained. She found fascination within ruins and vanished places—what she once called "lost worlds." That's what she called Goose Pond, a "lost world." We were walking at sunset across the field where the waters had formerly lapped in the breezes, where reeds and cattails to this day grow in the former shallows. That was the time I showed her the old Huber Steam Traction Engine. She said, "Tristan, it's like a lost world out here. Lost and gone forever."

Personally, I would scarcely call Goose Pond a "lost world," though perhaps it was to the unfortunate creatures that inhabited its waters and to the geese and ducks and such that rested there as they journeyed north and south, on their long circuits up and down the world. Thanks to my Grandfather Hamilton, the pond is, as Mitzy said, "Lost and gone forever."

Goose Pond Farm was never much of a farm. It was part of a vast area that Grandfather Hamilton called "The Wilderness Lands." He had high hopes for the area, though things did not turn out as he wanted. As far as I know, the endeavor was the only major failure in his roster of otherwise successful undertakings. Sometime in the 1870s—I believe along about 1876 or '77, when Colonel Hamilton & Son was building many of the houses and business blocks of present-day Marion—he purchased nearly four thousand acres of wasteland in the northwestern regions of Marion County and the southwestern parts of Wyandot County. I do not know what he paid, but I believe no more than an average of thirty cents an acre and possibly far less for some of it. Grandfather's idea was to drain the ponds and wetlands, clear the forests, pull the sod from the prairies, and thereafter establish farms. He would build roads, houses, and barns and out buildings; he would dig wells and even plant crops. Once these ready-made farms were up and running, he would sell them to modern newcomers from the East who wanted to farm, but not pioneer. He even planned to advertise in rural newspapers across New England and the northeast. Grandfather Hamilton planned to keep the first farm for himself and name it Goose Pond Farm, which he did. In theory his idea was sound, but the land he bought so cheaply turned out to be altogether too wet and marshy for farming and far less yielding than he had hoped.

I read in one of the old histories of Marion County that Goose Pond was once well known to sportsmen in every city west of the Allegany

Mountains. Frankly, I do not buy into that inflated statement; nevertheless, the pond certainly was once an extensive body of water where the fishing and hunting were excellent. I have always been sorry that Grandfather drained the pond. Even my father said it was a foolish thing to do and that he had no "right" to do it. Mind you, Dad said that only in the later years of his life, after he had jumped onto the conservation bandwagon, quite a few years after Grandfather Hamilton was in his grave. In 1904 my father, inspired by Teddy Roosevelt, donated all of that wasteland except Goose Pond Farm to the State of Ohio with the stipulation that it remain in perpetuity a reserve for wildlife.

Hence my grandfather's flop became the Sanctuary Lands.

Today what was once Goose Pond is now nothing more than a dreary godforsaken expanse of nothingness. Not even trees grow there, much less corn or soybeans or winter wheat. Geese, ducks, and cranes no longer stop there, though I have seen pheasant, quail, and wild turkey in the vicinity. Legend has it that back in Indian days so many waterfowl alighted on the pond that the Indians could kill two birds with a single arrow. In later days, the wind carried the honking miles away to the settlers along Broken Sword Creek, where Johnny Appleseed planted an orchard that was still bearing fruit in my youth. Supposedly, for years and years after the waters were drained, befuddled flocks still flew over honking and circling the vanished pond.

Now all is quiet and desolate there and has been for nearly a hundred years.

Mitzy and I first visited Goose Pond Farm on a summer afternoon about two weeks after her first visit to Tioga. That was the visit when the Buick had a blowout in front of the little white schoolhouse where Warren Harding taught at the age of seventeen, after graduating from Iberia College. I believe I may have already mentioned the fact that, during the gubernatorial campaign of 1910, I passed many a long evening in Mr. Harding's parlor. I remember an evening when Mr. Harding mentioned teaching at the white schoolhouse and I distinctly recall him telling me, "Lordy, Trey, that was the awfulest year of my life."

When I asked him why, he looked away and after a moment said, "I guess it was humiliating and lots of other things, none of them good. For one, it was just so damn far out there. Rode the mule out on Sundays and rode her back on Fridays. Most nights I had to sleep on a pallet beside the stove, with the mice running all around and the wind rattling through the windows and me all alone. It was just awful. A real learning experience, though—least for me it was. I learned I wasn't cut out to be a teacher. Can't say if my pupils learned anything other than that either."

I said, "Rode out on a mule, slept on a pallet, probably chopped your own wood too. Sounds a bit like Abe Lincoln to me."

"Abe Lincoln," he muttered, surprisingly annoyed. "What a bunch of phooey you come up with. I was no Abe Lincoln, not then, not now. Why, nowadays when I travel past there, I look the other way so as not to look at that damned, accursed place."

Mr. Harding left one or two things out of his explanation that my dad later filled in for me.

Apparently, Mr. Harding was too young and too docile to handle rambunctious farm boys and girls, some a few years older than he and no doubt bigger and stronger as well; I doubt very much if he ever took a strap to a single one of them, perhaps out of fear that they might take it from him and do the same to him. And as I understood it, they called him "Nigger Warren." To his face. And the parents complained to the mayor about their children having to learn their three Rs from a "nigger boy."

On that hot summer afternoon in 1912, the Buick had a front blowout that nearly put Mitzy and me in the ditch, not fifty feet from the schoolhouse. I was taking her to the Goose Pond Farm to display my handiwork, which is to say, to show her the shed I was building for my father. I had worked for Colonel Hamilton & Son ever since I was taken out of school and Dad got it in his head that he wanted me to build a "well-made shed" and to do so completely on my own, from the foundation in the earth to the shingles on the roof. It was my very first exercise and a test of my carpentry and building skills as he prepared me for the eventual takeover of the family business. That was, by the way, the same summer when I began attempting to learn Classical Greek, as my mother would have wished; however, I had to master it on my own, or rather I had to *attempt* to master it on my own. But it was useless without someone to tutor and guide me, and the texts seemed to leave much unsaid—as texts will. Eventually, I gave up in complete exasperation, vindictively casting the Greek grammars I had received via mail order into the furnace. I may have failed at Greek, but as for the shed, if I may say so, I believe I did a pretty good job. Dad thought so too and was genuinely proud of me. I remember him climbing onto the roof with a level, and finding it true.

"Couldn't have done better myself," he said.

And so with a shed I began my career as a so-called "master builder."

Anyway, on that hot summer afternoon, I was driving Mitzy out to the Farm so she could ostensibly admire my handiwork, in one form or another.

It was July, so the grass at the schoolhouse had grown long, probably not having been mown since before Decoration Day. Under ordinary circumstances jacking up a Buick Model 10 and popping the wheel would have been no great chore for me, but the day was so hot that my shirt clung to my skin. Dust devils swarmed along the road, and every one seemed to make a beeline straight for me. After I popped the wheel off, I sat in the long grass under the big oak and patched the tube, while Mitzy lay beside me, admiring the sky through the high canopy of leaves. She stretched a hand heavenward, like she was trying to grasp those faraway leaves and bits of cloud floating by in the summer sky. She said, "Tristan, I am ever so pleased you had that little blowout, poor thing. If not, I should never have seen the summer sky on this particular day through this particular tree."

I laughed at her ever unique and charming way of viewing the world. Being young and full of spunk, I jumped atop her, situating myself on all fours, like a wrestler pinning her arms to the ground, my face not two inches from hers, my belly on hers.

"Now what do you see?"

She laughed at my horseplay, "A lunatic boy."

I started to kiss her lips but she dodged my kiss, and then when she was of a mind, she turned back and stole a kiss from me, and turned away again, in her playful way.

Back in those days traffic out there was less than nil. We lay in the shade for a while longer, and after a time, I said, "Mitzy, you notice the dumpy little schoolhouse over there?"

Without looking, she said, "What of it?"

"That's where Mr. Harding taught, back when he was seventeen."

"Really!" She raised her head and looked through the long grass. "Are you sure?"

"What's to be sure of? He taught there."

She pushed herself up, "Let's go look."

"Go look! Look at what?"

"I want to go see."

I suddenly regretted having said a word about the dump. "Let's not."

"Just for a minute. I've never been inside a country schoolhouse."

"It's a schoolhouse. So what?"

She was now up and lifting her hem, brushing the bits of grass from her skirt. I grabbed the bare calf of her leg and squeezed. She told me to let go but I squeezed even tighter. When she screamed a mock scream, I released her.

"Brute! Brute insolence!"

I watched her pretty figure sashaying through the grass towards that shabby schoolhouse. Out in the sunlight, she turned and shaded her eyes. "Are you coming or not?"

"Get lost!" I shouted.

"Suit yourself, little boy. I'll just go by myself."

"And maybe I'll just drive off without you!"

Without turning, she made a gesture with her hand, as if brushing an annoying dog behind her.

I flung a stick in her direction and screamed, "You're entering the devil's workshop."

Once on the step, she opened the door a crack and peeked inside. She looked back at me and then disappeared into the shadows.

After a few minutes I found myself peering through the doorway. She was running her fingers over the teacher's pulpit-like desk, as if inspecting its smoothness. As I entered, I tried to imagine Mr. Harding sitting there in his teaching suit, day after merciless day.

I did not realize that Mitzy was aware of my presence, as her back was to me and she had not turned, but she said, "Tristan, you'll never guess what I found in here."

"What?"

"Treasure!"

One of her seemingly countless games. "You did, did you?"

She turned and said, "Yes, I did. Come see, Sir Tristan, and you shall receive a most princely reward."

The schoolhouse had the deep abandoned quiet of summer and the scent of old, unpainted wood. As I approached, she made a show of clutching her hands tightly in the hollow between her breasts, which pressed the fabric tightly to her breasts.

I said, "So show me this treasure you found. Gold or diamonds?"

"Nearer to diamonds, I'd say. Open your hand and close your eyes, and you shall see."

I obeyed.

She placed an object in my open palm and then closed my fingers upon it. "Now, Sir Tristan, behold your princely reward."

I opened my eyes and my hand, A lump of coal lay in my palm.

"That's all the treasure bad boys get. That—and a kiss!"

I DO NOT WANT YOU TO THINK ill of us—or at least not of Mitzy—but the truth is we used the excuse of the blowout to spend the night at Goose Pond Farm. I have made a point of not remembering the embarrassment I suffered upon facing her mother again—the way she bit her lip and that look in her eyes. Frankly, I think Mrs. von Leuckel was a bit too distracted by the dearth of their circumstances to have been much appalled by our accidental waywardness. She liked me. More to the point, I believe she considered me a "good catch" (even if her daughter, ultimately, did not). The most Mrs. von Leuckel did was tell us not to mention our night at the Farm to others as they might "get the wrong idea." As for my father, he mystified me (at least at the time) by saying, "If you're going to go sowing your wild oats, Trey, then the least you can do is take along some galoshes."

I showed Mitzy the shed I was building and pointed out little details that would not be obvious to the untrained eye. That evening at sunset I also showed her the remnants of Goose Pond. Long ago a broad drive wended its way from the barn doors into the backfields. By 1912 prairie grass and dandelions had reclaimed most of the path that snaked its way along the riparian woodlands on the late pond's western shore. To this day tiny springs bubble up and sinuous narrow streams cut through the grass on their way to what was once Goose Pond. I remember how, as Mitzy and I walked along the old drive, the setting sun cast its ruby-gold light over the scattered cattail marshes glinting like sheets of copper. Shadows gathered in the sedge meadows and in the faraway forests—where timber wolves and panthers roamed during pioneer days, where Indians hunted deer and black bear, wild boar and buffalo. Only the deer remained into my grandfather's day. We walked through one of those cool spots that you find abroad near woodlands at nightfall, and I said, "Ghosts! You feel that Mitzy? We just passed through ghosts!"

"Yes, I felt them too. Indian spirits. I could sense them before I felt them. We mustn't be out after dark or they might not let us return."

I had meant my words as a joke, but her words spooked me. The sun was sinking into the far-off mists and so we picked up our pace.

A manmade declivity descends from where the drive ends in the emptiness of the vanished pond. I remember my grandfather telling me that gangs of day-laboring tramps built the earthen ramp. Tramps had also dug the channel to drain the waters. The ramp was made for the enormous Huber Steam Traction Engine—an early specimen of the tractor, one that resembled a modest-sized locomotive. At some time in the late 1880s, the massive giant foundered up to its boiler in a sinkhole, never departing from the shallow grave created by its own tremendous weight. Even in ruins the thing looked like a monster from prehistory sleeping in a bed of tall yellow flowers and milkweeds. As children, Adeline and I kept our distance, until the day when I read a fairytale about a daring little boy who climbed onto the back of a sleeping dragon and became its friend. Thus once in the 1890s I forged my courage and began shimming up the spokes of the enormous wheels, but as I pushed and pulled my way upward, onto the top tread, a sliver of rust pierced my leg. By some miracle, I did not die of lockjaw. Mother told us we were never, ever to go near the engine again, though she hardly needed to; after that the monster took on an even more sinister air that warned us away.

Of course it held no such sway over time and the elements. Dampness leached through the old iron and a decade and a half later, when Mitzy and I ventured there, the traction engine was considerably reduced. Daylight appeared through fissures in the boiler and an owl had built its nest atop the chimney. By mid century, it had melted and been swallowed so far into the earth that it was not much taller than a basket of apples. Today no one would ever know that anything enormous and manmade once stood in that patch of prairie roses, milkweed, and trillium growing through that gravelike area of rust flakes and earth.

As Mitzy and I stood marveling at the colossal wreck, lightning bugs passed through its fissures as they would through dead branches. After a short spell of quiet, Mitzy said, "Makes me think of the *Titanic*, Trey. Do you see it too?"

I gave a little laugh, but checked myself, and said nothing. The great White Star liner had gone down in the spring, and something about its mystery and the folly of its tragedy—its profound presumptions and arrogance toward nature, toward God—seemed to haunt even those of us who lived in the hinterland, who had never laid eyes on the sea.

Gazing at the colossal wreck, Mitzy said, "It certainly has abundant—" She paused with wonder. "Abundant what, Trey?"

"Rust," I said, "abundant rust."

"Stupid. That's not at all what I mean. I mean something like—like presence. Yes, it has great and brooding presence."

"Several tons worth," I reflected.

"And secrets too, like this whole country out here has secrets, lots and lots of secrets." We looked away towards the prairies and scattered ponds and bogs, the shadowy land filling with night, and she said, "Land filled with ghosts."

Miles to the north, mists and shadows drew a shroud over the woods and the north breeze winnowed through the prairie grass and leaves. I told her about the Indian burial mounds and the remains of wigwams that Grandfather found along the banks of the Little Scioto, and the great conical mound back in the woods crowned by a sycamore. And then I said, "Mitzy, you see that patch of trees way yonder in the mists?" They seemed to pass in and out of view. "That's where the Indians killed Colonel Crawford."

She gasped at the thought.

"My father and I hiked out there a long time ago, when I was a boy. You could still find musket balls stuck in the tree bark. Dad dug one out for me with his knife. I still have it on my dresser. And we think we found the clearing where the Injuns roasted him alive on the coals, after they flayed and scalped him, and blinded him with burning sticks."

"Oh, Tristan, how horrible! How absolutely cruel and abominable!" Her voice trailed into pity. "How could human beings do such a thing to man or beast? Why, it's incomprehensible! Evil beyond all telling."

"Then the wolves made a meal of him," I said. "Maybe the first and last time they ever had cooked meat."

"Oh, Tristan! What an irregular thing to say! What a shameful, irregular boy!"

In spite of my admittedly off-color remark, she pressed herself to me, and I to her. I felt the sinew of my young manhood and a strong urge to prove my gallantry in some heroic, antique way. We stood looking toward the distant woods, unchanged since Indian days.

"Grandfather told me that the men he hired to drain Goose Pond, the tramps who turned it into a giant field, one night were sitting 'round their fires, and they heard—or they thought they heard—a man's screams blowing in from way out there in the dark of night. Grandfather said they swore to it, up and down, every last one of them—horrific, blood-curdling screams on the wind, and at sunrise three or four who'd been soldiers in the Civil War hiked out with their pistols and Bowie knives at the ready, thinking they'd find mischief, or signs of it, but the only thing they found were trees and birds chirping and fluttering through the leaves. None of them had ever heard of Colonel Crawford—that is until Grandfather told them."

"Tristan," she whispered, "it's spooky out here. Let's head in."

Mitzy had been thoughtful enough to pack a basket of food. Her little brother Cedric brought home "day-olds" from his all-night bakery job, and so we had an ample supply of slightly stale cinnamon rolls, along with meat sandwiches made with bread that had hardened at the crust. On the way out, after the blowout, we had passed a field of sweet corn growing ramrod straight in the afternoon sun, guarded by a scarecrow. We saved the farmer the trouble of picking a dozen or so ears. My father— like Adeline—was a great lover of wine so he kept an ample store in the cellar. Thus, Mitzy and I were neither imperiled by hunger nor thirst as we endured our night of isolation at Goose Pond Farm, exquisitely far from the known world.

VII

"A Fine Place to Slay Isaac"

THE CORN WAS ABOUT AS HIGH AS DANDELIONS when we drove out on that June afternoon thirty five years later to drop off Matthias Mende at the Farm. As I recall, Dana basically invited himself—not that I think any of us really minded. And we certainly had plenty of room in the car. As a rule, I usually did the driving, but for some reason Addy drove her car that afternoon. Maybe she wanted to "stretch its legs" as she used to say, but then again, she was going to be driving to Cincinnati at the crack of dawn the next morning to attend an annual function of the Ohio Orchid Society, of which she was an avid member. Matt had a hitchhiker's appreciation for other people's automobiles and he was quite taken with my sister's enormous 1938 Cadillac. He even nicknamed it "The Flying Fortress" and joked that it had enough metal for three bombers. We took a decidedly roundabout course to the Farm—I guess just for the simple pleasure of motoring in the country on a June afternoon. Dana rode up front with Addy, while Matt rode in the back between Lucy and me, almost as if this former fighter pilot were a little boy snuggled between two oldsters. I think he was quite pleased with himself regarding the cushy setup he made for himself amongst the remnants of the old "Ohio Gang." We headed southwest through Oakland Heights, and as we drew near to Dr. Sawyer's place, Addy said, "Matthias, you see that place back there?—that's the once famous White Oaks Farm, the Surgeon General's residence. Lloyd George once visited the First Lady there, bearing greetings

430

from the King of England. One of the Edwards, I believe. Now it's just another old place out in the middle of nowhere."

"George V," he corrected.

I noticed that Matt had already been looking quite intently at the house even before Adeline pointed it out. I had the feeling that someone else had brought him out this way before. As we passed White Oaks Farm, I said, "Matt, I met Babe Ruth right there, where the fish pond is, just this side of it. Why, I can still see him standing in his Yankees uniform, surrounded by little orphans in ball caps and knickers. The Sawyers had a picnic for the boys and girls from the children's home and the Babe was giving them batting lessons. Even the girls were trying to have at it. They all seemed to have great fun."

Lucy said, "Trey always remembers that day. I think meeting the Babe meant more to him than meeting all the others combined, and mind you, all the others includes the likes of Thomas Edison, Henry Ford, and Douglas Fairbanks. The list goes on and on. Al Jolson, too."

"Well," I said, "meeting Mrs. Fairbanks, Mary Pickford, now that was something! Let's not forget her. Lucy and I and Addy met her and Douglas Fairbanks at a dinner party in the fall of 1920. They were real movie stars, weren't they, Lucy?—carried themselves like royalty, but as kind and personable and as gracious as they could be."

"Neighborly," Lucy said.

Mitzy floated into my mind and I saw her in a blue cloak in the lush gardens. I was prepared to tell Matt more about the movie stars and Mr. Harding, and who knows—I may have actually opened up and touched on the Chancellor story, in a marginal sort of way. But instead he said, "The Sawyer farm back there, I believe that's where Mrs. Harding died, isn't it?"

He knew that already, I *knew* he knew that already.

Dana chimed in from up front, "And Dr. Sawyer too, don't forget. Flossie fixed him supper, he felt a bit woozy, left the table, and lay down on his bed and died. Just like that. And not long after that, she was dead too."

Through the rearview mirror I saw Addy's eyes shift towards the backseat. Our eyes met for a moment, and then hers shifted for a split second to Matt before settling again on the road ahead. She was wearing white gloves, as she always did when she drove.

She said, "Flossie did *not* fix him supper, you *imbecile*. Flossie would not have been caught dead in the kitchen. Count on it. And in that household the housekeeper did the cooking." Addy had seemed troubled of late, but then again, calling Dana names was nothing out of the ordinary, certainly not like calling someone else an "imbecile"; something in his nature seemed to solicit disparagement, which rolled right off of him when tendered.

"And Dana," I said, "Sorry to point it out, old boy, but I'm afraid you've erred on a second point too. The Surgeon General did *not* lie down on his bed and die. He lay down on the horsehair couch in his office, at the back of the house, and that's where he died. You see, Matt, all the misinformation, small and large, that gets spread about anything associated with the Harding story? Starts small, ends big, usually through inference. The pity of it is that even people who've lived in Marion all their lives can't seem to get the simplest facts straight—two facts wrong in one little sentence—from that chatty fellow up front. And then we wonder why it is that outsiders, historians and the like, can't get the facts straight either. Well, I'll tell you why—it's because they listen to the wrong people, that's why."

Dana said, "Well, correct me if I'm wrong . . ."

"You're wrong," Addy said, and then she added, "Lovely afternoon isn't it?"

Dana continued, casting a sidelong glance towards the backseat, "Charming, isn't she? Correct me if I'm wrong . . ."

Addy said, "Dana, do you want to ride back to Marion? Or *walk*?"

Her little comment lightened things up, and we all got a chuckle out of that.

"Ride. I wore the wrong shoes for walking." Dana turned to us, "You see, Matt, what the Harding story does? Divides lifelong friends and threatens to make pedestrians of us all."

In retrospect his comment was weirdly prescient in at least one way.

Matt was clever enough to elicit information more by interjecting and then listening rather than asking. Thus having raised the topic, he now simply sat mum, letting us go at it like squabbling children. Dana said, "At any rate, the First Lady and the Surgeon General dined together and then he got up and lay down and died, just like that." He snapped his fingers, for the dramatic effect. "Just like the President died. Same symptoms, same everything, entirely."

"Correct," I said, "More or less. And just like countless other stroke victims—very similar symptoms. Stroke symptoms."

"And no autopsy," he added, "Just like the President. And yes, just like millions of others, the vast majority of humanity, no doubt. No autopsy."

"No need," I said. "A stroke is a stroke is a stroke."

Addy said, "Lovely afternoon to be talking about death, isn't it?"

As we rode along, I was newly certain that a certain someone had been bending Matt's ear about all sorts of things, including Mitzy and Mr. Harding, and maybe about Mitzy and me—though it is to Matt's credit that he never once even hinted an interest in knowing about failed courtships, love affairs, adultery and the like, presidential or nonpresidential. With the exception of the poison rumor, Matt eschewed gossip of all sorts and kept his focus. For that I admire him anew, and presently I regret his unfinished work anew. I am sure he could have made a difference in people's perception of President Harding.

We passed through Green Camp village before wending our way northward, straying through lonely, marginal regions of Marion County where the roads are so unfrequented that here and there tall weeds grow through cracks in the pavement. I pointed out remnants of one of the orchards in the area planted by Johnny Appleseed, and I told Matt about the little family of pioneers that built a cabin nearby but soon died in a cabin fire, during Andrew Jackson's Administration. That story was new to Dana as well. Farther northward the land takes on a sort of privacy and loneliness, a verdant desolation. As we sped along I imagined far off in the woods and high grasses deer and bobcats, gray foxes and meadowlarks watching, startled, as our gleaming behemoth roared along the outskirts of their world. Northward, when we neared the western precincts of the Sanctuary Lands, I noted the solitary Indian trail marker standing on the prairie, the massive oak bent as a sapling, hundreds of years ago, its trunk pointing like an arrowhead towards Goose Pond, now decades and decades vanished.

There is nothing special about our old farmhouse. It is a plain white two-story affair with a broad porch, spacious parlor, dining room, a big kitchen and pantry hidden away at the back, and five bedrooms, four upstairs and one down for the aged. The house predates Tioga by about thirty years and so it was only in later years that my father installed indoor plumbing, pulling down the outhouse and filling in the hole. Mind you, in spite of the house's comparative simplicity and plainness—no mansard roof or colored glass above the bay windows—it is not wholly lacking in charms. I would compare the house to a country lady both pretty and plain, a lady who is what she is, gracefully, without striving to be more. Maples, buckeyes, and an Indian cigar tree shade the house, though we long ago lost the big chestnut tree to blight, and since then several of the elms have gone too. Abundant lilacs and forsythia, roses of Sharon, and beds of hosta and lemon lilies, tulips and poppies are the house's only adornment, along with the ornate birdhouse, since dilapidated, where the purple martins once lived. And then for some years after 1947, the new garden in the back managed to push up a few flowers. "Matt's garden," Addy once said, with a touch of seeming sadness. But there was never much to it, and she never seemed to take an interest in that garden, not like the gardens at Tioga. Maybe she associated that little patch with his going away, his work unfinished, promises unkept—a violation of our trust, and of our many kindnesses and generosity towards him, of our faith in his aims and abilities. Perhaps to her, at last, the garden became an emblem of his desertion and betrayal, his (and our) lost cause.

I cannot tell you how deeply disappointed I have always been in that young man, indeed, even *hurt* that he never wrote his book, that he apparently allowed events to intercede between himself and his endeavor, even if perhaps, by fate or by folly, he allowed himself to be drowned during a midnight swim in Lake Erie. I warned him in no uncertain terms not to go swimming off the cliffs at Indian Rock, just as I warned him about his midnight swims in Lake Etowah. I warned him that, away from her gentle beaches, Lake Erie is a perilous maw, a cunning and opportunistic killer; she spots her prey and then strikes, secretly and mysteriously. And once she strikes, she is loath to yield her dead. Even if misfortune took Matthias Mende, I still hold him accountable for his unfinished work. What business had he, risking his life when his book on the President was still unwritten? He *owed* it to the President. He owed it to me—to us. I suppose his haughtiness got the best of him. I suppose he thought that if he could survive Hitler's Luftwaffe, then he could survive his own folly and escapades into peaceful, perilous territory. And besides, sometimes I had the feeling that he inhabited a sort of labyrinthine night-world of drinking and strange goings-on and midnight swims in dangerous waters. He ought to have stayed his course and kept clear of the lot of them.

Anyway, I smile again as I remember how, as we pulled into the long, maple-shaded drive, he sort of cooed, "Ooo-la-la!"

I laughed at his Frenchy gibberish. "So you think you'll like it here, young man? Think you'll be able to put up with Goose Pond for a week or so, do you?"

"Do I ever, Mr. Hamilton!" He gave a sort of delighted laugh, "Why, you made it sound like some kind of shack in Appalachia or something! Looks more like a bit of heaven to me, heaven plopped right down here in Nowhereville, Ohio—I should've known, should've known."

Dana of course had to get in his two cents' worth. "Limbo's more like it," he quipped. "Not heaven. If this is heaven then, please—"

I ignored his remark. "I don't know about heaven, but it's pretty quiet out here. You'll have no neighbors knocking on the door asking for a cup of sugar out here. Nothing like that."

I had already filled him in on the history of the place, and I pointed out the remnants of Goose Pond, to the east of the house, and the stand of trees far in the north where Colonel Crawford was tortured and burnt. I knew he would be visiting these places before he left the Farm.

Rob Roy generally drove out on Fridays at that time of year (still does, in fact), to mow the yard, and so the place looked pretty trim. Indeed, to this day Rob does a pretty good job, even trimming around the trees, where the grass grows through the roots, which all too many mowers neglect.

As Adeline pulled the car to a stop, Lucy said, "You think this is something, Matt, wait till you see Indian Rock! Now that's a good, old-fashioned summer place, isn't it Trey, isn't it Addy?"

"You bet it is!" I said.

"It's quite comfortable," Addy said.

I held the door for Matt. Sometimes he had to use his hands to lift his left leg out of the car. I think it got stiff after longish rides in an automobile. Mind you, that young fellow was no cripple. Nevertheless, I grabbed his portfolio for him along with his tray of colored pencils. Dana made the mistake of trying to take his arm, as one might take the arm of an old man, but Matt jerked it away and shot him a violent look. There had been something overly chummy in Dana's gesture and I pretended I did not see any of it.

I added, "Ah, the lake, the cliffs, the sunsets! The sunsets over Lake Erie! Now that's a sight to see! Dad loved it up there, didn't he Addy?"

"He did. I think it was his favorite place in the whole wide world. Mind you, Daddy's whole wide world consisted mostly of Marion County and Lake Erie. Pretty much like his daughter's, I suppose."

"His son's as well," I added.

My sister wore her straw sunhat with a lavender bow and one of her Sunday dresses; I was struck anew, out there in the open country, by her natural feminine grace. Far in the back of my mind, Momma rose in my thoughts and then slipped away like a spirit. "As for sunsets," she continued, "well, I've seen some pretty fine ones right here at the old Farm." We were in the backyard and she glanced westward, the light still golden and well above the distant treetops. "Not like Tioga," she said, "all hemmed in by trees."

Dana carried the box of documents into the kitchen and placed them on the harvest table, where Matt would have more than enough room to spread out. The little trove of documents that I allowed him to cart along to the Farm was surely more than enough to occupy his days in the country. I believe that, at that time, he was concentrating his research—or I should say *trying* to concentrate his research—on the Washington Conference. I am very pleased to repeat myself and say once again that President Harding conceived and initiated the first disarmament conference in the entire history of the world, in his noble attempt to reduce global tensions after the Great War.

The day before we drove out, Lucy went shopping and cooked up plenty of food, a ham and pot of mashed potatoes, a couple of pounds of chocolate chip cookies (a favorite of Matt's) and who knows what else, so I can assure you that the young man was in no danger of starvation. Inside the house, Lucy put these in good order for him, in the icebox, the cupboards, and the cookie jar. And I carried his satchel upstairs to the room he had picked out for his stay. It is none of my business, but I had the feeling that he also stashed a bottle or two of Jim Beam in his satchel. I say that because when

I carried it upstairs, it seemed to me by the sheer heft of the thing that he had more than socks and underwear stuffed inside. Besides, I heard a bit of sloshing around in there, and I do not think it was after-shave.

After I showed him around the place and told him about the quirks in the plumbing, and after Addy staked out in the grass the lines for her new garden and laid out the tools, we ventured off, the five of us, back along the Indian trail to the ancient sites. These lie nestled in a hollow to the northwest of the house, across the prairie, hidden away in a stand of trees a good mile or so from the road and utterly apart from the world. As we headed into the high grasses, the chill of evening began seeping into the day, and the western sky took on the whitish, yellow glow of late afternoon. Now and then the "peepers"—the baby frogs off along the winding banks of the Tymochtee Creek and out in the scattered ponds and bogs—began to cut through the quiet with their short metallic notes. Later on, after the sun was well gone, their peaceful little song would fill the night, like a lullaby of myriad little bells ringing far off in the night. I have never heard the nightingale, probably never will, and the loons left Ohio years before my time, thus for me, the song of the peepers is one of my favorites in all of nature.

In spite of the Indian trail's utter lack of use in modern times, its tracing nonetheless remained (at least back in '47) visible across the prairie, right into the distant citadel of trees. As we followed the path, I said, "You realize, Matt, that Indians in their moccasins walked this very trail back in olden times."

I felt a bit like my own father talking to me when I was a boy.

I continued, "In fact, they're the ones who made the trail, the Wyandot and Delaware peoples—their moccasins tamped down these grasses over hundreds of years. And here it remains, and here we are, following in their footsteps."

"Yes, sir, Mr. Hamilton, I do realize that. They used it till they were rounded up—men, women, and children, the young and the very elderly—and driven into exile west of the Mississippi, 'long about 1838 or so. Sort of our homegrown version of the Bataan Death March, when you think of it. But instead of eighty miles, it was a thousand."

Frankly, I do not think I had ever once in my life heard anyone say anything like that. I almost said, *Well, Matt, but they were Indians.*

But my soul shushed me. My sister, walking ahead, gave a sharp, half-glance back, but said nothing. If Adeline and I had been facing each other, she would have given me a telling look—maybe one that says, *See what I mean? A loose cannon.* For a startled moment, I sensed she was right. I gave a little laugh and said, "Well, Matt, I don't know about that!"

"I do, sir, begging your pardon. I *do* know about that. And I know very well about it. Presidents Jackson and Van Buren, Federal troops, state militias, and vigilantes coming out of the trees, evicting those people from their homelands. The truth is the truth, sir. Time does not annul the truth. Tries to hide it, maybe, tries to bury it, but doesn't annul it. It all comes out someday, sooner or later. As you folks say out here in Ohio, 'Sooner or later the birds always come home to roost.' All of the roads that lead out here have their graves beneath them."

Dana and Matt were walking a few steps behind Lucy and me. I told myself that maybe Matt had already partaken of a shot or two of Jim Beam—maybe when he stepped into the bathroom back at the house. For a split second, as I glanced at the woods around me, I thought, *Stolen lands. But how could it be otherwise?*

Dana jumped in and changed the topic. "Say, Tristan, you remember that summer day when you and me hiked back here, along this very trail? Your dad bought us moccasins for my birthday and we came out to Goose Pond Farm and painted our faces like Red Chief and hiked back to the mounds—'yonder,' as Colonel Hamilton used to say. Remember that? It was on a Saturday."

I laughed—I suppose in part in relief at having the aforementioned topic dropped "like a hot potato," and in part because it was, indeed, a warm memory. "I sure do, Dana. We stuck hawk's feathers in our hair and munched rhubarb and papaws as we sat 'neath the old hickory tree, up top of the big mound—thought we could see the whole wide world from up there. Thought we could see Lake Erie. Probably was just blue mists far off. And then when we came back and told Dad about it, that we'd seen Lake Erie, he said, 'Well, boys, maybe you did, maybe you did!' That was Dad, ne'er a discouraging word."

Addy laughed at our little story. "Oh, Daddy!" she said, "Dear, dear Daddy!"

"And Mother, too," I added, "Mustn't forget Mom, just 'cause she was so early called away."

"Yes, and dear, dear Momma as well."

Mother had been dead for so very, very long that Addy and I were almost the only ones in this world who remembered anything about her. Lucy knew her only vicariously—and not well at that, owing to the fact that Momma died so early in our lives.

A breeze parted the grasses like a comb moving through hair. The prairie and scattered trees, and the freshness of the air and all the waters rippling through the land, gave the afternoon an early summer fragrance, fleeting and heavenly. Adeline, walking before us, kept her eyes peeled for baby toads loitering on the path. As we passed near the little bog, she warned us, "Careful, careful now!" We slowed our pace while she swished the hem of her dress to send the babies scurrying. "Hurry away, little ones," she said. "Hop, hop, hurry away, or else!"

Dana said, "That was forty years ago, Trey, when you and me climbed that mound, forty years if it was a day."

He added, "You do know, Matt, don't you, that you're an honored fellow, coming back here. These mounds are a family secret. And to think— they don't even have anything to do with Warren Harding! Why, even I haven't been back here, since—well, not since World War I, I believe. The Kaiser was still in Potsdam and Hitler was busy flunking out of art school, last time I was back here."

Addy said, "Not since your hair was black as coal, Dana, and mine was 'brown as chestnuts,' as Daddy used to say."

Dana said, "And Trey's was as golden as gold. And shiny like gold too."

"Once again, your memory is faulty," I said. "On two counts, no less. My hair was *never* golden. Plain ol' yellow's more like it, not golden . . ."

"Dana's right, golden like corn silk," Addy said.

I continued, "And we came back here other times too. Lucy and me and you and Margaret and the boys, first when they were little, then again when Jason and Brendan were . . ."

"Ah, yes, the Fourth of July. Forgot, as usual."

"Between the wars," I added. I was reaching back in time for the years and I could have dug them up, too, but Lucy said, "We do sort of keep the place secret, Matt. Trey and Addy, they don't want every Tom, Dick, and

Harry traipsing back here leaving beer bottles and cigarette butts and who knows what else."

"Hint, hint," Dana said. He and Matt were smoking cigarettes.

Lucy continued, "Or worse yet, digging things up."

"Hint, hint," Dana repeated.

For a moment, silence fell upon us. I took that as a possible allusion to the President's remains. I am certain that Addy took it that way, especially knowing the way her mind worked, with all its twists and turns.

Matt said, "I won't tell a soul, Mrs. Hamilton. I promise I won't. On my honor!"

"You honor's good enough for me, Matthias, and then some." Lucy paused and then added, "You know, Matt, we're going to miss you 'round here when you head back east. You'll have to think of us now and then, out there."

"I will, Mrs. Hamilton, I will. That's a promise too. And I'll miss you folks aplenty, but don't you fret 'bout that right now. That probably won't be till the leaves fall, or maybe not till the snow flies. I just hope I don't wear out my welcome 'fore then."

Lucy said, "I know I speak for all of us when I say you don't need to worry about that."

I thought of Matt not sitting at his table in the bungalow anymore, of not having him to check on, and I cast a glance over my shoulder. His blond head was bowed and he was drawing on his Lucky Strike—like he was deep in thought, or suddenly troubled, saddened by the thoughts of going.

Suddenly, I wondered about Dana too—what was *he* thinking? What was *he* feeling? I happened to catch sight of a jackrabbit darting off in the distance away into the grasses and for some inexplicable reason that old adage came to mind: *Love goes where love is bidden, even into the tall grasses.* With that, my hand flew up, seemingly of its own volition, and covered my eyes as a deep and mysterious unease pierced me—almost like I had stumbled upon a massasauga, the deeply reclusive rattler of these parts, coiled before me on the path, its satanic eyes shining and fastened on mine, its forked tongue flashing.

Lucy took notice and whispered, in her private voice, "Trey, what is it? What's wrong, dear?"

I waved my hand and gave a little laugh. "Nothing. Mosquito, I guess. Darn things."

Lucy was *never* to be fooled. She squeezed my hand, my fingers, tightly, as if to drive away that which was vexing me.

Dana had always, rather proudly, made himself a bit like a brother to me—albeit a black sheep of a brother. And yet a black sheep who had dutifully played by all the rules, so far as I knew, and he had done very well indeed: lovely wife; beautiful, well-raised sons; pleasant house—on Vernon Heights Boulevard, no less; office job at the Shovel—but still a black sheep, of sorts. I think Dana had more or less stumbled, almost by luck, into his good standing within the community. He had chosen his associates well, as if by "animal instincts," as if his keen intelligence were incidental to the connections by which his success came about. My father was quite fond of Dana, I believe. But once late at night, as Dad and I talked in the library, as we sipped scotch (I was a grown man then), Dad said, "You know, Trey, now and again I think there's something not quite right about Dana."

He cast me an indecipherable look and took another sip.

I shrugged. "Well, Dad, Dana is Dana."

He savored his scotch—smuggled by relatives into the country from County Perth, for Prohibition was then in force—and he said, "Yes. Dana is Dana. No doubt about it. Fine fellow, all in all."

We left it at that.

I often wished that Dana was not there.

I wished that Dana was not there now.

More to the point, I wished that he had never met Matthias Mende.

At Goose Pond Farm, the woods surrounding the mound soar from the prairie like the walls of an ancient citadel. When I was a child my mother gave me an illustrated volume of the legends of King Arthur and the Knights of the Round Table. I am sorry to say that it was lost somewhere in the shuffle when we moved from the brick house on Vine Street. I remember many of the drawings, but in particular I remember one of the knights, I believe Percival, riding his white horse through a flowered meadow towards the soaring, gate-like opening in a dark forest. As we entered into the trees we passed through one of those chilly pockets in the air which, as children, we believed were ghosts. Perhaps quite appropriately such spaces had become the final, most substantial mementos of my long ago courtship with Mitzy von Leuckel. During the ensuing years, long after our mutual, romantic adventures, on those occasions when I happened to pass through such exhalations, I might find the young Miss von Leuckel flitting through my thoughts. And her quaint line would ever return to me, "Land filled with ghosts."

And so I was amused when, just as we passed through that particular sentinel-like pocket, Matt said, "Say, you got any ghosts out here, Mr. Hamilton?"

I gave a little laugh. "Oh, do we got ghosts! We've got a land *filled* with ghosts! You felt that cool spot back there? What do you think that was!"

"Tristan," Lucy said, "you'll scare him."

Matt and I both laughed.

"Matt," she said, "don't you let Mr. Hamilton pull your leg like that. I been coming out here since before we were married and I've never seen nor heard a single ghostly thing in all those years. Mr. Hamilton does that, you know—teases people. So pay him no mind."

"Mrs. Hamilton, even if there are a few spooks roaming 'round out here, I don't think they could hold a candle to a Kraut barreling out of the clouds in a Messerschmitt."

"That's what you think," Dana said. "You're in Harding Country. Watch your back."

Lucy said, "Trey and I haven't been back here since the day the Japs surrendered. We drove out here tooting our horn, and then we climbed the mound and drank a bottle of Champagne—from the bottle!"

I added, "And we sang *America the Beautiful*. We sang and drank and laughed. It was a day unlike any other in the world."

"We were mad with joy—delirious, just like everyone else, from sea to shining sea."

The woods felt damp and cool and birds twittered in the high treetops, some taking wing at the noise of our approach. All sorts of exotic characters make themselves at home at Goose Pond Farm and the adjacent Sanctuary Lands. I am no "birder" and so must plead ignorance on the more unusual species, but I do know that warblers, terns, thrushes, orioles, and kinglets inhabit these parts. Of course I recognize sparrows and robins and the like that inhabit the trees, as well as the starlings at nightfall, the cranes standing on their spindly, twig-like legs along the creeks and in the bogs, and the owls perched in the treetops after sunset. Suffice it to say that quite a feathered menagerie lives in those secret, tucked-away lands, unnoticed by mankind.

Our mound is a few hundred yards into the woods, so you would never know it is out there, though someone from afar might notice a very high hickory towering above the other trees. But more likely, someone from the road would take no notice of it.

I have lived all of my days in country where Indian lore is as palpable as their "ghosts." Thus the mound does not strike in me the wonder that it might in outsiders—and so far as I know, Matthias Mende was the last outsider to set foot in those precincts. Now mind you, lest you think I am making a mountain out of our mound, let me say outright that it is not exactly a place worthy of seeking out, even if one could find it. Basically, it is a pile of dirt and nothing more. In fact, in these parts mounds every bit as high are stashed away in plain sight—for instance, in the remnants of the Old Forest behind Harding High School—and those mounds are much easier to find. But differences exist. My theory is that the builders of our mound, clever fellows that they were, used a small glacial hillock to give their little mound a great boost heavenwards, making it appear to be upwards of seventy feet in height.

And before I proceed, I wish to compliment our savage builder—our foreman, as I like to think of him—the fellow who no doubt walked about the place, perhaps with a hawk's feather in his hair, scanning and surveying by eye, instructing his fellow savages to dump another bushel of dirt here, another there, to tamp it down a bit more in one place and even it out a bit in another—all the while making improvements and alterations so as to conform the hillock more smoothly to his mound, to his vision. At last, the two became one; nature's hillock became his mound.

So dense am I that I was well into manhood before I even realized the essence shared by that fellow and me. We were both fabricators, we both dragged earth from earth—be it soil, stone, or wood—and reshaped it, thrusting it upwards, using our vision to fill an emptiness.

I am sure my savage builder had a name. And what I would give simply to know his name! Alas, it has vanished as thoroughly as a coin dropped from the railing of a ship into the high seas. I regard it as our mutual lot to remain in permanent evanescence. My name too will fall into the perpetual oblivion of vanished things.

The surrounding area of the mound precinct is circular—peaceful, mysterious, and beautiful. When we came into the clearing, Matt stopped in his tracks, "Holy cow! Would you look at that!"

After a moment, newly astonished, Dana said, "Well, I'll be! Odd, isn't it? I'd almost forgotten."

The mound soared before us in conical simplicity, like a pyramid without edges faced with weeds and billowing grasses, dandelions and wildflowers, along with a scattering of stunted trees—all green and dark. Afternoon was advancing, the sun declining; here and there within the precincts mists seeped into the clearing in from shadowy places in the woods. At the flattened peak, the hickory's leaves flickered in the golden light of declining day. Somehow the tree has defied centuries of lightning strikes and twisters swirling across these wide, untrammeled prairies. Why, even the tornado that plowed through the woods in my grandfather's day, leaving a now-vanished avenue of mayhem, supposedly passed without even rustling the leaves of "Old Hickory."

Matt said, "Why, you folks got all kinds of things stashed away 'round here, don't you?"

I anticipated a remark from Dana, but he stood mum, surveying the mound.

"I don't know about that," I said, "but we do have this, for what it's worth, which of course isn't much. Just a queer curiosity, that's all it is, when you think of it."

"But how'd it get here? How'd they get all this, this soil, this *earth* back here? Where the hell'd it come from? Why, it's like a pyramid or something, like someone's giant sandcastle. I don't get it."

"Well, not to shatter illusions," I said, "but it's about 90 percent natural and only 10 percent mound, I believe. Or maybe 70/30, if that. My theory is that they built it on top of a little glacial hill and then made adjustments accordingly, so it looks like it's all mound, but I'm almost sure it isn't. Much of it's glacial, from the last ice. That's my theory."

"How do you know that?"

"Well, because it is. It's only logical. Glacial hillocks are a dime a dozen in these parts. The savages turned this one into a mound, that's all. Very clever of them."

We stood for an admiring moment.

"So," I said, "are we going to stand here all day all agog or go up top and get a gander of the countryside?"

Addy said, "I'm going to stay right here, thank you. As it is my calves will file a complaint tonight, with all this walking."

"Me too," Lucy said. "I'll stay with Addy. Though if you gentlemen see Lake Erie, give a holler. I'll be up in a flash."

She gave Dana a chiding wink.

My grandmother placed a stone bench in a little grove off the path, facing the mound. Parts of the seat were covered with moss and lichen, making it very antique and pretty looking. And it is surprisingly comfortable—a good place to sit and read of a summer afternoon. Once or twice a year, usually in July and August, Lucy and I would pack a picnic lunch and venture back with our books. We were known (at least to the birds) to steal little kisses there too. Lucy and Addy settled themselves on this bench.

And so we trudged up the slope, Matt, Dana and I through the sun-warmed grasses, the buttercups and daisies, the prairie orchids and forget-me-nots and, of course, the dandelions. I do not know if it is true, as I have not the curiosity to look it up, but Addy once said that our most populous weed, the dandelion, was an immigrant from the steppes of Asia—though she was at a loss as to how on earth it got here—or perhaps I should say here, there, and everywhere. The climb up our little mound is not terribly steep, and to this day I can ascend in a minute or so flat, faster if I wish. But I remember that on that particular day poor Dana had to lag behind, to pause and catch his breath midway up. Matt and I reached the top and, when I turned around, Dana was a still good thirty paces behind, florid in the face and standing with his hands on his hips, like an exhausted runner at the end of a very long race.

Frankly, something in me was glad to see his manly humiliation and I called out, with a derisive laugh, "Say there, old man, too many Lucky Strikes?"

He shook his head in lieu of a remark, but then he mustered enough breath to answer, rather, "Not enough."

At the time I did not appreciate the seriousness of his condition. Only in looking back did I realize that Dana's windedness likely had to do with the heart problem that would cripple him and then claim him within a few years—more than a bit like President Harding climbing the steps at Tioga in July of 1922.

The top of our mound is flat and circular, about nineteen feet across in most places, with the hickory soaring from the center. I have no idea who planted the tree; I only know that it was already ancient on the day my grandfather discovered the mound, nearly a hundred years ago. Matt seemed more interested in the level area at the top than the view itself, which admittedly is not spectacular, especially, I am sure, if one has flown thousands of feet above Europe in a Mustang. He said, "I wonder what they did up here, why it's flat."

"Who knows? Probably don't want to know."

"I want to know, Mr. Hamilton." And then, looking about, he mused, "A fine place to slay Isaac."

Matt was pushing the toe of his new "penny loafer" into the grass beneath the hickory, as if probing.

"No digging up here, young man, if that's what you're thinking. You save all your digging for down there, in the backyard."

He blushed. "Sir, you know I wouldn't do that. That is I *hope* you know. Though I'd like to."

Just then, Dana dragged himself onto the summit. Apparently, my chiding had reminded him of his needs, and he was already taking long drags on another Lucky Strike, as if that would help him catch his breath. He seemed embarrassed by his delay. "What do you expect?" he said. "I live in a ranch house."

I believe that Matt and I both cast bemused looks his way.

"Don't have any stairs to climb," he explained, "not used to it." As he said that, he scanned the northern vistas, searching for that fabled boyhood view of Lake Erie, sixty some miles away. The horizon, already hinting of night, faded into shadows and blue-gray mists.

Dana said, "So here we are, Trey, like when we were boys."

"Yes, here we are, Dana."

And he added, "At least some places never change, even as we grow old."

The hickory leaves rustled and breezes combed through the prairie grasses. To the north, the far reaches of Marion County stretched into Crawford County, and in all directions—Ohio, resplendent in her deep and varied greens of early summer, the late afternoon sun sparkling on far-off ponds and wetlands, the ripples like the wings of golden butterflies. And Tymochtee Creek to the west, winding like a serpent through the long billowing grasses. Miles before us, the dome of the Wyandot County Courthouse rose seemingly tiny from the cluster of trees marking the village of Upper Sandusky, and to the south, even more distant, our own Courthouse dome, like a miniscule silver knob on the horizon. Had I the presence of mind, I would have brought my binoculars so we could have viewed the crowning bronze statue of Lady Justice, blindfolded and holding her scales.

I pointed to the woods where Captain Pipe and his Indians flayed Colonel William Crawford and roasted him alive on a bed of red-hot embers. That's when I told Matt of the skirmish and the musket balls embedded in the tree bark and still visible when I was growing up. I knew his curiosity would lead him there by week's end.

I have long noted that the view from our mound, while not spectacular, nevertheless seems to impart a sort of inner quiet. Thus we found ourselves standing in silence, looking off into the distance—"musing," as Lucy used to say.

Why, even Dana kept his trap shut for a change.

In the west, Venus shimmered through the fiery glow of that fading Sunday afternoon in June 1947.

After some minutes, I said, "Gentlemen, I suppose we best be off. Addy has to get up at the crack of dawn, and tomorrow *is* another day."

Back at the house, Matt walked the four of us to the car.

I wished him well and teased him not to burn the place down, and bade him to enjoy his stay and his trip to Lake Erie, if I did not see him before.

We shook hands. He and Dana did the same. And then we rode away in Addy's big '38 Cadillac, the Flying Fortress.

Once out on the road, I glanced back. Matt was standing in the yard beneath the old buckeye, watching us depart. We exchanged a wave.

I never saw nor heard from him again.

VIII

❧

"My Earthly Days Are Done,
Yours Go On. Live"

ALREADY DAY LEANS TOWARD NIGHT and any moment now Mitzy and her son will pull into the drive. Rob Roy was over a while ago clearing snow for the second time today, and said he would come back, if need be. Earlier, I was listening to my transistor as I shaved. President Johnson has issued a Thanksgiving Day proclamation that Cape Canaveral will henceforth be known as the John F. Kennedy Space Center, in honor of our late President's keen interest in the space program. WMRN carried the speech live and Mr. Johnson said, "From this midnight of tragedy, we shall move forward to an America of greatness."

Rather articulate for a Texan, though I suspect someone put the words in his mouth.

As we all know, President Kennedy wrote his own speeches.

On this day my heart goes out to Mrs. Kennedy and to her two little ones—*our* little ones, since they are now the fatherless children of our beloved, martyred President, and thus of our nation. I think of Mrs. Kennedy, of little Caroline and John-John, and their sorrowful Thanksgiving dinner, said by the radioman to be going on at this very moment in Hyannis Port. Here in Marion the snow falls quite peacefully but, as the reporter said, dismal rains pelt Cape Cod and seventy mile an hour winds blow from Nantucket Sound, ripping at the flag that flies half-mast at the Kennedy Compound.

448

I believe all of us everywhere today share the same Thanksgiving board: one of mixed plenty and emptiness.

From this week forward, nothing shall ever be the same.

After the fires in the parlor and dining room grates were burning good and strong, I descended into the cellar and dusted off the very last of my father's winemaking efforts—what Dad called, with a wink, his "Catawba port." In other words, his own Ohio wine fortified with fine, strong brandy. The year penciled on the label is 1912.

For long years after Dad's death, Adeline, Lucy, and I opened a bottle each Thanksgiving and then again on Christmas Day. Addy always had Stilton shipped in from England and pears from the Northwest. And so every Christmas the Hamiltons enjoyed a real English-style dessert. When we finally came down to the last bottle, the bottle I dusted off today, we decided to set it aside for some future, appropriate occasion. That future outlived both Addy and Lucy. And here I am. Suffice it to say, when one reaches one's proverbial three score years and ten, one's appropriate future occasions have narrowed to a precious few. So in spite of Dr. Sawyer's remarks, I shall forego the presumption of a long stretch of future years and simply be done with it.

Earlier today Mrs. Christian telephoned Heidi Blakely, to inquire about Carl and to check as to whether Mrs. Blaine and her son (both guests at the Blakely house) still intend to venture forth in this snowfall. Heidi said, "Mom says she'll be there come hell or high water, by snowshoe if need be. And Arrian's looking forward to it too."

I smiled when I heard "come hell or high water" and "by snowshoe if need be." Just like something Mitzy would have said fifty years ago. Something essential always persists in each of us, something present in youth and abiding long after youth is gone.

Now as you can imagine, I am a bit edgy about all of this, and I suppose that is to be expected. No doubt Mrs. Blaine is a little nervous too.

I am sure she has greatly changed—and I do not simply mean the inevitable gray hair and wrinkles; I mean in her thoughts, in her ways of looking at the world, in who she has become as opposed to who she was, before her marriage and her children, before the inevitable disappointments and gratifications of life on earth. What worries me is, after fifty years, will we have much to say to each other?

Thank heavens Arrian will be here. I have not seen him in years and I wonder to what extent, in middle age, he will resemble his father. When he was young, he was a dead ringer for his mother.

Anyway, I can assure you, I shall have *much* to tell him. I am sure his mother has told him how very well I knew the President. And Mrs. Harding as well. I have personal knowledge and recollections of Mr. Harding that no one living could possibly possess—knowledge derived, to some extent, from those long summer evenings in 1910—the year of Mr. Harding's failed gubernatorial bid. George Christian and Harry Daugherty and I used to sit with Mr. Harding in his parlor planning his campaign, drafting speeches and such—"scheming," as Mr. Harding called it. But we also passed those evenings just plain old talking. And sometimes, long after dark, after George moseyed home across the yard, and after Harry grabbed his hat and "hoofed it" (as he used to say) back down Mt. Vernon Avenue towards Hotel Marion, after they were gone, Mr. Harding would sometimes encourage me to stay and "not rush off." By then the hour was usually pretty late and Mrs. Harding, of course, had already retired to their room above us.

His mother died a couple of months before and he seemed a little lost and nostalgic—fully understandable, of course, especially considering how very close they were. Warren Harding loved his mother as much as any son ever. Once or twice, when it was just Mr. Harding and I, I saw tears well up in his eyes when he talked about her. That summer he reminisced a lot about his boyhood days in Blooming Grove and about his early years with the *Star*—things like that; "happy days" as he called them. If I may say so, I know more about the twenty-ninth President of the United States than anyone alive, including Arrian's mother, Nan Britton, and anyone else. Things large and small, like what the President's mother's favorite flower was (the lemon lily). According to Mr. Harding's memory, Phoebe somehow coaxed her beautiful lemon lilies into bloom weeks before their ordained time and managed to keep them blooming weeks after. Apparently, they were especially beautiful and lavish in her garden at Blooming Grove. And who else still walking this earth knows about the time in the early 1870s, when Warren was a little boy, when the Seventh Day Adventists got it into their heads that the world would end on such and such a day, precisely at sunset. Mr. Harding said that his mother made for them white robes out of bed sheets. (Tryon, Warren's father, refused to wear a robe or to take part.) Dressed like angels, the faithful stood in a field somewhere over in Blooming Grove singing hymns and looking westward, trembling as the sun began to set, as they waited for that blast from Gabriel's trumpet, when Jesus and all His angels would descend on a cloud from Heaven to cast the lost into Hell and bring the saved into Heaven.

I bet not even Arrian's mother ever heard *that* particular story. And I bet Warren never told Mitzy the racy details of his first sexual encounter, which took place in a grove along the Whetstone Creek, with an older girl—a teacher, no less.

But he told me. As Mr. Harding remembered with a smile, "As far as I was concerned, she was just doing her job."

That is one story I shall be sure *not* to include tonight in our dinner table conversation.

In spite of his fondness for snuggling with "the girlies," as he sometimes called them, Mr. Harding preferred the camaraderie and social company of men. I think that, as much as anything, was probably why he had all those poker parties in the White House, for which he has been much maligned by history. Mr. Harding liked to pass long hours at a time with "the fellas." Poker chips and whiskey were just aspects of that camaraderie that he loved so much. Obviously, that impulse played into his undoing, simply because of the sorts of men he gathered around him.

I have the impression that Arrian is a very straight-laced man, and I do hope he understands that his father was merely trying to alleviate his loneliness, out there in Washington, via the poker parties and whiskey in the White House. And likewise, I hope he understands that, aside from the adultery, his father was a highly decent fellow. *And* he remains the most under-credited President in American history—thanks to the blind spots and shallow thinking of historians; thanks also to malicious tongue wagging by the likes of H. L. Mencken and company. Granted, unfortunately, Mr. Harding did drag a few too many of his poker buddies with him into high places. But if you look past the adultery, then President Warren G. Harding's personal integrity was of the highest.

And not only was he a good President, why, he was learning quickly and he was poised to become nothing short of majestic—had destiny not robbed him of his term.

I do hope that Arrian is able to understand that his father was a decent man, as well as an exemplary and *honest* President.

That, more than anything, he shall learn this day from this visit.

It has been occurring to me that perhaps I have spoken overmuch of Mitzy in the past few days, and I simply wish to assure you, again, that through the many long years of my marriage to Lucy, Mrs. Blaine scarcely crossed my mind. Indeed, I would venture to say that she was every bit as remote to me as Hezekiah Neil was to Lucy.

I was wondering, a little while ago, what Lucy might say if her spirit returned to comment upon my Thanksgiving Day plans with Mrs. Blaine, my long-lost first sweetheart. Upon considering this, I imagined most vividly the two of us seated side by side on our sofa back at home, down the avenue in the house where we spent our long years together. The fire crackled in the grate, this very same snow fell past our windows, and Lucy leaned forward, rested her cheek in her hand, and said, "Trey, don't be an old stick in the mud. My earthly days are done, yours go on. *Live.* When the time comes, we'll be together again."

I was watching through the lace of the parlor windows when an enormous forest green Lincoln Continental appeared on the snowy avenue. It slowed as its front, whitewall tires approached the carriage drive, and then it paused, as if hesitant. I glimpsed through the passenger window an attractive, gray-haired lady, her gaze turned this way, and then the Lincoln swung into the drive.

A pang of hollowness pierced me, and the sudden unexpected threat of tears.

Most unaccountably, I muttered, "Oh, Lucy, dear sweet Lucy, help me."

The crunch of snow beneath the Lincoln's tires merged with the crackling flames in the hearth. The sedan stopped beside the walkway. After a moment, I heard the opening of car doors, and then the closing.

In the foyer's gilt-framed mirror, I once again smoothed my hair and straightened my lapels and the black tie that I wore in respect for President Kennedy.

And then I turned to open the front door and welcome my guests.

BOOK V

The Return

I

SATURDAY NIGHT
30 NOVEMBER 1963
TIOGA

Goose Pond Farm

NEVER BEFORE in my seventy years of life have I had so many thoughts and feelings to sort through. Never before—until this week beyond all reckoning—has so much simultaneously occurred, both in my personal life and in the world at large. One remarkable turn has followed another, much—though certainly not all—having been unleashed by the Pandora's Box of President Kennedy's assassination; though even that to which it is wholly unconnected seems somehow inextricably entwined with the tragedy. And yet in spite of November 22nd, I feel within myself the gratitude and calm of a new beginning.

A few nights ago Chet Long, my favorite Ohio TV commentator (and my contemporary), noted that those three shots fired in Dallas will echo down through the years in the most unaccountable ways, causing a whole string of events that will likely still be unfolding for the next fifty or one hundred years, whether those events seem connected or not. We shall see, or rather, we and our children and grandchildren shall see—not that I doubt Chet. Indeed, I have seen firsthand countless times how the past stubbornly resists being left behind, how it unceasingly colonizes the future, determining the remote twists and turns of distant years. In fact, already in my imagination, the world after November 22nd somehow feels a bit like the world after the first Great War. By that I mean one sensed

454

in a vague sort of way that some immense shift had altered *everything*. One felt as if the entire world and one's puny life within it had passed through a keyhole, and there would be no going back. The quieter, more innocent earth was no more, and something vast lurked in the offing. One sensed its presence "just around the corner." After the Great War, that *something* was the 20th century—the *everything thereafter* unleashed when that young fanatic in Sarajevo killed the Archduke, the spark that ignited the ever-burning conflagration of continuously unfolding events.

Let me say though that I have a feeling, especially today, that not all will be bad—indeed, far from it. Sort of like a forest fire—vast and all-consuming, horrifying as it rages, but afterwards, new growth, green and pure, and before you know it, birds chirp amid the ashes. In all, I suppose that we can do little more than accept what life sends our way, good or bad, or more likely, both mixed in an intricate, inescapable mesh of tragedies and blessings.

Well, I see that I am nattering on again like some less-than-mediocre "sage"—and mind you, one who did not even finish high school. But as I have made clear, my lack of "education" is hardly my fault. And frankly, I have always liked remembering what my beloved Lucy once told me. I remember I had made one of my self-demeaning comments regarding my lack of education, and she said, "But Trey, it didn't cost you a penny, did it? Made you richer, I'd say. Made you work harder. Made you smarter."

"Smarter?" I said.

"Yes, smarter. You wouldn't have read all those books every night of your life, if you'd been 'educated.' Maybe a few of them in college and such, but not your whole life long, night after night, underlining and jotting notes in the margins. Who else goes to Wiants all the time and orders books that the ladies at the library have never even heard of?"

As usual, my dear wife had a point, and to this day I thank her for that little kindness, for that little illumination, that affirmation. No man on earth ever had a finer, more loving wife than my beloved Lucy and even today I thank God that events long ago unfolded as they did.

Anyway, if you will allow me to carry on a bit longer in my meandering, then I would like to say that I continue to see striking similarities between the deaths of President Kennedy and President Harding. Each died in the West with the First Lady at his side. For each, the crossing of the continent and the lying in state, first in the East Room of the White House and then in the great Rotunda of the Capital, with thousands filing past the coffin—each of which, by the way, rested on the same catafalque that supported the coffin of Abraham Lincoln. Still other similarities exist. According to the *Star*, forty thousand people visited President Kennedy's grave yesterday in the pouring rain—and his widow, before she took her little brood to Hyannis Port, paid a midnight visit to her husband's grave, where she left a sprig of lilies of the valley. For days and weeks after President Harding's death, an almost endless stream of mourners made their way through the gates of Marion Cemetery to stand before the holding crypt where the President's coffin was plainly visible (before I enclosed it in a burial vault, which I in turn encased in asphalt, along about October—something I should have had the sense to do the moment the funeral ended). Mrs. Harding too, in her enormous Pierce-Arrow limousine, made a midnight visit to her husband's resting place, just after the funeral, bearing flowers. And obviously, conspiracy rumors began flying almost immediately after President Harding's death, just as they are flying fast and furious at this very moment.

I must admit, though, that some of the current rumors, or at least questions, demand strong consideration by the FBI and the appropriate authorities. According to a long article in the *Star*, much speculation is occurring both here and abroad that neither Lee Harvey Oswald nor Jack Ruby acted alone. And lots of military and firearms experts, including trained Army snipers, are wondering how Oswald could have so accurately fired three shots within five seconds from one hundred yards—with a twelve dollar bolt-action Italian rifle that he bought through mail order. Records of his Marine service are said not to indicate any such training or ability. Of course one wonders: If Lee Harvey Oswald was working for a foreign power, or even a homegrown extremist group, then why did they not provide him with a high-quality rifle, instead of the cheapest rifle on the market? And I will grant that it is very odd that Jack Ruby could simply walk up to Oswald, in the parking garage of the municipal building, and fire point-blank into his liver, when the assassin (or alleged assassin, if you wish) was surrounded by detectives.

And if Jack Ruby, with his gangster connections, loved and admired President Kennedy and his family so very much, so much that he would personally take it upon himself to avenge his murder, then why did he skip the opportunity of simply walking down the side street, from his seedy little strip joint, to watch the President's motorcade pass?

I suspect that by this time tomorrow, even more questions will bubble to the surface—and in this case, I think many should be given consideration. If the example of our dear and long-forgotten President Harding is any indication, then each question asked will sprout other questions, and each of those, still more, like the multiple heads of some mythical beast. And as Chet Long indicated, many of those questions may persist for decades to come.

I do hope though that none of the rumors are so ludicrous as to implicate Mrs. Kennedy. But with so many nuts out there . . . just wait and see. Put it this way: The Dana Yosts of this world are legion, and they will concoct something.

Before I tell you of my utterly extraordinary visit with Arrian and his mother, let me first say that I had to get out of the house today, not having set foot out of here since my visit to Dr. Sawyer and my errands on Wednesday. And so, aside from making a pass by the Harding Memorial, I also took a drive out to Goose Pond Farm on this cold, gray, final day of November 1963. I guess I desired something simple and my curiosity got the best of me. For one thing, I wanted to see if the shed I built in my youth had managed to withstand our Thanksgiving snowfall. I am pleased to say that it did. Though I shall take no more chances. I managed to pull some of the snow off the roof with a rake. And the moment I arrived back home, I picked up the telephone and arranged for a couple of fellows who used to work for me to go out next week, in this slow season before Christmas, and prop up the rotted beams before the next snowfall. And then come spring, they will replace the roof—basic maintenance that I ought to have attended to along about the summer of '53.

Frankly, I was driven to that "land filled with ghosts" by something else as well, something in the revelations and ambiguity lacing through these busy days of recollection. Fortunately, our efficient county road crews had already plowed Goose Pond Road; otherwise I could not have driven within miles of the place. I did have to leave the car out on the road. Now you can imagine how stark and lonely that old farmhouse looked standing way off in the distance, its windows dark amid blowing snow and skeletal, leafless trees. The snow-covered yard stretched into the lonely prairies and these vanished into the emptiness of endless white. I had already donned my field boots and dug Dad's plaid shirt from the back of the cedar closet, not to mention my heaviest car coat. Matt—both eclipsed and magnified by yesterday—has remained very much on my mind since I found his ring. As I stepped from my car, I again saw him standing in the shade of the old buckeye tree sixteen years and six months ago, on that late Sunday afternoon in June, giving me that long wave good-bye. He was there and then gone. I traipsed up the buried drive through drifts and blowing snow, the only sounds, the crunch of my footsteps and the icy wind whipping out of the north.

I do not know why, but we have always used the back door at Goose Pond Farm; Grandma and Grandpa Hamilton did the same. Thus I dutifully trudged around back, following decades of vanished footsteps, my own and my mother's and the footsteps of others I have loved. When I first saw my old shed standing firm and indomitable under its thick white "hat" of snow, I laughed aloud and called out, "Hey, well done, old man!"

The garden that Matt prepared during the summer of '47 has long since been reclaimed by prairie grass and wildflowers, and nowadays, come summer, Rob Roy mows right over it, so no shrubs or ornaments of any kind hint at its vanished whereabouts, especially in the snow. Far off in the distance, in the unbroken white, the woods rose trimmed with snow, shadows darkening into shadows, and above the treetops, the barren uppermost limbs of the old hickory rose from that great, pyramid-sized Indian mound, concealed by dense woods within its inner circle. For a fleeting moment I imagined Matt and me, and Arrian too, standing at the snowy summit looking across the vast desolation stretching toward Lake Erie, white landscape vanishing into windswept white and gray. But I would not have ventured back there today for the world, not after all that has transpired. Out at the Farm my imagination plays tricks on me, and I had the strangest feeling that if I hiked back there now, alone, then I would vanish from the known world, never to return and no trace of me would ever be found.

This too will sound "imaginative," but sometimes I am half-afraid to enter my own farmhouse. Like today. I found myself pushing open the door, but then simply pausing at the threshold, peering into the shadows. As I stood there, the cold seeped down my back like an icy breath, and I listened for I know not what. I coughed, as if to announce myself, and nudged myself in. Needless to say, all was exactly as I had left it—and yet, something . . . well, once again my imagination was whispering, inaudibly, through veils of unanswered questions.

Now I know what you must be thinking, based on my apprehensions and such: that mysterious incidents took place out there, that perhaps secret pages of the Harding history had been written (and simultaneously expunged) at Goose Pond Farm.

I understand your suspicions and I sympathize with them, especially after all of the cards I have laid on the table—not the least being the admission of my own bewilderment.

But before I go on with today, let me lay before you a few more cards from the past.

I took a trip to Goose Pond Farm in mid-June of 1947, on Saturday afternoon to be precise, six days after Addy and Lucy and me, and Dana Yost too, dropped Matthias Mende off out there.

I simply wanted to check up on things, meaning on Matt and the Harding papers. Lucy made sandwiches for our young guest. I also brought along a couple of bottles of Jim Beam, which I intended not to make an issue of; indeed, I laid them at the bottom of the basket, covering them with some clean bath towels that Lucy had included. Were he not there, then I would discreetly leave them for him in the bungalow, upon his return from Indian Rock.

The assigned patch of ground out back had been broken and nicely tilled, in short, beautifully prepared for Adeline's new garden. I knew she would be very pleased when she saw it, upon her return from the south. She had spoken of planting lavender, though I never really paid attention as to whether she did or not. Personally, I would not know lavender from parsley. Anyway, Matt had obviously been busy. There was no denying he was a good worker—a "real toiler in the vineyards" as Lucy used to say of hard workers, especially those toiling towards a vision.

I knocked on the back door, but received no answer, so I opened it a crack and called, "Hey, Matt. Hello in there."

But the house answered back with the silence of emptiness. I waited, somehow knowing that our friend was *gone*, and not just on a local excursion, off in the countryside, say, pursuing ghosts and history.

"Matthias? Hello in there."

No answer.

I glanced out across the prairies behind me, towards the stand of trees where Colonel Crawford had been flayed and burned alive, thinking that perhaps he had gone for a hike, maybe to examine those ancient trees still faintly scared by musket balls.

I entered the house, laden with the young man's sandwiches and whiskey. I placed these on the counter, wondering at the deep stillness of the place, the emptiness.

I found on the kitchen table a nicely executed charcoal drawing of the farmhouse, with its shade trees. I realized then that, almost certainly, he had already headed for the Lake. The drawing was exquisite and I conjured in my mind an image of our young friend sitting Indian-style in the front yard, rendering this image for Addy and Lucy and me. To this day the drawing hangs in the parlor out there, infused with moody darkness and mystery—elements that seemed inevitably to creep into Matthias Mende's drawings, at least the ones that I saw.

Everything was neat as a pin.

The Harding documents were back in their box on the kitchen table.

I checked to see, and sure enough, the historic and highly valuable Washington Naval Conference treaty was in that box, with the signatures of President Harding, Secretary of State Charles Evans Hughes, Lord Balfour, Barron Kato of the Japanese Empire, and numerous other luminaries of the day, including representatives from Italy, France, New Zealand, et cetera.

That document, worth thousands upon thousands of dollars even back then, was dutifully tucked back in its musty yellow folder—just as I knew, in my heart, that it would be.

I climbed the stairs and entered Matt's room at the back of the house, quite empty of his presence, and I stood by his empty bed, perplexed and personally disappointed that he was already gone, but his efficiency never surprised me. Personally, I was missing him already. He had made his bed very neatly. One could tell that he had slept in a barrack, that he had once had officers thundering about such things, looking for wrinkles in the blankets and such.

The gist of the matter is that he had apparently labored day and night during his stay at the Farm, completed his work, and then hitched to Lake Erie, just as planned. I miscalculated, thinking his work would take him longer.

I felt a little bad for Lucy, for the trouble she had gone to, fixing him sandwiches and cookies and such.

A couple of weeks later, when Matt still had not come back to Marion, Lucy and I took a drive up to Indian Rock to check up on him. That would have been on the 4th of July 1947.

The only evidence of his visit there was an unfinished cup of coffee on the kitchen counter, with spots of powdery white mold floating on top. And a bottle of sour milk in the icebox.

On the counter lay the set of keys I had leant him to the farmhouse and the cottage.

Alas, there was no drawing of Indian Rock with its tower and widow's watch looking out upon Lake Erie, far more picturesque than the stark whiteness and plain lines of Goose Pond Farm.

That day, Lucy took a stroll along East Cliff Road to ask folks if they had seen a young man coming and going from our place.

No one had noticed a thing, no comings, no goings, no lights burning on June evenings.

We drove the seventy miles home in silence.

NOW IN CASE YOUR MIND is following the same thread as Dana Yost's thinking, conjuring the idea of "foul play," as the police blotters say, then allow me to tell you about my sister Addy during that exact same week in time.

She departed for Cincinnati at the crack of dawn on the Monday after we dropped Matt off at the Farm.

In fact, a few days after that, perhaps on Thursday or Friday, Lucy and I received a picture postcard from Addy sent from Hamilton County, one hundred and twenty-some miles to the south. I still have it; instinct told me to keep it in the letterbox.

Indeed, I dug it out early this morning and read it again for the first time since 1947—not that it says much. The picture, in that soft glowing color of old postcards, appearing like a cross between a painting and a photograph, depicts the monolithic tomb of William Henry Harrison, on Mt. Nebo, overlooking the Ohio River. On the back, Addy jotted:

> *Arrived Cin. Mon. in time for supper. Exhausted. Meeting with the O.O.S. [Ohio Orchid Society] this morn then three ladies and I visited Pres. Harrison's tomb. Forgot how pretty Ohio is down in this neck of the woods. The old Cadillac does well. Except a rear flat outside Vandalia. Negro gentleman stopped to fix it. Refused payment, but I got his address. Will send him and his family a nice basket come Christmas. See you soon.*

The card is postmarked June 11, 1947.

Later in the week—the second week of June—Addy called Lucy and me from the Vernon Manor Hotel in Cincinnati to say that, instead of returning to Marion directly, she had decided to take a drive south and pay a visit to the Smokey Mountains.

To tell you the truth, Lucy and I were quite surprised and pleased.

In spite of her youthful years in France, my reclusive sister seldom ventured beyond the outskirts of Marion, excepting her excursions to the Farm and Indian Rock—which we always regarded as extensions of home, of Tioga.

Adeline may have been driving south to the Smokeys on the very afternoon when I drove out to Goose Pond Farm to check on Matt and drop off his sandwiches and Jim Beam.

Why, even Dana received a postcard from Addy. Only later did he seem to forget this telling fact and allow his imagination to run into the deep thickets and the quicksand beyond.

The point is, Adeline was hundreds of miles away during that entire week.

And indeed, during much of the following week as well.

And to think that that dimwitted blabbermouth and fool, that ass, Dana Yost, knew *all of this*!

I tell you, my father and I set him up in life—without us, he would have spent his life clerking in Woolworths, keeping inventory of the bubblegum, balsawood planes, and dollies.

In the weeks and months to come, his mind ran wild. His tongue too, and soon he betrayed us—our lifelong friendship crumbled into the channeled madness of his suspicions and weird, unspeakable affections for Matthias Mende.

And that idiot even embarrassed us and made a further perverse ass of himself by going to the police.

As if he, of all people, had any right filing a missing persons report on behalf of a drifter he barely knew and yet slobbered over and, perhaps, drove away with his own disgusting attentions.

But then again, as I have said before, Matt very well may have simply drowned in the tempestuous and covetous waters of Lake Erie.

By the same token, if Matt did go swimming off the cliffs, and if by some unlucky fate misfortune struck, then what became of his satchel? What became of his portfolio? And the tins with his charcoal and his drawing utensils?

What became of the notebooks that he so diligently kept on President Harding?

Nothing was ever accounted for. At least not by any of us.

Personally, I think the man in him sickened of Dana's weird attentions and the fellow hightailed it out of Ohio, instead of simply telling Dana to go to hell.

Understandably, Matt was too embarrassed to speak of this matter to me—and, frankly, I am grateful that he did not.

The reasons and particulars of his going have obviously slipped into the dark landscape of lost, unknowable things.

TO CONTINUE on with the events of today—at Goose Pond Farm we have always kept the green blinds in the downstairs rooms drawn when we are not there, so you can imagine the inner bleakness of the house today—shadows fleeing into shadows and the vapor of my breath vanishing into them. The house inside was as cold as the outside, albeit cold with an inner dimension and stillness—with the exception of the blinds that seemed to breathe when the wind gusts pounded at the north- and west-facing panes. In the kitchen hangs a sampler from the time of my mother's death; I believe it was a gift from the wife of one of my father's foremen. The embroidered roses are now faded, but the dictum remains quite legible: *Precious hours have perished here.* But on such a day as this, one could scarcely imagine the sun streaming through the windows on summer mornings, the clatter of plates as Lucy set the table, the dogs whining at the back door, wanting their fair share of the meat sizzling on the iron stove, the flies buzzing at the screens, and one or two sneaking in, and Lucy and me pursuing them with our swatters.

In the parlor I paused before Matt's drawing of the farmhouse, displayed in its golden frame. He had executed the picture in the late afternoon or early evening. I can tell because the shadows run long and eastward.

After Matt was some months gone, in the autumn of '47, when I gave up all hope of his return, I traveled to the Farm alone one Saturday afternoon, with the newly framed drawing. Before hanging it, I carried the drawing into the front yard, the leaves falling around me, and I tried to ascertain the exact spot where Matt sat in the grass, executing his sketch. I never told anyone other than Lucy this, but on that day, after I thought I found the spot, I sat Indian-style in the deep cushion of grass and fallen leaves with his drawing on my lap.

And I sat there for the longest time.

When I told Lucy of this incident, she said, "Oh, Trey"—and she pulled me close and kissed my cheek.

This morning I climbed the stairs as softly as possible, the wood creaking in the cold under foot. Sometimes in the house I have the oddest feeling that listeners inhabit dimensions to which no earthly access exists. As I have said, Goose Pond Farm does that sort of thing to one's imagination, especially during the bleakest times of year.

I followed the shadowy hall into the back and paused before the closed door. The white porcelain knob was frigid in my gloveless hand, and in my thoughts were Mitzy's words at Thanksgiving dinner, "In the room at the back of the house, Tristan, upstairs at Goose Pond Farm. There."

Her face was lined but still beautiful in the dinner table candlelight and the flickering glow from the hearth at my back.

"That warm spring weekend," she continued. "You remember. A few months before the first war. You and I, we went out for a weekend. Before Mr. Harding, more or less. Before Lucy. Back when the two of us were one."

And then my astonished gaze at her son—Arrian's gray-blue eyes, Mr. Harding's gray-blue eyes, his nod, his glance away, as if in shame.

His mother touched my hand. She too, like me, had removed her wedding band at sometime during her widowhood.

The hinges creaked in the cold as I shoved open the door. The panes rattled violently in their frames, as if protesting my intrusion, until I closed the door behind me. Then came the affronted peace, the impermeable stillness of a summer place in winter. I heard from above, groaning through the beams and plaster, the creek of the weather vane on the north gable turning in the riotous wind. The very air seemed gray with muted daylight and the plainness of the white walls and wooden floors. The iron-frame bed in the corner by the windows, stripped to the faded blue and white of its mattress. And now, more vividly than before, that long-buried memory of Mitzy and me returned—1914, the two of us stealing out here of a Friday morning, staying till Sunday evening, lying low in the country (the Buick stashed in the backyard, hidden by the house, though I do not think a single wagon or automobile rolled by the entire time). Since Thanksgiving dinner, I have managed to conjure in my mind (or at least my imagination) that visit pretty clearly. I remember the back windows open to the screens, and at night, off in the ponds and wetlands, the songs of the whip-poor-wills and spring peepers, the tree frogs and the hoot of an owl calling through the darkness. The flame of the oil lamp turned low, we stretched glowing and youthful in the golden light. To this day, the same lamp occupies the same nightstand.

When Sunday morning came, I lay with my hand resting on the flat of Mitzy's belly. Her eyes turned toward the ceiling, her thoughts wandering elsewhere. "A penny for your thoughts."

She did not answer, so after a minute or so, I started to repeat, "A penny for your . . ."

"Nothing, Tristan. I'm thinking of nothing."

But after a moment she turned to me, "Tristan, what do you think of me?"

"What do I think of you!?"

"Yes, what do you *really* think of me?"

I kissed her lips. "I think the world of you. You can't tell?"

"What kind of girl do you think I am?"

"The best! The cat's pajamas, the best of the best. You're swell, Mitzy. And on top of that, you're the kitty's mittens."

She laughed at my corniness and gave me a sudden squeeze that made me gasp.

"Oh, don't do that," I said, in pain. "Not down there."

She laughed at my pain and said, "You'll live, silly boy." And then, "I think you're swell too, Tristan."

A tone of seriousness returned to her voice as she said, "Remember that I said that; remember forever and a day that I think you're swell."

I thought something was on her mind and we lay quiet in the morning light and then she said, "No one will ever think me a maiden, will they?"

"What? Mitzy! What are you saying? I never talk about what we do. I never brag, not like other boys do."

"I know you don't. You're different. Ordinary in your way, but different too. As Momma says, 'Honorable. A gentleman.'"

I laughed. "And if she saw us *now?*" I kissed her cheek and snuggled my face into her face and, truth to tell, I cupped her breast in my youthful, grasping hand. "You're mine," I whispered, "all mine." I nibbled her earlobe. "And I'm yours, all yours, forever and a day. We'll marry, when you're done with college, since that's the way you want it, or the way you say you want it, or we'll marry tomorrow, if you'd like it that way. And I'll build you a nice big house. Dad said I can. You pick out the plans. You pick out the land. And then we'll raise a family. Just the way it's supposed to be."

She turned her head towards the window and we lay in silence. "Marion," she said.

"We'll take trips. We can sail to France and see Addy in Paris, and I'm sure you'll want to add Heidelberg and Dresden to your list. We'll hop a night train to Berlin, and sail on that river down to Bavaria and see the big fairytale castle you've always wanted to see, whatever it's called."

She did not answer, but lay looking through the window, into the vast distance, morning sunlight lying across the land.

Mitzy always liked poetry, so I had memorized poems on her behalf; in truth, I had even written a few (none of my copies survived the termination of our courtship). In an attempt to shift her mood, I began, "How do I love thee? Let me count the ways. I love thee to the depth and breadth and height . . ."

"Oh, Tristan, please, not now! I can't listen to that crap now."

Frankly, I felt as if she had slapped my face; nevertheless, after a stunned moment or two, I lay my head on her shoulder, attributing her sudden burst of bad temper to the legendary fickleness of the weaker sex. I looked across the shapely mounds of breasts, through the window and out upon the rolling land, the young world teeming with springtime and sunlight.

BUT TODAY of course, forty-nine and a half years later, the view through the same window swept into billowing white, into the indistinguishable horizon in the north. Words from a reading last Sunday in church returned to me: "In that place where the ends of the earth and the ends of the sky meet."

And as I turned from the window an image of Matt flickered into my thoughts, him in the same bed on a night many decades later, propped on a pillow, reading whatever library book he may have had, maybe a few of the Harding papers spread beside him on the sheets, a glass of whiskey glittering on the night table, himself wiry like me in my youth, shirtless and handsome in the golden lamplight.

I do not know what possessed me, but before I left the bedroom I opened the closet door—as if perhaps Matt had maybe left something behind, something other than his ring, perhaps a long overlooked jacket, or one of those nice new shirts he had bought at Jim Dugan's. And I wondered again whatever had happened to that wool Air Corp coat, the one draped upon his shoulders like a cape, out at the Memorial, on the day when I first laid eyes upon him, the one he wore until the cool days abated.

But the closet contained only the familiar age-old contents—three hopelessly fragile and old-fashioned summer dresses from Grandmother Hamilton's day hung on the wooden rod, suspended by their ancient wooden hangers, as if still awaiting her return, more than half a century after she had passed both from and into the earth. Why those dresses had never been given to the poor long, long ago, when they would have been of use to someone is utterly beyond me. I only keep them because my father and sister kept them, and because they have always been there. A couple of bandboxes occupy the lone shelf, also from Grandma's day, and several ancient books, including two Bibles and a hymnal from the Crawford Community Church—"Christmas 1873" inscribed on the inner cover in Grandmother Hamilton's hand.

I stood on my tiptoes and felt around the shelf, behind bandboxes and Bibles, and felt the deep corners, though frankly, I do not know what I was looking for. What I found was the dust of decades encrusting my fingers.

I even opened the top couple of drawers in the chest, finding only stacks of musty bed linens that have not been slept on for years.

Thus, finding nothing, I departed the house. Using the footprints I had made in the snow upon my arrival, I fled across the frigid land toward the warmth of my trusty Lincoln.

But at the risk of sounding a bit loony, I must confess that I did something peculiar out there. It happened when I opened the car door. With one leg in, I paused, looking across the car roof to the bare, ancient tree and the farmhouse, the vast and darkening desolation stretching away. Without a moment of forethought, I heard myself calling out, "Matt?"

I listened.

Just the silence of winds.

I called again, "Matthias!"

I listened as deeply as I could.

And yet again, I hurled his name into oblivion, "Matthias!"

The snow swarmed from the whiteness and, far-off and not so far-off, atop the Indian mound, the bare limbs of the hickory stood black against the leaden sky. The world is freighted with mysteries, and Marion has more than its share. We shall never know what became of Matthias Mende or how my sister came into possession of his beloved ring. We shall never know what secrets Adeline took to her grave; the same can be said of Mrs. Harding. We shall never know if there was more to President Harding's death than apoplexy. These are unknowable things, everlasting secrets.

Too much has come to pass this week. I am ashamed to admit (nevertheless, I shall) that, as I stepped into my car, tears began welling in my eyes and running down my cheeks.

As I drove away, I vowed not to return to Goose Pond Farm until the peepers and the whip-poor-wills begin to sing again, come spring.

II

🌹

The New Leaf

SO LET ME TELL YOU ABOUT YESTERDAY, how I stood at the front door peering through the lace curtains and lightly falling snow as my guests came along the walkway. At first, I scarcely noted Arrian. As for Mrs. Blaine, I must say she has aged considerably, albeit gracefully. I seem to have no vivid recollections of her from those long middle decades when she was married to Jim, though she was living, for many of those years, right here in Marion. Thus it was Mitzy von Leuckel, the girl I knew during the earlier century, from whom I took my references, the pretty girl who lifted her skirt above her knees to avoid thickets during our summer walk through the Old Forest; the girl who ran her probing fingers over my father's desk and the curlicues of his bookcase, murmuring, "Yes—yes, exactly like this"; and the young lady standing in the gardens at Lake Etowah in a cloak of royal blue, her hand caressing the snout of a stone leopard, before she turned to me, as if startled. It was this sensual girl upon whom I superimposed the older woman coming along the walkway. She glanced a bit warily (or so it seemed to me) towards the house she had not entered for half a century. The Lake Erie storm was beginning to abate and the snowflakes were drifting somewhat more lightly now, settling upon her "pillbox" hat and in her abundant gray hair, which she still wore in the Gibson Girl fashion of her youth. The long dark cloak and black gloves gave her a sweeping, aristocratic look. I was watching from the inner shadows, behind lace. She paused at the bottom of the steps and said something to her son, perhaps about Tioga. They paused, arm-in-arm, looking up, their eyes moving over the house.

469

Only then did I glance at the President's son, expecting to see some reminder of Mr. Harding. Arrian has always favored his mother, but instead of seeing in his face either his mother or his father, I was startled to find myself facing yet another uncanny reminder of Matthias Mende. Granted, if I had not found his ring that very morning, then I do not think the similarity would have struck me so quickly. Arrian is, after all, several years older than Matthias would be now. Besides, Arrian is presently about twice the age that Matt was during his time in Marion, more than sixteen years ago. Nevertheless, I assure you, the reminder that I glimpsed in his features could not be wholly attributed to my imagination. Something coincidental in his facial features struck up the reminder, something in the cut of his hair or the trim frame of a youthful man in middle age.

A new wave of anxiety swept through me, along with a sort of inexplicable sorrow, and suddenly I regretted not fortifying myself with a comforting glass of scotch. There was a hollowness in the pit of my stomach, like a hermit might feel when confronted with an unexpected journey into the *terra incognito*, in the company of others.

As my guests mounted the stairs, I opened the door.

Mrs. Blaine stopped as if startled. No doubt she was feeling her own sense of disquiet.

I held the door open wide and announced, as I had rehearsed in my thoughts, "Mrs. Blaine, Dr. Lang, welcome to Tioga. I would wish you a Happy Thanksgiving, but I hardly think it is in order this year. Perhaps a Reflective Thanksgiving is more like it."

Mrs. Blaine smiled slightly, perhaps finding a bit of humor in my little prepared speech. In the back of my mind I thought of her chiding me in my youth for supposedly wearing "starched underwear."

"Oh, Tristan," she smiled, "dear Tristan, how very good to see you. And thank you for having us."

The warmth of her words and voice touched me. "Thank you for joining me."

Surely she was superimposing the old man before her with the lithesome and malleable boy she had romped with in her girlhood days, and to whom she had taught so very many worldly things. I had planned for a simple handshake. In fact, as I welcomed Mrs. Blaine, I extended my hand and she clasped it, but we somehow mutually dissolved into a long embrace. I could smell the old-fashioned rose water. "How good to see you, too, Mrs. Blaine," I softly said in her ear. I did not mean to, but I kissed her cheek.

The last human being with whom I had shared an embrace was Lucy and so perhaps I held her a moment longer than I should have. Perhaps it was the same for her—we two former, youthful lovers in the embrace of widowhood and old age.

I noticed that Dr. Lang had a certain watchfulness—something like wonder—and I would have given plenty to have read his thoughts.

"You remember Arrian."

"Indeed, I do, though it's been a very long time."

As we shook hands I thought I could see the President's gray-blue eyes in his.

"Dr. Lang," I said, "I'm not sure if you favor more your father or your mother."

"His father," Mrs. Blaine said, "if you spent time with him, you'd know."

"Ah then, let that get you into high places—but not into mischief."

They both laughed. He said, "I'll do my best, sir."

The homey aromas of Thanksgiving Day seeped beyond the closed doors of the distant kitchen and crept lightly through the house, the roasting turkey, the sweet spices, the chestnuts on their tray in the oven, not to mention the light fragrance from the cherry logs, with which I had built the fire. I wondered if Emma Linda had heard the car doors from way off in the back of the house. I knew for a fact that her mother had not. "What a wonderful aroma," Mrs. Blaine said. "The first whiff of the holidays."

Arrian concurred.

As I took their wraps, I said, "I am sure that you're quite aware, Dr. Lang ..."

"Arrian, sir, please call me Arrian."

"Arrian, I am sure you are quite aware that my entire family knew President Harding very, very well. Perhaps I'll tell you later how Dad saved your father, when he was a young man, from the wrath of Mr. Amos Kling, his future father-in-law. Specifically, from bankruptcy."

But as I hung their coats in the closet, I regretted my offer. After all, there was no telling that particular story without making references to his father's Negro blood. So I add, "But I have lots of stories. Perhaps that one's not the place to begin."

Mrs. Blaine stood gazing into the shadows at the top of the staircase, remembering heaven knows what. She appeared as if straining to listen to something far off.

I too glanced into those distant shadows. The early darkness of late November gathered in the upper hall, the balustrade of birdseye maple marching up the stairs with progressive dimness; nevertheless, I imagined again in that moment, in my recollections, President and Mrs. Harding, and Addy and me, climbing those stairs on the bright sunny morning of July 3rd, 1922. When I first showed Mitzy the upper rooms on that summer afternoon in 1912, we sneaked up the back staircase (I suppose to add intrigue to our adventure)—in spite of the fact that we were alone in the house.

"Why, it's amazing," Mrs. Blaine said, gazing about her, "Tioga seems not to have changed at all. It's as if—why, it's as if time simply passed it by."

I laughed at the naïve and charming incorrectness of her view. "For the house, maybe, but it certainly marched on for the rest of us. Now it's just me and Mrs. Christian. Everyone else—gone, years gone."

"And this mirror—" Mrs. Blaine said, her voice trailing off as she studied her reflection.

I wondered if she was remembering that afternoon when she and I stood right there, exactly in that same place, my hands caressing her shoulders, on her first visit to Tioga—though maybe that was just a moment that had permanently settled into my mind, not hers.

"That mirror," I said, "has seen its share of faces. Including, if you don't mind me saying so, Thomas Edison, Henry Ford, and Harvey Firestone. It hung in the foyer on Vine Street—we lived in a brick house there, before Dad built Tioga. Why, even my mother's young and beautiful face glided over its surface. Developed its own age spots, as you can see. So time *has* stolen into Tioga, though we've done our best to keep the place up. Especially Addy. She was meticulous in its care. Me a bit less so."

Arrian seemed to keep studying me, a most quizzical look in his eyes, as if he were simultaneously searching for something and witnessing it too. I said, "Arrian, more than once your father stood right there, before that very mirror touching up his hair and tie before dinner."

He nodded.

"You know," I added, "President Harding was every bit as meticulous about his appearance as President Kennedy was. And every bit as handsome too, just older. They have quite a few things in common, you know. Not only the fact that exactly—well, almost exactly—forty years separate their Inaugurations *and* their deaths."

I wondered if Arrian was a Democrat, like his mother and me, or a Republican, like his father.

I gestured toward the parlor, though even as I did, Mrs. Blaine glanced back through the double doors of the library. Bulbs in the chandelier glimmered like tiny candle flames and the room glowed darkly on the curlicues of my father's desk. The bookshelves, massive and silent, stood like giant palisades looming in the shadows. Evening had gathered in the eastern bay windows and the distant trees of the Old Forest stood stark in late day wintry shadows. For a moment in my thoughts Mitzy circled again beneath the chandelier, gazing up at her youthful reflection in the golden ball. I wondered if Mrs. Blaine (or anyone) had ever told Arrian the long-forgotten story of Orrin de Pue.

The parlor was all aglow—crackling fire in the hearth and two small lamps glowing on the tables. An hour before, Mrs. Christian had come in and lit the candles, including the stout candle that the Sawyers brought from Bavaria—with the Cross glowing between the stag's horns in bas-relief, and the hunter, on one knee, his musket cast aside. The last time I used this room to entertain some cousins on my mother's side, Mr. Christian noted after their departure that some figurines belonging to my grandmother had vanished from our possession, including my little white statue of a soldier of the Grand Army of the Republic, leaning against his horse. My grandmother had given that memento to me in my boyhood. Never again shall I consort with those thieves, "family" or not. Anyway, I had already arranged three chairs around the coffee table, facing the fireplace, and the fire flickered upon polished glass over polished black walnut. The cherry wood logs burning in the fireplace added a sweet, subtle fragrance and my father's bronze statue of an Indian warrior, on horseback, bow in hand, gleamed in the corner with its secrets. As Mrs. Blaine took a seat, she said, "What a momentous week it has been!"

"You can say that again. Like the sneak attack on Pearl Harbor, albeit without the war." I feared that my words, in spite of their gravity, somehow sounded trivial. I added, "Nothing will ever be the same. I suspect we could all use a drink."

I told my guests of the liquors and such that we keep (much of it in the cabinet since Adeline's day), and as I did, I pressed the hidden wall button that Addy had installed back in the '20s or '30s, buzzing the kitchen—the first time I have ever used this little convenience, though I now feel that it may not be the last.

As I was pouring drinks—a glass of sherry for Mrs. Blaine, a highball for her son, the usual scotch for me—I added, "Wait and see. Another Pandora's Box has opened—that's what November 22nd is, one of those rare—I don't know quite how to say it," (though I knew perfectly well how to say it) "one of those rare, everlasting days. November 22nd will never go away, even when we think it's long faded. It will still be here. Anyway, we shall see what Lyndon Baines Johnson does with his presidency, what he does with us. I just hope he leaves his cowboy hat in Texas."

My guests laughed at my comment, though I did not mean it in lightness, and then we sat for a moment in the quiet of sobering reflections. I thought of telling Arrian that his father was the one responsible for making Pearl Harbor the great naval base that it was on that other momentous day, December 7, 1941, that more than any President in the 20th century, Mr. Harding had organized the superstructure for the Navy, even as it is today, and that, indeed, he militarily prepared the United States for the 20th century, whilst remaining true to the disarmament conference that he himself convened in Washington. In short, I thought about further illuminating Arrian in regards to the President's many, many accomplishments during his brief tenure, regarding peace and war, but I did not want to distract from President Kennedy's sacrifice, so for the time being, I decided to keep mum. I sensed that other occasions would unfurl for us.

Mrs. Blaine said, "I not only feel sympathy for Mrs. Kennedy and little Carolyn and John-John, but also for Mrs. Oswald and her two little ones."

"Oh, absolutely. Talk about the most innocent of bystanders!"

"Can you imagine! Twenty-two years old, a sweet, shy-looking thing. Pretty too. And her life ruined—and those poor little girls, their lives ruined. How will they be treated in the schoolroom, not to mention the playground? Children can be cruel, sometimes even more so than adults."

"Ha!" I said, remembering.

"I hope she has the good sense to change all their names and move to someplace far, far away. Maybe even back to Russia. To think of it—four children left fatherless, two young mothers widowed, the President and his assassin, dead. And poor Officer Tippet."

She sighed and glanced into the shadows in sorrow.

Arrian said, "Some people feel grateful to Jack Ruby. Want to pin a medal on him or something, but there's going to be lots and lots of unanswered questions now. We'll probably never get to the bottom of this. Or even if we do, people'll still have their doubts. It has conspiracy written all over it, even if it wasn't."

I thought of mentioning the rumors surrounding his father's death, but most of those rumors encompassed my sister, so I kept mum.

Mrs. Blaine was saying that Mrs. Oswald and her two baby girls had been placed under Secret Service protection, when Emma Linda rounded the corner with a tray of fancy whipped cream cheese, mixed with chopped parsley and other delights, spread on Ritz crackers.

Mrs. Christian was so pleased that guests were returning to Tioga that, last week she went to Uhler's and purchased, for herself and her daughter, identical dark blue dresses with white collars and white aprons. "Uniforms," she called them—"like the 'help' wear in the movies." I believe that she saw them as imparting an almost Hollywood glamour to the occasion.

Emma Linda looked quite pretty in her uniform.

"Emma Linda," I said, "You remember Mrs. Blaine, don't you? And this is her son, Dr. Arrian Lang, from Battelle Memorial Institute."

"I sure do. Welcome to Tioga. And Happy Thanksgiving. Or as Mr. Hamilton said this morning, in this most saddest of years, a 'Thoughtful Thanksgiving.'"

Emma Linda had been very keen on laying eyes on the President's son, but you would never have known it. By her response, one would have thought that Dr. Lang was just an average Joe.

After Emma Linda and our guests exchanged courtesies, Mrs. Blaine said, "Tristan, I was telling Arrian today, as we drove past the Memorial, that someone out in Washington should get in touch with you about building a monument for President Kennedy. I bet you're the only man alive who has experience building something as colossal as that."

"Hmm," I thought for a moment, or rather pretended to, as I already knew. "Not really. Remember, the Jefferson Memorial came after ours. It wasn't there in President Harding's day."

"Ah," she seemed to look off, perhaps remembering. "Come to think of it, there were cherry trees over there, back in Warren's day. I used to walk there; nevertheless, Tristan—"

"Arrian," I said, "I'll bet you a dollar you never knew this, but the design for the Jefferson Memorial was first intended for the *Harding* Memorial. The design was submitted to us in competition by Mr. John Russell Pope, though in a slightly different form. He later added a portico or something. It was absolutely beautiful, but we gave it a reluctant thumbs-down. The historians say we did so because we thought we'd be hearing off-color remarks about 'adding a spout and a handle and we'd have a teapot'. As in Teapot Dome, of course. Nonsense, just lies and nonsense. We chose the Hornbostel design simply because it accommodated a tree and gardens. I do not know if you know this, but your father once expressed a desire to be buried beneath a tree—thus he got his wish, a willow."

Mrs. Blaine said, "Yes, Tristan, but in regards to a memorial for President Kennedy, I suspect the Jefferson Memorial was probably made by committee, rather than by a—by a *presence*. I have little doubt that you're the only man alive who has the personal hands-on experience of building such a huge monument in the here and now, and building it from the ground up, every little feature. Tristan, I don't think you're aware of the magnitude of your achievement. You not only got the ball rolling, you put the capstone in place."

I shrugged. "Well, they're welcome to contact me, if they wish. But those clever Harvard fellows, they don't need me. They'd laugh at the thought of me—'Marion, Ohio! Where's that? What's that?' That's what they'd say. And Warren Harding—!" I caught myself and fell mum, so as not to offend the President's son.

Mrs. Blaine said, "They wouldn't laugh if I sent them a couple of picture postcards. Perhaps I'll do that. Perhaps I'll write them and tell them about you, if you don't mind. I saw some names in the *Star* about the committee that's being set up. I cut the article out and kept it."

Again, I shrugged, "I'd help in any way I can, but to tell you the truth, I doubt anything like the Harding Memorial will ever be built again. Not even for President Kennedy. That sort of thing belongs to the ages, just like the President himself. Like President Harding too. The Jefferson Monument was probably the last gasp of the classical in our century."

One could hear the distant rumble of a locomotive approaching the Jefferson Street crossing far to the north, its whistle a tiny wail piercing the snowy quiet, making these warm, pleasant rooms seem, I think, a world apart from the world.

During a lull in the conversation, I said, "I trust your life has gone well, Mrs. Blaine."

She seemed to think for a moment, as if appraising her life. "I suppose it's gone well enough, as lives go. Yes, five wonderful children, decades with a devoted husband. Years of wonderful pupils, well, some of them wonderful, if only in their own mediocre way. We never had much, Jim and I, but when he was gone, he surprised me with an extravagant insurance policy. He never said boo about it, just that I was to be sure to open that envelope, in the security box, after he was gone. He seemed to always know that he would go first. And suddenly, at the age of 66, I found myself wealthy. So I would shame myself by complaining. Whatever I'd wanted in my girlhood—" She glanced toward the fire. "Our lives turn out, one way or another, don't they? Perhaps I was foolish back then, but all in all, I wouldn't change much, even if I could."

I nodded.

We sat quietly for a moment, with our own thoughts. I said, "So it sounds as if you've had a good life."

"Good enough for this world." Mrs. Blaine sipped her sherry, which already was down to the stem, the firelight glinting golden upon the crystal. I refreshed her glass. Arrian's drink was barely touched. After I returned to my chair, Mrs. Blaine said, "You and Lucy, Tristan, you never had any children, did you?"

I believe I shifted in my chair and took a sip of scotch. For one thing, I thought the question quite odd, something she already knew. "Well, we had one."

She stared at me in blank amazement. I could tell that I had startled Arrian too, I believe, judging from the intensity of his gaze, which I took in from the periphery of my vision.

"Eric," I said. "He miscarried. Personally, I never laid eyes on him, but he was my son."

Mrs. Blaine looked away and touched her hair. I think for a fleeting moment, tears came into her eyes. That would not have happened fifty years ago, in her youth. "Oh, yes, I'm sorry. I simply wasn't thinking." I felt her son studying me. In the back of my mind, I recalled the conversation that Matthias Mende and I had regarding Eric, back in the Harding press bungalow, when the forsythia were in bloom.

I did not want my guests to be saddened by our perpetual loss of decades ago, so I said, "Other than that, Lucy and I had a good marriage. I was blessed with her love for me, her kindness, her patience, and her humility. And I tried to be a good husband, and I believe I succeeded, however modestly."

"I'm sure you did. How could you not?"

"I shall ever remember our long, countless evenings together, reading together in our living room, in our house down the avenue. I scarcely remember a bad day with her. We lost a housekeeper back in the '20s, Nora—she died young, not that long after Eric. Those two events, those two losses combined, put Lucy out of sorts for a long time to come, for a year or so. I remember days when she didn't even want to eat or get out of bed. Couldn't. She simply couldn't. Dr. Sawyer told me to have patience with her, to be kind, which I hope I was. And little by little, sure enough, life slowly returned, and when our lives finally got back to normal—thereafter we had decades of contented life, contented and happy."

And then, for some reason, I added, "But Adeline, my sister, now she was—she was a cipher."

I felt the lump of gold, of Matt's Alexander the Great ring in my pants pocket. I added, "Other than a couple of years in Paris, my younger sister spent virtually her entire life alone, right here in this very house. Seems she may have had a young French beau over in Paris, Bernart; I gather that we would say 'Bernard.' But he died in the war of 1914. Addy had left right after the Archduke was killed and came back to Marion. After Dad died, she ended up living here all alone, till she died in '59." As much to myself as my guests, I conjectured, "Seems no one was ever quite good enough for her, not around here anyways. I guess Paris was a different story. If it hadn't been for the war, then who knows. Everything may have been different."

I sipped my scotch and glanced into the peaceful flames, the crackling firelight and murmured, "This accursed, godforsaken century. And its barely half over."

And then I added, "In some ways, I can't make heads or tails of her, of Addy. And she was my own sister, my only sibling, and she lived right here, right down the avenue from me. Saw her a couple times a week throughout our lifetimes, for the most part, but—"

In the privacy of my thoughts, and for the umpteenth time, I saw Orrin de Pue plunging to his death and heard my tiny little sister's screams. Her screams and wails as she fled, as fast as her little feet would carry her, deep into the Old Forest, with me fleeing after her, with her.

I resumed, "Who knows why someone becomes so lonely. Or at least so *alone*." And then I added, "Well, I certainly didn't mean to sound so glum. Begging your pardon."

"Not at all," Mitzy said. "I think the entire country is looking inward, now."

Arrian said, "Little towns are so interesting."

I laughed at his understatement. "Well! Interesting and then some. You have no idea, Arrian, *no idea*."

His mother added, "I always thought there was something a bit, I don't know—fascinating about your sister. Though for some reason, I was always vaguely afraid of her."

I glanced away.

She hastened to add, "I don't mean that in a bad way, Tristan." And then, "Arrian, I think I've told you that Miss Hamilton was a very beautiful woman."

"Yes."

"Even when she got older."

"And very clever too," I said. "Dana Yost once told me, said to me very, very much on the sly—he did both of our taxes, you know—he whispered in my ear, 'You know, Trey, that sister of yours, she makes damn near as much money as you *not* working.' He found it amusing. He assured me he could not go into details. Dana meant Addy's real estate and such. Dad was very generous to her, maybe he sensed she would never marry and was not the working sort of girl, and so she'd have to live on her own. Then she met Mr. Oppenheimer, a stockbroker in that little office in the Hotel Harding. Well, let me tell you, the two of them hit it off royally, *royally*. He had big-city intuitions, in a little bitty office, in a little bitty town. They were a good team. She had the wherewithal and he had the instincts, the knowledge. They lined each other's pockets. Though she never dropped a pin. Wasn't till she was gone that I saw the lay of the land. Not that I ever thought she was hurting." I paused, the fire crackled in the hearth with its own quietness. "I guess some people are like that, living in their own high castle walls. Invisible, more or less, even when they're standing right in front of you."

I could hear Mrs. Christian and Emma Linda making their final arrangements in the dining room down the hall, and the aroma of our Thanksgiving feast filling the house.

"So Dr. Lang, Arrian—tell me about yourself."

"Well, sir, not much to tell, really. I have a wonderful family. My wife Kate—Katherine—and then there's Gordon and Tristan and little Amelia, they're all down at her folks' house in Gallipolis. Though they'll be up for Christmas and we'll all be together. Mom'll be there."

I was a bit startled at the coincidence that one of his sons and I shared names, and I wondered if, perhaps, his mother had once spoken of me with more esteem than I might imagine.

Arrian seemed to hesitate, as if he wanted to say something more.

When he didn't, I said, "You're one of those smart Battelle fellows, aren't you?"

He smiled. "My colleagues are smart, believe you me. As for me—I slipped in through the back door."

His mother blew a breath through her lips and waved her hand. "Modesty forces him to fib. He's brilliant, Tristan, *brilliant*. He's pulling your leg."

I smiled, "I'm sure he is!" I was delighted in thinking of this, considering the fact that all too often President Harding has been thought of (and even referred to, in history books), as a "buffoon"—as if a buffoon could bring brilliance into this world.

I said, "I think your colleagues would be fascinated to know that your father was on the founding Board of Trustees at Battelle. Did you know that, do they?"

"Yes, sir, an oil portrait of President Harding hangs in one of the conference rooms."

"Ah, I didn't know! I wonder when he sat for it. Wonder who painted it?"

He shrugged, unknowing. I sensed indifference on his part, and in a way I understood. Mr. Harding bore two known children, both during his Washington years. (There may have been others from his years as a young man, and as a not so young man, gadding about, sowing his wild oats.) Mr. Harding refused to acknowledge either Elizabeth Ann or Arrian and supposedly on one occasion, when Nan visited Washington, he refused to even look from a White House window to see his own daughter sitting on a park bench, with Nan's sister. Not exactly what you would call neighborly, much less fatherly.

Anyway, I continued, "About the Battelle connection, Mr. Harding was a good friend of Gordon Battelle. I knew Gordon. He sat in this very room, had dinner at the same table where we're going to have dinner tonight. That would have been during the Campaign Summer of 1920. Gordon died the same year the President died. Died young. Couldn't have been more than forty. A burst appendix, I believe. A real shame, too. Decades of promise lay ahead of him."

As happens so often in my life, a fleeting vision of my mother in her coffin passed through me: Momma and my baby brother uncorrupted down there in the earth, dimly glowing in supernatural light.

And then I added, "Lots of early deaths like that back then, wouldn't be as likely to happen nowadays, thank heavens."

Mrs. Blaine said, "Arrian, tell Tristan about the coins."

"The coins?" I asked, thinking maybe he was some kind of collector. I have never been impressed with collectors, though heaven only knows why.

"Yes," he said, "coinage." He leaned my way, as if to impart something dear and confidential. "You see, sir, there's a problem. A problem with coins as we know them. Something called seignorage—that's the difference between the cost of bullion and the value of the coins themselves. The thing is this, it's getting so that a quarter costs more to make than a quarter's worth. Same as a dime, half dollar, and silver dollar. Because of our reputation with metallurgy, the U.S. Mint contacted us and asked if we could figure out some new kind of alloyed coin. That's my staff's project. To come up with a new kind of coin."

Mrs. Blaine said, "In two or three years, Tristan, the coins we carry in our pockets—Arrian, he'll have designed them, excepting the pennies."

"And the nickels. Metallurgically designed them, that is. In the sense of the coins' blend of copper and nickel components and binding them together into a solid, adhesive wafer, or coin. Copper core, nickel cladding. Design-wise, they'll look the same. We have nothing to do with that. That's the mint, obviously, or Congress. Except I've been told that they're already drawing up plans for a Kennedy half-dollar. We have a WATTS line, and I was talking to a fellow yesterday morning in D.C. and that's what he said. So anyway, the fifty-cent piece is going to change, or so they say. We'll see."

"Well," I said, "I think I'll miss the idea of having real silver jangling in my change purse, but other than that, rather impressive. I'm sure your father would be proud of you. And," I added, "*I am* proud of you, on the President's behalf."

I took a sip of scotch. Neither of my guests replied, so I said, "Say listen Arrian, you know people in the Mint, right? I wouldn't want them to think you were indulging in nepotism or anything, but you ought to put a bug in their ear about putting your father's image on something."

Mrs. Blaine sighed, "Oh, Tristan—" her same exact tone of occasional annoyance from fifty years ago—as when I proposed that the two of us elope and marry in Argentina (though I no longer have any memory as to why a young stay-at-home like me would have ever conjured such an outlandish folly).

I added, "But they talked about it after he died. They just never did anything about it. Maybe Arrian, with his influence and all—"

They both sat there, looking at me. Arrian glanced at the fire.

"And put Warren's image on *what*?" Mrs. Blaine asked. "A three-dollar bill?"

I believe I reddened, taken aback. "Well, maybe a stamp then."

"Tristan, you have to be the most loyal person alive. Warren used to say the same thing himself. In fact, the constancy and sheer intensity of your devotion baffled him. Sometimes I think it even unnerved him."

"But I had to remain devoted to Warren Harding. We helped create him, made him who he was. Now I tend his flame."

"No doubt about it."

Dinnertime was quite near; nevertheless, I got up to refresh our drinks. We could carry them to the dinner table with us. Wine or no wine, I have never been one to have qualms about bringing cocktails to the dinner table. As I was pouring, I said, "Speaking of flames, I do like Mrs. Kennedy's idea of an 'eternal flame.' Wish I'd thought of it, though frankly, I'm not sure how *eternal* eternal is. Or perhaps I should say, will be. I mean the practicality of it, of maintaining the gas jets, the piping and such through the vagaries of time and centuries, though maybe you read that article in the *Star*—the flame in Paris, at the Arch of Triumph's, it's supposedly been burning unquenched since 1921. Not even the Nazis tampered with it. One of the few things they seemed to respect was tradition. But forty-two years is not eternity. Be that as it may, as far as I'm concerned, in the end, stone, and what we make from it, is as close as we get to *eternal*. I mean that strictly in the worldly, material way. And even that will fall."

Mrs. Christian's soft footsteps came padding along the hallway. And then you could hear her pause on the other side of the wall, before she sort of peeked around the corner, in the shy way of her girlhood days. "Excuse me, Mr. Hamilton," she half-spoke/half-whispered, "Dinner is—" Her eyes settled on Dr. Lang and perhaps astonishment at seeing the President's son in the flesh seemed to take the words out of her. She stared at him for an odd and startled moment. She looked at me and her face reddened, and then she regained herself. "Dinner is served." And then with a timid smile, she added, "Hello everyone."

My guests returned her salutation.

I said, "Smells wonderful, Mrs. Christian, so good to have the aroma of a real holiday dinner in the house again. You remember Mrs. Blaine, of course, and this is her son Dr. Arrian Lang. President Harding's son."

She was staring at Dr. Lang and then she nodded their way. "Welcome to Tioga. Good to have folks to cook for again. Come along when you're ready." She turned to go down the hall, but then paused and, looking at me, she said, "But let's not let the peas get cold, okay?"

"Of course, Mrs. Christian, we'll be right along. Thank you."

My housekeeper/commander disappeared down the hallway. Mrs. Blaine and Arrian found a measure of humor in our marching orders.

"Well," I said, "I think we better heed our summons."

For the first time in ages the wide double doors of the dining room were rolled into their casements and the end of the hall, usually dark, now glowed with soft golden light, the aroma of Thanksgiving permeating the warmth.

Frankly, I was taken aback by the sight of this welcoming room, particularly by the table laid out for guests, as in olden days. I paused in the doorway. All was as it had been during now distant occasions and holiday times: my mother's golden damask tablecloth, the roasted turkey on its silver tray cooked to perfection and encircled by shiny red apples and fresh sprigs of parsley and mint; and the delectables of the day brimming in their bowls—mashed potatoes, creamed onions, buttered snow peas, yam pudding, and sundry old favorites of the harvest season. Two old-fashioned, cut crystal decanters—one with the very last of my father's wine, his "Catawba port," the other with sherry—stood waiting at the long table's end, their facets glittering darkly. I had placed the port bottle aside, upon which my father had written 1912 on the label, so that I could show my guests this quaint relic from a distant time. I had selected four dinner wines, not knowing my guests' preferences: a Riesling and a Gewürztraminer, a pink Catawba and a Côte d'Or, each on a sterling coaster. Emma Linda had made a centerpiece of orange daises and yellow chrysanthemums, gourds and Indian corn, wheat and cattails. The darkest shadows had fled into their nooks and crannies, driven off by the chandelier's rose-colored globes, by the candles flickering in sterling and the firelight crackling in the hearth. The room had the feeling of a special place removed from the world. Mrs. Christian and her daughter had posted themselves on either side of the fireplace, quite official-looking in their new uniforms, waiting and at our service. I had not seen this half-forgotten room, as it was now laid out, for many long years, and something unaccountable arose within me; I became filled with—I do not know what to say—with more than mere nostalgia, with poignancy, with feelings of loss and richness, with keen sorrow and gratitude mixing into a sweeping moment. Literally, I believe my breath fled me, and several seconds passed before it returned. Mind you, I think my odd, emotional reaction had just as much to do with the long week past as with the setting of the table or the lustrous room. This has been one of the longest weeks in my three score years and ten, and too much has happened too quickly—President Kennedy in his grave at Arlington; the countless reminders of President and Mrs. Harding, and all those long, buried years, returning; the discovery of Matt's ring this very morning; and now Mitzy's return to Tioga, after fifty years. And then, to come into this room once again where, of a Sunday afternoon in the summer of 1914, we sat at this very table, alone together in this big house, and she told me, in a voice I had never heard before, that our courtship was off, forever. She had laid her head on the table and wept. I had vanished through the back door, wandering through the Old Forest until nightfall. When at last I returned, I watched my dad through the library's bay windows, sitting at his desk, reading.

Pausing for a long moment in the doorway, these memories of other times passed through me like ghosts through walls.

Frankly, the scotch may have imposed its own spirits.

Mrs. Christian nodded with a sad smile, sensing some of my thoughts.

"Well, Mrs. Christian, I see you've outdone yourself yet again, another blue-ribbon job! And thank you, Emma Linda, for helping us out this week." And I added with a little laugh, "Frankly, for a moment there I guess you could say I was 'startled' by the table's beauty."

With a glance to my guests, I said, "Everything looks beautiful, doesn't it?"

"Oh, absolutely," Mrs. Blaine said, "Just like a picture from a magazine."

"A veritable feast," her son added.

Mrs. Christian said, "It's a joy to cook again. I mean to *really* cook, just like in the old days. And to have folks in the house again. Life returns, even if time does not."

Laying hands on the back of my chair, I gestured to the two place settings to either side of me and, with the fire playing at my back, I said, "Please."

Arrian pulled the chair to my right for his mother, and then came 'round to my left.

Seated now, I said, "I believe grace is in order."

We bowed our heads: "For each new morning with its light, For rest and shelter of the night, For health and food, For love and friends, For everything Thy goodness sends, we thank Thee, Lord. Bless us Dear Lord, along with the souls of all who once joined us on this day, but join us no more. And especially, we ask Thee to bless the soul of our beloved countryman, John Fitzgerald Kennedy, gathered with you into eternity, and bless this day and all future days of Mrs. Kennedy and her fatherless little ones, *our* fatherless little ones, Caroline and John, Jr. Amen."

Those with me remained silent for a moment, and then the voices around me softly spoke, "Amen."

I realized, as surely as if I had eyes in the back of my head, that Mrs. Christian was wiping her eyes. I did not mean for it to be like that; I had merely wanted to prepare a grace befitting Thanksgiving Day, in the year of Our Lord, 1963.

"Well," I said, determined to lift our spirits, "Let's eat, drink, and enjoy this wonderful feast. Joy is gratitude, gratitude, joy." We had not yet poured the wine but we had our drinks from the parlor, so I raised my scotch and said, "God bless us all. God bless and keep President Lyndon Baines Johnson and the United States of America, the best and greatest nation on earth!"

"Here, here," Arrian said.

"Happy Thanksgiving!" I added.

And we toasted, "Happy Thanksgiving!"

And for no reason at all, we laughed.

Mrs. Christian carved the turkey—I'd told her earlier that I was afraid I might bungle it—and Emma Linda poured the wine: Riesling for Mrs. Blaine and Dr. Lang, "for starters," and the Côte d'Or for me.

After the turkey and cranberry-apple dressing were served, and plenty more placed on the platter, and after all of the delectables had made their rounds, I said, "Now Mrs. Christian, you and Emma Linda can forget about us for a while. I want you ladies to go have yourselves a well-deserved break. We'll be just fine."

"Very well, Mr. Hamilton. You remember where the buzzer is?"

I felt around under the table, left side, "Ah, yes, here it is. If it still works."

"It works. And don't forget to save room for dessert."

"We'll do our best."

As the ladies withdrew into the kitchen, we "dug in."

Arrian said, "Quite a setup you have here, sir."

I gave a little laugh. "Well, you can be sure that Lucy and I lived much more simply. No electronic buzzers and such. Lucy and I lived for decades down the Avenue, and from our dining room table you could look straight through the kitchen and right out the back door. You could hear the pots and pans banging around plain as day."

I believe each of us relished our little feast. The mashed potatoes—one of my personal lifelong favorites—were as creamy and smooth as they could be, and the turkey breast, nicely carved into slabs, was succulent and flavorful.

For a few moments, the only sound was the delicate clatter of forks and knives. In the large oil above the credenza, oblivious of our feast, two pioneers were forever raising their muskets somewhere in the Old Forest, and the stag was forever turning startled toward them, while a lone Indian, with his sad countenance, peeked from behind an ancient oak.

The room glowing warm and mellow whilst we passed through, by my estimate, one of those fleeting, memorable moments in a lifetime that one returns to in thoughts, again and again.

After we were served, Mitzy said, "Tristan, I've been thinking lately of Goose Pond Farm."

I laughed at the irony, "Goose Pond Farm! Funny you should say that. I've been thinking of it too. For one thing, remember the shed I built for Dad, my first building? Well, I should have had the roof replaced years ago and I'm wondering if the poor thing survived this snowfall. Besides—" In a fleeting moment, with the scotch in my veins, I thought of Matt's disappearance from the place and of his mother and "kid sister" coming here to look for him, months later. I thought of the Missing Persons Report that Dana filed with the police, and of Officer Evans calling on Lucy and me, and then Addy. Later, he would note on the report: *Drifter. No physical evidence of foul play.* My guests were looking at me oddly, as if the specter of his disappearance had flitted across my face. I resumed, "Besides, I don't go to the farm much this time of year, pretty desolate out there, though I sort of miss the old place."

"And Tioga?" Arrian said, "How old is Tioga, sir? And what's it mean, 'Tioga'?"

"The gate, it means the gate. Dad built it in 1900 and we moved in, in 1901."

I sipped the Côte d'Or—both subtle and luscious, and was charmed by Dr. Lang's interest in this peculiar old place at the edge of our forgotten little town. I added, "*Tioga* comes from the lost language of the Wyandot Indians who lived in these parts since time immemorial." Matt flitted through my mind, and I said, "That is until President Andrew Jackson drove them into exile. Dad said he got the name from an old book of some sort, one on the old Indian tongues, though I'll be darned if I've ever been able to find it, neither the book nor any other reference to the name."

I paused and then, no doubt telling them more than they needed to know, I added, "I remember running through the long upstairs hallway and Addy and me playing 'neath this very table. She liked to hide under here. If you called her, she wouldn't answer. But you knew where to find her. You can imagine what it was like for children, moving into a place like this. Tioga was brand new then, but I think it felt just like it does now— like it went way, way back before its own time, somehow embodying secrets from the first. Secrets from history."

"Interesting," Arrian said. "Our house in Upper Arlington is nothing like this. Roomy and bright, but without the kind of character Tioga has. You'll see." Arrian spoke like an admiring, modern visitor to an antique land.

His mother said, "He's being modest, Tristan. Arrian and Margaret's house is lovely."

"Oh, I'm quite sure."

Arrian said, "Lovely, maybe, but new. On Elgin Road, if you know where that is."

"Can't say as I do, but I assure you, there's nothing wrong with new. New wood, new wires, new pipes, new roof—excellent combination. My family earned its bread and butter from *new*—as in new houses."

"Tristan, I remember you saying something in our youth about 'new antiquity.'"

I laughed. "I did? 'New antiquity!' About Tioga?"

"I don't remember, maybe, but 'new antiquity,' nonetheless. Those exact two words. Never forgot them. They sum you up, in a sense."

I thought back, trying to fish the phrase from the deep pond of my past. Unable to do so, I said, "Well, lots in my life has constituted 'new antiquity,' in one form or another."

"Mine too." A momentary silence descended, and then she added, "Now where shall we go from here?"

On that note, Mrs. Blaine finished her sherry.

"One thing's for certain," I said, "Someday Tioga will be 'gone with the wind,' just like Tara, though more so. Come back in 1983 or '93, or who knows when—and you can bet your life, Tioga will be long gone, barely remembered, eventually altogether *unremembered*. You'll find a filling station here, gasoline pumps where the bronze deer now stand. Or maybe an apartment house, folks sitting in drywall rooms, where we're sitting now, eating pizza and watching a future equivalent of *The Beverly Hillbillies*. As for whatever inhabits this place in distant years to come, you can be sure of one thing, it will have something to do with asphalt. Count on it. After all, this *is* Marion, Ohio."

"But tear down Tioga!" Arrian said, "That would be a crime. A crime against—"

His mother provided the word for which he was searching, "History. A crime against history, and beauty."

"Yes," I said, "it will be a crime, but it will be a crime that shall happen, rest assured. Or unrest assured." I downed the last of my scotch, feeling its mellowness in my veins. I continued, "In my time, in my father's and grandfather's time, which is to say in *our* time, we built solidly for the future, with one eye toward beauty and another towards service and *progress*—and we expected what we bequeathed to be used accordingly. As for folks nowadays, at least folks 'round here, why, if this were England, they'd tear down Stonehenge and put up a laundromat. Tioga will be torn down, count on it."

Mrs. Blaine said, "Unfortunately, you're probably right."

"I am right, no 'probably' about it."

She added, "When I think of the Marion of my girlhood, and the Marion of today, why, the changes are shameful. Build new buildings, yes, but do so in their own place. Don't go tearing down the beautiful and the old to throw up the ugly and the new."

"Here, here!" I said, "And you'll remember Amos Kling's house. Gone. Replaced by a Sunoco station. Mr. Kling had a copula that seemed to float above the treetops. He used to sit up there and smoke cigars and watch the world go by, till he got too old to climb the stairs. And he had a beautiful, octagonal orchidarium in the backyard, an extension of the house, where he raised orchids that came from places like Costa Rica and Madagascar. The orchidarium was plate glass and copper. Nowadays derelict cars are parked on asphalt where the orchidarium stood. That's Marion, Ohio in a nutshell, then and now."

I continued, "And then there's Mr. and Mrs. Huber's place on Greenwood and East Center Street. Their house was as solid as a medieval fortress, and just as big. My grandfather built it to stand forever and a day. They tore it down a few years back, and that puny little Sinclair station is there now, with its used car lot. They whitewash the prices on the windshields so you can see them as you drive by or wait at the traffic light.

"And the list goes on and on—the magnificent old—*old* that's a laugh—the magnificent, *lost* High School building on West Center, where you used to teach, Mitzy—" (I had not meant to call her "Mitzy;" a name with which I had not addressed her in fifty years, though there was no summoning the utterance back, and I believe I saw surprise and appreciation flash in her eyes.) "That building was one of the most beautiful in all of old Ohio! It had arches and bays and soaring gables, and inside, burled walnut banisters and woodwork, and classrooms and an assembly hall and dining hall that Harvard or Oxford might have envied. Built to last for centuries. Torn down less than fifty years after it opened. That's Marion. Replaced by a five and dime store, J.C. Penney's, and a row of other lesser stores. And lots and lots of asphalt, of course. Can't do without asphalt around here. The more the better.

"Hotel Marion and the old jailhouse on State Street are slated soon to go. Thus as I say, Tioga shall follow in the pathways of the architecturally doomed."

I paused in my quiet tirade, and then, "Why, I wouldn't put it past Marion to tear down the Courthouse. They've already cut down its ancient sycamores. Blamed it on the starlings, said they were untidy. But birds had been roosting in those trees for hundreds of years. And since when are birds calling the shots?

"Why, Arrian, I'm half-afraid that when I'm out of here, they'll set their sights on your father's tomb. It'd be a perfect place for a gas station, you know. Folks could pull in for fill up before they head for Columbus. Very convenient."

Mitzy said, "Strange to hear you talk like this, Tristan. I always thought of you as Marion's biggest booster."

"I *was* Marion's biggest booster, back when Marion was Marion, back when it was filled with ideals and possibilities, or so we thought, back when 'progress,' as I understood it, meant the enrichment and betterment of our lives and surroundings, not their depletion, not their uglification— if that's a word. Back then, we stood for something. And it always worked out for us. Always.

"Arrian, during that famous summer of 1920, when your dad stood on his Front Porch, *The New York Times* did a profile on Marion and said we were one of the most beautiful and forward-looking towns in America, the 'epitome of America,' they called us. Ha! Why, can you imagine anyone saying something like that today?"

I caught my breath, feeling the effects of the scotch and the wine. "Well," I said quietly, "I'm really sorry to go on like this."

"Not at all," Mitzy said. "I think you're right on the mark."

"I am on the mark. That's the sad thing. I expected more, I expected better." Again I paused in my tirade, "It's been a hell of a week, a hell of a century; everything, absolutely *everything* past and future, gathering in the fullness of time."

My guests studied me, and saw whatever they saw in me. And what did they see? An embittered old man? Perhaps. Odd, never would I have perceived myself so meanly, but I was hoping that I did not come across as such.

Mrs. Blaine said, almost gently, "And more of *everything* will gather, Tristan. More past, more future. Indeed, it's already waiting in the wings."

"I am more prepared than I may sound. I think I should drink up and shut up."

I took another sip of the good Côte d'Or, after which Arrian topped my glass. I found some humor in his gesture, as if he were saying, *Drink up and calm down, old man*. I added, "Speaking of the past, you see that decanter of port?" I nodded toward the end of the table. "That's the last of my father's wine, the last he made in his lifetime. The very, very last bottle. 'Catawba port 1912.' Dad was a winemaker by avocation, among other things. There stands the end of his earthly spirits."

"1912," Arrian said. "Amazing! I feel as if I've stepped into history."

"You have."

"Yes," Mitzy said. "1912!"

"The year we built the Wyandot Popcorn plant, the year the *Titanic* went down." I thought of my first visit with Mitzy to Goose Pond Farm and of her first visit to Tioga. I added, "Mrs. Christian and I gave the wine a taste test. It's aged beautifully, I assure you."

"You should have kept it, sir." Arrian said.

I gave a sharp laugh, "For what? I turn 71, come January!"

"You should have kept it for today," his mother said, "which is exactly what happened. Today is the perfect occasion."

"Yes, today!" And I added, "You know, Arrian, your father was most careful not to allow liquor bottles to gather dust, or for wine to turn to vinegar."

I thought my remark rather humorous, but that seemed not to be the case; indeed, a measure of seriousness seemed to descend upon my guests at the mere mention of the President and his drinking (though I wish to append categorically that, yes, while the President enjoyed his whiskey, nevertheless, Warren G. Harding was *not* a drunkard—and any historian who says or implies that he was, is an out-and-out *liar*).

Mitzy said, "For many long years now, Tristan, I have hoped that neither of us would die before the three of us had a chance to sit together, as we're doing now, this evening."

Her remark, with its sudden gravity, encompassing our lifetimes, took me slightly aback. I simply said, "Why, yes. I'm happy that it's so."

She added, "I am grateful to Divine Providence for providing the occasion, at last. And Colonel Hamilton's 'earthly spirits,' as you say, are the perfect accompaniment for the occasion."

"I agree. Dad would be delighted to know that on a Thanksgiving night, forty-one years after his death, we would be drinking the last of his wine, fifty-one years after he bottled it."

In my slightly inebriated imagination, I saw my Mitzy, a girl again, my betrothed, walking up the carriage path in dappled sunlight, and Senator Harding lurking in the shadows, looking up, over his hands as he struck a match and lit his cigarette.

I heard myself say, "Love goes where love is bidden, even into the high grasses."

Mrs. Blaine laughed, "That it does, in spite of snakes lurking in the brambles."

"If Mrs. Harding had died, as planned, you would have become the Jacqueline Kennedy of the '20s. Your fame may have persisted to this very day, like Alice Roosevelt's."

"Then thank heavens Mrs. Harding *didn't* die, no matter what I said or thought I wanted at the time. All the circumstances of my life would have changed. And for what? For a long-forgotten White House wedding. For a couple of glamorous years with Warren, though who knows who else he would have been with. And I'd be without my children, with the wonderful exception of Arrian."

Her son gave a slight smile.

I kept my council, for I wondered if her gladness was not at least somewhat mitigated by regret. I used to think that Mitzy von Leuckel might have become another Gloria Swanson or Mary Pickford, had she become the President's wife and used her White House fame as a stepping-stone to Hollywood. But who knows where that in turn may have led, had Pearl Street been Sunset Boulevard instead.

"Same as if *we* had married, Tristan. You and Lucy would never have been; no Jim and me either, nor the children and the life we both had."

"Granted," I said, "all was exactly as it should have been, no matter what we felt or considered at the time."

I thought of those once seemingly endless nights, now long gone: Lucy and me upstairs in each other's arms, and the summer evenings on the porch swing as we grew older, side by side, reading together by the same lamp in the parlor. "Yes," I added, "all was as it should have been." I thought of Eric, and added, "Including the losses, I suppose. At the very least, all was as it *was*. Time has come and gone, with us and without us."

We dined in silence. And then I recommended second helpings—the turkey and mashed potatoes being the favorites.

Arrian said, "You've never met my children, sir, have you?"

"No, I haven't, and that would be a pleasure, Arrian, that and getting to know you better."

Frankly, more than once it had occurred to me to invite (quietly, without any measure of fuss) Dr. Arrian Lang to become a member of the Board of Directors of the Harding Commemorative Society. I pictured

Dr. Lang attending our annual dinner in the banquet room at the Hotel Harding. Older folks in the town, those "in the know," would smile to themselves at the secret recognition of his name and whisper, "The President's son!" I would have extended the invitation long ago, if not for his seeming indifference to the Harding legacy, or maybe it was just plain old embarrassment over the old scandals, not to mention the possible stigma of his illegitimate birth.

I said, "I have often thought, I wish a genealogist or someone of that ilk would do a little research and find out who our nation's presidential descendants are and where they're living. They could publish a sort of 'who's who directory of presidential relatives'—who they are and what they've done or what they're doing. Mind you, it wouldn't have to have street addresses or even towns. Maybe just the state you folks live in. That couldn't do any harm, could it? I read in the Sunday supplement, not long ago, that Abraham Lincoln's last descendant lives in Vermont, an elderly man with no heirs to his credit." I thought of myself, alone in this big empty house with no heirs to my credit either, and I added, "Once that fellow's gone, the Lincoln family will vanish from the face of the earth."

I took a sip of wine and continued, "I have always thought it would be interesting to organize a gathering of Presidential descendants. Everyone could wear a name tag, one with their name as well as their Presidential ancestor. Maybe President Johnson would host it. Maybe in the East Room. The White House could use a happy occasion again, maybe sometime next year, to dispel some measure of all of that sorrow that's descended upon the nation."

In my mind, Mrs. Kennedy once again walked into the East Room wearing one of her French dresses, the flash bulbs popping as she smiled again—with the President's little ones in tow. And I thought of the Lincoln descendant having his picture taken, with his elderly arms draped around little Caroline and John-John, perhaps with the crystal chandelier glowing above them.

Arrian said, "That would be a fine idea, sir. You could propose it."

"You should," Mitzy said.

"Perhaps I can suggest it to someone, though who knows who. Arrian, I'm sure you're well aware that you have a half-sister out there, somewhere, though who knows where. I know for a fact that Elizabeth Ann Britton

once lived in Chicago, though I've since heard she's somewhere out West."
I paused, expecting a reply, but Arrian did not offer one, so I continued.
"I was thinking the other day, remembering that along about 1951 or '52,
one of the groundskeepers out at the Memorial found a bouquet of white
roses that someone had left by the bronze gate, at the President's tomb.
I made inquiries among the local florists. Mrs. Hemmerly had sold just
such a bouquet to a thirtyish year old woman, not from these parts. She
had no idea who she was. I have often wondered—was that Elizabeth
Ann passing through, visiting her father's tomb? I guess we'll never know,
unless she gets in touch with us, which seems doubtful. She wants nothing
to do with us, as if we're irrelevant. The President should have paid her
more mind, ever so discreetly, of course, but he didn't."

In my mind's eye, I pictured Elizabeth Ann and Arrian and their
children in the East Room, off to the side, apart from the Kennedys,
Roosevelts, and the Eisenhowers, but nonetheless, among them. And I
thought of all the presidential descendants, many (if not most) no doubt
hidden away in ordinary lives, most, like Arrian and Elizabeth Ann, not
even bearing the names of their White House ancestors. I said, "Can you
imagine tracking all those folks down, or trying to? Why, we'd not only
need genealogists, we'd need J. Edgar Hoover and his FBI."

My guests concurred.

"It was just a thought," I said, "a penny-notion that I've toyed with
for years. Maybe sooner or later someone in Washington will think of it,
someone who's in a position to actually do something about it. Maybe
you know someone, Arrian, through your Battelle connections."

"I'm sorry, sir, I don't."

I had always wondered one thing about Arrian and Elizabeth Ann,
and so I added, "Arrian, I hope you don't mind me asking, but do people
know?"

He looked at me, clearly puzzled.

"Do they know about your paternity? Do your neighbors and the folks
at Battelle *know* that you are President Warren G. Harding's son? What do
you tell them?"

I could not help but notice the troubled look that came upon him, as
if I had truly crossed a line outside of my own business. He cast a glance
across the table to his mother.

496 ✹ Vincent Nicolosi

Only then did I realize that the scotch and wine had nudged me a bit too far across the line of propriety. "Oh, what am I saying! I beg your pardon. I have no right to be so forward, and truly I didn't mean to be. I beg your pardon."

"Not at all, sir."

To cover my faux pas, I said, "I seem to assume that everything and anything having to do with President Harding likewise has to do with me—I mean as founder and lifelong president of the Harding Commemorative Society, the keeper of his flame, the executor of his estate; but obviously, there are exceptions. After all, Warren Harding wasn't just *history*; he was a man, a private individual, and I sometimes forget that."

"It's not that, sir."

His mother said (or rather started to say), "Tristan, there's—"

Just then, Mrs. Christian came through the door bearing the antique pitcher to refill our water goblets and to check on our progress, bringing with her the aroma of perking coffee. I was relieved to have a sudden distraction from my faux pas and I suppose my guests were as well. I said, "Ah, here's the lady to whom we owe this splendid feast! My dear and faithful Mrs. Christian! God bless her!"

I applauded her and my guests, of course, followed suit, and we supplemented our applause with a little chorus of compliments about the moistness of the turkey, the creaminess of the mashed potatoes, and the heartiness of the other delicacies. In former times, back in the days of Adeline and Lucy, and even further back, in the days of my father and the Hardings and the other guests who once crowded this table, back then Mrs. Christian would have stood blushing by the door, but now she accepted our praise with the polite, albeit world-weary indifference of the old—more interested in getting on with things than in the praise, which, nevertheless, she was gracious enough to accept, with a little smile of gratitude.

Mitzy said, "Thank you, Mrs. Christian, for all the trouble you've gone to, you and Emma Linda. Why to think, such lavish fare, and only for three!"

"It's an honor, Mrs. Blaine."

And I added, by way of correction, "Mrs. Christian and Emma Linda get what they want of the leftovers. And there'll be plenty, so it's more than just for three."

As Mrs. Christian refreshed our water goblets, she said, "It's a pleasure to cook again. You folks should come more often. This house needs a little life in it."

"Couldn't agree more," I said. "Old age brings its—" I was searching for a word that was not too dispiriting.

"Its surprises," Mrs. Blaine said. "Old age brings its surprises."

"Ah, yes," I said, not quite in agreement, "that too, I suppose. Old age brings its surprises, every day's potential."

"Tonight is for the better," Mrs. Christian said, as she began removing our plates. "With that said, I hope you folks saved room for dessert."

"I saved room for a sliver," I said.

"When you see what Emmy managed to bring for you, Mr. Hamilton, you'll want a smidgen more than a sliver, I'll bet my bottom dollar on it."

"Oh?" I said, glancing toward my guests with a surprised and playful air. With a little laugh I added, "Well, maybe old age *does* bring its surprises."

As if summoned, Emma Linda came from the kitchen bearing a tray.

"We were just telling your mother, Emma Linda, what an excellent dinner you ladies prepared for us. Couldn't be better. You and your mom make the perfect team."

Emma Linda said, "I'm happy to be here, Mr. Hamilton. Mom and I'll gladly plan on coming back for the next—" she seemed to scan her mind for an appropriate number, and then she said, "For all the Thanksgivings in the world."

We laughed at her charming phrase, and I said, "I for one will gladly take you up on that offer."

Emma Linda placed the tray on the credenza, the cream and sugar on the table, and then she came 'round to pour our coffees.

A satisfied quiet settled upon us, though Mrs. Blaine seemed to have something restless on her mind. I felt the warmth of the fire at my back, and outside, in my thoughts, I stood for a ghostly moment on the snowbound summits of the Indian mound at Goose Pond Farm searching the northern darkness where the wild waves of Lake Erie crashed upon the cliffs at Indian Rock, the spray freezing upon the jagged stone. I thought of Matt. I glanced at Arrian. The unwritten book of deliverance for his father.

Mrs. Christian was saying, "Emma Linda, show Mr. Hamilton what you brought him for dessert, for you folks too, if you're brave enough to venture."

"Oh?" I said again, suddenly sensing what it might be.

To my guests Mrs. Christian said, as if an aside, "Don't fuss, we have mincemeat and pumpkin pie à la mode, if you prefer."

In the middle of the table before me, before us, Emma Linda placed a tray with a wheel of Stilton cheese, along with sliced pears—a rare delicacy from my parents' day, and from our Anglo-Saxon roots.

"Stilton! Why, where on earth—and in Marion, Ohio!?"

"Columbus," Mrs. Christian corrected. "You'll recall Emmy went Christmas shopping last Friday, to Lazarus, or started to."

"Ah, of course I remember."

And she added, with appropriate gravity, "On November 22nd."

Emma Linda said, "I was on the sixth floor, in the toy department, when a colored man came dashing from the back hollering out, 'President Kennedy's been shot! President Kennedy's been shot!' For a moment I thought they turned a lunatic loose. But he shouted, 'Out in Dallas. President Kennedy's been shot out in Dallas and it's all over the radio. It's true!'"

"Just then the music from the PA stopped in an awful way, and then it was a newscaster's voice on the radio, all frantic saying the same thing as the colored fellow." She paused, "But he seemed confused. A horrible silence fell over the place. And then, like someone shouted 'Fire,' hysteria, everyone rushing for the escalators. Folks tossing their selections on the display counters and hurrying away.

"Of course I knew Mom was here at Tioga and so when I got outside I managed to call you folks from a phone booth by the parking lot. Had to wait in line to make that call. Cost me thirty-five cents. By then the church bells were tolling, people wandering along crying. A young man was running down the street, beside Lazarus, running towards the river, as if he had a demon on his tail, shouting, 'Kennedy's dead. Kennedy's dead.'"

A hush had fallen over the table.

Emma Linda continued, "To make a long story short, I saw the Stilton that morning in the window of the cheese shop on High Street, up from the RKO Theatre. Good thing I picked it up when I did or it wouldn't be here."

I said, "Well, I'm pleased to hear that one good thing came from that dreadful day."

Our narrator added, with a kind of faraway wonderment, "It's as if something changed course that day. Something big. As Dad would say, 'Something in the offing.'"

We agreed.

I said, "Nothing will ever be the same."

Both of my guests opted for Stilton and pears over pie and ice cream and, while Emma Linda arranged our dessert plates, her mother bore the decanter of my father's darkly gleaming Catawba port from the far end of the table, placing it with almost religious reverence before me. In my imagination, Dad's wine had assumed a ghostly, celestial presence, the facets of its crystal decanter emitting little prisms of refracted candlelight, emanations from another world. For a fleeting instant, I thought of Addy and me, when small, helping Dad in the cool shadows of the long grape arbor outback at Goose Pond Farm, dappled green sunlight flickering through the broad, grape leaves into the arbor's little cloistered and tunnel-like walkway, on a bright September afternoon now buried under sixty odd years.

I lifted the decanter's crystal stopper and said, "Vintage 1912, from grapes picked from the long-vanished arbor at Goose Pond Farm. No doubt on a radiant September day," and I added with a bit of awe, "the year the *Titanic* went down."

"Mrs. Blaine," I offered.

She proffered her glass and I filled it.

"Arrian."

After filling his glass, I poured mine.

Stillness had fallen over the table. I raised my Catawba port. "A second toast, if I may: To the maker of this wine, to the builder of this house, to the living and the dead in our families, to our beloved President Kennedy, to our beloved President Harding, dear in personal memory to each of us. God bless us all, the living and the dead."

We touched our glasses. They rang with their quick, fleeting crystalline notes.

I sipped Dad's wine, closing my eyes, savoring the smooth, dark ancientness of ripening sun filtered through broad leaves and grape clusters of a long ago summer.

After a moment, Mrs. Blaine, in a hushed voice, said, "My lord, Tristan! It's astonishing! It's magical! Heavens!"

Her son let out a long breath of delight and amazement. "Why who would have thought! Ohio? From a back yard in Ohio! Now this *is* extraordinary!"

His mother added, "And to think, the grapes were pressed before you were even born, Arrian." And then she added, "You certainly have a way with words, Tristan."

"A way with words?"

"Your beautiful toast! You have *always* had a way with words. You used to help me with my essays, remember? Long after you left school. You used to 'burnish' them for me—your word. Why, in your old age you should write a book."

"Ha!" I laughed, though I felt quite flattered. "I'm afraid I have nothing to say. I've lived a wholly uneventful life. Nothing to write about, only Marion."

"'Nothing to write about!' 'Only Marion!' Please! Only the world! What about your family? What about Ohio? And Warren? And the building of that vast marble sepulcher at the edge of town! Like something from another world, and yet from this world. Why, there's so much to tell, so much to write. You call that nothing? I call it a bit of everything, and then some. You want all that to die with you, Tristan?"

I shrugged as the past week flitted through my mind: President Kennedy and President Harding; Lucy and Mitzy; Flossie, sitting in this very chair at this very hour, exactly forty Thanksgivings ago; my sister and Matt. And for a fleeting instant, that wily old goat Professor Chancellor haunted the shadows of my backyard with his two schoolboys, coming to taunt me, and then running scared. And I thought of his schoolmarm daughter watching me through falling leaves and of shimmying through the basement window at the Holcomb Museum; Orrin de Pue falling through the spring air again and again, as he had in my life, and my little sister's scream as she ran into the Old Forest. And all the lives and deaths along the way, the orchids and the printers' plates.

I glanced at Dr. Arrian Lang, studying me. I finally replied, to his mother's suggestion, "Well, maybe someday I'll do that—in spite of all that I lack in a formal sense. But don't make too much of me. Basically, I'm just a glorified carpenter, living in a rambling old house, beyond where the sidewalk ends, at the edge of this forgotten little town."

Mitzy smiled and touched my hand. "Tristan, you are one of the cleverest, most discerning men I have ever known. Wholly self-taught, as we teachers say. And I assure you, people with diplomas have no monopoly on intelligence."

I squeezed Mitzy's hand, hearing a lifelong teacher so generously say what I had figured out through the lonesomeness of self-teaching, even if I was still hounded by what I lacked.

The warmth I felt for Mitzy, in that instant, bridged fifty years.

Arrian said, "Momma's right. People with diplomas don't have a monopoly on intelligence, take my word for it."

Suddenly, I had a feeling he knew all about my lost education, and maybe he knew a bit more than I might have expected, and I was pleased to think that I had, perhaps, maintained a larger part in his mother's life than I may have heretofore expected.

"Thank you both for your kindness," I said, "for saying and understanding what I have long felt with, I am sorry to say, a touch of bitterness." I paused and added, mostly to myself, "Education meant a great deal to my mother. *My* education."

But after a moment Mitzy said, as if out of the blue, "Tristan, how you must have hated me back then!"

As you can imagine, the comment came like cold water in the face. "What!" I gave an astonished little laugh and shifted in my chair. "All of that was so very long ago."

"Perhaps you did hate me."

My face flushing, I am certain, I glanced at her son. "Well—"

The fire suddenly felt hot on the back of my neck. I said, "Perhaps I did for a time, Mitzy, but what of it? And only for a time." I felt my way cautiously with my words, and added, "Or maybe it wasn't hatred, just lost love, resentment, a long-ago affront to my young manhood. But all of that ended decades ago, didn't it? And truthfully, until this past week or so, it was as if all remembrance of the two of us had ceased. But then it all came flooding back. Not just because I saw Heidi, not just because she said you were in town, but somehow because of President Kennedy's death, because in some unaccountable way those shots fired out in Dallas threw open the floodgates and the entire past and everything else came flooding through—President Harding's death, the Summer Campaign. Why even you, Arrian, I've thought of you and your mother."

And I added, "And now the future's coming. Whatever days or years God may grant us. One way or another, here we are in the here and now of this snowy Thanksgiving evening, munching on Stilton and pears and sipping Dad's Catawba port, vintage 1912."

"Life is deceiving," Mrs. Blaine said.

"Ah," I said, not knowing what else to say.

"And where shall we go from here!"

"To the moon," I joked. "Just like President Kennedy planned for us—to the moon."

Mitzy was looking off elsewhere, into a distance far beyond the coziness of this warm room. She turned back to me, her eyes glistening. "Tristan, there's something I must tell you, something I must confess, yet another of my unforgivable sins—this one the worst of all, though I plead for consideration, for some little understanding of the difficult choices I had to make, long, long ago, and of the choices I felt I had to maintain, even in more recent decades."

I gave a little laugh. "Mitzy, I doubt that you can possibly have anything so weighty to confess. Whatever you think you may have to admit could not possibly go unredeemed by the passage of fifty years."

"You think so? Let's see. But where to begin—? You remember that Sunday afternoon in the summer of 1914? We were seated at this very table, you and me, exactly where we're seated now, and I ended our courtship mostly because I wanted more than anything to leave Marion—or at least I thought I did, back then, and because you were content to stay and make your life here, even determined to do so. I thought of you as a bit of a stick in the mud, Tristan, which in fact you were, albeit a stick-in-the-mud that blossomed into a great oak. Warren was on the verge of fame and the Senate, and I had an eye for him and he certainly had an eye for me. For other girls too, of course."

I glanced (a little uncomfortably) at Arrian, not that he was hearing anything that he did not already know.

"I guess I liked older men; Momma said it was because I barely knew Papa, like you barely knew your mother. Anyway, there was more to tell that day—"

As she paused, perhaps searching for words for difficult things to say, I wondered why she was opening this ancient grave. I said, "We all make our choices, Mitzy. My life was in Marion with Lucy. Yours was elsewhere, for a time, with Warren, more or less—though I gather it was a bit *less* than more—and then you were back in Marion, eventually with Jim. Our lives took their courses based on our decisions, which I've always thought, at any given time, are probably less solely *our* decisions than we may think. And our lives took their courses based on the events and occasions about us. I guess you could say based on destiny too, or what-have-you. I harbor no resentment, not so much as an ounce, if that's what you're getting at. No regrets. And I hope you harbor none either. It's just the way our lives were. And I think it's safe to say we've both had pretty good lives, all in all, in spite of the inevitable disappointments and sorrows along the way."

"Yes, we have. I'm sure of it, but I still have regrets, one or two. For one, I feel like a robber, the worst kind of robber of all, though considering the choices I had to make and the circumstances at the time, I can at least accept my own past decisions and not fault myself too harshly. But circumstances have changed and we've lived to see this day—the time has come, at last."

She drew a breath, took a sip of my father's wine. "Anyway, to that summer's day in 1914 when I told you our courtship was off and that I had to get out of here. I remember I laid my head on this very table and cried my eyes out. I did love you Tristan, really, really I did. Never doubt that. Ever. I don't know what happened then. I fell asleep, I think, right here in this very spot. And when I awoke and looked about, you had vanished and I was alone in this great big house with all its—its whispers. Your sister was in Europe; your dad—who knows where he was? And you, Tristan, may I now ask out of curiosity, fifty years on, where did you go that day? Maybe you don't even remember such a little point, but I had something more to tell you, though to this day I'm not sure if I would've."

It took me a moment to answer, so perplexing did I find this unexpected turn of the conversation. "Into the Old Forest," I said. "I think I wanted to lose myself and so I walked and walked along the Indian trails. It was like I wanted to lose my way and end up in some entirely unknown place, impossibly far, far away, some place from which I could never return. But I knew the woods like the back of my hand. I came back at nightfall and waited in the yard until long after dark. I could see Dad sitting in his leather chair in the library, reading one of his books. I crept in the back door and up the kitchen stairs to my room, closed the door, and fell asleep. I remember I woke up the next morning still dressed in my Sunday clothes and I think I remember feeling refreshed. I don't know, sort of like a shipwrecked sailor who wakes up on the shore, surprised to find himself alive."

I paused and then added, "You wasted no time in hightailing it out of Marion, did you, Mitzy? I didn't see you for years after that Sunday afternoon, so *you* were the one who wandered off and lost yourself. It was only by an act of will that I never made a single inquiry about you. Not even to your mother, when I occasioned upon her. I'd ask about her and Cedric, but pointedly, not about you. I know that was mean-spirited and rude of me, but that's how I felt at the time. And your mother always looked half-ashamed when she saw me. During that time, Lucy's first husband was killed on the rails, the Neil boy, and after a while, we married—best thing that ever happened." I took a sip of Dad's wine. "And then we were in the war and, *voilà*, you were back in Marion. I never was sure where you went off to. I'd gone into the Old Forest for the better part of a day. You wandered off for years. I know you eventually ended up in Washington to be near to Senator Harding."

"I went to Aunt Dora's, on Geneva-on-the-Lake, Aunt Dora Lang's. I went there until—" She glanced at her son.

I glanced at him too, embarrassed that Arrian had to listen to this unexpected discussion. I felt like saying to him, *Sorry, Arrian, carrying on like this, with and without you.* But I said nothing.

He nodded to his mother. "Go on, Momma, continue."

She did: "I lived there for about a year. Warren and I corresponded. He liked pale blue stationery—"

I knew very well that they wrote to each other and I remembered Mitzy saying once, a long time ago, that she had burnt all of Mr. Harding's letters; nevertheless, just to be sure, I interrupted, "You have letters?"

She gave me what I thought was an odd look, and so I add, "I'm only asking as president of the Harding Commemorative Society, nothing personal. I'm interested in anything and everything having to do with the President. And rest assured, I am *not* a burner of documents, not even private ones, no matter their content. I preserve and maintain. I'm not Flossie."

"No, I have no letters. I destroyed them all in 1920, I think, along with those that came my way thereafter. I was afraid that someone like that—you remember that old geezer-professor that came to Marion? I came to see you about him when you were having dinner at Kings' Mansion. Why, I can't remember his name for the life of me."

"Chancellor. William Chancellor."

"Why, yes! That's it, Chancellor."

"How odd," I said, "I was thinking of him just the other day." Through my mind flashed the face of his homely daughter, sitting on her horsehair couch in the gray light of that shadowy house in Wooster, autumn leaves blowing past the window. As far I know, the poor, lonely thing went to her grave a childless spinster.

Mitzy said, "I was living in an apartment on Windsor Street. You came to see me there once during the War, remember? Well, I was afraid someone like him would break in and root through my things and steal the letters and use them against Warren. So they're all gone and have been for decades."

"You should have kept them at your mother's. They would have been safe there. So I guess there were none after that, during his Presidency?"

She shrugged. "To continue, Tristan—in the summer of 1915, Warren and I secretly met in Erie, Pennsylvania. He rented a charming, secluded cottage there for the two of us on the shores of Lake Erie. Harry Daugherty made the arrangements. I never liked that man. He never seemed to take notice of me, scarcely even when I was sitting across the table from him. It was almost like I was hired help. Though his friend Jess Smith was a perfect gentleman. Jess would stand up and kiss my hand when I entered the room. A nod was the most I ever got from Harry, or 'There she is' if he was in good humor—that, or maybe, 'Howdy-do.' I guess he thought I was—I don't know." She glanced away even as she continued. "I cried when poor Jess blew his brains out. I always sensed that he and Harry had a peculiar friendship. But that was *not* the sort of thing you raised with Warren.

"That summer, Warren and I spent ten days on Lake Erie. Warren thought there'd be less chance of him being recognized in Pennsylvania than Ohio, not that we went out much. That's when our romance finally began, our *liaison d'amour*. The words are much prettier in French than in German, to be sure. Two months later, I was living in Washington, attending George Washington University, a female student of history. There weren't many of us then. Senator Harding paid for everything. All the while I'd left Arrian in Geneva-on-the-Lake to be raised by my aunt. I'm sorry to say that I wasn't a very good mother."

Arrian assured me, "Believe me, Momma has done her best to make up for any lapses in those early days. She did her best thereafter. And I seem to have turned out pretty okay."

"Yes," I said, sensing something in all of this, though I knew not what.

"Do you grasp what I'm saying, Tristan?"

"I'm sorry?"

"That was the summer of 1915. I left Arrian in Geneva-on-the-Lake. Aunt Dora raised him. As you used to say, Tristan, 'Run the numbers.'"

I glanced at Arrian, as if for a clue; he was looking at me most intently. Again, I thought of Matt.

Mitzy continued, "Arrian's birth certificate states that he was born in Geneva-on-the-Lake, Ohio, on February 11, 1915. What it does not state is that he was conceived on a weekend in May of 1914, in northern Marion County, in the upstairs bedroom at the back of Goose Pond Farm. Tristan, *you* are Arrian's father, *not* Warren Harding. Arrian is your son, not the President's. That is God's truth."

I lack the power to tell you, to even begin to tell you the jolt flung through my being by those words.

I turned to the middle-aged man beside me. Suddenly I saw myself and, I believe, my parents in his wistful eyes. "My son?"

"Yes, Tristan, Arrian is your son. Not Warren's."

For a moment, I thought I would weep. I glanced away, but only for a moment—as I attempted to align myself between my seventy years before this moment and our lives hereafter.

"Sir," he added, "I want you to understand that Mom always thought the truth might compromise your life, your marriage to Mrs. Hamilton. We knew we weren't doing the right thing, but we never knew if we were doing the wrong thing either, by simply leaving well enough alone. It wasn't only Momma's doing, it was mine. We talked about it now and then, and the years went by and things stayed as they were. So now you know. And now we're all here, together."

"Tristan"—Mitzy's eyes had filled with tears—"Forgive me."

Let me just say that I reached for Mitzy's hand. And my son reached for mine.

EPILOGUE

Tomorrow

NOW AS THE LAST HOUR of this last day of November hastens towards midnight, as this extraordinary week sweeps us like a whirlwind into history, and as this old, calamitous year slowly draws to its close, I am sitting again at my father's desk, one world passing away, a new world looming in the near distance. The nation has lost its President and I have gained a son, and who knows what the future may hold for any of us. In the here and now of this fleeting hour, I am sipping the last of my father's Catawba "port," and presently my mind seems especially attuned to the ticking of the clocks throughout Tioga.

After Mitzy's revelation, after she and our son and I had gathered our collective wits about us and after our feast, she requested to visit the library once again. I had seen by her long glance through the wide double doors, upon her arrival, that for her the library still held its old allure. Once again she ran her fingers over the desk and the bronze griffin, just as she did over fifty years ago. She touched the curlicues and the edges of shelves, pausing here and there before this or that volume. She and Arrian studied the engravings of ancient monuments hanging near the door, the temple of Assos in Asia Minor and the Tholos at Delphi. Below these, matted in a mutual frame, hang the drawings of the four finalists for the Harding Memorial Competition.

And there too hangs the charcoal sketch of the President's tomb, executed by Matthias Mende, on or near Easter Monday in April of 1947.

As Mitzy and Arrian leaned near to this drawing, I touched the gold lump of Matt's Alexander the Great ring in my pocket.

"How curious," Mitzy said. "The tomb almost looks haunted."

"It is." I said. "It *is* haunted."

Without turning towards me, she nodded and murmured, "Yes, it would be, wouldn't it?"

Here too from the wall of the library, Adeline's collection of Venetian masks and sculpted faces gaze silently into the room with their mute, coquettish stillness, their smiles and their sneers.

Beneath the rug woven in Persia by anonymous hands over a century ago, beneath the parquet and the thick underlayer of hardwood, lie the rough-hewn timbers upon which blood pooled during that spring morning in 1900, the stain ever blossoming rose-like across the wood grain, ever hidden and ever here, like the past itself, endlessly absent, endlessly present.

At one point in the library, Arrian said to me, "I want you to know—" He paused, I would say, almost timid, and frankly, for an instant I feared he would call me "Father" or worse yet "Dad," which would have been like a consummation far too soon. Arrian continued, "I want you to know, sir, that my family and I, *your* family, we want nothing from you, so please don't ever think, don't think—" His voice trailed off yet again.

His mother finished for him, "Don't ever think that Arrian or his children will make material claims upon you. As he says, his family, *your* family, Tristan, our family, we want for nothing—and they want nothing from you, except to have you now as part of their lives. Even if they were poor, they would not stoop so low."

"Yes," Arrian said. "That's it. You can trust us, sir."

And his mother added, "Arrian can stand on his own two feet—in fact, stand rock solid."

"Yes," he added again, "Yes. Rock solid."

WELL, I THINK IT IS BEST I TURN IN NOW. Tomorrow morning I am to pick Mitzy up at her daughter's place. From there we head for the Epworth Methodist Church to attend Sunday services together. No doubt this will cause quite a sensation amongst the oldster set, at least those who remember the intimacies of former days. Dr. and Mrs. Sawyer are generally there and I smile to think of the look on their faces. Thereafter, Mitzy and I will drive south along Main Street, past the Harding Memorial, as we head for our son's house in Upper Arlington. I guess poor, old Warren gets left out of this one.

Soon, for the first time in my life, I shall meet my daughter-in-law Katherine and my grandchildren Gordon, Amelia, and Tristan. The children's ages range from seventeen to thirteen, Amelia being fifteen. Their grandmother assures me that they are bright, beautiful, pleasant, and well-mannered children, though Tristan, unlike his father and his namesake grandfather, is pleasantly rambunctious and high-spirited. As Mitzy said, "Like a young colt."

Apparently, the children have heard oblique references to their "Grandpa" throughout their young lives and Arrian is preparing them for our meeting.

Soon, ever so soon, my grandchildren shall know me and I shall know them.

Thus an entire volume of my life comes to its close and, at the age of seventy, the unwritten book of my new future begins.